From the Pages of
The Canterbury Tales

(In Chaucer's Middle English. See modern English translation on next page.)

> Whan that Aprille with his shoures sote
> The droghte of Marche hath perced to the rote,
> And bathed every veyne in swich licour,
> Of which vertu engendred is the flour;
> Whan Zephirus eek with his swete breeth
> Inspired hath in every holt and heeth
> The tendre croppes and the yonge sonne
> Hath in the Ram his halfe cours y-ronne,
> And smale fowles maken melodye,
> That slepen al the night with open yë,
> (So priketh him nature in hir corages):
> Than longen folke to goon on pilgrimages.
>
> (from "The Prologue," page 2)

> Thou mightest wene that this Palamoun
> In his fighting were a wood leoun,
> And as a cruel tygre was Arcite:
> As wilde bores gonne they to smyte,
> That frothen whyte as foom for ire wood.
> Up to the ancle foghte they in hir blood.
>
> (from "The Knightes Tale," page 88)

> "Thou shalt na-more, thurgh thy flaterye,
> Do me to singe and winke with myn yë.
> For he that winketh, whan he sholde see,
> Al wilfully, god lat him never thee!"
>
> (from "The Nonne Preestes Tale," page 570)

From the Pages of
The Canterbury Tales

(In modern English. See Chaucer's original Middle English on previous page.)

When April with his showers sweet
The drought of March has pierced to the root,
And rain, like virtue
Made those flowers grow;
When West Wind with his sweet breath has
Blown through every wood and heath
The tender buds, and the young sun
In Aries has his half-course run;
And little birds make melody,
That sleep all night with open eye—
So pricks them Nature in their souls—
Then folks yearn to go on pilgrimages.
                              (from "The General Prologue," page 3)

You may be sure that this Palamon
In his fighting was an enraged lion,
And as a cruel tiger was Arcita;
They proceeded to smite like wild boars
That froth white with foam in wild anger.
Up to the ankle fought they in their blood.
                              (from "The Knight's Tale," page 89)

"You shall no more, through your flattery,
Cause me to sing and close my eyes.
For he who blinks when he should look,
All willfully, may God not give him luck!"
                              (from "The Nun's Priest's Tale," page 571)

The
CANTERBURY TALES

Geoffrey Chaucer

In Original Chaucerian English with a Facing-Page
Modern Translation by Peter Tuttle

Selected, with an Introduction and Notes
by Robert W. Hanning

George Stade
Consulting Editorial Director

JB
BARNES & NOBLE CLASSICS
NEW YORK

JB

BARNES & NOBLE CLASSICS

NEW YORK

Published by Barnes & Noble Books
122 Fifth Avenue
New York, NY 10011

www.barnesandnoble.com/classics

Geoffrey Chaucer worked on his *Canterbury Tales* from 1386 or 1387 until his death in 1400. The current edition presents Chaucer's original English, as edited by W. W. Skeat (Clarendon Press, 1900), and a new, modern English translation by Peter Tuttle.

Published in 2007 by Barnes & Noble Classics with new modern English translation, Introduction, A Note on the Text and the Translation, Notes, Biography, Chronology, Inspired By, Comments & Questions, and For Further Reading.

The Canterbury Tales
ISBN-13: 978-1-59308-080-8
ISBN-10: 1-59308-080-8
LC Control Number 2006937723

Produced and published in conjunction with:
Fine Creative Media, Inc.
322 Eighth Avenue
New York, NY 10001

Michael J. Fine, President and Publisher

Printed in the United States of America

WCM

7 9 11 13 15 14 12 10 8

Geoffrey Chaucer

Geoffrey Chaucer, author of one of the greatest—and earliest—poems written in English, was born in London in the early 1340s. His father was a successful vintner and deputy chief butler to King Edward III. Little is known of Chaucer's early years. He most likely attended a grammar school but did not study at a university. He learned Latin and French, and perhaps some Italian, the latter probably from wine traders with whom his father did business. Around 1356 he became a page in the household of Elizabeth, countess of Ulster and wife of Lionel, one of Edward III's sons.

In 1359 Chaucer journeyed to France in the service of Prince Lionel and Edward III on one of the many campaigns fought during the Hundred Years' War; when Chaucer was captured, Edward provided the money for his ransom. Little is known of Chaucer during the decade following his return from France. In the early 1360s he entered Edward III's household as a yeoman and soon became an esquire; as such, he probably lived at court and performed duties for the crown. He married Philippa Roet, who was descended from a powerful family, in 1366. During the same period, Edward III awarded him a lifetime annuity, one among many Chaucer and his wife received.

Chaucer served Edward III, John of Gaunt, and Richard II in a variety of capacities, including diplomat, justice of the peace, and translator. Beginning in 1374 he was controller of wool customs for the port of London; around this time he and his family moved into comfortable, rent-free quarters above one of London's seven city gates. He traveled frequently on royal business; in the late 1370s, during a trip to Italy, he may have obtained copies of the works of Dante, Boccaccio, and Petrarch.

Possibly in response to political pressures, Chaucer resigned his position as controller of customs and left his London apartment in 1386; that same year he was elected to Parliament from the county of Kent, and in 1387 his wife is reported to have died. In 1391 he retired to Kent, presumably to write. A year or two before his death, he returned to London to live.

Chaucer is thought to have begun *The Canterbury Tales*, his masterpiece, in the late 1380s. While he drew on French and Italian forms of prose, and on the work of Dante, Ovid, and Virgil, his poetry was innovative—written in his native tongue, while most writers of the day composed in Latin or French. He produced some of the most renowned verse in the history of the English language, particularly in *The Canterbury Tales*. Geoffrey Chaucer died in 1400 and was buried in Westminster Cathedral.

masterpiece, in the late 1380s. While he drew on French and Italian forms of prose, and on the work of Dante, Ovid, and Virgil, his poetry was innovative—written in his native tongue, while most writers of the day composed in Latin or French. He produced some of the most renowned verse in the history of the English language, particularly in *The Canterbury Tales*. Geoffrey Chaucer died in 1400 and was buried in Westminster Cathedral.

Geoffrey Chaucer

Geoffrey Chaucer, author of one of the greatest—and earliest—poems written in English, was born in London in the early 1340s. His father was a successful vintner and deputy chief butler to King Edward III. Little is known of Chaucer's early years. He most likely attended a grammar school but did not study at a university. He learned Latin and French, and perhaps some Italian, the latter probably from wine traders with whom his father did business. Around 1356 he became a page in the household of Elizabeth, countess of Ulster and wife of Lionel, one of Edward III's sons.

In 1359 Chaucer journeyed to France in the service of Prince Lionel and Edward III on one of the many campaigns fought during the Hundred Years' War; when Chaucer was captured, Edward provided the money for his ransom. Little is known of Chaucer during the decade following his return from France. In the early 1360s he entered Edward III's household as a yeoman and soon became an esquire; as such, he probably lived at court and performed duties for the crown. He married Philippa Roet, who was descended from a powerful family, in 1366. During the same period, Edward III awarded him a lifetime annuity, one among many Chaucer and his wife received.

Chaucer served Edward III, John of Gaunt, and Richard II in a variety of capacities, including diplomat, justice of the peace, and translator. Beginning in 1374 he was controller of wool customs for the port of London; around this time he and his family moved into comfortable, rent-free quarters above one of London's seven city gates. He traveled frequently on royal business; in the late 1370s, during a trip to Italy, he may have obtained copies of the works of Dante, Boccaccio, and Petrarch.

Possibly in response to political pressures, Chaucer resigned his position as controller of customs and left his London apartment in 1386; that same year he was elected to Parliament from the county of Kent, and in 1387 his wife is reported to have died. In 1391 he retired to Kent, presumably to write. A year or two before his death, he returned to London to live.

Chaucer is thought to have begun *The Canterbury Tales*, his

Table of Contents

The World of Geoffrey Chaucer and The Canterbury Tales

1340– 1345	Geoffrey Chaucer is born in London, the son of John Chaucer, a prominent wine importer, and his wife, Agnes.
1346	The English triumph at Crecy, one of many bloody battles fought between England and France during the Hundred Years' War.
1348– 1349	The Black Death (the plague) sweeps through England, reportedly killing one-third of the population.
1349– 1351	Giovanni Boccaccio writes the *Decameron*.
1356	The English are victorious at the battle of Poitiers; Edward III captures the French king, John II.
1357	The first known mention of Chaucer is a record of a purchase of clothing, possibly suggesting he was a page in the household of Elizabeth, countess of Ulster and wife of Lionel, the second son of Edward III.
1359– 1360	Chaucer serves in the English army and travels to the battlefields of France with Edward III and his sons, including the eldest, known as the Black Prince.
1360	Chaucer is captured by the French and held for ransom until he is released for the sum of £16; Edward III provides the sum. With the Treaty of Brétigny, England establishes peace with France that will last nine years.
1361– 1362	The plague returns, again devastating the population. Wages for laborers increase, as there are more jobs available than workers to perform them. The use of English in courts of law is formalized.
1366	Chaucer marries Philippa Roet. His father dies.
1367	Chaucer is given a lifetime annuity of £20 per year by Edward III. Chaucer will serve the royal household in various capacities until his death. His son, Thomas, is born. Richard II, the son of the Black Prince, is born.
c.1367– 1370	William Langland's *Piers Plowman* appears.

1368   Chaucer travels overseas on royal missions, perhaps to France or Italy.

1369–
1372   Chaucer writes *The Book of the Duchess*, an elegy for Blanche of Lancaster, who died in 1368. Edward III's wife, Queen Philippa, dies. A third major plague spreads throughout England.

1370   John Lydgate, a writer remembered as an imitator of Chaucer, is born.

1371   John of Gaunt, another son of Edward III and Blanche of Lancaster's widower, marries Constance of Castile. Philippa Chaucer serves in their household.

1372   Chaucer makes his first known journey to Italy on a diplomatic mission.

1374   Chaucer moves to Aldgate and is appointed the port of London's controller of customs for wool, skins, and hides. King Edward awards Chaucer a gallon pitcher of wine daily for life for loyal service. Petrarch dies.

1375   Boccaccio dies.

1376   The Black Prince dies.

1377   Edward III dies, and Richard II becomes king. Chaucer makes several top-secret journeys to France on behalf of Richard II to negotiate for peace. The first poll tax is instituted.

1378   Chaucer travels to Milan on a diplomatic mission to see the Lord of Milan, Bernabo Visconti. Their meeting inspires Chaucer to include Visconti as a tragic figure in "The Monk's Tale."

1378–
1381   Chaucer's comic poem *The House of Fame* appears. He also writes *Palamon and Arcita*, a poem based on Boccaccio's *Teseida* that is later adapted to become "The Knight's Tale."

1380   Cecily Champain accuses Chaucer of rape, then settles with him out of court. Chaucer begins writing *Troilus and Criseyde*, a tragic love story set against the backdrop of the Trojan War.

1381   In honor of the King's upcoming marriage, Chaucer writes *The Parliament of Fowls*, a dream-vision poem in which a group of birds choose their mates. He begins to write *Boece*, a translation of Roman philosopher Boethius' *The*

Consolation of Philosophy. Workers of various economic and social strata gather in London to protest the poll tax; this civilian rebellion, known as the Great Rising or the Peasants' Revolution, causes extensive damage and upheaval.

1382   Richard II marries Anne of Bohemia. John Wycliffe translates the Bible into English.

1385   French poet Eustache Deschamps praises Chaucer for his skill as a translator. Chaucer becomes justice of the peace for the county of Kent.

1386   He resigns from his customs duties and serves as a member of Parliament for Kent. He begins writing *The Legend of Good Women*, a collection of stories that will remain unfinished.

1387   Around this time, Chaucer begins writing *The Canterbury Tales*. Opponents of Richard II, known as the Lords Appellant, curtail the King's authority. Several of the King's supporters, including poet Thomas Usk, are executed.

1389   Richard II appoints Chaucer clerk of the King's Works.

1390   Chaucer supervises the building of the scaffolding to be used for the Smithfield jousts.

1394   Richard II awards Chaucer an annuity of £20 per year.

1396   John of Gaunt marries his longtime mistress, Katherine Swynford, Philippa Chaucer's sister.

1399   Richard II is deposed, and Henry Bolingbroke accedes to the throne as Henry IV. John of Gaunt dies.

1400   Geoffrey Chaucer dies, leaving *The Canterbury Tales* unfinished, and is buried at Westminster Abbey.

Introduction

Geoffrey Chaucer's *Canterbury Tales* is undeniably one of the English language's greatest literary achievements. However, despite the apparent accessibility of many of its unforgettable characters, and the continued relevance of some of its main themes and concerns, this collection of tales, ostensibly told to each other by a group of late-fourteenth-century English pilgrims while on their way to the shrine of Saint Thomas Becket at Canterbury, offers the twenty-first-century reader many problems of interpretation and understanding; among these, its (to us) archaic language is perhaps the least formidable. The following pages, after a brief rehearsal of information about Chaucer's life, times, social placement, and other works, will consider some of the major critical questions that have swirled around the form and content of *The Canterbury Tales* during the last century or so and propose, however hesitantly, answers to some of them.

Life and Times

Chaucer was born in London in the early 1340s, the son of a prosperous vintner (wine merchant). With its population of 50,000 (the largest in England but small compared to Paris, Florence, or Venice), London had recently established itself as the commercial, intellectual, and cultural capital of the English kingdom; its port was a major center of wool exports (England's most important product) and wine imports, and its close relations with the nearby city of Westminster (the seat of the royal government and its national legal and financial bureaucracy) gave it additional prominence because of its political and economic importance to the monarchy.

Men such as Chaucer's father were entrepreneurs who tended to trade in any commodities that offered profits; in London, as in the other major cities of the realm, they formed an oligarchy exercising, through their associations, or guilds, predominant authority in the political life of the city. One of the consequences (and sources) of London merchants' power was their often close relations with the king, to whose court they were purveyors of victuals and luxury goods (including spices from the East), and to whom they sometimes lent money for use in his prosecution of the war with France (the so-called Hundred Years' War) over his supposed right to the French throne as well as his own.

It is presumably as a result of such contacts that John Chaucer, Geoffrey's father, obtained for his son around 1356 a place, probably as a page (a quite menial servant), in the household of Elizabeth, countess of Ulster and wife of Lionel, second surviving son of King Edward III (1327–1377). Before this, Chaucer was presumably educated in one of London's many "grammar schools" attached to parish churches or other religious establishments; and perhaps at the Almonry School attached to Saint Paul's Cathedral (near Chaucer's presumed home on Thames Street). He did not attend university, although several of his works make it clear that he knew the town and schools of Oxford and Cambridge well. He also knew Latin, French (both the continental variety and the "insular," Anglo-French variety, the latter used for legal purposes), and presumably some Italian, which he could have learned from the many Italian merchants with whom his father probably had business dealings.

In 1359 Chaucer became a *valettus* (yeoman) in Prince Lionel's service; in that capacity he fought in the latter's army in France, where he was captured in battle and ransomed in March 1360. Sometime after the end of 1360 he passed into the King's household, first as a yeoman but later in the decade attaining the higher rank of esquire, along with a life annuity (a standard reward for services rendered). By 1366 he was married to Philippa, a member of the Queen's household, and in the following year a son, Thomas, was born. In royal service—to the King, to John of Gaunt, duke of Lancaster, and perhaps to Edward III's eldest son, the Black Prince—Chaucer made repeated trips abroad in the coming years, on public and secret diplomatic missions, to France, Spain, and Italy, while also participating in court life and entertainments in England. He was dispatched to Genoa and Florence on royal business at the end of 1372, and spent several months in Italy, where he is often thought by modern scholars to have met Boccaccio and Petrarch, or at least become familiar with many of their works.

In 1374 Chaucer was appointed controller of wool customs for the port of London, a civil service position that he held for the next twelve years; at the same time he received a rent-free lifetime lease on spacious quarters above Aldgate, one of London's seven cit gates, and a further annuity from John of Gaunt, in honor of whose dead wife, Blanche, he had written *The Book of the Duchess* (see below). At the time Chaucer's wife was a member of the household of John's new wife, Constance of Castille, a situation in which she continued until her death in 1387.

Chaucer's job as controller was to keep an accurate record of wool and other goods being exported, in order to ensure that that accurate duties on them might be charged by the collectors of customs. These worthies tended to be rich and powerful London merchants (many became lord mayors) who obtained their positions as favors from the king, and did not hesitate to use them for personal profit, a situation that put the much less powerful controller in an awkward position. Halfway through his term as controller Chaucer became involved in a court case that has created controversy among modern Chaucerians: In May 1380 Cecily Champain released Chaucer from all legal reprisals concerning her *raptus*. Other court documents and debts called in by Chaucer at this time suggest an expensive settlement, but the actual details of the rape (for that, not abduction, is what the Latin term means in this legal context) are lost.

From time to time, Chaucer was temporarily excused from the obligations of his controller's position to make further trips abroad on royal business, some in connection with peace negotiations with France and Richard's search for a suitable wife. On a second (at least) trip to Italy in 1378, he may have spent time in the Visconti library in Milan, and there obtained copies of works by Dante, Petrarch, and Boccaccio.

The 1380s were a decade of major political tensions and upheavals in London and in England as a whole. The merchant oligarchy that controlled London politics was challenged (successfully for a time) by an alliance of lesser guilds led by John of Northampton. In 1381 there was the Great Rising (formerly known as the Peasants' Revolution), a mass and often violent protest by peasants, urban artisans, and minor gentry against the radically unequal distribution of power and resources in English society. In the latter part of the decade, frequent threats of French invasion agitated Londoners. Above all, young King Richard II (Edward III's grandson, who had inherited the throne at age eleven) was caught up in power struggles with Parliament and with several of the great barons of the realm. The climax came in 1387 and 1388, when Richard was almost deposed by an alliance of his opponents, the so-called Lords Appellant (that is, accusers), who, acting in conjunction with Parliament, managed to have several of the King's friends and confidants (some of whom were also Chaucer's friends or associates) executed, and others exiled and stripped of their lands.

Chaucer's reputation as a poet grew during the 1380s, both at court and in the London literary circles in which he doubtless also moved (more about this shortly). The French poet Eustache Deschamps praised him as a "grand translateur," and his London contemporary Thomas Usk called him a "noble philosophical poet." Concurrently, in what might be seen as the height of his public career, Chaucer was elected to the Commons in the so-called Wonderful Parliament of October–November 1386. In a session that initiated some of the anti-Ricardian legislation mentioned above, Parliament also requested (without success) that controllers of customs appointed for life be removed from office and no further life appointments made; shortly after the session ended, Chaucer resigned his position as controller of customs and vacated his Aldgate residence. It is hard not to see this as a precautionary move, though some scholars regard the timing as coincidental and see the decision as no more than a sign that Chaucer was tired of a time-consuming job and wanted to live in the country. Since 1385 he had been serving as a justice on the commission of the peace for the county of Kent, which investigated and prosecuted minor crimes and offenses.

In 1388 Chaucer sold the rights to his annuities, perhaps to repay debts (he was sued for debt more than once in this period) or simply because the "Merciless Parliament" of 1388 attacked the practice of granting life annuities as part of its campaign against Richard's supposed malfeasance. Chaucer's return to royal service, and a regular stipend, came in May 1389, when he was appointed clerk of the King's Works, responsible for the building and repair of royal properties, an important and demanding job that involved obtaining building materials and paying contractors, supervisory craftsmen, and laborers. Relieved of this position in June 1391, he retired to Kent, presumably to continue work on *The Canterbury Tales*, which most scholars believe he had begun in the late 1380s. From 1394 onward his financial situation improved due to grants from the crown (presumably rewards for past service), and in 1398 he may have moved back to London; it is certain that late in 1399, not long a

Richard's deposition by Henry Bolingbroke (Henry IV), he leased a house on the grounds of Westminster Abbey and had his latest annuity from Richard renewed by Henry (who also gave Chaucer a substantial gift, perhaps, as has been suggested, because he recognized the potential usefulness of a well-known poet to his new and shaky reign). Chaucer died the following year—probably on October 25, 1400—and was buried in Westminster Abbey. In 1556 his remains were moved to their present tomb, and the area surrounding his burial spot became known as Poets' Corner.

Audience and Sources

Chaucer moved in several milieux during his adult life, among them the royal court at Westminster; the mercantile world of the London docks and customs houses; and the literate cohort of court functionaries (household knights and squires, many of whom Chaucer knew well), government clerks (of chancery, the exchequer, and the law courts), scribes, notaries, lawyers, and men of letters that probably formed his most challenging, and preferred, audience. To many such listeners or readers of Chaucer's poetry, themselves placed peripherally or ambiguously with respect to major centers of power or patronage, the ironies, obliquities, and downright silences that distinguish the Chaucerian narrative voice might strike a familiar, self-preserving, and deferential chord.

The poetry that Chaucer created for his varied audiences reveals wide knowledge and keenly honed appropriative skills. He was thoroughly conversant in the lyric and narrative forms of French court poetry; he is the earliest known English poet to have been familiar with, and to adapt, texts written by the three great Tuscan authors, Dante, Petrarch, and Boccaccio. He translated or paraphrased several Latin texts of classical antiquity, and was also familiar with influential medieval-Latin philosophical poetry. His knowledge of insular literature in English (his own natal tongue) was expectably great if not always respectful: The jogging meters of Middle English popular romances are the butt of the poetic joke in the tedious tale of Sir Thopas,* told by Chaucer's alter ego, the narrator of *The Canterbury Tales*. Whatever he borrowed from another language or culture he stamped in his poetry with the unmistakable marks of

---

*This tale and others marked with an asterisk do not appear in this edition.

Chaucerian style: wit, complexity, and what the late E. Talbot Donaldson characterized as a habitual "elusion of clarity."

Canon

That Chaucer wrote almost entirely in English for the audiences I have enumerated above suggests the headway that English (marginalized socially, intellectually, and politically after the Norman Conquest of England in 1066) had made by the later fourteenth century in being accepted as a medium for serious expression in a wide range of cultural situations. French had been considered the language of genteel society for almost three centuries after the Conquest, although even the upper nobility was English-speaking within a few generations of that event, and French (in its insular form, commonly known as Anglo-Norman) was increasingly a language that had to be learned, as opposed to spoken from birth. In Chaucer's day French continued to be the language of legal and Parliamentary written records, and Latin the language of the Church and higher education, but both tongues were increasingly invaded by the vocabulary and syntax of the language native to everyone born in England.

Chaucer's first substantial poetic efforts are innovative versions of an established French literary form, the dream vision, in which a narrator, while dreaming, observes or takes part in discussions or debates about love among characters who may be allegorical abstractions (Youth, Age, Beauty, Pride, etc.) or who may represent, in idealized form, powerful noble folk who are the poet's patrons and members of their court. *The Book of the Duchess*, written around 1369 to honor Blanche, the recently deceased duchess of Lancaster, offers stylized sympathy and consolation to her husband, John of Gaunt (who later granted Chaucer a life annuity, possibly in thanks for the poem). *The House of Fame*, written in the late 1370s, inspired by the poet's reading of Virgil, Ovid, and Dante, stresses comedy rather than pathos in depicting the arbitrary and amoral judgments handed down by the goddess Fame; it is a cynical commentary on the untrustworthiness of all communication—especially by poets. In *The Parliament of Fowls* (written around 1381), birds of all kinds meet on Saint Valentine's day to choose mates, and in their arguments demonstrate the stereotypical ideas that people (here represented as birds) have of each other.

Abandoning the dream vision, between 1380 and 1386 Chaucer composed *Troilus and Criseyde*, his most fully realized poetic achievement. Set against the background of the Trojan War, the poem depicts a passionate and ultimately tragic love affair. Chaucer created in Criseyde a woman whose complexity of character and motive has fascinated and disturbed modern readers. She may also have disturbed some of Chaucer's contemporaries, or at least he pretended that she did, for in *The Legend of Good Women*—a collection of short tales about women betrayed by men, preceded by a prologue in the form of a dream vision—the poet must defend himself against an angry God of Love (depicted as a king, sharing some traits with Chaucer's sovereign, Richard II), who accuses him of slandering women by his portrait of Criseyde. After (or while) composing the unfinished *Legend*, Chaucer began writing *The Canterbury Tales*.

Problems: Unity, Coherence, Authenticity

The twenty-first-century reader of *The Canterbury Tales* experiences Chaucer's tale collection in a manner very different from any the poet could have imagined. What we read today in carefully prepared printed editions may not correspond to what Chaucer wanted his poem to look like; indeed, it seems doubtful that he even had a final plan for its contents and order. He probably began to compose a collection of tales quite different from the monothematic, classically oriented stories comprising *The Legend of Good Women*—but like it, a collection headed by a considerable prologue—sometime in the late 1380s, before or after he left London for Kent. How long he worked on *The Canterbury Tales* is unknown—perhaps until illness or death interrupted his labors, but he may have abandoned the project much earlier. Other unanswerable questions: Did he ever really contemplate writing 120 tales, as is implied by the Host's suggestion to the Canterbury-bound pilgrims that each of the thirty travelers tell two tales on the road to the shrine and two more on the way back to the celebratory dinner at his inn, the Tabard? (Elsewhere in the framing fiction there are suggestions that one tale will suffice from each pilgrim.) And how many of the tales had been written and either circulated in writing or performed orally before the poet had the idea of incorporating them within a frame? (A list of his works included by Chaucer in the prologue to the *Legend* suggests that "The Knight's Tale" and "The Second Nun's Tale of Saint Cecilia"* preexisted the *Canterbury* collection, and various scholars have conjectured an earlier composition for a number of others.)

What modern presentations of *The Canterbury Tales* hide behind their neatness and precision is the state in which Chaucer's *Canterbury* project actually comes down to us. More than eighty extant manuscripts contain all or part of the text; each has variants and errors because, as with all textual reproduction before the invention of printing, manuscripts were copied one at a time by scribes in differing states of attentiveness or fatigue. Scholars have been unable to work out a system that organizes the manuscripts in such a way as to discover, behind all the variant readings, exactly what Chaucer wrote.

Only one manuscript of *The Canterbury Tales* (the so-called Hengwrt manuscript, now in the National Library of Wales) may date from Chaucer's lifetime; it contains a highly accurate text but lacks a tale (that of the Canon's Yeoman) and several passages linking tales that appear in other manuscripts written within a decade of Chaucer's death. The most famous manuscript, and until recently the one accorded highest authority because of its completeness and illustrations of all the pilgrims, is the Ellesmere manuscript, now in the Huntington Library in San Marino, California. What emerges from these and other manuscripts is that Chaucer gathered many of the tales into groups, or fragments, by means of interstitial dialogue between the pilgrims. There is no agreed order for these fragments, and some manuscripts omit genuine linking dialogues, while others contain obviously spurious links. So except for the first fragment (containing the so-called "General Prologue," the Knight's, Miller's, and Reeve's tales, and the Cook's unfinished tale*—which comes first in all manuscripts that contain it), we cannot be absolutely sure about how Chaucer intended to order his stories—if indeed he ever settled on an order or, for that matter, on a text. All the evidence suggests that when he died, or abandoned work on *The Canterbury Tales*, he left behind piles of papers containing versions of the tales, but that he had also, during his years of composing them, circulated individual stories among his readership that he may later have revised, leaving different versions in circulation to be copied after his death into the manuscripts we now possess. It follows that a cloud of uncertainty, varying in extent and density, must hang over all critical judgments about the meaning and effect of this radically incomplete, but still quite brilliant, collection of tales within their framing fiction.

Analysis

The *Canterbury Tales* as we possess it contains twenty-four tales—some incomplete—gathered into ten fragments (at least according to the Ellesmere text), headed by a prologue that establishes the pilgrimage to Canterbury as the occasion for a tale-telling contest, and offers the narrator's more or less detailed descriptions of almost all the pilgrims. The tales themselves fall into a wider variety of story types than is characteristic of other European tale collections Chaucer may have known, including Boccaccio's *Decameron*: saints' lives, miracle stories, romances of various types, pathetic tales of victimized women, fortune tragedies, fabliaux (brief, irreverent, and often sexually explicit tales mocking marriage, the Church, and all social ranks), even an animal fable. There are two long prose tales: one an allegory opposing anger and prudence as bases for political action, the other (not really a tale at all) a concluding exercise in the dominant late-medieval discourse of penance and confession, attributed to one of the priests on the pilgrimage, but considered by some scholars a separate Chaucerian text that accidentally became attached to *The Canterbury Tales* after the poet's death. Appended to "The Parson's Tale"* is a statement of retraction in which Chaucer, speaking in some version of his own voice, expresses regret for the irreligious nature of much of his poetry and prays for forgiveness; it too has been judged by some a mistaken addition.

Chaucer's treatment of *The Canterbury Tales*' framing fiction is as innovative as the variety of literary genres it encloses and interconnects. He uses the frame to expose social and political tensions that are manifested in interpersonal rivalries and in resistance to the authority of the self-appointed "monarch" of the pilgrimage, Harry Bailly, innkeeper of the Tabard Inn, from which the pilgrimage begins and to which, thanks to Harry's intervention, it will return. In this way, Chaucer shapes frame and tales into a social model of ongoing competition for success and mastery.

The key to the dramatic impact of *The Canterbury Tales* is to be found succinctly stated in these lines from early in "The General Prologue," initial component of Fragment I: "At night was come in-to that hostelrye / Wel nyne and twenty in a companye / Of sondry folk, by aventure y-falle / In felawshipe, and pilgrims were they alle" (p. 2; see translation on facing page). The characters who will tell Chaucer's tales are "sondry"—that is, of widely differing ranks and professions or trades—and they have come together accidentally, united solely by their decision (or, as the poem more precisely puts it, their shared desire: "Than longen folk to goon on pilgrimages"; p. 2). Hence no ties of class solidarity and antecedent friendship or association bind them. The mix of personalities and statuses (soon to be described by the narrator) is potentially volatile, and the match to set it ablaze is supplied by the Host of the Tabard when he suggests to his guests that since they will undoubtedly pass the time on their journey by telling stories and playing games, they can increase the pleasure derivable from storytelling by making a contest out of it, the winner to receive a free meal "at our aller cost" (p. 42)—not just Harry's—on their return to the Tabard. He will accompany them in order to serve as judge of the tales told, and anyone who disobeys or challenges him "shal paye al that we spenden by the weye" (p. 42), a heavy penalty indeed.

Harry's ostensibly friendly suggestion, and volunteering of himself as judge, has political and economic dimensions the burly innkeeper does not acknowledge. Southwark, the suburb across London Bridge (later home to Shakespeare's Globe Theatre), was a rowdy place of brothels, bearbaiting, and bars; there was plenty of competition for travelers on their way to Canterbury, and by proposing his storytelling contest to the pilgrims, the Host is obviously thinking about how he can secure the custom of this group, as a group, after the conclusion of their pilgrimage. By installing himself as leader and judge, whose word is law, Harry is also transforming a "felawshipe" into a de facto monarchy (hence comparable, however obliquely, to Chaucer's England under its embattled ruler, Richard II).

That the Host, though only an urban bourgeois, will prove a monarch who embraces both narrative and social decorum becomes clear when, after the conclusion of the first tale (told by the Knight, the highest-ranking secular pilgrim), he asks the Monk,* an analogously respectable Churchman, to tell the next story, "sumwhat, to quyte with the Knightes tale" (p. 166)—that is, a tale as elevated in style and subject as its predecessor (albeit presumably on a religious subject). ("Quyte" can mean to pay back, redeem, achieve balance, or get even, depending on the context.) But at this point the social and rhetorical journey of *The Canterbury Tales* turns sharply in new directions. Robin, the drunken Miller, insists on speaking next and, in response to the Host's articulation of his program for the tale-telling contest: "Abyd, Robin, my leve brother, / Som bettre man shal telle us first another" (p. 166), calls the latter's bluff by asserting that he will speak now or leave the company. Harry, in a pinch more businessman than king, gives in rather than lose a customer, and the result torpedoes his proposed top-down telling order; the Miller, who has already announced, "I can a noble tale for the nones, / With which I wol now quyte the Knightes tale" (p. 166), brings class-based anger into the pilgrimage, expressed via the discursive weapon of corrosive irony: His sarcastic descriptor, "noble tale," echoes, and in echoing mocks, the earlier reported judgment of the pilgrims (but especially of the "gentils everichoon," those far above the Miller in status) that the Knight has told "a noble storie, / And worthy for to drawen to memorie" (p. 166). His rejoinder will be anything but noble in content, and with it he will "quyte" the Knight's epic romance of classical antiquity, not by matching it, but by exposing to ridicule its pretensions and class biases.

The Miller announces that he will tell a "legende and a lyf" of how a clerk cuckolded a carpenter, a raunchy fabliau with blasphemous echoes of the Gospel narrative of Joseph and Mary, "a Carpenter, and . . . his wyf" (p. 166). But another pilgrim, the Reeve (an estate manager who is also a carpenter by craft) becomes incensed at what he perceives to be an insult to women and to himself. He confronts the Miller, who rebuffs the attack with more vicious humor, this time equating the divine providence ("goddes privetee") with the private parts of a wife and arguing facetiously that a husband should not attempt to know too much about either, as long as he has access to "goddes foyson" ("God's bounty") on both fronts.

By this point it is clear that the tale-telling competition proposed and refereed by Harry Bailly has metamorphosed into a contest of a very different, much less sociable nature. Language has begun to demonstrate its capacity to annoy and destroy as well as to create and delight, and its availability as an instrument of both inter-class warfare (Miller versus Knight, in a dim and discreet echo of the Great Rising of 1381) and intra-class rivalry (the respective positions of Millers and Reeves within the manorial economy would tend to make them frequent opponents, though both of humble status). As important, tale-telling will receive its impetus not only, or even primarily, from the choices of the pilgrimage's "monarch," but also from the desire or need of one pilgrim to reply to inaccuracies or insults perceived in another's story; tale follows tale not as a manifestation of social decorum but as an ongoing process of reception, interpretation, judgment, and reciprocation.

I have thus far omitted from this analysis of Fragment I of *The Canterbury Tales* the role of the narrator, which is crucial to the process I have outlined because it is through the narrator's act of supposedly memorial reconstruction that we know what we do about the status, character, and appearance of his fellow pilgrims: "Whiche they weren, and of what degree; / And eke in what array that they were inne" (p. 4). The series of "portraits" of the pilgrims are perhaps the single most famous part of the poem, and it is important to state at once that they are not portraits drawn from life—not, that is, descriptions of Chaucer's contemporaries as he carefully observed them in their respective professional, vocational, or artisanal capacities. Instead the portraits enact something more complex: The narrator's "erotics of memory"—that is, his recollection of particular things he especially liked or disliked about the pilgrims—fitted into an overall taxonomy of "estates" (social statuses) that he (and behind him Chaucer the poet) gleaned from the popular literary form called "estates satire," which purported to reveal and excoriate the characteristic vices (or, less often, praise the ideal virtues) of the different estates. The problem with the narrator's descriptions is that they sometimes reveal the erotics of memory and the classifications of estates satire pulling in opposite directions (as, for example, with the Monk,* Prioress, and Friar, all of whom the narrator likes while giving us abundant, if stereotypical, reasons why he, and we, should not). To complicate matters further, characters such as the Monk,* Friar, Pardoner, and Wife of Bath show signs of being themselves thoroughly familiar with the accusations directed at their respective cohorts by estates satire, and of gleefully mouthing or enacting them in a spirit of holiday fun, or to outrage the simple souls who take seriously such categorizations. One effect of the portraits in "The General Prologue" is to impose on us a double task of interpretation: On the one hand we're invited to judge the pilgrims, and on the other to judge the narrator's representation of them, to seek out inconsistencies and obvious instances where attraction (for example, to the Prioress' dainty mouth) or repulsion (such as to the Miller's big mouth and the wart on the tip of his nose) support or subvert estates satire commonplaces.

So much for the frame into which Chaucer put the opening tales of his collection. The tales themselves form a brilliant sequence featuring radically different narrative styles and social points of view, but also thematic interconnections and a progressive revelation of language's efficacy as an instrument of mastery in a competitive world. "The Knight's Tale," based on Boccaccio's early epic romance *Il Teseida*, is a serious meditation on the uses and limits of unfettered political power when it is threatened by external enemies, by the irrationality of erotic passion, by the unpredictable, irresistible actions of Fortune, and above all by the provocations to intemperate, tyrannical behavior that the just ruler must resist in exercising his authority. Theseus, duke of Athens and mighty conqueror, is faced with the dilemma of how to deal with Palamon and Arcita, two Theban princes who fall into his hands after he has defeated Creon, ruler of Thebes, and destroyed his city. The tale chronicles the continual policy adjustments he must make in attempting to solve this problem (even as the Host will have to make analogous adjustments to keep the Miller in the pilgrimage), thanks to his prisoners' being enamored with his ward, Emily, and their resultant dispute over her, which leads to escapes, disguises, potentially deadly duels, and finally, under the Duke's supervision, a tournament battle between the two lovers, each with one hundred followers, in an arena built for the occasion by Theseus. (The circumstances surrounding this battle provide the Knight an occasion to offer a distinctly nonidealized depiction of chivalry—that is, professional combat—in action.) As the tale's narrative unfolds, it contrasts the struggle between mortal anger and prudential restraint that the Duke must wage within himself with the extravagant, unrestrained rhetoric and deeds of Palamon and Arcita, whose desires and flights of eloquence about their unjust fate as Theseus' prisoners serve to emphasize both the imprudence and the powerlessness of their situation.

When the gods (representing both human passions and the universal forces that radically restrict humanity's control over its fate) thwart Theseus' plan by destroying Arcita, the tournament victor, the Duke must finally rely on language's persuasive power to achieve politically satisfactory closure. His final speech to the grieving Palamon and Emily (adapted by Chaucer from Boethius' influential, late-classical treatise *The Consolation of Philosophy*), after justifying Arcita's untimely death as the working of Divine Providence, urges the young couple to marry, thus making "of sorwes two / O parfyt joye" (p. 162)—and, in the process, insuring that the Duke will "have fully of Thebans obeisaunce" (p. 156).

The Miller's parody of "The Knight's Tale" reconceives the rivalry of Palamon and Arcita for Emily's hand as a competition— between Nicholas, a clever, fast-talking, and entirely self-interested university student, and Absolon, a dandified parish cleric with a delusory attachment to the ridiculous rituals of romantic love—for the body of Alison, beautiful and earthy young wife of John, who is Theseus reimagined as a foolish old carpenter with whom Nicholas boards in Oxford. The Knight's depiction of power politics in ancient Athens is thus reduced to a town/gown squabble in contemporary Oxford, a university town famous for such tensions. Their passion for Alison leads all three men to painful fates that the Miller clearly believes they deserve; his tale presents each as seduced not only by her but by an uncritically embraced literary genre. Gullible John's acceptance of the depiction of Noah's flood in medieval mystery plays allows Nicholas to convince him that a new flood is about to engulf the world, and that he must hang separate tubs inside the roof of his house for himself, Alison, and Nicholas, in which they will weather the storm. (Nicholas' persuasive speech parodies Theseus' more elevated but equally self-interested words to Palamon and Emily at the end of "The Knight's Tale.") Nicholas, in turn, is so enamored of the role of the tricky cleric who cuckolds unsuspecting husbands in dozens of medieval fabliaux that, after having sex with Alison in John's bed while the carpenter snores in his tub—the Miller's tart version of Theseus sitting on a high throne towering above his worshipful subjects—he can't resist improving on his scheme by sticking his buttocks out the window for Absolon to kiss, only to have them badly burned when that worthy man, frustrated and furious over having been tricked into kissing Alison's "naked ers" at the same window earlier that night, buggers Nicholas with a hot coulter (a phallus-shaped plow blade).

Absolon's mistreatment by Alison results from his assumption that he could win her by reciting plaintive love lyrics outside her bedroom; his resulting indignation leads him to forswear such "paramours" and to undertake the red-hot vengeance that constitutes one of English literature's great comic climaxes: When wounded Nicholas cries out for water, John awakes and, thinking that "Nowélis flood"

(p. 202) has come, cuts loose his tub and falls to the ground, breaking his arm.

The epic struggle in "The Knight's Tale" between ancient city-states degenerates in the Miller's hands into Oxford intergroup antagonism and stereotyping. Early in the tale, Nicholas, promising Alison that he will find a way for them to have sex without John's knowledge, declares scornfully, "A clerk had litherly biset his whyle, / But-if he coude a carpenter bigyle!" (p. 176). John returns the favor when he thinks Nicholas' (phony) coma results from his prying into "goddes privetee" (p. 184), and berates scholars for lacking the good sense of working people like himself. At the end, when the wounded John tries to tell his neighbors the truth about his fall, he is successfully contradicted by all the students present, who stick together in unanimously pronouncing the carpenter mad.

As the Miller "quytes" the Knight, so "The Reeve's Tale" enacts revenge for the latter's perceived mistreatment in the Miller's prologue and tale. A further coarsening of language results: When the Reeve is not showering words of sarcastic contempt on Simkin, the vicious, scoundrelly, and ridiculously proud miller of Trumpington, the latter is sassing his victims—Allen and John, two Cambridge students, further degraded versions of Palamon and Arcita, whom he has just cheated—by suggesting that since they must stay overnight in his narrow dwelling they should use the hocus-pocus of philosophy to make it bigger. Even Allen and John (yokels whose northern dialect Chaucer reproduces in the first known instance of English dialect comedy) respond to their misadventures by insulting each other, and when Allen decides to get even by raping the Miller's daughter, he chides his companion as a "swynes-heed" and a "coward" (p. 226) for not joining in (John then rapes the wife). When language finally yields to violence—the students beat the Miller to a pulp and get their stolen flour back—the reader feels that the descent has not been very great.

The last part of *The Canterbury Tales*, Fragment I, is the ninety-eight-line snippet of "The Cook's Tale,"* all that is extant and probably all Chaucer wrote. It's preceded by a prologue featuring a brief, sharp dialogue between the Host and the Cook, natural rivals for Southwark customers, suggesting future (if not present) "quytyng," but in the few lines of the tale that we have, its inhabitants (London low-lifes) meet to "hoppe and synge and maken swich disport" ("dance and sing and make sport") rather than tell stories; the preferred form of intercourse (because of the money it can supply) is sexual rather than verbal or commercial: As the fragment ends we learn of a wife "that heeld for countenance / A shoppe, and swyved for hir sustenaunce" ("that kept, for countenance, / A shop, and whored to gain her sustenance").

In another instance of "quytyng," the Friar and the Summoner—two clerical con men who prey on their victims by means of opportunistic preaching and flattery (the Friar) or threats of punishment by ecclesiastical courts (the Summoner, or process server)—square off with the anger of competitors, not for a free dinner but for a free ride at the expense of the gullible or the vulnerable. The Friar, a university-trained intellectual, adapts to his purpose a widely diffused preacher's parable about a notoriously predatory official (in this case a summoner, of course) who is carried off to hell by a devil because his victims really mean it when they wish him there for his crimes. To his appropriation of the medieval "theology of intention" the Friar adds a dialogue between the summoner and his diabolical companion that emphasizes the former's prying nature (necessary for one who makes a living by blackmail as well as coercion) in the way he grills the devil about his life in Hell and his methods of trapping sinners. The Friar's implication is clear: The summoner's curiosity—his meddling in other people's *pryvetee*—is setting him up for his final, infernal destination, where he will learn plenty about the wages of sin.

The Summoner's reply counters the Friar's theological language with a dose of the well-established anti-fraternal discourse that took shape in thirteenth-century Parisian university circles (where it was sponsored by opponents of mendicant scholars such as the Dominican Thomas Aquinas) and became popular among fourteenth-century critics of the increasingly worldly and prosperous fraternal orders, which originally intended to support themselves by begging. The outrageously greedy and hypocritical friar of "The Summoner's Tale" suffers a double humiliation. First, Thomas, the sick householder from whom the friar relentlessly solicits a monetary offering, farts into the latter's hand after inviting him to "grope" behind him for a gift that, however, the mendicant must share with the other eleven members of his convent. ("Grope" was a word widely applied to a priest's quizzing of a penitent in confession—"groping" his conscience in order to discover all his sins—and friars were popular confessors because, according to their detractors, they assigned easy penances in return for gifts; hence Thomas's use of the term has a satirical edge.) Thomas's angry, flatulent riposte to his tormentor sets up the friar's second comeuppance: the solution to the problem of how to divide a fart in twelve parts proposed by Jankin, a squire of the local lord to whom the friar goes to complain about his mistreatment. Jankin's ingenious suggestion, involving a cartwheel along the spokes of which the fart's sound and odor can be dispensed equally to the other members of the convent, with the friar himself occupying a privileged position at the hub of the wheel immediately below farting Thomas, has parodic overtones of Pentecost (when the gift of the Holy Spirit showed itself divided into tongues of flame over the head of each apostle), and thus makes a satiric comment on the pride taken by the mendicant orders as preachers of the Word, which, in their hypocritical mouths, becomes no better than a fart.

Several *Canterbury Tales* besides "The Knight's Tale" explore the problem of making appropriate decisions in situations where there can be no certainty about the best choice. In such cases careful deliberation, based on the wisdom to be garnered from prior experience and trustworthy counselors, leads to prudent decision-making, while imprudent choices, driven by the passions of the moment and applauded by sycophantic subordinates, can issue in folly and disaster. The long prose "Tale of Melibee"* told by the pilgrimage narrator (hence some version of Chaucer) consists of an extended dialogue between Melibee, a mighty lord outraged by an assault on his home and intent on vengeance, and his wife, Prudence, who, true to her name, argues for patience, good counsel (especially hers), and full consideration of possible consequences before Melibee takes action.

More purely narrative than the "Melibee,"* but like it seriously concerned with the processes and outcomes of decision-making by those who possess domestic or political power (and in some cases those who do not), are the tales told by the Clerk (graduate student) of Oxford, the Merchant, and the Franklin. "The Clerk's Tale" is the great enigma of *The Canterbury Tales*; its story of Griselda, the humble peasant girl chosen as wife by Walter, a rich marquis, who then brutally tests her obedience to him, even to the point of her acquiescing when she's told of his apparent murder of their young children, was one of the most widely known stories of fourteenth-century Western Europe. Each version of the story differs in how it seeks to explain Walter's behavior, his motivation for testing Griselda, and her choices in obeying him. The happy ending, in which Griselda is reunited with her children and her husband (who had also feigned divorcing her so he could marry someone of a more appropriate social rank), does nothing to efface the air of psychological mystery and extreme human imprudence that hangs over the story. In the end, the greatest mystery is whether Walter or Griselda has the greater power in their relationship—he by his ability to impose harsh trials on her, or she by her ability to endure the trials and to force him finally to suspend them.

"The Merchant's Tale" is a quasi-allegorical fable about the high price of imprudence. Lecherous old January decides to marry beautiful young May, ignoring the reservations of his counselor, Justinus, in favor of the enthusiastic support given by his time-serving lackey, Placebo (literally, "I will please"). When January cannot satisfy May sexually, she decides to accept the importunate advances of his squire, Damyan. January, long blinded by his imprudent passion, is suddenly struck literally blind and seeks, in his jealousy, to enjoy his wife in exclusivity in a beautiful walled garden he has built—a symbol of the paradise he has expected his marriage to be. But his garden harbors a serpent, Damyan, hidden by May in a tree into which she climbs with her blind husband's assistance, a symbolic enactment of how his imprudence and impercipience have contributed to his being cuckolded. The ensuing argument between the god Pluto and his consort Proserpina, improbable residents of the garden, over May's culpability leads Pluto to give January back his sight, an advantage that Proserpina immediately neutralizes by giving May the persuasive speech she needs to convince January that his restored vision in fact results from her "strugle with a man up-on a tree."

So if the tale's message is that January's imprudence makes him the certain victim of May's schemes and mendacity, it seems also to be saying that blind or sighted (that is, imprudent or prudent), men cannot escape the wiles of women (especially their verbal wiles). Justinus and Pluto know the bitter truth about women and marriage, but they cannot open January's eyes to his folly; by implication, the misogynistic, misogamous message of "The Merchant's Tale" will go similarly unheeded. This is the ultimate cynicism of the tale: Its teller has ultimately wasted his time telling it.

"The Franklin's Tale" uses the kind of short romance called a *lai Breton* (Breton lay) to pose several questions. The first is what prudent choice a wife should make when her earlier imprudence (setting a supposedly impossible task for a would-be lover in order to discourage him) comes back to torment her (when he accomplishes the task and asks for his reward)? Should she acquiesce? Refuse? Commit suicide? This leads to the second question: What prudent choice can the husband make when he learns of the wife's situation? Should he allow her to leave him, in order to fulfill her imprudent promise, or forbid her to go, thus saving his honor as her husband while simultaneously ruining hers as a breaker of contracts? The Franklin's resolution of this double dilemma reflects a point of view grounded in his social status as a wealthy, but not gently born, landholder: Acts of generosity, reflecting nobility of spirit that is not the exclusive property of any one class, can solve even the most difficult problem and, in effect, efface the contrast between prudence and imprudence, but from an idealistic, rather than a cynical, perspective. The three such acts he depicts save the chastity of Dorigen, the wife; the honor of Averagus, the husband; and the money that Aurelius, the would-be lover, had contracted to pay to the magician who accomplished, for a hefty fee, the impossible task. This improbable ending leads to the tale's last, unanswerable question: Which man (husband, lover, or magician) was the most "free" (generous)?

Having showcased domestic prudence in action, Chaucer parodies it in "The Nun's Priest's Tale," a barnyard fable about Chauntecleer, a colorful, libidinous rooster with seven hen-wives. Chauntecleer's terrifying dream (a strange animal grabs him with murderous intent) prompts a debate between himself and his number one paramour, Pertelote, over the veracity of dreams, with exemplary stories, recipies for herbal laxatives, and mutual recriminations flying thick and fast. Having rejected his wife's counsel, only to reject his own rejection out of lust for her body, Chauntecleer encounters a fox, who tricks the vain rooster by challenging him to sing as well as (that is, compete with) his dead father (eaten by the same fox). The fox is outwitted in turn by heeding some very bad advice from his captive. This is a world in which, despite immense expenditures of learning and counsel, prudence is very little in evidence.

The other tale besides that of the Nun's Priest to use avian protagonists to offer a tart commentary on human, especially domestic, relationships is that of the Manciple. There a bird distinguished by its bright plumage and ability to communicate directly with humans runs afoul of its powerful owner, Phoebus Apollo, by revealing that his wife is cuckolding him with a lover of much lower status; the distraught god kills his wife in jealous anger, too late experiences remorse for his hasty reaction, and wreaks vengeance on the tattletale by stripping him of his voice and colorful feathers. The lesson usually drawn from this exemplary tale, of which several versions exist, is not to be the bearer of bad news, even if it is true. Other obvious morals—don't take pleasure in revealing other peoples' faults; don't allow your emotions to get the better of you in ways you'll later regret; don't blame others for your own lack of self-control—seem rarely, if ever, to be drawn. Chaucer takes the cynical and incomplete nature of this tale's traditional moralization as the starting point for his placement of it within his Canterbury collection. He gives it to the Manciple, a dubiously honest purchasing agent, who, after verbally trashing another pilgrim (the helplessly drunken Cook) and being warned by the Host of the latter's potential retaliation (he could reveal some of the Manciple's shady dealings), tells the tale as a caution against plain speaking, but in a manner so parodically excessive as to make clear his scorn for the story's traditional exemplary function. Phoebus's jealous near-imprisonment of his wife (she is almost as caged as his bird) and his behavior in first killing and then idealizing her cost him our sympathy, while the bird, although speaking truth to power, does it with such obvious malice and pleasure that it too forfeits the consideration it might otherwise earn as the innocent victim of a distraught husband's misdirected violence. Along the way, the narrating Manciple reveals his misogyny, comparing women to animals in heat, and his complete disenchantment about the role of language in perpetuating class distinctions and protecting the powerful from the opprobrium they deserve for their wrongdoing: An adulterous wife of the upper classes is someone's "mistress," while her equivalent of humbler status is a mere "wench" or "lemman." His final exhortation to silence, put in the mouth of his loquacious mother, puts the seal of insincerity on the supposed moral dimension of the tale.

Various *Canterbury Tales* are connected by, but also contrasted within, shared literary types, rhetorical modes, and thematic elements. For instance, both "The Squire's Tale" and the Chaucerian narrator's "Tale of Sir Thopas"* are loosely structured adventure tales, or "romances"; they also share a dubious distinction as two of the three tales rendered incomplete thanks to interruptions by other pilgrims (the Squire by the Franklin, who clothes his disruptive move in flattering words; the narrator by the Host, who minces no words in telling the narrator, "Thy drasty ryming is nat worth a tord"). The respective matters and settings of the two tales diverge widely; the Squire evokes an "orientalized," exotic Mongolian court where rituals of courtesy familiar to all readers of French chivalric romance provide a setting for marvelous happenings and artifacts, including a ring that allows its wearer to understand animal speech and a mechanical, flying horse whose movements are governed by a kind of control panel. The Mongolian courtiers, unaware of this simple mechanism for putting the horse into orderly motion, offer a range of opinions, all irrelevant, as to the creature's nature and function; the result is a sly metaphor of the young Squire's inability, through inexperience, to shape his own miscellaneous fund of romance motifs and conventions into an effective narrative trajectory. Analogously—and with thoroughly Chaucerian irony—the poet's surrogate narrator shows his complete inability to construct a credible tale about a Flemish knight whose feminized appearance and pointless wanderings constitute Chaucer's parody of many popular English romances of his day, and also (as William Askins has recently argued) a sharp satire on the economic and military policies of a duchy (Flanders) whose rulers at that time were bitter rivals of the English monarch and English merchants.

A very different kind of romance narrative, known since classical antiquity and based on the many risks and perils inherent in Mediterranean travel and commerce, organizes "The Man of Law's Tale," in which Custance, the beautiful and pious daughter of a Roman emperor, endures hardship and victimization in places as far apart as Muslim Syria and Anglo-Saxon England, but is protected throughout her trials by the Divine Providence. The special agents of her persecution are the stereotypically cruel and jealous mothers of the two men she marries and converts to Christianity: the Syrian Sultan and the English king.

Narratives that repeatedly place a beautiful woman (like the famous Pauline of silent movie serials) in situations of great personal danger, often involving or suggesting rape, appeal to their audience by evoking feelings of compassion (and, by extension, of self-pity), but also, and less overtly, sado-masochistic responses to the spectacle of a virtuous heroine threatened with violation and destruction. The Man of Law's version of this story attempts further to manipulate its audience's response by embracing a form of rhetorical expansion quite divergent from the irrelevancies and ineptitudes of "Thopas" or "The Squire's Tale": an amalgam of apostrophe, lament, and other forms of self-conscious narratorial intrusion that demonstrates both the lawyer's forensic skill in defending his "client," Custance, against her persecutors, and the learning, wisdom, and moral stature that should (in his own opinion) earn him the storytelling prize.

"The Physician's Tale" of the Roman maiden, Virginia, killed by her father to prevent her ravishment by a lustful and corrupt judge, and "The Prioress's Tale" of an innocent Christian child brutally murdered by Jews, who object to his singing a song in praise of the Virgin as he passes through their ghetto each day on his way to and from school, share with "The Man of Law's Tale" reliance on situations of helpless, victimized virtue and a narratorial voice designed to manipulate audience emotions. The anti-Semitism and bloodthirstiness of "The Prioress's Tale"—the Jews cut the child's throat and throw him in a privy, and are themselves later punished by being torn apart by wild horses, then hung—has occasioned much controversy about Chaucer's attitude toward Jews (who had been expelled from England in 1290 and were thus not part of his normal experience) and toward his character, the Prioress, whose refined behavior (as described in her "General Prologue" portrait) may disguise strong feelings of resentment toward, and victimization by, men that surface in the sado-masochistic elements of her tale.

"The Canon's Yeoman's Tale" is absent from the earliest extant manuscript of *The Canterbury Tales*, leading some recent scholars to question its place in the Chaucer canon. It may represent a late entry into Chaucer's plan for his collection, a fact perhaps alluded to in the belated arrival among the pilgrims of the Canon and his servant, whose frantic haste to overtake the *compaignye* leaves the master so perspired as to prompt the narrator's almost admiring comment, "But it was joye for to seen him swete." The tale proper, a fairly conventional story of how a phony alchemist runs a con on a priest whose greed matches his gullibility, is preceded by two more unusual segments, an introduction and a prologue. (Unfortuntely, these have been mislabeled, respectively, "Prologue" and "Part One" [of the tale].) The former of these is a reconception of "The General Prologue" in which the narrator, instead of recalling the impression made on him by specific pilgrims over the whole course of their journey together, vividly recapitulates the appearance of Canon and Yeoman at the precise moment of their arrival on the scene and the Host's penetrating interrogation of the Yeoman, which forces the latter to confess that the initial salvo of praise he delivered to the *compaignye* on his master's behalf is a tissue of lies, since he and the Canon are failures in their alchemical quest to turn base metals into gold. His inhibitions destroyed and frustrations liberated by Harry Bailly's cross-examination, the Yeoman proceeds, in his prologue, to launch into an obsessive cataloguing of the materials (mostly noxious) among which he passes his days in the Canon's laboratory, in the process reducing himself to a barely human piece of alchemical detritus. The pandemonium of regrets and mutual accusations that ensues, according to the Yeoman, when an experiment misfires, spewing broken crockery and its contents across the room, would have strongly reminded the tale's medieval audiences of the panic and recriminations among the devils when Christ comes in glory before his Resurrection to liberate the virtuous dead from hell, a popular scene in the English mystery plays.

Perhaps the most striking feature of *The Canterbury Tales* is the "confessional" prologues that precede (and dominate) the tales told by the Wife of Bath and the Pardoner. Both these monologues contain so many outrageous and mutually inconsistent statements that making secure judgments about their speakers becomes extremely difficult. As a result, much ink has been spilled, through the twentieth century and into the twenty-first, about their motivations and moral status, and about Chaucer's goal(s) in creating them: Is the Wife of Bath a protofeminist or simply an anthology of misogynist and misogamous stereotypes? Does she represent Chaucer's indirect comment on the contention of religious reformers that women should be allowed to teach and preach, and if so, on which side of the question? Is the Pardoner a eunuch, or what we would today call a homosexual? When, after having revealed the tricks and phony relics by which he takes money from congregations, he invites the pilgrims to come and pay to kiss what are presumably those same relics, is he drunk? Or just adding a final twist to his deliberately over-the-top performance as stage villain? Or is he moved by some deep impulse of self-loathing that desires the cruel rejoinder of the Host, who proposes to cut off what the Pardoner may already lack, his "coillons"?

To ask such questions seems appropriate, even inevitable. On the other hand, to seek clear-cut answers to them risks misunderstanding, and diminishing, Chaucer's achievement. The nature of that achievement is to explore, seriously but also comically, the important role of self-construction and performance as strategies of successful participation in the competition for justification and mastery central to social existence. In creating his great prologues, Chaucer in effect anticipated the theorization of social behavior as performance in the works of sociologists such as Erving Goffman (whose books include *The Presentation of Self in Everyday Life*). Chaucer was, of course, familiar with the performative rituals and spectacles—tournaments, royal entries, coronations and crown wearings, state banquets, etc.—by which nobility and royalty constructed images of their power and hegemony. But the Wife of Bath and the Pardoner undertake their respective self-constructions and self-presentations from much less powerful and secure positions. As a woman, Alison of Bath played the game of life on a distinctly unleveled playing field; as for the Pardoner, both his body and his profession made him suspect: the first because of widely (but not universally) recognized medical and physiognomic theories that equated physical "deformity" with moral failings, and the second because the offer of indulgences (guarantees of the diminution or elimination of purgatorial suffering after death for sins committed during life) in return for acts of piety, including contributions to the building of bridges and the maintenance of hospitals, was widely regarded in late-medieval Europe as an ecclesiastical practice rife with corruption—nothing less than the selling of salvation.

The question then becomes, what are we to make of these self-constructions? Where and how, if at all, does virtuoso performance intersect with reality? This seems to me the other significant achievement of the prologues of the Wife of Bath and the Pardoner: They put the reader (or listener, if Chaucer ever read them aloud to his contemporaries) in the same position of trying to separate fact from fiction, or of discovering the psychological truths

that lie beneath the most extravagant or self-delusory masquer-
ades, which we experience in our social or professional interactions
with our friends, acquaintances, superiors, colleagues, or subordi-
nates.

It's important to realize that in crafting their pilgrimage personae
the Wife of Bath and Pardoner make use of readily available, dom-
inant discourses, as they (and the other pilgrims) do in their tales.
For example, the later, larger portion of the Wife's prologue utilizes
two major bodies of textuality—misogynist and misogamous—by
which men have justified their continuing social and political hege-
mony over women. Classical, clerical, and popular literary strands
intermingle in these discourses, and Chaucer, by putting these ste-
reotypes in the Wife's mouth, has seemed to some readers to be en-
dorsing, however playfully, their points of view. At least as likely is
the view of other critics that Alison, by constructing herself as a
compendium of male fears about female sexuality and aggressive-
ness, is enjoying the paradoxical power that such discourses unin-
tentionally grant their victims: the power to induce shock and anger
by their overt, hyperbolical embrace, in word and deed, of the sup-
posedly debilitating stereotypes. Chaucer suggests the success of this
strategy by his depiction of the responses of male pilgrims (Friar,
Clerk, Merchant, Franklin, perhaps Nun's Priest) whose tales, or
comments in links between tales, reveal their need to respond to,
and dispute, the Wife's outrageous claim to have achieved complete
mastery over her five husbands (albeit, in the case of the last one, not
without a fight).

The Pardoner's strategy is similar. Faced with the knowledge that
his physical features—high voice, lack of facial hair, glaring eyes—
suggested to adherents of physiognomic analysis an absent or de-
viant sexuality (as witnessed by the narrator's assessment in "The
General Prologue": "I trowe he were a gelding or a mare"; p. 36), he
plays with, and seeks to provoke, his fellow pilgrims by singing
"Com hider, love, to me" with the Summoner (suggesting what me-
dievals would have called a sodomitic relationship), but also claim-
ing, when he interrupts the Wife of Bath, that he was about to
marry, and then declaring, as proof of his villainy, that he will "have
a joly wenche in every toun" (p. 490). That both the Pardoner's ap-
pearance and his profession suggest an immoral character is under-
scored when the Host (who salutes him insolently as "thou bel

amy") asks him to "tel us som mirth or japes" (an off-color story), and there is an outcry from the pilgrims of upper rank—"Nay, lat him telle us of no ribaudye!"—who obviously fear the kind of filth such a man might be capable of uttering. As part of his strategy of exacerbating (and thus in a sense controlling) such negative reactions to him, the Pardoner implies that it will be a stretch for him to think of "som honest thing" to tell, and that he will need strong drink to help him!

The "honest thing" he chooses to tell in his tale is a hair-raising story of evil's self-destructive nature, the quasi-allegorical quest for Death by three young scoundrels who start out on their "pilgrimage" from a tavern and end up killing each other over a cache of gold to which they are directed by an old man whom they meet (and verbally abuse) along the way. It's fairly easy to see this story as the Pardoner's tart comment on the pilgrimage that began at the Tabard and on some of his self-righteous detractors, who have treated him as the young wastrels treat the old man who responds by sending them to their death.

But before we get to this grisly tale, which demonstrates the Pardoner's command of the exemplary stories so important to medieval preaching (especially that of the mendicants), the Pardoner performs a different kind of honesty (or fictitious honesty): an exposé of the pulpit trickery by which he defrauds gullible congregations of their hard-earned money by hawking phony relics. He does not just reveal his hypocrisy—he preaches against greed, the very sin that motivates him—he revels in it: Although a sinner, he saves others by his preaching, but that is not his intention; as long as the money rolls in, its donors can go to hell for all he cares.

In crafting the Pardoner's prologue, Chaucer synthesizes contemporary concerns about the fraudulent selling of pardons with two other areas of discontent: the traffic in false relics and the problem of sinful priests who do not practice what they preach. The last of these three abuses contributes most to the Pardoner's melodramatic "confession" of his misdeeds, and it's no surprise that Chaucer lifts the Pardoner's description of his hypocritical preaching from an established discourse on the subject that circulated in late-medieval preaching manuals and treatises, which besides offering advice on effective preaching contained warnings that such preaching required of its practitioners a virtuous life, as well as discussions about whether a priest guilty of mortal sin should be allowed in the pulpit. That the poet should have converted the manuals' warnings and condemnations into the self-description of a *Canterbury Tales* character can mean one of two things: Either Chaucer raided the discourse of the hypocritical preacher in order to give, in the Pardoner, an example of clerical villainy, or the Pardoner is himself fully conversant with the preaching manuals and from them has constructed two voices: one, that of the effective preacher (as shown in his tale); the other, that of the hypocritical, evil preacher (as shown in the prologue). By showing his mastery of both discourses, the Pardoner not only manages to upset and outrage his critics on the pilgrimage; he also makes a good case for winning the supper for the best tale. After all, he boasts that "my entente is nat but for to winne" (p. 488), which could refer not only to his quest for wealth, but also to the storytelling contest, and indeed to his ongoing battle against being physically and professionally stereotyped—or to all three.

The self-constructing performances of the Wife of Bath and the Pardoner may represent the pinnacle of Chaucer's art in *The Canterbury Tales*, but they share with many other moments in that incomplete collection of stories told on a pilgrimage that never reaches either of its announced goals—Becket's shrine or Harry Bailly's dinner table—a power to delight, engage, and mystify their readers that shows no sign of lessening more than 600 years after their author's death.

Robert W. Hanning is Professor of English at Columbia University, where he has taught since 1961. He holds degrees from Columbia and Oxford Universities, and has also taught at Yale, Princeton, Johns Hopkins, and New York University. Recipient of fellowships from the Guggenheim Foundation, the American Council of Learned Societies, and the National Endowment for the Humanities, he has published *The Vision of History in Early Britain, The Individual in Twelfth-Century Romance, The Lais of Marie de France* (co-translated with Joan Ferrante), and *Castiglione: The Ideal and the Real in Renaissance Culture* (co-edited with David Rosand), as well as many articles on Chaucer's poetry and other medieval and Renaissance subjects.

A Note on the Text
and the Translation

The Middle English text of *The Canterbury Tales* used in this edition is that of W. W. Skeat (1835–1912), the great Victorian scholar of medieval English literature. Skeat's editions of Chaucer's complete works and of many other Old and Middle English texts, including *Piers Plowman*, by Chaucer's contemporary, William Langland, established new standards of textual accuracy, thanks to the extensive study of medieval manuscripts on which they were based. A fellow of Christ's College, Cambridge, Skeat was an indefatigable worker who played a major role in the Early English Text Society, the Philological Society, and the British Academy, and in the establishment of English language and literature as subjects of serious study at the university level. He also published a widely used *Etymological Dictionary*.

—Robert W. Hanning

The American scholar Jacques Barzun once wrote that, unlike French written some 600 years ago, English of that era—that is, Chaucer's English—is still comprehensible to the modern reader.

But while it is true that, as Barzun pointed out, the structure of the language is the same, then and now, and many of the words are the same, only the most studious and patient modern reader will get the meaning of every line in Chaucer's Middle English. The spelling is different than ours, and in Chaucer every sixth or seventh word refers to something medieval and not in our modern vocabulary. The result is that, between stopping to sound out the differently spelled words and looking up those words in Chaucer that are no longer in use today, it's very slow going. In the process, we lose the poetry.

So for this modernization of Chaucer's language, I've changed all the Middle English spellings to modern English and substituted, wherever possible, words or phrases we use today for those in Chaucer we no longer recognize. What I have not tried to do is make Chaucer sound like a modern man, using modern, idiomatic speech. Many of Chaucer's lines are structured so that the key phrase or word—the word or phrase that reveals the meaning or outcome—is held back until the end of the line. To rearrange the parts of these lines would remove both the rhythmic and dramatic tension in the poetry. There is not much fun in knowing the end of the line—or story—ahead of time, especially if it has been turned from the silver or gold of rhyme and meter into a leaden paraphrase.

So what you have here, I hope, is still Chaucer, with all his brilliance, subtlety, and sense of drama, and as much of the rhythm and meter integral to it that I could conserve—but written in English readily comprehensible to the contemporary reader. I would like to think that, as you read along, enough of Chaucer's tone and feel is still present that you lose yourself in the tale, hear Chaucer speaking directly to you, and forget that it is a translation.

—Peter Tuttle

Peter Tuttle's most recent poetry is *Looking for a Sign in the West*, published by Back Shore in 2003.

The
CANTERBURY TALES

The General Prologue

Whan that Aprille with his shoures sote
The droghte of Marche hath perced to the rote,
And bathed every veyne in swich licour,
Of which vertu engendred is the flour;
Whan Zephirus eek with his swete breeth
Inspired hath in every holt and heeth
The tendre croppes, and the yonge sonne
Hath in the Ram his halfe cours y-ronne,
And smale fowles maken melodye,
That slepen al the night with open yë,
(So priketh hem nature in hir corages):
Than longen folk to goon on pilgrimages
(And palmers for to seken straunge strondes)
To ferne halwes, couthe in sondry londes;
And specially, from every shires ende
Of Engelond, to Caunterbury they wende,
The holy blisful martir for to seke,
That hem hath holpen, whan that they were seke.
　　Bifel that, in that seson on a day,
In Southwerk at the Tabard as I lay
Redy to wenden on my pilgrimage
To Caunterbury with ful devout corage,
At night was come in-to that hostelrye
Wel nyne and twenty in a companye,
Of sondry folk, by aventure y-falle
In felawshipe, and pilgrims were they alle,
That toward Caunterbury wolden ryde;
The chambres and the stables weren wyde,
And wel we weren esed atte beste.
And shortly, whan the sonne was to reste,
So hadde I spoken with hem everichon,
That I was of hir felawshipe anon,
And made forward erly for to ryse,
To take our wey, ther as I yow devyse.
　　But natheles, whyl I have tyme and space
Er that I ferther in this tale pace,
Me thinketh it acordaunt to resoun,

The General Prologue

W HEN A PRIL WITH HIS showers sweet
The drought of March has pierced to the root,
And rain, like virtue
Made those flowers grow;
When West Wind with his sweet breath has
Blown through every wood and heath
The tender buds, and the young sun
In Aries has his half-course run;
And little birds make melody,
That sleep all night with open eye—
So pricks them Nature in their souls—
Then folks yearn to go on pilgrimages,
And pilgrims for to seek strange strands,
To faraway shires in sundry lands;
And specially from every shire's end
Of England to Canterbury they wend,
The holy blissful martyr[1] for to seek,
Who helped them, when they were sick.
    So in that season on a day,
In Southwark at the Tabard[2] as I lay
Ready to wend on my pilgrimage
To Canterbury with full devout courage,
At night was come into that hostelry
Well nine and twenty in a company
Of sundry folk, by sheer chance fallen
Into fellowship, and pilgrims were they all,
Who toward Canterbury would ride.
The rooms and stables were goodsized,
And they gave us among the best.
And shortly, when the sun was to rest,
So had I spoken with them every one
That I was of their fellowship anon,[3]
And agreed early to arise,
To head out, as I say.
    But nevertheless while I have time and space,
Before I further in this tale ride,
Methinks it according to reason

3

To telle yow al the condicioun
Of ech of hem, so as it semed me,
And whiche they weren, and of what degree;
And eek in what array that they were inne:
And at a knight than wol I first biginne.

A KNIGHT ther was, and that a worthy man
That fro the tyme that he first bigan
To ryden out, he loved chivalrye,
Trouthe and honour, fredom and curteisye.
Ful worthy was he in his lordes werre,
And therto hadde he riden (no man ferre)
As wel in Cristendom as hethenesse,
And ever honoured for his worthinesse.

At Alisaundre he was, whan it was wonne;
Ful ofte tyme he hadde the bord bigonne
Aboven alle naciouns in Pruce.
In Lettow hadde he reysed and in Ruce,
No Cristen man so ofte of his degree.
In Gernade at the sege eek hadde he be
Of Algezir, and riden in Belmarye.
At Lyeys was he, and at Satalye,
Whan they were wonne; and in the Grete See
At many a noble aryve hadde he be.
At mortal batailles hadde he been fiftene,
And foughten for our feith at Tramissene
In listes thryes, and ay slayn his fo.
This ilke worthy knight had been also
Somtyme with the lord of Palatye,
Ageyn another hethen in Turkye:
And evermore he hadde a sovereyn prys.
And though that he were worthy, he was wys,
And of his port as meke as is a mayde.
He never yet no vileinye ne sayde
In al his lyf, un-to no maner wight.
He was a verray parfit gentil knight.
But for to tellen yow of his array,
His hors were gode, but he was nat gay.
Of fustian he wered a gipoun
Al bismotered with his habergeoun;

To tell you all the calling
Of each of them, so as it seemed to me,
And who they were, and of what character,
And what raiment they were in;
And at a Knight then will first begin.

　　A Knight there was,[4] and he a worthy man,
Who from the time that he first began
To ride out, he loved chivalry,
Truth and honor, freedom and courtesy.
He fought bravely in his lords' wars,
And in them had he ridden, no other man so far,
As well in Christendom as in heathen places,
And ever honored for his worthiness.

　　At Alexandria he was when it was won;
Full often time he'd sat at head of table
Above all the knights of Prussia.
In Lithuania he'd fought and in Russia,
More often than any other Christian man his rank.
In Grenada also had he been at the siege
Of Algeciras, and ridden in Benmarin.
At Ayeas was he and at Adalia
When they were won; and in the Mediterranean
At many a noble crusade had he been.
In duels to the death had he been fifteen,
And fought for our faith in Tlemecen
In tournaments thrice, and slain his foe.
This same worthy knight had been also
Sometime with the lord of Palatia,
Against another heathen in Turkey;
And evermore he had a sterling name.
And though he was brave, he was wise,
And of his manner as meek as is a maid.
He was never rude
In all his life to any sort of person.
He was a true, perfect, noble knight.
But to tell you of his attire,
His horses were good, but his clothes not bright.
Of rough cloth he wore a tunic
All ruststained by his coat of mail,

For he was late y-come from his viage,
And wente for to doon his pilgrimage.
　With him ther was his sone, a yong SQUYER,
A lovyere, and a lusty bacheler,
With lokkes crulle, as they were leyd in presse
Of twenty yeer of age he was, I gesse.
Of his stature he was of evene lengthe,
And wonderly deliver, and greet of strengthe.
And he had been somtyme in chivachye,
In Flaundres, in Artoys, and Picardye,
And born him wel, as of so litel space,
In hope to stonden in his lady grace.
Embrouded was he, as it were a mede
Al ful of fresshe floures, whyte and rede.
Singinge he was, or floytinge, all the day;
He was as fresh as is the month of May.
Short was his goune, with sleves longe and wyde.
Wel coude he sitte on hors, and faire ryde.
He coude songes make and wel endyte,
Juste and eek daunce, and wel purtreye and wryte.
So hote he lovede, that by nightertale
He sleep namore than dooth a nightingale.
Curteys he was, lowly, and servisable,
And carf biforn his fader at the table.
　A YEMAN hadde he, and servaunts namo
At that tyme, for him liste ryde so;
And he was clad in cote and hood of grene;
A sheef of pecok-arwes brighte and kene
Under his belt he bar ful thriftily;
(Wel coude he dresse his takel yemanly:
His arwes drouped noght with fetheres lowe),
And in his hand he bar a mighty bowe.
A not-heed hadde he, with a broun visage.
Of wode-craft wel coude he al the usage.
Upon his arm he bar a gay bracer,
And by his syde a swerd and a bokeler,
And on that other syde a gay daggere,
Harneised wel, and sharp as point of spere;
A Cristofre on his brest of silver shene.

For he'd no sooner returned from his voyage,
Than he set out to make his pilgrimage.
    With him there was his son, a young SQUIRE,
A lover, and a knight he would become,
With locks so curly, you'd think them curling-ironed.
Of twenty years of age he was, I guess.
Of his stature he was average height,
And wonderfully agile, and of great strength.
And he had spent some time in combat
In Flanders, Artois and Picardy,[5]
And carried himself well, for a beginner,
In hope to stand in his lady's grace.
Embroidered was he, as if a meadow
All full of fresh flowers, white and red.
Singing he was, or piping all the day;
He was as fresh as is the month of May.
Short was his gown, with sleeves long and wide.
Well could he sit a horse and well ride.
He could songs make and poetry indite,
Joust and dance, draw well and write.
So hotly he loved all through the night
He slept no more than a nightingale.
Courteous he was, humble and himself useful made,
And carved meat for his father at the table.
    A YEOMAN had he, and servants no more
At that time, for it pleased him to ride so;
And he was clad in coat and hood of green.
A sheaf of peacock-arrows sharp and bright
Under his belt he carried with care.
Well could he keep his gear:
His arrows drooped not with feathers low,
And in his hand he bore a mighty bow.
A close-cropped head had he, with a sun-browned face.
Of woodcraft he knew all the skills.
Upon his arm he bore a fine wrist guard,
And by his side a buckler and sword,
And on his other side a shining dagger,
Hafted well, and sharp as point of spear:
A silver Saint Christopher on his breast shone.

An horn he bar, the bawdrik was of grene;
A forster was he, soothly, as I gesse.
    Ther was also a Nonne, a PRIORESSE,
That of hir smyling was ful simple and coy:
Hir gretteste ooth was but by sëynt Loy;
And she was cleped madame Eglentyne.
Ful wel she song the service divyne,
Entuned in hir nose ful semely;
And Frensh she spak ful faire and fetisly,
After the scole of Stratford atte Bowe,
For Frensh of Paris was to hir unknowe.
At mete wel y-taught was she with-alle;
She leet no morsel from hir lippes falle,
Ne wette hir fingres in hir sauce depe.
Wel coude she carie a morsel, and wel kepe,
That no drope ne fille up-on hir brest.
In curteisye was set ful muche hir lest.
Hir over lippe wyped she so clene,
That in hir coppe was no ferthing sene
Of grece, whan she dronken hadde hir draughte.
Ful semely after hir mete she raughte,
And sikerly she was of greet disport,
And ful plesaunt, and amiable of port,
And peyned hir to countrefete chere
Of court, and been estatlich of manere,
And to ben holden digne of reverence.
But, for to speken of hir conscience,
She was so charitable and so pitous,
She wolde wepe, if that she sawe a mous
Caught in a trappe, if it were deed or bledde.
Of smale houndes had she, that she fedde
With rosted flesh, or milk and wastel-breed,
But sore weep she if oon of hem were deed,
Or if men smoot it with a yerde smerte:
And al was conscience and tendre herte.
Ful semely hir wimpel pinched was;
Hir nose tretys; hir eyen greye as glas;
Hir mouth ful smal, and ther-to softe and reed;
But sikerly she hadde a fair forheed;

A horn he carried, with strap of green;
A forester was he in fact, as I guess.
　　There was also a Nun, a PRIORESSE,
Whose smile was full simple and modest—
Her greatest oath was but *by Saint Eligius!*—
And she was called Madame Eglentyne.
Full well she sang the service divine,
Intoning in her nose full seemly;
And French she spoke with elegant fluency,
After the School of Stratford at Bow, [6]
For French of Paris was to her unknown.
At table well taught was she withal:
She let no morsel from her lips fall,
Nor wet her fingers in her sauce too deep.
Well could she convey a spoonful, and take care
That no drop fell upon her breast.
She took much pleasure in etiquette.
Her upper lip she wiped so clean,
That in her cup was no drop seen
Of grease, when she had drunk her draft.
Full politely for her food she reached,
And certainly she was a cheerful sort,
And full pleasant, nice deportment,
And she took pains to reflect the manners
Of court, and to be stately in her carriage,
And to be held worthy of reverence.
But, for to speak of her compassion,
She was so charitable and kind,
She would weep if she saw a mouse
Caught in a trap, or if it were dead or bleeding.
Some small hounds had she, that she fed
With roasted flesh, or milk and fine white bread.
But sorely wept she if one of them were dead,
Or if someone beat it with a stick;
She was all feeling and tender heart.
Full seemly her wimple pleated was,
Her nose graceful, her eyes gray as glass,
Her mouth full small, lips soft and red,
But certainly she had a fair forehead—

It was almost a spanne brood, I trowe;
For, hardily, she was nat undergrowe.
Ful fetis was hir cloke, as I was war.
Of smal coral aboute hir arm she bar
A peire of bedes, gauded al with grene;
And ther-on heng a broche of gold ful shene,
On which ther was first write a crowned A,
And after, *Amor vincit omnia.*

    Another NONNE with hir hadde she,
That was hir chapeleyne, and PREESTES THREE.

    A MONK ther was, a fair for the maistrye,
An out-rydere, that lovede venerye;
A manly man, to been an abbot able.
Ful many a deyntee hors hadde he in stable:
And, whan he rood, men mighte his brydel here
Ginglen in a whistling wind as clere,
And eek as loude as dooth the chapel-belle
Ther as this lord was keper of the celle.
The reule of seint Maure or of seint Beneit,
By-cause that it was old and som-del streit,
This ilke monke leet olde thinges pace,
And held after the newe world the space.
He yaf nat of that text a pulled hen,
That seith, that hunters been nat holy men;
Ne that a monk, whan he is cloisterlees,
Is lykned til a fish that is waterlees;
This is to seyn, a monk out of his cloistre.
But thilke text held he nat worth an oistre;
And I seyde, his opinioun was good.
What sholde he studie, and make himselven wood,
Upon a book in cloistre alwey to poure,
Or swinken with his handes, and laboure,
As Austin bit? How shal the world be served?
Lat Austin have his swink to him reserved.
Therefore he was a pricasour aright,
Grehoundes he hadde, as swifte as fowel in flight
Of priking and of hunting for the hare
Was al his lust, for no cost wolde he spare.
I seigh his sleves purfiled at the hond

It was almost a span broad, I believe—
For in no way was she undersized.
Full elegant was her cloak, as I was aware.
About her arm she bore a coral rosary,
The beads set off with stones green;
And thereon hung a broach, of shining gold,
On which there was first written a crowned *A*,
And after, *Amor vincit omnia.* [7]

    Another Nun with her had she,
Who was her chaplain, and Priests three.

    A Monk there was, and a good one too,
An estate manager, who also loved to hunt:
A manly man, and an abbot able.
Full many a fine horse had he in stable,
And when he rode men might his bridle hear
Jingling in a whistling wind as clear
And loud as doth the chapel bell,
There where this lord ran a priory.
The rule of Saint Maurus or of Saint Benedict, [8]
Because it was old and somewhat strict,
This same monk let slide,
And held after the new world for his guide.
He gave not for that text a plucked hen,
That said hunters should not be holy men,
Nor that a monk when he neglects his vows,
Is like a fish out of water
(That is to say a monk out of his cloister);
But that doctrine held he not worth an oyster.
And I said his opinion was good:
Why should he study, and make himself a nut,
Upon a book in cloister always to pore,
Or work with his hands and labor,
As Augustine[9] bid? How shall the world be served?
Let Augustine have his work for him reserved!
So he rode energetically all right:
Greyhounds he had, as swift as birds in flight;
Of riding and of hunting for the hare
Was all his lust, for it no cost would he spare.
I saw his sleeves trimmed at the cuff

With grys, and that the fyneste of a lond;
And, for to festne his hood under his chin
He hadde of gold y-wroght a curious pin:
A love-knotte in the gretter end ther was.
His heed was balled, that shoon as any glas,
And eek his face, as he had been anoint.
He was a lord ful fat and in good point;
His eyen stepe, and rollinge in his heed,
That stemed as a forneys of a leed;
His botes souple, his hors in greet estat.
Now certeinly he was a fair prelat;
He was nat pale as a for-pyned goost.
A fat swan loved he best of any roost.
His palfrey was as broun as is a berye.

    A FRERE ther was, a wantown and a merye,
A limitour, a ful solempne man.
In alle the ordres foure is noon that can
So muche of daliaunce and fair langage.
He hadde maad ful many a mariage
Of yonge wommen, at his owne cost.
Un-to his ordre he was a noble post.
Ful wel biloved and famulier was he
With frankeleyns over-al in his contree,
And eek with worthy wommen of the toun:
For he had power of confessioun,
As seyde him-self, more than a curat,
For of his ordre he was licentiat.
Ful swetely herde he confessioun,
And plesaunt was his absolucion;
He was an esy man to yeve penaunce
Ther as he wiste to han a good pitaunce;
For unto a povre ordre for to yive
Is signe that a man is wel y-shrive.
For if he yaf, he dorste make avaunt,
He wiste that a man was repentaunt.
For many a man so hard is of his herte,
He may nat wepe al-thogh him sore smerte.
Therfore, in stede of weping and preyeres,
Men moot yeve silver to the povre freres.

With gray fur and that the finest in the land;
And to fasten his hood under his chin,
He had of gold crafted a full curious pin:
A love-knot in the larger end there was.
His head was bald, and shone like glass,
And his face as well, as if anointed.
He was a lord full fat and yet his muscles fit:
His eyes protruding, and rolling in his head,
That glowed like the fire under a cauldron;
His boots supple, his horse in great condition—
Now certainly he was a fair prelate.
He was not pale as a tortured ghost;
A fat swan loved he best of any roast.
And brown as a berry was his horse.

    A FRIAR[10] there was, a lecher and a merry,
A licensed beggar, with his own territory.
Among the orders four was none who knew
So much of dalliance and fair language.
He had arranged full many a marriage
Of young women, at his own cost.
Unto his order he was a noble post.
Full well beloved and familiar was he
With rich franklins throughout his territory,
And with the worthy women of the town;
For he had power of confession,[11]
As he said himself, more than a local curate,
For of his order he was licentiate.
Full sweetly he heard confession,
And pleasant was his absolution;
He was an easy man to make penance
Wherever he could expect a nice remembrance.
For unto a poor order to give
Is a sign that a man is well shriven—
For if he gave something, the Friar could be content,
That a man was truly repentant.
For many a man is so hard of heart,
He may not weep though it sore smarts:
Therefore instead of weeping and prayers,
Men may give silver to the poor freres.

His tipet was ay farsed ful of knyves
And pinnes, for to yeven faire wyves.
And certeinly he hadde a mery note;
Wel coude he singe and pleyen on a rote.
Of yeddinges he bar utterly the prys.
His nekke whyt was as the flour-de-lys;
Ther-to he strong was as a champioun.
He knew the tavernes wel in every toun,
And everich hostiler and tappestere
Bet than a lazar or a beggestere;
For un-to swich a worthy man as he
Acorded nat, as by his facultee,
To have with seke lazars aqueyntaunce.
It is nat honest, it may nat avaunce
For to delen with no swich poraille,
But al with riche and sellers of vitaille.
And over-al, ther as profit sholde aryse,
Curteys he was, and lowly of servyse.
Ther nas no man no-wher so vertuous.
He was the beste beggere in his hous;
And yaf a certeyn ferme for the graunt;
Noon of his bretheren cam ther in his haunt;
For thogh a widwe hadde noght a sho,
So plesaunt was his "*In principio*,"
Yet wolde he have a ferthing, er he wente.
His purchas was wel bettre than his rente.
And rage he coude, as it were right a whelpe.
In love-dayes ther coude he muchel helpe.
For there he was nat lyk a cloisterer,
With a thredbar cope, as is a povre scoler,
But he was lyk a maister or a pope.
Of double worsted was his semi-cope,
That rounded as a belle out of the presse.
Somwhat he lipsed, for his wantownesse,
To make his English swete up-on his tonge;
And in his harping, whan that he had songe,
His eyen twinkled in his heed aright,
As doon the sterres in the frosty night.
This worthy limitour was cleped Huberd.

His cape was always full of knives
And pins for to give fair wives.
And certainly he had a nice voice;
Well could he sing and pluck the strings:
For ballad singing he was first choice.
His neck white was as the lily flower;
Plus he had a champion's muscle power.
He knew the taverns well in every town,
And every innkeeper and every bargirl
Better than he knew any leper or lady beggar,
For such a worthy man as he
Should not, in his belief,
Have acquaintance with sick lepers:
It was not dignified and did him no good
To deal with such poor suffering souls,
But always with rich folk and food purveyors.
And everywhere—anywhere—profit promised to arise,
Courteous he was, and humble in service.
There was no man anywhere near so virtuous.
He was the best beggar in his order's house,
(And gave a certain payment for the grant:[12]
None of his brothers trespassed on his haunts.)
For though a widow had not a shoe,
So pleasant was his *In principio*,[13]
That he would have a farthing before he went.
His income was well better than his rent.
And he could be charming as a pup.
To resolve disputes he could often help,
For he was not like a cloisterer,
With threadbare cape, as is a poor scholar.[14]
But he was like a master or a pope:
Of double-worsted was his half-cape,
That swelled around him like a bell.
Somewhat he lisped, in affectation,
To make his English sweet upon his tongue;
And when he had played his harp and sung,
His eyes twinkled in his head aright
As do the stars on a frosty night.
This worthy friar was called Huberd.

A MARCHANT was ther with a forked berd,
In mottelee, and hye on horse he sat,
Up-on his heed a Flaundrish bever hat;
His botes clasped faire and fetisly.
His resons he spak ful solempnely,
Souninge alway th'encrees of his winning.
He wolde the see were kept for any thing
Bitwixe Middelburgh and Orewelle.
Wel coude he in eschaunge sheeldes selle.
This worthy man ful wel his wit bisette;
Ther wiste no wight that he was in dette,
So estatly was he of his governaunce,
With his bargaynes, and with his chevisaunce.
For sothe he was a worthy man with-alle,
But sooth to seyn, I noot how men him calle.

A CLERK ther was of Oxenford also,
That un-to logik hadde longe y-go.
As lene was his hors as is a rake,
And he nas nat right fat, I undertake;
But loked holwe, and ther-to soberly.
Ful thredbar was his overest courtepy;
For he had geten him yet no benefyce,
Ne was so worldly for to have offyce.
For him was lever have at his beddes heed
Twenty bokes, clad in blak or reed,
Of Aristotle and his philosophye,
Than robes riche, or fithele, or gay sautrye.
But al be that he was a philosophre,
Yet hadde he but litel gold in cofre;
But al that he mighte of his freendes hente,
On bokes and on lerninge he it spente,
And bisily gan for the soules preye
Of hem that yaf him wher-with to scoleye.
Of studie took he most cure and most hede.
Noght o word spak he more than was nede,
And that was seyd in forme and reverence,
And short and quik, and ful of hy sentence.
Souninge in moral vertu was his speche,
And gladly wolde he lerne, and gladly teche.

A MERCHANT there was with forked beard,
In patterned cloth, and high on his horse he sat;
Upon his head a Flemish beaverfur hat,
His boots well tied and neat.
His opinions he pompously offered,
Proclaiming always the increase of his profit.
He wanted the pirates at any price expelled
Between Middleburgh and Orowelle.[15]
Well could he exchange French coins.
This worthy man full well his wit employed:
No one knew he was in debt,
So careful was he of his outward impression,
With his bargains and his (perhaps) shady lending.
He was a worthy man, all the same;
But in truth I do not know his name.

A SCHOLAR there was of Oxford also,
Who unto logic had himself devoted,
All lean was his horse as is a rake,
And he was not fat, I undertake,
But looked hollow and also soberly.
Full threadbare was his over cloak,
For he had received yet no benefice,
Nor did he worldly work for his daily bread;
For he would rather have at his bed's head
Twenty books clad in black or red,
Of Aristotle and his philosophy,
Than robes rich, psaltery or harp.
Albeit that he was a philosopher,
Yet had he but little gold in his coffer;
And all that his friends might him lend,
On books and learning he it spent,
And busily did for the souls pray
Of those who for his tuition gave.
Of study took he most care and most heed.
Not one word spoke he more than was needed,
And that was said in correct form and respect,
And short and quick, and full of high intellect.
Resounding in moral virtue was his speech,
And gladly would he learn, and gladly teach.

A SERGEANT OF THE LAWE, war and wys,
That often hadde been at the parvys,
Ther was also, ful riche of excellence.
Discreet he was, and of greet reverence:
He semed swich, his wordes weren so wyse.
Justyce he was ful often in assyse,
By patente, and by pleyn commissioun;
For his science, and for his heigh renoun
Of fees and robes hadde he many oon.
So greet a purchasour was no-wher noon.
Al was fee simple to him in effect,
His purchasing mighte nat been infect.
No-wher so bisy a man as he ther nas,
And yet he semed bisier than he was.
In termes hadde he caas and domes alle,
That from the tyme of king William were falle.
Therto he coude endyte, and make a thing,
Ther coude no wight pinche at his wryting;
And every statut coude he pleyn by rote.
He rood but hoomly in a medlee cote
Girt with a ceint of silk, with barres smale;
Of his array telle I no lenger tale.

A FRANKELEYN was in his companye;
Whyt was his berd, as is the dayesye.
Of his complexioun he was sangwyn.
Wel loved he by the morwe a sop in wyn.
To liven in delyt was ever his wone,
For he was Epicurus owne sone,
That heeld opinioun, that pleyn delyt
Was verraily felicitee parfyt.
An housholdere, and that a greet, was he;
Seint Julian he was in his contree.
His breed, his ale, was alwey after oon;
A bettre envyned man was no-wher noon.
With-oute bake mete was never his hous,
Of fish and flesh, and that so plentyous,
It snewed in his hous of mete and drinke,
Of alle deyntees that men coude thinke.
After the sondry sesons of the yeer,

A SERGEANT OF THE LAW,[16] alert and wise,
Who had often been at the parvis,[17]
There was also, full rich of excellence.
Discreet he was and worthy of great respect:
He seemed such, his words were so wise.
Judge he was full often in assizes cases,[18]
With full authority from the king;
For his knowledge and for his high renown,
Of fees and robes had he many a one.
So sharp a wheeler-dealer was nowhere known:
All contracts were with no strings attached;
His ownership might not be attacked.
Nowhere so busy a man as he there was;
And yet he seemed busier than he was.
He knew the details of all the cases,
That from the time of King William had taken place.
Thereto he could write and draw up papers;
No one could find fault with his writing,
And every statute he knew by heart.
He rode unfancily in a multicolored coat,
Girt with a cinch of silk with stripes narrow;
Of his outfit I will no more tell.
 A FRANKLIN[19] was in his company.
White was his beard as is the daisy;
Of his temperament he was sanguine.[20]
Well he loved a breakfast cake soaked in wine.
To live in delight was ever his custom,
For he was Epicurus' own son,
Who held opinion that complete delight
Was the true measure of perfection.
A householder, and a great one, was he;
Saint Julian[21] he was in his country.
His bread, his ale were always good;
A better wine-cellared man was nowhere known.
Without meat pies was never his house,
Of fish and flesh, and that so plenteous
It rained in his house of meat and drink.
Of all delicacies that men could think,
According to the sundry seasons of the year,

So chaunged he his mete and his soper.
Ful many a fat partrich hadde he in mewe,
And many a breem and many a luce in stewe.
Wo was his cook, but-if his sauce were
Poynaunt and sharp, and redy al his gere.
His table dormant in his halle alway
Stood redy covered al the longe day.
At sessiouns ther was he lord and sire;
Ful ofte tyme he was knight of the shire.
An anlas and a gipser al of silk
Heng at his girdel, whyt as morne milk.
A shirreve hadde he been, and a countour;
Was no-wher such a worthy vavasour.

    An HABERDASSHER and a CARPENTER,
A WEBBE, a DYERE, and a TAPICER,
Were with us eek, clothed in o liveree,
Of a solempne and greet fraternitee.
Ful fresh and newe hir gere apyked was;
Hir knyves were y-chaped noght with bras,
But al with silver, wroght ful clene and weel,
Hir girdles and hir pouches every-deel.
Wel semed ech of hem a fair burgeys,
To sitten in a yeldhalle on a deys.
Everich, for the wisdom that he can,
Was shaply for to been an alderman.
For catel hadde they y-nogh and rente,
And eek hir wyves wolde it wel assente;
And elles certein were they to blame.
It is ful fair to been y-clept "*ma dame*,"
And goon to vigilyës al bifore,
And have a mantel royalliche y-bore.

    A COOK they hadde with hem for the nones,
To boille the chiknes with the marybones,
And poudre-marchant tart, and galingale.
Wel coude he knowe a draughte of London ale.
He coude roste, and sethe, and broille, and frye,
Maken mortreux, and wel bake a pye.
But greet harm was it, as it thoughte me,
That on his shine a mormal hadde he;

So varied his dinner and his supper.
Full many a fat partridge had he in coop,
And many a bream and many a pike in pond.
Woe to his cook, unless his sauces were
Pungent and sharp, and ever-ready all his pans and pots.
His table in his dining hall
Stood always for his dinner set.[22]
At meetings of local justices there he was lord and sire;
Full often time he was MP for the shire.
A dagger and a purse all of silk
Hung at his waist, white as morning milk.
A sheriff had he been, and an auditor;
Was nowhere such a worthy landowner.

  A HABERDASHER and a CARPENTER,
A WEAVER, a DYER and a TAPESTRY-MAKER,
Were with us also, all clothed in the livery
Of a distinguished and great parish guild.[23]
Full fresh and new their dress uniform was;
Their knives were mounted not with brass,
But all with silver, full well made and brightly
Polished, as were their belts and purses.
Well seemed each of them a fair burgher
To sit in guildhall in a place of honor.
Each one of them could have been
An alderman.
For property had they enough and income,
And their wives would say the same;
Or else certain were they to blame.
It is full fair to be called "*Madame*,"
And go to church at procession's head,
And have a mantle like royalty carried.

  A COOK they had with them for their travel,
To boil the chickens with the marrowbones
And spices—poudre-marchant tart and galingale.
Well could he identify a draught of London ale.
He could roast and boil and broil and fry,
Make stews and well bake a pie.
But great misfortune was it, as it seemed to me,
That on his shin an open sore had he.

For blankmanger, that made he with the beste.
    A SHIPMAN was ther, woning fer by weste:
For aught I woot, he was of Dertemouthe.
He rood up-on a rouncy, as he couthe,
In a gowne of falding to the knee.
A daggere hanging on a laas hadde he
Aboute his nekke under his arm adoun.
The hote somer had maad his hewe al broun;
And, certeinly, he was a good felawe.
Ful many a draughte of wyn had he y-drawe
From Burdeux-ward, whyl that the chapman sleep.
Of nyce conscience took he no keep.
If that he faught, and hadde the hyer hond,
By water he sente hem hoom to every lond.
But of his craft to rekene wel his tydes,
His stremes and his daungers him bisydes,
His herberwe and his mone, his lode-menage,
Ther nas noon swich from Hulle to Cartage.
Hardy he was, and wys to undertake;
With many a tempest hadde his berd been shake.
He knew wel alle the havenes, as they were,
From Gootlond to the cape of Finistere,
And every cryke in Britayne and in Spayne;
His barge y-cleped was the Maudelayne.
    With us ther was a DOCTOUR OF PHISYK,
In al this world ne was ther noon him lyk
To speke of phisik and of surgerye;
For he was grounded in astronomye.
He kepte his pacient a ful greet del
In houres, by his magik naturel.
Wel coude he fortunen the ascendent
Of his images for his pacient.
He knew the cause of everich maladye,
Were it of hoot or cold, or moiste, or drye,
And where engendred, and of what humour;
He was a verrey parfit practisour.
The cause y-knowe, and of his harm the rote,
Anon he yaf the seke man his bote.
Ful redy hadde he his apothecaries,

For blancmange, that made he with the best.
      A SHIPMAN[24] was there, living far to the west:
For all I know, he was of Dartmouth.
He rode upon a sturdy little horse, as best he could,
In a heavy wool gown reaching to the knee.
A dagger hanging on a cord had he
About his neck and down beneath his arm.
The high summer had made his hue all brown;
And certainly he was a good fellow.
Full many a draught of wine had he tapped
En route from Bordeaux, while the wine merchant slept.
Of nice conscience he took no heed:
In a fight, if he had the upper hand,
He sent them overboard, far from land.
But of navigation, to reckon well his tides,
His currents and his hazards him nearby,
His harbor and his moon, his compass use,
There was none such from Hull to Carthage.
Hardy he was, and careful in risks taken;
With many a tempest had his beard been shaken.
He knew well all the harbors, as they were,
From Gotland to the Cape of Finisterre,
And every creek in Brittany and Spain;
His ship was called the Magdalen.
      With us there was a PHYSICIAN;
In all the world there was none like him
To speak of medicine and of surgery
For he was grounded in astrology.
He tended his patient at just the right
Hours, guided by his magical powers.
Well could he determine the ascendent
Of the signs for his patient.[25]
He knew the cause of every malady,
Were it hot or cold or moist or dry,
And where engendered and of what humor;
He was a truly perfect practitioner.
The cause known, and of the malady its origin,
Quickly he gave the sick man his medicine.
Full ready had he his apothecaries,

To sende him drogges and his letuaries,
For ech of hem made other for to winne;
Hir frendschipe nas nat newe to biginne.
Wel knew he th' olde Esculapius,
And Deiscorides, and eek Rufus,
Old Ypocras, Haly, and Galien;
Serapion, Razis, and Avicen;
Averrois, Damascien, and Constantyn;
Bernard, and Gatesden, and Gilbertyn.
Of his diete mesurable was he,
For it was of no superfluitee,
But of greet norissing and digestible.
His studie was but litel on the bible.
In sangwin and in pers he clad was al,
Lyned with taffata and with sendal;
And yet he was but esy of dispence;
He kepte that he wan in pestilence.
For gold in phisik is a cordial,
Therfore he lovede gold in special.

    A good WYF was ther of bisyde BATHE,
But she was som-del deef, and that was scathe.
Of clooth-making she hadde swiche an haunt,
She passed hem of Ypres and of Gaunt.
In al the parisshe wyf ne was ther noon
That to th' offring bifore hir sholde goon;
And if ther dide, certeyn, so wrooth was she,
That she was out of alle charitee.
Hir coverchiefs ful fyne were of ground;
I dorste swere they weyeden ten pound
That on a Sonday were upon hir heed.
Hir hosen weren of fyn scarlet reed,
Ful streite y-teyd, and shoos ful moiste and newe.
Bold was hir face, and fair, and reed of hewe.
She was a worthy womman al hir lyve,
Housbondes at chirche-dore she hadde fyve,
Withouten other companye in youthe;
But therof nedeth nat to speke as nouthe.
And thryes hadde she been at Jerusalem;
She hadde passed many a straunge streem;

To send him drugs and potions,
For each helped the other to make a profit,
Their friendship was not new to begin.
Well he knew the old Aesculapius,
Dioscorides, and Rufus,
Old Hippocrates, Hali and Galen,
Serapion, Rhazes and Avicenna, Averroes,
Damascenus and Constantine,
Bernard and Gatesden and Gilbert.[26]
Of his diet moderate was he,
For it was of no great quantity
But of great nourishment and digestible.
His study was but little on the Bible.
In blood red and blue he clad was all,
Lined with taffeta and fine silk;
And yet he was not quick to spend,
He kept what he earned in time of plague,
For gold is good for the heart in medicine;
Therefore gold he loved especially.

    A good WIFE there was, from near Bath,
But she was somewhat deaf, and that was too bad.
Of clothmaking she had such a talent,
She surpassed that of Ypres and of Ghent.[27]
In all the parish a wife was there none
Who gave more at the church offering;
And if they did, certain so angry was she,
That she was all out of charity.[28]
Her Sunday shawls were of full fine hand;
I daresay that they weighed ten pounds
That on a Sunday were upon her head.
Her hose were of fine scarlet red,
Full tightly tied, and shoes full soft and new.
Bold was her face, and fair and red of hue.
She was a worthy woman all her life:
Husbands at church door[29] she'd had five,
Not counting other company in youth—
But we need not speak of them right now—
And thrice had she been to Jerusalem.
She had crossed many a foreign stream:

At Rome she hadde been, and at Boloigne,
In Galice at seint Jame, and at Coloigne.
She coude muche of wandring by the weye:
Gat-tothed was she, soothly for to seye.
Up-on an amblere esily she sat,
Y-wimpled wel, and on hir heed an hat
As brood as is a bokeler or a targe;
A foot-mantel aboute hir hipes large,
And on hir feet a paire of spores sharpe.
In felawschip wel coude she laughe and carpe.
Of remedyes of love she knew perchaunce,
For she coude of that art the olde daunce.

  A good man was ther of religioun,
And was a povre PERSOUN of a toun;
But riche he was of holy thoght and werk.
He was also a lerned man, a clerk,
That Cristes gospel trewely wolde preche;
His parisshens devoutly wolde he teche.
Benigne he was, and wonder diligent,
And in adversitee ful pacient;
And swich he was y-preved ofte sythes.
Ful looth were him to cursen for his tythes,
But rather wolde he yeven, out of doute,
Un-to his povre parisshens aboute
Of his offring, and eek of his substaunce.
He coude in litel thing han suffisaunce.
Wyd was his parisshe, and houses fer a-sonder,
But he ne lafte nat, for reyn ne thonder,
In siknes nor in meschief, to visyte
The ferreste in his parisshe, muche and lyte,
Up-on his feet, and in his hand a staf.
This noble ensample to his sheep he yaf,
That first he wroghte, and afterward he taughte;
Out of the gospel he tho wordes caughte;
And this figure he added eek ther-to,
That if gold ruste, what shal iren do?
For if a preest be foul, on whom we truste,
No wonder is a lewed man to ruste;
And shame it is, if a preest take keep,

To Rome she had been,[30] and to Boulogne,
In Galicia to Saint James, and to Cologne;
She knew much of wandering along the road.
Gap-toothed she was, the truth to say.
Upon an easyriding horse she easily sat,
Wimpled well, and on her head a hat
As broad as is a buckler or a targe;
An overskirt about her hips large,
And on her feet a pair of spurs sharp.
She was full of laughter and of gossip.
Of love remedies she knew by chance,
For she knew the steps of that old dance.

    A good man was there of religion,
And he was a poor PARSON of a town,
But rich he was in holy thought and work.
He was also a learned man, a scholar
Who Christ's gospel truly would preach,
His parishioners devotedly would he teach.
Kindly he was, and very diligent,
And in adversity full patient,
And he proved to be such oftentimes.
Full loath was he to excommunicate for his tithes,[31]
But rather would he give, without a doubt,
Unto his poor parishioners out of
His offerings and his income.
He knew how to have enough with not much.
Wide was his parish, and houses far apart,
But he neglected none, for rain nor thunder,
In sickness nor in misfortune, to visit
The furthest in his parish, great and humble,
Travelling by foot, and in his hand a staff.
This noble example to his sheep he gave,
That first he wrought, and afterward he taught.
From the gospel he these words took,
And this metaphor he added thereto:
That if gold rusts, what should iron do?
For if a priest be corrupt, upon whom we trust,
No wonder is an unlearned man to rust;
And shame it is if a priest be seen,

A shiten shepherde and a clene sheep.
Wel oghte a preest ensample for to yive,
By his clennesse, how that his sheep shold live.
He sette nat his benefice to hyre,
And leet his sheep encombred in the myre,
And ran to London, un-to sëynt Poules,
To seken him a chaunterie for soules,
Or with a bretherhed to been withholde;
But dwelte at hoom, and kepte wel his folde,
So that the wolf ne made it nat miscarie;
He was a shepherde and no mercenarie.
And though he holy were, and vertuous,
He was to sinful man nat despitous,
Ne of his speche daungerous ne digne,
But in his teching discreet and benigne.
To drawen folk to heven by fairnesse
By good ensample, was his bisinesse:
But it were any persone obstinat,
What-so he were, of heigh or lowe estat,
Him wolde he snibben sharply for the nones.
A bettre preest, I trowe that nowher noon is.
He wayted after no pompe and reverence,
Ne maked him a spyced conscience,
But Cristes lore, and his apostles twelve,
He taughte, and first he folwed it himselve.

    With him ther was a PLOWMAN, was his
      brother,
That hadde y-lad of dong ful many a fother,
A trewe swinker and a good was he,
Livinge in pees and parfit charitee.
God loved he best with al his hole herte
At alle tymes, thogh him gamed or smerte,
And thanne his neighebour right as himselve.
He wolde thresshe, and ther-to dyke and delve,
For Cristes sake, for every povre wight,
Withouten hyre, if it lay in his might.
His tythes payed he ful faire and wel,
Bothe of his propre swink and his catel.
In a tabard he rood upon a mere.

As a shitcovered shepherd with clean sheep.
Well ought a priest example for to give,
By his cleanliness, how his sheep should live.
He rented not his benefice out to hire,
And left his sheep encumbered in the mire,
And ran into London to Saint Paul's
To seek him a sinecure as a chantry-priest,
Or a retainer as chaplain for a guild,[32]
But dwelt at home and kept well his fold.
So that the wolf didn't make it come to grief;
He was a shepherd and not a mercenary.
And though he holy was, and virtuous,
He was to sinful men not despising,
Nor in speech haughty or disdainful,
But in his teaching discreet and benign.
To draw folk to heaven by fairness,
By good example, that was his business;
But were there any person obstinate,
Whoever he was, of high or low estate,
He would him rebuke sharply in that instance.
A better priest I believe there nowhere is.
He yearned not for pomp and reverence,
Nor made a show of righteousness,
But Christ's teaching and his apostles twelve,
He taught, and first he followed it himself.
   With him there was a PLOWMAN,[33] who was his
      brother,
Who had hauled of dung full many a cart.
An honest worker, and a good one was he,
Living in peace and perfect charity.
God loved he best with his whole heart
At all times, both happy and tough,
And his neighbor much as himself.
He would thresh and ditch and shovel,
For Christ's sake, for every poor soul,
Without payment, if it lay in his power.
His tithes he paid full fair and well,
Both of his work and his property.
In a smock he rode upon a mare.

Ther was also a Reve and a Millere,
A Somnour and a Pardoner also,
A Maunciple, and my-self; there were namo.
    The MILLER was a stout carl, for the nones,
Ful big he was of braun, and eek of bones;
That proved wel, for over-al ther he cam,
At wrastling he wolde have alwey the ram.
He was short-sholdred, brood, a thikke knarre,
Ther nas no dore that he nolde heve of harre,
Or breke it, at a renning, with his heed.
His berd as any sowe or fox was reed,
And ther-to brood, as though it were a spade.
Up-on the cop right of his nose he hade
A werte, and ther-on stood a tuft of heres,
Reed as the bristles of a sowes eres;
His nose-thirles blake were and wyde.
A swerd and bokeler bar he by his syde;
His mouth as greet was as a greet forneys.
He was a janglere and a goliardeys,
And that was most of sinne and harlotryes.
Wel coude he stelen corn, and tollen thryes;
And yet he hadde a thombe of gold, pardee.
A whyt cote and a blew hood wered he.
A baggepype wel coude he blowe and sowne,
And ther-with-al he broghte us out of towne.
    A gentil MAUNCIPLE was ther of a temple;
Of which achatours mighte take exemple
For to be wyse in bying of vitaille
For whether that he payde, or took by taille,
Algate he wayted so in his achat,
That he was ay biforn and in good stat.
Now is nat that of God a ful fair grace,
That swich a lewed mannes wit shal pace
The wisdom of an heep of lerned men?
Of maistres hadde he mo than thryes ten,
That were of lawe expert and curious;
Of which there were a doseyn in that hous
Worthy to been stiwardes of rente and lond
Of any lord that is in Engelond,

There was also a Reeve[34] and a Miller,
A Summoner[35] and a Pardoner[36] also,
A Manciple,[37] and myself—there were no more.
    The MILLER was indeed a stout fellow;
Full big he was of muscle and bones—
Who proved himself, for wherever he went,
At wrestling he would always win the ram.
He was short-shouldered, a broad, thick cudgel:
There was no door he couldn't yank off its hinges,
Or go through by ramming it with his noggin.
His beard as any sow or fox was red,
And thereto broad, as though it were a spade.
Upon the tip of his nose he had
A wart, and thereon stood a tuft of hairs,
Red as the bristles of a sow's ears;
His nostrils were black and wide.
A sword and buckler bore he by his side.
His mouth gaped big as a furnace;
He was a talker and a joke teller,
And those mostly of sin and off-color.
Well could he steal wheat, and grind it thrice,
And yet he had a thumb of gold, by God.
A white coat and blue hood wore he.
A bagpipe well could he blow and sing,
And with it he brought us out of town.
    A worthy MANCIPLE was there of a law school,
From whom buyers might take example
To be smart in purchasing their needs,
For whether he paid, or put on account,
Always he so carefully watched his pennies
That he was always ahead, and in the black.
Now is that not of God a full fair grace,
That such an uneducated man should surpass
The wisdom of a heap of graduates?
Of masters had he thrice ten
Who were of law expert and skillful,
Among whom there were a dozen in that house
Worthy to be stewards of money and land
For any lord that is in England,

To make him live by his propre good,
In honour dettelees, but he were wood,
Or live as scarsly as him list desire;
And able for to helpen al a shire
In any cas that mighte falle or happe;
And yit this maunciple sette hir aller cappe.
    The REVE was a sclendre colerik man,
His berd was shave as ny as ever he can.
His heer was by his eres round y-shorn.
His top was dokked lyk a preest biforn.
Ful longe were his legges, and ful lene,
Y-lyk a staf, ther was no calf y-sene.
Wel coude he kepe a gerner and a binne;
Ther was noon auditour coude on him winne.
Wel wiste he, by the droghte, and by the reyn,
The yelding of his seed, and of his greyn.
His lordes sheep, his neet, his dayerye,
His swyn, his hors, his stoor, and his pultrye,
Was hoolly in this reves governing,
And by his covenaunt yaf the rekening,
Sin that his lord was twenty yeer of age;
Ther coude no man bringe him in arrerage.
Ther nas baillif, ne herde, ne other hyne,
That he ne knew his sleighte and his covyne;
They were adrad of him, as of the deeth.
His woning was ful fair up-on an heeth,
With grene trës shadwed was his place.
He coude bettre than his lord purchace.
Ful riche he was astored prively,
His lord wel coude he plesen subtilly,
To yeve and lene him of his owne good,
And have a thank, and yet a cote and hood.
In youthe he lerned hadde a good mister;
He was a wel good wrighte, a carpenter.
This reve sat up-on a ful good stot,
That was al pomely grey, and highte Scot.
A long surcote of pers up-on he hade,
And by his syde he bar a rusty blade.
Of Northfolk was this reve, of which I telle,

Able to make him live within his means
In honor, debt free, unless he had big dreams,
Or to live as frugally as he desired,
And the same dozen were able to help an entire shire,
In any situation that might happen or befall,
And yet this manciple made fools of them all.
    The REEVE was a slender choleric man.
His beard was shaved as close as he could;
His hair was by his ears closely shorn,
His top was cut short like a priest's in front.
Full long were his legs, and full lean,
Like a staff; there was no calf to be seen.
Well could he keep a granary and a bin—
There was no auditor who could catch him short.
Well judged he by the drought and by the rain
The yielding of his seed and of his grain.
His lord's sheep, his cattle, his dairy herd,
His swine, his horses, his livestock, and his poultry,
Were wholly in this reeve's governing,
And by his contract he kept the reckoning,
Since his lord was in age but twenty years.
There could no man bring him in arrears.
There was no bailiff, nor herdsman, nor other servant,
But that he knew their tricks and their deceit;
They were afraid of him as of the Death.
His dwelling was full fair upon a heath;
With green trees shadowed was his place.
Better than his lord he could his goods increase.
Full rich he was with private stock;
His lord could he please full subtly,
To give and lend him of his own goods,
And receive thanks, and a gift coat and hood.
In youth he had learned a good trade:
He was a fine craftsman, a carpenter.
This reeve sat upon a full good farm horse
That was all dappled gray and named Scot.
A long coat of blue upon him he had,
And by his side he wore a rusty blade.
Of Norfolk was this reeve of whom I tell,

Bisyde a toun men clepen Baldeswelle.
Tukked he was, as is a frere, aboute,
And ever he rood the hindreste of our route.
    A Somnour was ther with us in that place,
That hadde a fyr-reed cherubinnes face,
For sawcefleem he was, with eyen narwe.
As hoot he was, and lecherous, as a sparwe;
With scalled browes blake, and piled berd;
Of his visage children were aferd.
Ther nas quik-silver, litarge, ne brimstoon,
Boras, ceruce, ne oille of tartre noon,
Ne oynement that wolde clense and byte,
That him mighte helpen of his whelkes whyte,
Nor of the knobbes sittinge on his chekes.
Wel loved he garleek, oynons, and eek lekes,
And for to drinken strong wyn, reed as blood.
Than wolde he speke, and crye as he were wood.
And whan that he wel dronken hadde the wyn,
Than wolde he speke no word but Latyn.
A fewe termes hadde he, two or three,
That he had lerned out of som decree;
No wonder is, he herde it al the day;
And eek ye knowen wel, how that a jay
Can clepen "Watte," as well as can the pope.
But who-so coude in other thing him grope,
Thanne hadde he spent al his philosophye;
Ay *"Questio quid iuris"* wolde he crye.
He was a gentil harlot and a kinde;
A bettre felawe sholde men noght finde.
He wolde suffre, for a quart of wyn,
A good felawe to have his concubyn
A twelf-month, and excuse him atte fulle:
Ful prively a finch eek coude he pulle.
And if he fond o-wher a good felawe,
He wolde techen him to have non awe,
In swich cas, of the erchedeknes curs,
But-if a mannes soule were in his purs;
For in his purs he sholde y-punisshed be.
"Purs is the erchedeknes helle," seyde he.

From near a town men call Bawdeswell.
Belted he was as is a friar;
And he rode always the hindmost of our group.
    A SUMMONER was there with us in that place,
Who had a fire-red cherubim's face,
For pimpled he was, with eyes narrow.
As hotblooded he was and lecherous as a sparrow,
With scabby black eyebrows, and scraggly beard;
Of his face children were afraid.
There was no quicksilver, lead oxide nor brimstone,
Borax, white lead, nor oil of tartar lotion,
Nor ointment that would cleanse and bite,
That might help him of his pimples cure,
Nor of the bumps sitting on his cheeks.
Well loved he garlic, onions and also leeks,
And for to drink strong wine, red as blood.
Then would he speak, and shout as if he were deranged;
And when he had drunk enough wine,
Then would he speak no word but in Latin.
A few phrases had he, two or three,
That he had learned out of some decree—
No wonder it is, he heard it all the day;
And you know well, how a bird
Can call *Walter!* as well as can the Pope.
But if you would in other things him query,
Then he'd used up all his philosophy;
Ever *Questio quid iuris*[38] would he cry.
He was a worthy rascal and also kind;
A better pal could no man find:
He would allow, for a quart of wine,
A buddy to have his concubine
For a year, and excuse him in full;
Full secretly a young thing could he seduce.
And if he found somewhere a pal,
He would teach him to have no fear
With regard to the Archdeacon's curse,[39]
Unless a man's soul were in his purse,
For then in his purse should he punished be.
"Purse is the Archdeacon's hell," said he.

But wel I woot he lyed right in dede;
Of cursing oghte ech gilty man him drede—
For curs wol slee, right as assoilling saveth—
And also war him of a *significavit.*
In daunger hadde he at his owne gyse
The yonge girles of the diocyse,
And knew hir counseil, and was al hir reed.
A gerland hadde he set up-on his heed,
As greet as it were for an ale-stake;
A bokeler hadde he maad him of a cake.

    With him ther rood a gentil PARDONER
Of Rouncival, his freend and his compeer,
That streight was comen fro the court of Rome.
Ful loude he song, "Com hider, love, to me."
This somnour bar to him a stif burdoun,
Was never trompe of half so greet a soun.
This pardoner hadde heer as yelow as wex,
But smothe it heng, as dooth a strike of flex;
By ounces henge his lokkes that he hadde,
And ther-with he his shuldres overspradde;
But thinne it lay, by colpons oon and oon;
But hood, for jolitee, ne wered he noon,
For it was trussed up in his walet.
Him thoughte, he rood al of the newe jet;
Dischevele, save his cappe, he rood al bare.
Swiche glaringe eyen hadde he as an hare.
A vernicle hadde he sowed on his cappe.
His walet lay biforn him in his lappe,
Bret-ful of pardoun come from Rome al hoot.
A voys he hadde as smal as hath a goot.
No berd hadde he, ne never sholde have,
As smothe it was as it were late y-shave;
I trowe he were a gelding or a mare.
But of his craft, fro Berwik into Ware,
Ne was ther swich another pardoner.
For in his male he hadde a pilwe-beer,
Which that, he seyde, was our lady veyl:
He seyde, he hadde a gobet of the seyl
That sëynt Peter hadde, whan that he wente

But well I know he lied indeed:
Excommunication each man should dread—
For curse will slay, as absolution saves—
And also avoid a warrant for arrest.
In his power in his own way had he
The young wenches of the diocese,
And knew their secrets, and gave them advice.
A garland had he set upon his head,
As big as if it were for a tavern sign;
A buckler had he made with a loaf of bread.
    With him there rode a gentle PARDONER
Of Rouncival,[40] his friend and his companion,
Who straight was come from the court of Rome.
Full loud he sang, "Come hither, love, to me."
The summoner joined in with a strong bass voice,
No trumpet made half so much noise.
This pardoner had hair as yellow as wax,
But in truth it hung, as does a spray of flax;
In thin strands hung the locks that he had,
And therewith his shoulders overspread;
But thin it lay in small locks one by one;
But hood, for fashion's sake, wore he none,
For it was packed up in his bag.
He thought he rode in the newest style;
With hair loose, save his cap, he rode with head bare.
Such staring eyes had he as a hare.
A veronica[41] had he sewn on his cap.
His bag lay before him in his lap,
Brimful of pardons, fresh and hot from Rome.
A voice he had as small as a goat.
No beard had he, nor ever should have,
His face was smooth as if it were just shaved:
I believe he was a gelding or a mare.
But of his profession, from Berwick to Ware,
Never was there such another pardoner.
For in his bag he had a pillowcase,
That he said was Our Lady's veil.
He said he had a piece of the sail
That Saint Peter had, when he strode

Up-on the see, til Jesu Crist him hente.
He hadde a croys of latoun, ful of stones,
And in a glas he hadde pigges bones.
But with thise relikes, whan that he fond
A povre person dwelling up-on lond,
Up-on a day he gat him more moneye
Than that the person gat in monthes tweye.
And thus, with feyned flaterye and japes,
He made the person and the peple his apes.
But trewely to tellen, atte laste,
He was in chirche a noble ecclesiaste.
Wel coude he rede a lessoun or a storie,
But alderbest he song an offertorie;
For wel he wiste, whan that song was songe
He moste preche, and wel affyle his tonge,
To winne silver, as he ful wel coude;
Therfore he song so meriely and loude.
      Now have I told you shortly, in a clause,
Th'estat, th'array, the nombre, and eek the cause
Why that assembled was this companye
In Southwerk, at this gentil hostelrye,
That highte the Tabard, faste by the Belle.
But now is tyme to yow for to telle
How that we baren us that ilke night,
Whan we were in that hostelrye alight.
And after wol I telle of our viage,
And al the remenaunt of our pilgrimage.
But first I pray yow, of your curteisye,
That ye n'arette it nat my vileinye,
Thogh that I pleynly speke in this matere,
To telle yow hir wordes and his chere;
Ne thogh I speke hir wordes properly.
For this ye knowen al-so wel as I,
Who-so shal telle a tale after a man,
He moot reherce, as ny as ever he can,
Everich a word, if it be in his charge,
Al speke he never so rudeliche and large;
Or elles he moot telle his tale untrewe,
Or feyne thing, or finde wordes newe.

Upon the sea, till Jesus Christ of him took hold.
He had a cross of metal, full of gems,
And in a glass jar he had pig's bones.
But with these relics, when he found
A poor parson dwelling in the country
In one day he made himself more money
Than that parson got in two months.
And thus, with feigned flattery and tricks
He made the parson and the people his fools.
But truth to tell, at last,
He was in church a noble preacher.
Well could he read a devotional lesson or story,
But best of all he sang an offertory;
For well he knew, when that song was sung,
He must preach, and file smooth his tongue
To win silver, as he full well could—
Therefore he sang both merrily and loud.

    Now have I told you truly, in brief,
The calling, the appearance, the number and the reason
Why assembled was this company
In Southwark, at this good hostelry,
By name of the Tabard, nearby the Bell.[42]
But now is the time for me to tell
How we conducted ourselves that same night,
When we were in that hostelry settled;
And after will I tell of our journey,
And all the remainder of our pilgrimage.
But first I pray you, of your courtesy,
That you not take it as my bad manners
Even though I speak plainly in this matter,
To tell you their words and their behavior
Even though I speak their words verbatim.
For this you all know as well as I:
Whoso shall tell a tale heard from another man
He must repeat closely as he can
Every word, if it be in his charge,
However rough or rude,
Or else he must tell his tale untrue,
Or make it up, or find words new.

He may nat spare, al-thogh he were his brother;
He moot as wel seye o word as another.
Crist spake him-self ful brode in holy writ,
And wel ye woot, no vileinye is it.
Eek Plato seith, who-so that can him rede,
The wordes mote be cosin to the dede.
Also I prey yow to foryeve it me,
Al have I nat set folk in hir degree
Here in this tale, as that they sholde stonde;
My wit is short, ye may wel understonde.

    Greet chere made our hoste us everichon,
And to the soper sette us anon;
And served us with vitaille at the beste.
Strong was the wyn, and wel to drinke us leste.
A semely man our hoste was with-alle
For to han been a marshal in an halle;
A large man he was with eyen stepe,
A fairer burgeys is ther noon in Chepe:
Bold of his speche, and wys, and wel y-taught,
And of manhod him lakkede right naught.
Eek therto he was right a mery man,
And after soper pleyen he bigan,
And spak of mirthe amonges othere thinges,
Whan that we hadde maad our rekeninges;
And seyde thus: "Now, lordinges, trewely,
Ye been to me right welcome hertely:
For by my trouthe, if that I shal nat lye,
I ne saugh this yeer so mery a companye
At ones in this herberwe as is now.
Fayn wolde I doon yow mirthe, wiste I how.
And of a mirthe I am right now bithoght,
To doon yow ese, and it shal coste noght.

    Ye goon to Caunterbury; God yow spede,
The blisful martir quyte yow your mede.
And wel I woot, as ye goon by the weye,
Ye shapen yow to talen and to pleye;
For trewely, confort ne mirthe is noon
To ryde by the weye doumb as a stoon;
And therfore wol I maken yow disport,

He may not hold back, even to spare his brother,
He must say as well one word as another.
Christ himself spoke down-to-earth in Holy Writ,
And well you know, no vulgarity is in it.
And Plato says, who can him read,
The words must be cousin to the deed.[43]
Also I pray you to forgive me,
That I have not described the folk
Here in this tale, in order of their rank;
My wit is short, you may well understand.

Very welcome our Host made us everyone,
And to the supper he set us anon;
He served us the best of food.
Strong was the wine, and it pleased us to drink.
Perfect for his work was our host withal
For he'd presided over a noble's great hall;
A large man he was with protruding eyes—
No better burgher was there in all Cheapside.
Bold of his speech, and wise, and well-taught,
And of manhood he lacked right nought.
And also he was truly a merry man,
And after supper to jest he began,
And spoke of mirth among many other things—
After we had paid our bills—
And said thus, "Now lords, truly,
You are to me right welcome, heartily.
For by my troth, I shall not lie,
I've not seen this year so merry a company
At one time in this inn as is now.
Happily would I offer some merriment, knew I how,
And of such I have just now thought
To give you pleasure, and it shall cost nought.

You go to Canterbury—God you speed;
And may the blissful martyr reward your deed.
And well I know, as you go your way,
That you make plans to share some tales;
For truly, pleasure or merriment is there none
To ride along as dumb as stone;
And therefore will I make you a game,

As I seyde erst, and doon you som confort.
And if yow lyketh alle, by oon assent,
Now for to stonden at my judgment,
And for to werken as I shal yow seye,
To-morwe, whan ye ryden by the weye,
Now, by my fader soule, that is deed,
But ye be merye, I wol yeve yow myn heed.
Hold up your hond, withouten more speche."
    Our counseil was nat longe for to seche;
Us thoughte it was noght worth to make it wys,
And graunted him withouten more avys,
And bad him seye his verdit, as him leste.
    "Lordinges," quod he, "now herkneth for the beste;
But tak it not, I prey yow, in desdeyn;
This is the poynt, to speken short and pleyn,
That ech of yow, to shorte with your weye,
In this viage, shal telle tales tweye,
To Caunterbury-ward, I mene it so,
And hom-ward he shal tellen othere two,
Of aventures that whylom han bifalle.
And which of yow that bereth him best of alle,
That is to seyn, that telleth in this cas
Tales of best sentence and most solas,
Shal have a soper at our aller cost
Here in this place, sitting by this post,
Whan that we come agayn fro Caunterbury.
And for to make yow the more mery,
I wol my-selven gladly with yow ryde,
Right at myn owne cost, and be your gyde.
And who-so wol my jugement withseye
Shal paye al that we spenden by the weye.
And if ye vouche-sauf that it be so,
Tel me anon, with-outen wordes mo,
And I wol erly shape me therfore."
    This thing was graunted, and our othes swore
With ful glad herte, and preyden him also
That he wold vouche-sauf for to do so,
And that he wolde been our governour,
And of our tales juge and reportour,

As I said before, and have some fun.
And if it pleases you all, with one voice,
Now to abide by my judgement,
And to proceed as I will now say,
Tomorrow, when you set out on your way—
Now by my father's soul who is dead—
Unless you be merry, I will give you my head.
Hold up your hands, without more speech."

We needed not long to agree;
We thought it not worth too long a ponder,
And granted his terms without thinking longer,
And bade him say his verdict as he pleased.

"Lords," said he, "now listen well,
But take it not, I pray you, wrong.
This is the point, to speak short and plain:
That each of you, to shorten our journey,
In this journey shall tell tales two,
Toward Canterbury, that is,
And homeward each another two shall tell
Of adventures that once upon a time you befell.
And whichever of you does best of all,
That is to say, who tells to this end
Tales of best wisdom, instruction and delight,
Shall have a supper on the rest of us
Here in this place, this same site,
When we come again from Canterbury.
And for to make you the more merry,
I will myself gladly with you ride,
Right at my own cost, and be your guide.
And whoso will my judgement naysay
Shall pay all we spend along the way.
And if you grant that it be so,
Tell me anon, without words more,
And I will myself quickly prepare."

This thing was agreed, and our oaths sworn
With full glad heart, and we begged him also
That he would be willing to do so,
And that he would be our governor
And of our tales judge and referee,

And sette a soper at a certeyn prys;
And we wold reuled been at his devys,
In heigh and lowe; and thus, by oon assent,
We been acorded to his jugement.
And ther-up-on the wyn was fet anon;
We dronken, and to reste wente echon,
With-outen any lenger taryinge.

A-morwe, whan that day bigan to springe,
Up roos our host, and was our aller cok,
And gadrede us togidre, alle in a flok,
And forth we riden, a litel more than pas,
Un-to the watering of seint Thomas.
And there our host bigan his hors areste,
And seyde; "Lordinges, herkneth, if yow leste.
Ye woot your forward, and I it yow recorde.
If even-song and morwe-song acorde,
Lat see now who shal telle the firste tale.
As ever mote I drinke wyn or ale,
Who-so be rebel to my jugement
Shal paye for al that by the weye is spent.
Now draweth cut, er that we ferrer twinne;
He which that hath the shortest shal biginne.
Sire knight," quod he, "my maister and my lord
Now draweth cut, for that is myn acord.
Cometh neer," quod he, "my lady prioresse;
And ye, sir clerk, lat be your shamfastnesse,
Ne studieth noght; ley hond to, every man."

Anon to drawen every wight bigan,
And shortly for to tellen, as it was,
Were it by aventure, or sort, or cas,
The sothe is this, the cut fil to the knight,
Of which ful blythe and glad was every wight;
And telle he moste his tale, as was resoun,
By forward and by composicioun,
As ye han herd; what nedeth wordes mo?
And whan this gode man saugh it was so,
As he that wys was and obedient
To kepe his forward by his free assent,
He seyde: "Sin I shal beginne the game,

And set a supper at a certain price;
And we would be governed by his word
In every way; and thus, by one assent,
We agreed to his judgement.
And thereupon the wine was fetched anon;
We drank, and to bed went each one,
Without any longer tarrying.

  In the morning, when day began to spring,
Up rose our host, and was for all our rooster,
And gathered us together, all in a flock;
And forth we rode, at a trot,
To Saint Thomas a Watering,[44]
And there our host stopped his horse,
And said, "Lords, harken, if you please.
You know our agreement, and so
If evensong and morningsong agree,
Let's see now who shall tell the first tale.
And surely as I may ever drink wine or ale,
Whoso rebels against my judgement
Shall pay for all that on the road we spend.
Now draw lots, before we further go;
He that has the shortest shall begin.
Sir Knight," said he, "my master and my lord
Now draw your straw, for that is my word.
Come nearer," said he, "my lady Prioress;
And you, sir Scholar, forget your shyness,
And study not. Lay hand to, every man!"

  At once to draw every person began,
And shortly to tell it as it was,
Were it by chance, or fortune or fate,
The truth is, the lot fell to the Knight,
Of which full blithe and glad was every person;
And tell he must his tale, as was right,
By agreement and arrangement,
As you have heard. Who needs more words?
And when this good man saw it was so,
As he was wise and willing
To keep his word
He said, "Since I shall begin the game,

What, welcome be the cut, a Goddes name!
Now lat us ryde, and herkneth what I seye."
    And with that word we riden forth our weye;
And he bigan with right a mery chere
His tale anon, and seyde in this manere.

Why, welcome be my lot, in God's name!
Now let us ride, and hear what I say."
    And with that we rode forth on our way:
And he began with right merry cheer
His tale anon, and said as you may hear.

The Knightes Tale

Iamque domos patrias, Scithice post aspera gentis Prelia,
laurigero, &c.

[Statius, THEB. xii. 519.]

Part One

WHYLOM, AS OLDE STORIES tellen us,
Ther was a duk that highte Theseus;
Of Athenes he was lord and governour,
And in his tyme swich a conquerour,
That gretter was ther noon under the sonne.
Ful many a riche contree hadde he wonne;
What with his wisdom and his chivalrye,
He conquered al the regne of Femenye,
That whylom was y-cleped Scithia;
And weddede the quene Ipolita,
And broghte hir hoom with him in his contree
With muchel glorie and greet solempnitee,
And eek hir yonge suster Emelye.
And thus with victorie and with melodye
Lete I this noble duk to Athenes ryde,
And al his hoost, in armes, him bisyde.

And certes, if it nere to long to here,
I wolde han told yow fully the manere,
How wonnen was the regne of Femenye
By Theseus, and by his chivalrye;
And of the grete bataille for the nones
Bitwixen Athenës and Amazones;
And how asseged was Ipolita,
The faire hardy quene of Scithia;
And of the feste that was at hir weddinge,
And of the tempest at hir hoom-cominge;
But al that thing I moot as now forbere.
I have, God woot, a large feeld to ere,
And wayke been the oxen in my plough.

The Knight's Tale

And now Theseus, drawing near to his native land in laurel-bedecked chariot after fierce battle with the Scythian folk, etc.

[Statius, THEBAID, 12.519]

Part One

ONCE UPON A TIME, as old stories tell us,
There was a duke named Theseus;
Of Athens he was a lord and governor,
And in his time such a conqueror,
That greater was there none under the sun.
Full many a rich country had he won;
What with his wisdom and his ability,
He had conquered all the Amazons' realm,
That once was called Scythia,
And wedded the queen Hyppolyta,
And brought her home with him to his country
With much glory and great ceremony,
And also her young sister Emily.
And thus with victory and with melody
Let I this noble duke to Athens ride,
And all his host, in arms, him beside.

And certainly, if it were not too long to hear,
I would have told you fully the manner
How won was the Amazons' realm
By Theseus, and by his fellow knights
And of the decisive, great battle
Between Athens and the Amazons;
And how besieged was Hyppolyta,
The fair, brave queen of Scythia;
And of the feast at their wedding,
And of the tempest at their homecoming;
But all that I must for now forebear.
I have, God knows, a large field to harrow,
And weak be the oxen in my plough.

The remenant of the tale is long y-nough.
I wol nat letten eek noon of this route;
Lat every felawe telle his tale aboute,
And lat see now who shal the soper winne;
And ther I lefte, I wol ageyn biginne.

This duk, of whom I make mencioun,
When he was come almost unto the toun,
In al his wele and in his moste pryde,
He was war, as he caste his eye asyde,
Wher that ther kneeled in the hye weye
A companye of ladies, tweye and tweye,
Ech after other, clad in clothes blake;
But swich a cry and swich a wo they make,
That in this world nis creature livinge,
That herde swich another weymentinge;
And of this cry they nolde never stenten,
Til they the reynes of his brydel henten.

"What folk ben ye, that at myn hoom-cominge
Perturben so my feste with crying?"
Quod Theseus, "have ye so greet envye
Of myn honour, that thus compleyne and crye?
Or who hath yow misboden, or offended?
And telleth me if it may been amended;
And why that ye ben clothed thus in blak?"

The eldest lady of hem alle spak,
When she hadde swowned with a deedly chere,
That it was routhe for to seen and here,
And seyde: "Lord, to whom Fortune had yiven
Victorie, and as a conquerour to liven,
Noght greveth us your glorie and your honour;
But we biseken mercy and socour.
Have mercy on our wo and our distresse.
Som drope of pitee, thurgh thy gentilesse,
Up-on us wrecched wommen lat thou falle.
For certes, lord, ther nis noon of us alle,
That she nath been a duchesse or a quene;
Now be we caitifs, as it is wel sene:
Thanked be Fortune, and hir false wheel,

The rest of the tale is long enough.
I will not hinder any of this company;
Let every fellow tell his tale in turn,
And let us see who shall the supper win;
And where I left off, I shall again begin.

    This duke, of whom I made mention,
When he was come almost to the town,
In all his happy success and in his pride,
He was aware, as he cast his glance aside,
That there knelt in the highway
A group of ladies, two by two,
Each after the other, clad in clothes black;
But such a cry and such a woe they made
That in this world there is no creature living
Who has heard such lamenting;
And of this crying they would not cease,
Till the reins of his bridle they had seized.

    "What folk be you, that at my homecoming
You disturb so my parade with crying?"
Said Theseus. "Have you so great envy
Of my honor, that you thus complain and cry?
Or who has you harmed, insulted or offended?
And tell me if it may be amended,
And why you thus be clothed in black."

    The eldest lady of them all spoke,
After almost fainting—she so looked like death
That it was a pity to see and hear.
She said, "Lord, to whom Fortune has given
Victory, and as a conqueror to live,
We don't begrudge your glory and your honor,
But we beseech mercy and succor.
Have mercy on our woe and our distress.
Let fall some drop of pity, through your nobility,
Upon us wretched women.
For surely, lord, there is none of us all,
Who has not been a duchess or a queen;
Now we be wretches, as is well seen,
Thanked be Fortune and her false wheel[1]

That noon estat assureth to be weel.
And certes, lord, t'abyden your presence,
Here in the temple of the goddesse Clemence
We han been waytinge al this fourtenight;
Now help us, lord, sith it is in thy might.
    I wrecche, which that wepe and waille thus,
Was whylom wyf to king Capaneus,
That starf at Thebes, cursed be that day!
And alle we, that been in this array,
And maken al this lamentacioun,
We losten alle our housbondes at that toun,
Whyl that the sege ther-aboute lay.
And yet now th' olde Creon, weylaway!
The lord is now of Thebes the citee,
Fulfild of ire and of iniquitee,
He, for despyt, and for his tirannye,
To do the dede bodyes vileinye,
Of alle our lordes, whiche that ben slawe,
Hath alle the bodyes on an heep y-drawe,
And wol nat suffren hem, by noon assent,
Neither to been y-buried nor y-brent,
But maketh houndes ete hem in despyt."
And with that word, with-outen more respyt,
They fillen gruf, and cryden pitously.
"Have on us wrecched wommen som mercy,
And lat our sorwe sinken in thyn herte."
    This gentil duk doun from his courser sterte
With herte pitous, whan he herde hem speke.
Him thoughte that his herte wolde breke,
Whan he saugh hem so pitous and so mat,
That whylom weren of so greet estat.
And in his armes he hem alle up hente,
And hem conforteth in ful good entente;
And swoor his ooth, as he was trewe knight,
He wolde doon so ferforthly his might
Up-on the tyraunt Creon hem to wreke,
That al the peple of Grece, sholde speke
How Creon was of Theseus y-served,
As he that hadde his deeth ful wel deserved.

Who makes sure that no life will always be secure.
And indeed, lord, for your return,
Here in this temple of the goddess Mercy
We have been waiting all this fortnight;
Now help us, lord, since it is in your might.
    I, wretch, who weep and wail thus,
Was once wife to king Capaneus,[2]
Who died at Thebes—cursed be that day!
And all we who be in this state
And make all this lamentation,
We lost all our husbands at that town
While under siege it lay.
And yet now old Creon, wellaway,
Who lord is now of Thebes the city,
Brimful of malice and spite,
He, for spite and tyranny,
To dishonor the dead bodies
Of all our lords who were slain,
Has piled up all the bodies in a heap,
And would not allow them, by his leave,
To be buried or be burned,
But maliciously set the dogs on them to eat."
And with those words, and without more said,
They fell forward face down and cried piteously,
"Have on us wretched women some mercy,
And let our sore sink in your heart."
    This gentle duke down from his horse leapt
With heart merciful, pitying, when he heard them speak.
He thought that his heart would break,
When he saw them so pitiful and so bleak,
Who once were of so great estate.
And in his arms he them each took,
And comforted them as best he could;
And swore his oath, as he was a true knight,
He would use all his might
Upon the tyrant Creon him to wreak,
That all the people of Greece should speak
How Creon was by Theseus well-served
And he his death full well deserved.

And right anoon, with-outen more abood,
His baner he desplayeth, and foorth rood
To Thebes-ward, and al his host bisyde;
No neer Athenës wolde he go ne ryde,
Ne take his ese fully half a day,
But onward on his wey that night he lay;
And sente anoon Ipolita the quene,
And Emelye hir yonge suster shene,
Un-to the toun of Athenës to dwelle;
And forth he rit; ther nis namore to telle.
    The rede statue of Mars, with spere and targe,
So shyneth in his whyte baner large,
That alle the feeldes gliteren up and doun;
And by his baner born is his penoun
Of gold ful riche, in which ther was y-bete
The Minotaur, which that he slough in Crete.
Thus rit this duk, thus rit this conquerour,
And in his host of chivalrye the flour,
Til that he cam to Thebes, and alighte
Faire in a feeld, ther as he thoghte fighte.
But shortly for to speken of this thing,
With Creon, which that was of Thebes king,
He faught, and slough him manly as a knight
In pleyn bataille, and putte the folk to flight;
And by assaut he wan the citee after,
And rente adoun bothe wal, and sparre, and rafter;
And to the ladyes he restored agayn
The bones of hir housbondes that were slayn,
To doon obséquies, as was tho the gyse.
But it were al to long for to devyse
The grete clamour and the waymentinge
That the ladyes made at the brenninge
Of the bodyes, and the grete honour
That Theseus, the noble conquerour,
Doth to the ladyes, whan they from him wente;
But shortly for to telle is myn entente.
Whan that this worthy duk, this Theseus,
Hath Creon slayn, and wonne Thebes thus,
Stille in that feeld he took al night his reste,

And right anon, without more delay,
His banner he displayed, and forth rode
Thebesward, and all his host of men beside.
No nearer Athens would he walk nor ride,
Nor take his ease even half a day,
But onward on his way that night he lay,
And sent anon Hyppolyta the queen
And Emily, her young sister fair,
Unto the town of Athens to dwell;
And forth he rode, there is no more to tell.
    The red statue of Mars, with spear and shield,
So shines in his white banner large
That all the fields glitter up and down;
And by his banner borne is his pennant
Of gold full rich, and embroidered in it
The Minotaur,[3] that he slew in Crete.
Thus rode this duke, thus rode this conqueror
And in his host rode knighthood's flower,
Till that he came to Thebes, and alighted
In a field, where he thought to fight.
But to make a long story short
With Creon, who was Thebes' king,
He fought, and slew him manly, boldly as a knight
In open battle, and put the rest to flight;
And by assault he won the city after,
And tore down wall and beam and rafter;
And to the ladies he restored again
The bones of their husbands who were slain,
To do obsequies, as then was the custom.
But it would take too long to relate
The great clamor and the lamentation
That the ladies made at the burning
Of the bodies, and the great honor
That Theseus, the noble conqueror,
Did to the ladies, when they from him went;
But to make it short is my intent.
When that this worthy duke, this Theseus,
Had Creon slain and won Thebes thus,
Still in that field he took all night his rest,

And dide with al the contree as him leste.
    To ransake in the tas of bodyes dede,
Hem for to strepe of harneys and of wede,
The pilours diden bisinesse and cure,
After the bataille and disconfiture.
And so bifel, that in the tas they founde,
Thurgh-girt with many a grevous blody wounde,
Two yonge knightes ligging by and by,
Bothe in oon armes, wroght ful richely,
Of whiche two, Arcita hight that oon,
And that other knight hight Palamon.
Nat fully quike, ne fully dede they were,
But by hir cote-armures, and by hir gere,
The heraudes knewe hem best in special,
As they that weren of the blood royal
Of Thebes, and of sustren two y-born.
Out of the tas the pilours han hem torn,
And han hem caried softe un-to the tente
Of Theseus, and he ful sone hem sente
To Athenës, to dwellen in prisoun
Perpetuelly, he nolde no raunsoun.
And whan this worthy duk hath thus y-don,
He took his host, and hoom he rood anon
With laurer crowned as a conquerour;
And there he liveth, in joye and in honour,
Terme of his lyf; what nedeth wordes mo?
And in a tour, in angwish and in wo,
Dwellen this Palamoun and eek Arcite,
For evermore, ther may no gold hem quyte.
    This passeth yeer by yeer, and day by day,
Til it fil ones, in a morwe of May,
That Emelye, that fairer was to sene
Than is the lile upon his stalke grene,
And fressher than the May with floures newe—
For with the rose colour stroof hir hewe,
I noot which was the fairer of hem two—
Er it were day, as was hir wone to do,
She was arisen, and al redy dight;
For May wol have no slogardye a-night.

And did with all the country as he wished.
　To go through the mound of bodies dead,
Them to strip of armor and clothes,
The pillagers worked fast and well
After the battle and defeat.
And so befell, that in that mound they found,
Pierced through with many a grievous bloody wound,
Two young knights lying side by side,
Both with the same coat of arms, wrought full richly,
Of which two, one was named Arcita,
And the other knight was called Palamon.
Not fully alive nor fully dead they were,
But by their emblems and their gear,
The heralds knew especially well
That they were of the blood royal
Of Thebes, and of two sisters born.
Out of the mound the pillagers tore them
And carried them gently into the tent
Of Theseus, and he full soon them sent
To Athens, to dwell in prison
Perpetually: taking no ransom.
And when this worthy duke had thus done,
He took his men, and home he rode anon
With laurel crowned as a conqueror;
And there he lived in joy and honor
The rest of his life; who need say more?
And in a tower, in anguish and in woe,
Dwelt Palamon and Arcita
For evermore, held without ransom.
　This went on year by year and day by day,
Till it so happened, one morning in May,
That Emily, who fairer was to see
Than is the lily upon its stalk of green,
And fresher than May with its flowers new—
For with the rose's color strove her complexion's hue,
I know not which was the fairer of the two—
Before daylight, as was her wont to do,
She was arisen and promptly dressed,
For May at night will have no laziness.

The sesoun priketh every gentil herte,
And maketh him out of his sleep to sterte,
And seith, "Arys, and do thyn observaunce."
This maked Emelye have remembraunce
To doon honour to May, and for to ryse.
Y clothed was she fresh, for to devyse;
Hir yelow heer was broyded in a tresse,
Bihinde hir bak, a yerde long, I gesse.
And in the gardin, at the sonne up-riste,
She walketh up and doun, and as hir liste
She gadereth floures, party whyte and rede,
To make a sotil gerland for hir hede,
And as an aungel hevenly she song.
    The grete tour, that was so thikke and strong,
Which of the castel was the chief dongeoun,
(Ther-as the knightes weren in prisoun,
Of whiche I tolde yow, and tellen shal)
Was evene joynant to the gardin-wal,
Ther as this Emelye hadde hir pleyinge.
Bright was the sonne, and cleer that morweninge,
And Palamon, this woful prisoner,
As was his wone, by leve of his gayler,
Was risen, and romed in a chambre on heigh,
In which he al the noble citee seigh,
And eek the gardin, ful of braunches grene,
Ther-as this fresshe Emelye the shene
Was in hir walk, and romed up and doun.
This sorweful prisoner, this Palamoun,
Goth in the chambre, roming to and fro,
And to him-self compleyning of his wo;
That he was born, ful ofte he seyde, "alas!"
And so bifel, by aventure or cas,
That thurgh a window, thikke of many a barre
Of yren greet, and square as any sparre,
He caste his eye upon Emelye,
And ther-with-al he bleynte, and cryde "a!"
As though he stongen were un-to the herte.
And with that cry Arcite anon up-sterte,
And seyde, "Cosin myn, what eyleth thee,

The season pricks every gentle heart,
And makes each out of sleep to start
And says, "Arise, and do your observance."
This made Emily have remembrance
To do honor to May, and to arise.
Clothed was she fresh, as I may tell:
Her yellow hair was braided in a tress
Behind her back, a yard long, I guess.
And in a garden, just at sunrise
She walked up and down, as she pleased
She gathered flowers, white and red,
To deftly weave a garland for her head
And as an angel heavenly she sang.

    The great tower, that was so thick and strong,
Which of the castle was the chief dungeon
(There the knights were in prison,
Of whom I told you and shall tell)
Was just beside the garden wall
There where Emily had her garden walk.
Bright was the sun and clear that morning,
And Palamon, this woeful prisoner,
As was his wont, by leave of his jailer,
Was risen and roamed in a chamber on high,
In which he all the noble city saw,
And also the garden, full of branches green,
Where this fresh Emily the fair
Was in her walk, and roamed up and down.
This sorrowful prisoner, this Palamon,
Goes in the chamber roaming to and fro,
And to himself complaining of his woe.
That he was born, full oft he said, "Alas!"
And so it happened, by accident or chance
That through a window, thickset with many a bar
Of iron great and round as any spar,
He cast his eye upon Emily,
And therewith he flinched and cried "Ah!"
As though he were stung into the heart.
And with that cry Arcita anon upstarted
And said, "Cousin mine, what ails you,

That art so pale and deedly on to see?
Why crydestow? who hath thee doon offence?
For Goddes love, tak al in pacience
Our prisoun, for it may non other be;
Fortune hath yeven us this adversitee.
Som wikke aspect or disposicioun
Of Saturne, by sum constellacioun,
Hath yeven us this, al-though we hadde it sworn;
So stood the heven whan that we were born;
We moste endure it: this is the short and pleyn."
    This Palamon answerde, and seyde ageyn,
"Cosyn, for sothe, of this opinioun
Thou hast a veyn imaginacioun.
This prison caused me nat for to crye.
But I was hurt right now thurgh-out myn yë
In-to myn herte, that wol my bane be.
The fairnesse of that lady that I see
Yond in the gardin romen to and fro,
Is cause of al my crying and my wo.
I noot wher she be womman or goddesse;
But Venus is it, soothly, as I gesse."
And ther-with-al on kneës doun he fil,
And seyde: "Venus, if it be thy wil
Yow in this gardin thus to transfigure
Bifore me, sorweful wrecche creature,
Out of this prisoun help that we may scapen.
And if so be my destinee be shapen
By eterne word to dyen in prisoun,
Of our linage have som compassioun,
That is so lowe y-broght by tirannye."
And with that word Arcite gan espye
Wher-as this lady romed to and fro.
And with that sighte hir beautee hurte him so,
That, if that Palamon was wounded sore,
Arcite is hurt as muche as he, or more.
And with a sigh he seyde pitously:
"The fresshe beautee sleeth me sodeynly
Of hir that rometh in the yonder place;
And, but I have hir mercy and hir grace,

That you're such a pale and deathly hue?
Why did you cry? Who has offended you?
For God's love, take all in patience
Our prison, for it may not otherwise be;
Fortune has given us this adversity.
Some wicked aspect or disposition
Of Saturn, by some constellation,[4]
Has given us this, there's nothing we could have done.
So stood the stars when we were born.
We must endure it; this is the short and plain."
    This Palamon answered and said again,
"Cousin, forsooth, in this opinion
You have a mistaken imagination.
This prison caused me not to cry,
But I was so hurt right now through my eye
Into my heart, that it will me destroy.
The fairness of that lady that I see
Yonder in that garden roaming to and fro
Is cause of all my crying and my woe.
I don't know if she is a woman or a goddess,
But Venus is she truly, as I guess."
And therewithal on his knees down he fell,
And said: "Venus, if it be your will
Yourself in the garden thus to transfigure
Before me, sorrowful wretched creature,
Out of this prison help that we may escape.
And if so be my destiny shaped
By eternal word to die in prison,
Of our lineage have some compassion,
That is so low brought by tyranny."
And with that word Arcita did espy
Where this lady roamed to and fro;
And with that sight her beauty hurt him so,
That, if Palamon was wounded sore,
Arcita was hurt as much as he, or more.
And with a sigh he said piteously:
"The fresh beauty slays me suddenly
Of her who roams in yonder place;
And, unless I have her mercy and her grace,

That I may seen hir atte leeste weye,
I nam but deed; ther nis namore to seye."
    This Palamon, whan he tho wordes herde,
Dispitously he loked, and answerde:
"Whether seistow this in ernest or in pley?"
    "Nay," quod Arcite, "in ernest, by my fey!
God help me so, me list ful yvele pleye."
    This Palamon gan knitte his browes tweye:
"It nere," quod he, "to thee no greet honour
For to be fals, ne for to be traytour
To me, that am thy cosin and thy brother
Y-sworn ful depe, and each of us til other,
That never, for to dyen in the peyne,
Til that the deeth departe shal us tweyne,
Neither of us in love to hindren other,
Ne in non other cas, my leve brother;
But that thou sholdest trewely forthren me
In every cas, and I shal forthren thee.
This was thyn ooth, and myn also, certeyn;
I wot right wel, thou darst it nat withseyn.
Thus artow of my counseil, out of doute.
And now thou woldest falsly been aboute
To love my lady, whom I love and serve,
And ever shal, til that myn herte sterve.
Now certes, fals Arcite, thou shalt nat so.
I loved hir first, and tolde thee my wo
As to my counseil, and my brother sworn
To forthre me, as I have told biforn.
For which thou are y-bounden as a knight
To helpen me, if it lay in thy might,
Or elles artow fals, I dar wel seyn."
    This Arcite ful proudly spak ageyn,
"Thou shalt," quod he, "be rather fals than I;
But thou art fals, I telle thee utterly;
For *par amour* I loved ir first er thow.
What wiltow seyn? thou wistest nat yet now
Whether she be a womman or goddesse!
Thyn is affeccioun of holinesse,
And myn is love, as to a creature;

That I may see her at least,
I am good as dead; there is no more to say."
    Then Palamon, when he those words heard,
Angrily he looked and answered:
"Are you saying this in earnest or in jest?"
    "No," said Arcita, "in earnest, by my faith!
God help me so, I have no desire to joke with you."
    Then Palamon knitted his brows two:
And said he, "It is not to you any great honor
To be false, nor to be traitor
To me, your own cousin and brother
Sworn in blood, and each of us to the other,
That never, not even under torture's pain,
To the death shall we two part,
Nor in love shall we hinder the other,
Nor in any other way, my dear brother;
But that you should stand by me truly
In every way, as I shall you.
This was your oath, and mine also, for sure;
I know right well, you dare not it deny.
Thus you know my secrets, without doubt,
And now you would falsely set out
To love my lady, whom I love and serve,
And ever shall, till my heart quits.
Now surely, false Arcita, you won't do it.
I loved her first, and told you my woe
As my confidant and my brother sworn
To stand by me, as I have said before.
For which you're bound as a knight
To help me, if it lies in your might,
Or else you're false, I dare well say."
    This Arcita full proudly spoke again:
"You shall," said he, "be sooner false than I;
But you are false, I tell you straight;
For as flesh and blood I loved her before you.
What would you say? You don't yet know
Whether she's a woman or a goddess!
Yours is affection spiritual,
And mine is love, as to a creature,

For which I tolde thee myn aventure
As to my cosin, and my brother sworn.
I pose, that thou lovedest hir biforn;
Wostow nat wel the olde clerkes sawe,
That 'who shal yeve a lover any lawe?'
Love is a gretter lawe, by my pan,
Than may be yeve to any erthly man.
And therefore positif lawe and swich decree
Is broke al-day for love, in ech degree.
A man moot nedes love, maugree his heed.
He may nat fleen it, thogh he sholde be deed,
Al be she mayde, or widwe, or elles wyf.
And eek it is nat lykly, al thy lyf,
To stonden in hir grace; namore shal I;
For wel thou woost thy-selven, verraily,
That thou and I be dampned to prisoun
Perpetuelly; us gayneth no raunsoun.
We stryve as dide the houndes for the boon,
They foughte al day, and yet hir part was noon;
Ther cam a kyte, whyl that they were wrothe,
And bar awey the boon bitwixe hem bothe.
And therfore, at the kinges court, my brother,
Ech man for him-self, ther is non other.
Love if thee list; for I love and ay shal;
And soothly, leve brother, this is al.
Here in this prisoun mote we endure,
And everich of us take his aventure."

Greet was the stryf and long bitwixe hem tweye,
If that I hadde leyser for to seye;
But to th' effect. It happed on a day,
(To telle it yow as shortly as I may)
A worthy duk that highte Perotheus,
That felawe was un-to duk Theseus
Sin thilke day that they were children lyte,
Was come to Athenes, his felawe to visyte,
And for to pleye, as he was wont to do,
For in this world he loved no man so:
And he loved him as tenderly ageyn.
So wel they loved, as olde bokes seyn,

For which I told you my adventure
As to my cousin and my brother sworn.
But let us say that you loved her first:
Don't you know the old scholar's saw:
'Who shall give a lover any law?'
Love is a greater law, in my mind,
Than may be given to any earthly man.
And therefore man's law and such decrees
Are broken for love every day by everybody.
A man must love, though his head says no.
He may not escape it, even if it means dying,
Whether she's a maid, a widow or else a wife.
And you're not likely for all your life
To stand in her grace; no more shall I;
For well you know yourself, verily,
That you and I be condemned to prison
Perpetually; we shall have no ransom.
We strive as did the hounds for the bone:
They fought all day, and yet their part was none;
There came a bird, while they were fighting so,
And bore away the bone from them both.
And therefore, at the king's court, my brother,
Each man for himself: there is no other.
Love if you will, for I love and always shall;
And truly, dear brother, this is all.
Here in this prison must we endure,
And each of us take what to him comes."
        Great was the strife and long between the two,
And would that I had time to describe—
But to the outcome. It happened on a day,
To make it short as I can,
A worthy duke named Perotheus,[5]
Who was a friend to duke Theseus
Since the days when they were children little,
Was come to Athens his friend to visit,
And to play as he was wont to do;
For in this world he loved no man so,
And Theseus loved him as tenderly in turn.
So well they loved, as old books say,

That whan that oon was deed, sothly to telle,
His felawe wente and soghte him doun in helle;
But of that story list me nat to wryte.
    Duk Perotheus loved wel Arcite,
And hadde him knowe at Thebes yeer by yere;
And fynally, at requeste and preyere
Of Perotheus, with-oute any raunsoun,
Duk Theseus him leet out of prisoun,
Freely to goon, wher that him liste over-al,
In swich a gyse, as I you tellen shal.
    This was the forward, pleynly for t'endyte,
Bitwixen Theseus and him Arcite:
That if so were, that Arcite were y-founde
Ever in his lyf, by day or night or stounde
In any contree of this Theseus,
And he were caught, it was acorded thus,
That with a swerd he sholde lese his heed;
Ther nas non other remedye ne reed,
But taketh his leve, and homward he him spedde;
Let him be war, his nekke lyth to wedde!
    How greet a sorwe suffreth now Arcite!
The deeth he feleth thurgh his herte symte;
He wepeth, wayleth, cryeth pitously;
To sleen him-self he wayteth prively.
He seyde, "Allas that day that I was born!
Now is my prison worse than biforn;
Now is me shape eternally to dwelle
Noght in purgatorie, but in helle.
Allas! that ever knew I Perotheus
For elles hadde I dwelled with Theseus
Y-fetered in his prisoun ever-mo.
Than hadde I been in blisse, and nat in wo.
Only the sighte of hir, whom that I serve,
Though that I never hir grace may deserve,
Wolde han suffised right y-nough for me.
O dere cosin Palamon," quod he,
"Thyn is the victorie of this aventure,
Ful blisfully in prison maistow dure;
In prison? certes nay, but in paradys!

That when one was dead, truly to tell,
His friend went and sought him down in hell;
But of that story I don't want to write.
    Duke Perotheus loved Arcita well,
And had known him at Thebes for many years;
And finally, at request and prayer
Of Perotheus, without any ransom,
Duke Theseus let him out of prison
Free to go wherever he pleased,
In such a way as I shall you tell.
    This was the agreement, to plainly write,
Between Theseus and Arcita:
That if it happened, that Arcita were found
Ever in his life, by day or night, for one moment
In any country of this Theseus,
And he were caught, it was agreed thus,
That with a sword he should lose his head;
With no other choice or remedy
But to take his leave, and homeward he him speed;
Let him be warned, his neck lies as a pledge.
    How great a sorrow suffered now Arcita!
The death he felt through his heart strike,
He wept, wailed, cried piteously;
To slay himself he intended secretly.
He said, "Alas that day that I was born!
Now is my prison worse than before!
Now is my destiny eternally to dwell
Not in purgatory but in hell.
Alas, that ever I knew Perotheus!
For otherwise had I dwelled with Theseus
Fettered in his prison evermore.
Then had I been in bliss, and not in woe.
Only the sight of her whom that I serve,
Though that I never her grace may deserve,
Would have sufficed right enough for me.
O dear cousin Palamon," said he,
"Yours is the victory of this adventure
Full blissfully in prison must you endure.
In prison? surely not, but in paradise!

Wel hath fortune y-turned thee the dys,
That hast the sighte of hir, and I th'absence.
For possible is, sin thou hast hir presence,
And art a knight, a worthy and an able,
That by som cas, sin fortune is chaungeable,
Thou mayst to thy desyr som-tyme atteyne.
But I, that am exyled, and bareyne
Of alle grace, and in so greet despeir,
That ther nis erthe, water, fyr, ne eir,
Ne creature, that of hem maked is,
That may me helpe or doon confort in this:
Wel oughte I sterve in wanhope and distresse;
Farwel my lyf, my lust, and my gladnesse!

    Allas, why pleynen folk so in commune
Of purveyaunce of God, or of fortune,
That yeveth hem ful ofte in many a gyse
Wel bettre than they can hem-self devyse?
Som man desyreth for to han richesse,
That cause is of his mordre or greet siknesse.
And som man wolde out of his prison fayn,
That in his hous is of his meynee slayn.
Infinite harmes been in this matere;
We witen nat what thing we preyen here.
We faren as he that dronke is as a mous;
A dronke man wot wel he hath an hous,
But he noot which the righte wey is thider;
And to a dronke man the wey is slider.
And certes, in this world so faren we;
We seken faste after felicitee,
But we goon wrong ful often, trewely.
Thus may we seyen alle, and namely I,
That wende and hadde a greet opinioun,
That, if I mighte escapen from prisoun,
Than hadde I been in joye and perfit hele,
Ther now I am exyled fro my wele.
Sin that I may nat seen you, Emelye,
I nam but deed; ther nis no remedye."

    Up-on that other syde Palamon,
Whan that he wiste Arcite was agon,

Well has Fortune turned the dice,
That you have the sight of her face, and I her absence.
For possible is, since you have her presence,
And are a knight, worthy and able,
That by some chance, since Fortune is changeable,
You may your desire sometime attain.
But I, who am exiled and barren
Of all grace, and in so great despair
That there is neither earth, water, fire nor air,
Nor any creature that of them made is
That may help me or give me comfort in this,
Well ought I die in despair and distress.
Farewell my life, my joy, and my gladness!
   Alas, why complain folk so often
About Divine Providence, or of Fortune,
That gives them full often in many a guise
Well better than they can themselves devise?
One man may desire to have riches,
That cause his murder or great sickness.
Another man would out of his prison gladly be,
Who in his own house is slain by his enemy.
Infinite harms be in this matter;
We know not what thing we pray for.
We act like someone as drunk as a mouse,
A drunk man knows well he has a house,
But he knows not the right way there;
And to a drunk man the road is all ice.
And certainly, in this world so fare we;
We seek always after happiness,
But we go wrong full often, truly.
Thus may we all say, and especially I
Who thought and had a great opinion
That if I might escape from prison,
Then I would have been in joy and perfect health,
Whereas now I am exiled from my felicity.
Since I may not see you, Emily,
I am but dead; there is no remedy."
   Upon that other side Palamon,
When he knew Arcita was gone,

Swich sorwe he maketh, that the grete tour
Resouneth of his youling and clamour.
The pure fettres on his shines grete
Weren of his bittre salte teres wete.
"Allas!" quod he, "Arcita, cosin myn,
Of al our stryf, God woot, the fruyt is thyn.
Thow walkest now in Thebes at thy large,
And of my wo thou yevest litel charge.
Thow mayst, sin thou hast wisdom and manhede,
Assemblen alle the folk of our kinrede,
And make a werre so sharp on this citee,
That by som aventure, or some tretee,
Thou mayst have hir to lady and to wyf,
For whom that I mot nedes lese my lyf.
For, as by wey of possibilitee,
Sith thou art at thy large, of prison free,
And art a lord, greet is thyn avauntage,
More than is myn, that sterve here in a cage.
For I mot wepe and wayle, whyl I live,
With al the wo that prison may me yive,
And eek with peyne that love me yiveth also,
That doubleth al my torment and my wo."
Ther-with the fyr of jelousye up-sterte
With-inne his brest, and hente him by the herte
So woodly, that he lyk was to biholde
The box-tree, or the asshen dede and colde.
Tho seyde he; "O cruel goddess, that governe
This world with binding of your word eterne,
And wryten in the table of athamaunt
Your parlement, and your eterne graunt,
What is mankinde more un-to yow holde
Than is the sheep, that rouketh in the folde?
For slayn is man right as another beste,
And dwelleth eek in prison and areste,
And hath siknesse, and greet adversitee,
And ofte tymes giltelees, pardee!
   What governaunce is in this prescience,
That giltelees tormenteth innocence?
And yet encreseth this al my penaunce,

Made such sorrow that the great tower
Resounded with his yowling and his clamor.
The very fetters on his swollen limbs
Were of his bitter salt tears wet.
"Alas!" said he, "Arcita, cousin mine,
Of all our strife, God knows, the fruit is yours.
You walk freely now in Thebes,
And to my woe you give little heed.
You may, since you have wisdom and manhood,
Assemble all the folk of our kindred,
And make a war so sharp on this city,
That by some chance, or some treaty,
You may have her as your lady and wife,
For whom that I must needs lose my life.
For, as by way of possibility,
Since you are at large, of prison free,
And are a lord, great is your advantage
More than mine, dying here in a cage.
For I must weep and wail, while I live,
With all the woe that prison may me give,
And with the pain that love me gives also,
That doubles all my torment and my woe."
Therewith the fire of jealousy upstarted
Within his breast, and seized him by the heart
So tightly, that he was like to behold
Boxwood blossoms white or ashes dead and cold.
Then said he, "O cruel goddess, who governs
This world with binding of your word eternal,
And writes in the tablet of adamantine
Your decision and your eternal decree,
How is mankind more to you
Than the sheep that cowers in the fold?
For slain is man as any other beast,
And dwells also in prison and arrest,
And has sickness and great adversity.
And oftentimes guiltless, certainly!

   What purpose is there in this prescience
That torments guiltless innocence?
And yet this increases all my penance,

That man is bounden to his observaunce,
For Goddes sake, to letten of his wille,
Ther as a beest may al his lust fulfille.
And whan a beest is deed, he hath no peyne;
But man after his deeth moot wepe and pleyne,
Though in this world he have care and wo:
With-outen doute it may stonden so.
Th' answere of this I lete to divynis,
But wel I woot, that in this world gret pyne is.
Allas! I see a serpent or a theef,
That many a trewe man hath doon mescheef,
Goon at his large, and wher him list may turne.
But I mot been in prison thurgh Saturne,
And eek thurgh Juno, jalous and eek wood,
That hath destroyed wel ny al the blood
Of Thebes, with his waste walles wyde.
And Venus sleeth me on that other syde
For jelousye, and fere of him Arcite."

Now wol I stinte of Palamon a lyte,
And lete him in his prison stille dwelle,
And of Arcita forth I wol yow telle.

The somer passeth, and the nightes longe
Encresen double wyse the peynes stronge.
Bothe of the lovere and the prisoner.
I noot which hath the wofullere mester.
For shortly for to seyn, this Palamoun
Perpetuelly is dampned to prisoun,
In cheynes and in fettres to ben deed;
And Arcite is exyled upon his heed
For ever-mo as out of that contree,
Ne never-mo he shal his lady see.

Yow loveres axe I now this questioun,
Who hath the worse, Arcite or Palamoun?
That oon may seen his lady day by day,
But in prison he moot dwelle alway.
That other wher him list may ryde or go,
But seen his lady shal he never-mo.
Now demeth as yow liste, ye that can,
For I wol telle forth as I bigan.

That man is bound to the obligation,
For God's sake, to restrain his will,
While a beast may all his desire fulfill.
And when a beast is dead, he has no pain;
But man after his death must weep and complain,
Though in this world he have care and woe.
Without doubt it may stand so.
The answer to this I leave to divines,
But well I know, that in this world great pain is.
Alas! I see a serpent or a thief,
That to many a true man has done mischief,
Go freely, wherever he wishes to turn.
But I must be in prison through Saturn,
And through Juno, jealous, angry and wild,[6]
Who have destroyed nearly all the blood
Of Thebes, with its wasted walls wide.
And Venus slays me on the other side
For jealousy, and fear of Arcita."
    Now will I let go of Palamon a little
And let him in his prison still dwell,
And of Arcita more I will you tell.

    The summer passed, and the nights long
Increased doubly the pains strong of
Both the lover and the prisoner.
I do not know who had the woefuller place.
For, to make it brief, this Palamon
Perpetually is condemned to prison,
In chains and fetters until his death;
And Arcita is exiled upon pain of beheading
Forevermore out of that country,
Nor evermore shall his lady see.
    Of you lovers I now ask this question:
Who had the worse, Arcita or Palamon?
That one may see his lady day by day
But in prison he must dwell always.
The other where he wishes may ride or go,
But see his lady shall he nevermore.
Now judge as you will, you who understand,
For I will continue as I began.

Part Two

Whan that Arcite to Thebes comen was,
Ful ofte a day he swelte and seyde "allas,"
For seen his lady shal he never-mo.
And shortly to concluden al his wo,
So muche sorwe had never creature
That is, or shal, whyl that the world may dure.
His sleep, his mete, his drink is him biraft,
That lene he wex, and drye as is a shaft.
His eyen holwe, and grisly to biholde;
His hewe falwe, and pale as asshen colde,
And solitarie he was, and ever allone,
And wailling al the night, making his mone.
And if he herde song or instrument,
Then wolde he wepe, he mighte nat be stent;
So feble eek were his spirits, and so lowe,
And chaunged so, that no man coude knowe
His speche nor his vois, though men it herde.
And in his gere, for al the world he ferde
Nat oonly lyk the loveres maladye
Of Hereos, but rather lyk manye
Engendered of humour malencolyk,
Biforen, in his celle fantastyk.
And shortly, turned was al up-so doun
Bothe habit and eek disposicioun
Of him, this woful lovere daun Arcite.
        What sholde I al-day of his wo endyte?
Whan he endured hadde a yeer or two
This cruel torment, and this peyne and wo,
At Thebes, in his contree, as I seyde,
Up-on a night, in sleep as he him leyde,
Him thoughte how that the winged god Mercurie
Biforn him stood, and bad him to be murye.
His slepy yerde in hond he bar uprighte;
An hat he werede up-on his heres brighte.
Arrayed was this god (as he took keep)
As he was whan that Argus took his sleep;
And seyde him thus: "T' Athénës shaltou wende;

Part Two

When Arcita was come to Thebes,
Full often a day he sighed and said "alas,"
For his lady shall he see nevermore.
And to sum up briefly all his woe,
So much sorrow had never a creature
That is or will be so long as the world endures.
His sleep, his appetite, his thirst was him bereft,
That lean he waxed and dry as is a shaft.
His eyes hollow, and grim to behold
His color faded and pale as ashes cold;
And solitary he was and ever alone,
And wailing all night, making his moan.
And if he heard song or instrument,
Then would he weep, he could not be stopped.
So feeble were his spirits, and so low,
And he changed so, that no man could know
His speech nor his voice, though men it heard.
And in his woe for all the world he had
Not only the pain of
Love sickness,
But also the anguish
Of a spirit by love torn.
And shortly, was turned all upside down
Both habit and disposition
Of him, this woeful lover lord Arcita.
      Why should I all day of his woe write?
When he had endured a year or two
This cruel treatment and this pain and woe,
At Thebes, in his country, as I said,
Upon a night, in sleep as he lay
He dreamed that the winged god Mercury
Before him stood and bade him to be merry.
His sleepwand in hand he bore upright;
And helmet he wore upon his hair bright.
Dressed was this god, as Arcita saw
As when he had sent Argus to sleep;
And told him thus, "To Athens you shall wend:

Ther is thee shapen of thy wo an ende."
And with that word Arcite wook and sterte.
"Now trewely, how sore that me smerte,"
Quod he, "t' Athénës right now wol I fare;
Ne for the drede of deeth shal I nat spare
To see my lady, that I love and serve;
In hir presence I recche nat to sterve."
      And with that word he caughte a greet mirour,
And saugh that chaunged was al his colour,
And saugh his visage al in another kinde.
And right annon it ran him in his minde,
That, sith his face was so disfigured
Of maladye, the which he hadde endured,
He mighte wel, if that he bar him lowe,
Live in Athénes ever-more unknowe,
And seen his lady wel ny day by day.
And right anon he chaunged his array,
And cladde him as a povre laborer,
And al allone, save oonly a squyer,
That knew his privetee and al his cas,
Which was disgysed povrely, as he was,
T' Athénës is he goon the nexte way.
And to the court he wente up-on a day,
And at the gate he profreth his servyse,
To drugge and drawe, what so men wol devyse.
And shortly of this matere for to seyn,
He fil in office with a chamberleyn,
The which that dwelling was with Emelye;
For he was wys, and coude soon aspye
Of every servaunt, which that serveth here.
Wel coude he hewen wode, and water bere,
For he was yong and mighty for the nones,
And ther-to he was strong and big of bones
To doon that any wight can him devyse.
A yeer or two he was in this servyse,
Page of the chambre of Emelye the brighte;
And "Philostrate" he seide that he highte.
But half so wel biloved a man as he
Ne was ther never in court, of his degree;

There be destined your woe to end."
And with that word Arcita woke and gave a start.
"Now truly, however sore it may me hurt,"
Said he, "to Athens right now I will head;
Even dread of death will not keep me from
Seeing my lady, whom I love and serve.
In her presence I care not if I end up dead."
    And with that word he seized a great mirror,
And saw that changed was all his color,
And saw his face looking like someone else.
And right away it went through his mind
That, since his face was so disfigured
By the lovesickness that he'd endured,
He might well, if he took a station low,
Live in Athens evermore unknown,
And see his lady well nigh every day.
And right away he changed his clothes,
And clad himself as a poor laborer,
And all alone, save for a squire
Who knew his private life and situation,
Who was disguised as poor as he was,
To Athens did he go the shortest way.
And to the court he went upon a day,
And at the gate he proffered his service
To drudge and carry, whatever was needed.
And shortly of this matter for to say,
He got a place with a chamberlain,
Who worked for Emily,
For he was quick, and could soon learn
From every servant, who served her there.
Well could he hew wood and water bear,
For he was young and worked with a will,
And he was strong and bigboned
To do whatever anyone wanted.
A year or two he was in this service,
Page of the chamber of Emily the bright;
And Philostrate he said that he was called.
But half so well beloved a man as he
Never was there ever in court at his station;

He was so gentil of condicioun,
That thurghout al the court was his renoun.
They seyden, that it were a charitee
That Theseus wolde enhauncen his degree,
And putten him in worshipful servyse,
Ther as he mighte his vertu excercyse.
And thus, with-inne a whyle, his name is spronge
Bothe of his dedes, and his goode tonge,
That Theseus hath taken him so neer
That of his chambre he made him a squyer,
And yaf him gold to mayntene his degree;
And eek men broghte him out of his contree
From yeer to yeer, ful prively, his rente;
But honestly and slyly he it spente,
That no man wondred how that he it hadde.
And three yeer in this wyse his lyf he ladde,
And bar him so in pees and eek in werre,
Ther nas no man that Theseus hath derre.
And in this blisse lete I now Arcite,
And speke I wol of Palamon a lyte.

    In derknesse and horrible and strong prisoun
This seven yeer hath seten Palamoun,
Forpyned, what for wo and for distresse;
Who feleth double soor and hevinesse
But Palamon? that love destreyneth so,
That wood out of his wit he gooth for wo;
And eek therto he is a prisoner
Perpetuelly, noght oonly for a yeer.
Who coude ryme in English properly
His martirdom? for sothe, it am nat I;
Therefore I passe as lightly as I may.

    It fel that in the seventhe yeer, in May,
The thridde night, (as olde bokes seyn,
That al this storie tellen more pleyn,)
Were it by aventure or destinee,
(As, whan a thing is shapen, it shal be,)
That, sone after the midnight, Palamoun,
By helping of a freend, brak his prisoun,
And fleeth the citee, faste as he may go;

He was so gentle of disposition
That throughout all the court was his renown.
They said it would be a charity
If Theseus would increase his rank
And put him in honorable service,
There as he might his virtue exercise.
And thus within awhile his name became so well-known,
Both for his deeds and his good tongue,
That Theseus brought him so near
That of his chamber he made him a squire,
And gave him gold to maintain his position;
And also men brought from his own country
From year to year, full secretly, his income;
But so fittingly and discreetly he spent,
That no man wondered how he had it.
And three years in this way his life he led,
And bore himself so in peace and in war,
There was no man whom Theseus held more dear.
And in this bliss I leave now Arcita,
And speak I will of Palamon a little.

    In darkness and horrible and strong prison
Those seven years had lived Palamon,
Wasted, what for woe and for distress.
Who but Palamon felt double sorrow and heaviness,
And who but Palamon whom love sickened so
That out of his head he went for woe?
And besides that he was a prisoner
Perpetually, not only for a year.
Who could rhyme in English properly
His martyrdom? Forsooth, it is not I;
Therefore I pass over it briefly as I may.

    It befell that in the seventh year, of May
The third night, as old books say,
That all this story tell more fully,
Were it by chance or destiny—
As, when a thing is fated, it shall be—
That soon after midnight Palamon,
By helping of a friend, escaped his prison
And fled the city fast as he could go;

For he had yive his gayler drinke so
Of a clarree, maad of a certeyn wyn,
With nercotikes and opie of Thebes fyn,
That al that night, thogh that men wolde him shake,
The gayler sleep, he mighte nat awake;
And thus he fleeth as faste as ever he may.
The night was short, and faste by the day,
That nedes-cost he moste him-selven hyde,
And til a grove, faste ther besyde,
With dredful foot than stalketh Palamoun.
For shortly, this was his opinioun,
That in that grove he wolde him hyde al day,
And in the night than wolde he take his way
To Thebes-ward, his freendes for to preye
On Theseus to helpe him to werreye;
And shortly, outher he wolde lese his lyf,
Or winnen Emelye un-to his wyf;
This is th' effect and his entente pleyn.

   Now wol I torne un-to Arcite ageyn,
That litel wiste how ny that was his care,
Til that fortune had broght him in the snare.

   The bisy larke, messager of day,
Saluëth in hir song the morwe gray;
And fyry Phebus ryseth up so brighte,
That al the orient laugheth of the lighte,
And with his stremes dryeth in the greves
The silver dropes, hanging on the leves.
And Arcite, that is in the court royal
With Theseus, his squyer principal,
Is risen, and loketh on the myrie day.
And, for to doon his observaunce to May,
Remembring on the poynt of his desyr,
He on a courser, sterting as the fyr,
Is riden in-to the feeldes, him to pleye,
Out of the court, were it a myle or tweye;
And to the grove, of which that I yow tolde
By aventure, his wey he gan to holde,
To maken him a gerland of the greves,
Were it of wodebinde or hawethorn-leves,

For he had given his jailer a draught
Of claret made of a certain wine,
With narcotics and opium of Thebes fine,
That all that night, though you would him shake,
The jailer slept, he would not awaken;
And thus he fled as fast as ever he might.
The night was short and just before break of day,
He needs must hide,
And into a grove nearby,
With fearful foot then slipped Palamon.
For, to make it short, this was his opinion:
That in that grove he would him hide all day,
And in the night then would he take his way
Thebesward, his friends to beg
To help him make war on Theseus;
And shortly, either he would lose his life
Or win Emily unto his wife.
This was the essence and his sole intent.

   Now will I turn to Arcita again,
Who little knew that trouble was so near,
Till Fortune had brought him in the snare.

   The busy lark, messenger of day,
Saluted in her song the morning gray;
And fiery Phoebus rose up so bright
That all the eastern sky laughed in the light,
And with his beams dried in the brush
The silver drops hanging on the leaves.
And Arcita, who in the court royal
Of Theseus is squire principal,
Has risen and looked on the merry day.
And to do his observance of May,
Keeping in mind the object of his desire,
He on a courser, leaping as the fire,
Has ridden into the fields to play,
Out of the court, were it a mile or two;
And to the grove of which that I you told,
As it happened his course he began to hold,
To make himself a garland from the grove,
Were it of woodbine or hawthorne leaves,

And loude he song ageyn the sonne shene:
"May, with alle thy floures and thy grene,
Wel-come be thou, faire fresshe May,
I hope that I som grerre gete may."
And from his courser, with a lusty herte,
In-to the grove ful hastily he sterte,
And in a path he rometh up and doun,
Ther-as, by aventure, this Palamoun
Was in a bush, that no man mighte him see,
For sore afered of his deeth was he.
No-thing ne knew he that it was Arcite:
God wot he wolde have trowed it ful lyte.
But sooth is seyd, gon sithen many yeres,
That "feeld hath eyen, and the wode hath eres."
It is ful fair a man to bere him evene,
For al-day meteth men at unset stevene.
Ful litel woot Arcite of his felawe,
That was so ny to herknen al his sawe,
For in the bush he sitteth now ful stille.

    Whan that Arcite had romed al his fille,
And songen al the roundel lustily,
In-to a studie he fil sodeynly,
As doon thise loveres in hir queynte geres,
Now in the croppe, now doun in the breres,
Now up, now doun, as boket in a welle.
Right as the Friday, soothly for to telle,
Now it shyneth, now it reyneth faste,
Right so can gery Venus overcaste
The hertes of hir folk; right as hir day
Is gerful, right so chaungeth she array.
Selde is the Friday al the wyke y-lyke.

    Whan that Arcite had songe, he gan to syke,
And sette him doun with-outen any more:
"Alas" quod he, "that day that I was bore!
How longe, Juno, thurgh thy crueltee,
Woltow werreyen Thebes the citee?
Allas! y-broght is to confusioun
The blood royal of Cadme and Amphioun;
Of Cadmus, which that was the firste man

And loud he sang to the sun bright:
"May, with all your flowers and your green,
Welcome be you, fair fresh May,
In hope that I something green may get."[7]
And from his courser, with a lusty heart,
Full hastily into the grove he leapt,
And in a path he roamed up and down,
Where, by chance, this Palamon
Was in the brush, that no man might him see,
For sore afraid of his death was he.
Nor knew he that it was Arcita;
God knows he would have believed it full little.
But truly it has been said, for many years,
That "field has eyes and the wood has ears."
It is desirable for a man to carry himself on guard,
For every day you meet men at moments unexpected.
Full little knew Arcita of his fellow,
Who was near enough to hear all he said,
For in the brush he sat now full still.

　　When Arcita had roamed all his fill,
And lustily sung his song,
Into a pensive mood he suddenly fell,
As do these lovers with their changing moods,
Now in the treetops, now in the briars,
Now up, now down, as a bucket in a well.
Right like Friday, truly for to tell,
Now it's sunshine, now it rains hard,
So can variable Venus overcast
The hearts of her folk, just as her day
Is changeable, just so she changes her arrangements.
Seldom is Friday like the week's other days.[8]

　　After Arcita had sung, he began to sigh,
And sat him down without further delay.
"Alas!" said he, "the day that I was born!
How long, Juno, through your cruelty,
Will you make war on Thebes city?
Alas! brought is to confusion
The blood royal of Cadmus and Amphion—
Of Cadmus, who was the first man

That Thebes bulte, or first the toun bigan,
And of the citee first was crouned king,
Of his linage am I, and his of-spring
By verray ligne, as of the stok royal:
     And now I am so caitif and so thral,
That he, that is my mortal enemy,
I serve him as his squyer povrely.
And yet doth Juno me wel more shame,
For I dar noght biknowe myn owne name;
But ther-as I was wont to highte Arcite,
Now highte I Philostrate, noght worth a myte.
Allas! thou felle Mars, allas! Juno,
Thus hath your ire our kindrede all fordo,
Save only me, and wrecched Palamoun,
That Theseus martyreth in prisoun.
And over al this, to sleen me utterly,
Love hath his fyry dart so brenningly
Y-stiked thurgh my trewe careful herte,
That shapen was my deeth erst than my sherte.
Ye sleen me with your eyen, Emelye;
Ye been the cause wherfor that I dye.
Of al the remenant of myn other care
Ne sette I nat the mountaunce of a tare,
So that I coude don aught to your plesaunce!"
And with that word he fil doun in a traunce
A long tyme; and after he up-sterte.
     This Palamoun, that thoughte that thurgh his herte
He felt a cold swerd sodeynliche glyde,
For ire he quook, no lenger wolde he byde.
And whan that he had herd Arcites tale,
As he were wood, with face deed and pale,
He sterte him up out of the buskes thikke,
And seyde: "Arcite, false traitour wikke,
Now artow hent, that lovest my lady so,
For whom that I have al this peyne and wo,
And art my blood, and to my counseil sworn,
As I ful ofte have told thee heer-biforn,
And hast by-japed here duk Theseus,
And falsly chaunged hast thy name thus;

To build at Thebes, or first the town began,
And of the city was first crowned king.
Of his lineage am I, and of his offspring
By direct descent, as of the stock royal;
    And now I am so wretched and enslaved
That he who is my mortal enemy,
I serve him as his squire lowly,
And yet Juno does me more shame,
For I dare not make known my own name;
But though I was once called Arcita,
Now I'm Philostrate, not worth a mite.
Alas, you cruel, deadly Mars! alas Juno!
Thus has your ire our lineage all destroyed,
Save only me and wretched Palamon,
Whom Theseus martyred in prison.
And over all this, to slay me utterly,
Love has his fiery dart so burningly
Stabbed through my woeful heart,
That my fate was woven before my first shirt.
You slay me with your eyes, Emily!
You be the cause wherefore that I die.
On all the remnants of my other woes
I would not set the worth of a single weed,
If I could do anything for your pleasure!"
And with that word he fell down in a trance
A long time; and after he up started.
    This Palamon, who thought that through his heart
He felt a cold sword suddenly glide,
For anger he shook, no longer would he bide.
And when he had heard Arcita's tale,
As if he were insane, with face deathly and pale,
He started up out of the brush thick,
And said, "Arcita, false traitor wicked,
Now are you caught, who loves my lady so,
For whom I have all this pain and woe,
And you are my blood, and to my secrets sworn,
As I full often have told you before,
And you have tricked her duke Theseus,
And falsely changed your name thus!

I wol be deed, or elles thou shalt dye.
Thou shalt nat love my lady Emelye,
But I wol love hir only, and namo;
For I am Palamoun, thy mortal fo.
And though that I no wepne have in this place,
But out of prison am astert by grace,
I drede noght that outher thou shalt dye,
Or thou ne shalt nat loven Emelye.
Chees which thou wilt, for thou shalt nat asterte."
    This Arcite, with ful despitous herte,
Whan he him knew, and hadde his tale herd,
As fiers as leoun, pulled out a swerd,
And seyde thus: "by God that sit above,
Nere it that thou art sik, and wood for love,
And eek that thou no wepne hast in this place,
Thou sholdest never out of this grove pace,
That thou ne sholdest dyen of myn hond.
For I defye the seurtee and the bond
Which that thou seyst that I have maad to thee.
What, verray fool, think wel that love is free,
And I wol love hir, maugre al thy might!
But, for as muche thou art a worthy knight,
And wilnest to darreyne hir by batayle,
Have heer my trouthe, to-morwe I wol nat fayl
With-outen witing of any other wight,
That here I wol be founden as a knight,
And bringen harneys right y-nough for thee;
And chees the beste, and leve the worste for me
And mete and drinke this night wol I bringe
Y-nough for thee, and clothes for thy beddinge.
And, if so be that thou my lady winne,
And slee me in this wode ther I am inne,
Thou mayst wel have thy lady, as for me."
This Palamon answerde: "I graunte it thee."
And thus they been departed til a-morwe,
When ech of hem had leyd his feith to borwe.
    O Cupide, out of alle charitee!
O regne, that wolt no felawe have with thee!
Ful sooth is seyd, that love ne lordshipe

I will be dead, or else you shall die.
You shall not love my lady Emily,
But I will love her only, and no one else;
For I am Palamon, your mortal foe.
And though I no weapon have in this place,
But out of prison am escaped by grace,
I doubt not that either you shall die
Or you shall not love Emily.
Choose which you would, for you shall not escape."
 This Arcita, with full scornful heart,
When he him knew, and had his tale heard,
As fierce as a lion pulled out his sword
And said: "By God who sits above,
Were it not that you are sick and mad with love,
And that you no weapon have in this place,
You would never leave this grove alive,
You would never my hand survive.
For I scorn the pledge and the bond
That you say I have made to you.
Why, you true fool, know well that love is free,
And I will love her despite all your might!
But, inasmuch as you are a worthy knight,
And want to decide who claims her by battle,
Have here my vow: tomorrow I will not fail,
Without telling any other person,
Here I will be armed as a knight,
And bring armor right enough for you;
And you may choose the best, and leave the worst for me.
And food and drink this night I will bring
Enough for you, and clothes for your bedding.
And if so be it that you my lady win,
And slay me in this wood where I am in,
You may well have the lady, so far as concerns me."
This Palamon answered, "I grant it to you."
And thus they were departed until morning tomorrow,
When each of them had laid his faith as a pledge.
 Oh Cupid, devoid of unselfish love!
Oh sovereign rule, who does not want to share!
Full truly it's said that neither love nor lordship

Wol noght, his thankes, have no felaweshipe;
Wel finden that Arcite and Palamoun.
Arcite is riden anon un-to the toun,
And on the morwe, er it were dayes light,
Ful prively two harneys hath he dight,
Bothe suffisaunt and mete to darreyne
The bataille in the feeld bitwix hem tweyne.
And on his hors, allone as he was born,
He carieth al this harneys him biforn;
And in the grove, at tyme and place y-set,
This Arcite and this Palamon ben met.
Tho chaungen gan the color in hir face;
Right as the hunter in the regne of Trace,
That stondeth at the gappe with a spere,
Whan hunted is the leoun or the bere,
And hereth him come russhing in the greves,
And breketh bothe bowes and the leves,
And thinketh, "heer cometh my mortel enemy,
With-oute faile, he moot be deed, or I;
For outher I mot sleen him at the gappe,
Or he mot sleen me, if that me mishappe:"
So ferden they, in chaunging of hir hewe,
As fer as everich of hem other knewe.
Ther nas no good day, ne no saluing;
But streight, with-outen word or rehersing,
Everich of hem halp for to armen other,
As freendly as he were his owne brother;
And after that, with sharpe speres stronge
They foynen ech at other wonder longe.
Thou mighest wene that this Palamoun
In his fighting were a wood leoun,
And as a cruel tygre was Arcite:
As wilde bores gonne they to smyte,
That frothen whyte as foom for ire wood.
Up to the ancle foghte they in hir blood.
And in this wyse I lete hem fighting dwelle;
And forth I wol of Theseus yow telle.

  The destinee, ministre general,
That executeth in the world over-al

Will willingly share their domain;
And so found that true, both Arcita and Palamon.
Arcita then returned to the town,
And on the morrow, before daylight
Full secretly two armor suits did he prepare,
Both sufficient and suitable to decide
The battle in the field between the two.
And on his horse, alone as he was born,
He carried with him all this armor;
And in the grove, at the time and place set,
This Arcita and Palamon did meet.
The color in their faces began to change,
Just as the hunters in the Kingdom of Thrace,
Who stood in the clearing with a spear,[9]
When hunted was the lion or the bear,
And heard him come rushing in the bushes
And breaking both branches and the leaves,
And thought, "Here comes my mortal enemy!
Without fail, he must be dead or I;
For either I slay him at the clearing,
Or he must slay me, if it goes ill for me,"—
So behaved they in changing of their raiment.
Although they knew each other well,
There was no "good day," nor greetings,
But straight without word or their pact restating,
Each of them helped to arm the other
As friendly as if he were his own brother;
And after that, with sharp spears strong
They thrust at each other wondrous long.
You may be sure that this Palamon
In his fighting was an enraged lion,
And as a cruel tiger was Arcita;
They proceeded to smite like wild boars
That froth white with foam in wild anger.
Up to the ankle fought they in their blood.
And in this state I leave them still fighting;
And forth I will of Theseus you tell.
　　Destiny, the minister general
Who executes in the world everywhere

The purveyaunce, that God hath seyn biforn,
So strong it is, that, though the world had sworn
The contrarie of a thing, by ye or nay,
Yet somtyme it shal fallen on a day
That falleth nat eft with-inne a thousand yere.
For certeinly, our appetytes here,
Be it of werre, or pees, or hate, or love,
Al is this reuled by the sighte above.
This mene I now by mighty Theseus,
That for to honten is so desirous,
And namely at the grete hert in May,
That in his bed ther daweth him no day,
That he nis clad, and redy for to ryde
With hunte and horn, and houndes him bisyde.
For in his hunting hath he swich delyt,
That it is al his joye and appetyt
To been him-self the grete hertes bane:
For after Mars he serveth now Diane.
   Cleer was the day, as I have told er this,
And Theseus, with alle joye and blis,
With his Ipolita, the fayre quene,
And Emelye, clothed al in grene,
On hunting be they riden royally.
And to the grove, that stood ful faste by,
In which ther was an hert, as men him tolde,
Duk Theseus the streighte wey hath holde.
And to the launde he rydeth him ful right,
For thider was the hert wont have his flight,
And over a brook, and so forth on his weye.
This duk wol han a cours at him, or tweye,
With houndes, swiche as that him list comaunde.
   And whan this duk was come un-to the launde,
Under the sonne he loketh, and anon
He was war of Arcite and Palamon,
That foughten breme, as it were bores two;
The brighte swerdes wenten to and fro
So hidously, that with the leeste strook
It seemed as it wold feele an ook;
But what they were, no-thing he ne woot.

The providential plan that God has foreseen,
Is so strong that, though the world had sworn
The contrary of a thing by yes or no,
Yet at some time it will happen on a day
And will happen not again in a thousand years.
For certainly, our appetites here,
Be it of war, or peace, or hate, or love,
All is ruled by the foresight above.
This mean I now as it relates to mighty Theseus,
Who to hunt is so desirous,
And especially for the great hart in May,
That before the dawn of every day
He is clad and ready to ride
With huntsmen and horn and hounds him beside.
For in his hunting has he such delight
That it is all his joy and appetite
To be himself the great hart's slayer;
For after Mars he served Diana.

　　Clear was the day, as I have said before this,
And Theseus, with all joy and bliss,
With his Hyppolyta, the fair queen,
And Emily, clothed all in green,
To the hunt did they royally ride.
And to the grove that stood full fast by,
In which there was a hart, as men him told,
Duke Theseus the straight course did hold.
And to the clearing he rode straight,
For there was the hart wont to have his flight,
And over a brook and so forth on his way.
This duke will have a chase at him or two,
With hounds such as it pleases him to command.

　　And when this duke was come into the clearing,
Into the sunlight he looked, and anon
He was aware of Arcita and Palamon,
Who fought furiously as if they were boars two.
The bright swords went to and fro
So hideously that with the least stroke
It seemed as if it would fell an oak;
But who they were, he did not know.

This duk his courser with his spores smoot,
And at a stert he was bitwix hem two,
And pulled out a swerd and cryed, "ho!
Namore, up peyne of lesing of your heed.
By mighty Mars, he shal anon be deed,
That smyteth any strook, that I may seen!
But telleth me what mister men ye been,
That been so hardy for to fighten here
With-outen juge or other officere,
As it were in a listes royally?"
 This Palamon answerde hastily
And seyde: "sire, what nedeth wordes mo?
We have the deeth deserved bothe two.
Two woful wrecches been we, two caytyves,
That been encombred of our owne lyves;
And as thou art a rightful lord and juge,
Ne yeve us neither mercy ne refuge,
But slee me first, for seynte charitee;
But slee my felawe eek as wel as me.
Or slee him first; for, though thou knowe it lyte,
This is thy mortal fo, this is Arcite,
That fro thy lond is banished on his heed,
For which he hath deserved to be deed.
For this is he that cam un-to thy gate,
And seyde, that he highte Philostrate.
Thus hath he japed thee ful many a yeer,
And thou has maked him thy chief squyer:
And this is he that loveth Emelye.
For sith the day is come that I shal dye,
I make pleynly my confessioun,
That I am thilke woful Palamoun,
That hath thy prison broken wikkedly.
I am thy mortal fo, and it am I
That loveth so hote Emelye the brighte,
That I wol dye present in hir sighte.
Therfore I axe deeth and my juwyse;
But slee my felawe in the same wyse,
For bothe han we deserved to be slayn."
 This worthy duk answerde anon agayn,

This duke his horse with his spurs struck,
And in a moment he was between the two,
And pulled out a sword and cried, "Halt!
No more, upon pain of losing your head!
By mighty Mars, he shall anon be dead
Who strikes any stroke that I may see.
But tell me what kind of men you be,
Who have been so bold to fight here
Without judge or other officer,
As if in the lists of a tournament royal?"
  This Palamon answered hastily,
And said: "Sire, who needs words more?
We have the death deserved both two.
Two woeful wretches be we, two captives,
Who have been weary of our own lives;
And as you are a rightful lord and judge,
Give us neither mercy nor refuge,
But slay me first, for holy charity.
But slay my companion as well as me,
Or slay him first: for though you know it little,
This is your mortal foe, this is Arcita,
Who from your land is banished or lose his head,
For which he has deserved to be dead.
For this is he who came up to your gate
And said that he was called Philostrate.
Thus has he tricked you full many a year,
And you have made him your chief squire;
And this is he who loves Emily.
For since the day is come that I shall die,
I make plainly my confession
That I am that woeful Palamon
Who has from your prison broken.
I am your mortal foe, and it is I
Who loves with such passion Emily the bright
That I will die now in her sight.
Wherefore I ask death and my justice,
But slay my companion in the same way,
For both have we deserved to be slain."
  This worthy duke answered anon again,

And seyde, "This is a short conclusioun:
Youre owne mouth, by your confessioun,
Hath dampned you, and I wol it recorde,
It nedeth noght to pyne yow with the corde
Ye shul be deed, by mighty Mars the rede!"
 The quene anon, for verray wommanhede,
Gan for to wepe, and so dide Emelye,
And alle the ladies in the compayne.
Gret pitee was it, as it thoughte hem alle,
That ever swich a chaunce sholde falle;
For gentil men they were, of greet estat,
And no-thing but for love was this debat;
And sawe hir blody woundes wyde and sore;
And alle cryden, bothe lasse and more,
"Have mercy, lord, up-on us wommen alle!"
And on hir bare knees adoun they falle,
And wolde have kist his feet ther-as he stood,
Til at the laste aslaked was his mood;
For pitee renneth sone in gentil herte.
And though he first for ire quook and sterte,
He hath considered shortly, in a clause,
The trespas of hem bothe, and eek the cause:
And al-though that his ire hir gilt accused
Yet in his reson he hem bothe excused;
As thus: he thoghte wel, that every man
Wol helpe him-self in love, if that he can,
And eek delivere him-self out of prisoun;
And eek his herte had compassioun
Of wommen, for they wepen ever in oon;
And in his gentil herte he thoghte anoon,
And softe un-to himself he seyde: "fy
Up-on a lord that wol have no mercy,
But been a leoun, bothe in word and dede,
To hem that been in repentaunce and drede
As wel as to a proud despitous man
That wol maynteyne that he first bigan!
That lord hath litel of discrecioun,
That in swich cas can no divisioun,
But weyeth pryde and hum blesse after oon."

And said, "This is quickly decided.
Your own mouth, by your confession,
Has damned you, and I will make it my verdict;
It needs not to torture you with the cord.
You shall be dead, by mighty Mars the red!"
      The queen soon, for true womanhood,
Began to weep, and so did Emily,
And all the ladies in the company.
Great pity was it, as they thought all,
That ever such a chance should befall;
For gentlemen they were of great estate,
And nothing but for love was this debate;
And saw their bloody wounds wide and sore,
And all cried, both the lesser and greater in estate,
"Have mercy, lord, upon us women all!"
And on their bare knees down they fell,
And would have kissed his feet there as he stood,
Until at last quenched was his anger,
For pity runs soon in a gentle heart.
And though he first for anger shook and started,
He had considered quickly, in a short while,
The trespass of them both, and also the cause,
And although his anger their guilt blamed,
Yet in his reason he both them excused
As thus: he thought well that every man
Will help himself in love, if he can,
And deliver himself out of prison.
And also his heart had compassion
For the women, for they went on weeping every one.
And in his gentle heart he thought anon,
And soft unto himself he said: "Fie
Upon a lord who would have no mercy,
But be a lion, both in word and deed,
To those repentant and in fear and need
As well as to a proud and scornful man
Who would persevere in what he first began!
That lord has little of discernment
Who in such case sees no difference
But weighs pride and humbleness as one."

And shortly, whan his ire is thus agoon,
He gan to loken up with eyen lighte,
And spak thise same wordes al on highte:—
"The god of love, *a! benedicite,*
How mighty and how greet a lord is he!
Ayeins his might ther gayneth none obstacles,
He may be cleped a god for his miracles;
For he can maken at his owne gyse
Of everich herte, as that him list devyse.
Lo heer, this Arcite and this Palamoun,
That quitly weren out of my prisoun,
And mighte han lived in Thebes royally,
And witen I am hir mortal enemy,
And that hir deeth lyth in my might also;
And yet hath love, maugree hir eyen two,
Y-broght hem hider bothe for to dye!
Now loketh, is nat that an heigh folye?
Who may been a fool, but-if he love?
Bihold, for Goddes sake that sit above,
Se how they blede! be they noght wel arrayed?
Thus hath hir lord, the god of love, y-payed
Hir wages and hir fees for hir servyse!
And yet they wenen for to been ful wyse
That serven love, for aught that may bifalle!
But this is yet the beste game of alle,
That she, for whom they han this jolitee,
Can hem ther-for as muche thank as me:
She woot namore of al this hote fare,
By God, than woot a cokkow or an hare!
But al mot been assayed, hoot and cold;
A man mot been a fool, or yong or old;
I woot it by my-self ful yore agoon:
For in my tyme a servant was I oon.
And therfore, sin I knowe of loves peyne,
And woot how sore it can a man distreyne,
As he that hath ben caught ofte in his las,
I yow foryeve al hoolly this trespas,
At requeste of the quene that kneleth here,
And eek of Emelye, my suster dere.

And shortly, when his ire was thus gone,
He began to look up with eyes cheerful,
And spoke these same words aloud:
"The god of love—ah, *benedicite*[10]—
How mighty and great a lord is he!
Against his might there prevail no obstacles.
He may be called a god for his miracles,
For he can make as he chooses
Of every heart whatever he decides.
Look here, this Arcita and Palamon,
Who were well gone out of my prison,
And might have lived in Thebes royally,
And know I am their mortal enemy
And that their death lies in my might also;
And yet has love, despite their eyes open wide,
Brought them here both to die!
Now look, is not that a great folly?
Are we not all but fools for love?
Behold, for God's sake who sits above,
See how they bleed! be they not so well-decorated?
Thus has their lord, the god of love, paid
Their wages and their fees for their service!
And yet they think themselves to be full wise
Who serve love, no matter what occurs.
But this is yet the best jest of all:
That she, for whom they have this passion,
Has no more to thank them for than I do;
She knows no more of this madness,
By God, than does a hare or a cuckoo!
But all must be tried, hot and cold,
A man must be a fool, either young or old;
I know that of myself in time long gone,
For in my time as love's servant was I one.
And therefore, since I know of love's pain,
And know how sore it can a man torment,
And as one who has been caught often in its net,
I forgive you all wholly this trespass,
At request of the queen who kneels here,
And of Emily, my sister dear.

And ye shul bothe anon un-to me swere,
That never-mo ye shul my contree dere,
Ne make werre up-on me night ne day,
But been my freendes in al that ye may;
I yow foryeve this trespas every del."
And they him swore his axing fayre and wel,
And him of lordshipe and of mercy preyde,
And he hem graunteth grace, and thus he seyde:
     "To speke of royal linage and richesse,
Though that she were a quene or a princesse,
Ech of yow bothe is worthy, doutelees,
To wedden whan tyme is, but nathelees
I speke as for my suster Emelye,
For whom ye have this stryf and jelousye;
Ye woot your-self, she may not wedden two
At ones, though ye fighten ever-mo:
That oon of yow, al be him looth or leef,
He moot go pypen in an ivy-leef;
This is to seyn, she may nat now han bothe,
Al be ye never so jelous, ne so wrothe.
And for-thy I yow putte in this degree,
That ech of yow shal have his destinee
As him is shape; and herkneth in what wyse;
Lo, heer your ende of that I shal devyse.
     My wil is this, for plat conclusioun,
With-outen any replicacioun,
If that yow lyketh, tak it for the beste,
That everich of yow shal gon wher him leste
Frely, with-outen raunson or daunger;
And this day fifty wykes, fer ne ner,
Everich of yow shal bringe an hundred knightes,
Armed for listes up at alle rightes,
Al redy to darreyne hir by bataille.
And this bihote I yow, with-outen faille,
Up-on my trouthe, and as I am a knight,
That whether of yow bothe that hath might,
This is to seyn, that whether he or thou
May with his hundred, as I spak of now,
Sleen his contrarie, or out of listes dryve,

And you shall both anon unto me swear
That nevermore you shall my country harm,
Nor make war upon me night or day,
But be my friends in all that you may.
I forgive you this trespass in every way."
And they him swore his request fair and well,
And for his protection and his mercy as their lord prayed,
And he them granted grace, and thus he said—
　　"To speak of royal lineage and riches,
Though that she were a queen or a princess,
Each of you both is worthy, doubtless,
To wed when the time comes, but nevertheless—
I speak as for my sister Emily,
For whom you have this strife and jealousy—
You know yourself she may not wed two
At once, though you fight evermore:
That one of you, like it or not
Must go whistle in an ivy leaf;
That is to say, she may not now have both,
Though you be ever so jealous or so wroth.
And therefore I will arrange matters so
That each of you shall have your destiny
As it is meant to be, and listen now in what way;
Hear how your fate's unfolding I shall devise.
　　My will is this, to put it plainly,
And unconditionally—
So if you agree, take it for the best:
That each of you shall go where you will
Freely, without ransom or control;
And this day fifty weeks, not sooner or later,
Each of you shall bring a hundred knights
Armed for tournament in every way,
And ready to decide your claim to her in battle.
And this I promise you without fail,
Upon my troth, and as I am a knight,
That whichever of you has the might—
This is to say, that whether he or you
May with his hundred, as I spoke of now,
Slay his opponent or from the battleground drive—

Him shal I yeve Emelya to wyve,
To whom that fortune yeveth so fair a grace.
The listes shal I maken in this place,
And God so wisly on my soule rewe,
As I shal even juge been and trewe.
Ye shul non other ende with me maken,
That oon of yow ne shal be deed or taken.
And if yow thinketh this is wel y-sayd,
Seyeth your avys, and holdeth yow apayd.
This is your ende and your conclusioun."
    Who loketh lightly now but Palamoun?
Who springeth up for joye but Arcite?
Who couthe telle, or who couthe it endyte,
The joye that is maked in the place
Whan Theseus hath doon so fair a grace?
But doun on knees wente every maner wight,
And thanked him with al her herte and might,
And namely the Thebans ofte sythe.
And thus with good hope and with herte blythe
They take hir leve, and hom-ward gonne they ryde
To Thebes, with his olde walles wyde.

Part Three

I trowe men wolde deme it necligence,
If I foryete to tellen the dispence
Of Theseus, that goth so bisily
To maken up the listes royally;
That swich a noble theatre as it was,
I dar wel seyn that in this world ther nas.
The circuit a myle was aboute,
Walled of stoon, and diched al with-oute.
Round was the shap, in maner of compas,
Ful of degrees, the heighte of sixty pas,
That, whan a man was set on o degree,
He letted nat his felawe for to see.
    Est-ward ther stood a gate of marbel whyt,
West-ward, right swich another in the opposit.
And shortly to concluden, swich a place
Was noon in erthe, as in so litel space;

Then shall I give Emily to wife
To whom Fortune gives so fair a grace.
The battleground shall I make in this place,
And God so surely on my soul have pity
As I shall be impartial judge and true.
You shall no other compact with me make,
Unless one of you shall be dead or captive taken.
And if you think this is well said,
Say your opinion, and be content.
This is your end and your conclusion."

Who looks lightly now but Palamon?
Who springs up for joy but Arcita?
Who could tell, or who could write,
The joy that is made in the place
When Theseus had done so fair a grace?
But down on knees went every manner of person,
And thanked him with all their heart and might,
And especially the Thebans time and again.
And thus with good hope and with hearts blithe
They take their leave, and homeward did they ride
To Thebes, with its old walls wide.

Part Three

I believe men would deem it negligence
If I forget to tell the expenditure
Of Theseus, who goes so busily
To make up the battleground royally,
That such a noble arena as it was
I dare well say that in the world there was never.
The circuit a mile was about,
Walled of stone, and ditched all without.
Round was the shape, in manner of a compass,
Full of steps, the height of sixty paces,
That when a man was set on any one step
He hindered not his fellow's view.

Eastward there stood a gate of marble white,
Westward right such another opposite.
And shortly to conclude, such a place
Was ere none built on earth, and in so little time;

For in the lond ther nas no crafty man,
That geometrie or ars-metrik can,
Ne purtreyour, ne kerver of images,
That Theseus ne yaf him mete and wages
The theatre for to maken and devyse.
And for to doon his ryte and sacrifyse,
He est-ward hath, up-on the gate above,
In worship of Venus, goddesse of love,
Don make an auter and an oratorie;
And west-ward, in the minde and in memorie
Of Mars, he maked hath right swich another,
That coste largely of gold a fother.
And north-ward, in a touret on the wal,
Of alabastre whyt and reed coral
An oratorie riche for to see,
In worship of Dyane of chastitee,
Hath Theseus don wroght in noble wyse.

But yet hadde I foryeten to devyse
The noble kerving, and the portreitures,
The shap, the countenaunce, and the figures,
That weren in thise oratories three.

First in the temple of Venus maystow see
Wroght on the wal, ful pitous to biholde,
The broken slepes, and the sykes colde;
The sacred teres, and the waymenting;
The fyry strokes of the desiring,
That loves servaunts in this lyf enduren;
The othes, that hir covenants assuren;
Pleasaunce and hope, desyr, fool-hardinessee,
Beautee and youthe, bauderie, richesse,
Charmes and force, lesinges, flaterye,
Dispense, bisynesse, and jelousye,
That wered of yelwe goldes a gerland,
And a cokkow sitting on hir hand;
Festes, instruments, caroles, daunces,
Lust and array, and alle the circumstaunces
Of love, whiche that I rekne and rekne shal,
By ordre weren peynted on the wal,
And mo than I can make of mencioun.

For in the land there was no craftsman
Who knew geometry or arithmetic,
Nor painter, nor carver of images,
To whom Theseus did not give food and wages
The arena to make and devise.
And to do his rite and sacrifice,
He eastward, upon the gate above,
In worship of Venus, goddess of love,
Had made an altar and an oratory;
And on the gate westward, in memory
Of Mars, he had made another,
That cost a generous lading of gold.
And northward, in a turret on the wall,
Of alabaster white and red coral,
An oratory rich to see,
In worship of Diana of chastity,
Had Theseus wrought in noble fashion.

    But yet had I forgotten to describe
The noble carving and portraitures,
The shape, the countenance, and the figures,
That were in these oratories three.

    First in the temple of Venus you may see
Wrought on the wall, full piteous to behold,
The broken sleeps and chilling sighs cold,
The sacred tears and the lamenting,
The fiery strokes of the desiring
That love's servants in this life endure,
The oaths that their vows ensure;
Pleasure and Hope, Desire, Foolhardiness,
Beauty and Youth, Bawdry, Riches,
Charms and Force, Deceits, Flattery,
Expense, Business and Jealousy,
Who wore of yellow marigolds a garland,
And a cuckoo sitting on her hand;[11]
Feasts, instruments, songs and dances,
Joy and fancy dress, and all the circumstances
Of love, that I recounted and recount shall,
By order were painted on the wall,
And more than I can make of mention.

For soothly, al the mount of Citheroun,
Ther Venus hath hir principal dwelling,
Was shewed on the wal in portreying,
With al the gardin, and the lustinesse.
Nat was foryeten the porter Ydelnesse,
Ne Narcisus the faire of yore agon,
Ne yet the folye of king Salamon,
Ne yet the grete strengthe of Hercules—
Th' enchauntementes of Medea and Circes—
Ne of Turnus, with the hardy fiers corage,
The riche Cresus, caytif in servage.
Thus may ye seen that wisdom ne richesse,
Beautee ne sleighte, strengthe, ne hardinesse,
Ne may with Venus holde champartye;
For as hir list the world than may she gye.
Lo, alle thise folk so caught were in hir las,
Til they for wo ful ofte seyde "allas!"
Suffyceth heer ensamples oon or two,
And though I coude rekne a thousand mo.

The statue of Venus, glorious for to see,
Was naked fleting in the large see,
And fro the navele doun all covered was
With wawes grene, and brighte as any glas.
A citole in hir right hand hadde she,
And on hir heed, ful semely for to see,
A rose gerland, fresh and wel smellinge;
Above hir heed hir dowves flikeringe.
Biforn hir stood hir sone Cupido,
Up-on his shuldres winges hadde he two;
And blind he was, as it is ofte sene;
A bowe he bar and arwes brighte and kene.

Why sholde I noght as wel eek telle yow al
The portreiture, that was up-on the wal
With-inne the temple of mighty Mars the rede?
Al peynted was the wal, in lengthe and brede,
Lyk to the estres of the grisly place,
That highte the grete temple of Mars in Trace,
In thilke colde frosty regioun,
Ther-as Mars hath his sovereyn mansioun.

For truly, all the mount of Cythaeron,[12]
Where Venus has her principal dwelling,
Was shown on the wall in portraying,
With all the garden and the lustiness.
Not was forgotten the porter, Idleness,
Nor Narcissus the fair of long ago,
Nor yet the folly of King Solomon,
Nor yet the great strength of Hercules,
The enchantments of Medea and Circe,[13]
Nor of Turnus,[14] with the bold fierce courage,
The rich Croesus,[15] wretched in bondage.
Thus may you see that neither wisdom nor riches,
Beauty nor cleverness, strength nor boldness,
May with Venus hold equal force,
For as she wishes the world so may she coerce.
Lo, all these folk were so caught in her net,
Till they full often said "Alas!"
Suffice here examples one or two,
Although I could recount a thousand more.
　　The statue of Venus, glorious to see,
Was naked floating in the large sea,
And from the navel down all covered was
With waves green, and bright as any glass.
A cithara in her right hand had she,
And on her head, full comely to see,
A rose garland, fresh and sweet-smelling;
Above her head her doves fluttering.
Before her stood her son Cupid,
Upon his shoulders wings had he two,
And blind he was, as it is often seen.
A bow he bore and arrows bright and keen.
　　Why should I not also tell you all
The portraiture that was upon the wall
Within the temple of mighty Mars the red?
All painted was the wall, in length and breadth,
Like the inside of the grisly place
That is called the great temple of Mars in Thrace,
In that cold frosty region
There where Mars has his sovereign mansion.

First on the wal was peynted a foreste,
In which ther dwelleth neither man ne beste,
With knotty knarry bareyn treës olde
Of stubbes sharpe and hidous to biholde;
In which ther ran a rumbel and a swough,
As though a storm sholde bresten every bough:
And downward from an hille, under a bente,
Ther stood the temple of Mars armipotente,
Wroght al of burned steel, of which thentree
Was long and streit, and gastly for to see.
And ther-out cam a rage and such a vese,
That it made al the gates for to rese.
The northern light in at the dores shoon,
For windowe on the wal ne was ther noon,
Thurgh which men mighten any light discerne.
The dores were alle of adamant eterne,
Y-clenched overthwart and endelong
With iren tough; and, for to make it strong,
Every piler, the temple to sustene,
Was tonne-greet, of iren bright and shene.
　　Ther saugh I first the derke imagining
Of felonye, and al the compassing;
The cruel ire, reed as any glede;
The pykepurs, and eek the pale drede;
The smyler with the knyf under the cloke;
The shepne brenning with the blake smoke;
The treson of the mordring in the bedde;
The open werre, with woundes al bibledde;
Contek, with blody knyf and sharp manace;
Al ful of chirking was that sory place.
The sleere of him-self yet saugh I ther,
His herte-blood hath bathed al his heer;
The nayl y-driven in the shode a-night;
The colde deeth, with mouth gaping upright.
Amiddes of the temple sat meschaunce,
With disconfort and sory contenaunce.
Yet saugh I woodnesse laughing in his rage;
Armed compleint, out-hees, and fiers outrage.
The careyne in the bush, with throte y-corve:

First on the wall was painted a forest,
In which there dwelt neither man nor beast,
With knotty gnarled barren trees old,
Of shattered trunks hideous to behold,
Through which there ran a rumble in a wind,
As though a storm should break every bough,
And downward from a hill, under a bluff,
There stood the temple of Mars, strong in war,
Wrought of burnished steel, of which the entrance
Was long and straight, and ghastly to see.
And therefrom came a wind roar and such a blast
That it made all the gate to shudder.
The northern light in the doors shone,
For window on the wall there was none
Through which men might any light discern.
The door was all of adamant eternal
Reinforced crosswise and endlong
With iron tough; and to make it strong,
Every pillar, the temple to sustain,
Was barrel-thick, of iron bright and shining.

There saw I first the dark imagining
Of Crime, Treachery, and all the plotting;[16]
The cruel Ire, red as any coal burning,
The pickpocket, and also the pale Dread;
The smiler with the knife under the cloak;
The stable burning with the black smoke;
The treason of the murdering in the bed;
The open warfare, with the wounds all bled,
Conflict, with bloody knife and sharp menace.
All full of clamor was that sorry place.
The suicide saw I there:
His heart blood had bathed all his hair;
The nail driven in the head at night;
The cold death, with mouth gaping upright.
At the temple center sat Mischance,
With discouraged and sorry countenance.
Yet saw I Madness laughing in his rage,
Armed Grievance, Outcry and fierce Outrage;
The corpse in the brush, with throat slashed;

A thousand slayn, and nat of qualm y-storve;
The tiraunt, with the prey by force y-raft;
The toun destroyed, ther was no-thing laft.
Yet saugh I brent the shippes hoppesteres;
The hunte strangled with the wilde beres:
The sowe freten the child right in the cradel;
The cook y-scalded, for al his longe ladel.
Noght was foryeten by th'infortune of Marte;
The carter over-riden with his carte,
Under the wheel ful lowe he lay adoun.
Ther were also, of Martes divisioun,
The barbour, and the bocher, and the smith
That forgeth sharpe swerdes on his stith.
And al above, depeynted in a tour,
Saw I conquest sittinge in greet honour,
With the sharpe swerde over his heed
Hanginge by a sotil twynes threed.
Depeynted was the slaughtre of Julius,
Of grete Nero, and of Antonius;
Al be that thilke tyme they were unborn,
Yet was hir deeth depeynted ther-biforn,
By manasinge of Mars, right by figure;
So was it shewed in that portreiture
As is depeynted in the sterres above,
Who shal be slayn or elles deed for love.
Suffyceth oon ensample in stories olde,
I may not rekne hem alle, thogh I wolde.
    The statue of Mars up-on a carte stood,
Armed, and loked grim as he were wood;
And over his heed ther shynen two figures
Of sterres, that been cleped in scriptures,
That oon Puella, that other Rubeus.
This god of armes was arrayed thus:—
A wolf ther stood biforn him at his feet
With eyen rede, and of a man he eet;
With sotil pencel was depeynt this storie,
In redoutinge of Mars and of his glorie.
    Now to the temple of Diane the chaste
As shortly as I can I wol me haste,

A thousand slain, and of plague not dead;
The tyrant, with the plunder by force seized;
The town destroyed, there was nothing left.
Yet saw I burnt the ships as on the waves they danced,
The hunter killed by the wild bears;
The sow devouring the child right in the cradle;
The cook scalded, for all his long ladle—
Nought was forgotten by the evil of Mars—
The carter run over by his cart,
Under the wheel full low he lay down.
There were also, of Mars' cohort,
The barber and the butcher and the blacksmith,
Who forged sharp swords on his anvil.
And all above, depicted in a tower,
Saw I Conquest, sitting in great honor,
With the sharp sword over his head
Hanging by a twine's thin thread.
Depicted was the slaughter of Julius,
Of great Nero, and of Antonius;
Although they were at that time unborn,
Yet were their deaths depicted there before
By malignity of Mars prefigured.
So it was shown in that portraiture,
As depicted in the stars above
Who shall be slain or else dead for love.
Suffice one example in stories old:
I may not recount them all, though I would.
  The statue of Mars upon a chariot stood
Armed, and looked grim as if he were mad;
And over his head there shone two figures
Of stars, who had been called in books
The one Puella, that other Rubeus:[17]
This god of arms was displayed thus.
A wolf there stood before him at his feet
With eyes red, and of a man he ate.
With subtle brush was depicted this story
In reverence and fear of Mars and his glory.
  Now to the temple of Diana the chaste,
As briefly as I can, I will make haste

To telle yow al the descripcioun.
Depeynted been the walles up and doun
Of hunting and of shamfast chastitee.
Ther saugh I how woful Calistopee,
Whan that Diane agreved was with here,
Was turned from a womman til a bere,
And after was she maad the lode-sterre;
Thus was it peynt, I can say yow no ferre;
Hir sone is eek a sterre, as men may see.
Ther saugh I Dane, y-turned til a tree,
I mene nat the goddesse Diane,
But Penneus doughter, which that highte Dane.
Ther saugh I Attheon an hert y-maked,
For vengeaunce that he saugh Diane al naked;
I saugh how that his houndes have him caught,
And freten him, for that they knewe him naught.
Yet peynted was a litel forther-moor,
How Atthalante hunted the wilde boor,
And Meleagre, and many another mo,
For which Diane wroghte him care and wo.
Ther saugh I many another wonder storie,
The whiche me list nat drawen to memorie.
This goddesse on an hert ful hye seet,
With smale houndes al aboute hir feet;
And undernethe hir feet she hadde a mone,
Wexing it was, and sholde wanie sone.
In gaude grene hir statue clothed was,
With bowe in honde, and arwes in a cas.
Hir eyen caste she ful lowe adoun,
Ther Pluto hath his derke regioun.
A womman travailinge was hir biforn,
But, for hir child so longe was unborn,
Ful pitously Lucyna gan she calle,
And seyde, "help, for thou mayst best of alle."
Wel couthe he peynten lyfly that it wroghte,
With many a florin he the hewes boghte.
    Now been thise listes maad, and Theseus,
That at his grete cost arrayed thus
The temples and the theatre every del,

To tell you all the description.
Depicted were the walls up and down
Of hunting and of blameless chastity.
There saw I how woeful Callisto,[18]
When that Diana aggrieved was with her,
Was turned from a woman into a bear,
And after was she made the North Star;
Thus it was painted, I can tell you no more;
Her son is also a star, as men may see.
There saw I Daphne,[19] turned into a tree—
I mean not the goddess Diana,
But Peneus' daughter, who was called Daphne.
There I saw Actaeon[20] into a hart made;
For vengeance that he saw Diana all naked;
I saw how that his hounds have him caught
And upon him feasted, for they knew him not.
Yet painted along a little further,
How Atalanta hunted the wild boar,
And Meleager, and many another more,
For which Diana brought him care and woe.
There saw I many another wonderful story,
That I cannot now draw to memory.
This goddess on a hart full high sat,
With small hounds all about her feet;
And underneath her feet she had a moon,
Waxing it was, and should wane soon.
In yellow-green her statue clothed was,
With bow in hand, and arrows in a case.
Her eyes cast she full low down,
Where Pluto had his dark region.
A woman in labor was her before,
But because her child was so long unborn,
Full piteously Lucina[21] began she to call,
And said, "Help, for you may help best of all."
Well could he who wrought it paint like life;
With many a florin he the pigments bought.

　　Now was the arena made, and Theseus,
Who at his great cost adorned thus
The temples and battleground in every detail,

Whan it was doon, him lyked wonder wel.
But stinte I wol of Theseus a lyte,
And speke of Palamon and of Arcite.

The day approcheth of hir retourninge,
That everich sholde an hundred knightes bringe,
The bataille to darreyne, as I yow tolde;
And til Athénes, hir covenant for to holde,
Hath everich of hem broght an hundred knightes
Wel armed for the werre at alle rightes.
And sikerly, ther trowed many a man
That never, sithen that the world bigan,
As for to speke of knighthod of hir hond,
As fer as God hath maked see or lond,
Nas, of so fewe, so noble a companye.
For every wight that lovede chivalrye,
And wolde, his thankes, han a passant name,
Hath preyed that he mighte ben of that game;
And wel was him, that ther-to chosen was.
For if ther fille to-morwe swich a cas,
Ye knowen wel, that every lusty knight,
That loveth paramours, and hath his might,
Were it in Engelond, or elles-where,
They wolde, hir thankes, wilnen to be there.
To fighte for a lady, *ben'cite!*
It were a lusty sighte for to see.

And right so ferden they with Palamon.
With him ther wenten knightes many oon;
Som wol ben armed in an habergeoun,
In a brest-plat and in a light gipoun;
And somme woln have a peyre plates large;
And somme woln have a Pruce shield, or a targe;
Somme woln ben armed on hir legges weel,
And have an ax, and somme a mace of steel.
Ther nis no newe gyse, that it nas old.
Armed were they, as I have you told,
Everich after his opinioun.

Ther maistow seen coming with Palamoun
Ligurge him-self, the grete king of Trace;
Blak was his berd, and manly was his face.

When done it pleased him wonderfully well.
But for now I will cease to speak of Theseus,
And speak of Palamon and Arcita.

The day approached of their returning,
When each should a hundred knights bring
For the battle, as I you told;
And to Athens, their covenant to hold,
Had each of them brought a hundred knights
Well armed for the war at every point.
And surely, there believed many a man
That never, since the world began,
Among all knighthood's epitome,
As far as God had made land or sea,
Was there among so few so much nobility.
For every man who loved chivalry,
And would gladly have a puissant name,
Had prayed that he might be of that game;
And well was him who thereto chosen was.
For if there befell tomorrow such a case,
You know well that every lusty knight
Who loves passionately and has the power,
Were he in England or elsewhere,
He would, above all, wish to be there.
To fight for a lady, *benedicite!*
It would be a joyful sight to see.

And right so fared they with Palamon.
With him there went knights many a one;
One would be armed with a coat of mail,
And a breastplate and a light tunic;
And one would have a suit of armor plates large;
And some would have a light or Prussian shield;
Some would be armed on his legs well,
And have an axe, and some a mace of steel.
There is no new fashion that is not old.
Armed were they, as I have you told,
Each after his opinion.

There may you have seen, coming with Palamon,
Lycurgus himself, the great king of Thrace.
Black was his beard, and manly was his face.

The cercles of his eyen in his heed,
They gloweden bitwixe yelow and reed:
And lyk a griffon loked he aboute,
With kempe heres on his browes stoute;
His limes grete, his braunes harde and stronge,
His shuldres brode, his armes rounde and longe.
And as the gyse was in his contree,
Ful hye up-on a char of gold stood he,
With foure whyte boles in the trays.
In-stede of cote-armure over his harnays,
With nayles yelwe and brighte as any gold,
He hadde a beres skin, col-blak, for-old.
His longe heer was kembd bihinde his bak,
As any ravenes fether it shoon for-blak:
A wrethe of gold arm-greet, of huge wighte,
Upon his heed, set ful of stones brighte,
Of fyne rubies and of dyamaunts.
Aboute his char ther wenten whyte alaunts,
Twenty and mo, as grete as any steer,
To hunten at the leoun or the deer,
And folwed him, with mosel faste y-bounde,
Colers of gold, and torets fyled rounde.
An hundred lordes hadde he in his route
Armed ful wel, with hertes sterne and stoute.

    With Arcita, in stories as men finde,
The grete Emetreus, the king of Inde,
Up-on a stede bay, trapped in steel,
Covered in cloth of gold diapred weel,
Cam ryding lyk the god of armes, Mars.
His cote-armure was of cloth of Tars,
Couched with perles whyte and rounde and grete
His sadel was of brend gold newe y-bete;
A mantelet upon his shuldre hanginge
Bret-ful of rubies rede, as fyr sparklinge.
His crispe heer lyk ringes was y-ronne,
And that was yelow, and glitered as the sonne.
His nose was heigh, his eyen bright citryn,
His lippes rounde, his colour was sangwyn,
A fewe fraknes in his face y-spreynd,

The irises of his eyes in his head,
They glowed between yellow and red;
And like a griffin looked he about,
With shaggy hairs on his brows stout;
His limbs great, his muscles hard and strong,
His shoulders broad, his arms round and long;
And as the fashion was in his country,
Full high upon a chariot of gold stood he,
With four white bulls in the traces.
Instead of a coat of arms over his armor,
With nails yellow and bright as any gold
He had a bearskin, coal black and old.
His long hair was combed behind his back—
As any raven's feather it shone very black;
A wreath of gold, arm-thick and of huge weight,
Upon his head, set full of stones bright,
Of fine rubies and of diamonds.
About his chariot there went white wolfhounds,
Twenty and more, as great as any steer,
To hunt the lion or the deer,
And followed him with muzzles fastbound,
Collars of gold, and leash-rings filed round.
A hundred lords had he in his retinue,
Armed full well, with hearts stern and stout.
  With Arcita, in stories as men find,
The great Emetreus, the king of India,
Upon a baycolored steed with trappings of steel,
Covered in cloth of gold that was patterned well,
Came riding like the god of arms, Mars.
His coat of armor was of Tarsia cloth,
Set with pearls white and round and great,
His saddle was of burnished gold newly wrought;
A short cloak upon his shoulder hanging
Brimful of rubies red as fire sparkling.
His curly hair like rings hung down,
And that was yellow, and glittered as the sun.
His nose was high, his eyes bright citron,
His lips round, his complexion red;
A few freckles on his face scattered,

Betwixen yelow and somdel blak y-meynd,
And as a leoun he his loking caste.
Of fyve and twenty yeer his age I caste.
His berd was wel bigonne for to springe;
His voys was as a trompe thunderinge.
Up-on his heed he wered of laurer grene
A gerland fresh and lusty for to sene.
Up-on his hand he bar, for his deduyt,
An egle tame, as eny lilie whyt.
An hundred lordes hadde he with him there,
Al armed, sauf hir heddes, in al hir gere,
Ful richely in alle maner thinges.
For trusteth wel, that dukes, erles, kinges,
Were gadered in this noble companye,
For love and for encrees of chivalrye.
Aboute this king ther ran on every part
Ful many a tame leoun and lepart.
And in this wyse thise lordes, alle and some,
Ben on the Sonday to the citee come
Aboute pryme, and in the toun alight.

This Theseus, this duk, this worthy knight,
Whan he had broght hem in-to his citee,
And inned hem, everich in his degree,
He festeth hem, and dooth so greet labour
To esen hem, and doon hem al honour,
That yet men weneth that no mannes wit
Of noon estat ne coude amenden it.
The minstralcye, the service at the feste,
The grete yiftes to the moste and leste,
The riche array of Theseus paleys,
Ne who sat first ne last up-on the deys,
What ladies fairest been or best daunsinge,
Or which of hem can dauncen best and singe,
Ne who most felingly speketh of love:
What haukes sitten on the perche above,
What houndes liggen on the floor adoun:
Of al this make I now no mencioun;
But al th'effect, that thinketh me
    the beste;

Between yellow and almost black mingled;
And as a lion his glance he cast.
Of five and twenty years his age I guess:
His beard was well begun to fill.
His voice was as a trumpet thundering.
Upon his head he wore of laurel green
A garland fresh and lusty for to see.
Upon his hand he bore for his delight
An eagle tame, as any lily white.
A hundred lords had he with him there,
All armed, except their heads, in all their gear,
Full richly in all manner of things.
For trust well that dukes, earls, kings
Were gathered in this noble company
For love and for the increase of chivalry.
About this king there ran on every side
Full many a tame lion and leopard.
And in this way these lords, all and one,
Were on the Sunday to the city come
About prime, and in this town alighted.

    This Theseus, this duke, this worthy knight,
When he had brought them into his city,
And housed them, each according to his rank,
He feasted them, and did so great labor
To make them comfortable and do them all honor,
That yet men think that no man's wit
Of any rank could improve on it.
The minstrelsy, the service of the feast,
The great gifts to the guests highest and least,
The rich decor of Theseus' palace,
Who sat first and last upon the dais,
What ladies were fairest or best at dancing,
Or which of them could both dance best and sing,
Who most movingly spoke of love;
What hawks sat on the perch above,
What hounds lay on the floor below—
Of all this I make no mention now;
But only the heart of the matter—that seems to me
    the best.

Now comth the poynt, and herkneth if yow leste.
The Sonday night, er day bigan to springe,
When Palamon the larke herde singe,
Although it nere nat day by houres two,
Yet song the larke, and Palamon also.
With holy herte, and with an heigh corage
He roos, to wenden on his pilgrimage
Un-to the blisful Citherea benigne,
I mene Venus, honurable and digne.
And in hir houre he walketh forth a pas
Un-to the listes, ther hir temple was,
And doun he kneleth, and with humble chere
And herte soor, he seyde as ye shul here.
"Faireste of faire, o lady myn, Venus,
Doughter to Jove and spouse of Vulcanus,
Thou glader of the mount of Citheroun,
For thilke love thou haddest to Adoun,
Have pitee of my bittre teres smerte,
And tak myn humble preyer at thyn herte.
Allas! I ne have no langage to telle
Th'effectes ne the torments of myn helle;
Myn herte may myne harmes nat biwreye;
I am so confus, that I can noght seye.
But mercy, lady bright, that knowest weel
My thought, and seest what harmes that I feel,
Considere al this, and rewe up-on my sore,
As wisly as I shal for evermore,
Emforth my might, thy trewe servant be,
And holden werre alwey with chastitee;
That make I myn avow, so ye me helpe.
I kepe noght of armes for to yelpe,
Ne I ne axe nat to-morwe to have victorie,
Ne renoun in this cas, ne veyne glorie
Of pris of armes blowen up and doun,
But I wolde have fully possessioun
Of Emelye, and dye in thy servyse;
Find thou the maner how, and in what wyse.
I recche nat, but it may bettre be,
To have victorie of hem, or they of me,

Now comes the point, and listen if you please.
　　The Sunday night, before day began to spring,
When Palamon the lark heard sing
(Although it was not day by hours two,
Yet sang the lark) and Palamon,
With holy heart and with a high courage,
He arose to wend on his pilgrimage
Unto the blissful Cytherea benign—
I mean Venus, honorable and divine.
And in her hour[22] he walked slowly forth
Unto the arena where her temple was,
And down he knelt, and with humble spirit
And heart lovesore, he said as you shall hear:
　　"Fairest of fair, O lady mine, Venus,
Daughter to Jove and spouse of Vulcanus,
You gladdener of the mount of Cythaeron,
For the love you had for Adonis,
Have pity on my bitter, stinging tears,
And take my humble prayer to your heart.
Alas! I have no language to tell
The effects nor the torments of my hell;
My heart may my hurts not reveal;
I am so confused that I cannot say.
But mercy, lady bright, who knows well
My thought, and sees what hurt I feel,
Consider this, and have pity on my pain,
As surely as I shall for evermore,
With all my might, your true servant be,
And make war always with chastity.
That I make my vow, so you me help.
I dare not of arms for to boast,
Nor do I ask tomorrow to have victory,
Nor renown in this event, nor vain glory
Of reputation of arms sounded up and down,
But I would have full possession
Of Emily, and die in your service.
Find you the manner how, and in what way:
I care not whether it may better be
To have victory of them, or they of me,

So that I have my lady in myne armes.
For though so be that Mars is god of armes,
Your vertu is so greet in hevene above,
That, if yow list, I shal wel have my love.
Thy temple wol I worshipe evermo,
And on thyn auter, wher I ryde or go,
I wol don sacrifice, and fyres bete.
And if ye wol nat so, my lady swete,
Than preye I thee, to-morwe with a spere
That Arcita me thurgh the herte bere.
Thanne rekke I noght, whan I have lost my lyf,
Though that Arcita winne hir to his wyf.
This is th'effect and ende of my preyere,
Yif me my love, thou blisful lady dere."
    Whan th'orisoun was doon of Palamon,
His sacrifice he dide, and that anon
Ful pitously, with alle circumstaunces,
Al telle I noght as now his observaunces.
But atte laste the statue of Venus shook,
And made a signe, wher-by that he took
That his preyere accepted was that day.
For thogh the signe shewed a delay,
Yet wiste he wel that graunted was his bone;
And with glad herte he wente him hoom ful sone.
    The thridde houre inequal that Palamon
Bigan to Venus temple for to goon,
Up roos the sonne, and up roos Emelye,
And to the temple of Diane gan hye.
Hir maydens, that she thider with hir ladde,
Ful redily with hem the fyr they hadde,
Th'encens, the clothes, and the remenant al
That to the sacrifyce longen shal;
The hornes fulle of meth, as was the gyse;
Ther lakked noght to doon hir sacrifyse.
Smoking the temple, ful of clothes faire,
This Emelye, with herte debonaire,
Hir body wessh with water of a welle;
But how she dide hir ryte I dar not telle,
But it be any thing in general;

So that I have my lady in my arms.
For though Mars is god of arms,
Your virtue is so great in heaven above,
That if you will, I shall well have my love.
Your temple will I worship evermore,
And on your altar. Whether I walk or ride,
I will do sacrifice and fires light.
And if you will it not so, my lady sweet,
Then pray I you, tomorrow with a spear
That Arcita through my heart pierce.
Then care I not, when I have lost my life,
Though that Arcita wins her to his wife.
This is the essence and end of my prayer:
Give me my love, you blissful lady dear."

    When the prayer was done by Palamon,
His sacrifice he did, and that anon
Full humbly, in every detail complete,
Although I tell not now his observances.
But at last the statue of Venus shook,
And made a sign, whereby he understood
That his prayer accepted was that day.
For though the sign showed a delay
Yet knew he well that granted was his wish
And with glad heart he went home anon.

    Three hours after Palamon
Began to Venus' temple for to go,
Up rose the sun, and up rose Emily,
And to the temple of Diana hurried.
Her maidens, that she there with her led,
Full readily the fire with them they had,
The incense, the vestments and tapestries
That to the sacrifice should belong;
The horns full of mead, as was the fashion;
There lacked nothing to do her sacrifice.
Incensing the temples, full of tapestries fair,
This Emily, with heart humble and gracious,
Her body washed with water of a spring;
But how she did her rite I dare not tell,
At least not in detail;

And yet it were a game to heren al;
To him that meneth wel, it were no charge:
But it is good a man ben at his large.
Hir brighte heer was kempt, untressed al;
A coroune of a grene ook cerial
Up-on hir heed was set ful fair and mete.
Two fyres on the auter gan she bete,
And dide hir thinges, as men may biholde
In Stace of Thebes, and thise bokes olde.
Whan kindled was the fyr, with pitous chere
Un-to Diane she spak, as ye may here.
        "O chaste goddesse of the wodes grene,
To whom bothe heven and erthe and see is sene,
Quene of the regne of Pluto derk and lowe,
Goddesse of maydens, that myn herte hast knowe
Ful many a yeer, and woost what I desire,
As keep me fro thy vengeaunce and thyn ire,
That Attheon aboughte cruelly.
Chaste goddesse, wel wostow that I
Desire to been a mayden al my lyf,
Ne never wol I be no love ne wyf.
I am, thou woost, yet of thy companye
A mayde, and love hunting and venerye,
And for to walken in the wodes wilde,
And noght to been a wyf, and be with childe.
Noght wol I knowe companye of man.
Now help me, lady, sith ye may and can,
For tho thre formes that thou hast in thee.
And Palamon, that hath swich love to me,
And eek Arcite, that loveth me so sore,
This grace I preye thee with-oute more,
As sende love and pees bitwixe hem two;
And fro me turne awey hir hertes so,
That al hir hote love, and hir desyr,
And al hir bisy torment, and hir fyr
Be queynt, or turned in another place;
And if so be thou wolt not do me grace,
Or if my destinee be shapen so,
That I shal nedes have oon of hem two,

And yet it would be a pleasure to hear all,
For him for whom it be not too much;
For it is good for a man be free to speak or keep silence.
Her bright hair was combed, unbraided all;
A garland of evergreen oak
Upon her head was set full fair and fitting.
Two fires on the altar began she to light,
And did her rites, as men may behold
In Statius of Thebes and those books old.
When kindled was the fire, with piteous mien
Unto Diana she spoke as you may hear:
   "O chaste goddess of the woods green,
To whom both heaven and earth and sea is seen,
Queen of the realm of Pluto dark and low,
Goddess of maidens, whom my heart has known
Full many a year, and knowing what I desire,
Keep me from your vengeance and your ire,
That Actaeon suffered for cruelly.
Chaste goddess, well know you that I
Desire to be a maiden for all my life
And never wish to be a lover nor a wife.
I am, you know, yet of your company,
A maid, and love hunting and the chase,
And to walk in the woods wild,
And not to be a wife and be with child.
Not will I know company of man.
Now help me lady, if you may and can,
As Diana, Luna, and Persephone.
And Palamon, who has such love for me,
And Arcita, who loves me so sore,
This grace I pray you without more:
Send love and peace between them two,
And from me turn away their hearts so
That all their hot love and their desire,
And all their sharp torment and their fire,
Be quenched or turned toward another place.
Or if so be your will to not do me grace,
Or if my destiny be determined so,
That I must have one of the two,

As sende me him that most desireth me.
Bihold, goddesse of clene chastitee,
The bittre teres that on my chekes falle.
Sin thou are mayde, and keper of us alle,
My maydenhede thou kepe and wel conserve,
And whyl I live a mayde, I wol thee serve."
    The fyres brenne up-on the auter clere,
Whyl Emelye was thus in hir preyere;
But sodeinly she saugh a sighte queynte,
For right anon oon of the fyres queynte,
And quiked agayn, and after that anon
That other fyr was queynt, and al agon;
And as it queynte, it made a whistelinge,
As doon thise wete brondes in hir brenninge,
And at the brondes ende out-ran anoon
As it were blody dropes many oon;
For which so sore agast was Emelye,
That she was wel ny mad, and gan to crye,
For she ne wiste what it signifyed;
But only for the fere thus hath she cryed,
And weep, that it was pitee for to here.
And ther-with-al Diane gan appere,
With bowe in hond, right as an hunteresse,
And seyde: "Doghter, stint thyn hevinesse
Among the goddes hye it is affermed,
And by eterne word write and confermed,
Thou shalt ben wedded un-to oon of tho
That han for thee so muchel care and wo;
But un-to which of hem I may nat telle.
Farwel, for I ne may no lenger dwelle.
The fyres which that on myn auter brenne
Shul thee declaren, er that thou go henne,
Thyn aventure of love, as in this cas."
And with that word, the arwes in the cas
Of the goddesse clateren faste and ringe,
And forth she wente, and made a vanisshinge;
For which this Emelye astoned was,
And seyde, "What amounteth this, allas!
I putte me in thy proteccioun,

Send me he who most desires me.
Behold, goddess of clean chastity,
The bitter tears that on my cheeks fall.
Since you are a virgin and guardian of us all,
My maidenhood you keep and well conserve,
And while I live a maid, I will you serve."
    The fires burned upon the altar brightly,
While Emily was thus in her prayer.
But suddenly she saw a strange sight,
For right anon one of the fires died,
And flamed again, and after that anon
The other fire died, all gone;
And as it died, it made a whistling,
As do those wet firebrands burning,
And at the firebrand ends out ran anon
What looked like many bloody drops;
For which so sore aghast was Emily
That she was well nigh distraught, and began to cry,
For she knew not what it signified;
But only for the fear thus had she cried,
And wept, that it was pity for to hear.
And therewithal Diana began to appear,
With bow in hand, right as a huntress,
And said, "Daughter, stop your sorrow.
Among the gods high it is affirmed,
And by eternal word written and confirmed,
You shall be wedded unto one of those
Who have for you so much care and woe;
But unto which of them I may not tell.
Farewell, for I may here no longer dwell.
The fires that on my altar burn
Shall you tell, before you go hence,
Your fate in love, as in this case."
And with that word, the arrows in the case
Of the goddess clattered fast and rang,
And forth she went, and made a vanishing;
For which this Emily astonished was,
And said, "What means this, alas!
I put me in your protection,

Diane, and in thy disposicioun."
And hoom she gooth anon the nexte weye.
This is th'effect, ther is namore to seye.
    The nexte houre of Mars folwinge this,
Arcite un-to the temple walked is
Of fierse Mars, to doon his sacrifyse,
With alle the rytes of his payen wyse.
With pitous herte and heigh devocioun,
Right thus to Mars he seyde his orisoun:
    "O stronge god, that in the regnes colde
Of Trace honoured art, and lord y-holde,
And hast in every regne and every lond
Of armes al the brydel in thyn hond,
And hem fortunest as thee list devyse,
Accept of me my pitous sacrifyse.
If so be that my youthe may deserve,
And that my might be worthy for to serve
Thy godhede, that I may been oon of thyne,
Than preye I thee to rewe up-on my pyne.
For thilke peyne, and thilke hote fyr,
In which thou whylom brendest for desyr,
Whan that thou usedest the grete beautee
Of fayre yonge fresshe Venus free,
And haddest hir in armes at thy wille,
Al-though thee ones on a tyme misfille
Whan Vulcanus had caught thee in his las,
And fond thee ligging by his wyf, allas!
For thilke sorwe that was in thyn herte,
Have routhe as wel up-on my peynes smerte.
I am yong and unkonning, as thou wost,
And, as I trowe, with love offended most,
That ever was any lyves creature;
For she, that dooth me al this wo endure,
Ne reccheth never wher I sinke or flete.
And wel I woot, er she me mercy hete,
I moot with strengthe winne hir in the place;
And wel I woot, withouten help or grace
Of thee, ne may my strengthe noght availle.
Than help me, lord, to-morwe in my bataille,

Diana, and at your disposing."
And home she went anon the quickest way.
This is the result, there is no more to say.
    The next hour of Mars following this,
Arcita unto the temple walked
Of fierce Mars, to do his sacrifice,
With all the customs of his pagan rites.
With piteous heart and with high devotion,
Right thus to Mars he said his prayer:
    "O strong god, who in the realms cold
Of Thrace honored are and lordship held,
And has in every realm and every land
Of arms all the bridle reins in your hand,
And dispenses fortune as you decide,
Accept of me my piteous sacrifice.
If my youth may deserve,
And my might be worthy to serve
Your godhead, that I may be one of yours,
Then I pray you to take pity upon my pain.
For that same pain and that hot fire
In which you once burned for desire,
When you enjoyed the beauty
Of fair, generous, young fresh Venus,
And had her in arms at your will—
Although you one time went wrong
When Vulcan caught you in his net,[23]
And found you lying by his wife, alas!—
For such sorrow that was in your heart,
Have pity as well upon my pains sharp.
I am young and ignorant, as you know,
And, I believe, by love assailed more
Than ever was any living creature;
For she who makes me all this woe endure,
Cares not whether I sink or float.
And well I know, before she mercy promises,
I must with strength win her in the arena;
And well I know, without help or grace
Of you, no way may my strength avail.
Then help me, lord, tomorrow in my battle,

For thilke fyr that whylom brente thee,
As wel as thilke fyr now brenneth me,
And do that I to-morwe have victorie.
Myn be the travaille, and thyn be the glorie!
Thy soverein temple wol I most honouren
Of any place, and alwey most labouren
In thy plesaunce and in thy craftes stronge,
And in thy temple I wol my baner honge,
And alle the armes of my companye;
And evere-mo, un-to that day I dye,
Eterne fyr I wol biforn thee finde.
And eek to this avow I wol me binde:
My berd, myn heer that hongeth long adoun,
That never yet ne felte offensioun
Of rasour nor of shere, I wol thee yive,
And been thy trewe servant whyl I live.
Now lord, have routhe up-on my sorwes sore,
Yif me victorie, I aske thee namore."
       The preyere stint of Arcita the stronge,
The ringes on the temple-dore that honge,
And eek the dores, clatereden ful faste,
Of which Arcita som-what him agaste.
The fyres brende up-on the auter brighte,
That it gan al the temple for to lighte;
And swete smel the ground anon up-yaf,
And Arcita anon his hand up-haf,
And more encens in-to the fyr he caste,
With othere rytes mo; and atte laste
The statue of Mars bigan his hauberk ringe.
And with that soun he herde a murmuringe
Ful lowe and dim, that sayde thus, "Victorie":
For which he yaf to Mars honour and glorie.
And thus with joye, and hope wel to fare,
Arcite anon un-to his inne is fare,
As fayn as fowel is of the brighte sonne.
       And right anon swich stryf ther is bigonne
For thilke graunting, in the hevene above,
Bitwixe Venus, the goddesse of love,
And Mars, the sterne god armipotente,

For that fire that once burned you,
As well as that fire that now burns me;
And make it so tomorrow I have victory.
Mine be the labor, and yours be the glory!
Your sovereign temple will I most honor
Of any place, and always most labor
For your pleasure and in your arts strong,
And in your temple I will my banner hang,
And all the arms of my company;
And evermore, unto that day I die,
Eternal fire I will before you provide.
And also to this vow I will me bind:
My beard, my hair, that hangs long down
That has never yet felt damage
Of razor nor of shears, I will you give,
And be your true servant while I live.
Now lord, have pity upon my sorrows sore:
Give me the victory, I ask no more."

    The prayer being ended of Arcita the strong,
The rings on the temple door that hung,
And also the doors, clattered full fast,
Of which Arcita somewhat took fright.
The fires burned up on the altar bright,
That it began all the temple to light;
And sweet smell the ground anon gave up,
And Arcita anon his hand up lifted,
And more incense into the fire he cast,
With other rites more; and at last
The statue of Mars began his coat of mail to ring.
And with that sound he heard a murmuring
Full low and dim, that said thus, "Victory,"
For which he gave to Mars honor and glory.
And thus with joy and hope to fare well,
Arcita anon into his dwelling is gone,
As glad as is a bird of the bright sun.

    And right anon such strife there is begun,
For that granting, in the heaven above,
Between Venus, the goddess of love,
And Mars, the stern god strong in arms,

That Jupiter was bisy it to stente;
Til that the pale Saturnus the colde,
That knew so manye of aventures olde,
Fond in his olde experience an art,
That he ful sone hath plesed every part.
As sooth is sayd, elde hath greet avantage
In elde is bothe wisdom and usage;
Men may the olde at-renne, and noght at-rede.
Saturne anon, to stinten stryf and drede,
Al be it that it is agayn his kynde,
Of al this stryf he gan remedie fynde.
    "My dere doghter Venus," quod Saturne,
"My cours, that hath so wyde for to turne,
Hath more power than wot any man.
Myn is the drenching in the see so wan;
Myn is the prison in the derke cote;
Myn is the strangling and hanging by the throte;
The murmure, and the cherles rebelling,
The groyning, and the pryvee empoysoning:
I do vengeance and pleyn correccioun
Whyl I dwelle in the signe of the Leoun.
Myn is the ruine of the hye halles,
The falling of the toures and of the walles
Up-on the mynour or the carpenter.
I slow Sampsoun in shaking the piler;
And myne be the maladyes colde,
The derke tresons, and the castes olde;
My loking is the fader of pestilence.
Now weep namore, I shal doon diligence
That Palamon, that is thyn owne knight,
Shal have his lady, as thou hast him hight.
Though Mars shal helpe his knight, yet nathelees
Bitwixe yow ther moot be some tyme pees,
Al be ye noght of o complexioun,
That causeth al day swich divisioun.
I am thin ayel, redy at thy wille
Weep thou namore, I wol thy lust fulfille."
    Now wol I stinten of the goddes above,
Of Mars, and of Venus, goddesse of love.

That Jupiter was busy to stop it;
Till pale Saturn, baleful and cold,[24]
Who knew of so many adventures old,
Found in his old experience an art
That he full soon had pleased every side.
As truth is said, old age has great advantage,
In age is both wisdom and experience;
Men may the old outrun yet not outwit them.
Saturn anon, to stop strife and dread,
Albeit that it was against his nature,
Of all this strife he began a remedy to find.
    "My dear daughter Venus," said Saturn,
"My orbit, that has a circuit so wide to turn,
Has more power than knows any man.
Mine is the drowning in the sea so pale;
Mine is the prison in the dark hut;
Mine is the strangling and hanging by the throat;
The murmur and the peasants rebelling,
The grumbling and secret poisoning.
I do vengeance and full punishment
While I dwell in the sign of the lion.
Mine is the ruin of the high halls,
The falling of the towers and the walls
Upon the miner or the carpenter.
I slew Sampson, shaking the pillar;
And mine be the maladies cold,
The dark treasons, and the castles old;
My aspect is the father of pestilence.
Now weep no more, I shall do diligence
That Palamon, who is your own knight,
Shall have his lady, as you him promised.
Though Mars shall help his knight, yet nevertheless
Between you there must be at some time peace,
Albeit you are not of the same temperament,
That causes all day such division.
I am your grandfather, ready at your will;
Weep now no more, I will your desire fulfill."
    Now will I stop telling of the gods above,
Of Mars and Venus, goddess of love,

And telle yow, as pleynly as I can,
The grete effect, for which that I bigan.

Part Four

Greet was the feste in Athenes that day,
And eek the lusty seson of that May
Made every wight to been in swich plesaunce,
That al that Monday justen they and daunce,
And spenden it in Venus heigh servyse.
But by the cause that they sholde ryse
Erly, for to seen the grete fight,
Unto hir reste wente they at night.
And on the morwe, whan that day gan springe,
Of hors and harneys, noyse and clateringe
Ther was in hostelryes al aboute;
And to the paleys rood ther many a route
Of lordes, up-on stedes and palfreys.
Ther maystow seen devysing of herneys
So uncouth and so riche, and wroght so weel
Of goldsmithrie, of browding, and of steel;
The sheeldes brighte, testers, and trappures;
Gold-hewen helmes, hauberks, cote-armures;
Lordes in paraments on hir courseres,
Knights of retenue, and eek squyeres
Nailinge the speres, and helmes bokelinge,
Gigginge of sheeldes, with layneres lacinge;
Ther as need is, they weren no-thing ydel;
The fomy stedes on the golden brydel
Gnawinge, and faste the armurers also
With fyle and hamer prikinge to and fro;
Yemen on fote, and communes many oon
With shorte staves, thikke as they may goon;
Pypes, trompes, nakers, clariounes,
That in the bataille blowen blody sounes;
The paleys ful of peples up and doun,
Heer three, ther ten, holding hir questioun,
Divyninge of thise Theban knightes two.
Somme seyden thus, somme seyde it shal be so;
Somme helden with him with the blake berd,

And tell you as plainly as I can
The great outcome for which that I began.

Part Four

Great was the festival in Athens that day,
And also the lusty season of May
Made every person want to be in such pleasure,
That all that Monday jousted they and danced,
And spent it in Venus' high service.
But because they should rise
Early, for to see the great fight,
Unto their rest went they at night.
And on the morrow, when day began to spring,
Of horse and armor noise and clattering
There was in hostelries all about;
And to the palace rode there many a company
Of lords upon chargers and palfreys.
There may you have seen fitting of armor
So unusual and so rich, and wrought so well
Of goldsmithery, of embroidery, and of steel;
The shields bright, headpieces and trapping;
Gold-hued helmets, coats of mail, coats of arms;
Lords in stately robes on their chargers,
Knights in service, and also squires
Nailing points to the spear shafts, and helmets buckling;
Strapping of shields with leather thongs lacing—
Wherever needed, they were in no way idle;
The foamy steeds on the golden bridle
Gnawing, and fast the armorers also
With file and hammer riding to and fro;
Yeomen on foot and commoners many a one
With short staves, in close formation;
Pipes, trumpets, kettledrums, clarions
That in battle blow bloody sounds;
The palace full of people up and down,
Here three, there ten, holding their question,
Guessing about these Theban knights two.
Some said thus, some said it shall be so;
Some sided with him with the black beard,

Somme with the balled, somme with the thikke-herd;
Somme sayde, he loked grim and he wolde fighte;
He hath a sparth of twenty pound of wighte.
Thus was the halle ful of divyninge,
Longe after that the sonne gan to springe.

The grete Theseus, that of his sleep awaked
With minstralcye and noyse that was maked,
Held yet the chambre of his paleys riche,
Til that the Thebane knightes, bothe y-liche
Honoured, were into the paleys fet.
Duk Theseus was at a window set,
Arrayed right as he were a god in trone.
The peple preesseth thider-ward ful sone
Him for to seen, and doon heigh reverence,
And eek to herkne his hest and his sentence.

An heraud on a scaffold made an ho,
Til al the noyse of peple was y-do;
And whan he saugh the peple of noyse al stille,
Tho showed he the mighty dukes wille.

"The lord hath of his heigh discrecioun
Considered, that it were destruccioun
To gentil blood, to fighten in the gyse
Of mortal bataille now in this empryse;
Wherfore, to shapen that they shul not dye,
He wol his firste purpos modifye.
No man therfor, up peyne of los of lyf,
No maner shot, ne pollax, ne short knyf
Into the listes sende, or thider bringe;
Ne short swerd for to stoke, with poynt bytinge,
No man ne drawe, ne bere it by his syde.
Ne no man shal un-to his felawe ryde
But o cours, with a sharp y-grounde spere;
Foyne, if him list, on fote, him-self to were.
And he that is at meschief, shal be take,
And noght slayn, but be broght un-to the stake
That shal ben ordeyned on either syde;
But thider he shal by force, and ther abyde.
And if so falle, the chieftayn be take
On either syde, or elles slee his make,

Some with the bald, some with the thickhaired;
Some said that one looked grim, and he would fight—
"He has a battle-axe of twenty pounds weight."
Thus was the hall full of speculation,
Long after the sun began to spring.
     The great Theseus, who from his sleep awakened
With minstrelsy and noise that was made,
Held yet the chamber of his palace rich,
Till the Theban knights, both equally
Honored, were into the palace summoned.
Duke Theseus was sitting at a window
Looking as if he were a god enthroned.
The people pressed forward full soon
Him to see, and do high reverence,
And also to hear his command and his decision.
     A herald on a scaffold made a "Tadum!"
Till all the noise of the people was done;
And when he saw the people's noise all still,
Thus showed he the mighty duke's will:
     "The lord hath of his high acumen
Considered that it were destruction
To gentle blood to fight in the manner
Of mortal battle in this enterprise.
Wherefore, to ensure that they do not die,
He will his first purpose modify.
No man therefore, upon pain of loss of life,
Any manner of projectile, nor short knife
Onto the battleground shall send, or there bring;
Nor short sword, for to stab with point biting,
Nor may any man draw it or bear it by his side.
No man shall against his opponent ride
But one charge with a sharp ground spear;
He may parry, if he wishes, on foot, himself to defend.
And he who is in trouble shall be captured,
And not slain, but be brought unto the stake
That shall be set up on either side;
There brought by force, and there abide.
And if it so happens the chieftain be taken
On either side, or slain the other chieftain,

No lenger shal the turneyinge laste.
God spede yow; goth forth, and ley on faste.
With long swerd and with maces fight your fille.
Goth now your wey; this is the lordes wille."
     The voys of peple touchede the hevene,
So loude cryden they with mery stevene:
"God save swich a lord, that is so good,
He wilneth no destruccioun of blood!"
Up goon the trompes and the melodye.
And to the listes rit the companye
By ordinaunce, thurgh-out the citee large,
Hanged with cloth of gold, and nat with sarge.
     Ful lyk a lord this noble duk gan ryde,
Thise two Thebanes up-on either syde;
And after rood the quene, and Emelye,
And after that another companye
Of oon and other, after hir degree.
And thus they passen thurgh-out the citee,
And to the listes come they by tyme.
It nas not of the day yet fully pryme,
Whan set was Theseus ful riche and hye,
Ipolita the quene and Emelye,
And other ladies in degrees aboute.
Un-to the seetes preesseth al the route.
And west-ward, thurgh the gates under Marte,
Arcite and eek the hundred of his parte,
With baner reed is entred right anon;
And in that selve moment Palamon
Is under Venus, est-ward in the place,
With baner whyt, and hardy chere and face.
In al the world, to seken up and doun,
So even with-outen variacioun,
Ther nere swiche companyes tweye.
For ther nas noon so wys that coude seye,
That any hadde of other avauntage
Of worthinesse, ne of estaat, ne age,
So even were they chosen, for to gesse.
And in two renges faire they hem dresse.
     Whan that hir names rad were everichoon,

No longer shall the tourney last.
God speed you! Go forth, and lay on fast.
With long sword and mace fight your fill.
Go now your way—this is the lord's will."
    The voice of people touched the heaven,
So loud cried they with merry voice:
"God save such a lord, who is so good,
He desires no destruction of blood!"
Up went the trumpets and the melody,
And to the arena rode the company,
In order, throughout the city large,
Hung with cloth of gold and not with serge.
    Full like a lord this noble duke began to ride,
These two Thebans on either side;
And after rode the queen and Emily,
And after that another company
Of one and other, according to their rank.
And thus they passed throughout the city,
And to the arena come they promptly.
It was not of the day fully prime[25]
When sat this Theseus full rich and high,
Hyppolyta the queen and Emily,
And other ladies in tiers about.
Unto the seats pressed all the crowd.
And westward, through the gates under Mars,
Arcita, and the hundred of his side,
With banner red is entered right anon;
And in that same moment Palamon
Is under Venus, eastward in the place,
With banner white, and bold countenance and face.
In all the world, to seek up and down,
Matched so equally,
There never were such companies two.
For there was none so wise who could say
That either had of the other advantage
In worthiness, nor of estate nor age,
So even were they chosen, for to guess.
And in two rows fair they place themselves.
    Then every one of their names was read,

That in hir nombre gyle were ther noon,
Tho were the gates shet, and cryed was loude:
"Do now your devoir, yonge knightes proude!"
    The heraudes lefte hir priking up and doun;
Now ringen trompes loude and clarioun;
Ther is namore to seyn, but west and est
In goon the speres ful sadly in arest;
In goth the sharpe spore in-to the syde.
Ther seen men who can juste, and who can ryde;
Ther shiveren shaftes up-on sheeldes thikke;
He feleth thurgh the herte-spoon the prikke.
Up springen speres twenty foot on highte;
Out goon the swerdes as the silver brighte.
The helmes they to-hewen and to-shrede;
Out brest the blood, with sterne stremes rede.
With mighty maces the bones they to-breste.
He thurgh the thikkeste of the throng gan threste.
Ther stomblen stedes stronge, and doun goth al.
He rolleth under foot as dooth a bal.
He foyneth on his feet with his tronchoun,
And he him hurtleth with his hors adoun.
He thurgh the body is hurt, and sithen y-take,
Maugree his heed, and broght un-to the stake,
As forward was, right ther he moste abyde;
Another lad is on that other syde.
    And som tyme dooth hem Theseus to reste,
Hem to refresshe, and drinken if hem leste.
Ful ofte a-day han thise Thebanes two
Togidre y-met, and wroght his felawe wo;
Unhorsed hath ech other of hem tweye.
Ther nas no tygre in the vale of Galgopheye,
Whan that hir whelp is stole, whan it is lyte,
So cruel on the hunte, as is Arcite
For jelous herte upon this Palamoun:
Ne in Belmarye ther nis so fel leoun,
That hunted is, or for his hunger wood,
Ne of his praye desireth so the blood,
As Palamon to sleen his fo Arcite.
The jelous strokes on hir helmes byte;

So that there was no doubt of their equal numbers,
Then the gates were shut, and cried was loud:
"Do now your duty, young knights proud!"
    The heralds left their riding up and down;
Now rang trumpets loud and clarion.
There is no more to say, but west and east
In go the spears full solidly into the spear rests;
In go the sharp spurs into the side.
There see men who can joust and who can ride;
There shatter shafts upon shields thick;
One feels through the breastbone the prick.
Up spring spears twenty feet on high;
Out go the swords as the silver bright.
The helmets they hew and to pieces shred;
Out bursts the blood, with gushing streams red.
With mighty maces the bones they smash,
He through the thickest of the throng can press;
There strong steeds stumble, and down go all;
He rolls under foot as does a ball.
He parries on foot with his shattered spear,
And knocks horse and rider to the ground.
He through the body is hurt and then taken,
Despite all he could do, and brought to the stake.
As agreement was, there he must abide;
Another carried off on the other side.
    And from time to time Theseus causes them to rest,
Them to refresh and drink, if they wish.
Full often through the day have these Thebans two
Together met, and wrought his fellow woe;
Unhorsed has each the other of them twice.
There was no tiger in the vale of Gargaphie,
When its little cub was taken,
So cruel toward the hunter was Arcita
For jealous heart toward this Palamon.
Nor in Benmarin was there so fierce a lion
That hunted was, or crazed by hunger,
Nor of his prey desired so the blood,
As Palamon to slay his foe Arcita.
The jealous strokes on their helmets bite;

Out renneth blood on both hir sydes rede.
    Some tyme an ende ther is of every dede;
For er the sonne un-to the reste wente,
The strange king Emetreus gan hente
This Palamon, as he faught with Arcite,
And made his swerd depe in his flesh to byte;
And by the force of twenty is he take
Unyolden, and y-drawe unto the stake.
And in the rescous of this Palamoun
The stronge king Ligurge is born adoun;
And king Emetreus, for al his strengthe,
Is born out of his sadel a swerdes lengthe,
So hitte him Palamon er he were take;
But al for noght, he was broght to the stake.
His hardy herte mighte him helpe naught;
He moste abyde, whan that he was caught
By force, and eek by composicioun.
    Who sorweth now but woful Palamoun,
That moot namore goon agayn to fighte?
And whan that Theseus had seyn this sighte,
Un-to the folk that foghten thus echoon
He cryde, "Ho! namore, for it is doon!
I wol be trewe juge, and no partye.
Arcite of Thebes shal have Emelye,
That by his fortune hath hir faire y-wonne."
Anon ther is a noyse of peple bigonne
For joye of this, so loude and heigh withalle,
It seemed that the listes sholde falle.
    What can now faire Venus doon above?
What seith she now? what dooth this quene of love?
But wepeth so, for wanting of hir wille,
Til that hir teres in the listes fille;
She seyde: "I am ashamed, doutelees."
Saturnus seyde: "Doghter, hold thy pees.
Mars hath his wille, his knight hath al his bone,
And, by myn heed, thou shalt ben esed sone."
    The trompes, with the loude minstralcye,
The heraudes, that ful loude yolle and crye,
Been in hir wele for joye of daun Arcite.

Out runs blood on both their sides red.
　　At some time an end there is of every deed.
For before the sun unto its rest went,
The strong king Emetreus seized
This Palamon, as he fought with Arcita,
And made his sword deep in his flesh to bite;
And by the force of twenty is Palamon taken
Unyielding, and dragged unto the stake.
And in the attempted rescue of this Palamon
The strong king Licurgus is borne down;
And King Emetreus, for all his strength,
Was knocked out of his saddle a sword's length,
So hit him Palamon before he was taken.
But all for nought: he was brought to the stake.
His bold heart might help him not;
He must abide, when he was caught,
By necessity and also by agreement.
　　Who sorrows now but woeful Palamon,
Who must no more go again to fight?
And when Theseus had seen this sight,
Unto the folk who fought thus every one
He cried, "Halt! no more, for it is done!
I will be true judge, and not partisan.
Arcita of Thebes shall have Emily,
Who by his fortune has her fairly won."
Anon there is a noise of people begun
For joy of this, so loud and great withal,
It seemed that the arena should fall.
　　What now could fair Venus do above?
What says she now? what does this queen of love?
But weep so, for lacking of her will,
Till that her tears on the battleground fell?
She said, "I am ashamed, doubtless."
Saturn said, "Daughter, hold your peace.
Mars has his will, his knight has all his request;
And by my head, you shall be satisfied soon."
　　The trumpeters with the loud music,
The heralds who full loud yell and cry,
Were in their happiness for joy of sir Arcita.

But herkneth me, and stinteth now a lyte,
Which a miracle ther bifel anon.
        This fierse Arcite hath of his helm y-don,
And on a courser, for to shewe his face,
He priketh endelong the large place,
Loking upward up-on this Emelye;
And she agayn him caste a freendlich yë,
(For wommen, as to speken in comune,
They folwen al the favour of fortune);
And she was al his chere, as in his herte.
Out of the ground a furie infernal sterte,
From Pluto sent, at requeste of Saturne,
For which his hors for fere gan to turne,
And leep asyde, and foundred as he leep;
And, er that Arcite may taken keep,
He pighte him on the pomel of his heed,
That in the place he lay as he were deed,
His brest to-brosten with his sadel-bowe.
As blak he lay as any cole or crowe,
So was the blood y-ronnen in his face.
Anon he was y-born out of the place
With herte soor, to Theseus paleys.
Tho was he corven out of his harneys,
And in a bed y-brought ful faire and blyve,
For he was yet in memorie and alyve,
And alway crying after Emelye.
        Duk Theseus, with al his companye,
Is comen hoom to Athenes his citee,
With alle blisse and greet solempnitee.
Al be it that this aventure was falle,
He nolde noght disconforten hem alle.
Men seyde eek, that Arcite shal nat dye;
He shal ben heled of his maladye.
And of another thing they were as fayn,
That of hem alle was ther noon y-slayn,
Al were they sore y-hurt, and namely oon,
That with a spere was thirled his brest-boon.
To othere woundes, and to broken armes,
Some hadden salves, and some hadden charmes;

But listen to me now, and cease your noise a little,
To hear what a miracle there befell anon.
   This bold Arcita has off his helmet taken,
And on a courser, to show his face,
He spurred the length of the battleground,
Looking upward upon this Emily;
And she toward him cast a friendly eye
(For women, to speak in general,
Follow all the favor of fortune)
And she was all his happiness, as in his heart.
Then out of the ground a fury infernal leaped,
From Pluto sent at request of Saturn,
For which his horse for fear began to turn
And leapt aside, and fell back on him as he leapt;
And before Arcita could take heed,
He pitched on the crown of his head,
And in the place he lay as if he were dead,
His breast shattered by his saddlebow.
As black he lay as any coal or crow,
So was the blood suffusing his face.
Anon he was borne out of the place,
With heart sore, to Theseus' palace.
Then was he cut out of his armor,
And in a bed brought full fair and soon,
For he was yet conscious and alive,
And always crying after Emily.
   Duke Theseus, with all his company,
Is come home to Athens his city,
With all bliss and great solemnity.
Albeit that this accident had occurred,
He did not want to discomfort them all.
Men said also that Arcita shall not die;
He shall be healed of his malady.
And of another thing they were as glad,
That of them all was there none slain,
Although were they sore hurt and especially one,
Who by a spear was pierced through his breast bone.
For other wounds and for broken arms
Some had salves, and some had charms;

Fermacies of herbes, and eek save
They dronken, for they wolde hir limes have.
For which this noble duk, as he wel can,
Conforteth and honoureth every man,
And made revel al the longe night,
Un-to the straunge lordes, as was right.
Ne ther was holden no disconfitinge,
But as a justes or a tourneyinge;
For soothly ther was no disconfiture,
For falling nis nat but an aventure;
Ne to be lad with fors un-to the stake
Unyolden, and with twenty knightes take.
O persone allone, with-outen mo,
And haried forth by arme, foot, and to,
And eek his stede driven forth with staves,
With footmen, bothe yemen and eek knaves,
It nas aretted him no vileinye,
Ther may no man clepen it cowardye.
      For which anon duk Theseus leet crye,
To stinten alle rancour and envye,
The gree as wel of o syde as of other,
And either syde y-lyk, as otheres brother;
And yaf hem yiftes after hir degree,
And fully heeld a feste dayes three;
And conveyed the kinges worthily
Out of his toun a journee largely.
And hoom wente every man the righte way.
Ther was namore, but "far wel, have good day!"
Of this bataille I wol namore endyte,
But speke of Palamon and of Arcite.
      Swelleth the brest of Arcite, and the sore
Encreesseth at his herte more and more.
The clothered blood, for any lechecraft,
Corrupteth, and is in his bouk y-laft,
That neither veyne-blood, ne ventusinge,
Ne drinke of herbes may ben his helpinge.
The vertu expulsif, or animal,
Fro thilke vertu cleped natural
Ne may the venim voyden, ne expelle.

Medicines of herbs, and also an herb potion
They drank, for they would their limbs preserve.
For which this noble duke, as well as he knew,
Comforted and honored every man,
And made revel all the long night
With the foreign lords, as was right.
Nor was there held any bad blood
For it was a joust or tourneying;
For truly there was no discomfiture,
For falling was not but an accident.
Nor to be led with force unto the stake
Unyielding, and by twenty knights taken,
One person alone, without more,
And dragged forth by arm, foot and toe,
And also his steed driven forth with sticks
By foot soldiers, both yeomen and servants—
It was assigned to him no disgrace;
There may no man call it cowardice.

    For which anon duke Theseus had declared,
To stop all rancor and bad blood,
The worth of one side as equal to the other,
And each side alike as if the other's brother;
And gave them gifts after their rank,
And fully held a feast for days three;
And conveyed the kings worthily
Out of his town a day's ride fully.
And home went every man the right way.
There was no more but "Farewell, have a good day!"
Of this battle I will no more write,
But speak of Palamon and Arcita.

    Swelled the breast of Arcita, and the sore
Increased at his heart more and more.
The clotted blood, despite all medicine,
Corrupted and was in his body left,
Neither bloodletting, nor cupping,
Nor drink of herbs may be his helping.
His spirit's virtue could not compel
His body's virtue the bad
Blood to expel

The pypes of his longes gonne to swelle,
And every lacerte in his brest adoun
Is shent with venim and corrupcioun.
Him gayneth neither, for to gete his lyf,
Vomyt upward, ne dounward laxatif;
Al is to-brosten thilke regioun,
Nature hath now no dominacioun.
And certeinly, ther nature wol nat wirche,
Far-wel, phisyk! go ber the man to chirche!
This al and som, that Arcita mot dye,
For which he sendeth after Emelye,
And Palamon, that was his cosin dere;
Than seyde he thus, as ye shul after here.
    "Naught may the woful spirit in myn herte
Declare o poynt of alle my sorwes smerte
To yow, my lady, that I love most;
But I biquethe the service of my gost
To yow aboven every creature,
Sin that my lyf may no lenger dure.
Allas, the wo! allas, the peynes stronge,
That I for yow have suffred, and so longe!
Allas, the deeth! allas, myn Emelye!
Allas, departing of our companye!
Allas, myn hertes quene! allas, my wyf!
Myn hertes lady, endere of my lyf!
What is this world? what asketh men to have?
Now with his love, now in his colde grave
Allone, with-outen any companye.
Far-wel, my swete fo! myn Emelye!
And softe tak me in your armes tweye,
For love of God, and herkneth what I seye.
    I have heer with my cosin Palamon
Had stryf and rancour, many a day a-gon,
For love of yow, and for my jelousye.
And Jupiter so wis my soule gye,
To speken of a servant proprely,
With alle circumstaunces trewely,
That is to seyn, trouthe, honour, and knighthede,
Wisdom, humblesse, estaat, and heigh kinrede,

And the pipes of his lungs began to swell.
And every muscle in his breast
Is damaged by venom and corruption.
Him helped neither, to save his life,
Vomit upward nor downward laxative;
All is shattered in that region.
Nature had now no healing power;
And certainly, where nature will not work,
Farewell, medicine, go bear the man to church.
This is all there is, that Arcita must die;
For which he sent after Emily
And Palamon, who was his cousin dear.
Then said he thus, as you shall after hear:
    "May the woeful spirit in my heart
Not declare one part of all my sores sharp
To you, my lady, whom I love most;
But I bequeath the service of my spirit
To you above every creature,
Since my life may no longer endure.
Alas, the woe! alas, the pains strong,
That for you I have suffered, and so long!
Alas, the death! alas, my Emily!
Alas, that we must part!
Alas, my heart's queen! alas, my wife!
My heart's lady, ender of my life!
What is this world? What do men ask to have?
Now with his love, now in his cold grave
Alone, without any company.
Farewell, my sweet foe, my Emily!
And soft take me in your arms two,
For love of God, and listen to what I say:
    I have here with my cousin Palamon
Had strife and rancor many a day gone by,
For love of you and for my jealousy.
And Jupiter wisely guide me
To speak about a servant of love properly,
With all necessary qualities truly—
That is to say, fidelity, honor, knighthood,
Wisdom, humility, rank and kindred,

Fredom, and al that longeth to that art,
So Jupiter have of my soule part,
As in this world right now ne knowe I non
So worthy to ben loved as Palamon,
That serveth yow, and wol don al his lyf.
And if that ever ye shul been a wyf,
Foryet nat Palamon, the gentil man."
And with that word his speche faille gan,
For from his feet up to his brest was come
The cold of deeth, that hadde him overcome
And yet more-over, in his armes two
The vital strengthe is lost, and al ago.
Only the intellect, with-outen more.
That dwelled in his herte syk and sore,
Gan failen, when the herte felte deeth,
Dusked his eyen two, and failled breeth.
But on his lady yet caste he his yë;
His laste word was, "mercy, Emelye!"
His spirit chaunged hous, and wente ther,
As I cam never, I can nat tellen wher.
Therfor I stinte, I nam no divinistre;
Of soules finde I nat in this registre,
Ne me ne list thilke opiniouns to telle
Of hem, though that they wryten wher they dwelle.
Arcite is cold, ther Mars his soule gye;
Now wol I speken forth of Emelye.

   Shrighte Emelye, and howleth Palamon,
And Theseus his suster took anon
Swowninge, and bar hir fro the corps away.
What helpeth it to tarien forth the day,
To tellen how she weep, bothe eve and morwe?
For in swich cas wommen have swich sorwe,
Whan that hir housbonds been from hem ago,
That for the more part they sorwen so,
Or elles fallen in swich maladye,
That at the laste certeinly they dye.

   Infinite been the sorwes and the teres
Of olde folk, and folk of tendre yeres,
In al the toun, for deeth of this Theban;

Generosity, and all that belongs to that art—
As Jupiter shall receive my soul when I depart,
So in this world right now I know no one
So worthy to be loved as Palamon,
Who serves you and will do all his life.
And if ever you shall be a wife,
Forget not Palamon, the noble, virtuous man."
And with that word his speech to fail began,
For from his feet up to his breast was come
The cold of death, that had him overcome,
And yet moreover, in his arms two
The vital strength is lost and all gone.
Only then the intellect, without delay,
That dwelled in his heart sick and sore,
Began failing when the heart felt death.
Dimmed his eyes two, and failed breath,
But on his lady yet cast he his eye,
His last word was, "Mercy, Emily!"
His spirit changed houses and went there
Where I travelled never; I cannot compare.
Therefore I stop, I am no diviner;
Of souls I find not in this register,
It pleases me not to tell
Of those who write of where they dwell.
Arcita is cold, so Mars may his soul guide.
Now will I speak forth of Emily.

    Shrieked Emily and howled Palamon,
And Theseus his sister took anon
Swooning, and bore her from the corpse away.
What does it accomplish to while away the day
To tell how she wept both eve and morn?
For in such case women have such sorrow,
When their husbands from them go,
That many of them sorrow so,
Or else fall in such a malady
That at last certainly they die.

    Infinite were the sorrows and the tears
Of old folk and folk of tender years
In all the town, for death of this Theban;

For him ther wepeth bothe child and man;
So greet a weping was ther noon, certayn,
Whan Ector was y-broght, al fresh y-slayn,
To Troye; allas! the pitee that was ther,
Cracching of chekes, rending eek of heer.
"Why woldestow be deed," thise wommen crye,
"And haddest gold y-nough, and Emelye?"
No man mighte gladen Theseus,
Savinge his olde fader Egeus,
That knew this worldes transmutacioun,
As he had seyn it chaungen up and doun,
Joye after wo, and wo after gladnesse:
And shewed hem ensamples and lyknesse.
    "Right as ther deyed never man," quod he,
"That he ne livede in erthe in som degree,
Right so ther livede never man," he seyde,
"In al this world, that som tyme he ne deyde.
This world nis but a thurghfare ful of wo,
And we ben pilgrimes, passinge to and fro;
Deeth is an ende of every worldly sore."
And over al this yet seyde he muchel more
To this effect, ful wysly to enhorte
The peple, that they sholde hem reconforte.
    Duk Theseus, with al his bisy cure,
Caste now wher that the sepulture
Of good Arcite may best y-maked be,
And eek most honurable in his degree.
And at the laste he took conclusioun,
That ther as first Arcite and Palamoun
Hadden for love the bataille hem bitwene,
That in that selve grove, swote and grene,
Ther as he hadde his amorous desires,
His compleynt, and for love his hote fires,
He wolde make a fyr, in which th'office
Funeral he mighte al accomplice;
And leet comaunde anon to hakke and hewe
The okes olde, and leye hem on a rewe
In colpons wel arrayed for to brenne;
His officers with swifte feet they renne

For him there wept both child and man.
So great weeping was there none, certain,
When Hector was brought, all freshly slain,
To Troy. Alas, the pity that was there:
Scratching of cheeks, rending of hair.
"Why did you wish to be dead?" these women cry,
"And had gold enough, and Emily?"
No man might gladden Theseus
Save his old father Egeus,
Who knew this world's mutation,
And had seen it change both up and down—
Joy after woe, and woe after gladness—
And showed him analogies and examples.
    "Just as there never died a man," said he,
"Who never lived on earth in some degree,
Right so there never lived a man," he said,
"In all this world, who some time did not die.
This world is nought but a thoroughfare full of woe,
And we be pilgrims, passing to and fro;
Death is an end of every worldly sorrow."
And beyond all this said he much more
To this effect, full wisely to exhort
The people that they should be comforted.
    Duke Theseus, with all his diligent concern,
Considered now where the burial
Of good Arcita may best made be,
And also most honorable in his rank.
And at last he took conclusion,
That there where Arcita and Palamon
For love first battled;
In that same grove, sweet and green,
There where he had his amorous desires,
His lament, and for love his hot fires,
He would make a fire, in which the rites
Funereal he might all conduct;
And gave command anon to hack and hew
The oaks old, and lay them in a row
In pieces well arranged to burn.
His officers with swift feet they ran

And ryde anon at his comaundement.
And after this, Theseus hath y-sent
After a bere, and it al over-spradde
With cloth of gold, the richest that he hadde.
And of the same suyte he cladde Arcite;
Upon his hondes hadde he gloves whyte;
Eek on his heed a croune of laurer grene,
And in his hond a swerd ful bright and kene.
He leyde him bare the visage on the bere,
Therwith he weep that pitee was to here.
And for the peple sholde seen him alle,
Whan it was day, he broghte him to the halle,
That roreth of the crying and the soun.
    Tho cam this woful Theban Palamoun,
With flotery berd, and ruggy asshy heres,
In clothes blake, y-dropped al with teres;
And, passing othere of weping, Emelye,
The rewfulleste of al the companye.
In as muche as the service sholde be
The more noble and riche in his degree,
Duk Theseus leet forth three stedes bringe,
That trapped were in steel al gliteringe,
And covered with the armes of daun Arcite.
Up-on thise stedes, that weren grete and whyte,
Ther seten folk, of which oon bar his sheeld,
Another his spere up in his hondes heeld;
The thridde bar with him his bowe Turkeys,
Of brend gold was the cas, and eek the harneys;
And riden forth a pas with sorweful chere
Toward the grove, as ye shul after here.
The nobleste of the Grekes that ther were
Upon hir shuldres carieden the bere,
With slakke pas, and eyen rede and wete,
Thurgh-out the citee, by the maister-strete,
That sprad was al with blak, and
    wonder hye
Right of the same is al the strete y-wrye.
Up-on the right hond wente old Egeus,
And on that other syde duk Theseus,

And rode at his commandment.
And after this, Theseus had sent
For a bier, and it all covered
With cloth of gold, the richest that he had,
And in some of the same material he clad Arcita.
Upon his hands he had gloves white,
And on his head a crown of laurel green,
And in his hand a sword full bright and keen.
He lay him, with face uncovered, on the bier;
Therewith he wept that pity was to hear.
And so that the people should him see all,
When it was that day he brought him to the hall,
That roared with the crying and the sound.
    Then came this woeful Theban Palamon,
With fluttering beard and unkempt, ashy hair,
In clothes black, all wet with tears;
And surpassing others in weeping, Emily,
The sorrowfulest of all the company.
Inasmuch as the service should be
The more noble and rich according to his rank,
Duke Theseus caused three steeds to be brought,
That outfitted were in steel all glittering
And covered with the coat of arms of lord Arcita.
Upon these steeds, that were great and white,
There sat folk, of whom one bore his shield,
Another his spear up in his hands held,
The third bore with him his bow Turkish—
Of refined gold was the quiver and also the fittings;
And they rode forth at a walk with sorrowful look
Toward the grove, as you shall after hear.
The noblest of the Greeks that there were
Upon their shoulders carried the bier,
With slow pace and eyes red and wet,
Throughout the city by the main street,
That was all spread with shrouding black; and
    wondrous high
Right of the same was the street lined.
Upon the right hand went old Egeus,
And on the other side Duke Theseus,

With vessels in hir hand of gold ful fyn,
Al ful of hony, milk, and blood, and wyn;
Eek Palamon, with ful greet companye;
And after that cam woful Emelye,
With fyr in honde, as was that tyme the gyse,
To do th'office of funeral servyse.

    Heigh labour, and ful greet apparaillinge
Was at the service and the fyr-makinge,
That with his grene top the heven raughte,
And twenty fadme of brede the armes straughte;
This is to seyn, the bowes were so brode.
Of stree first ther was leyd ful many a lode.
But how the fyr was maked up on highte,
And eek the names how the treës highte,
As ook, firre, birch, asp, alder, holm, popler,
Wilow, elm, plane, ash, box, chasteyn, lind, laurer,
Mapul, thorn, beech, hasel, ew, whippel-tree,
How they weren feld, shal nat be told for me;
Ne how the goddes ronnen up and doun,
Disherited of hir habitacioun,
In which they woneden in reste and pees,
Nymphes, Faunes, and Amadrides;
Ne how the bestes and the briddes alle
Fledden for fere, whan the wode was falle;
Ne how the ground agast was of the light,
That was nat wont to seen the sonne bright;
Ne how the fyr was couched first with stree,
And than with drye stokkes cloven a three,
And than with grene wode and spycerye,
And than with cloth of gold and with perrye,
And gerlandes hanging with ful many a flour,
The mirre, th'encens, with al so greet odour;
Ne how Arcite lay among al this,
Ne what richesse aboute his body is;
Ne how that Emelye, as was the gyse,
Putte in the fyr of funeral servyse;
Ne how she swowned whan men made the fyr,
Ne what she spak, ne what was hir desyr;
Ne what jeweles men in the fyr tho caste,

With vessels in their hands of gold full fine,
All full of honey, milk, and blood, and wine;
And Palamon, with full great company;
And after that came woeful Emily,
With fire in hand, as was that time the rite,
To do the office of funeral service.
    Great labor and full great preparation
Was at the service and the firemaking,
That with its green top to heaven reached,
And twenty fathoms in breadth the sides stretched—
That is to say, the boughs were so broad.
Of straw first there was laid many a load;
But how the fire was made in height,
Nor the names how the trees were called—
As oak, fir, birch, aspen, alder, holly, poplar,
Willow, elm, plane, ash, box, chestnut, linden, laurel,
Maple, thorn, beech, hazel, yew, dogwood—
How they were felled shall not be told by me;
Nor how the tree spirits ran up and down,
Disinherited of their habitation,
In which they dwelt in rest and peace—
Nymphs, fauns and hamadryads;
Nor how the beasts and birds all
Fled for fear when the wood was felled;
Nor how the ground aghast was of the light,
That was not accustomed to see the sun bright;
Nor how the fire was laid first with straw,
And then with dry sticks split in three,
And then with green wood and spices,
And then with cloth of gold and with jewels,
And garlands hanging with full many a flower,
The myrrh, the incense, with all so great odor;
Nor how Arcita lay among all this,
Nor what riches about his body were;
Nor how Emily, as was the rite,
Lit the fire of funeral service;
Nor how she swooned when men made the fire,
Nor what she spoke, nor what was her desire;
Nor what jewels men in the fire cast;

Whan that the fyr was greet and brente faste;
Ne how som caste hir sheeld, and som hir spere,
And of hir vestiments, whiche that they were,
And cuppes ful of wyn, and milk, and blood,
Into the fyr, that brente as it were wood;
Ne how the Grekes with an huge route
Thryës riden al the fyr aboute
Up-on the left hand, with a loud shoutinge,
And thryës with hir speres clateringe;
And thryës how the ladies gonne crye;
Ne how that lad was hom-ward Emelye;
Ne how Arcite is brent to asshen colde;
Ne how that liche-wake was y-holde
Al thilke night, ne how the Grekes pleye
The wake-pleyes, ne kepe I nat to seye;
Who wrastleth best naked, with oille enoynt,
Ne who that bar him best, in no disjoynt.
I wol nat tellen eek how that they goon
Hoom til Athenes, whan the pley is doon;
But shortly to the poynt than wol I wende,
And maken of my longe tale an ende.

By processe and by lengthe of certeyn yeres
Al stinted is the moorning and the teres.
Of Grekes, by oon general assent,
Than semed me ther was a parlement
At Athenes, up-on certeyn poynts and cas;
Among the whiche poynts y-spoken was
To have with certeyn contrees alliaunce,
And have fully of Thebans obeisaunce.
For which this noble Theseus anon
Leet senden after gentil Palamon,
Unwist of him what was the cause and why;
But in his blake clothes sorwefully
He cam at his comaundemente in hye.
Tho sente Theseus for Emelye.
Whan they were set, and hust was al the place,
And Theseus abiden hadde a space
Er any word cam from his wyse brest,
His eyen sette he ther as was his lest,

When the fire was great and burned fast;
Nor how some cast their shields, and some their spears,
And some of the clothing that they wore,
And cups full of milk and wine and blood,
Into the fire that burned as if it were mad;
Nor how the Greeks with a huge company
Thrice rode all the fire about
Upon the left hand, with a loud shouting,
And thrice with their spears clattering;
And thrice how the ladies cried out;
Nor how Emily was homeward led;
Nor how Arcita was burnt to ashes cold;
Nor how the funeral wake was held
All that night; nor how the Greeks played
The funeral games, nor care I to say—
Who wrestled best naked with oil anointed,
Nor who bore himself best in every difficulty.
I will not tell how they went
Home to Athens when the games were done;
But quickly to the point then will I wend,
And make of my long tale an end.
     After the passage of a certain number of years
All ceased was the mourning and the tears
Of Greeks, by one general assent.
Then seems it to me there was a parliament
At Athens, upon certain points and matters;
Among which points discussed was
To have with certain countries alliance,
And to have fully of the Thebans submission.
For which this noble Theseus anon
Caused to be sent for gentle Palamon,
Unknown to him of what cause and why;
But in his black clothes sorrowfully
He came at his commandment quickly.
Then sent Theseus for Emily.
When they were sat, and hushed was all the place,
And Theseus had a space of time abided
Before any word came from his wise breast,
His eyes set he there as was his pleasure,

And with a sad visage he syked stille,
And after that right thus he seyde his wille.
　　"The firste moevere of the cause above,
Whan he first made the faire cheyne of love,
Greet was th'effect, and heigh was his entente;
Wel wiste he why, and what ther-of he mente;
For with that faire cheyne of love he bond
The fyr, the eyr, the water, and the lond
In certeyn boundes, that they may nat flee;
That same prince and that moevere," quod he,
"Hath stablissed, in this wrecched world adoun,
Certeyne dayes and duracioun
To al that is engendred in this place,
Over the whiche day they may nat pace,
Al mowe they yet tho dayes wel abregge;
Ther needeth non auctoritee allegg,
For it is preved by experience,
But that me list declaren my sentence.
Than may men by this ordre wel discerne,
That thilke moevere stable is and eterne.
Wel may men knowe, but it be a fool,
That every part deryveth from his hool.
For nature hath nat take his beginning
Of no party ne cantel of a thing,
But of a thing that parfit is and stable,
Descending so, til it be corrumpable.
And therfore, of his wyse purveyaunce,
He hath so wel biset his ordinaunce,
That speces of thinges and progressiouns
Shullen enduren by successiouns,
And nat eterne be, with-oute lyë:
This maistow understonde and seen at yë.
　　"Lo the ook, that hath so long a norisshinge
From tyme that it first biginneth springe,
And hath so long a lyf, as we may see,
Yet at the laste wasted is the tree.
Considereth eek, how that the harde stoon
Under our feet, on which we trede and goon,
Yit wasteth it, as it lyth by the weye.

And with a sad visage he sighed quietly,
And after that right thus he spoke his will:
    "The First Mover of the cause above,
When he first made the fair chain of love,[26]
Great was the effect, and noble was his intent.
Well knew he why, and what thereof he meant;
For with that fair chain of love he bound
The fire, the air, the water, and the land
In certain bounds, that they may not flee.
That same Prince and that Mover," said he,
"Has established in this wretched world below
Certain days and duration
To all that is engendered in this place,
Beyond which day they may not pass,
Although they yet may those days well shorten.
There needs no authority to cite,
For it is proved by experience,
But it pleases me to declare my thought.
Then may men by this order well discern
That the Mover is stable and eternal.
Well may men know, except the fool,
That every part derives from its whole.
For nature has not taken his beginning
Of any part or portion of a thing,
But from a thing that is perfect and stable,
Descending from heaven until it becomes corruptible.
And therefore, of his wise foresight and providence,
He has so well arranged his plan and ordinance
That species of things and natural changes
Shall endure by succession of generations
And not by being eternal, without any lie.
This you may understand and see with your own eye:
    "Lo, the oak that has so long a growth
From the time that it to life first began to spring,
And has so long a life, as we may see,
Yet at last wasted is the tree.
Consider also, how the hard stone
Under our feet, on which we tread and go,
Yet it wastes, as it lies by the way.

The brode river somtyme wexeth dreye.
The grete tounes see we wane and wende.
Than may ye see that al this thing hath ende.
    "Of man and womman seen we wel also,
That nedeth, in oon of thise termes two,
This is to seyn, in youthe or elles age,
He moot ben deed, the king as shal a page;
Som in his bed, som in the depe see,
Som in the large feeld, as men may se;
Ther helpeth noght, al goth that ilke weye.
Thanne may I seyn that al this thing moot deye.
What maketh this but Jupiter the king?
The which is prince and cause of alle thing,
Converting al un-to his propre welle,
From which it is deryved, sooth to telle.
And here-agayns no creature on lyve
Of no degree availleth for to stryve.
    "Thanne is it wisdom, as it thinketh me,
To maken vertu of necessitee,
And take it wel, that we may nat eschue,
And namely that to us alle is due.
And who-so gruccheth ought, he dooth folye,
And rebel is to him that al may gye.
And certeinly a man hath most honour
To dyen in his excellence and flour,
Whan he is siker of his gode name;
Than hath he doon his freend, ne him, no sham.
And gladder oghte his freend ben of his deeth,
Whan with honour up-yolden is his breeth,
Than whan his name apalled is for age;
For al forgeten is his vasselage.
Than is it best, as for a worthy fame,
To dyen whan that he is best of name.
The contrarie of al this is wilfulnesse.
Why grucchen we? why have we hevinesse,
That good Arcite, of chivalrye flour
Departed is, with duetee and honour,
Out of this foule prison of this lyf?
Why grucchen heer his cosin and his wyf

The broad river sometimes runs dry;
The great towns see we wane and die.
Then may you see that all these things have an end.
   "Of man and woman see we well also
That by necessity, in one of these two times,
That is to say, in youth or else age,
He must be dead, king as well as page;
One in his bed, one in the deep sea,
One in the large field, as men may see.
There helps nothing: all go that same way.
Then may I say that all these things must die.
Who made this but Jupiter the king,
Who is prince and cause of all things,
Converting everything to its proper source
From which it is derived, truth to tell?
And it avails no creature alive,
Against him to strive.
   "Then it is wisdom, it seems to me,
To make virtue of necessity,
And take well what we may not avoid,
And especially that which to us is due.
And whoso grouches in any way, he does folly,
And is rebel to him who governs all.
And certainly a man has most honor
To die in his excellence and flower,
When he is sure of his good name;
Then has he done neither his friend nor himself shame.
And gladder ought his friend be of his death
When with honor upyielded is his breath,
Than when his name faded is by age,
For all forgotten is his courage.
Then it is best, for a worthy fame,
To die when he is best of name.
The contrary of all this is wilfulness.
Why grouch we, why have we sorrow,
That good Arcita, of chivalry the flower,
Departed is with due respect and honor
Out of this foul prison of this life?
Why grouch here his cousin and his wife

Of his wel-fare that loved hem so weel?
Can he hem thank? nay, God wot, never a deel
That bothe his soule and eek him-self offende,
And yet they mowe hir lustes nat amende.

    "What may I conclude of this longe serie,
But, after wo, I rede us to be merie,
And thanken Jupiter of al his grace?
And, er that we departen from this place,
I rede that we make, of sorwes two,
O parfyt joye, lasting ever-mo;
And loketh now, wher most sorwe is herinne,
Ther wol we first amenden and biginne.

    "Suster," quod he, "this is my fulle assent,
With al th'avys heer of my parlement,
That gentil Palamon, your owne knight,
That serveth yow with wille, herte, and might,
And ever hath doon, sin that ye first him knewe,
That ye shul, of your grace, up-on him rewe,
And taken him for housbonde and for lord:
Leen me your hond, for this is our acord.
Lat see now of your wommanly pitee.
He is a kinges brother sone, pardee;
And, though he were a povre bacheler,
Sin he hath served yow so many a yeer,
And had for yow so greet adversitee,
It moste been considered, leveth me;
For gentil mercy oghte to
      passen right."

    Than seyde he thus to Palamon ful right;
"I trowe ther nedeth litel sermoning
To make yow assente to this thing.
Com neer, and tak your lady by the hond."
Bitwixen hem was maad anon the bond,
That highte matrimoine or mariage,
By al the counseil and the baronage.
And thus with alle blisse and melodye
Hath Palamon y-wedded Emelye.
And God, that al this wyde world hath wroght,
Sende him his love, that hath it dere a-boght.

Over his fate, who loved him so well?
Can he them thank? No, God knows, not a bit,
Who both his soul and themselves offend,
And yet they can their happiness not amend.

  "What may I conclude of this long argument,
But after would I advise us to be merry,
And thank Jupiter for all his grace;
And before we depart from this place,
I advise that we make of sorrows two
One perfect love, lasting evermore;
And look now, where most sorrow is herein,
There will we first amend and begin.

  "Sister," said he, "this is my full desire,
With all the advice here of my parliament:
That gentle Palamon, your own knight,
Who serves you with will, heart and might,
And ever has done so since you first him knew,
That you shall of your grace upon him take pity,
And take him for husband and for lord.
Give me your hand, for this is our concord.
Let us see now of your womanly pity.
He is a king's brother's son, indeed;
And even if he were a poor young knight,
Since he has served you for so many a year,
And has had in your service such great adversity,
It must be considered, believe me;
For gentle mercy ought to prevail over strictly
    legal right."

  Then said he thus to Palamon the knight:
"I believe there needs little preaching
To make you assent to this thing.
Come near, and take your lady by the hand."
Between them was made at once the bond
Of high matrimony, or marriage,
By all the council and the baronage.
And thus with all bliss and melody
Has Palamon wedded Emily.
And God, who all this wide world has wrought,
Send him his love who has it dearly bought.

For now is Palamon in alle wele,
Living in blisse, in richesse, and in hele;
And Emelye him loveth so tendrely,
And he hir serveth al-so gentilly,
That never was ther no word hem bitwene
Of jelousye, or any other tene.
Thus endeth Palamon and Emelye;
And God save al this faire companye!—Amen.

For now is Palamon in all happiness,
Living in bliss, in riches, and in health;
And Emily loves him so tenderly,
And he serves her so gently
That there never was a word between them
Of jealousy or any other trouble.
Thus ends Palamon and Emily;
And God save all this fair company! Amen.

The Milleres Tale

The Prologue

WHAN THAT THE KNIGHT had thus his tale y-told,
In al the route nas ther yong ne old
That he ne seyde it was a noble storie,
And worthy for to drawen to memorie;
And namely the gentils everichoon.
Our Hoste lough and swoor, "so moot I goon,
This gooth aright; unbokeled is the male;
Lat see now who shal telle another tale:
For trewely, the game is wel bigonne.
Now telleth ye, sir Monk, if that ye conne,
Sumwhat, to quyte with the Knightes tale."
The Miller, that for-dronken was al pale,
So that unnethe up-on his hors he sat,
He nolde avalen neither hood ne hat,
Ne abyde no man for his curteisye,
But in Pilates vois he gan to crye,
And swoor by armes and by blood and bones,
"I can a noble tale for the nones,
With which I wol now quyte the Knightes tale."
   Our Hoste saugh that he was dronke of ale,
And seyde: "abyd, Robin, my leve brother,
Som bettre man shal telle us first another:
Abyd, and lat us werken thriftily."
   "By goddes soul," quod he, "that wol nat I;
For I wol speke, or elles go my wey."
Our Hoste answerde: "tel on, a devel wey!
Thou art a fool, thy wit is overcome."
   "Now herkneth," quod the Miller, "alle and some!
But first I make a protestacioun
That I am dronke, I knowe it by my soun;
And therfore, if that I misspeke or seye,
Wyte it the ale of Southwerk, I yow preye;
For I wol telle a legende and a lyf
Bothe of a Carpenter, and of his wyf,
How that a clerk hath set the wrightes cappe."

The Miller's Tale

The Prologue

WHEN THE KNIGHT HAD his tale told,
In all the company there was neither young nor old
Who said not that it was a noble story,
And worthy for to keep in memory,
And so spoke the genteel pilgrims especially.
Our Host laughed and swore, "As I may hope to live,
This goes well, the bag is opened.
Let see now who should tell another tale,
For truly, the game is well begun.
Now tell you, sir Monk, if you know how,
Something to match the Knight's tale."
The Miller, who quite drunk was all pale,
So that with trouble upon his horse he sat,
Nor bothered to doff his hood or hat,
Nor deferred to anyone out of courtesy,
But in Pilate's voice[1] he began to harangue,
And swore, "By Christ's arms and by blood and bones,
I know a noble tale for this occasion,
With which I will now repay the Knight's tale."

Our Host saw that he was drunk on ale,
And said, "Wait, Robin, my dear brother,
Some better man shall tell us first another:
Wait, and let us go in proper order."

"By God's soul," said he, "that I will not;
For I will speak or else go my way."
Our Host answered, "Tell on, what the devil!
You are a fool, your wit is overcome."

"Now listen," said the Miller, "all and some!
But first I make a protestation
That I am drunk, I know by my voice's sound.
And therefore, if I misspeak or say,
Blame it on the ale of Southwark, I you pray;
For I will tell a legend and a life
Both of a carpenter and of his wife,
How that a student made of the carpenter a fool."

The Reve answerde and seyde, "stint thy clappe,
Lat be thy lewed dronken harlotrye.
It is a sinne and eek a greet folye
To apeiren any man, or him diffame,
And eek to bringen wyves in swich fame.
Thou mayst y-nogh of othere thinges seyn."
This dronken Miller spak ful sone ageyn,
And seyde, "leve brother Osewold,
Who hath no wyf, he is no cokewold.
But I sey nat therfore that thou art oon;
Ther been ful gode wyves many oon,
And ever a thousand gode ayeyns oon badde,
That knowestow wel thy-self, but-if thou madde.
Why artow angry with my tale now?
I have a wyf, pardee, as well as thou,
Yet nolde I, for the oxen in my plogh,
Taken up-on me more than y-nogh,
As demen of my-self that I were oon;
I wol beleve wel that I am noon.
And housbond shal nat been inquisitif
Of goddes privetee, nor of his wyf.
So he may finde goddes foyson there,
Of the remenant nedeth nat enquere."
What sholde I more seyn, but this Millere
He nolde his wordes for no man forbere,
But tolde his cherles tale in his manere;
M'athynketh that I shal reherce it here.
And ther-fore every gentil wight I preye,
For goddes love, demeth nat that I seye
Of evel entente, but that I moot reherce
Hir tales alle, be they bettre or werse,
Or elles falsen som of my matere.
And therfore, who-so list it nat y-here,
Turne over the leef, and chese another tale;
For he shal finde y-nowe, grete and smale,
Of storial thing that toucheth gentillesse,
And eek moralitee and holinesse;
Blameth nat me if that ye chese amis.
The Miller is a cherl, ye knowe wel this;

The Reeve answered and said, "Shut your trap!
Forget your rude drunken smut.
It is a sin and also a great folly
To injure any man, or him defame,
And to bring wives into ill-repute.
You may enough of other things say."

This drunken Miller spoke full soon again,
And said, "Dear brother Oswald,
Who has no wife, he is no cuckold.
But I say not therefore that you are one;
There be full good wives many a one,
And even a thousand good for every one bad.
You know that yourself, unless you're mad.
Why are you angry with my tale now?
I have a wife, by God, as well as you,
Yet would I not, for the oxen in my plow,
Take upon me more worries than enough,
As to imagine myself a cuckold;
I well believe that I am not one.
A husband shall not be inquisitive
Of God's secrets, nor of his wife.
So he may find God's bounty there,
Of the rest he need not inquire."

What should I say more, but this Miller
He would his words no man spare,
But told his churl's tale in his manner.
I regret I must repeat it here.
And therefore every genteel person I pray,
For God's love, deem it not that I speak
From evil intent, but that I must retell
His tales all, be they better or worse,
Or else falsify my subject matter.
And therefore, whoso wishes it not to hear,
Turn over the page, and choose another tale;
For he shall find enough, great and small,
Of historical things that touch on the genteel,
And also morality and holiness.
Blame me not if you choose amiss.
The Miller is a churl, you know well this;

So was the Reve, and othere many mo,
And harlotrye they tolden bothe two.
Avyseth yow and putte me out of blame;
And eek men shal nat make ernest of game.

The Tale

Whylom ther was dwellinge at Oxenford
A riche gnof, that gestes heeld to bord,
And of his craft he was a Carpenter.
With him ther was dwellinge a povre scoler,
Had lerned art, but al his fantasye
Was turned for to lerne astrologye,
And coude a certeyn of conclusiouns
To demen by interrogaciouns,
If that men axed him in certein houres,
Whan that men sholde have droghte or elles shoures,
Or if men axed him what sholde bifalle
Of every thing, I may nat rekene hem alle.
  This clerk was cleped hende Nicholas;
Of derne love he coude and of solas;
And ther-to he was sleigh and ful privee,
And lyk a mayden meke for to see.
A chambre hadde he in that hostelrye
Allone, with-outen any companye,
Ful fetisly y-dight with herbes swote;
And he him-self as swete as is the rote
Of licorys, or any cetewale.
His Almageste and bokes grete and smale,
His astrelabie, longinge for his art,
His augrim-stones layen faire a-part
On shelves couched at his beddes heed:
His presse y-covered with a falding reed.
And al above ther lay a gay sautrye,
On which he made a nightes melodye
So swetely, that al the chambre rong;
And *Angelus ad virginem* he song;
And after that he song the kinges note;
Ful often blessed was his mery throte.
And thus this swete clerk his tyme spente

So was the Reeve and others more,
And ribaldry they told both two.
Be advised and put me out of blame;
And do not take in earnest what is a game.

The Tale

Once upon a time there was dwelling at Oxford
A rich churl, who took in lodgers,
And by trade he was a carpenter.
With him there was dwelling a poor scholar,
Who studied the liberal arts, but all his fancy
Was turned to learn astrology,
And he knew a number of operations
With which to provide explanations,
If men asked him in certain hours
When men should have drought or showers,
Or if men asked him what should befall
Of every thing, I cannot count them all.

    This scholar was called polite Nicholas.
Of secret love he knew and of pleasure;
And thereto he was sly and secretive,
And like a maiden meek to look upon.
A room had he in that boardinghouse
Alone, without any company,
Full neatly arranged with herbs sweet;
And he himself as sweet as is the root
Of licorice, or any ginger spice.
His treatise by Ptolemy on astronomy,
His astrolabe,[2] belonging to his art,
His augrim-stones[3] lay fair apart
On shelves placed at his bed's head;
His clothes chest covered with wool cloth red.
And on it lay a pretty zither,
On which he made nightly melody
So sweetly, that all the chamber rang,
And an Annunciation hymn he sang,
And after that he sang the king's note,[4]
Full often blessed was his merry throat.
And thus this sweet student his living spent

After his freendes finding and his rente.
    This Carpenter had wedded newe a wyf
Which that he lovede more than his lyf;
Of eightetene yeer she was of age.
Jalous he was, and heeld hir narwe in cage,
For she was wilde and yong, and he was old,
And demed him-self ben lyk a cokewold.
He knew nat Catoun, for his wit was rude,
That bad man sholde wedde his similitude.
Men sholde wedden after hir estaat,
For youthe and elde is often at debaat.
But sith that he was fallen in the snare,
He moste endure, as other folk, his care.
    Fair was this yonge wyf, and ther-with-al
As any wesele hir body gent and smal.
A ceynt she werede barred al of silk,
A barmclooth eek as whyt as morne milk
Up-on hir lendes, ful of many a gore.
Whyt was hir smok and brouded al bifore
And eek bihinde, on hir coler aboute,
Of col-blak silk, with-inne and eek with-oute.
The tapes of hir whyte voluper
Were of the same suyte of hir coler;
Hir filet brood of silk, and set ful hye:
And sikerly she hadde a likerous yë.
Ful smale y-pulled were hir browes two,
And tho were bent, and blake as any sloo.
She was ful more blisful on to see
Than is the newe pere-jonette tree;
And softer than the wolle is of a wether.
And by hir girdel heeng a purs of lether
Tasseld with silk, and perled with latoun.
In al this world, to seken up and doun,
There nis no man so wys, that coude thenche
So gay a popelote, or swich a wenche.
Ful brighter was the shyning of hir hewe
Than in the tour the noble y-forged newe.
But of hir song, it was as loude and yerne
As any swalwe sittinge on a berne.

From a private income and gifts from friends.
   This carpenter had newly wedded a wife
Whom he loved more than his life;
Of eighteen years she was of age.
Jealous he was, and held her as in a cage,
For she was wild and young, and he was old
And deemed himself likely to be a cuckold.
He knew not Cato, for he was untaught,
Who bade man should wed his counterpart.
Men should wed according to their condition,
For youth and age often are in opposition.
But since he was fallen in the snare,
He must endure, as other folk, his care.
   Fair was this young wife, and all in all
As any weasel her body graceful and small.
A belt she wore striped all of silk;
An apron also as white as morning milk
Upon her loins, very fully cut.
White was her dress, and embroidered all before
And also behind, on her collar about,
Of coal-black silk, within and without.
The strings of her white bonnet
Were of the same kind as her collar;
Her headband broad of silk, and set full high.
And certainly she had a lecherous eye:
Full small plucked were her brows two,
And they were arched, and black as any berry.
She was full more blissful for to see
Than is the blossoming pear-jonette tree;
And softer than the wool is of a wether.
And by her waist hung a purse of leather
Tasseled with silk, and studded with metal.
In all this world, to seek up and down,
There is no man so wise who could imagine
So gay a baby doll, or such a wench.
Full brighter was the shining of her complexion
Than in the Tower the coin of new-forged gold.
But as to her song, it was lively and loud
As any swallow sitting on a barn.

Ther-to she coude skippe and make game,
As any kide or calf folwinge his dame.
Hir mouth was swete as bragot or the meeth
Or hord of apples leyd in hey or heeth.
Winsinge she was, as is a joly colt,
Long as a mast, and upright as a bolt.
A brooch she baar up-on hir lowe coler,
As brood as is the bos of a bocler.
Hir shoes were laced on hir legges hye;
She was a prymerole, a pigges-nye
For any lord to leggen in his bedde,
Or yet for any good yeman to wedde.

    Now sire, and eft sire, so bifel the cas,
That on a day this hende Nicholas
Fil with this yonge wyf to rage and pleye,
Whyl that hir housbond was at Oseneye,
As clerkes ben ful subtile and ful queynte;
And prively he caughte hir by the queynte,
And seyde, "y-wis, but if ich have my wille,
For derne love of thee, lemman, I spille."
And heeld hir harde by the haunche-bones,
And seyde, "lemman, love me al at-ones,
Or I wol dyen, also god me save!"
And she sprong as a colt doth in the trave,
And with hir heed she wryed faste awey,
And seyde, "I wol nat kisse thee, by my fey,
Why, lat be," quod she, "lat be, Nicholas,
Or I wol crye out 'harrow' and 'allas.'
Do wey your handes for your curteisye!"

    This Nicholas gan mercy for to crye,
And spak so faire, and profred hir so faste,
That she hir love him graunted atte laste,
And swoor hir ooth, by seint Thomas of Kent,
That she wol been at his comandement,
Whan that she may hir leyser wel espye.
"Myn housbond is so ful of jalousye,
That but ye wayte wel and been privee,
I woot right wel I nam but deed," quod she.
"Ye moste been ful derne, as in this cas."

Thereto she could skip and gambol,
As any kid or calf following his mother.
Her mouth was sweet as honeyed ale
Or hoard of apples laid in hay or heather.
Skittish she was, as is a jolly colt,
Long as a mast, and straight as an arrow.
A brooch she bore upon her collar low,
As broad as is the boss of a shield;
Her shoes were laced on her legs high.
She was a primrose, a cuckooflower,
For any lord to lay in his bed,
Or yet for any good yeoman to wed.

   Now sir, and again sir, so befell the case,
That on a day this polite, clever Nicholas
Happened with this young wife to flirt and play,
While her husband was at Osney,[5]
As scholars be full subtle and slippery.
And in private he caught her by her quack,[6]
And said, "Unless I have my will,
My love for you will make me crack."
And held her hard by the bum,
And said, "Sweetheart, love me at once,
Or I will die, as God me save!"
And she sprang as a colt does from the shoeing stall,
And with her head she twisted fast away,
And said, "I will not kiss you, by my faith.
Why, leave off," said she, "leave off, Nicholas,
Or I will cry 'help, help' and 'alas.'
Take your hands away, for your courtesy!"

   This Nicholas began mercy for to cry,
And spoke so fair, and offered himself so fast,
That she her love granted him at last,
And swore her oath, by Saint Thomas of Kent,
That she would be at his commandment,
When she may her chance espy.
"My husband is so full of jealousy,
That unless you wait well and be discreet,
I am as good as dead," said she. "You must be
Completely secret in this case."

"Nay ther-of care thee noght," quod Nicholas,
"A clerk had litherly biset his whyle,
But-if he coude a carpenter bigyle."
And thus they been acorded and y-sworn
To wayte a tyme, as I have told biforn.
Whan Nicholas had doon thus everydeel,
And thakked hir aboute the lendes weel,
He kist hir swete, and taketh his sautrye,
And pleyeth faste, and maketh melodye.

Than fil it thus, that to the parish-chirche,
Cristes owne werkes for to wirche,
This gode wyf wente on an haliday;
Hir forheed shoon as bright as any day,
So was it wasshen whan she leet hir werk.

Now was ther of that chirche a parish-clerk,
The which that was y-cleped Absolon.
Crul was his heer, and as the gold it shoon,
And strouted as a fanne large and brode;
Ful streight and even lay his joly shode.
His rode was reed, his eyen greye as goos;
With Powles window corven on his shoos,
In hoses rede he wente fetisly.
Y-clad he was ful smal and proprely,
Al in a kirtel of a light wachet;
Ful faire and thikke been the poyntes set.
And ther-up-on he hadde a gay surplys
As whyt as is the blosme up-on the rys.
A mery child he was, so god me save,
Wel coude he laten blood and clippe and shave,
And make a chartre of lond or acquitaunce.
In twenty manere coude he trippe and daunce
After the scole of Oxenforde tho,
And with his legges casten to and fro,
And pleyen songes on a small rubible;
Ther-to he song som-tyme a loud quinible;
And as wel coude he pleye on his giterne.
In al the toun nas brewhous ne taverne
That he ne visited with his solas,
Ther any gaylard tappestere was.

"Nay, thereof care you not," said Nicholas.
"A scholar has poorly used his time awhile,
If he cannot a carpenter beguile."
And thus they were accorded and sworn
To wait awhile, as I have told before.
When Nicholas had done this all,
And stroked her about her loins well,
He kissed her sweet, and took his zither,
And played hard, and made melody with her.

    Then befell it thus, that to the parish church,
To perform Christ's own works,
This good wife went on a holy day;
Her forehead shone as bright as any day,
So was it washed when she left her work.

    Now there was of that church a parish clerk,[7]
Who was called Absolon.
Curly was his hair, and as the gold it shone,
And spread out as a fan broad and large;
Full straight and even lay his hair parted.
His complexion was red, his eyes gray as a goose;
With Saint Paul's windows cut in his shoes,[8]
In stockings red he went trimly.
Clad he was full tightly and properly,
All in a coat of a light blue;
Neatly tied were the laces,
And thereupon he had a gay surplice
As white as the blossom upon the twig.
A merry young man he was, so God me save.
Well could he let blood[9] and cut hair and shave,
And make a charter of land or a deed of release.
In twenty ways could he trip and dance
After the fashion of Oxford then,
With his legs cast to and fro,
And play songs on a small fiddle;
Thereto he sang sometime in a high treble;
As well could he play on a guitar.
In all the town there was no brewhouse or tavern
That he did not visit with his play,
Where there was any gay barmaid.

But sooth to seyn, he was somdel squaymous
Of farting, and of speche daungerous.
    This Absolon, that jolif was and gay,
Gooth with a sencer on the haliday,
Sensinge the wyves of the parish faste;
And many a lovely look on hem he caste,
And namely on this carpenteres wyf.
To loke on hir him thoughte a mery lyf,
She was so propre and swete and likerous.
I dar wel seyn, if she had been a mous,
And he a cat, he wolde hir hente anon.
    This parish-clerk, this joly Absolon,
Hath in his herte swich a love-longinge,
That of no wyf ne took he noon offringe;
For curteisye, he seyde, he wolde noon.
The mone, whan it was night, ful brighte shoon,
And Absolon his giterne hath y-take,
For paramours, he thoghte for to wake.
And forth he gooth, jolif and amorous,
Til he cam to the carpenteres hous
A litel after cokkes hadde y-crowe;
And dressed him up by a shot-windowe
That was up-on the carpenteres wal.
He singeth in his vois gentil and smal,
"Now, dere lady, if thy wille be,
I preye yow that ye wol rewe on me,"
Ful wel acordaunt to his giterninge.
This carpenter awook, and herde him singe,
And spak un-to his wyf, and seyde anon,
"What! Alison! herestow nat Absolon
That chaunteth thus under our boures wal?"
And she answerde hir housbond ther-with-al,
"Yis, god wot, John, I here it every-del."
    This passeth forth; what wol ye bet than wel?
Fro day to day this joly Absolon
So woweth hir, that him is wo bigon.
He waketh al the night and al the day;
He kempte hise lokkes brode, and made him gay;
He woweth hir by menes and brocage,

But truth to say, he was somewhat squeamish
Of farting, and of speech fastidious.
  This Absolon, who amorous was and gay,
Went with a censer on the holy day,
Censing the wives of the parish with care,
And many a loving look on them he cast,
And namely on this carpenter's wife:
To look on her he thought a merry life.
She was so sweet and flirtatious,
I dare well say, if she had been a mouse,
And he a cat, he would have pounced.
  This parish clerk, this jolly Absolon,
Had in his heart such a love-longing,
That from no wife he took an offering;
For courtesy, he said, he wanted none.
The moon, when it was night, full bright shone,
And Absolon his guitar had taken—
For paramours he would stay awake.
And forth he went, jolly and amorous,
Till he came to the carpenter's house
A little after cocks had crowed,
And took his place near an open window
That was upon the carpenter's wall.
He sang in his voice thin and high,
"Now, dear lady, if your will be,
I pray that you will have pity on me,"
In nice harmony with his guitar.
This carpenter awoke and heard him sing,
And spoke unto his wife, and said anon,
"What, Alison, do you hear Absolon
Who sings thus under our bedroom wall?"
And she answered her husband forthwith,
"Yes, God knows, John, I hear it all."
  So this went on. What more can I say?
From day to day this jolly Absolon
So wooed her that he was woebegone.
He stayed awake all night and all the day;
He combed his locks broad, and made him gay;
He wooed her through intercessors,

And swoor he wolde been hir owne page;
He singeth, brokkinge as a nightingale;
He sente hir piment, meeth, and spyced ale,
And wafres, pyping hote out of the glede;
And for she was of toune, he profred mede.
For som folk wol ben wonnen for richesse,
And som for strokes, and som for gentillesse.
    Somtyme, to shewe his lightnesse and maistrye,
He pleyeth Herodes on a scaffold hye.
But what availleth him as in this cas?
She loveth so this hende Nicholas,
That Absolon may blowe the bukkes horn;
He ne hadde for his labour but a scorn;
And thus she maketh Absolon hir ape,
And al his ernest turneth til a jape.
Ful sooth is this proverbe, it is no lye,
Men seyn right thus, "alwey the nye slye
Maketh the ferre leve to be looth."
For though that Absolon be wood or wrooth,
By-cause that he fer was from hir sighte,
This nye Nicholas stood in his lighte.
    Now bere thee wel, thou hende Nicholas!
For Absolon may waille and singe "allas."
And so bifel it on a Saterday
This carpenter was goon til Osenay;
And hende Nicholas and Alisoun
Acorded been to this conclusioun,
That Nicholas shal shapen him a wyle
This sely jalous housbond to bigyle;
And if so be the game wente aright,
She sholde slepen in his arm al night,
For this was his desyr and hir also.
And right anon, with-outen wordes mo,
This Nicholas no lenger wolde tarie,
But doth ful softe un-to his chambre carie
Bothe mete and drinke for a day or tweye,
And to hir housbonde bad hir for to seye,
If that he axed after Nicholas,
She sholde seye she niste where he was,

And he swore he would be her own page;
He sang, trilling like a nightingale;
And sent her spiced wine, mead, and spiced ale,
And wafer cakes, piping hot out of the oven;
And he also offered money.
For some folk will be won by riches,
And some by blows, and some by kindness.
   Sometime, to show his agility and skill,
He played Herod[10] on the high stage.
But what did it avail him in this case?
She loved so this sweet Nicholas,
That Absolon didn't have a hope;
For his labor he got nothing but scorn.
And thus she made Absolon her monkey,
And all his earnestness turned into a joke.
For truth is in this proverb, it is no lie,
Men say right thus, "A bird in the hand
Is worth two in the bushes."
For no matter that Absolon might be undone,
By cause that he was far from her sight,
This nearby Nicholas stood in his light.
   Now bear you well, you sweet Nicholas!
For Absolon may wail and sing "alas."
And so befell it on a Saturday,
This carpenter was gone to Osney,
And sweet Nicholas and Alison
Agreed to this conclusion,
That Nicholas shall invent a wile
This silly husband to beguile;
And if the game went aright,
She should sleep in his arms all night,
For this was his desire and hers also.
And right anon, without words more,
This Nicholas no longer would tarry,
But secretly into his chamber carries
Both meat and drink for a day or two,
And to her husband bade her to say,
If that he asked after Nicholas,
She should say she didn't know where he was,

Of al that day she saugh him nat with yë;
She trowed that he was in maladye,
For, for no cry, hir mayde coude him calle;
He nolde answere, for no-thing that mighte falle.

    This passeth forth al thilke Saterday,
That Nicholas stille in his chambre lay,
And eet and sleep, or dide what him leste,
Til Sonday, that the sonne gooth to reste.

    This sely carpenter hath greet merveyle
Of Nicholas, or what thing mighte him eyle,
And seyde, "I am adrad, by seint Thomas,
It stondeth nat aright with Nicholas.
God shilde that he deyde sodeynly!
This world is now ful tikel, sikerly;
I saugh to-day a cors y-born to chirche
That now, on Monday last, I saugh him wirche.

    "Go up," quod he un-to his knave anoon,
"Clepe at his dore, or knokke with a stoon,
Loke how it is, and tel me boldely."

    This knave gooth him up ful sturdily,
And at the chambre-dore, whyl that he stood,
He cryde and knokked as that he were wood:—
"What! how! what do ye, maister Nicholay?
How may ye slepen al the longe day?"

    But al for noght, he herde nat a word;
An hole he fond, ful lowe up-on a board,
Ther as the cat was wont in for to crepe;
And at that hole he looked in ful depe,
And at the laste he hadde of him a sighte,
This Nicholas sat gaping ever up-righte,
As he had kyked on the newe mone.
Adoun he gooth, and tolde his maister sone
In what array he saugh this ilke man.

    This carpenter to blessen him bigan,
And seyde, "help us, seinte Frideswyde!
A man woot litel what him shal bityde.
This man is falle, with his astromye,
In som woodnesse or in som agonye;
I thoghte ay wel how that it sholde be!

During all that day she saw him not with eye,
She believed he had a malady,
For although she called him a lot
He wouldn't answer, no matter what.

This went on all that Saturday,
That Nicholas still in his chamber lay,
And ate and slept, or did what he pleased,
Till Sunday, when the sun went to rest.

This silly carpenter had greatly marvelled
At Nicholas, or what thing might him ail,
And said, "I am afraid, by Saint Thomas,
Something is wrong with Nicholas.
God forbid that he should die suddenly!
This world is now unstable, surely:
I saw today a corpse borne to church
Who now, on Monday last, I saw him work.

"Go up," said he to his servant anon,
"Call at his door, or knock with a stone,
Look how he is, and tell me straightaway."

This servant went up full sturdily,
And at the chamber door, while that he stood
He cried and knocked as if he were crazy:
"What! How are you, master Nicholay?
How can you sleep all the long day?"

But all for nought, he heard not a word.
A hole he found, full low upon a board,
There where the cat was wont to creep;
And at that hole he looked in full deep,
And at last he had of him a sight.
This Nicholas sat ever staring upward,
As if half gone he gazed at the new moon.
Down he went, and told his master soon
In what shape he saw this same man.

This carpenter to cross himself began,
And said, "Help us, Saint Frideswide!¹¹
A man knows little what shall him betide.
This man is fallen, with his astronomy,¹²
Into some madness or in some fit;
I knew well all along what might happen!

Men sholde nat knowe of goddes privetee.
Ye, blessed be alwey a lewed man,
That noght but only his bileve can!
So ferde another clerk with astromye;
He walked in the feeldes for to prye
Up-on the sterres, what ther sholde bifalle,
Til he was in a marle-pit y-falle;
He saugh nat that. But yet, by seint Thomas,
Me reweth sore of hende Nicholas.
He shal be rated of his studying,
If that I may, by Jesus, hevene king!
Get me a staf, that I may underspore,
Whyl that thou, Robin, hevest up the dore.
He shal out of his studying, as I gesse"—
And to the chambre-dore he gan him dresse.
His knave was a strong carl for the nones,
And by the haspe he haf it up atones;
In-to the floor the dore fil anon.
This Nicholas sat ay as stille as stoon,
And ever gaped upward in-to the eir.
This carpenter wende he were in despeir,
And hente him by the sholdres mightily,
And shook him harde, and cryde spitously,
"What! Nicholay! what, how! what! loke adoun!
Awake, and thenk on Cristes passioun;
I crouche thee from elves and
    fro wightes!"
Ther-with the night-spel seyde he anon-rightes
On foure halves of the hous aboute,
And on the threshfold of the dore with-oute:—
    "Jesu Crist, and sëynt Benedight,
    Blesse this hous from every wikked wight,
    For nightes verye, the white *paternoster!*—
    Where wentestow, seynt Petres soster?"
And atte laste this hende Nicholas
Gan for to syke sore, and seyde, "allas!
Shal al the world be lost eftsonnes now?"
    This carpenter answerde, "what seystow?
What! thenk on god, as we don, men that swinke."

Men should not know God's secrets.
Yes, blessed be always an unlearned man
Who nought but his religion knows!
So fared another scholar with astromony:
He walked in the fields for to spy
Upon the stars, to learn what the future would hold,
Till he was in a clay pit fallen—
He saw not that. But yet, by Saint Thomas,
I pity greatly sweet Nicholas.
He shall be berated for his studying,
If that I may, by Jesus, heaven's king!
Get me a staff, that I may pry up,
While that you, Robin, push on the door.
He shall come out of his studying, as I guess."
And the chamber door he began to address.
His knave was a strong fellow for this task,
And by the hasp he heaved it off at once;
Onto the floor the door fell anon.
This Nicholas sat ever as still as a stone,
And ever stared upward into the air.
This carpenter thought he was in despair,
And seized him by the shoulders mightily,
And shook him hard, and cried violently,
"What, Nicholay! What, how! What, look adown!
Awake, and think on Christ's passion!
This sign of the cross will protect you from elves
     and such!"
Therewith the night charm said he at once
On all four sides of the house about,
And on the threshhold of the front door without:
     "Jesus Christ, and Saint Benedict,
     Bless this house from every creature wicked,
     For nights, the white *paternoster*![13]
     Where did you go, Saint Peter's sister?"
And at last this sweet Nicholas
Began to sigh deeply, and said, "Alas!
Shall all the world be lost again so soon?"
     This carpenter answered, "What say you?
What! Think on God, as we do, men who labor!"

This Nicholas answerde, "fecche me drinke;
And after wol I speke in privetee
Of certeyn thing that toucheth me and thee;
I wol telle it non other man, certeyn."

This carpenter goth doun, and comth ageyn,
And broghte of mighty ale a large quart;
And when that ech of hem had dronke his part,
This Nicholas his dore faste shette,
And doun the carpenter by him he sette.

He seyde, "John, myn hoste lief and dere,
Thou shalt up-on thy trouthe swere me here,
That to no wight thou shalt this conseil wreye;
For it is Cristes conseil that I seye,
And if thou telle it man, thou are forlore;
For this vengaunce thou shalt han therfore,
That if thou wreye me, thou shalt be wood!"
"Nay, Crist forbede it, for his holy blood!"
Quod tho this sely man, "I nam no labbe,
Ne, though I seye, I nam nat lief to gabbe.
Sey what thou wolt, I shal it never telle
To child ne wyf, by him that harwed helle!"

"Now John," quod Nicholas, "I wol nat lye;
I have y-founde in myn astrologye,
As I have loked in the mone bright,
That now, a Monday next, at quarter-night,
Shal falle a reyn and that so wilde and wood,
That half so greet was never Noës flood.
This world," he seyde, "in lasse than in an hour
Shal al be dreynt, so hidous is the shour;
Thus shal mankynde drenche and lese hir lyf."

This carpenter answerde, "allas, my wyf!
And shal she drenche? allas! myn Alisoun!"
For sorwe of this he fil almost adoun,
And seyde, "is ther no remedie in this cas?"

"Why, yis, for gode," quod hende Nicholas,
"If thou wolt werken after lore
    and reed;
Thou mayst nat werken after thyn owene heed.
For thus seith Salomon, that was ful trewe,

This Nicholas answered, "Fetch me drink;
And after will I speak in secrecy
Of certain things that touch upon you and me;
I will tell it to no other man, certainly."

This carpenter went down and came again,
And brought of mighty ale a large quart,
And when each of them had drunk his part,
This Nicholas his door fast shut,
And down he sat, the carpenter by him.

He said, "John, my host beloved and dear,
You shall upon your honor swear me here,
That to no person you will this secret betray;
For it is Christ's counsel that I say,
And if you to any man tell it, you are lost;
For this vengeance you shall have therefore,
That if you betray me you shall go cuckoo!"
"No, Christ forbid it, by his holy blood!"
Said this silly man, "I am no blabber,
Though I admit I like to chatter.
Say what you will, I shall it never tell
To child nor wife, by him who harrowed hell!"

"Now John," said Nicholas, "I will not lie.
I have found in my astrology,
As I have looked in the moon bright,
That now, on Monday next, at quarter night,[14]
Shall fall a rain and that so furious and wild,
That not half so great was Noah's flood.
This world," he said, "in less than an hour
Shall be drowned, so hideous will be the shower;
Thus shall mankind drown and lose its life."

This carpenter answered, "Alas, my wife!
And shall she drown? alas, my Alison!"
For sorrow of this he fell almost adown,
And said, "Is there no remedy in this case?"

"Why yes, by God," said nice Nicholas,
"If you will work according to learning and good
    advice;
You may not follow your own mind;
For Solomon said, who was trustworthy,

'Werk al by conseil, and thou shalt nat rewe.'
And if thou werken wolt by good conseil,
I undertake, with-outen mast and seyl,
Yet shal I saven hir and thee and me.
Hastow nat herd how saved was Noë,
Whan that our lord had warned him biforn
That al the world with water sholde be lorn?"
       "Yis," quod this carpenter, "ful yore ago."
       "Hastow nat herd," quod Nicholas, "also
The sorwe of Noë with his felawshipe,
Er that he mighte gete his wyf to shipe?
Him had he lever, I dar wel undertake,
At thilke tyme, than alle hise wetheres blake,
That she hadde had a ship hir-self allone.
And ther-fore, wostou what is best to done?
This asketh haste, and of an hastif thing
Men may nat preche or maken tarying.

       Anon go gete us faste in-to this in
A kneding-trogh, or elles a kimelin,
For ech of us, but loke that they be large,
In whiche we mowe swimme as in a barge,
And han ther-inne vitaille suffisant
But for a day; fy on the remenant!
The water shal aslake and goon away
Aboute pryme up-on the nexte day.

       But Robin may nat wite of this, thy knave,
Ne eek thy mayde Gille I may nat save;
Axe nat why, for though thou aske me,
I wol nat tellen goddes privetee.
Suffiseth thee, but if thy wittes madde,
To han as greet a grace as Noë hadde.
Thy wyf shal I wel saven, out of doute,
Go now thy wey, and speed thee heeraboute.

       But whan thou hast, for hir and thee and me,
Y-geten us thise kneding-tubbes three,
Than shaltow hange hem in the roof ful hye,
That no man of our purveyaunce spye.
And whan thou thus hast doon as I have seyd,
And hast our vitaille faire in hem y-leyd,

'Work all by advice, and you shall not be sorry.'
And if you will work by good counsel,
I promise, without mast and sail,
Yet shall I save her and you and me.
Have you not heard how saved was Noah,
When that Our Lord had warned him before
That all the world with water should be lost?"

"Yes," said the carpenter, "full long ago."

"Have you not heard," said Nicholas, "also
The troubles of Noah and his fellows
Before he might get his wife to ship?[15]
He would have rather, I dare remark,
That she had for herself alone a ship
Than to have kept all his fine black sheep.
And therefore, do you know what is best to do?
This requires haste, and for an urgent thing
Men may not preach or shilly-shally.

Anon go get us fast into this dwelling
A kneading trough or else a shallow tub
For each of us, but look that they be large,
In which we may float as in a barge,
And have therein victuals sufficient
But for a day, fie on the remainder!
The water shall slake and go away
About prime on the next day.

But Robin may not know of this, your servant,
Nor your maid Jill, whom I may not save.
Ask not why, for though you ask me,
I will not tell God's secret things.
Suffice it for you, unless you are mad,
To have as great a grace as Noah had.
Your wife shall I well save, without doubt.
Now get going—and make it snappy.

But when you have, for her and you and me,
Gotten us these kneading tubs three,
Then shall you hang them in the roof full high,
That no man our preparations may espy.
And when you thus have done, as I have said,
And have our provisions in them laid,

And eek an ax, to smyte the corde atwo
When that the water comth, that we may go,
And broke an hole an heigh, up-on the gable,
Unto the gardin-ward, over the stable,
That we may frely passen forth our way
Whan that the grete shour is goon away—
Than shaltow swimme as myrie, I undertake,
As doth the whyte doke aftir hir drake.
Than wol I clepe, 'how! Alison! how! John!
Be myrie, for the flood wol passe anon.'
And thou wolt seyn, 'hayl, maister Nicholay!
Good morwe, I se thee wel, for it is day.'
And than shul we be lordes al our lyf
Of al the world, as Noë and his wyf.

But of o thyng I warne thee ful right,
Be wel avysed, on that ilke night
That we ben entred in-to shippes bord,
That noon of us ne speke nat a word,
Ne clepe, ne crye, but been in his preyere;
For it is goddes owne heste dere.

Thy wyf and thou mote hange fer a-twinne,
For that bitwixe yow shal be no sinne
No more in looking than ther shal in dede;
This ordinance is seyd, go, god thee spede!
Tomorwe at night, whan men ben alle aslepe,
In-to our kneding-tubbes wol we crepe,
And sitten ther, abyding goddes grace.
Go now thy wey, I have no lenger space
To make of this no lenger sermoning.
Men seyn thus, 'send the wyse, and sey no-thing;'
Thou art so wys, it nedeth thee nat teche;
Go, save our lyf, and that I thee biseche."

This sely carpenter goth forth his wey.
Ful ofte he seith "allas" and "weylawey,"
And to his wyf he tolde his privetee;
And she was war, and knew it bet than he,
What al this queynte cast was for to seye.
But nathelees she ferde as she wolde deye,
And seyde, "allas! go forth thy wey anon,

And also an axe, to smite the cord in two
When the water comes, that we may go,
And break a hole on high upon the gable
Toward the garden, over the stable,
That we may freely pass forth our way
When that great shower is gone away—
Then shall you float as merry, I dare say,
As does the white duck after her drake.
Then will I call, 'How, Alison! How, John!
Be merry, for the flood will pass anon!'
And you will say, 'Hail, master Nicholay!
Good morrow, I see you well, for it is day.'
And then shall we be lords all our lives
Of all the world, as Noah and his wife.

But of one thing I warn you full right:
Be well advised on that same night
Once we be our ships aboard
Then none of us shall speak a word,
No call, no cry, but be at prayer;
For it is God's own commandment dear.

Your wife and you must hang far apart,
So that between you shall be no sin
No more in looking than there shall be in deed;
This ordinance is said, go, God you speed!
Tomorrow at night, when men be all asleep,
Into our kneading tubs will we creep,
And sit there, awaiting God's grace.
Go now your way, I have no more time
To make of this a longer sermonizing.
Men say thus, 'Send the wise, and say no thing.'
You are wise, and don't need teaching;
Go save our lives, and that I you beseech."

This silly carpenter went forth his way.
Full often he said "alas" and "wellaway,"
And to his wife he told his secret;
And she was aware, and knew better than he,
The point of all this crackpot strategy.
But nevertheless she acted as if she would die,
And said, "Alas! go forth your way anon,

Help us to scape, or we ben lost echon;
I am thy trewe verray wedded wyf;
Go, dere spouse, and help to save our lyf."
    Lo! which a greet thyng is affeccioun!
Men may dye of imaginacioun,
So depe may impressioun be take.
This sely carpenter biginneth quake;
Him thinketh verraily that he may see
Noës flood come walwing as the see
To drenchen Alisoun, his hony dere.
He wepeth, weyleth, maketh sory chere,
He skyeth with ful many a sory swogh.
He gooth and geteth him a kneding-trough,
And after that a tubbe and a kimelin,
And prively he sente hem to his in,
And heng hem in the roof in privetee.
His owne hand he made laddres three,
To climben by the ronges and the stalkes
Un-to the tubbes hanginge in the balkes,
And hem vitailled, bothe trogh and tubbe,
With breed and chese, and good ale in a jubbe,
Suffysinge right y-nogh as for a day.
But er that he had maad al this array,
He sente his knave, and eek his wenche also,
Up-on his nede to London for to go.
And on the Monday, whan it drow to night,
He shette his dore with-oute candel-light,
And dressed al thing as it sholde be.
And shortly, up they clomben alle three;
They sitten stille wel a furlong-way.
    "Now, *Pater-noster*, clom!" seyde Nicholay,
And "clom," quod John, and "clom" seyde Alisoun.
This carpenter seyde his devocioun,
And stille he sit, and biddeth his preyere,
Awaytinge on the reyn, if he it here.
    The dede sleep, for wery bisinesse,
Fil on this carpenter right, as I gesse,
Aboute corfew-tyme, or litel more;
For travail of his goost he groneth sore,

Help us to escape, or we'll be dead soon.
I am your true wedded wife;
Go, dear spouse, and help to save our life."
　　Behold, what a great thing is emotion!
Men may die of what they imagine,
So deep may impression be taken.
This silly carpenter began to quake;
He thought verily that he might see
Noah's flood come rolling as the sea
To drown Alison, his honey dear.
He weeps, he wails, makes a long face,
He sighs with full many a sorry groan.
He goes and gets himself a kneading trough,
And after that a tub and another,
And secretly he sent them to his home,
And hung them in the roof in secrecy.
With his own hand he made ladders three,
To climb by the rungs and the shafts
Unto the tubs hanging in the beams,
And them provisioned, both trough and tub,
With bread and cheese, and good ale in a jug,
Sufficient right enough for a day.
But before he had made all this array,
He sent his servant and his maid also
Upon his business up to London to go.
And on the Monday, when it drew to night,
He shut his door without candlelight,
And arranged everything as it should be.
And shortly, up they climbed all three;
They sat still a short time that way.
　　"Now, *Paternoster*, then mum!" said Nicholay,
And "mum," said John, and "mum" said Alison.
This carpenter said his devotion,
And still he sat, and offered his prayer,
All the while waiting the rain to hear.
　　The sleep of the dead, from all his labor,
Fell on this carpenter right as I guess
About curfew-time,[16] or a little more;
For travail of his soul he groaned sore,

And eft he routeth, for his heed mislay.
Doun of the laddre stalketh Nicholay,
And Alisoun, ful softe adoun she spedde;
With-outen wordes mo, they goon to bedde
Ther-as the carpenter is wont to lye.
Ther was the revel and the melodye;
And thus lyth Alison and Nicholas,
In bisinesse of mirthe and of solas,
Til that the belle of laudes gan to ringe,
And freres in the chauncel gonne singe.

    This parish-clerk, this amorous Absolon,
That is for love alwey so wo bigon,
Up-on the Monday was at Oseneye
With compayne, him to disporte and pleye,
And axed up-on cas a cloisterer
Ful prively after John the carpenter;
And he drough him a-part out of the chirche,
And seyde, "I noot, I saugh him here nat wirche
Sin Saterday; I trow that he be went
For timber, ther our abbot hath him sent;
For he is wont for timber for to go,
And dwellen at the grange a day or two;
Or elles he is at his hous, certeyn;
Wher that he be, I can nat sothly seyn."

    This Absolon ful joly was and light,
And thoghte, "now is tyme wake al night;
For sikirly I saugh him nat stiringe
Aboute his dore sin day bigan to springe.
So moot I thryve, I shal, at cokkes crowe,
Ful prively knokken at his windowe
That stant ful lowe up-on his boures wal.
To Alison now wol I tellen al
My love-longing, for yet I shal nat misse
That at the leste wey I shal hir kisse.
Som maner confort shal I have, parfay,
My mouth hath icched al this longe day;
That is a signe of kissing atte leste.
Al night me mette eek, I was at a feste.
Therfor I wol gon slepe an houre or tweye,

And he snored as his head crooked in the tub lay.
Down from the ladder crept Nicholay,
And Alison, full soft adown she sped;
Without words more, they went to bed
There where the carpenter was wont to lie.
There was revelry and melody;
And thus lie Alison and Nicholas
In business of pleasure and mirth,
Till that the chapel bell[17] began to ring,
And friars in the chancel began to sing.

    This parish clerk, this amorous Absolon,
Who was for love always so woebegone,
Upon the Monday was at Osney
With company himself to disport and play,
And happened to ask a friar
Full discreetly about John the carpenter;
And he drew him aside out of the church,
And said, "I don't know, I haven't seen him
Since Saturday. I believe that he went
For timber, where our abbot had him sent,
For he is wont for timber for to go,
And dwell at the monastery's farmhouse a day or two;
Or else he is at his house, for certain.
Where he may be, I cannot truly say."

    This Absolon full jolly was and joyous,
And thought, "Now is time to stay awake all night;
For surely I saw him not stirring
About his door since day began to spring.
So may I thrive, I shall, at cock's crow,
Full secretly knock at his window
That stands full low upon his bedroom wall.
To Alison now will I tell all
My love-longing, for yet I shall not miss
That at the least I shall her kiss.
Some kind of comfort shall I have, by my faith.
My mouth has itched all this long day;
That is a sign of kissing at least.
Also I dreamt all night I was at a feast.
Therefore I will go on and sleep an hour or two,

And al the night than wol I wake and pleye."
    Whan that the firste cok hath crowe, anon
Up rist this joly lover Absolon,
And him arrayeth gay, at point-devys.
But first he cheweth greyn and lycorys,
To smellen swete, er he had kembd his heer.
Under his tonge a trewe love he beer,
For ther-by wende he to ben gracious.
He rometh to the carpenteres hous,
And stille he stant under the shot-windowe;
Un-to his brest it raughte, it was so lowe;
And softe he cogheth with a semi-soun—
"What do ye, hony-comb, swete Alisoun?
My faire brid, my swete cinamome,
Awaketh, lemman myn, and speketh to me!
Wel litel thenken ye up-on my wo,
That for your love I swete ther I go.
No wonder is thogh that I swelte and swete;
I moorne as doth a lamb after the tete.
Y-wis, lemman, I have swich love-longinge,
That lyk a turtel trewe is my moorninge;
I may nat ete na more than a mayde."
    "Go fro the window, Jakke fool," she sayde,
"As help me god, it wol nat be 'com ba me,'
I love another, and elles I were to blame,
Wel bet than thee, by Jesu, Absolon!
Go forth thy wey, or I wol caste a ston,
And lat me slepe, a twenty devel wey!"
    "Allas," quod Absolon, "and weylawey!
That trewe love was ever so yvel biset!
Than kisse me, sin it may be no bet,
For Jesus love and for the love of me."
    "Wiltow than go thy wey ther-with?" quod she.
    "Ye, certes, lemman," quod this Absolon.
    "Thanne make thee redy," quod she, "I come anon;"
And un-to Nicholas she seyde stille,
"Now hust, and thou shalt laughen al thy fille."
    This Absolon doun sette him on his knees,
And seyde, "I am a lord at alle degrees;

And all the night will I wake and play."
    When that the first cock crowed, anon
Up rose this jolly lover Absolon,
And dressed himself up to perfection.
But first he chewed cardamom and licorice,
To smell sweet, before he combed his hair.
Under his tongue a true-love leaf he bore,
And thereby thought he to be gracious.
He roamed to the carpenter's house,
And still he stood under the open window—
Up to his breast it reached, it was so low—
And soft he coughed with a small sound:
"What do you, honeycomb, sweet Alison,
My fair bird, my sweet cinnamon?
Awaken, sweetheart mine, and speak to me!
Well little think you upon my woe,
That for your love I sweat wherever I go.
No wonder it is that I swelter and sweat;
I yearn as does a lamb after the teat.
Truly, sweetheart, I have such love-longing,
That like a turtledove true is my mourning;
I may not eat more than a maid."
    "Go from the window, Jack fool," she said,
"As help me God, it will not be 'come kiss me.'
I love another, and otherwise I would be to blame,
Much better than you, by Jesu, Absolon!
Go forth your way or I will cast a stone,
And let me sleep, in the devil's name!"
    "Alas," said Absolon, "and wellaway,
That true love was ever so ill-bestowed!
Then kiss me, since it may be no better,
For Jesus' love and for the love of me."
    "Will you then get out of here?" said she.
    "Yes, truly," said this Absolon.
    "Then make you ready," said she, "Here I come!"
And to Nicholas she said quietly,
"Now hush, and you shall laugh all your fill."
    This Absolon down set him on his knees,
And said, "I am a lord in all ways;

For after this I hope ther cometh more!
Lemman, thy grace, and swete brid, thyn ore!"
　　The window she undoth, and that in haste,
"Have do," quod she, "com of, and speed thee faste,
Lest that our neighebores thee espye."
　　This Absolon gan wype his mouth ful drye;
Derk was the night as pich, or as the cole,
And at the window out she putte hir hole,
And Absolon, him fil no bet ne wers,
But with his mouth he kiste hir naked ers
Ful savourly, er he was war of this.
　　Abak he sterte, and thoghte it was amis,
For wel he wiste a womman hath no berd;
He felt a thing al rough and long y-herd,
And seyde, "fy! allas! what have I do?"
　　"Tehee!" quod she, and clapte the window to;
And Absolon goth forth a sory pas.
　　"A berd, a berd!" quod hende Nicholas,
"By goddes corpus, this goth faire and weel!"
　　This sely Absolon herde every deel,
And on his lippe he gan for anger byte;
And to him-self he seyde, "I shal thee quyte!"
　　Who rubbeth now, who froteth now his lippes
With dust, with sond, with straw, with clooth, with
　　　chippes,
But Absolon, that seith ful ofte, "allas!
My soule bitake I un-to Sathanas,
But me wer lever than al this toun," quod he,
"Of this despyt awroken for to be!
Allas!" quod he, "allas! I ne hadde y-bleynt!"
His hote love was cold and al y-queynt;
For fro that tyme that he had kiste hir ers,
Of paramours he sette nat a kers,
For he was heled of his maladye;
Ful ofte paramours he gan deffye,
And weep as dooth a child that is y-bete.
A softe paas he wente over the strete
Un-til a smith men cleped daun Gerveys,
That in his forge smithed plough-harneys;

For after this I hope there will be more.
Sweetheart, your grace, and sweet bird, your mercy!"
     The window she wide opened, and that in haste,
"Have do," said she, "come on, and hurry,
Lest our neighbors you espy."
     This Absolon wiped his mouth full dry:
Dark was the night as pitch, or as the coal,
And out the window she put her hole,
And Absolon, fared no better or worse,
But with his mouth he kissed her naked arse
Full savourly, before he was aware of this.
     Aback he started, and thought it was amiss,
For well he knew a woman had no beard;
He felt a thing all rough and long-haired,
And said, "Fie! alas, what have I done?"
     "Teehee," said she, and clapped the window shut;
And Absolon went forth with sorry step.
     "A beard, a beard!" said nice Nicholas,
"By God's body, this goes fair and well!"
     This poor Absolon heard every word,
And on his lip he began for anger to bite;
And to himself he said, "I shall you requite."
     Who rubs now, who chafes now his lips
With dirt, with sand, with straw, with cloth, with
     bark chips,
But Absolon, who says full often, "Alas!
My soul I commit to Satan,
If I would rather own this town," said he,
"Than be avenged of this insult to me.
Alas!" said he, "alas, that I did not abstain!"
His hot love was cold and quenched and quashed;
For from that time that he had kissed her arse,
For paramours he cared not a watercress,
For he was cured of his illness.
Full often paramours he began to decry,
And wept as does a beaten child.
With a soft step he went across the street
To a blacksmith called Gervase,
Who in his smithy forged plough hardware:

He sharpeth shaar and culter bisily
This Absolon knokketh al esily,
And seyde, "undo, Gerveys, and that anon."
　　"What, who artow?" "It am I, Absolon."
"What, Absolon! for Cristes swete tree,
Why ryse ye so rathe, ey *ben'cite!*
What eyleth yow? som gay gerl, god it woot,
Hath broght yow thus up-on the viritoot;
By sëynt Note, ye woot wel what I mene."
　　This Absolon ne roghte nat a bene
Of al his pley, no word agayn he yaf;
He hadde more tow on his distaf
Than Gerveys knew, and seyde, "freend so dere,
That hote culter in the chimenee here,
As lene it me, I have ther-with to done,
And I wol bringe it thee agayn ful sone."
　　Gerveys answerde, "certes, were it gold,
Or in a poke nobles alle untold,
Thou sholdest have, as I am trewe smith;
Ey, Cristes foo! what wol ye do therwith?"
　　"Therof," quod Absolon, "be as be may;
I shal wel telle it thee to-morwe day"—
And caughte the culter by the colde stele.
Ful softe out at the dore he gan to stele,
And wente un-to the carpenteres wal.
He cogheth first, and knokketh ther-with-al
Upon the windowe, right as he dide er.
　　This Alison answerde, "Who is ther
That knokketh so? I warante it a theef."
　　"Why, nay," quod he, "god woot, my swete leef,
I am thyn Absolon, my dereling!
Of gold," quod he, "I have thee broght a ring;
My moder yaf it me, so god me save,
Ful fyn it is, and ther-to wel y-grave;
This wol I yeve thee, if thou me kisse!"
　　This Nicholas was risen for to pisse,
And thoghte he wolde amenden al the jape,
He sholde kisse his ers er that he scape.
And up the windowe dide he hastily,

He busily sharpened both coulter and ploughshare.
This Absolon knocked all quietly,
And said, "Open up, Gervase, and that anon."
     "What, who are you?" "It is I, Absolon."
"What, Absolon! For Christ's sweet cross,
Why rise you so early, aye, *benedicite!*
What ails you? Some pretty girl, God knows,
Has brought you out upon first cock crow;
By Saint Neot,[18] you know well what I mean."
     This Absolon cared not beans
For all his joking. No word he gave in reply;
He had more on his mind
Than Gervase knew, and said, "Friend so dear,
That hot coulter[19] in the forge here,
Do lend it me: I have therewith to do,
And I will bring it to you again full soon."
     Gervase answered, "Truly, were it gold,
Or sack of coins in number untold,
You should have it, as I am a true smith.
Hey, Devil take it, what will you do with it?"
     "Thereof," said Absolon, "be it as it may:
I shall tell you tomorrow day,"
And caught the coulter by the handle's cold steel.
Full soft out the door he began to steal,
And went unto the carpenter's wall.
He coughed first, and knocked therewithal
Upon the window, just as he did before.
     And Alison answered, "Who is there
Who knocks so? I warrant it's a thief."
     "Why, nay," said he, "God knows, my dear sweet one,
I am your Absolon, my darling.
Of gold," said he, "I have brought you a ring—
My mother gave it to me, so God me save—
Full fine it is, and well-engraved.
This will I give you, if you me kiss!"
     This Nicholas was risen for to piss,
And thought he would improve upon the caper;
He should kiss his arse before he escapes.
And up the window put he hastily,

And out his ers he putteth prively
Over the buttok, to the haunche-bon;
And ther-with spak this clerk, this Absolon,
"Spek, swete brid, I noot nat wher thou art."
     This Nicholas anon leet flee a fart,
As greet as it had been a thonder-dent,
That with the strook he was almost y-blent;
And he was redy with his iren hoot,
And Nicholas amidde the ers he smoot.
Of gooth the skin an hande-brede aboute,
The hote culter brende so his toute,
And for the smert he wende for to dye.
As he were wood, for wo he gan to crye—
"Help! water! water! help, for goddes herte!"
     This carpenter out of his slomber sterte,
And herde oon cryen "water" as he were wood,
And thoghte, "Allas! now comth Nowélis flood!"
He sit him up with-outen wordes mo,
And with his ax he smoot the corde a-two,
And doun goth al; he fond neither to selle,
Ne breed ne ale, til he cam to the selle
Up-on the floor; and ther aswowne he lay.
     Up sterte hir Alison, and Nicholay,
And cryden "out" and "harrow" in the strete.
The neighebores, bothe smale and grete,
In ronnen, for to guaren on this man,
That yet aswowne he lay, bothe pale and wan;
For with the fal he brosten hadde his arm;
But stonde he moste un-to his owne harm.
For whan he spak, he was anon bore doun
With hende Nicholas and Alisoun.
They tolden every man that he was wood,
He was agast so of "Nowélis flood"
Thurgh fantasye, that of his vanitee
He hadde y-boght him kneding-tubbes three,
And hadde hem hanged in the roof above;
And that he preyed hem, for goddes love,
To sitten in the roof, *par companye.*
     The folk gan laughen at his fantasye;

And out his arse he put secretly
Over the buttock, to the haunch-bone;
And therewith spoke this clerk, this Absolon,
"Speak, sweet bird, I know not where you are."
   This Nicholas anon let fly a fart,
As great as had it been a thunderclap,
And with that stroke Absolon was almost blinded;
And he was ready with his iron hot;
And Nicholas amid the arse he smote.
Off went the skin a handsbreath across,
The hot coulter burned so his bum,
And for the smart he expected for to die.
As if he were gone berserk, he began to cry—
"Help! water! water! Harrow,[20] for God's heart!"
   This carpenter out of his slumber started,
And heard someone crying 'water' as if gone mad,
And thought, "Alas, now comes Noel's flood!"[21]
He sat him up without words more,
And with his axe he smote the cord in two,
And down went all, he found time neither to sail
Nor for bread or ale, till he came to the boards
Upon the floor; and there in a faint he lay.
   Up leapt Alison and Nicholay,
And cried "help" and "help" in the street.
The neighbors, both small and great,
In ran to stare at this man,
Who still fainted lay, both pale and wan;
For with the fall he had broken his arm.
But bear the burden he must for his own harm.
For when he spoke, he was at once shouted down
By both Nicholas and Alison.
They told every man that he was crazy,
He was so afraid of "Noel's flood"
Through delusion, that of his foolish pride
He had bought him kneading tubs three,
And had them hanged in the roof above;
And that he prayed them, for God's love,
To sit in the roof, for the sake of company.
   The folk laughed hard at his fantasy;

In-to the roof they kyken and they gape,
And turned al his harm un-to a jape.
For what so that this carpenter answerde,
It was for noght, no man his reson herde;
With othes grete he was so sworn adoun,
That he was holden wood in al the toun;
For every clerk anon-right heeld with other.
They sede, "the man is wood, my leve brother;"
And every wight gan laughen of this stryf.

    Thus swyved was the carpenteres wyf,
For al his keping and his jalousye;
And Absolon hath kist hir nether yë;
And Nicholas is scalded in the toute.
This tale is doon, and god save al the route!

Into the roof they gazed and gawked,
And turned all his misfortune into a joke.
For whatsoever that this carpenter answered,
It was for nought; no man his reasons heard.
With oaths great he was so sworn down,
That he was thought mad in all the town.
For every scholar agreed at once with the other:
They said, "The man is unhinged, my dear brother;"
And every person laughed at this strife.

    Thus screwed by another was the carpenter's wife
For all his guarding and his jealousy;
And Absolon had kissed her nether eye;
And Nicholas is scalded in the bum.
This tale is done, and God save all the company!

The Reves Tale

The Prologue

WHAN FOLK HAD LAUGHEN at this nyce cas
Of Absolon and hende Nicholas,
Diverse folk diversely they seyde;
But, for the more part, they loughe and pleyde,
Ne at this tale I saugh no man him greve,
But it were only Osewold the Reve,
By-cause he was of carpenteres craft.
A litel ire is in his herte y-laft,
He gan to grucche and blamed it a lyte.
    "So thee'k," quod he, "ful wel coude I yow quytë
With blering of a proud milleres yë,
If that me liste speke of ribaudye.
But ik am old, me list not pley for age;
Gras-tyme is doon, my fodder is now forage,
This whyte top wryteth myne olde yeres,
Myn herte is al-so mowled as myne heres,
But-if I fare as dooth an open-ers;
That ilke fruit is ever leng the wers,
Til it be roten in mullok or in stree.
We olde men, I drede, so fare we;
Til we be roten, can we nat be rype;
We hoppen ay, whyl that the world wol pype.
For in oure wil ther stiketh ever a nayl,
To have an hoor heed and a grene tayl,
As hath a leek; for thogh our might be goon,
Our wil desireth folie ever in oon.
For whan we may nat doon, than wol we speke;
Yet in our asshen olde is fyr y-reke.
    Foure gledes han we, whiche I shal devyse,
Avaunting, lying, anger, coveityse;
Thise foure sparkles longen un-to elde.
Our olde lemes mowe wel ben unwelde,
But wil ne shal nat faillen, that is sooth.
And yet ik have alwey a coltes tooth,
As many a yeer as it is passed henne

The Reeve's Tale

The Prologue

WHEN FOLK HAD LAUGHED at this foolish case
Of Absolon and nice Nicholas,
Diverse folk diverse things they said,
But, for the most part, they laughed and jested;
Nor at this tale I saw any man peeved,
Except for only Oswald the Reeve.
Because he was of carpenter's trade,
A little anger in his heart remained:
He began to grouch and blamed it a little.

"So," said he, "full well could I you requite
By sticking it in a proud miller's eye,
If I wanted to speak of ribaldry.
But I am old; I won't because of age;
Grass-time is done, my fodder is now forage;
This white top writes of my old years.
My heart is also moldy as my hairs,
Unless I fare as a medlar fruit;[1]
Which ripens only as it rots,
Till it be rotten in mud or straw.
We old men, I fear, so fare we:
Till we be rotten, we cannot be ripe;
We dance as long as the world plays the pipe.
For in our desire there always sticks a nail,
To have a hoary head and a green tail,
As has a leek, for though our strength be gone,
Our will desires folly all the same.
For when we may not act, then we will speak;
Yet within our ashes old is fire banked.

Four burning coals have we, which I shall list:
Boasting, lying, anger, avarice.
These four sparks belong to old age.
Our old limbs may be weak,
But will does not fail, that is the truth.
Yet still I have always a colt's tooth,
As many a year has gone

Sin that my tappe of lyf bigan to renne.
For sikerly, whan I was bore, anon
Deeth drogh the tappe of lyf and leet it gon;
And ever sith hath so the tappe y-ronne,
Til that almost al empty is the tonne.
The streem of lyf now droppeth on the chimbe;
The sely tonge may wel ringe and chimbe
Of wrecchednesse that passed is ful yore;
With olde folk, save dotage, is namore."
      Whan that our host hadde herd this sermoning,
He gan to speke as lordly as a king;
He seide, "what amounteth al this wit?
What shul we speke alday of holy writ?
The devel made a reve for to preche,
And of a souter a shipman or a leche.
Sey forth thy tale, and tarie nat the tyme,
Lo, Depeford! and it is half-way pryme.
Lo, Grenewich, ther many a shrewe is inne;
It wer al tyme thy tale to biginne."
      "Now, sires," quod this Osewold the Reve,
"I pray yow alle that ye nat yow greve,
Thogh I answere and somdel sette his howve;
For leveful is with force of-showve.
      This dronke millere hath y-told us heer,
How that bigyled was a carpenteer,
Peraventure in scorn, for I am oon.
And, by your leve, I shal him quyte anoon;
Right in his cherles termes wol I speke.
I pray to god his nekke mote breke;
He can wel in myn yë seen a stalke,
But in his owne he can nat seen a balke."

Since my tap of life began to run.
For truly, when I was born, anon
Death drew the tap of life and let it flow;
And ever since so has run the tap,
Till almost empty is the cask.
The stream of life now drops on the rim.
The foolish tongue may well chime and ring
Of wretchedness that passed long ago;
With old folk, dotage excepted, there is no more."
        When that our Host had heard this preaching,
He began to speak as lordly as a king.
He said, "What amounts to all this wit?
Why must we speak all day of Holy Writ?
The devil made a reeve into a preacher,
Or into a cobbler, sailor, or a doctor.
Tell forth your tale, and lose not the time,
Lo, Deptford, and it is half-way prime!
Lo, Greenwich, where many a rascal is in!
It's high time now your tale to begin."
        "Now, sires," said this Oswald the Reeve,
"I pray you all that you don't take it amiss,
Though I answer and somewhat his cap twist;
For lawful is it to answer force with force.
        This drunk miller has told us here
How that beguiled was a carpenter,
Perhaps in scorn, for I am one.
And by your leave, I shall requite him anon;
Right in his churl's words I will speak.
I pray to God his neck may break—
He can well in my eye see a straw,
But in his own he can't see a log."

The Tale

At Trumpington, nat fer fro Cantebrigge,
Ther goth a brook and over that a brigge,
Up-on the whiche brook ther stant a melle;
And this is verray soth that I yow telle.
A Miller was ther dwelling many a day;
As eny pecok he was proud and gay.
Pypen he coude and fisshe, and nettes bete,
And turne coppes, and wel wrastle and shete;
And by his belt he baar a long panade,
And of a swerd ful trenchant was the blade.
A joly popper baar he in his pouche;
Ther was no man for peril dorste him touche
A Sheffeld thwitel baar he is his hose;
Round was his face, and camuse was his nose.
As piled as an ape was his skulle.
He was a market-beter atte fulle.
Ther dorste no wight hand up-on him legge,
That he ne swoor he sholde anon abegge.
A theef he was for sothe of corn and mele,
And that a sly, and usaunt for to stele.
His name was hoten dëynous Simkin.
A wyf he hadde, y-comen of noble kin;
The person of the toun hir fader was.
With hir he yaf ful many a panne of bras,
For that Simkin sholde in his blood allye.
She was y-fostred in a nonnerye;
For Simkin wolde no wyf, as he sayde,
But she were wel y-norissed and a mayde,
To saven his estaat of yomanrye.
And she was proud, and pert as is a pye.
A ful fair sighte was it on hem two;
On haly-dayes biforn hir wolde he go
With his tipet bounden about his heed,
And she cam after in a gyte of reed;
And Simkin hadde hosen of the same.
Ther dorste no wight clepen hir but "dame."
Was noon so hardy that wente by the weye

The Tale

At Trumpington, not far from Cambridge,
There goes a brook and over that a bridge,
Upon which brook there stands a mill;
And this is a true story that I you tell.
A miller was there dwelling many a day;
As any peacock he was proud and gay.
Play bagpipes he could and fish, and mend nets,
And make wooden cups, and wrestle well, and shoot;
And by his belt he bore a long sword,
And full sharp was the blade.
A jolly dagger bore he in his pouch—
Every man for fear dared not him touch—
A Sheffield knife he bore in his hose.
Round was his face, and pug was his nose;
As bald as an ape was his skull.
He swaggered in the market towns.
No man dared to a hand upon him lay,
For he would swear him to repay.
A thief he was in truth of wheat and meal,
And that a sly one, and wont to steal.
His name was called scornful Simkin.
A wife he had, come from noble kin:
The priest of the town her father was.
For dowry he gave full many a pan of brass,
That Simkin should with his blood ally.
She was raised in a nunnery
For Simkin wanted no wife, as he said,
Unless she were well brought up and a maid,
To preserve his rank as a yeoman free.
And she was proud, and pert as a magpie.
A full fair sight was it to look upon the two;
On holidays before her he would go
With his scarf wound round his head,
And she came after in a gown of red;
And Simkin had stockings of the same.
There dared no one call her but "Madame."
And there was none so bold who went by the way

That with hir dorste rage or ones pleye,
But-if he wolde be slayn of Simkin
With panade, or with knyf, or boydekin.
For jalous folk ben perilous evermo,
Algate they wolde hir wyves wenden so.
And eek, for she was somdel smoterlich,
She was as digne as water in a dich;
And ful of hoker and of bisemare.
Hir thoughte that a lady sholde hir spare,
What for hir kinrede and hir nortelrye
That she had lerned in the nonnerye.

A doghter hadde they bitwixe hem two
Of twenty yeer, with-outen any mo,
Savinge a child that was of half-yeer age;
In cradel it lay and was a propre page.
This wenche thikke and wel y-growen was,
With camuse nose and yën greye as glas;
With buttokes brode and brestes rounde and hye,
But right fair was hir heer, I wol nat lye.

The person of the toun, for she was feir,
In purpos was to maken hir his heir
Bothe of his catel and his messuage.
And straunge he made it of hir mariage.
His purpos was for to bistowe hir hye
In-to som worthy blood of auncetrye;
For holy chirches good moot been despended
On holy chirches blood, that is descended.
Therfore he wolde his holy blood honoure,
Though that he holy chirche sholde devoure.

Gret soken hath this miller, out of doute,
With whete and malt of al the land aboute;
And nameliche ther was a greet collegge,
Men clepen the Soler-halle at Cantebregge,
Ther was hir whete and eek hir malt y-grounde.
And on a day it happed, in a stounde,
Sik lay the maunciple on a maladye;
Men wenden wisly that he sholde dye.
For which this miller stal bothe mele and corn
An hundred tyme more than biforn;

Who with her dared dally or play,
Unless he wanted to by Simkin be slain
With cutlass, or with knife, or dagger,
For jealous folk be dangerous evermore—
At least, they want their wives to believe so.
And also, for she was somewhat besmirched,
She was worthy as water in a ditch,
And full of hauteur and disdain.
He thought that a lady should remain aloof,
Thanks to her kindred and the refinement
That she had learned in the convent.

A daughter they had between the two
Of twenty years, without any more,
Except a child who was six months old;
In cradle it lay and was a fine boy.
This wench stout and well grown was,
With pug nose and eyes gray as glass,
With buttocks broad and breasts round and high;
But right fair was her hair, I will not lie.

The priest of the town, because she was fair,
Proposed to make her his heir
Both of his property and his house,
And particular he was about her espousal.
His purpose was to marry her high
Into some worthy old blood line;
For holy churchmen's goods must be spent
On holy churchmen's blood, that is descended.
Therefore he would his holy blood honor,
Though that he the holy church should devour.

Great monopoly had this miller, without doubt,
In wheat and malt of ale the land about;
And namely there was a great college
Men called Solar Hall at Cambridge;[2]
There was their wheat and also their malt ground.
And on a day it happened, at one time,
Sick lay the manciple with a malady:
Men thought for certain that he would die,
From whom this miller stole both meal and wheat
A hundred times more than before;

For ther-biforn he stal but curteisly,
But now he was a theef outrageously,
For which the wardeyn chidde and made fare.
But ther-of sette the miller nat a tare;
He craketh boost, and swoor it was nat so.

    Than were ther yonge povre clerks two,
That dwelten in this halle, of which I seye.
Testif they were, and lusty for to pleye,
And, only for hir mirthe and revelrye,
Up-on the wardeyn bisily they crye,
To yeve hem leve but a litel stounde
To goon to mille and seen hir corn y-grounde;
And hardily, they dorste leye hir nekke,
The miller shold nat stele hem half a pekke
Of corn by sleighte, ne by force hem reve;
And at the laste the wardeyn yaf hem leve.
John hight that oon, and Aleyn hight that other;
Of o toun were they born, that highte Strother,
Fer in the north, I can nat telle where.

    This Aleyn maketh redy al his gere,
And on an hors the sak he caste anon.
Forth goth Aleyn the clerk, and also John,
With good swerd and with bokeler by hir syde.
John knew the wey, hem nedede no gyde,
And at the mille the sak adoun he layth.
Aleyn spak first, "al hayl, Symond, y-fayth;
How fares thy faire doghter and thy wyf?"

    "Aleyn! welcome," quod Simkin, "by my lyf,
And John also, how now, what do ye heer?"

    "Symond," quod John, "by god, nede has na peer;
Him boës serve him-selve that has na swayn,
Or elles he is a fool, as clerkes sayn.
Our manciple, I hope he wil be deed,
Swa werkes ay the wanges in his heed.
And forthy is I come, and eek Alayn,
To grinde our corn and carie it ham agayn;
I pray yow spede us hethen that ye may."

    "It shal be doon," quod Simkin, "by my fay;
What wol ye doon whyl that it is in hande?"

For heretofore he stole but in a polite way,
But now he was a thief outrageously.
For which the warden chided him as he dared,
But thereof cared the miller not a tare;
He talked loud, and swore it was not so.
    Then were there young poor scholars two
Who dwelt in this hall of which I speak.
Headstrong they were, and in high spirits,
And, only for their mirth and revelry,
They pestered the warden
To give them leave but a little while
To go to the mill and see wheat ground;
And boldly, they dare risk their necks,
The miller should not steal from them half a peck
Of wheat by sleight, nor by force them rob;
And at last the warden gave them leave.
John was named one, and Allen named the other;
Of one town were they born, that was called Strother,
Far in the north, I cannot tell where.
    This Allen made ready all his gear,
And on a horse the sack of grain he cast anon.
Forth went Allen the scholar, and also John,
With good swords and shields by their sides.
John knew the way, they needed no guide,
And at the mill the sack adown he laid it.
Allen spoke first, "All hail, Simon, in faith!
How fares your daughter and your wife?"
    "Allen, welcome," said Simkin, "by my life!
And John also, how now, what do you here?"
    "Simon," said John, "by God, who has no peer,
He who has no servant should serve himself,
Or else he is a fool, as scholars say.
Our manciple, I expect, he will be dead,
So ache the molars in his head.
And therefore am I come, and also Allen,
To grind our wheat and carry it home again;
I pray you take care of us soon as you may."
    "It shall be done," said Simkin, "by my faith.
What will you do while it is in hand?"

"By god, right by the hoper wil I stande,"
Quod John, "and se how that the corn gas in;
Yet saugh I never, by my fader kin,
How that the hoper wagges til and fra."
    Aleyn answerde, "John, and wiltow swa,
Than wil I be bynethe, by my croun,
And se how that the mele falles doun
In-to the trough; that sal be my disport.
For John, in faith, I may been of your sort;
I is as ille a miller as are ye."
    This miller smyled of hir nycetee,
And thoghte, "al this nis doon but for a wyle;
They wene that no man may hem bigyle;
But, by my thrift, yet shal I blere hir yë
For al the sleighte in hir philosophye.
The more queynte crekes that they make,
The more wol I stele whan I take.
In stede of flour, yet wol I yeve hem bren.
'The gretteste clerkes been noght the wysest men,'
As whylom to the wolf thus spak the mare;
Of al hir art I counte noght a tare."
    Out at the dore he gooth ful prively,
Whan that he saugh his tyme, softely;
He loketh up and doun til he hath founde
The clerkes hors, ther as it stood y-bounde
Bihinde the mille, under a levesel;
And to the hors he gooth him faire and wel;
He strepeth of the brydel right anon.
And whan the hors was loos, he ginneth gon
Toward the fen, ther wide mares renne,
Forth with wehee, thurgh thikke and thurgh thenne.
    This miller smyled of hir nycetee,
But dooth his note, and with the clerkes pleyde,
Til that hir corn was faire and wel y-grounde.
And whan the mele is sakked and y-bounde,
This John goth out and fynt his hors away,
And gan to crye "harrow" and "weylaway!
Our hors is lorn! Alayn, for goddes banes,
Step on thy feet, com out, man, al at anes!

"By God, right by the hopper will I stand,"
Said John, "and see how the wheat goes in.
Yet saw I never, by my father's kin,
How that the hopper wags to and fro."
     Allen answered, "John, and will you do so?
Then will I be beneath, by my head,
And see how the meal falls down
Into the trough; that shall be my disport.
For John, in faith, I may be of your sort:
I am as bad a miller as are you."
     This miller smiled at their foolishness,
And thought, "all this is done but as a trick.
They think no man can them beguile,
But, by my thrift, yet will I blur their eyes
For all the sleight in their philosophy.
The more sly moves that they make,
The more will I steal when I take.
Instead of flour, yet will I give them bran.
'The greatest scholars be not the wisest men,'
As once to the wolf thus spoke the mare;
Of all their art count I not a tare."
     Out at the door he went full stealthily,
When that he saw his time, softly;
He looked up and down till he had found
The scholars' horse, there where it stood bound
Behind the mill, under a trellis.
And to the horse he went fair and well;
He stripped off the bridle right anon.
And when the horse was loose, it was gone
Toward the meadow, where the wild mares run,
Forth with "whinny," through thick and through thin.
     This miller went in again, no word he said,
But did his job, and with the scholars joked,
Till that their flour was fair and well ground.
And when the flour was sacked and bound,
This John went out and found his horse away,
And began to cry "help" and "wellaway!
Our horse is lost! Allen, for God's bones,
Step on it! come on, man, and at once!

Allas, our wardeyn has his palfrey lorn."
This Aleyn al forgat, bothe mele and corn,
Al was out of his mynde his housebondrye.
"What? whilk way is he geen?" he gan to crye.

The wyf cam leping inward with a ren,
She seyde, "allas! your hors goth to the fen
With wilde mares, as faste as he may go.
Unthank come on his hand that bond him so,
And he that bettre sholde han knit the reyne."

"Allas," quod John, "Aleyn, for Cristes peyne,
Lay doun thy swerd, and I wil myn alswa;
I is ful wight, god waat, as is a raa;
By goddes herte he sal nat scape us bathe.
Why nadstow pit the capul in the lathe?
Il-hayl, by god, Aleyn, thou is a fonne!"

Thic sely clerkes han ful faste y-ronne
To-ward the fen, bothe Aleyn and eek John.

And whan the miller saugh that they were gon
He half a busshel of hir flour hath take,
And bad his wyf go knede it in a cake.
He seyde, "I trowe the clerkes were aferd;
Yet can a miller make a clerkes berd
For al his art; now lat hem goon hir weye.
Lo wher they goon, ye, lat the children pleye;
They gete him nat so lightly, by my croun!"

Thise sely clerkes rennen up and doun
With "keep, keep, stand, stand, jossa, warderere,
Ga whistle thou, and I shal kepe him here!"
But shortly, til that it was verray night,
They coude nat, though they do al hir might,
Hir capul cacche, he ran alwey so faste,
Til in a dich they caughte him atte laste.

Wery and weet, as beste is in the reyn,
Comth sely John, and with him comth Aleyn.
"Allas," quod John, "the day that I was born!
Now are we drive til hething and til scorn.
Our corn is stole, men wil us foles calle,
Bathe the wardeyn and our felawes alle,
And namely the miller; weylaway!"

Alas, our warden has his palfrey gone!"
This Allen forgot both flour and grain;
All was out of his mind his careful plan.
"What, which way is he gone?" he began to cry.

The wife came leaping inside at a run;
She said, "Alas! Your horse went to the fen
With wild mares, as fast as he may go.
No thanks to the hand that hitched him so,
And he who better should tie the reins."

"Alas," said John, "Allen, for Christ's pain,
Lay down your sword, I will mine also.
I am full swift, God knows, as is a deer;
By God's heart he shall not escape us both!
Why didn't you put him in the barn?
Bad luck, by God, Allen, you are a fool!"
These foolish scholars have full fast run
Toward the meadow, both Allen and also John.

And when the miller saw that they were gone,
He half a bushel of their flour has taken,
And bade his wife go knead it into a cake.[3]
He said, "I believe the scholars were suspicious,
Yet can a miller outsmart a scholar
For all their art, now let them go their way.
Lo, where he goes! Yes, let the children play.
They won't easily catch him, by my head!"
These silly scholars ran up and down
With "Keep! keep! stand! down here! look out behind!
Go whistle you, and I shall keep him here!"
But in short, until it was truly night,
They could not, though they tried with all their might,
Catch their horse, he ran away so fast,
Till in a ditch they caught him at last.

Weary and wet, as creatures in the rain,
Comes silly John, and with him comes Allen.
"Alas," said John, "the day that I was born!
Now are we driven into mockery and scorn.
Our wheat is stolen, men will us fools call,
Both the warden and our companions all,
And especially the miller, wellaway!"

Thus pleyneth John as he goth by the way
Toward the mille, and Bayard in his hond.
The miller sitting by the fyr he fond,
For it was night, and forther nighte they noght;
But, for the love of god, they him bisoght
Of herberwe and of ese, as for hir peny.

The miller seyde agayn, "if ther be eny,
Swich as it is, yet shal ye have your part.
Myn hous is streit, but ye han lerned art;
Ye conne by argumentes make a place
A myle brood of twenty foot of space.
Lat see now if this place may suffyse,
Or make it roum with speche, as is youre gyse."

"Now, Symond," seyde John, "by seint Cutberd,
Ay is thou mery, and this is faire answerd.
I have herd seyd, man sal taa of twa thinges
Slyk as he fyndes, or taa slyk as he bringes.
But specially, I pray thee, hoste dere,
Get us some mete and drinke, and make us chere,
And we wil payen trewely atte fulle.
With empty hand men may na haukes tulle;
Lo here our silver, redy for to spende."

This miller in-to toun his doghter sende
For ale and breed, and rosted hem a goos,
And bond hir hors, it sholde nat gon loos;
And in his owne chambre hem made a bed
With shetes and with chalons faire y-spred,
Noght from his owne bed ten foot or twelve.
His doghter hadde a bed, al by hir-selve,
Right in the same chambre, by and by;
It might be no bet, and cause why,
Ther was no roumer herberwe in the place.
They soupen and they speke, hem to solace,
And drinken ever strong ale atte beste.
Aboute midnight wente they to reste.

Wel hath this miller vernisshed his heed;
Ful pale he was for-dronken, and nat reed.
He yexeth, and he speketh thurgh the nose
As he were on the quakke, or on the pose.

Thus complained John as he went by the way
Toward the mill, and horse Bayard in his hand.
The miller sitting by the fire they found,
For it was night, and go further they might not.
But for the love of God they him besought
Of lodging and rest, and offered their penny.

The miller said to them, "If there be any,
Such as it is, yet shall you have your part.
My house is small, but you have learned art:
You know how by arguments to make a place
A mile broad from twenty foot of space.
Let's see now if this place may suffice—
Or make it roomy with talk, as is your way."

"Now, Simon," said John, "by Saint Cuthbert,[4]
You're a funny man, and that's a good answer.
I have heard said, 'man shall take of two things:
Such as he finds, or such as he brings.'
But specially, I pray you, host dear,
Get us some meat and drink and make us good cheer,
And we will pay truly at full;
With empty hand men may not hawks lure.
Lo, here is our silver, ready for to spend."

This miller into town his daughter sent
For ale and bread, and roasted them a goose,
And hitched their horse, it should no more get loose;
And in his own chamber them made a bed
With sheets and blankets fairly spread,
Not far from his own bed ten foot or twelve.
His daughter had a bed, all by herself,
Right in the same chamber, side by side.
It might be no better arranged, was the reason why,
There was no larger lodging in the place.
They supped and they talked, themselves to enjoy,
And drank very strong ale of the best.
About midnight went they to rest.

Well had this miller plastered his head:
So drunk he was full pale, not red;
He hiccupped, and he spoke through the nose
As if he were hoarse, or had a cold.

To bedde he gooth, and with him goth his wyf.
As any jay she light was and jolyf,
So was hir joly whistle wel y-wet.
The cradel at hir beddes feet is set,
To rokken, and to yeve the child to souke.
And whan that dronken al was in the crouke,
To bedde went the doghter right anon;
To bedde gooth Aleyn and also John;
Ter nas na more, hem nedede no dwale.
This miller hath so wisly bibbed ale,
That as an hors he snorteth in his sleep,
Ne of his tayl bihinde he took no keep.
His wyf bar him a burdon, a ful strong,
Men mighte hir routing here two furlong;
The wenche routeth eek par companye.
    Aleyn the clerk, that herd this melodye,
He poked John, and seyde, "slepestow?
Herdestow ever slyk a sang er now?
Lo, whilk a compline is y-mel hem alle!
A wilde fyr up-on thair bodyes falle!
Wha herkned ever slyk a ferly thing?
Ye, they sal have the flour of il ending.
This lange night ther tydes me na reste;
But yet, na fors; al sal be for the beste.
For John," seyde he, "als ever moot I thryve
If that I may, yon wenche wil I swyve.
Som esement has lawe y-shapen us;
For John, ther is a lawe that says thus,
That gif a man in a point be y-greved,
That in another he sal be releved.
Our corn is stoln, shortly, it is na nay,
And we han had an il fit al this day.
And sin I sal have neen amendement,
Agayn my los I wil have esement.
By goddes saule, it sal neen other be!"
    This John answerde, "Alayn, avyse thee,
The miller is a perilous man," he seyde,
"And gif that he out of his sleep abreyde
He mighte doon us bathe a vileinye."

To bed he went, and with him went his wife—
As any jay she was cheerful and jolly,
So was her whistle well-wetted.
The cradle at their bed's foot is set,
To rock, and to give the child to suck.
And when they had drunk all in the jug,
To bed went the daughter right anon;
To bed went Allen and also John;
There was no more, they needed no sleeping potion.
This miller had so deeply imbibed ale,
That like a horse he snored in his sleep,
And of his tail behind he took no heed.
His wife sang bass, and full strong:
Men might their snoring hear from two furlongs;
The wench snored also to keep them company.
    Allen the scholar, who heard this melody,
He poked John, and said, "Are you asleep?
Heard you ever such a song before now?
Lo, such an evensong they sing all!
A fiery rash upon their bodies fall!
Who heard ever such a weird thing?
Yes, they shall have the flour of this bad ending.
This long night promises me no rest;
But yet, no matter, all shall be for the best.
For John," said he, "as ever may I thrive,
If that I may, to yon wench will I make love.
Some redress has law provided for us.
For John, there is a law that says thus,
That if a man in one point be aggrieved,
That in another he shall be relieved.
Our wheat is stolen, there's no denying,
And we've had a miserable time this day.
And since I shall have no amends
Against my loss, I will have redress.
By God's soul, it shall not otherwise be!"
    This John answered, "Allen, take heed,
This miller is a dangerous man," he said,
"And if he out of his sleep awakens,
He might do us both an injury."

Aleyn answerde, "I count him nat a flye;"
And up he rist, and by the wenche he crepte.
This wenche lay upright, and faste slepte,
Til he so ny was, er she mighte espye,
That it had been to late for to crye,
And shortly for to seyn, they were at on;
Now pley, Aleyn! for I wol speke of John.

    This John lyth stille a furlong-wey or two,
And to him-self he maketh routhe and wo:
"Allas!" quod he, "this is a wikked jape;
Now may I seyn that I is but an ape.
Yet has my felawe som-what for his harm;
He has the milleris doghter in his arm.
He auntred him, and has his nedes sped,
And I lye as a draf-sek in my bed;
And when this jape is tald another day,
I sal been halde a daf, a cokenay!
I wil aryse, and auntre it, by my fayth!
'Unhardy is unsely,' thus men sayth."
And up he roos and softely he wente
Un-to the cradel, and in his hand it hente,
And baar it softe un-to his beddes feet.

    Sone after this the wyf hir routing leet,
And gan awake, and wente hir out to pisse,
And cam agayn, and gan hir cradel misse,
And groped heer and ther, but she fond noon.
"Allas!" quod she, "I hadde almost misgoon;
I hadde almost gon to the clerkes bed.
Ey, *ben'cite!* thanne hadde I foule y-sped:"
And forth she gooth til she the cradel fond.
She gropeth alwey forther with hir hond,
And fond the bed, and thoghte noght but good,
By-cause that the cradel by it stood,
And niste wher she was, for it was derk;
But faire and wel she creep in to the clerk,
And lyth ful stille, and wolde han caught a sleep.
With-inne a whyl this John the clerk up leep,
And on this gode wyf he leyth on sore.
So mery a fit ne hadde she nat ful yore;

Allen answered, "I count him not a fly."
And up he rose, and by the wench he crept.
This wench lay on her back, and fast slept
Till he so close was, if she might him see,
That it would have been too late for her to cry,
And to make it short, they were at one;
Now play, Allen! For will I speak of John.

    This John lies still for a moment or two,
And to himself he makes lamentation and woe:
"Alas!" said he, "this is a wicked joke.
Now may I say that I am but an ape.
Yet has my fellow something for his harm:
He has the miller's daughter in his arm.
He took a risk, and has his needs fed,
And I lie like a straw sack in my bed.
And when this joke is told another day,
I shall be held a fool, a sap:
I will arise and risk it, by my faith!
Unbold is unlucky, thus men say."
And up he rose and softly he went
To the cradle, and in his hand it held,
And bore it softly to his bed's foot.

    Soon after this the wife her snoring ceased,
And began to wake, and went her out to piss,
And came again, and found her cradle missing,
And groped here and there, but it was gone.
"Alas!" said she, "I had almost stepped wrong;
I had almost gone to the scholars' bed—
Eh, *benedicite*, then had I wrong been!"
And forth she went until she the cradle found;
She groped ever further with her hand,
And found the bed, and thought nought but good,
By cause that the cradle by it stood,
And knew not where she was, for it was dark;
But fair and well she crept in with the scholar,
And lay full still, and would have asleep fallen.
Within a while this John the scholar up leapt,
And on this good wife he at it hard set.
So merry a bout she had not in a long time had;

He priketh harde and depe as he were mad.
This joly lyf han thise two clerkes lad
Til that the thridde cok bigan to singe.

Aleyn wex wery in the daweninge.
For he had swonken al the longe night;
And seyde, "far wel, Malin, swete wight!
The day is come, I may no lenger byde;
But evermo, wher so I go or ryde,
I is thyn awen clerk, swa have I seel!"

"Now dere lemman," quod she, "go, far weel!
But er thou go, o thing I wol thee telle,
Whan that thou wendest homward by the melle,
Right at the entree of the dore bihinde,
Thou shalt a cake of half a busshel finde
That was y-maked of thyn owne mele,
Which that I heelp my fader for to stele.
And, gode lemman, god thee save and kepe!"
And with that word almost she gan to wepe.

Aleyn up-rist, and thoughte, "er that it dawe,
I wol go crepen in by my felawe;"
And fond the cradel with his hand anon.
"By god," thoghte he, "al wrang I have misgon;
Myn heed is toty of my swink to-night,
That maketh me that I go nat aright.
I woot wel by the cradel, I have misgo,
Heer lyth the miller and his wyf also."
And forth he goth, a twenty devel way,
Un-to the bed ther-as the miller lay.
He wende have cropen by his felawe John;
And by the miller in he creep anon,
And caughte hym by the nekke, and softe he spak:
He seyde, "thou, John, thou swynes-heed, awak
For Cristes saule, and heer a noble game.
For by that lord that called is seint Jame,
As I have thryes, in this shorte night,
Swyved the milleres doghter bolt-upright,
Whyl thow hast as a coward been agast."

"Ye, false harlot," quod the miller, "hast?
A! false traitour! false clerk!" quod he,

He pricked long and deep as if he were mad.
This jolly life have these two scholars led
Till the third cock began to sing.

    Allen waxed weary at the dawning,
For he had worked all the long night,
And said, "Farewell, Molly, sweet one!
The day is come, I may no longer stay;
But evermore, wherever I ride or go,
I am your own scholar, as I hope for joy!"

    "Now, dear sweetheart," said she, "go, farewell!
But before you go, one thing I will you tell:
When that you wend home by the mill,
Right at the entry of the door behind,
You shall a cake of half a bushel find
That was made of your own meal,
Which I helped my sire to steal.
And, good sweetheart, God you save and keep!"
And with that word she almost began to weep.

    Allen up rose, and thought, "Before that it dawns,
I will go creep by my fellow,"
And found the cradle with his hand anon.
"By God," thought he, "All wrong have I gone.
My head is light from my work tonight:
That makes me go not aright.
I know well by the cradle I have gone wrong—
Here lie the miller and his wife also."
And forth he went, to the devil straight,
To the bed where the miller lay—
He meant to creep by his fellow John—
And by the miller in he crept anon,
And caught him by the neck, and soft he spoke.
He said, "You, John, you swine's head, awaken
For Christ's soul, and hear a great joke.
For by that lord who is called Saint James,
So I have thrice in this short night
Made love to the miller's daughter bolt upright,
While you have as a coward been afraid."

    "You, false rascal," said the miller, "have?
Ah! false traitor! false scholar!" said he,

"Thou shalt be deed, by goddes dignitee!
Who dorste be so bold to disparage
My doghter, that is come of swich linage?"
And by the throte-bolle he caughte Alayn.
And he hente hymn despitously agayn,
And on the nose he smoot him with his fest.
Doun ran the blody streem up-on his brest;
And in the floor, with nose and mouth to-broke,
They walwe as doon two pigges in a poke.
And up they goon, and doun agayn anon,
Til that the miller sporned at a stoon,
And doun he fil bakward up-on his wyf,
That wiste no-thing of this nyce stryf;
For she was falle aslepe a lyte wight
With John the clerk, that waked hadde al night.
And with the fal, out of hir sleep she breyde—
"Help, holy corys of Bromeholm," she seyde,
"*In manus tuas!* lord, to thee I calle!
Awak, Symond! the feend is on us falle,
Myn herte is broken, help, I nam but deed;
There lyth oon up my wombe and up myn heed;
Help, Simkin, for the false clerkes fighte."
      This John sterte up as faste as ever he mighte,
And graspeth by the walles to and fro,
To finde a staf; and she sterte up also,
And knew the estres bet than dide this John,
And by the wal a staf she fond anon,
And saugh a litel shimering of a light,
For at an hole in shoon the mone bright;
And by that light she saugh hem bothe two,
But sikerly she niste who was who,
But as she saugh a whyt thing in hir yë.
And whan she gan the whyte thing espye,
She wende the clerk hadde wered a volupeer.
And with the staf she drough ay neer and neer,
And wende han hit this Aleyn at the fulle,
And smoot the miller on the pyled skulle,
That doun he gooth and cryde, "harrow! I dye!"
Thise clerkes bete him weel and lete him lye;

"You shall be dead, by God's dignity!
Who would dare be so bold to dishonor
My daughter, who is come of such high birth?"
And by the Adam's apple he caught Allen;
And Allen held him fiercely in turn,
And on the nose he smote him with his fist—
Down ran the blood stream upon his breast.
And on the floor, with nose and mouth broken,
They wallowed as do two pigs in a poke.
And up they go, and down again anon,
Till that the miller tripped on a stone,
And down he fell backward upon his wife,
Who knew nothing of this silly strife,
For she had fallen asleep for a bit
With John the scholar, who waked had all night;
And with the fall, out of her sleep she started.
"Help, holy cross of Bromholm,"[5] she said,
"*In manus tuas!*[6] Lord, to you I call!
Awake, Simon! the fiend is on me fallen,
My heart is broken, help, I am almost dead:
There lies someone on my womb and on my head.
Help, Simkin, for the false scholars fight."
     This John leapt up as fast as ever he might,
And groped along the walls to and fro,
To find a staff; and she leapt up also,
And knew the place better than did this John,
And by the wall a staff she found anon,
And saw a little shimmering of a light—
For at a hole in shone the moon bright—
And by that light she saw them both two,
And truly she knew not who was who,
Except that she saw a white thing in her eye.
And when she did this white thing espy,
She thought the scholar had worn a nightcap,
And with the staff she drew ever near and nearer,
And thinking to hit Allen at the full,
And smote the miller on the bald skull
So down he went and cried, "Help! I die!"
These scholars beat him well and let him lie,

And greythen hem, and toke hir hors anon,
And eek hir mele, and on hir wey they gon.
And at the mille yet they tok hir cake
Of half a busshel flour, ful wel y-bake.

   Thus is the proude miller wel y-bete,
And hath y-lost the grinding of the whete,
And payed for the soper every-deel
Of Aleyn and of John, that bette him weel.
His wyf is swyved, and his doghter als;
Lo, swich it is a miller to be fals!
And therfore this proverbe is seyd ful sooth,
"Him thar nat wene wel that yvel dooth;
A gylour shal him-self bigyled be."
And God, that sitteth heighe in magestee,
Save al this companye grete and smale!
Thus have I quit the miller and my tale.

And gathered themselves, and took their horse anon,
And also their flour, and on their way they went.
And at the mill they took their cake
Of half a bushel flour, full well baked.
　　Thus is the proud miller well beaten,
And has lost the grinding of the wheat,
And paid for the supper complete
Of Allen and John, who beat him well;
His wife is enjoyed, and his daughter also.
Lo, so it goes for a miller false!
And therefore this proverb is said so true,
"He should not expect good who will evil do;
A beguiler shall himself beguiled be."
And God, who sits high in majesty,
Save all this company great and small!
Thus I have repaid the Miller in my tale.

The Tale of the Wyf of Bathe

The Prologue

"EXPERIENCE, THOUGH NOON AUCTORITEE
Were in this world, were right y-nough to me
To speke of wo that is in mariage;
For, lordinges, sith I twelf yeer was of age,
Thonked be god that is eterne on lyve,
Housbondes at chirche-dore I have had fyve
For I so ofte have y-wedded be;
And alle were worthy men in hir degree.
But me was told certeyn, nat longe agon is,
That sith that Crist ne wente never but onis
To wedding in the Cane of Galilee,
That by the same ensample taughte he me
That I ne sholde wedded be but ones.
Herke eek, lo! which a sharp word for the nones
Besyde a welle Jesus, god and man,
Spak in repreve of the Samaritan:
'Thou hast y-had fyve housbondes,' quod he,
'And thilke man, the which that hath now thee,
Is noght thyn housbond;' thus seyde he certeyn;
What that he mente ther-by, I can nat seyn;
But that I axe, why that the fifthe man
Was noon housbond to the Samaritan?
How manye mighte she have in mariage?
Yet herde I never tellen in myn age
Upon this nombre diffinicioun;
Men may devyne and glosen up and doun.
But wel I woot expres, with-oute lye,
God bad us for to wexe and multiplye;
That gentil text can I wel understonde.
Eek wel I woot he seyde, myn housbonde
Sholde lete fader and moder, and take me;
But of no nombre mencioun made he,
Of bigamye or of octogamye;
Why sholde men speke of it vileinye?
    Lo, here the wyse king, dan Salomon;

The Wife of Bath's Tale

The Prologue

"EXPERIENCE, THOUGH NO OTHER authority
Were in this world, is quite enough for me
To speak of woe that is in marriage:
For, lordings, since I twelve years was of age,
Thanks be to God who is eternally alive,
Husbands at church door have I had five
(If I so often might have wedded be)[1]
And all were worthy in their degree.[2]
But I was told, truly, not long ago,
That since Christ never went but once
To wedding in the Cana of Galilee,[3]
That by the same example taught he me
That I should not be wedded but once.
Harken, also, to the sharp word,
Beside a well, that Jesus, God and man,
Spoke in reproof to the Samaritan:[4]
'You have had five husbands,' said he,
'And that same man who now has you
Is not your husband;' thus said he certain.
What he meant thereby I cannot say,
Except I ask, why the fifth man
Was not husband to the Samaritan?
How many might she have in marriage?
Yet never have I heard tell in all my time
Of this number an explanation.
Men may interpret and gloss up and down,
But well I know especially, without lie,
God bade us for to increase and multiply:
That noble text can I well understand.
Also well I know he said, my husband
Should leave father and mother, and take to me;
But of no number mention made he,
Of in succession how many.
Why should men then speak of it reproachfully?
    Lo, here the wise king, Lord Solomon;

I trowe he hadde wyves mo than oon;
As, wolde god, it leveful were to me
To be refresshed half so ofte as he!
Which yifte of god hadde he for alle his wyvis!
No man hath swich, that in this world alyve is.
God woot, this noble king, as to my wit,
The firste night had many a mery fit
With ech of hem, so wel was him on lyve!
Blessed be god that I have wedded fyve!
Welcome the sixte, whan that ever he shal.
For sothe, I wol nat kepe me chast in al;
Whan myn housbond is fro the world y-gon,
Som Cristen man shal wedde me anon;
For thanne th'apostle seith, that I am free
To wedde, a godd's half, wher it lyketh me.
He seith that to be wedded is no sinne;
Bet is to be wedded than to brinne.
What rekketh me, thogh folk seye vileinye
Of shrewed Lameth and his bigamye?
I woot wel Abraham was an holy man,
And Jacob eek, as ferforth as I can;
And ech of hem hadde wyves mo than two;
And many another holy man also.
Whan saugh ye ever, in any maner age,
That hye god defended mariage
By expres word? I pray you, telleth me;
Or wher comanded he virginitee?
I woot as wel as ye, it is no drede,
Th'apostel, whan he speketh of maydenhede;
He seyde, that precept ther-of hadde he noon.
Men may conseille a womman to been oon
But conseilling is no comandement;
He putte it in our owene jugement
For hadde god comanded maydenhede,
Thanne hadde he dampned wedding with the dede;
And certes, if ther were no seed y-sowe,
Virginitee, wher-of than sholde it growe?
Poul dorste nat comanden atte leste
A thing of which his maister yaf noon heste.

I believe he had wives more than one.
Would to God it were allowed for me
To be refreshed half so often as he!
What a gift of God had he for all his wives!
No man has such, who in the world alive now is.
God knows this noble king, so far as I can see,
The first night had many a merry fight
With each of them, so lucky was his life!
Blessed be God that I have wedded five,
Welcome the sixth, whenever he arrives!
For in truth I will not keep myself all chaste.
When my husband is from this world gone
Some Christian man shall wed me anon;
For then the apostle says that I am free
To wed, on God's behalf, where it pleases me.
He says that to be wedded is no sin:
Better to be wedded than to burn.
What matters it to me though folk speak badly
Of cursed Lamech and his bigamy?
I know well that Abraham was a holy man,
And Jacob also, as far as I know;
And each of them had wives more than two,
And many another holy man also.
Where can you see, in whatever age,
That high God forbade marriage
By express word? I pray you, tell me.
Or where commanded he virginity?
I know as well as you, it is no doubt,
The Apostle, when he spoke of maidenhood,
He said commandment thereof had he none.
Men may counsel a woman to be one,
But counseling is no commandment:
He put it in our own judgement.
For had God commanded maidenhood,
Then he would have damned wedding in that deed.
And certainly, if there were no seed sown,
Virginity, then whereof should it grow?
Paul dared not in the least command,
A thing of which his master gave no behest.

The dart is set up for virginitee;
Cacche who so may, who renneth best lat see.
    But this word is nat take of every wight,
But ther as god list give it of his might.
I woot wel, that th'apostel was a mayde;
But natheless, thogh that he wroot and sayde,
He wolde that every wight were swich as he,
Al nis but conseil to virginitee;
And for to been a wyf, he yaf me leve
Of indulgence; so it is no repreve
To wedde me, if that my make dye,
With-oute excepcioun of bigamye.
Al were it good no womman for to touche,
He mente as in his bed or in his couche;
For peril is bothe fyr and tow t'assemble;
Ye knowe what this ensample may resemble.
This is al and som, he heeld virginitee
More parfit than wedding in freletee.
Freeltee clepe I, but-if that he and she
Wolde leden al hir lyf in chastitee.
    I graunte it wel, I have noon envye,
Thogh maydenhede preferre bigamye;
Hem lyketh to be clene, body and goost,
Of myn estaat I nil nat make no boost.
For wel ye knowe, a lord in his houshold,
He hath nat every vessel al of gold;
Somme been of tree, and doon hir lord servyse,
God clepeth folk to him in sondry wyse,
And everich hath of god a propre yifte,
Som this, som that,—as him lyketh shifte.
    Virginitee is greet perfeccioun,
And continence eek with devocioun.
But Crist, that of perfeccioun is welle,
Bad nat every wight he sholde go selle
All that he hadde, and give it to the pore,
And in swich wyse folwe him and his fore.
He spak to hem that wolde live parfitly;
And lordinges, by your leve, that am nat I.
I wol bistowe the flour of al myn age

The prize is set up for virginity:
Catch it who so may: who runs best let's see.
    But this word is not taken by every person,
But to whom God chooses, in his might.
I well know that the apostle was a maid;
But nevertheless, though he wrote and said
He would that every person were such as he,
All this just recommends virginity,
And for to be a wife, he gave me leave
By indulgence. So it is no reproach
To wed me, if that my mate die,
Without accusation of bigamy,
Although were it good no woman to touch—
He meant as in his bed or in his couch—
For peril is both spark and tinder to assemble;
You know what this example may resemble.
This all and some: he held virginity
More perfect than wedding in frailty.
'Frailty' I call it, unless he and she
Would lead all their lives in chastity.
    I grant it well, I have no envy
Though maidenhood be preferred to bigamy.
They wish to be clean, body and soul.
Of my condition I will make no boast:
For well you know, a lord in his household
Has not every vessel all of gold;
Some be of wood, and do their lord service.
God calls folk to him in sundry ways,
And everyone has from God his special virtue,
Some this, some that, as He chooses.
    Virginity is great perfection,
And continence also, if coupled with devotion.
But Christ, who of perfection is the source,
Bade not every person that he should go sell
All that he had and give it to the poor,
And in such way follow him and his footsteps.
He spoke to those who would live perfectly,
And lordings, by your leave, that is not I.
I will bestow the flower of my prime age

In th' actes and in fruit of mariage.
    Telle me also, to what conclusioun
Were membres maad of generacioun,
And for what profit was a wight y-wroght?
Trusteth right wel, they wer nat maad for noght.
Glose who-so wole, and seye bothe up and doun,
That they were maked for purgacioun
Of urine, and our bothe thinges smale
Were eek to knowe a femele from a male,
And for noon other cause: sey ye no?
The experience woot wel it is noght so;
So that the clerkes be nat with me wrothe,
I sey this, that they maked been for bothe,
This is to seye, for office, and for ese
Of engendrure, ther we nat god displese.
Why sholde men elles in hir bokes sette,
That man shal yelde to his wyf hir dette?
Now wher-with sholde he make his payement
If he ne used his sely instrument?
Than were they maad up-on a creature,
To purge uryne, and eek for engendrure.
    But I seye noght that every wight is holde,
That hath swich harneys as I to yow tolde,
To goon and usen hem in engendrure;
Than sholde men take of chastitee no cure.
Crist was a mayde, and shapen as a man,
And many a seint, sith that the world bigan,
Yet lived they ever in parfit chastitee.
I nil envye no virginitee;
Lat hem be breed of pured whete-seed,
And lat us wyves hoten barly-breed;
And yet with barly-breed, Mark telle can,
Our lord Jesu refresshed many a man.
In swich estaat as god hath cleped us
I wol persevere, I nam nat precious.
In wyfhode I wol use myn instrument
As frely as my maker hath it sent.
If I be daungerous, god yeve me sorwe!
Myn housbond shal it have bothe eve and morwe,

In the acts and in fruit of marriage.
    Tell me also, to what purpose
Were organs for procreation shaped
And by so perfect a workman wrought?
Trust right well, they were not made for nought.
Interpret who will, and say both up and down
That they were made for purgation
Of urine, and both our things small
Were also to tell a female from a male,
And for no other cause, say you no?
The experienced know well it is not so.
So that theologians be not with me wroth,
I say this, that they were made for the both—
That is to say, for purpose and pleasure
Of procreation, therefore we do not God displease.
Why should men otherwise in their books set
That man shall give to his wife her debt?
Now where should he make his payment
If he uses not his blessed instrument?
Therefore were they made upon a creature
To purge urine, and also to engender.
    But I say not that everyone is bound,
Who has such equipment that I to you told,
To go and use them in procreation:
Then should men take of chastity no concern.
Christ was a maid and formed as a man,
And many a saint, since the world began,
Lived ever in perfect chastity.
I will envy not virginity:
Let virgins be bread of the finest wheat,
And let us wives be barley-bread.
And yet with barley-bread, as Saint Mark tell can,
Our Lord Jesus refreshed many a man.
In such condition as God has called us
I will persevere, I am not fastidious.
In wifehood I will use my instrument
As generously as my Maker has it sent.
If I be reluctant, God give me sorrow!
My husband shall have it both eve and morrow,

Whan that him list com forth and paye his dette.
An housbonde I wol have, I nil nat lette,
Which shal be bothe my dettour and my thral,
And have his tribulacioun with-al
Up-on his flessh, whyl that I am his wyf.
I have the power duringe al my lyf
Up-on his propre body, and noght he.
Right thus th'apostel tolde it un-to me;
And bad our housbondes for to love us weel.
Al this sentence me lyketh every-deel"—
Up sterte the Pardoner, and that anon,
"Now dame," quod he, "by god and by seint John,
Ye been a noble prechour in this cas!
I was aboute to wedde a wyf; allas!
What sholde I bye it on my flesh so dere?
Yet hadde I lever wedde no wyf to-yere!"

    "Abyde!" quod she, "my tale is nat bigonne;
Nay, thou shalt drinken of another tonne
Er that I go, shal savoure wors than ale.
And whan that I have told thee forth my tale
Of tribulacioun in mariage,
Of which I am expert in al myn age,
This to seyn, my-self have been the whippe;—
Than maystow chese whether thou wolt sippe
Of thilke tonne that I shal abroche.
Be war of it, er thou to ny approche;
For I shal telle ensamples mo than ten.
Who-so that nil be war by othere men,
By him shul othere men corrected be.
The same wordes wryteth Ptholomee;
Rede in his Almageste, and take it there."

    "Dame, I wolde praye yow, if your wil it were,"
Seyde this Pardoner, "as ye bigan,
Telle forth your tale, spareth for no man,
And teche us yonge men of your praktike."

    "Gladly," quod she, "sith it may yow lyke.
But yet I praye to al this companye,
If that I speke after my fantasye,
As taketh not a-grief of that I seye;

When that he wishes to come forth, his debt to pay.
A husband will I have, I will not fail,
Who shall be both my debtor and my thrall,
And have his tribulation besides
Upon his flesh, while that I am his wife.
I have the power during all my life
Over his own body, and not he:
Right thus the Apostle told it unto me,
And bade our husbands for to love us well.
And that makes me happy, as you may tell."
Up started the Pardoner, and that anon:
"Now dame," said he, "by God and by Saint John,
You be a noble preacher in this case!
I was about to wed a wife. Alas,
Why should I pay for it with my flesh so dear?
Now would I prefer to wed no wife this year!"

   "Abide!" said she, "my tale is not begun.
Nay, you shall drink of another barrel
Before I go, which shall taste worse than ale.
And when that I have told you forth my tale
Of tribulation in marriage,
Of which I've been expert all my years—
This is to say, I myself have been the whip—
Then you choose whether or not to sip
Of that same cask I will broach.
Be wary of it, before you too near approach,
For I shall tell examples more than ten.
'He who won't be warned by other men,
By him shall other men corrected be.'
The same words wrote Ptolemy:
Read in his Almagest,[5] and take it there."

   "Dame, I would pray you, if you will it be,"
Said this Pardoner, "as you began,
Tell forth your tale, hold back for no man,
And teach us young men of your practice."

   "Gladly," said she, "since it may you please.
But yet I pray to all this company,
If I speak according to my fantasy,
Take it not badly what I say;

For myn entente nis but for to pleye.
    Now sires, now wol I telle forth my tale.—
As ever mote I drinken wyn or ale,
I shal seye sooth, tho housbondes that I hadde,
As three of hem were gode and two were badde.
The three men were gode, and riche, and olde;
Unnethe mighte they the statut holde
In which that they were bounden un-to me.
Ye woot wel what I mene of this, pardee!
As help me god, I laughe whan I thinke
How pitously a-night I made hem swinke;
And by my fey, I tolde of it no stoor.
They had me yeven hir gold and hir tresoor;
Me neded nat do lenger diligence
To winne hir love, or doon hem reverence.
They loved me so wel, by god above,
That I ne tolde no deyntee of hir love!
A wys womman wol sette hir ever in oon
To gete hir love, ther as she hath noon.
But sith I hadde hem hoolly in myn hond,
And sith they hadde me yeven all hir lond,
What sholde I taken hede hem for to plese,
But it were for my profit and myn ese?
I sette hem so a-werke, by my fey,
That many a night they songen 'weilawey!'
The bacoun was nat fet for hem, I trowe,
That som men han in Essex at Dunmowe.
I governed hem so wel, after my lawe,
That ech of hem ful blisful was and fawe
To bringe me gaye thinges fro the fayre.
They were ful glad whan I spak to hem fayre;
For god it woot, I chidde hem spitously.
    Now herkneth, how I bar me proprely,
Ye wyse wyves, that can understonde.
      Thus shul ye speke and bere hem wrong on honde;
For half so boldely can ther no man
Swere and lyen as a womman can.
I sey nat this by wyves that ben wyse,
But-if it be whan they hem misavyse.

For my intent is not but to play.
   Now sires, now will I tell forth my tale.
As ever might I drink wine or ale,
I shall say the truth of those husbands that I had,
As three of them were good and two were bad.
The three men were good, and rich, and old;
Just barely could they the statute uphold
By which they were bound to me.
You know well what I mean by this, by God!
So help me, I laugh when I think
How pitiably at night I made them work;
And by my faith, I set by it no store.
They had given me their land and their treasure;
I needed not to work at it any longer
To win their love, or do them honor.
They loved me so well, by God above,
That I took for granted all their love!
A prudent woman will busy herself every moment
To get herself beloved, where she has none.
But since I had them wholly in my hand,
And since they had given me all their land,
Why should I take care for them to please,
Unless it were for my profit and my ease?
I set them so to working, by my faith,
That many a night they sang 'wellaway!'
That reward in Essex,[6] I promise,
Went not to them for married bliss.
I governed them so well after my law
That each of them full happy was and eager
To bring me gay things from the fair.
They were full glad when I spoke to them nicely,
For God knows, I chided them with spite.
   Now listen how I handled myself:
You prudent wives, who can understand,
   Thus shall you speak and put them in the wrong,
For half so boldly can any man
Swear and lie as a woman can.
I say this not about wives who be careful,
Unless they do something not so wary.

A wys wyf, if that she can hir good,
Shal beren him on hond the cow is wood,
And take witnesse of hir owene mayde
Of hir assent; but herkneth how I sayde.
    'Sir olde kaynard, is this thyn array?
Why is my neighebores wyf so gay?
She is honoured over-al ther she goth;
I sitte at hoom, I have no thrifty cloth.
What dostow at my neighebores hous?
Is she so fair? artow so amorous?
What rowne ye with our mayde? *ben'cite!*
Sir olde lechour, lat thy japes be!
And if I have a gossib or a freend,
With-outen gilt, thou chydest as a fiend,
If that I walke or pleye un-to his hous!
Thou comest hoom as dronken as a mous,
And prechest on thy bench, with yvel preef!
Thou seist to me, it is a greet meschief
To wedde a povre womman, for costage;
And if that she be riche, of heigh parage,
Than seistow that it is a tormentrye
To suffre hir pryde and hir malencolye.
And if that she be fair, thou verray knave,
Thou seyst that every holour wol hir have;
She may no whyle in chastitee abyde,
That is assailled up-on ech a syde.
    Thou seyst, som folk desyre us for richesse,
Som for our shap, and som for our fairnesse;
And som, for she can outher singe or daunce,
And som, for gentillesse and daliaunce;
Som, for hir handes and hir armes smale;
Thus goth al to the devel by thy tale.
Thou seyst, men may nat kepe a castel-wal;
It may so longe assailled been over-al.
    And if that she be foul, thou seist that she
Coveiteth every man that she may see;
For as a spaynel she wol on him lepe,
Til that she finde som man hir to chepe;
Ne noon so grey goos goth ther in the lake,

A wise wife, if she knows her own good,
Shall assure him the talking bird is crazy,[7]
And take as witness her own maid
With her consent. But listen how I said:
　　'Sir old dotard, is this your idea of raiment?
Why is my neighbor's wife dressed so gaily?
She is honored wherever she goes:
I sit at home, I have no good clothes.
What do you at my neighbor's house?
Is she so fair? Are you so amorous?
What whisper you with our maid? *benedicite!*
Sir old lecher, let your pranks be!
And if I have a male confidant or a friend,
Not a paramour, you scold like a fiend,
If that I walk or play unto his house!
You come home drunk as a mouse,
And preach from your bench, bad luck to you!
You say to me, it is a great mischief
To wed a poor woman, due to expense.
And if that she be rich, of high parentage,
Then you say that it is a torment
To suffer her pride and temperament.
And if that she be fair, you, true knave,
You say that every lecher will her have:
She may no while in chastity abide
Who is assailed on every side.

　　You say some folk desire us for our money,
Some for our shape, and some for our beauty,
And some because she can either sing or dance,
And some for good breeding and coquetry,
Some for her hands and her arms slender;
Thus go all to the devil, by your account.
You say men may not defend a castle wall,
If it may be everywhere assailed.

　　And if that she be ugly, you say that she
Covets every man that she may see;
For as a spaniel she would on him leap,
Till that she find some man with her to sleep.
There swims no goose so gray in the lake

As, seistow, that wol been with-oute make.
And seyst, it is an hard thing for to welde
A thing that no man wol, his thankes, helde.
Thus seistow, lorel, whan thow goost to bedde;
And that no wys man nedeth for to wedde,
Ne no man that entendeth un-to hevene.
With wilde thonder-dint and firy levene
Mote thy welked nekke be to-broke!

Thow seyst that dropping houses, and eek smoke,
And chyding wyves, maken men to flee
Out of hir owene hous; a! *ben'cite!*
What eyleth swich an old man for to chyde?
Thow seyst, we wyves wol our vyces hyde
Til we be fast, and than we wol hem shewn;
Wel may that be a proverbe of a shrewe!
Thou seist, that oxen, asses, hors, and houndes,
They been assayed at diverse stoundes;
Bacins, lavours, er that men hem bye,
Spones and stoles, and al swich housbondrye,
And so been pottes, clothes, and array;
But folk of wyves maken noon assay
Til they be wedded; olde dotard shrewe!
And than, seistow, we wol oure vices shewe.

Thou seist also, that it displeseth me
But-if that thou wolt preyse my beautee,
And but thou poure alwey up-on my face,
And clepe me "faire dame" in every place;
And but thou make a feste on thilke day
That I was born, and make me fresh and gay,
And but thou do to my norice honour,
And to my chamberere with-inne my bour,
And to my fadres folk and his allyes;—
Thus seistow, olde barel ful of lyes!

And yet of our apprentice Janekyn,
For his crisp heer, shyninge as gold so fyn,
And for he squiereth me bothe up and doun,
Yet hastow caught a fals suspecioun;
I wol hym noght, thogh thou were deed to-morwe.

As, you say, that would be without a mate.
And you say, it is a hard thing to control
A thing that no man willingly will hold.
Thus say you, wretch, when you go to bed,
And that no wise man needs for to wed,
Nor any man who intends heaven to enter.
With wild thunderclap and fiery lightning
May your withered neck be broken!
    You say that leaking houses and smoke
And chiding wives make men flee
Out of their own house; ah, *benedicite!*
What ails such an old man for to chide?
You say we wives will our vices hide
Till we be married, and then we will them reveal—
Well may that be a proverb fit for a villain!
You say that oxen, asses, horses, and hounds,
They be tested at various times;
Basins, washbowls, before men them buy,
Spoons and stools, and all such household goods,
And so be pots, clothes and the rest;
But folk of wives make no test
Till they be wedded. Old nasty wretch!
And then, you say, we will our vices show.
    You say also that it displeases me
Unless you will praise my beauty,
And look with longing upon my face,
And call me "fair dame" in every place;
And unless you make a feast on that same day
That I was born, and make me fresh and gay,
And unless you do to my nurse honor,
And to my chambermaid within my bedchamber,
And to my father's folk and his cousins—
Thus say you, old barrel full of lies!
    And yet of our apprentice Jankin,
For his curly hair, shining as gold so fine,
And because he squires me both up and down,
Yet you have caught a false suspicion.
I want him not, though you were dead tomorrow.

But tel me this, why hydestow,
   with sorwe,
The keyes of thy cheste awey fro me?
It is my good as wel as thyn, pardee.
What wenestow make an idiot of our dame?
Now by that lord, that called is seint Jame,
Thou shalt nat bothe, thogh that thou were wood,
Be maister of my body and of my good;
That oon thou shalt forgo, maugree thyne yën;
What nedeth thee of me to enquere or spyën?
I trowe, thou woldest loke me in thy cheste!
Thou sholdest seye, "wyf, go wher thee leste,
Tak your disport, I wol nat leve no talis;
I knowe yow for a trewe wyf, dame Alis."
We love no man that taketh kepe or charge
Wher that we goon, we wol ben at our large.

   Of alle men y-blessed moot he be,
The wyse astrologien Dan Ptholome,
That seith this proverbe in his Almageste,
"Of alle men his wisdom is the hyeste,
That rekketh never who hath the world in honde."
By this proverbe thou shalt understonde,
Have thou y-nogh, what thar thee recche or care
How merily that othere folkes fare?
For certeyn, olde dotard, by your leve,
Ye shul have queynte right y-nough at eve.
He is to greet a nigard that wol werne
A man to lighte his candle at his lanterne;
He shal have never the lasse light, pardee;
Have thou y-nough, thee thar nat pleyne thee.

   Thou seyst also, that if we make us gay
With clothing and with precious array,
That it is peril of our chastitee;
And yet, with sorwe, thou most enforce thee,
And seye thise wordes in the apostles name,
"In habit, maad with chastitee and same,
Ye wommen shul apparaille yow," quod he,
"And noght in tressed heer and gay perree,
As perles, ne with gold, ne clothes riche;"

But tell me this, why do you hide—and you'll be
  sorry—
The keys of your treasure chest away from me?
It is my property as well as yours, by God.
Why, what do you mean making an idiot of our dame?
Now by that lord who is called Saint James,
You shall not both, though you were mad with rage,
Be master of all my goods and my body;
One of them shall you forfeit, no matter what you try.
What does it help you on me to inquire or spy?
I believe, you would lock me in your chest!
You should say, "Wife, go where you please;
Have your fun, I will not any tales believe.
I know you for a true wife, Dame Alice."
We love no man who keeps track or cares
Where that we go, when we tend to our affairs.

    Of all men blessed may he be,
The wise astrologer Lord Ptolemy,
Who says this proverb in his Almagest:
"Of all men his wisdom is the highest,
Who never cares who has this world in his hand."
By this proverb you shall understand,
If you have enough, why should you count or care
How merrily that other folks fare?
For certain, old dotard, by your leave,
You shall have quite enough at eve.
He is too great a niggard who would refuse
A man to light a candle at his lantern;
He shall not miss the light, by God.
If you have enough, you should not complain.

    You say also that if we make us gay
With clothing and jewelry,
That is risky for our chastity;
And further—may you regret it—you insist,
And say these words in the Apostle's name:[8]
"In clothing made with chastity and shame,
You women should yourselves attire," said he,
"And not in braided hair and jewelry,
Nor pearls, nor gold, nor garments fancy."

After thy text, ne after thy rubriche
I wol nat wirche as muchel as a gnat.
Thou seydest this, that I was lyk a cat;
For who-so wolde senge a cattes skin,
Thanne wolde the cat wel dwellen in his in;
And if the cattes skin be slyk and gay,
She wol nat dwelle in house half a day,
But forth she wole, er any day be dawed,
To shewe hir skin, and goon a-caterwawed;
This is to seye, if I be gay, sir shrewe,
I wol renne out, my borel for to shewe.

    Sire olde fool, what eyleth thee to spyën?
Thogh thou preye Argus, with his hundred yën,
To be my warde-cors, as he can best,
In feith, he shal nat kepe me but me lest;
Yet coude I make his berd, so moot I thee.

    Thou seydest eek, that ther ben thinges three,
The whiche thinges troublen al this erthe,
And that no wight ne may endure the ferthe;
O leve sir shrewe, Jesu shorte thy lyf!
Yet prechestow, and seyst, an hateful wyf
Y-rekened is for oon of thise meschances.
Been ther none othere maner resemblances
That ye may lykne your parables to,
But-if a sely wyf be oon of tho?

    Thou lykenest wommanes love to helle,
To bareyne lond, ther water may not dwelle.
Thou lyknest it also to wilde fyr;
The more it brenneth, the more it hath desyr
To consume every thing that brent wol be.
Thou seyst, that right as wormes shende a tree,
Right so a wyf destroyeth hir housbonde;
This knowe they that been to wyves bonde.'

    Lordinges, right thus, as ye have understonde,
Bar I stifly myne olde housbondes on honde,
That thus they seyden in hir dronkenesse;
And al was fals, but that I took witnesse
On Janekin and on my nece also.
O lord, the peyne I dide hem and the wo,

Neither by your text, nor your reading of it,
Will I live as much as would a gnat.
You said this, that I was like a cat:
For whoso would singe a cat's fur,
Then would the cat well dwell in his home;
And if the cat's fur be sleek and gay,
She will not dwell at home half a day,
But go forth she will, before day has dawned,
To show her fur and go caterwauling.
This is to say, if I be pretty, sir welladay,
I will go out, my wardrobe for to display.

    Sir old fool, how does it help you to spy?
Though you beg Argus,[9] with his hundred eyes,
To be my minder, as best he knows,
In faith, he shall follow only as I allow;
I could give him the slip, so may I thrive.

    You say also that there be things three,
Which trouble all this earth,
And that no person may endure the fourth.
Oh dear sir welladay, may Jesus shorten your life!
You're still preaching that a hateful wife
Is the cause of one of these mischances.
Be there no other resemblances
That you may liken to your parables,
Unless an innocent wife be one of those?

    You liken also woman's love to hell,
To barren land, where water may not dwell;
You liken it also to wild fire:
The more it burns, the more it has desire
To consume every thing that burned can be.
You say that just as worms damage a tree,
Right so a wife destroys her husband;
This know they who to wives be bound.'

    Lordings, right thus, as you have understood,
I led my old husbands so firmly by their snoots
That thus they said in their drunkenness;
And all was false, and yet I took witness
From Jankin and my niece also.
Oh Lord, the suffering I caused them and the woe,

Ful giltelees, by goddes swete pyne!
For as an hors I coude byte and whyne.
I coude pleyne, thogh I were in the gilt,
Or elles often tyme hadde I ben spilt.
Who-so that first to mille comth, first grint;
I pleyned first, so was our werre y-stint.
They were ful glad t'excusen hem ful blyve
Of thing of which they never agilte hir lyve.

Of wenches wolde I beren him on honde,
Whan that for syk unnethes mighte he stonde.
Yet tikled it his herte, for that he
Wende that I hadde of him so greet chiertee.
I swoor that al my walkinge out by nighte
Was for t'espye wenches that he dighte;
Under that colour hadde I many a mirthe.
For al swich wit is yeven us in our birthe;
Deceite, weping, spinning god hath yive
To wommen kindely, whyl they may live.
And thus of o thing I avaunte me,
Atte ende I hadde the bettre in ech degree,
By sleighte, or force, or by som maner thing,
As by continuel murmur or grucching;
Namely a-bedde hadden they meschaunce,
Ther wolde I chyde and do hem no plesaunce;
I wolde no lenger in the bed abyde,
If that I felte his arm over my syde,
Til he had maad his raunson un-to me;
Than wolde I suffre him do his nycetee.
And ther-fore every man this tale I telle,
Winne who-so may, for al is for to selle.
With empty hand men may none haukes lure;
For winning wolde I al his lust endure,
And make me a feyned appetyt;
And yet in bacon hadde I never delyt;
That made me that ever I wolde hem chyde.
For thogh the pope had seten hem bisyde,
I wolde nat spare hem at hir owene bord.
For by my trouthe, I quitte hem word for word.
As help me verray god omnipotent,

Full guiltless, by God's sweet suffering!
For like a horse could I bite and whinny.
I would complain, though I was guilty,
Otherwise oftentimes would I have been ruined.
Whoso to the mill first comes, first grinds.
I complained first, so was our strife concluded.
They were full glad to excuse full quickly themselves
Of things which they were never guilty of.

    Of wenches would I accuse them on every hand,
When that for illness they could scarcely stand.
Yet warmed I his heart, for all he
Thought I had for him this great charity.
I swore that all my walking out by night
Was to espy wenches that he might lay by.
Under that pretense had I many a mirth,
For all such cleverness is given us in our birth.
Deceit, weeping, spinning God has given
To women by nature while they may live.
And thus of one thing I boast:
In the end I got the better of them in every way,
By trickery, or force, or some other thing,
As by continual murmur or grouching.
Especially in bed had they misfortune:
There would I scold and give them no pleasure;
I would no longer in the bed abide,
If that I felt his arm over my side,
Till he had paid his ransom unto me;
Then would I suffer him to do his little folly.
And therefore to every man this tale I tell,
Profit whoso may, for all is for sale.
With empty hand men may no hawks lure.
For gain would I all his lust endure,
And make me a feigned appetite—
And yet in old meat never had I delight.
That is why that ever I would them chide.
For though the Pope had them sat beside,
I would not spare them at their own table.
For by my troth, I requited them word for word.
So help me true God omnipotent,

Thogh I right now sholde make my testament,
I ne owe hem nat a word that it nis quit.
I broghte it so aboute by my wit,
That they moste yeve it up, as for the beste;
Or elles we never been in reste.
For thogh he loked as a wood leoun,
Yet sholde he faille of his conclusioun.
　　Thanne wolde I seye, 'gode lief, tak keep
How mekely loketh Wilkin oure sheep;
Com neer, my spouse, let me ba thy cheke!
Ye sholde been al pacient and meke,
And han a swete spyced conscience,
Sith ye so preche of Jobes pacience.
Suffreth alwey, sin ye so wel can preche;
And but ye do, certein we shal yow teche
That it is fair to have a wyf in pees.
Oon of us two moste bowen, doutelees;
And sith a man is more resonable
Than womman is, ye moste been suffrable.
What eyleth yow to grucche thus and grone?
Is it for ye wolde have my queynte allone?
Why taak it al, lo, have it every-deel;
Peter! I shrewe yow but ye love it weel!
For if I wolde selle my *bele chose*,
I coude walke as fresh as is a rose;
But I wol kepe it for your owene tooth.
Ye be to blame, by god, I sey yow sooth.'
　　Swiche maner wordes hadde we on honde.
Now wol I speken of my fourthe housbonde.
　　My fourthe housbonde was a revelour,
This is to seyn, he hadde a paramour;
And I was yong and ful of ragerye,
Stiborn and strong, and joly as a pye.
Wel coude I daunce to an harpe smale,
And singe, y-wis, as any nightingale,
Whan I hade dronke a draughte of swete wyn.
Metellius, the foule cherl, the swyn,
That with a staf birafte his wyf hir lyf,
For she drank wyn, thogh I hadde been his wyf,

Though I right now should make my will and testament,
I left no word unreturned.
I brought it so about, by my cleverness,
That they must give it up, as for the best,
Or else had we never been in rest.
For though he looked like a lion maddened,
Yet should he fail in the end.
        Then would I say, 'Sweetheart, take heed
How meekly looks Wilkin our sheep!
Come near, my spouse, let me kiss your cheek!
You should be all patient and meek,
And have a disposition seasoned sweetly,
Since you so speak of Job's patience.
Endure always, since you so well can preach;
And unless you do, for certain we shall you teach
That it is nice to have a wife in peace.
One of us two must give in, doubtless,
And since a man is more reasonable
Than woman is, you must be patient.
What ails you to grouch and groan?
Is it that you would have my quack alone?
Why take it all! Lo, have it every bit!
By Saint Peter! I curse you but you love it well!
For if I would sell my *belle chose*,
I could walk as fresh as is a rose;
But I will keep it for your own appetite.
You be to blame, by God, I tell you the truth.'
        Like that back and forth we bandied.
Now will I speak of my fourth husband.
        My fourth husband was a reveler—
That is to say, he had a paramour—
And I was young and full of appetite,
Stubborn and strong, and jolly as a magpie.
Well could I dance to a harp small,
And sing, truly, as any nightingale,
When I had drunk a draught of sweet wine.
Metellius, the foul churl, the swine,
Who with a staff bereft his wife of her life
For she drank wine, though if I had been his wife,

He sholde nat han daunted me fro drinke;
And, after wyn, on Venus moste I thinke:
For al so siker as cold engendreth hayl,
A likerous mouth moste han a likerous tayl.
In womman vinolent is no defence,
This knowen lechours by experience.

But, lord Crist! whan that it remembreth me
Up-on my yowthe, and on my jolitee,
It tikleth me aboute myn herte rote.
Unto this day it dooth myn herte bote
That I have had my world as in my tyme.
But age, allas! that al wol envenyme,
Hath me biraft my beautee and my pith;
Lat go, fare-wel, the devel go therwith!
The flour is goon, ther is na-more to telle,
The bren, as I best can, now moste I selle;
But yet to be right mery wol I fonde.
Now wol I tellen of my fourthe housbonde.

I seye, I hadde in herte greet despyt
That he of any other had delyt.
But he was quit, by god and by seint Joce!
I made him of the same wode a croce;
Nat of my body in no foul manere,
But certeinly, I made folk swich chere,
That in his owene grece I made him frye
For angre, and for verray jalousye.
By god, in erthe I was his purgatorie,
For which I hope his soule be in glorie
For god it woot, he sat ful ofte and song
Whan that his shoo ful bitterly him wrong.
Ther was no wight, save god and he, that wiste,
In many wyse, how sore I him twiste.
He deyde whan I cam fro Jerusalem,
And lyth y-grave under the rode-beem,
Al is his tombe noght so curious
As was the sepulcre of him, Darius,
Which that Appelles wroghte subtilly;
It nis but wast to burie him preciously.
Lat him fare-wel, god yeve his soule reste,

He should not have frightened me from drink!
And after wine on Venus must I think,
For all so surely as cold engenders hail,
A thirsty mouth must have a thirsty tail.
In women full of wine there's no defence—
This know lechers by experience.

But, Lord Christ! When I think
Upon my youth, and on my gaiety,
It tickles me about my heart's root.
Unto this day it does my heart good
That in my time I have had my world.
But age, alas! that all will poison,
Has me bereft my beauty and my vigor.
Let it go, farewell! The devil with it go!
The flower is gone, there is no more to tell:
The husk, as best I can, now must I sell;
But yet to be right merry will I try.
Now will I tell of my fourth husband.

I say, I had in heart great spite
That he of any other had delight.
But he was repaid, by God and Saint Joce!
I made him of the same wood a cross—
Not of my body in an unclean manner,
But certainly, to other men I was so nice
That in his own grease I made him fry
For anger and for pure jealousy.
By God, on earth I was his purgatory,
For which I hope his soul be in glory.
For God it knows, he sat full often and sang
When that his shoe full bitterly fitted him wrong.
There was no person, save God and he, who knew
How many ways I sorely him tormented.
He died when I returned from Jerusalem,
And lies buried inside a chapel,
Although his tomb was not so ornamented
As was the sepulchre of old Darius,[10]
Which that Appelles skillfully wrought;
It would have been a waste to bury him at high cost.
May he fare well, God rest his soul!

He is now in the grave and in his cheste.
    Now of my fifthe housbond wol I telle.
God lete his soule never come in helle!
And yet was he to me the moste shrewe;
That fele I on my ribbes al by rewe,
And ever shal, un-to myn ending-day
But in our bed he was so fresh and gay,
And ther-with-al so wel coude he me glose,
Whan that he wolde han my *bele chose*,
That thogh he hadde me bet on every boon,
He coude winne agayn my love anoon.
I trowe I loved him beste, for that he
Was of his love daungerous to me.
We wommen han, if that I shal nat lye,
In this matere a queynte fantasye;
Wayte what thing we may nat lightly have,
Ther-after wol we crye al-day and crave.
Forbede us thing, and that desyren we;
Prees on us faste, and thanne wol we flee.
With daunger oute we al our chaffare;
Greet prees at market maketh dere ware,
And to greet cheep is holde at litel prys;
This knoweth every womman that is wys.
    My fifthe housbonde, god his soule blesse!
Which that I took for love and no richesse,
He som-tyme was a clerk of Oxenford,
And had left scole, and wente at hoom to bord
With my gossib, dwellinge in oure toun,
God have hir soule! hir name was Alisoun.
She knew myn herte and eek my privetee
Bet than our parisshe-preest, so moot I thee!
To hir biwreyed I my conseil al.
For had myn housbonde pissed on a wal,
Or doon a thing that sholde han cost his lyf,
To hir, and to another worthy wyf,
And to my nece, which that I loved weel,
I wolde han told his conseil every-deel.
And so I dide ful often, god it woot,
That made his face ful often reed and hoot

He is now in the grave and in his box.
   Now of my fifth husband will I tell—
God let his soul never come in hell!
And yet he was to me the worst rascal.
Soreness on my ribs I still feel from a scuffle,
And ever shall unto my dying day.
But in our bed he was so fresh and gay,
And therewithal so well could he me persuade
When he would have my *belle chose*,
That though he would have beaten me on every bone,
He could win again my love anon.
I believe I loved him best for that he
Was of his love grudging to me.
We women have, if that I shall not lie,
In this matter an odd fantasy:
Whatever thing we may not lightly have,
Thereafter we will cry all day and crave.
Forbid us something, and that desire we;
Pursue us hard, and then we will flee.
For the haughty we set out all our wares:
Great crowd at market makes things dear,
And for too good a bargain we little care.
This knows every woman who is wise.
   My fifth husband, God his soul bless!
Who that I took for love and no riches,
He was once a scholar at Oxford,
And had left school, and went home to board
With my close friend, dwelling in our town—
God save her soul, her name was Alison.
She knew my heart and also my secrets
Better than our parish priest,[11] so may I flourish!
To her revealed I my feelings all,
For had my husband pissed on a wall,
Or done a thing that should have cost his life,
To her and to another worthy wife,
And to my niece, whom I loved well,
I would tell his secrets in detail.
And so I did often, God well knows,
That made his face full often red and hot

For verray shame, and blamed him-self for he
Had told to me so greet a privetee.
    And so bifel that ones, in a Lente,
(So often tymes I to my gossib wente,
For ever yet I lovede to be gay,
And for to walke, in March, Averille, and May,
Fro hous to hous, to here sondry talis),
That Jankin clerk, and my gossib dame Alis,
And I my-self, in-to the feldes wente.
Myn housbond was at London al that Lente;
I hadde the bettre leyser for to pleye,
And for to see, and eek for to be seye
Of lusty folk; what wiste I wher my grace
Was shapen for to be, or in what place?
Therefore I made my visitaciouns,
To vigilies and to processiouns,
To preching eek and to thise pilgrimages,
To pleyes of miracles and mariages,
And wered upon my gaye scarlet gytes.
Thise wormes, ne thise motthes, ne thise mytes,
Upon my peril, frete hem never a deel;
And wostow why? for they were used weel.
    Now wol I tellen forth what happed me.
I seye, that in the feeldes walked we,
Til trewely we hadde swich daliance,
This clerk and I, that of my purveyance
I spak to him, and seyde him, how that he,
If I were widwe, sholde wedde me.
For certeinly, I sey for no bobance,
Yet was I never with-outen purveyance
Of mariage, n'of othere thinges eek.
I holde a mouses herte nat worth a leek,
That hath but oon hole for to sterte to,
And if that faille, thanne is al y-do.
    I bar him on honde, he hadde enchanted me;
My dame taughte me that soutiltee.
And eek I seyde, I mette of him al night;
He wolde han slayn me as I lay up-right,
And al my bed was ful of verray blood,

For pure shame, and blamed himself because he
Had told me so great a secrecy.
    And so it befell that once during Lent—
So oftentimes that to my friend I went,
For ever yet I loved to be gay,
And for to walk in March, April and May,
From house to house, to hear sundry tales—
That Jankin the scholar and my friend Alis
And I myself into the fields went.
My husband was at London all that Lent:
I had the better chance to play,
And for to see, and also to be seen
By lusty folk. What knew I where grace
Was meant for me, or in what place?
Therefore I made my visitations,
To feast day services and processions,
To preaching and to these pilgrimages,
To plays of miracles, and marriages,
And wore my gay scarlet gowns.
Those worms, nor moths, nor mites,
Upon my soul's peril, ate them not at all;
And you know why? For they were used well.
    Now will I tell forth what happened to me.
I say that in the fields walked we,
Till truly we were getting on so well,
This scholar and I, that in my foresight
I spoke to him and how that he,
If I were widowed, should wed me.
For certainly, I say for no boast,
Yet I was never without future provision
Of marriage, not to mention other things.
I hold a mouse's heart not worth a leek
That has but one hole for to run,
And if that fails, all is done.
    I had him believe he had enchanted me—
My mother taught me that subtlety—
And also I said I dreamed of him all night:
That he would me slay as on my back I lay,
And all my bed was full of wet blood;

But yet I hope that he shal do me good;
For blood bitokeneth gold, as me was taught.
And al was fals, I dremed of it right naught,
But as I folwed ay my dames lore,
As wel of this as of other thinges more.

But now sir, lat me see, what I shal seyn?
A! ha! by god, I have my tale ageyn.

Whan that my fourthe housbond was on bere,
I weep algate, and made sory chere,
As wyves moten, for it is usage,
And with my coverchief covered my visage;
But for that I was purveyed of a make,
I weep but smal, and that I undertake.

To chirche was myn housbond born a-morwe
With neighebores, that for him maden sorwe;
And Jankin oure clerk was oon of tho.
As help me god, whan that I saugh him go
After the bere, me thoughte he hadde a paire
Of legges and of feet so clene and faire,
That al myn herte I yaf un-to his hold.
He was, I trowe, a twenty winter old,
And I was fourty, if I shal seye sooth;
But yet I hadde alwey a coltes tooth.
Gat-tothed I was, and that bicam me weel;
I hadde the prente of sëynt Venus seel.
As help me god, I was a lusty oon,
And faire and riche, and yong, and wel bigoon;
And trewely, as myne housbondes tolde me,
I had the beste *quoniam* mighte be.
For certes, I am al Venerien
In felinge, and myn herte is Marcien.
Venus me yaf my lust, my likerousnesse,
And Mars yaf me my sturdy hardinesse
Myn ascendent was Taur, and Mars ther-inne.
Allas! allas! that ever love was sinne!
I folwed ay myn inclinacioun
By vertu of my constellacioun;
That made me I coude noght withdrawe
My chambre of Venus from a good felawe.

But yet I hoped that he should do me good,
For blood betokens gold, as I was taught.
And all was false—I dreamed of it right not,
But as I followed always my dame's lore
As well with this as other things more.

But now, sire, let me see, what was I saying?
Aha! By God, I have my tale again.

When that my fourth husband was on his bier,
I wept of course, and wore a sorry expression
As wives must, for it is the custom,
And with my kerchief covered my face;
But because I was provided with a mate,
I wept but little, and that I declare.

To church was my husband borne in the morning
With neighbors, who for him made sorrow;
And Jankin our scholar was one of those.
So help me God! When I saw him walk
After the bier, me thought he had a pair
Of legs and of feet so neat and fair,
That all my heart I gave to his hold.
He was, I believe, twenty winters old,
And I was forty, if I shall say right;
But yet I had always a colt's appetite.
Gap-toothed I was, and that became me well;
I had the birthmark of Saint Venus' seal.[12]
So help me God, I was a lusty one,
And fair, and rich, and young;
And truly, as my husbands told me,
I had the best *pudendum*[13] that might be.
For certainly, I am all Venerian
In feeling, and my heart is Martian:
Venus gave me my lust, my lecherousness,
And Mars gave me my sturdy boldness;
My ascendant was Taurus, and Mars therein.[14]
Alas! Alas! that ever love was sin!
I followed always my inclination
By virtue of my constellation;
So that I could not withhold
My chamber of Venus from a good fellow.

Yet have I Martes mark up-on my face,
And also in another privee place.
For, god so wis be my savacioun,
I ne loved never by no discrecioun,
But ever folwede myn appetyt,
Al were he short or long, or blak or whyt:
I took no kepe, so that he lyked me,
How pore he was, ne eek of what degree.
    What sholde I seye, but, at the monthes ende,
This joly clerk Jankin, that was so hende,
Hath wedded me with greet solempnitee,
And to him yaf I al the lond and fee
That ever was me yeven ther-bifore;
But afterward repented me ful sore.
He nolde suffre nothing of my list.
By god, he smoot me ones on the list,
For that I rente out of his book a leef,
That of the strook myn ere wex al deef.
Stiborn I was as is a leonesse,
And of my tonge a verray jangleresse,
And walke I wolde, as I had doon biforn,
From hous to hous, al-though he had it sworn.
For which he often tymes wolde preche,
And me of olde Romayn gestes teche,
How he, Simplicius Gallus, lefte his wyf,
And hir forsook for terme of al his lyf,
Noght but for open-heeded he hir say
Lokinge out at his dore upon a day.
    Another Romayn tolde he me by name,
That, for his wyf was at a someres game
With-oute his witing, he forsook hir eke.
And than wolde he up-on his Bible seke
That ilke proverbe of Ecclesiaste,
Wher he comandeth and forbedeth faste,
Man shal nat suffre his wyf go roule aboute;
Than wolde he seye right thus, withouten doute,
    'Who-so that buildeth his hous al of salwes,
    And priketh his blinde hors over the falwes,
    And suffreth his wyf to go seken halwes,

Yet I have Mars' mark upon my face,
And also in another private place.
For, God so wise be my salvation,
I never loved with any wisdom,
But ever followed my appetite:
Whether he were short or long or black or white,
I didn't care, so long as he pleased me,
How poor he was, nor of what level in society.
      What should I say but, at the month's end,
This jolly scholar Jankin, who was so nice,
Had wedded me with great solemnity,
And to him gave I all the land and property
That ever was given me therebefore.
But afterward I regretted it full sore;
He wouldn't give me anything I pleased.
By God, he hit me once on the ear
Because I tore from his book a leaf,
And from that stroke my ear went deaf.
Stubborn I was as is a lioness,
And with my tongue a true wasp,
And walked I would, as I had before done,
From house to house, although he had it forbidden.
For which he oftentimes would preach,
And me of old Roman stories teach,
How Simplicius Gallus[15] left his wife,
And her forsook the rest of his life,
Only because he her bareheaded saw
Looking out their door upon a day.
      Another Roman told he me by name,
Who, because his wife was at a summer's revel
Without his knowing, he too her forsook.
And then would he in his Bible seek
That same proverb of Ecclesiasticus
Where he commands and sternly forbids
Man should not allow his wife to roam about:
Then would he say right thus, without doubt:
      'Whoso builds his house of willow twigs,
      And spurs his blind horse over ploughed furrows,
      And his wife to go seek shrines allows,

Is worthy to been hanged on the galwes!'
But al for noght, I sette noght an hawe
Of his proverbes n'of his olde sawe,
Ne I wolde nat of him corrected be.
I hate him that my vices telleth me,
And so do mo, god woot! of us than I.
This made him with me wood al outrely;
I nolde noght forbere him in no cas.
      Now wol I seye yow sooth, by seint Thomas,
Why that I rente out of his book a leef,
For which he smoot me so that I was deef.
He hadde a book that gladly, night and day,
For his desport he wolde rede alway.
He cleped it Valerie and Theofraste,
At whiche book he lough alwey ful faste.
And eek ther was som-tyme a clerk at Rome,
A cardinal, that highte Seint Jerome,
That made a book agayn Jovinian;
In whiche book eek ther was Tertulan,
Crisippus, Trotula, and Helowys,
That was abbesse nat fer fron Parys;
And eek the Parables of Salomon,
Ovydes Art, and bokes many on,
And alle thise wer bounden in o volume.
And every night and day was his custume,
Whan he had leyser and vacacioun
From other worldly occupacioun,
To reden on this book of wikked wyves.
He knew of hem mo legendes and lyves
Than been of gode wyves in the Bible.
For trusteth wel, it is an impossible
That any clerk wol speke good of wyves,
But-if it be of holy seintes lyves,
Ne of noon other womman never the mo.
Who peyntede the leoun, tel me who?
By god, if wommen hadde writen stories,
As clerkes han with-inne hir oratories,
They wolde han writen of men more wikkednesse
Than al the mark of Adam may redresse.

Is worthy to be hanged on the gallows!'
But all for nought, I give not a hawthorne berry
For his proverbs nor for his old saw,
Nor would I by him corrected be.
I hate him who my vices describes to me,
And so do more of us, God knows, than I.
This made him with me angry completely:
I would not go along with him in any case.
    Now will I tell you the truth, by Saint Thomas,
Why I tore out of his book a leaf,
For which he smacked me so that I was deaf.
He had a book that gladly, night and day,
For his disport he would read always.
He called it Valerie and Theofraste,[16]
At which book he would laugh and laugh.
And also there was once a scholar at Rome,
A cardinal, who was called Saint Jerome,
Who made a book against Jovinian;
In which book there was Tertullian,
Chrysippus, Trotula,[17] and Heloise,
Who was the abbess not far from Paris;
And also the Proverbs of Solomon,
Ovid's Art of Love, and books many a one,
And all these were bound in one volume.
And every night and day was his custom,
When he had leisure and free time
From other worldly occupation,
To read in this book of wicked wives.
He knew of them more legends and lives
Than there are of good wives in the Bible.
For trust well, it is an impossibility
That any scholar will speak good of wives,
But unless it be of holy saints' lives,
Nothing of any other woman ever.
Who painted the lion,[18] tell me, who?
By God, if women had written stories,
As scholars have within their oratories,
They would have written of men more wickedness
Than all the sex of Adam may redress.

The children of Mercurie and of Venus
Been in hir wirking ful contrarious;
Mercurie loveth wisdom and science,
And Venus loveth ryot and dispence.
And, for hir diverse disposicioun,
Ech falleth in otheres exaltacioun;
And thus, god woot! Mercurie is desolat
In Pisces, wher Venus is exaltat;
And Venus falleth ther Mercurie is reysed;
Therfore no womman of no clerk is preysed.
The clerk, whan he is old, and may noght do
Of Venus werkes worth his olde sho,
Than sit he doun, and writ in his dotage
That wommen can nat kepe hir mariage!

    But now to purpos, why I tolde thee
That I was beten for a book, pardee.
Up-on a night Jankin, that was our syre,
Redde on his book, as he sat by the fyre,
Of Eva first, that, for hir wikkednesse,
Was al mankinde broght to wrecchednesse,
For which that Jesu Crist him-self was slayn,
That boghte us with his herte-blood agayn.
Lo, here expres of womman may ye finde,
That womman was the los of al mankinde.

        Tho redde he me how Sampson loste his heres,
Slepinge, his lemman kitte hem with hir sheres;
Thurgh whiche tresoun loste he bothe his yën.

        Tho redde he me, if that I shal nat lyen,
Of Hercules and of his Dianyre,
That caused him to sette himself a-fyre.

        No-thing forgat he the penaunce and wo
That Socrates had with hise wyves two;
How Xantippa caste pisse up-on his heed;
This sely man sat stille, as he were deed;
He wyped his heed, namore dorste he seyn
But 'er that thonder stinte, comth a reyn.'

        Of Phasipha, that was the quene of Crete,
For shrewednesse, him thoughte the tale swete;
Fy! spek na-more—it is a grisly thing—

The children of Mercury and of Venus[19]
Be in their behavior full contrarious:
Mercury loves science and wisdom,
And Venus loves revelry and to spend;
And, because of their diverse dispositions,
Each falls in the moment of the other's highest ascent,
And thus, God knows, Mercury is powerless
In Pisces where Venus is at her greatest,
And Venus falls there where Mercury has risen;
Therefore no woman by a scholar is prized.
The scholar, when he is old, and may not do
Of Venus' works worth his old shoe—
Then sits he down and writes in his dotage
That women cannot be faithful in marriage!

    But now to the purpose why I told you
That I was beaten for a book, by God.
Upon a night Jankin, who was my lord,
Read in his book as he sat by the fire
Of Eve first, who for her wickedness
Was all mankind brought to wretchedness,
For which that Jesus Christ himself was slain,
Who bought us with his heartblood again.
Lo, here specifically of woman may you find
Who caused the loss to all mankind.

    Then read he me how Samson lost his hair:
Sleeping, she cut it with her shears,
Through which treason lost he both his eyes.

    Then read he me, if that I shall not lie,
Of Hercules and his Deianira,[20]
Who caused him to set himself afire.

    Nothing forgot he the sorrow and the woe
That Socrates had with his wives two—
How Xantippe cast piss upon his head:
This poor man sat still, as if he were dead;
He wiped his head; no more dared he say
But 'Before thunder ceases, there comes a rain.'

    Of Pasiphae[21] who was the Queen of Crete
Out of meanness him thought the tale sweet—
Fie! Speak no more, it is a grisly thing,

Of hir horrible lust and hir lyking.
  Of Clitemistra, for hir lecherye,
That falsly made hir housbond for to dye,
He redde it with ful good devocioun.
  He tolde me eek for what occasioun
Amphiorax at Thebes loste his lyf;
Myn housbond hadde a legende of his wyf,
Eriphilem, that for an ouche of gold
Hath prively un-to the Grekes told
Wher that hir housbonde hidde him in a place,
For which he hadde at Thebes sory grace.
  Of Lyvia tolde he me, and of Lucye,
They bothe made hir housbondes for to dye;
That oon for love, that other was for hate;
Lyvia hir housbond, on an even late,
Empoysoned hath, for that she was his fo.
Lucya, likerous, loved hir housbond so,
That, for he sholde alwey up-on hir thinke,
She yaf him swich a maner love-drinke,
That he was deed, er it were by the morwe;
And thus algates housbondes han sorwe.
  Than tolde he me, how oon Latumius
Compleyned to his felawe Arrius,
That in his gardin growed swich a tree,
On which, he seyde, how that his wyves three
Hanged hem-self for herte despitous.
'O leve brother,' quod this Arrius,
'Yif me a plante of thilke blissed tree,
And in my gardin planted shal it be!'
  Of latter date, of wyves hath he red,
That somme han slayn hir housbondes in hir bed,
And lete hir lechour dighte hir al the night
Whyl that the corps lay in the floor up-right.
And somme han drive nayles in hir brayn
Whyl that they slepte, and thus they han hem slayn.
Somme han hem yeve poysoun in hir drinke.
He spak more harm than herte may bithinke.
And ther-with-al, he knew of mo proverbes
Than in this world ther growen gras or herbes.

Of her horrible lust and her liking.
    Of Clytemnestra,[22] for her lechery,
Who falsely made her husband for to die,
He read it with full good devotion.
    He told me also for what occasion
Amphiaraus[23] at Thebes lost his life.
My husband had a legend of his wife,
Eriphilem, who for a brooch of gold
Had secretly unto the Greeks told
Where her husband hid in a place,
For which he had at Thebes misfortune.
    Of Livia told he me, and of Lucilia.
They both made their husbands for to die,
That one for love, the other was for hate.
Livia her husband, on an evening late,
Poisoned him, for she was his foe.
Lucilia, lecherous, loved her husband so,
That, so he should always upon her think,
She gave him such a kind of love-drink,
That he was dead before it was the morrow;
And thus always husbands have sorrow.
    Then he told me how one Latumius
Complained unto his companion Arrius,[24]
Who in his garden grew a certain tree
On which he said how his wives three
Hanged themselves for spite.
'Oh dear brother,' said this Arrius,
'Give me a cutting of that blessed tree,
And in my garden planted shall it be!'
    Of later date, of wives had he read
Who some had slain their husbands in their beds,
And let their lovers lie with them all night
While the corpse lay on the floor with open eyes.
And some had driven nails in their brains
While they slept, and thus they had them slain.
Some had in their drink them given poison.
He spoke more harm than heart may imagine.
And in addition he knew of more proverbs
Than in this world there grow grass or herbs.

'Bet is,' quod he, 'thyn habitacioun
Be with a leoun or a foul dragoun,
Than with a womman usinge for to chyde.
Bet is,' quod he, 'hye in the roof abyde
Than with an angry wyf doun in the hous;
They been so wikked and contrarious;
They haten that hir housbondes loveth ay.'
He seyde, 'a womman cast hir shame away,
Whan she cast of hir smok;' and forthermo,
'A fair womman, but she be chaast also,
Is lyk a gold ring in a sowes nose.'
Who wolde wenen, or who wolde suppose
The wo that in myn herte was, and pyne?
　　And whan I saugh he wolde never fyne
To reden on this cursed book al night,
Al sodeynly three leves have I plight
Out of his book, right as he radde, and eke,
I wit my fist so took him on the cheke,
That in our fyr he fil bakward adoun.
And he up-stirte as dooth a wood leoun,
And with his fist he smoot me on the heed,
That in the floor I lay as I were deed.
And when he saugh how stille that I lay,
He was agast, and wolde han fled his way,
Til atte laste out of my swogh I breyde:
'O! hastow slayn me, false theef?' I seyde,
'And for my land thus hastow mordred me?
Er I be deed, yet wol I kisse thee.'
　　And neer he cam, and kneled faire adoun,
And seyde, 'dere suster Alisoun,
As help me god, I shal thee never smyte;
That I have doon, it is thy-self to wyte.
Foryeve it me, and that I thee biseke'—
And yet eft-sones I hitte him on the cheke,
And seyde, 'theef, thus muchel am I wreke;
Now wol I dye, I may no lenger speke.'
But atte laste, with muchel care and wo,
We fille acorded, by us selven two.
He yaf al the brydel in myn hond

'Better it is,' said he, 'your habitation
Be with a lion or a foul dragon,
Than with a woman accustomed for to chide.
Better it is,' said he, 'high on the roof abide
Than with an angry wife down in the house;
They be so wicked and contrarious
They hate what their husbands love ever.'
He said, 'A woman casts her shame away,
When she casts off her underclothes;' and furthermore,
'A fair woman, unless she be chaste also,
Is like a gold ring in a sow's nose.'
Who would guess, or who would suppose
The woe that in my heart was, and pain?

　　And when I saw that he would never finish
To read in this cursed book all night,
All suddenly three pages have I ripped
Out of his book, right as he read, and also
I with my fist so hit him on the cheek
That in our fire he fell backward down.
And he got up as does an angry lion,
And with his fist he struck me on the head
That on the floor I lay as if I were dead.
And when he saw how still that I lay,
He was aghast, and would have fled away,
Till at last out of my swoon I breathed:
'Oh! have you slain me, you thief?' I said,
'And for my land have you murdered me?
Before I be dead, yet will I kiss you.'

　　And near he came, and kneeled fair down,
And said, 'Dear sister Alison,
So help me God, I shall never you strike;
But for what I've done, you have yourself to blame.
Forgive it me, and that I you beseech—'
And yet again I hit him on the cheek
And said, 'Thief! thus much I am avenged.
Now will I die: I may no longer speak.'
But at last, with much care and woe,
We came to an agreement between us two.
He gave me the bridle completely in my hand,

To han the governance of hous and lond,
And of his tonge and of his hond also,
And made him brenne his book anon right tho.
And whan that I hadde geten un-to me,
By maistrie, al the soveraynetee,
And that he seyde, 'myn owene trewe wyf,
Do as thee lust the terme of al thy lyf,
Keep thyn honour, and keep eek myn estaat'—
After that day we hadden never debaat.
God help me so, I was to him as kinde
As any wyf from Denmark un-to Inde,
And also trewe, and so was he to me.
I prey to god that sit in magestee,
So blesse his soule, for his mercy dere!
Now wol I seye my tale, if ye wol here."

Biholde the wordes bitwene the Somonour and the Frere

The Frere lough, whan he hadde hend al this,
"Now, dame," quod he, "so have I joye or blis,
This is a long preamble of a tale!"
And whan the Somnour herde the Frere gale,
"Lo!" quod the Somnour, "goddes armes two!
A frere wol entremette him ever-mo.
Lo, gode men, a flye and eek a frere
Wol falle in every dish and eek matere.
What spekestow of preambulacioun?
What! amble, or trotte, or pees, or go sit doun;
Thou lettest our disport in this manere."

"Ye, woltow so, sir Somnour?" quod the Frere,
"Now, by my feith, I shal, er that I go,
Telle of a Somnour swich a tale or two,
That alle the folk shal laughen in this place."

"Now elles, Frere, I bishrewe thy face,"
Quod this Somnour, "and I bishrewe thy face,"
But-if I telle tales two or three
Of freres er I come to Sidingborne,
That I shal make thyn herte for to morne;
For wel I woot thy pacience is goon."

To have the governance of house and land,
And of his tongue and his hand also;
And made him burn his book anon right then.
And when that I had gotten for myself,
By mastery, all the sovereignty,
And that he said, 'My own true wife,
Do as you please for the rest of your life;
Preserve your honor, and keep my reputation—'
After that day we had never debate.
God help me so, I was to him as kind
As any wife from Denmark unto India,
And just as true, and so was he to me.
I pray to God who sits in majesty,
So bless his soul by his mercy dear!
Now will I say my tale, if you will hear."

Behold the words between the Summoner and the Friar

The Friar laughed when he had heard all this.
"Now dame," said he, "as I may have joy or bliss,
This is a long preamble for a tale!"
And when the Summoner heard the Friar say that aloud,
"Behold," said the Summoner, "God's two arms,
A friar will insinuate himself evermore!
Behold, good men, a fly and also a friar
Will fall in every dish and every topic.
Why do you speak of perambulation?
Behold! Amble, or trot, or walk, or go sit down!
You interrupt our fun in this manner."

      "So you'd say, sir Summoner?" said the Friar;
"Now by my faith, I shall, before I go,
Tell of a summoner such a tale or two
That all the folk shall laugh in this place."

      "Now otherwise, Friar, I will curse your face,"
Said this Summoner, "and I curse me
Unless I tell tales two or three
Of friars, before I come to Sittingbourne,[25]
So that I shall make your heart for to mourn—
For well I know your patience is gone."

Our hoste cryde "pees! and that anoon!"
And seyde, "lat the womman telle hir tale.
Ye fare as folk that dronken been of ale.
Do, dame, tel forth your tale, and that is best."

"Al redy, sir," quod she, "right as yow lest,
If I have licence of this worthy Frere."

"Yis, dame," quod he, "tel forth, and I wol here."

The Tale

In th'old dayes of the king Arthour,
Of which that Britons speken greet honour,
Al was this land fulfiled of fayerye.
The elf-queen, with hir joly companye,
Daunced ful ofte in many a grene mede;
This was the olde opinion, as I rede.
I speke of manye hundred yeres ago;
But now can no man see none elves mo.
For now the grete charitee and prayeres
Of limitours and othere holy freres,
That serchen every lond and every streem,
As thikke as motes in the sonne-beem,
Blessinge halles, chambres, kichenes, boures,
Citees, burghes, castels, hye toures,
Thropes, bernes, shipnes, dayeryes,
This maketh that ther been no fayeryes.
For ther as wont to walken was an elf,
Ther walketh now the limitour himself
In undermeles and in morweninges,
And seyth his matins and his holy thinges
As he goth in his limitacioun.
Wommen may go saufly up and doun,
In every bush, or under every tree;
Ther is noon other incubu but he,
And he ne wol doon hem but dishonour.

And so bifel it, that this king Arthour
Hadde in his hous a lusty bacheler,
That on a day cam rydinge fro river;
And happed that, allone as she was born,
He saugh a mayde walkinge him biforn,

Our Host cried "Peace! and that anon!"
And said, "Let the woman tell her tale.
You act as folk do who have had too much ale.
Do, dame, tell forth your tale, and that is best."

"All ready, sire," said she, "right as you wish,
If I have the permission of this worthy Friar."

"Yes, dame," said he, "tell forth, and I will hear."

The Tale

In the old days of King Arthur,
Of whom Britons speak great honor,
All was this land filled with fairies.
The elf-queen with her jolly company
Danced full often in many a green meadow.
This was the old opinion, as I read—
I speak of many hundred years ago—
But now can man see elves no more.
For now the great charity and prayers
Of beggars and other holy friars,[26]
Who visit every land and every stream,
As thick as dustmotes in the sunbeam,
Blessing halls, chambers, kitchens, bedrooms,
Cities, towns, castles, high towers,
Villages, barns, sheds, dairies—
This causes there to be no fairies.
For there where was wont to walk an elf,
There walks now the limitour[27] himself
In afternoons and in mornings,
And says his Matins and his holy things
As he goes in his territory.
Women may now go safely up and down:
In every bush or under every tree
There is no other incubus but he,
And he will only do them dishonor.

And so it happened that this King Arthur
Had in his house a lusty young knight,
Who on a day came riding from the river;
And it happened that, alone as he was born,
He saw a maid walking him before,

Of whiche mayde anon, maugree hir heed,
By verray force he rafte hir maydenheed;
For which oppressioun was swich clamour
And swich pursute un-to the king Arthour,
That dampned was this knight for to be deed
By cours of lawe, and sholde han lost his heed
Paraventure, swich was the statut tho;
But that the quene and othere ladies mo
So longe preyeden the king of grace,
Til he his lyf him graunted in the place,
And yaf him to the quene al at hir wille,
To chese, whether she wolde him save or spille.
    The quene thanketh the king with al hir might,
And after this thus spak she to the knight,
Whan that she saugh hir tyme, up-on a day:
"Thou standest yet," quod she, "in swich array,
That of thy lyf yet hastow no suretee.
I grante thee lyf, if thou canst tellen me
What thing is it that wommen most desyren?
Be war, and keep thy nekke-boon from yren.
And if thou canst nat tellen it anoon,
Yet wol I yeve thee leve for to gon
A twelf-month and a day, to seche and lere
An answere suffisant in this matere.
And suretee wol I han, er that thou pace,
Thy body for to yelden in this place."
    Wo was this knight and sorwefully he syketh;
But what! he may nat do al as him lyketh.
And at the laste, he chees him for to wende,
And come agayn, right at the yeres ende,
With swich answere as god wolde him purveye;
And taketh his leve, and wendeth forth his weye.
    He seketh every hous and every place,
Wher-as he hopeth for to finde grace,
To lerne, what thing wommen loven most;
But he ne coude arryven in no cost,
Wher-as he mighte finde in this matere
Two creatures accordingee in-fere.
    Somme seyde, wommen loven best richesse,

Of which maid anon, no matter what she did,
By force itself he took her maidenhead.
For which wrong was such clamor
And such pleading unto King Arthur,
That condemned was this knight for to be dead
By course of law, and should have lost his head—
As it happened such was the law then—
Except that the queen and other ladies more
So long begged the king for grace
Till he his life granted in the place,
And gave him to the queen entirely at her will,
To choose whether she would him save or kill.

The queen thanked the king with all her might,
And after this thus spoke she to the knight
When she saw her time, upon a day:
"You stand yet," said she, "in such danger
That of your life you have yet no guarantee.
I grant you life, if you can tell me
What thing it is that women most desire.
Be careful, and keep your neck from the blade of iron.
And if you cannot tell it now,
Yet will I give you leave to go
For twelve months and a day, to seek and learn
An answer sufficient in this matter.
And a surety bond will have, before you leave,
To guarantee your return to this place."

Woeful was this knight and sorrowfully he sighed.
But what! He may not do all as he liked,
And at last he chose to his way wend,
And come again, right at the year's end,
With such answer as God would him provide;
And he took his leave and wended forth his way.

He sought every house and every place
Where he hoped to have the good grace,
To learn what thing women love most;
But he could arrive at no country or coast
Where he might find in this matter
Two creatures agreeing with each other.

Some said women love best riches,

Somme seyde, honour, somme seyde, jolynesse;
Somme, riche array, somme seyden, lust abedde,
And ofte tyme to be widwe and wedde.
     Somme seyde, that our hertes been most esed,
Whan that we been y-flatered and y-plesed.
He gooth ful ny the sothe, I wol nat lye;
A man shal winne us best with flaterye;
And with attendance, and with bisinesse,
Been we y-lymed, bothe more and lesse.
     And somme seyn, how that we loven best
For to be free, and do right as us lest,
And that no man repreve us of our vyce,
But seye that we be wyse, and no-thing nyce.
For trewely, ther is noon of us alle,
If any wight wol clawe us on the galle,
That we nil kike, for he seith us sooth;
Assay, and he shal finde it that so dooth.
For be we never so vicious with-inne,
We wol been holden wyse, and clene of sinne.
     And somme seyn, that greet delyt han we
For to ben holden stable and eek secree,
And in o purpos stedefastly to dwelle,
And nat biwreye thing that men us telle.
But that tale is nat worth a rake-stele;
Pardee, we wommen conne no-thing hele;
Witnesse on Myda; wol ye here the tale?
     Ovyde, amonges othere thinges smale,
Seyde, Myda hadde, under his longe heres,
Growinge up-on his heed two asses eres,
The whiche vyce he hidde, as he best mighte,
Ful subtilly from every mannes sighte,
That, save his wyf, ther wiste of it na-mo.
He loved hir most, and trusted hir also;
He preyde hir, that to no creature
She sholde tellen of his disfigure.
     She swoor him "nay, for al this world to winne,
She nolde do that vileinye or sinne,
To make hir housbond han so foul a name;
She nolde nat telle it for hir owene shame."

Some said honor, some said jollyness;
Some rich adornment, some said lust abed,
And oftentime to be widowed and again then wed.
    Some said that our hearts have been most eased
When that we be flattered and pleased.
He got very near the truth, I will not lie:
A man shall win us best with flattery;
And with attention and with diligence
Be we snared, both more and less.
    And some said how that we love best
For to be free and do right as we wish,
And that no man reproach us for our vice,
But say that we be not foolish, but all wise.
For truly, there is none of us all,
If any person would scratch our sore wounds,
Who will not kick back if he tells the truth:
Try, and he who does shall find it so.
For be we ever so vicious within,
We want to be thought wise, and clean of sin.
    And some say that great delight have we
For to be thought steadfast and discreet,
And in one purpose steadfastly to dwell,
And not reveal things that men us tell—
But that tale is not worth a rake handle.
By God, we women know not how anything to conceal:
Witness on Midas—will you hear this tale?
    Ovid, among other things brief,
Said Midas[28] had under his long hairs,
Growing upon his head two asses' ears,
The which flaw he hid as best he might
Full cleverly from every man's sight.
So that, save his wife, there knew of it no one.
He loved her most, and trusted her also;
He begged her that to no creature
She should tell of his disfigure.
    She swore him that no, for all the world to win,
She would not do that bad deed or sin,
To make her husband have so foul a name.
She would not tell it to spare her own shame.

But nathelees, hir thoughte that she dyde,
That she so longe sholde a conseil hyde;
Hir thoughte it swal so sore aboute hir herte,
That nedely som word hir moste asterte;
And sith she dorste telle it to no man,
Doun to a mareys faste by she ran;
Til she came there, hir herte was a-fyre,
And, as a bitore bombleth in the myre,
She leyde hir mouth un-to the water doun:
"Biwreye me nat, thou water, with thy soun,"
Quod she, "to thee I telle it, and namo;
Myn housbond hath longe asses eres two!
Now is myn herte all hool, now is it oute;
I mighte no lenger kepe it, out of doute."
Heer may ye se, thogh we a tyme abyde,
Yet out it moot, we can no conseil hyde;
The remenant of the tale if ye wol here,
Redeth Ovyde, and ther ye may it lere.

        This knight, of which my tale is specially,
Whan that he saugh he mighte nat come therby,
This is to seye, what wommen loven moost,
With-inne his brest ful sorweful was the goost;
But hoom he gooth, he mighte nat sojourne.
The day was come, that hoomward moste he tourne,
And in his wey it happed him to ryde,
In al this care, under a forest-syde,
Wher-as he saugh up-on a daunce go
Of ladies foure and twenty, and yet mo;
Toward the whiche daunce he drow ful yerne,
In hope that som wisdom sholde he lerne.
But certeinly, er he came fully there,
Vanisshed was this daunce, he niste where.
No creature saugh he that bar lyf,
Save on the grene he saugh sittinge a wyf;
A fouler wight ther may no man devyse.
Agayn the knight this olde wyf gan ryse.
And seyde, "sir knight, heer-forth ne lyth no wey.
Tel me, what that ye seken, by your fey?
Paraventure it may the bettre be;

But nevertheless, she thought that she should die
If she should for long the secret hide.
Her thought it swelled so sore about her heart
That need be some word out of her must start,
And since she dared tell no man,
Down to a nearby marsh she ran.
Till she came there her heart was on fire,
And as a bittern's call booms in the mire,
She laid her mouth unto the water down:
"Betray me not, you water, with your sound,"
Said she, "to you I tell it, and else no one;
My husband has long asses' ears two!
Now is my heart again all whole, now is it out.
I might no longer keep it, with no doubt."
Here you may see, though we a while abide,
Yet out it must, we can no secret hide.
The ending of this tale if you will hear,
Read Ovid, and there you may it learn.

    This knight of which my tale is specially,
When he saw he might not get his answer,
That is to say, what women love most,
Within his breast full sorrowful was his soul,
But home he went, he might not linger.
The day was come that homeward must he turn,
And on his way it happened him to ride
In all this care by a forest side,
Where he saw engaged in a dance
Of ladies four and twenty and yet more;
Toward which dance he drew with yearning,
In hope that some wisdom he could learn.
But certainly, before he came fully there,
Vanished was this dance, he knew not where.
No creature saw he that bore life,
Save on the grass he saw sitting a woman—
An uglier person may no man imagine.
To meet the knight this old lady arose,
And said, "Sir knight, through here there's no way.
Tell me what you seek, by your faith!
Perhaps it may the better be:

Thise olde folk can muchel thing," quod she.
      "My leve mooder," quod this knight certeyn,
"I nam but deed, but-if that I can seyn
What thing it is that wommen most desyre;
Coude ye me wisse, I wolde wel quyte your hyre."
      "Plight me thy trouthe, heer in myn hand," quod she,
"The nexte thing that I requere thee,
Thou shalt it do, if it lye in thy might;
And I wol telle it yow er it be night."
"Have heer my trouthe," quod the knight, "I grante."
      "Thanne," quod she, "I dar me wel avante,
Thy lyf is sauf, for I wol stonde therby,
Up-on my lyf, the queen wol seye as I.
Lat see which is the proudeste of hem alle,
That wereth on a coverchief or a calle,
That dar seye nay, of that I shal thee teche;
Lat us go forth with-outen lenger speche."
Tho rouned she a pistel in his ere,
And bad him to be glad, and have no fere.
      Whan they be comen to the court, this knight
Seyde, "he had holde his day, as he hadde hight,
And redy was his answere," as he sayde.
Ful many a noble wyf, and many a mayde,
And many a widwe, for that they ben wyse,
The quene hir-self sittinge as a justyse,
Assembled been, his answere for to here;
And afterward this knight was bode appere.
      To every wight comanded was silence,
And that the knight sholde telle in audience,
What thing that worldly wommen loven best.
This knight ne stood nat stille as doth a best,
But to his questioun anon answerde
With manly voys, that al the court it herde:
      "My lige lady, generally," quod he,
"Wommen desyren to have sovereyntee
As wel over hir housbond as hir love,
And for to been in maistrie him above;
This is your moste desyr, thogh ye me kille,
Doth as yow list, I am heer at your wille."

We old folks know many things," said she.
    "My dear mother," said this knight, "for certain
I am good as dead, unless I can say
What thing it is that women most desire.
Could you tell me, I will repay your hire."
    "Pledge me your promise, here in my hand," said she,
"The next thing that I request of thee,
You shall do it, if it lies in your power,
And I will tell it you before it be night."
"Have here my promise," said the knight. "I grant it."
    "Then," said she, "I dare well boast
Your life is safe, for I will stand thereby.
Upon my life, the queen will say as well as I.
Let see which is the proudest of them all,
Who wears a kerchief or a crown,
Who dares to deny that which I teach.
Let us go forth without longer speech."
Then whispered she a message in his ear,
And bade him to be glad and have no fear.
    When they returned to the court, this knight
Said he had kept to his day, as he had pledged,
And ready was his answer, as he said.
Full many a noble wife, and many a maid,
And many a widow—because they be wise—
The queen herself sitting as a judge,
Assembled were, his answer for to hear;
And then this knight was bidden to appear.
    To every person commanded was silence,
And thus the knight should tell his audience
What thing that worldly women love best.
This knight stood not still as does a beast,
But to his question anon answered
With manly voice, so that all the court it heard:
    "My liege lady, generally," said he,
"Women desire to have sovereignty
As well over their husband as their lovers,
And for to be in mastery them above.
This is your greatest desire, though you me kill.
Do as you wish—I am here at your will."

In al the court ne was ther wyf ne mayde,
Ne widwe, that contraried that he sayde,
But seyden, "he was worthy han his lyf."
    And with that word up stirte the olde wyf,
Which that the knight saugh sitting in the grene:
"Mercy," quod she, "my sovereyn lady quene!
Er that your court departe, do me right.
I taughte this answere un-to the knight;
For which he plighte me his trouthe there,
The firste thing I wolde of him requere,
He wolde it do, if it lay in his might.
Bifore the court than preye I thee, sir knight,"
Quod she, "that thou me take un-to thy wyf;
For wel thou wost that I have kept thy lyf.
If I sey fals, sey nay, up-on thy fey!"
    This knight answerde, "allas! and weylawey!
I woot right wel that swich was my biheste.
For goddes love, as chees a newe requeste;
Tak al my good, and lat my body go."
    "Nay than," quod she, "I shrewe us bothe two!
For thogh that I be foul, and old, and pore,
I nolde for al the metal, ne for ore,
That under erthe is grave, or lyth above,
But-if thy wyf I were, and eek thy love."
    "My love?" quod he; "nay, my dampnacioun!
Allas! that any of my nacioun
Sholde ever so foule disparaged be!"
But al for noght, the ende is this, that he
Constreyned was, he nedes moste hir wedde;
And taketh his olde wyf, and gooth to bedde.
    Now wolden som men seye, paraventure,
That, for my necligence, I do no cure
To tellen yow the joye and al th'array
That at the feste was that ilke day.
To whiche thing shortly answere I shal;
I seye, ther nas no joye ne feste at al,
Ther nas but hevinesse and muche sorwe;
For prively he wedded hir on a morwe,
And al day after hidde him as an oule;

In all the court there was no wife, nor maid,
Nor widow who contraried what he said,
But said he was worthy to have his life.
    And with that upstarted the old lady,
Who that the knight saw sitting in the grass:
"Mercy!" said she, "my sovereign lady queen!
Before your court departs, do me right.
I taught this answer unto the knight;
For which he gave me his promise there,
The first thing I would of him require
He would it do, if it lay in his might.
Before the court then I pray thee, sir knight,"
Said she, "that you me take unto your wife,
For well you know that I have saved your life.
If I say false, say no, upon your faith!"
    This knight answered, "Alas and wellaway!
I know right well that such was my promise.
For God's love, choose a new request:
Take all my goods, and let my body go."
    "No then," said she, "I curse us both two!
For though I be ugly and old and poor,
I would not for all the metal nor the ore
That under the earth is buried or lies above
Be anything but your wife, and your love."
    "My love?" said he. "No, my damnation!
Alas! that any of my lineage
Should ever so foul degraded be!"
But all for nought, the end is this, that he
Constrained was: he must needs her wed,
And take his old wife and go to bed.
    Now would some men say, perhaps,
That out of my negligence I fail
To tell you the joy and all the show
That at the feast was that same day.
To which thing briefly answer I shall:
I say there was no joy nor feast at all;
There was but heaviness and much sorrow,
For privately he married her on the morrow,
And all day afterward hid himself like an owl,

So wo was him, his wyf looked so foule.

  Greet was the wo the knight hadde in his thoght,
Whan he was with his wyf a-bedde y-broght;
He walweth, and he turneth to and fro.
His olde wyf lay smylinge evermo,
And seyde, "o dere housbond, *ben'cite!*
Fareth every knight thus with his wyf as ye?
Is this the lawe of king Arthures hous?
Is every knight of his so dangerous?
I am your owene love and eek your wyf,
I am she, which that saved hath your lyf;
And certes, yet dide I yow never unright;
Why fare ye thus with me this firste night?
Ye faren lyk a man had lost his wit;
What is my gilt? for godd's love, tel me it,
And it shal been amended, if I may."

  "Amended?" quod this knight, "allas! nay, nay!
It wol nat been amended never mo!
Thou art so loothly, and so old also,
And ther-to comen of so lowe a kinde,
That litel wonder is, thogh I walwe and winde.
So wolde god myn herte wolde breste!"

  "Is this," quod she, "the cause of your unreste?"

  "Ye, certainly," quod he, "no wonder is."

  "Now, sire," quod she, "I coude amende al this,
If that me liste, er it were dayes three,
So wel ye mighte bere yow un-to me.

  But for ye speken of swich gentillesse
As is descended out of old richesse,
That therfore sholden ye be gentil men,
Swich arrogance is nat worth an hen.
Loke who that is most vertuous alway,
Privee and apert, and most entendeth ay
To do the gentil dedes that he can,
And tak him for the grettest gentil man.
Crist wol, we clayme of him our gentillesse,
Nat of our eldres for hir old richesse.
For thogh they yeve us al hir heritage,
For which we clayme to been of heigh parage,

For woe was with him, his wife looked so foul.
   Great was the woe the knight had in his thought,
When he was with his wife to bed brought;
He wallowed, and he turned to and fro.
His old wife lay smiling ever so,
And said, "Oh dear husband, *benedicite!*
Behaves every knight this way to his wife as you?
Is this the law of King Arthur's household?
Is every knight of his so cold?
I am your own love and also your wife;
I am she who has saved your life;
And certainly did I never you unright.
Why do you thus with me this first night?
You act like a man who has lost his wit!
What is my guilt? For God's love, tell me it,
And it shall be amended, if I may."
   "Amended?" said this knight, "alas! nay, nay!
It will not be amended ever more!
You are so ugly, and so old also,
And come from such lowly birth,
That little wonder is it that I toss and turn.
So would God my heart burst!"
   "Is this," said she, "the cause of your unrest?"
   "Yes, certainly," said he, "no wonder is."
   "Now sir," said she, "I could amend all this,
If that I wish, before it were days three,
So long as you behave well toward me.
   Though you speak of such gentleness
As is descended out of old riches—
Therefore you should be a gentle man—
Such arrogance is not worth a hen.
See who is most virtuous always,
In private and public, and who ever intends
To do the gentle deeds that he can,
And take him for the greatest gentleman.
Christ wills that we draw from him our gentleness,
Not of our ancestors from their old riches.
For though they give us all their heritage—
For which we claim to be of high parentage—

Yet may they nat biquethe, for no-thing,
To noon of us hir vertuous living,
That made hem gentil men y-called be;
And bad us folwen hem in swich degree.
 Wel can the wyse poete of Florence,
That highte Dant, speken in this sentence;
Lo in swich maner rym is Dantes tale:
'Ful selde up ryseth by his branches smale
Prowesse of man; for god, of his goodnesse,
Wol that of him we clayme our gentillesse;'
For of our eldres may we no-thing clayme
But temporel thing, that man may hurte and mayme.
Eek every wight wot this as wel as I,
If gentillesse were planted naturelly
Un-to a certeyn linage, doun the lyne,
Privee ne apert, than wolde they never fyne
To doon of gentillesse the faire offyce;
They mighte do no vileinye or vyce.

 Tak fyr, and ber it in the derkeste hous
Bitwix this and the mount of Caucasus,
And lat men shette the dores and go thenne;
Yet wol the fyr as faire lye and brenne,
As twenty thousand men mighte it biholde;
His office naturel ay wol it holde,
Up peril of my lyf, til that it dye.

 Heer may ye see wel, how that genterye
Is nat annexed to possessioun,
Sith folk ne doon hir operacioun
Alwey, as dooth the fyr, lo! in his kinde.
For, god it woot, men may wel often finde
A lordes sone do shame and vileinye:
And he that wol han prys of his gentrye
For he was boren of a gentil hous,
And hadde hise eldres noble and vertuous,
And nil him-selven do no gentil dedis,
Ne folwe his gentil auncestre that deed is,
He nis nat gentil, be he duk or erl;
For vileyns sinful dedes make a cherl.
For gentillesse nis but renomee

Yet may they not bequeath, in any way,
To any of us their virtuous living
That made them be called gentlemen,
Though they bade us follow them to such condition.
     We know the wise poet of Florence,
Called Dante,[29] speaks on this topic;
Behold, in such manner is Dante's tale:
'Seldom grows as shoots from his family tree
The excellence of man, for God in his goodness
Desires that from him we claim our gentleness;'
For of our elders we can make no claim
But of temporal things, that can hurt and maim.
And every person knows this as well as I,
That if gentleness were planted naturally
Within a certain lineage through its generations,
Privately and publicly, they would never cease
To do the fair office of virtue—
They could do no violence or villainy.
     Take fire, bear it into the darkest house
Between here and the Mount of Caucasus,
And let men shut the doors and go away,
Yet will the fire as fair lie and burn,
As when twenty thousand men might it behold:
Its nature will it retain,
Upon peril of my life, until it dies.
     Here may you see well how that gentility
Is not attached to possession,
Since folk do their work
Always, as does the fire, according to their natures.
For, God knows, men may often find
A lord's son doing shame and villainy;
And he who will have esteem for his gentility
Because he was born of a gentle house,
And had his elders noble and virtuous,
And will himself do no gentle deeds,
Nor follow his gentle ancestor who dead is,
He is not gentle, be he duke or earl;
For villainous sinful deeds make a churl.
For gentleness is nothing but the renown

Of thyne auncestres, for hir heigh bountee,
Which is a strange thing to thy persone.
Thy gentillesse cometh fro god allone;
Than comth our verray gentillesse of grace,
It was no-thing biquethe us with our place.
  Thenketh how noble, as seith Valerius,
Was thilke Tullius Hostilius,
That out of povert roos to heigh noblesse.
Redeth Senek, and redeth eek Boëce,
Ther shul ye seen expres that it no drede is,
That he is gentil that doth gentil dedis;
And therfore, leve housbond, I thus conclude,
Al were it that myne auncestres were rude,
Yet may the hye god, and so hope I,
Grante me grace to liven vertuously.
Thanne am I gentil, whan that I biginne
To liven vertuously and weyve sinne.
  And ther-as ye of povert me repreve,
The hye god, on whom that we bileve,
In wilful povert chees to live his lyf.
And certes every man, mayden, or wyf,
May understonde that Jesus, hevene king,
Ne wolde nat chese a vicious living.
Glad povert is an honest thing, certeyn;
This wol Senek and othere clerkes seyn.
Who-so that halt him payd of his poverte,
I holde him riche, al hadde he nat a sherte.
He that coveyteth is a povre wight,
For he wolde han that is nat in his might.
But he that noght hath, ne coveyteth have
Is riche, al-though ye holde him but a knave.
  Verray povert, it singeth proprely;
Juvenal seith of povert merily:
'The povre man, whan he goth by the weye,
Bifore the theves he may singe and pleye.'
Povert is hateful good, and, as I gesse,
A ful greet bringer out of bisinesse;
A greet amender eek of sapience
To him that taketh it in pacience.

Of your ancestors, for their great goodness,
Which is quite foreign to your person.
Your gentleness comes from God alone.
Thence comes our true gentleness of grace:
It was in no way bequeathed us with our status.

    Think how noble, as said Valerius,
Was that Tullius Hostilius,
Who out of poverty rose to high nobility.
Read Seneca, and read also Boethius:
There shall you see clearly that no doubt is
That he is gentle who does gentle deeds.
And therefore, dear husband, I must conclude:
Albeit that my ancestors were humble,
Yet may the high God, and so hope I,
Grant me grace to live virtuously.
Then I am gentle, when I begin
To live virtuously and waive sin.

    And there as you of poverty me reprove,
The high God, in whom we believe,
In willed poverty chose to live his life.
And certainly every man, maiden or wife,
May understand that Jesus, heaven's king,
Would not choose a vicious way of living.
Glad poverty is an honest thing, certainly;
This will Seneca and other scholars say.
Whoso with poverty is content,
I hold him rich, though he have no shirt.
He who covets is the person poor,
For he would have what is not in his power.
But he who nothing has, and nothing covets,
Is rich, though you hold him but of low estate.

    True poverty, it sings by its nature.
Juvenal said of poverty merrily:
'The poor man, when he goes by the way,
Even among thieves he may sing and play.'
Poverty is a hated good, and as I guess,
A great spur for hard work's dedication;
A great amender also of wisdom
To him who with patience it endures.

Povert is this, al-though it seme elenge:
Possessioun, that no wight wol chalenge.
Povert ful ofte, whan a man is lowe,
Maketh his god and eek him-self to knowe.
Povert a spectacle is, as thinketh me,
Thurgh which he may his verray frendes see.
And therfore, sire, sin that I noght yow greve,
Of my povert na-more ye me repreve.

    Now, sire, of elde ye repreve me;
And certes, sire, thogh noon auctoritee
Were in no book, ye gentils of honour
Seyn that men sholde an old wight doon favour,
And clepe him fader, for your gentillesse;
And auctours shal I finden, as I gesse.

    Now ther ye seye, that I am foul and old,
Than drede you noght to been a cokewold;
For filthe an elde, al-so mote I thee,
Been grete wardeyns up-on chastitee.
But nathelees, sin I knowe your delyt,
I shal fulfille your worldly appetyt.

    "Chees now," quod she, "oon of thise thinges tweye,
To han me foul and old til that I deye,
And be to yow a trewe humble wyf,
And never yow displese in al my lyf,
Or elles ye wol han me yong and fair,
And take your aventure of the repair
That shal be to your hous, by-cause of me,
Or in som other place, may wel be.
Now chees your-selven, whether that yow lyketh."

    This knight avyseth him and sore syketh,
But atte laste he seyde in this manere,
"My lady and my love, and wyf so dere,
I put me in your wyse governance;
Cheseth your-self, which may be most plesance,
And most honour to yow and me also.
I do no fors the whether of the two;
For as yow lyketh, it suffiseth me."

    "Thanne have I gete of yow maistrye," quod she,
"Sin I may chese, and governe as me lest?"

Poverty is this, although it seems misery,
A possession that no person will covet.
Poverty full often, when a man is low,
Makes him his God and himself know;
Poverty a pair of spectacles may be,
Through which he may his true friends see.
And therefore, sir, since with it I do not you trouble,
For my poverty no more should you me reprove.

Now sir, of old age you may blame me:
And certainly, sir, even if no authority
Were in any book, you who claim honor
Say that men should to an old person do favor
And call him father, out of your gentleness;
And authorities shall I find, as I guess.

Now when you say that I am ugly and old,
Then you need not to be a cuckold,
For filth and age, as I may prosper,
Be great protectors of chastity.
But nevertheless, since I know your delight,
I shall fulfill your worldly appetite.

"Choose now," said she, "one of these things two:
To have me foul and old till that I die
And be to you a true and humble wife,
And never you displease in all my life,
Or else you will have me young and fair,
And take your chances with the crowd
Who shall come to your house, because of me,
Or in some other place, as may well be.
Now choose whichever pleases you."

This knight thought hard and sorely sighed,
But at last he said in this manner:
"My lady and my love and my wife so dear,
I put me in your wise governance:
Choose yourself which may give the most pleasure
And most honor to you and me too.
I do not care which of the two you choose,
For as you like, so it suffices me."

"Then have I gotten over you mastery," said she,
"Since I may choose and govern as I please?"

"Ye certes, wyf," quod he, "I holde it best."
"Kis me," quod she, "we be no lenger wrothe;
For, by my trouthe, I wol be to yow bothe,
This is to seyn, ye, bothe fair and good.
I prey to god that I most sterven wood,
But I to yow be al-so good and trewe
As ever was wyf, sin that the world was newe.
And, but I be to-morn as fair to sene
As any lady, emperyce, or quene,
That is bitwixe the est and eke the west,
Doth with my lyf and deeth right as yow lest.
Cast up the curtin, loke how that it is."

And whan the knight saugh verraily al this,
That she so fair was, and so yong ther-to,
For joye he hente hir in his armes two,
His herte bathed in a bath of blisse;
A thousand tyme a-rewe he gan hir kisse.
And she obeyed him in every thing
That mighte doon him plesance or lyking.

And thus they live, un-to hir lyves ende,
In parfit joye; and Jesu Crist us sende
Housbondes meke, yonge, and fresshe a-beede,
And grace t'overbyde hem that we wedde.
And eek I preye Jesu shorte hir lyves
That wol nat be governed by hir wyves;
And olde and angry nigardes of dispence,
God sende hem sone verray pestilence.

"Yes, certainly, wife," said he, "I hold it best."
"Kiss me," said she, "we be no longer angry,
For by my troth, I will to you both be,
This is to say, yes, both fair and good.
I pray to God that I die dimwitted,
Unless I am to you both good and true
As ever was wife, since the world was new.
And unless I be tomorrow as fair to see
As any lady, empress, or queen,
Between east and west,
Do with my life and death just as you wish.
Cast up the curtain: look at me."

And when the knight did he saw in truth,
That she was fair and young also,
For joy he clasped her in his arms two;
His heart bathed in a bath of bliss.
A thousand times he began to her kiss,
And she obeyed him in every thing
That might give him pleasure or delight.

And thus they lived until their lives' end
In perfect joy. And Jesus Christ us send
Husbands meek, young, and fresh in bed,
And grace to outlive those that we wed.
And I pray Jesus to shorten their lives
Who not will be governed by their wives;
And old and angry niggards with their pence,
God send them soon true pestilence.

The Clerkes Tale

The Prologue

"Sir clerk of Oxenford," our hoste sayde,
"Ye ryde as coy and stille as dooth a mayde,
Were newe spoused, sitting at the bord;
This day ne herde I of your tonge a word.
I trowe ye studie aboute som sophyme,
But Salomon seith, 'every thing hath tyme.'

Fod goddes sake, as beth of bettre chere,
It is no tyme for to studien here.
Telle us some mery tale, by your fey;
For what man that is entred in a pley,
He nedes moot unto the pley assente.
But precheth nat, as freres doon in Lente,
To make us for our olde sinnes wepe,
Ne that thy tale make us nat to slepe.

Telle us som mery thing of aventures;—
Your termes, your colours, and your figures,
Kepe hem in stoor til so be ye endyte
Heigh style, as whan that men to kinges wryte,
Spekketh so pleyn at this tyme, I yow preye,
That we may understonde what ye seye."

This worthy clerk benignely answerde,
"Hoste," quod he, "I am under your yerde;
Ye han of us as now the governaunce,
And therfor wol I do yow obeisaunce,
As fer as reson axeth, hardily.
I wol yow telle a tale which that I
Lerned at Padowe of a worthy clerk,
As preved by his wordes and his werk.
He is now deed and nayled in his cheste,
I prey to god so yeve his soule reste!

Fraunceys Petrark, the laureat poete,
Highte this clerk, whos rethoryke sweete
Enlumined al Itaille of poetrye,
As Linian dide of philosophye
Or lawe, or other art particuler;

The Clerk's Tale

The Prologue

"Sir Scholar of Oxford," our Host said,
"You ride as shy and still as does a maid,
Who is just married, sitting at the wedding table.
This day I have not heard a word from your tongue.
I believe you're thinking of some sophistry,
But Solomon says, 'Everything has its time.'
    For God's sake, be of better cheer.
It is no time to study here.
Tell us some merry tale, by your faith!
For whosoever has entered in a game,
He needs must by the rules play.
But preach not, as friars do in Lent,
To make us of our old sins weep,
Nor should your tale lead us to sleep.
    Tell us some merry thing of adventures.
Your rhetorical devices, your figures of speech,
Keep them in store until you're called to indite
In high style, as when men to kings write.
Speak so plainly at this time, we you pray,
That we may understand what you say."
    This worthy Scholar graciously replied:
"Host," said he, "I am under your rule;
You have of us now the governance,
And therefore will I do you obedience
As far as reason requires, certainly.
I will tell you a tale that I
Learned at Padua of a worthy scholar,
As proven by his words and his work.
He is now dead and nailed in his coffin chest,
I pray to God give his soul rest!
    Francis Petrarch,[1] the laureate poet,
This scholar was called whose rhetoric sweet
Illuminated all Italy with poetry,
As Legnano[2] did of philosophy
Or law, or other art particular;

299

But deeth, that wol nat suffre us dwellen heer
But as it were a twinkling of an yë,
Hem bothe hath slayn, and alle shul we dyë.
    But forth to tellen of this worthy man,
That taughte me this tale, as I bigan,
I seye that first with heigh style he endyteth,
Er he the body of his tale wryteth,
A proheme, in the which discryveth he
Pemond, and of Saluces the contree,
And speketh of Apennyn, the hilles hye,
That been the boundes of West Lumbardye,
And of Mount Vesulus in special,
Where as the Poo, out of a welle smal,
Taketh his firste springing and his sours,
That estward ay encresseth in his cours
To Emelward, to Ferrare, and Venyse:
The which a long thing were to devyse.
And trewely, as to my jugement,
Me thinketh it a thing impertinent,
Save that he wol conveyen his matere:
But this his tale, which that ye may here."

The Tale

PART ONE

Ther is, at the west syde of Itaille,
Doun at the rote of Vesulus the colde,
A lusty playne, habundant of vitaille,
Wher many a tour and toun thou mayst biholde,
That founded were in tyme of fadres olde,
And many another delitable sighte,
And Saluces this noble contree highte.

A markis whylom lord was of that londe,
As were his worthy eldres him bifore;
And obeisant and redy to his honde

But death, that will not allow us here to dwell
But as it were the blink of an eye,
Them both has slain, as we all shall die.
    But to tell more of this worthy man
Who taught me this tale, as I began,
I say that first with high style he composed,
Before the body of his main tale he wrote,
A prologue, in which he described the
Piedmont and Saluzzo country,
And spoke of the Apennines, the hills high,
That be the bounds of West Lombardy,
And of Mount Viso especially,
Where the River Po, out of a spring small,
Takes its origin and its source,
Then eastward flows increasing in its course
To Emilia, to Ferrara and Venice:
Which would take a long time to relate,
And truly, in my judgement,
Methinks it a thing irrelevant,
Except to introduce his story.
But this is his tale, which you may now hear."

The Tale

PART ONE

There is, in the west of Italy,
Down at the foot of Mount Viso the cold,
A pleasant plain, abundant of food,
Where many a tower and town you may behold
That founded were in times of forefathers old,
And many another delightful sight,
And Saluzzo was this noble country called.

A marquis once upon a time was of that land
As were his worthy elders him before;
And obedient, ever ready to his hand

Were alle his liges, bothe lasse and more.
Thus in delyt he liveth, and hath don yore,
Biloved and drad, thurgh favour of fortune,
Bothe of his lordes and of his commune.

Therwith he was, to speke as of linage,
The gentilleste y-born of Lumbardye,
A fair persone, and strong, and yong of age,
And ful of honour and of curteisye;
Discreet y-nogh his contree for to gye,
Save in somme thinges that he was to blame,
And Walter was this yonge lordes name.

I blame him thus, that he considereth noght
In tyme cominge what mighte him bityde,
But on his lust present was al his thoght,
As for to hauke and hunte one every syde;
Wel ny alle othere cures leet he slyde,
And eek he nolde, and that was worst of alle,
Wedde no wyf, for noght that may bifalle.

Only that point his peple bar so sore,
That flokmele on a day they to him wente,
And oon of hem, that wysest was of lore,
Or elles that the lord best wolde assente
That he sholde telle him what his peple mente,
Or elles coude he shewe wel swich matere,
He to the markis seyde as ye shul here.

"O noble markis, your humanitee
Assureth us and yeveth us hardinesse,
As ofte as tyme is of necessitee
That we to yow mowe telle our hevinesse;
Accepteth, lord, now for your gentillesse,
That we with pitous herte un-to yow pleyne,
And lete your eres nat my voys disdeyne.

Al have I noght to done in this matere
More than another man hath in this place,

Were all his vassals, both less and more.
Thus in delight he lived, and had done of yore,
Beloved and feared, through Fortune's favor,
Both by his commoners and his lords.

Also he was, to speak of lineage,
The highest born of Lombardy,
A handsome person, and strong, and young of age,
And full of honor and of courtesy;
Wise enough to govern his country—
Save in some things wherein he was to blame—
And Walter was this young lord's name.

I blame him thus, that he considered not
In the future what might him betide,
But on his immediate pleasure was all his thought,
And to hunt and hawk on every side;
Well nigh all other cares let he slide,
And would not—and that was worst of all—
Wed a wife, no matter what may befall.

Only that point his people took so hard
That in crowds on a day they to him went,
And one of them, who was most learned,
Or because the lord would best assent
That he should tell him what his people meant,
Or because he best knew how to put it,
He to the marquis said as you shall hear.

"Oh noble marquis, your humanity
Assures us and gives us the boldness
As often as it is necessary,
That we may tell you our heaviness.
Accept, lord, of your gentleness,
That we with sorrowful heart to you complain,
And let your ears my voice not disdain.

Although I have no more to do in this matter
Than any other man in this place,

Yet for as muche as ye, my lord so dere,
Han alwey shewed me favour and grace,
I dar the better aske of yow a space
Of audience, to shewen our requeste,
And ye, my lord, to doon right as yow leste.

For certes, lord, so wel us lyketh yow
And al your werk and ever han doon, that we
Ne coude nat us self devysen how
We mighte liven in more felicitee,
Save o thing, lord, if it your wille be,
That for to been a wedded man yow leste,
Than were your peple in sovereyn hertes reste.

Boweth your nekke under that blisful yok
Of soveraynetee, noght of servyse,
Which that men clepeth spousaille or wedlok;
And thenketh, lord, among your thoghtes wyse,
How that our dayes passe in sondry wyse;
For though we slepe or wake, or rome, or ryde,
Ay fleeth the tyme, it nil no man abyde.

And though your grene youthe floure as yit,
In crepeth age alwey, as stille as stoon,
And deeth manaceth every age, and smit
In ech estaat, for ther escapeth noon:
And al so certein as we knowe echoon
That we shul deye, as uncerteyn we alle
Been of that day whan deeth shal on us falle.

Accepteth than of us the trewe entente,
That never yet refuseden your heste,
And we wol, lord, if that ye wol assente,
Chese yow a wyf in short tyme, atte leste,
Born of the gentilleste and of the meste
Of al this lond, so that it oghte seme
Honour to god and yow, as we can deme.

Yet inasmuch as you, my lord so dear,
Have always showed me favor and grace,
I dare the better ask of you a chance
For audience, to put forward our request,
And you, my lord, may do just as you wish.

For certainly, lord, so well do you us please
And all your work, and have always done, that we
Could not ourselves imagine how
We might live in more felicity,
Save one thing, lord, if it be your will,
And would please you to be a wedded man,
Then would your people rest in supreme happiness.

Bow your neck under that blissful yoke
Of sovereignty, not of service,
Which men call wedlock or marriage;
And think, lord, among your thoughts wise,
How our days pass in sundry ways;
For though we sleep or wake, or roam, or ride,
Still flees the time, for no man will it wait.

And though your green youth flowers as yet,
In creeps age always, silent as stone,
And death menaces every age, and smites
In every rank, for there escapes no one:
And even though certain as we each know
That we shall die, as uncertain we all
Be of that day when death shall on us fall.

Accept then of us this loyal good faith,
That never yet refused your wish,
And we will, lord, if you will assent,
Choose you a wife in short time, and at the least,
Born of the gentlest and of the best
Of this land, so that it will be an
Honor to God and you, as we can deem.

Deliver us out of al this bisy drede,
And take a wyf, for hye goddes sake;
For if it so bifelle, as god forbede,
That thurgh your deeth your linage sholde slake,
And that a straunge successour sholde take
Your heritage, o! wo were us alyve!
Wherfor we pray you hastily to wyve."

Hir meke preyere and hir pitous chere
Made the markis herte han pitee.
"Ye wol," quod he, "myn owene peple dere,
To that I never erst thoghte streyne me.
I me rejoysed of my libertee,
That selde tyme is founde in mariage;
Ther I was free, I moot been in servage.

But nathelees I see your trewe entente,
And truste upon your wit, and have don ay;
Wherfor of my free wil I wol assente
To wedde me, as sone as ever I may.
But ther-as ye han profred me to-day
To chese me a wyf, I yow relesse
That choys, and prey yow of that profre cesse.

For god it woot, that children ofte been
Unlyk her worthy eldres hem bifore;
Bountee comth al of god, nat of the streen
Of which they been engendred and y-bore;
I truste in goddes bountee, and therfore
My mariage and myn estaat and reste
I him bitake; he may don as him leste.

Lat me alone in chesinge of my wyf,
That charge up-on my bak I wol endure;
But I yow preye, and charge up-on your lyf,
That what wyf that I take, ye me assure
To worshipe hir, whyl that hir lyf may dure,
In word and werk, bothe here and everywhere,
As she an emperoures doghter were.

Deliver us out of this anxious dread
And take a wife, for high God's sake,
For if it so befell, may God forbid,
That through your death your line should end,
And that an unknown successor should take
Your heritage, Oh, woe were us alive!
Wherefore we pray you hastily take a wife."

Their meek prayer and their piteous looks
Made the marquis' heart have pity.
"You wish," said he, "mine own people dear,
What I never thought of doing before.
I rejoiced in a liberty
That seldom is found in marriage;
Where I was once free, I would be in service.

But nevertheless I see your true intent,
And trust your judgement, and have done ever,
Wherefore of my free will I will assent
To wed, as soon as ever I may.
But where you have offered me today
To choose me a wife, I release you from
That choice, and pray you withdraw that offer.

For, God knows, that children oft be
Unlike their worthy elders them before;
Goodness comes from God, not of the blood
Of which they be engendered and born.
I trust in God's goodness, and therefore
My marriage and my nobility and peace
I to Him entrust, to do as he pleases.

Let me alone in the choosing of my wife—
That burden upon my back I will endure;
But I you pray, and charge upon your life,
That whatever wife I take, you me assure
To revere her while her life may endure,
In word and work, both here and everywhere,
As if she an emperor's daughter were.

And forthermore, this shal ye swere, that ye
Agayn my choys shul neither grucche ne stryve;
For sith I shal forgoon my libertee
At your requeste, as ever moot I thryve,
Ther as myn herte is set, ther wol I wyve;
And but ye wole assente in swich manere,
I prey yow, speketh na-more of this matere."

With hertly wil they sworen, and assenten
To al this thing, ther seyde no wight nay;
Bisekinge him of grace, er that they wenten,
That he wolde graunten hem a certein day
Of his spousaille, as sone as ever he may;
For yet alwey the peple som-what dredde
Lest that this markis no wyf wolde wedde.

He graunted hem a day, swich as him leste,
On which he wolde be wedded sikerly,
And seyde, he dide al this at hir requeste;
And they, with humble entente, buxonly,
Knelinge up-on her knees ful reverently
Him thanken alle, and thus they han an ende
Of hir entente, and hoom agayn they wende.

And heer-up-on he to his officeres
Comaundeth for the feste to purveye,
And to his privee knightes and squyeres
Swich charge yaf, as him liste on hem leye;
And they to his comandement obeye,
And ech of hem doth al his diligence
To doon un-to the feste reverence.

And furthermore this shall you swear, that you
Against my choice shall neither grouch nor strive;
For since I shall forego my liberty
At your request, as I may thrive,
Where my heart is set, there will I take a wife.
And unless you will assent in such manner,
I pray you, speak no more of this matter."

With sincere hearts they swore and assented
To all this thing—there said no person nay—
Beseeching of him his grace, before they went,
That he would grant them a certain day
For his wedding, as soon as ever he may;
For yet still the people somewhat dreaded
Lest that this marquis no wife would wed.

He granted them a day, such as it him pleased,
On which he would be wedded surely,
And said he did all this at their request.
And they, with humble intent, submissively,
Kneeling upon their knees full reverently,
All thanked him; and thus they had an end
Of their purpose, and home again they went.

And hereupon he to his household
Commanded for the feast to provide,
And to his personal knights and squires
Such charge gave as upon them he chose to lay;
And they to the commandment obeyed,
And each of them did all his best
To do honor unto the feast.

Noght fer fro thilke paleys honurable
Ther-as this markis shoop his mariage,
Ther stood a throp, of site delitable,
In which that povre folk of that village
Hadden hir bestes and hir herbergage,
And of hir labour took hir sustenance
After that th'erthe yaf hem habundance.

Amonges thise povre folk ther dwelte a man
Which that was holden povrest of hem alle;
But hye god som tyme senden can
His grace in-to a litel oxes stalle:
Janicula men of that throp him calle.
A doghter hadde he, fair y-nogh to sighte,
And Grisildis this yonge mayden highte.

But for to speke of vertuous beautee,
Than was she oon the faireste under sonne;
For povreliche y-fostred up was she,
No likerous lust was thurgh hir herte y-ronne:
Wel ofter of the welle than of the tonne
She drank, and for she wolde vertu plese,
She knew wel labour, but non ydel ese.

But thogh this mayde tendre were of age,
Yet in the brest of hir virginitee
Ther was enclosed rype and sad corage;
And in greet reverence and charitee
Hir olde povre fader fostred she;
A fewe sheep spinning on feeld she kepte,
She wolde noght been ydel til she slepte.

And whan she hoomward cam, she wolde bringe
Wortes or othere herbes tymes ofte,
The whiche she shredde and seeth for hir livinge,
And made hir bed ful harde and no-thing softe;
And ay she kept hir fadres lyf on-lofte
With everich obeisaunce and diligence
That child may doon to fadres reverence.

PART TWO

Not far from this worthy place
Where the marquis prepared for marriage,
There stood a village, of site delightful,
In which poor folk of that village
Had their beasts and their habitations,
And by their labor took their sustenance
Such as provided their land's abundance.

Among these poor folk there dwelt a man
Who was held to be poorest of them all;
But high God sometimes can send
His grace into a little ox's stall.
Janicula men of that town him called;
A daughter had he, fair enough to the eye,
And Griselda was this young maiden's name.

But to speak of virtuous beauty,
Then was she one of the fairest under the sun;
Because she was raised in poverty,
No greed through her heart ran.
Water from the spring, not wine from the cask
She drank; and because she would virtue please,
She knew well labor, but not idle ease.

But though this maid tender was of age,
Yet in the breast of her virginity
There was enclosed a firm and mature heart;
And in great reverence and charity
Her old poor father cared for she.
A few sheep, while spinning, on watch she kept;
She would not be idle till she slept.

And when she homeward went, she would often bring
Plants or other herbs,
Which she shredded and boiled for her living,
And made her bed full hard and nothing soft;
And ever she her father's life sustained
With every obedience and diligence
That a child may do for her parent.

Up-on Grisilde, this povre creature,
Ful ofte sythe this markis sette his yë
As he on hunting rood paraventure;
And whan it fil that he mighte hir espye,
He noght with wantoun loking of folye
His yën caste on hir, but in sad wyse
Up-on hir chere he wolde him ofte avyse,

Commending in his herte hir wommanhede,
And eek hir vertu, passing any wight
Of so yong age, as wel in chere as dede.
For thogh the peple have no greet insight
In vertu, he considered ful right
Hir bountee, and disposed that he wolde
Wedde hir only, if ever he wedde sholde.

The day of wedding cam, but no wight can
Telle what womman that it sholde be;
For which merveille wondred many a man,
And seyden, whan they were in privetee,
"Wol nat our lord yet leve his vanitee?
Wol he nat wedde? allas, allas the whyle!
Why wol he thus him-self and us bigyle?"

But natheles this markis hath don make
Of gemmes, set in gold and in asure,
Broches and ringes, for Grisildis sake,
And of hir clothing took he the mesure
By a mayde, lyk to hir stature,
And eek of othere ornamentes alle
That un-to swich a wedding sholde falle.

The tyme of undern of the same day
Approcheth, that this wedding sholde be;
And al the paleys put was in array,
Bothe halle and chambres, ech in his degree;
Houses of office stuffed with plentee
Ther maystow seen of deyntevous vitaille,
That may be founde, as fer as last Itaille.

Upon Griselda, this poor creature,
Full oftentimes this marquis set his eye
As he while hunting by chance rode by;
And when it befell that he might her espy,
He not with wanton, foolish looks
His eyes cast upon her, but in a serious way
Upon her face he would often ponder,

Commending in his heart her womanhood,
And also her virtue, surpassing any person
Of so young age, as well in looks as deed.
For though common folk have no great insight
In virtue, he considered fully
Her goodness, and decided that he would
Wed her only, if wed he ever should.

The day of wedding came, but no one could
Tell what woman it would be;
For which wondered many a man
And said, when they were in private,
"Will not our lord yet leave his levity?
Will he not wed? alas, alas the while!
Why will he thus himself and us beguile?"

But nevertheless this marquis had ordered made
Of gems, set in gold and in azure
Brooches and rings, for Griselda's sake,
And of her clothing too he took the measure
By a maid, like to her stature,
And also of other adornments all
That unto such a wedding should fall.

As midmorning of the same day
Approached, that this wedding should be;
And all the palace was put in order,
Both hall and chambers, each in its degree;
Kitchens stuffed with plenty
There you could see, with dainty foods
That may be found as far as extends Italy.

This royal markis, richely arrayed,
Lordes and ladyes in his companye,
The whiche unto the feste were y-prayed,
And of his retenue the bachelrye,
With many a soun of sondry melodye,
Un-to the village, of the which I tolde,
In this array the righte wey han holde.

Grisilde of this, god woot, ful innocent,
That for hir shapen was al this array,
To fecchen water at a welle is went,
And cometh hoom as sone as ever she may.
For wel she hadde herd seyd, that thilke day
The markis sholde wedde, and, if she mighte,
She wolde fayn han seyn som of that sighte.

She thoghte, "I wol with othere maydens stonde,
That been my felawes, in our dore, and see
The markisesse, and therfor wol I fonde
To doon at hoom, as sone as it may be,
The labour which that longeth un-to me;
And than I may at leyser hir biholde,
If she this wey un-to the castel holde."

And as she wolde over hir threshfold goon,
The markis cam and gan hir for to calle;
And she set doun hir water-pot anoon
Bisyde the threshfold, in an oxes stalle,
And doun up-on hir knees she gan to falle,
And with sad contenance kneleth stille
Til she had herd what was the lordes wille.

This thoghtful markis spak un-to this mayde
Ful sobrely, and seyde in this manere,
"Wher is your fader, Grisildis?" he sayde,
And she with reverence, in humble chere,
Answerde, "lord, he is al redy here."
And in she gooth with-outen lenger lette,
And to the markis she hir fader fette.

This royal marquis, richly dressed,
Lords and ladies in his company,
Who unto the feast were asked,
And the young knights of his retinue,
With many a sound of various melodies,
Unto the village of which I spoke,
In their array the straight way took.

Griselda, full unaware
That all this parade was prepared for her,
Went to fetch water at the well,
And came home as soon as ever she could.
For well she had heard said that very day
The marquis should wed, and if she might,
She would gladly have seen some of that sight.

She thought, "I will with other maidens stand,
Who be my companions, in our door and see
The marchioness, and therefore will I try
To finish up at home as soon as may be
The labor that belongs to me;
And then I may at leisure her behold,
If she this way unto the castle goes."

And as she would over her threshold go,
The marquis came and began for her to call;
And she set down her pail anon
Beside the threshold, in an ox's stall,
And down on her knees she began to fall,
And with earnest countenance knelt still
Till she had heard what was the lord's will.

The thoughtful marquis spoke unto this maid
Full gravely, and said in this manner:
"Where is your father, Griselda?"
And she with reverence, in a humble way,
Answered, "Lord, he is here, ready to serve you."
And she went in without delay,
And to the marquis her father led.

He by the hond than took this olde man,
And seyde thus, whan he him hadde asyde,
"Janicula, I neither may ne can
Lenger the plesance of my herte hyde.
If that thou vouche-sauf, what-so bityde,
Thy doghter wol I take, er that I wende,
As for my wyf, un-to hir lyves ende.

Thou lovest me, I woot it wel, certyn,
And art my feithful lige man y-bore;
And al that lyketh me, I dar wel seyn
It lyketh thee, and specially therfore
Tel me that poynt that I have seyd bifore,
If that thou wolt un-to that purpos drawe,
To take me as for thy sone-in-lawe?"

This sodeyn cas this man astoned so,
That reed he wex, abayst, and al quaking
He stood; unnethes seyde he wordes mo,
But only thus: "lord," quod he, "my willing
Is as ye wole, ne ayeines your lyking
I wol no-thing; ye be my lord so dere;
Right as yow lust governeth this matere."

"Yet wol I," quod this markis softely,
"That in thy chambre I and thou and she
Have a collacion, and wostow why?
For I wol axe if it hir wille be
To be my wyf, and reule hir after me;
And al this shal be doon in thy presence,
I wol noght speke out of thyn audience."

And in the chambre whyl they were aboute
Hir tretis, which as ye shal after here,
The peple cam un-to the hous with-oute,
And wondred hem in how honest manere
And tentifly she kepte hir fader dere.
But outerly Grisildis wondre mighte,
For never erst ne saugh she swich a sighte.

He by the hand then took this old man,
And said when he had him aside,
"Janicula, I neither may nor can
Longer the pleasure of my heart hide.
If you will permit, whatever may betide,
Your daughter will I take, before I depart—
For my wife, until our lives end.

You love me, I know it well, certain,
And were my faithful vassal born;
And all that pleases me, I dare well say
Also pleases you; and especially therefore
Answer me that question I have said before:
If you will
Take me for your son-in-law."

This sudden turn this man bewildered so
That red he turned, abashed and all trembling
He stood. Scarcely said he words more,
But only thus: "Lord," said he, "my wish
Is as you will; against your liking
I wish no thing, you be my lord so dear.
Right as you please govern this matter."

"Then I would like," said this marquis softly,
"That in your chamber you and I and she
Have a talk, and do you know why?
For I will ask if her will it be
To be my wife, and govern herself after me.
And all this shall be done in your presence—
I will not speak out of your audience."

And in the chamber while they made
Their contract, as you shall after hear,
The people came to the house outside,
And wondered at how attentively
And tenderly she kept her father dear.
But especially Griselda might have wondered,
For never before had she seen such a sight.

No wonder is thogh that she were astoned
To seen so greet a gest come in that place;
She never was to swiche gestes woned,
For which she loked with ful pale face.
But shortly forth this tale for to chace,
Thise arn the wordes that the markis sayde
To this benigne verray feithful mayde.

"Grisilde," he seyde, "ye shul wel understonde
It lyketh to your fader and to me
That I yow wedde, and eek it may so stonde,
As I suppose, ye wol that it so be.
But thise demandes axe I first," quod he,
"That, sith it shal be doon in hastif wyse,
Wol ye assente, or elles yow avyse?

I seye this, be ye redy with good herte
To al my lust, and that I frely may,
As me best thinketh, do yow laughe or smerte,
And never ye to grucche it, night ne day?
And eek whan I sey 'ye,' ne sey nat 'nay,'
Neither by word ne frowning contenance;
Swer this, and here I swere our alliance."

Wondring upon this word, quaking for drede,
She seyde, "lord, undigne and unworthy
Am I to thilke honour that ye me bede;
But as ye wol your-self, right so wol I.
And heer I swere that never willingly
In werk ne thoght I nil yow disobeye,
For to be deed, though me were looth to deye."

"This is y-nogh, Grisilde myn!" quod he.
And forth he gooth with a ful sobre chere
Out at the dore, and after that cam she,
And to the peple he seyde in this manere,
"This is my wyf," quod he, "that standeth here,
Honoureth hir, and loveth hir, I preye,
Who-so me loveth; ther is na-more to seye."

No wonder that she was bewildered
To see so great a guest come in that place;
She never was to such guests accustomed,
And so she looked with full pale face.
But shortly, this matter to pursue,
These are the words that the marquis said
To this gracious, true, faithful maid.

"Griselda," he said, "you shall well understand
It pleases your father and me
That I you wed, and also it may be the case,
As I suppose, you will that it so be.
But these demands I ask first," said he,
"That since it shall be done in haste,
Will you assent, or else deliberate?

I say this, be you ready with good heart
To honor my every wish, and that I freely may,
As I think best, make you laugh or suffer,
And you never to complain about it, night or day?
And also when I say 'yes,' you say not 'nay,'
Neither by word nor frowning countenance?
Swear this, and here I swear our alliance."

Wondering upon this speech, trembling for dread,
She said, "Lord, undeserving and unworthy
Am I to that honor that you offer me;
But as you will it yourself, right so will I,
And here I swear that never willingly
In deed nor thought will I disobey you,
Even to die, though to die I loathe would be."

"This is enough, Griselda, mine!" said he.
And forth he went with a full sober face
Out at the door, and after that came she,
And to the people he said in this manner:
"This is my wife," said he, "who stands here.
Honor her and love her I pray
Whoso me loves; there is no more to say."

And for that no-thing of hir olde gere
She sholde bringe in-to his hous, he bad
That wommen sholde dispoilen hir right there;
Of which thise ladyes were nat right glad
To handle hir clothes wher-in she was clad.
But natheles this mayde bright of hewe
Fro foot to heed they clothed han al newe.

Hir heres han they kembd, that lay untressed
Ful rudely, and with hir fingres smale
A corone on hir heed they han y-dressed,
And sette hir ful of nowches grete and smale;
Of hir array what sholde I make a tale?
Unnethe the peple hir knew for hir fairnesse,
Whan she translated was in swich richesse.

This markis hath hir spoused with a ring
Broght for the same cause, and than hir sette
Up-on an hors, snow-whyt and wel ambling,
And to his paleys, er he lenger lette,
With joyful peple that hir ladde and mette,
Conveyed hir, and thus the day they spende
In revel, til the sonne gan descende.

And shortly forth this tale for to chace,
I seye that to this newe markisesse
God hath swich favour sent hir of his grace,
That it ne semed nat by lyklinesse
That she was born and fed in rudenesse,
As in a cote or in an oxe-stalle,
But norished in an emperoures halle.

To every wight she woxen is so dere
And worshipful, that folk ther she was bore
And from hir birthe knewe hir yeer by yere,
Unnethe trowed they, but dorste han swore
That to Janicle, of which I spak bifore,
She doghter nas, for, as by conjecture,
Hem thoughte she was another creature.

And so that none of her old clothes
She should bring into his house, he bade
That women should undress her right there;
Of which these ladies were not right glad
To handle her clothes wherein she was clad.
But nevertheless, this maid bright of hue
From foot to head they clothed all new.

Her hair they combed, that lay unbraided
Full artless, and with their fingers small
A crown on her head they placed,
And adorned her full of jewels great and small.
Of her apparel why should I make a tale?
Scarcely the people knew her for her fairness,
When she was transformed in such richness.

This marquis had her married with a ring
Brought for the same purpose, and then her set
Upon a horse, snow-white and soft-gaited,
And to his palace, with no further delay,
With joyful people who her met and led,
Conveyed her; and thus the day they spent
In revel, till the sun did set.

And shortly, this tale to pursue,
I say that to this new marquess
God had such favor sent her of his grace,
That it seemed not likely
That she was born and fed in lowliness,
As in a cottage or an ox stall,
But nourished in an emperor's hall.

To every person she grew so dear
And of honor worthy, that people where she was born
And from her birth knew her year by year,
Scarcely could believe—though they it would swear—
That to Janicula, of whom I spoke before,
She daughter was, for, as by conjecture,
To them she seemed another creature.

For thogh that ever vertuous was she,
She was encressed in swich excellence
Of thewes gode, y-set in heigh bountee,
And so discreet and fair of eloquence,
So benigne and so digne of reverence,
And coude so the peples herte embrace,
That ech hir lovede that loked on hir face.

Noght only of Saluces in the toun
Publiced was the bountee of hir name,
But eek bisyde in many a regioun,
If oon seyde wel, another seyde the same;
So spradde of hir heigh bountee the fame,
That men and wommen, as wel yonge as olde,
Gon to Saluce, upon hir to biholde.

Thus Walter lowly, nay but royally,
Wedded with fortunat honestetee,
In goddes pees liveth ful esily
At hoom, and outward grace y-nogh had he;
And for he saugh that under low degree
Was ofte vertu hid, the peple him helde
A prudent man, and that is seyn ful selde.

Nat only this Grisildis thurgh hir wit
Coude al the feet of wyfly hoomlinesse,
But eek, whan that the cas requyred it,
The commune profit coude she redresse.
Ther nas discord, rancour, ne hevinesse
In al that lond, that she ne coude apese,
And wysly bringe hem alle in reste and ese.

Though that hir housbonde absent were anoon,
If gentil men, or othere of hir contree
Were wrothe, she wolde bringen hem atoon;
So wyse and rype wordes hadde she,
And jugements of so greet equitee,
That she from heven sent was, as men wende,
Peple to save and every wrong t'amende.

For although ever virtuous was she,
She was increased in such excellence
Of qualities fine, set in high goodness,
And so wise and fair of speech,
So gracious and so worthy of reverence,
And could so the people's hearts hold fast,
That each loved her who looked upon her face.

Not only in the town of Saluzzo
Published was the goodness of her name,
But also in many another region:
If one spoke well, another said the same.
So spread of her high goodness the fame
That men and women, as well young as old,
Went to Saluzzo upon her to behold.

Thus Walter lowly—nay but royally—
Wedded with fortunate honor,
In God's peace lived full easily
At home, and outward grace enough had he;
And because he saw that under low degree
Was often virtue hid, the people held him
A prudent man, and that is full seldom seen.

Not only this Griselda through her wit
Knew all the tasks of a housewife's skill,
But also, when the case required it,
The common good could she amend.
There was no discord, rancor, nor heaviness
In all the land that she could not appease,
And wisely bring them all peace and ease.

Though her husband absent were,
If gentlemen or others of her country
Were angry, she would soon bring them into one;
So wise and mature words had she,
And judgements of so great even-handedness,
That she was sent from heaven, as men imagined,
People to save and every wrong to mend.

Nat longe tyme after that this Grisild
Was wedded, she a doughter hath y-bore,
Al had hir lever have born a knave child.
Glad was this markis and the folk therfore;
For though a mayde child come al bifore,
She may unto a knave child atteyne
By lyklihed, sin she nis nat bareyne.

PART THREE

Ther fil, as it bifalleth tymes mo,
Whan that this child had souked but a throwe,
This markis in his herte longeth so
To tempte his wyf, hir sadnesse for to knowe,
That he ne mighte out of his herte throwe
This merveillous desyr, his wyf t'assaye,
Needless, god woot, he thoughte hir for t'affraye.

He hadde assayed hir y-nogh bifore,
And fond hir ever good; what neded it
Hir for to tempte and alwey more and more?
Though som men preise it for a subtil wit,
But as for me, I seye that yvel it sit
T'assaye a wyf whan that it is no nede,
And putten her in anguish and in drede.

For which this markis wroghte in this manere;
He cam alone a-night, ther as she lay,
With sterne face and with ful trouble chere,
And seyde thus, "Grisild," quod he, "that day
That I yow took out of your povre array,
And putte yow in estaat of heigh noblesse,
Ye have nat that forgeten, as I gesse.

I seye, Grisild, this present dignitee,
In which that I have put yow, as I trowe,
Maketh yow nat foryetful for to be
That I yow took in povre estaat ful lowe
For any wele ye moot your-selven knowe.

Not long time after this Griselda
Was wedded, she a daughter had borne.
Although she'd rather have borne a son,
Glad was this marquis and the folk therefore;
For though a maid child came before,
She may unto a boy child attain
By likelihood, since she was not barren.

PART THREE

There happened, as it so often does,
When this child had nursed but a short while,
That this marquis in his heart longed so
To tempt his wife, her fidelity to know,
That he could not out of his heart throw
This strange desire, to test his wife;
Needlessly, God knows, he decided her to frighten.

He had tested her enough before
And found her ever good. Why should he need
To tempt her always more and more,
Though some men praised it for subtle wit?
But as for me, I say that it ill becomes a man
To test a wife when there is no need,
And put her in anguish and in dread.

For which this marquis wrought in this manner:
He came alone at night, where she lay,
With stern face and full troubled look,
And said thus: "Griselda, that day
That I you took out of your poor place
And put you in estate of high noblesse,
You have not that forgotten, as I guess.

I say, Griselda, this present dignity,
In which I have put you, as I believe,
Perhaps makes you forget
That I took you in poor estate full low.
For any happiness you may yourself know,

Tak hede of every word that I yow seye,
Ther is no wight that hereth it but we tweye.

Ye woot your-self wel, how that ye cam here
In-to this hous, it is nat longe ago,
And though to me that ye be lief and dere,
Un-to my gentils ye be no-thing so;
They seyn, to hem it is greet shame and wo
For to be subgets and ben in servage
To thee, that born art of a smal village.

And namely, sith thy doghter was y-bore,
Thise wordes han they spoken doutelees;
But I desyre, as I have doon bifore,
To live my lyf with hem in reste and pees;
I may nat in this caas be recchelees.
I moot don with thy doghter for the beste,
Nat as I wolde, but as my peple leste.

And yet, god wot, this is ful looth to me;
But nathelees with-oute your witing
I wol nat doon, but this wol I," quod he,
"That ye to me assente as in this thing.
Shewe now your pacience in your werking
That ye me highte and swore in your village
That day that maked was our mariage."

Whan she had herd al this, she noght ameved
Neither in word, or chere, or countenaunce;
For, as it semed, she was nat agreved;
She seyde, "lord, al lyth in your plesaunce,
My child and I with hertly obeisaunce
Ben youres al, and ye mowe save or spille
Your owene thing; werketh after your wille.

Ther may no-thing, god so my soule save,
Lyken to yow that may displese me;
Ne I desyre no-thing for to have,
Ne drede for to lese, save only ye;

Take heed of every word that I say to you:
There's no one who hears it but we two.

You know well yourself how you came here
Into this house, not long ago,
And though to me you be beloved and dear,
Unto my gentlefolk you be nothing so;
They say it is a great shame and woe
To be subjects and be in service
To you, who born art of a small village.

And especially since your daughter was born
These words have they spoken, doubtless;
But I desire, as I have done before,
To live my life with them in rest and peace;
I may not in this case be heedless.
I must do with your daughter for the best,
Not as I would, but as my people wish.

And yet, God knows, this is full loath to me.
But nevertheless without your knowing
I will not act, but this I wish," said he,
"That you to me assent in this thing.
Show now your patience in your deeds
That you me promised and swore in your village
That day that made was our marriage."

When she had heard all this, she no motion made
Neither in word nor manner nor countenance;
For as it seemed, she was not aggrieved.
She said, "Lord, all lies in your pleasure;
My child and I with heartfelt obedience
Be yours all, and you may save or destroy
Your own thing: do as you wish.

There may be no thing, God so my soul save;
That pleases you that displeases me;
Nor do I desire anything to have,
Nor dread to lose, save only you;

This wil is in myn herte and ay shal be.
No lengthe of tyme or deeth may this deface,
Ne chaunge my corage to another place."

Glad was this markis of hir answering,
But yet he feyned as he were nat so;
Al drery was his chere and his loking
Whan that he sholde out of the chambre go.
Sone after this, a furlong wey or two,
He prively hath told al his entente
Un-to a man, and to his wyf him sente.

A maner sergeant was this privee man,
The which that feithful ofte he founden hadde
In thinges grete, and eek swich folk wel can
Don execucioun on thinges badde.
The lord knew wel that he him loved and dradde;
And whan this sergeant wiste his lordes wille,
In-to the chambre he stalked him ful stille.

"Madame," he seyde, "ye mote foryeve it me,
Thogh I do thing to which I am constreyned;
Ye ben so wys that ful wel knowe ye
That lordes hestes mowe nat been y-feyned;
They mowe wel been biwailled or compleyned,
But men mot nede un-to her lust obeye,
And so wol I; ther is na-more to seye.

This child I am comanded for to take"—
And spak na-more, but out the child he hente
Despitously, and gan a chere make
As though he wolde han slayn it er he wente.
Grisildis mot al suffren and consente;
And as a lamb she siteth meke and stille,
And leet this cruel sergeant doon his wille.

Suspecious was the diffame of this man,
Suspect his face, suspect his word also;
Suspect the tyme in which he this bigan.

This will is in my heart and ever shall be.
No length of time or death may this deface,
Nor change my heart to another place."

Glad was this marquis for her answer,
But yet he feigned as he were not so;
All sad was his face and his look
When he left the chamber.
Soon after this, within a little while,
He secretly told all his plan
Unto a man, and sent him to his wife.

A sergeant-at-arms was this trusted man,
Whom often he had found faithful
In things great, and also such folk well know
How to perform in things bad.
The lord well knew that he him loved and feared;
And when this sergeant knew his lord's will,
Into the chamber he crept full silent and still.

"Madame," said he, "you must forgive me,
Though I do something to which I am constrained.
You be so wise that full well you know
That lords' wishes may not be avoided,
They may well be bewailed or lamented,
But men must unto their will obey,
And so will I; there is no more to say.

This child I am commanded for to take"—
And spoke no more, but the child he seized
Cruelly, and made
As though he would slay it before he left.
Griselda must all suffer and all consent;
And as a lamb she sat meek and still,
And let this cruel sergeant do his will.

Suspect was the reputation of this man,
Suspect his face, suspect his word also;
Suspect the time in which he this began.

Allas! hir doghter that she lovede so
She wende he wolde han slawen it right tho.
But natheles she neither weep ne syked,
Consenting hir to that the markis lyked.

But atte laste speken she bigan,
And mekely she to the sergeant preyde,
So as he was a worthy gentil man,
That she moste kisse hir child er that it deyde;
And in her barm this litel child she leyde
With ful sad face, and gan the child to kisse
And lulled it, and after gan it blisse.

And thus she seyde in hir benigne voys,
"Far weel, my child; I shal thee never see;
But, sith I thee have marked with the croys,
Of thilke fader blessed mote thou be,
That for us deyde up-on a croys of tree.
Thy soule, litel child, I him bitake,
For this night shaltow dyen for my sake."

I trowe that to a norice in this cas
It had ben hard this rewthe for to se;
Wel mighte a mooder than han cryed "allas!"
But nathelees so sad stedfast was she,
That she endured all adversitee,
And to the sergeant mekely she sayde,
"Have heer agayn your litel yonge mayde.

Goth now," quod she, "and dooth my lordes heste,
But o thing wol I preye yow of your grace,
That, but my lord forbad yow, atte leste
Burieth this litel body in som place
That bestes ne no briddes it to-race."
But he no word wol to that purpos seye,
But took the child and wente upon his weye.

This sergeant cam un-to his lord ageyn,
And of Grisildis wordes and hir chere

Alas! her daughter that she loved so,
She thought he would have slain it right then.
But nevertheless she neither wept nor sighed,
Conforming herself to what the marquis liked.

But finally to speak she began,
And meekly she to the sergeant begged,
So as he was a worthy gentleman,
That she might kiss her child before it died;
And in her lap this little child she laid
With a full sad face, and began the child to bless
And lulled it, and after began it to kiss.

And thus she said in her gracious voice,
"Farewell, my child; I shall you never see.
But since I have marked you with the cross
Of our Father, blessed may he be,
Who for us died upon a cross.
Your soul, little child, to him I commend,
For this night shall you die for my sake."

I believe that to a nurse in this case
It would have been hard this pitiful sight to see;
Well might a mother have then cried "alas!"
But nevertheless so firmly steadfast was she
That she endured all adversity,
And to the sergeant meekly she said,
"Have here again your little young maid.

Go now," said she, "and do my lord's wish.
But one thing will I pray you of your grace,
That, unless my lord forbid it you, at least
Bury this little body in some place
Where no beasts nor birds tear it to pieces."
But he no word to that purpose said,
But took the child and went upon his way.

This sergeant came unto his lord again,
And of Griselda's words and her behavior

He tolde him point for point, in short and playn,
And him presenteth with his doghter dere.
Somwhat this lord hath rewthe in his manere;
But nathelees his purpos heeld he stille,
As lordes doon, whan they wol han hir wille;

And bad his sergeant that he prively
Sholde this child ful softe winde and wrappe
With alle circumstances tendrely,
And carie it in a cofre or in a lappe;
But, up-on peyne his heed of for to swappe,
That no man sholde knowe of his entente,
Ne whenne he cam, ne whider that he wente;

But at Boloigne to his suster dere,
That thilke tyme of Panik was countesse,
He sholde it take, and shewe hir this matere,
Bisekinge hir to don hir bisinesse
This child to fostre in alle gentilesse;
And whos child that it was he bad hir hyde
From every wight, for oght that may bityde.

The sergeant gooth, and hath fulfild this thing;
But to this markis now retourne we;
For now goth he ful faste imagining
If by his wyves chere he mighte see,
Or by hir word aperceyve that she
Were chaunged; but he never hir coude finde
But ever in oon y-lyke sad and kinde.

As glad, as humble, as bisy in servyse,
And eek in love as she was wont to be,
Was she to him in every maner wyse;
Ne of hir doghter noght a word spak she.
Non accident for noon adversitee
Was seyn in hir, ne never hir doghter name
Ne nempned she, in ernest nor in game.

He told him point for point, in short and plain,
And presented to him his daughter dear.
This lord showed some pity in his manner,
But nevertheless his purpose held he still,
As lords do when they will have their will.

And bade this sergeant that he secretly
Should this child soft wind and wrap
Tenderly in every way,
And carry it in a box or a sling;
But upon pain of having his head chopped,
That no man should know of his intent,
Nor whence he came, nor whither he went;

But at Bologna to his sister dear,
Who at that time was of Panico countess,
He should take it, and explain to her this matter,
Beseeching her to do her best,
This child to foster in all gentleness;
And whose child it was he bade her hide
From every man, no matter what might betide.

The sergeant went, and had fulfilled this thing;
But to this marquis now return we.
For now he went full fast wondering
If by his wife's expression he might see,
Or by her word perceive, that she
Were changed; but he found her
Ever steadfast and kind.

As glad, as humble, as busy in service,
And also in love as she was accustomed to be,
Was she to him in every way;
Nor of her daughter a word spoke she.
No outward sign of any adversity
Was seen in her, nor ever her daughter's name
Spoke she, in earnest or in play.

In this estaat ther passed been foure yeer
Er she with childe was; but, as god wolde,
A knave child she bar by this Walter,
Ful gracious and fair for to biholde.
And whan that folk it to his fader tolde,
Nat only he, but al his contree, merie
Was for this child, and god they thanke and herie.

Whan it was two yeer old, and fro the brest
Departed of his norice, on a day
This markis caughte yet another lest
To tempte his wyf yet ofter, if he may.
O needles was she tempted in assay!
But wedded men ye knowe no mesure,
Whan that they finde a pacient creature.

"Wyf," quod this markis, "ye han herd er this,
My peple sikly berth our mariage,
And namely, sith my sone y-boren is,
Now is it worse than ever in al our age.
The murmur sleeth myn herte and my corage;
For to myne eres comth the voys so smerte,
That it wel ny destroyed hath myn herte.

Now sey they thus, 'whan Walter is agoon,
Then shal the blood of Janicle succede
And been our lord, for other have we noon;'
Swiche wordes seith my peple, out of drede,
Wel oughte I of swich murmur taken hede;
For certeinly I drede swich sentence,
Though they nat pleyn speke in myn audience.

I wolde live in pees, if that I mighte;
Wherfor I am disposed outerly,
As I his suster servede by nighte,
Right so thenke I to serve him prively;
This warne I yow, that ye nat sodeynly

PART FOUR

In this condition there passed four years
Before she with child was; but, as God willed,
A boy child she bore by this Walter,
Full gracious and handsome to behold.
And when his father learned of his birth,
Not only he, but all his country, was merry
For this child, and God they thanked and praised.

When it was two years old and from the breast
Departed of his nurse, on a day
This marquis conceived yet another desire
To tempt his wife again, if he may.
Oh, needlessly was she put to the test!
But wedded men know no measure
When that they find a patient creature.

"Wife," said this marquis, "you have heard before this,
My people bear ill our marriage,
And especially, since my son is born,
Now it is worse than ever in all our days.
The murmur slays my heart and spirit,
For to my ears comes the voice so sharp
That it has well nigh destroyed my heart.

Now they say thus, 'When Walter is gone,
Then shall the blood of Janicula succeed
And be our Lord, for other we have none;'
Such words say my people, without doubt.
Well ought I of such murmur take heed,
For certainly, I dread such opinion,
Though they speak it not in my hearing.

I would live in peace if I might;
Wherefore I am disposed entirely,
As I his sister dealt with by night,
Right so I think to take care of him in secret.
This I warn you, that you do not suddenly

Out of your-self for no wo sholde outraye;
Beth pacient, and ther-of I yow preye."

"I have," quod she, "seyd thus, and ever shal,
I wol no thing, ne nil no thing, certayn,
But as yow list; noght greveth me at al,
Thogh that my doghter and my sone be slayn,
At your comandement, this is to sayn.
I have noght had no part of children tweyne
But first siknesse, and after wo and peyne.

Ye been our lord, doth with your owene thing
Right as yow list; axeth no reed at me.
For, as I lefte at hoom al my clothing,
Whan I first cam to yow, right so," quod she,
"Lefte I my wil and al my libertee,
And took your clothing; wherfor I yow preye,
Doth your plesaunce, I wol your lust obeye.

And certes, if I hadde prescience
Your wil to knowe er ye your lust me tolde,
I wolde it doon with-outen necligence;
But now I woot your lust and what ye wolde,
Al your plesaunce ferme and stable I holde;
For wiste I that my deeth wolde do yow ese,
Right gladly wolde I dyen, yow to plese.

Deth may noght make no comparisoun
Un-to your love:" and, whan this markis sey
The constance of his wyf, he caste adoun
His yën two, and wondreth that she may
In pacience suffre al this array.
And forth he gooth with drery contenaunce,
But to his herte it was ful greet plesaunce.

This ugly sergeant, in the same wyse
That he hir doghter caughte, right so he,
Or worse, if men worse can devyse,
Hath hent hir sone, that ful was of beautee.

Lose control of yourself in sorrow:
Be patient, and thereof I pray you."

"I have," said she, "said thus, and ever shall,
I desire nothing, certainly,
Unless it pleases you; it grieves me not at all,
Though my daughter and my son be slain—
At your commandment, this is to say.
I have had no part of children two
But first childbearing, and after woe and pain.

You be our lord, do with your own thing
Right as you wish, ask no advice from me.
For as I left at home all my clothing
When I first came to you, right so," said she,
"Left I my will and all my liberty,
And took your clothing. Wherefore I you pray,
Do your pleasure, I will your desire obey.

And certainly, if I had prescience
Your will to know before you told it to me,
I would do it without negligence.
But now I know your pleasure and what you will,
All your desire firmly and steadfastly I hold;
For if I knew my death would do you ease,
Right gladly would I die, you to please.

Death may not make comparison
With your love." And when this marquis saw
The constancy of his wife, he cast down
His eyes two, and wondered that she could
In patience suffer all these events.
And forth he went with doleful countenance,
But to his heart it was full great pleasant.

This fearsome sergeant, in the same way
That he her daughter took away, right so he—
Or worse, if men can devise—
Had seized her son, who was full of beauty.

And ever in oon so pacient was she,
That she no chere made of hevinesse,
But kiste hir sone, and after gan it blesse;

Save this; she preyed him that, if he mighte,
Hir litel sone he wolde in erthe grave,
His tendre limes, delicat to sighte,
Fro foules and fro bestes for to save.
But she non answer of him mighte have.
He wente his wey, as him no-thing ne roghte;
But to Boloigne he tendrely it broghte.

This markis wondreth ever lenger the more
Up-on hir pacience, and if that he
Ne hadde soothly knowen ther-bifore,
That parfitly hir children lovede she,
He wolde have wend that of som subtiltee,
And of malice or for cruel corage,
That she had suffred this with sad visage.

But wel he knew that next him-self, certayn,
She loved hir children best in every wyse.
But now of wommen wolde I axen fayn,
If thise assayes mighte nat suffyse?
What coude a sturdy housbond more devyse
To preve hir wyfhod and hir stedfastnesse,
And he continuing ever in sturdinesse?

But ther ben folk of swich condicioun,
That, whan they have a certein purpos take,
They can nat stinte of hir entencioun,
But, right as they were bounden to a stake,
They wol nat of that firste purpos slake.
Right so this markis fulliche hath purposed
To tempte his wyf, as he was first disposed.

He waiteth, if by word or contenance
That she to him was changed of corage;
But never coude he finde variance;

And ever and always so patient was she
That she no expression made of heaviness,
But kissed her son, and after began him to bless.

Save this: she prayed the sergeant that he might
Her little son in the earth bury,
To save his tender limbs, delicate to see,
From birds and beasts.
But she no answer from him received.
He went on his way, as though he cared not at all,
But to Bologna he brought it tenderly.

This marquis wondered ever more
Upon her patience, and if he
Had not truly known before
How perfectly her children loved she,
He would have thought that it was by some trick,
Or through a cruel heart,
That she suffered this with unchanged face.

But well he knew that next to himself, certainly,
She loved her children best in every way.
But now of women would I like to ask,
If these trials might not suffice?
What could a cruel husband more devise
To test her wifehood and her steadfastness,
And he continuing even with cruelty?

But there be folk of such disposition
Who, when they have a certain course taken,
They cannot stop short of their destination;
But just as if they were bound to a stake,
They will not of that first purpose slake.
Right so this marquis fully has intended
To tempt his wife as he was first disposed.

He watched if by word or countenance
That she to him was changed in her heart,
But never could he find variance:

She was ay oon in herte and in visage;
And ay the forther that she was in age,
The more trewe, if that it were possible,
She was to him in love, and more penible.

For which it semed thus, that of hem two
Ther nas but o wil; for, as Walter leste,
The same lust was hir plesance also,
And, god be thanked, al fil for the beste.
She shewed wel, for no worldly unreste
A wyf, as of hir-self, no-thing ne sholde
Wille in effect, but as hir housbond wolde.

The sclaundre of Walter ofte and wyde spradde,
That of a cruel herte he wikkedly,
For he a povre womman wedded hadde,
Hath mordred bothe his children prively.
Swich murmur was among hem comunly.
No wonder is, for to the peples ere
Ther cam no word but that they mordred were.

For which, wher-as his peple ther-bifore
Had loved him wel, the sclaundre of his diffame
Made hem that they him hatede therfore;
To been a mordrer is an hateful name.
But natheles, for ernest ne for game
He of his cruel purpos nolde stente;
To tempte his wyf was set al his entente.

Whan that his doghter twelf yeer was of age,
He to the court of Rome, in subtil wyse
Enformed of his wil, sente his message,
Comaunding hem swiche bulles to devyse
As to his cruel purpos may suffyse,
How that the pope, as for his peples reste,
Bad him to wedde another, if him leste.

I seye, he bad they sholde countrefete
The popes bulles, making mencioun

She was ever unchanged in heart and visage.
And ever the older that she was in age,
The more true, if that were possible,
She was to him in love, and more painstaking.

For which it seemed thus, that for them both
There was but one will; for, as Walter wished,
That same desire was her pleasure also;
And, God be thanked, all turned out for the best.
She showed well that for no earthly distress
A wife, for her own sake, should nothing
Wish for but as her husband would.

The scandal of Walter wide and often spread
That of a cruel heart he wickedly,
Because he a poor woman had wed,
Had murdered both his children in secret.
Such murmur was commonly among them.
No wonder is, for to the people's ear
There came no word but that they murdered were.

For which, whereas his people heretofore
Had loved him well, the scandal of his ill repute
Made them hate him for it:
To be a murderer is a hateful name.
But nevertheless, neither in earnest nor play,
He of his cruel purpose would relent.
To tempt his wife was set all his intent.

When his daughter twelve years was of age,
He to the court of Rome, in secret ways
Informed of his will, sending his emissary,
Commanding them such papal bulls[3] to devise
As to his cruel purpose might suffice:
That the Pope, for his people's peace,
Bade him to wed another if he wished.

I say, he bade they should counterfeit
The Pope's bulls, making mention

That he hath leve his firste wyf to lete,
As by the popes dispensacioun,
To stinte rancour and dissencioun
Bitwixe his peple and him; thus seyde the bulle,
The which they han publiced atte fulle.

The rude peple, as it no wonder is,
Wenden ful wel that it had been right so;
But whan thise tydinges cam to Grisildis,
I deme that hir herte was ful wo.
But she, y-lyke sad for evermo,
Disposed was, this humble creature,
Th'adversitee of fortune al t'endure.

Abyding ever his lust and his plesaunce,
To whom that she was yeven, herte and al,
As to hir verray worldly suffisaunce;
But shortly if this storie I tellen shal,
This markis writen hath in special
A lettre in which he sheweth his entente,
And secrely he to Boloigne is sente.

To th'erl of Panik, which that hadde tho
Wedded his suster, preyde he specially
To bringen hoom agayn his children two
In honurable estaat al openly.
But o thing he him preyede outerly,
That he to no wight, though men wolde enquere,
Sholde nat telle, whos children that they were,

But seye, the mayden sholde y-wedded be
Un-to the markis of Saluce anon.
And as this erl was preyed, so dide he;
For at day set he on his wey is goon
Toward Saluce, and lordes many oon,
In riche array, this mayden for to gyde;
Hir yonge brother ryding hir bisyde.

That he had permission his first wife to leave,
By the Pope's dispensation,
To stop rancor and dissention
Between his people and him—thus said the bull,
Which they had published full well.

The common people, as it no wonder is,
Believed full well that it had been right so;
But when these tidings came to Griselda,
I am sure her heart was full of woe.
But she, constant evermore,
Disposed was, this humble creature,
The adversity of Fortune all to endure,

Serving ever his desire and his pleasure,
To whom she had given heart and all,
As being her true, earthly contentment.
But shortly of this story I tell shall,
This marquis had written in secret
A letter in which he revealed his intent,
And secretly he to Bologna it sent.

To the Earl of Panico, who had
Wedded his sister, he specially requested
To bring home again his children two
In honorable estate all openly.
But one thing he requested above all,
That he to no one, though men would inquire,
Should tell whose children that they were,

But say the maid should wedded be
Unto the Marquis of Saluzzo anon.
And as this earl was asked, so did he,
For on the appointed day he set on his way
Toward Saluzzo, with lords many a one
In rich display, this maiden to guide,
Her young brother riding her beside.

Arrayed was toward hir mariage
This fresshe mayde, ful of gemmes clere;
Hir brother, which that seven yeer was of age,
Arrayed eek ful fresh in his manere.
And thus in greet noblesse and with glad chere,
Toward Saluces shaping hir journey,
Fro day to day they ryden in hir wey.

PART FIVE

Among al this, after his wikke usage,
This markis, yet his wyf to tempte more
To the uttereste preve of hir corage,
Fully to han experience and lore
If that she were as stedfast as bifore,
He on a day in open audience
Ful boistously hath seyd hir this sentence:

"Certes, Grisilde, I hadde y-nough plesaunce
To han yow to my wyf for your goodnesse,
As for your trouthe and for your obeisaunce,
Nought for your linage ne for your richesse;
But now knowe I in verray soothfastnesse
That in gret lordshipe, if I wel avyse,
Ther is gret servitute in sondry wyse.

I may nat don as every plowman may;
My peple me constreyneth for to take
Another wyf, and cryen day by day;
And eek the pope, rancour for to slake,
Consenteth it, that dar I undertake;
And treweliche thus muche I wol yow seye,
My newe wyf is coming by the weye.

Be strong of herte, and voyde anon hir place,
And thilke dower that ye broghten me
Tak it agayn, I graunte it of my grace;
Retourneth to your fadres hous," quod he;
"No man may alwey han prosperitee;

Adorned for her marriage was
This fresh maid, covered with jewels shining;
Her brother who was seven years of age,
Dressed also full fresh in his manner.
And thus grandly and with glad aspect,
Toward Saluzzo on their journey,
From day to day they rode on their way.

PART FIVE

Meanwhile, in his wicked way,
This marquis yet his wife to test more
To the utmost of her soul and heart,
Fully to see and know
If she was as steadfast as before,
He on a day in open court
Full roughly had to her announced:

"Truly, Griselda, I had pleasure enough
To have you to my wife for your goodness—
And for your truth and your obedience—
Not for your lineage or your riches.
But now I know in certain truth
That in great lordship, if I well discern,
There is great servitude in sundry ways.

I may not do as any plowman may.
My people constrain me to take
Another wife, and call for it day by day;
And also the Pope, rancor to appease,
Consents to it, so I dare declare;
And truly this much I will to you say,
My new wife is coming along the way.

Be strong of heart, and vacate at once her place;
And that same dowry that you brought me
Take it again, I grant it of my grace.
Return to your father's house," said he.
"No man may always have prosperity;

With evene herte I rede yow t'endure
The strook of fortune or of aventure."

And she answerde agayn in pacience,
"My lord," quod she, "I woot, and wiste alway
How that bitwixen your magnificence
And my poverte no wight can ne may
Maken comparison; it is no nay.
I ne heeld me never digne in no manere
To be your wyf, no, ne your chamberere.

And in this hous, ther ye me lady made—
The heighe god take I for my witnesse,
And also wisly he my soule glade—
I never heeld me lady ne maistresse,
But humble servant to your worthinesse,
And ever shal, whyl that my lyf may dure,
Aboven every worldy creature.

That ye so longe of your benignitee
Han holden me in honour and nobleye,
Wher-as I was noght worthy for to be,
That thonke I god and yow, to whom I preye
Foryelde it yow; there is na-more to seye.
Un-to my fader gladly wol I wende,
And with him dwelle un-to my lyves ende.

Ther I was fostred of a child ful smal,
Til I be deed, my lyf ther wol I lede
A widwe clene, in body, herte, and al.
For sith I yaf to yow my maydenhede
And am your trewe wyf, it is no drede,
God shilde swich a lordes wyf to take
Another man to housbonde or to make.

And of your newe wyf, god of his grace
So graunte yow wele and prosperitee:
For I wol gladly yelden hir my place,
In which that I was blisful wont to be,

With steady heart I advise you to endure
This stroke of Fortune or of chance."

And she again answered in patience,
"My lord," said she, "I know and knew always,
That between your magnificence
And my poverty no man can
Make comparison; it cannot be denied.
I never held myself worthy in any way
To be your wife, nor your chambermaid.

And in this house where you made me a lady—
The high God I take for witness,
And also as surely as he my soul gladdens—
I never considered myself a lady or mistress,
But humble servant to your worthiness,
And ever shall, while that my life may last,
Above every worldly creature.

That you so long of your graciousness
Have held me in honor and nobility,
Where I was not worthy to be,
For that I thank God and you, and I pray God to
Repay you for it. There is no more to say.
Unto my father gladly will I wend,
And with him dwell until my life's end.

There I was raised from a child full small,
Till I be dead, my life there will I lead:
A widow pure, in body, heart and all.
For since I gave to you my maidenhood,
I am your true wife, there is no doubt.
God forbid such a lord's wife to take
Another man to husband or as mate.

And with your new wife, God by his grace
So grant you prosperity and happiness!
For I will gladly yield her my place,
In which I was blissful accustomed to be.

For sith it lyketh yow, my lord," quod she,
"That whylom weren al myn hertes reste,
That I shal goon, I wol gon whan yow leste.

But ther-as ye me profre swich dowaire
As I first broghte, it is wel in my minde
It were my wrecched clothes, no-thing faire,
The which to me were hard now for to finde.
O gode god! how gentil and how kinde
Ye semed by your speche and your visage
The day that maked was our mariage!

But sooth is seyd, algate I finde it trewe—
For in effect it preved is on me—
Love is noght old as whan that it is newe.
But certes, lord, for noon adversitee,
To dyen in the cas, it shal nat be
That ever in word or werk I shal repente
That I yow yaf myn herte in hool entente.

My lord, ye woot that, in my fadres place,
Ye dede me strepe out of my povre wede,
And richely me cladden, of your grace.
To yow broghte I noght elles, out of drede,
But feyth and nakednesse and maydenhede.
And here agayn my clothing I restore,
And eek my wedding-ring, for evermore.

The remenant of your jewels redy be
In-with your chambre, dar I saufly sayn;
Naked out of my fadres hous," quod she,
"I cam, and naked moot I turne agayn.
Al your plesaunce wol I folwen fayn;
But yet I hope it be nat your entente
That I smoklees out of your paleys wente.

Ye coude nat doon so dishoneste a thing,
That thilke wombe in which your children leye
Sholde, biforn the peple, in my walking,

For since it pleases you, my lord," said she,
"Who once was all my heart's rest,
That I shall go, I will go when you wish.

But though you offer me such dowry
As I first brought, it is well in my mind
It was my wretched clothes, in no way nice,
And which to me were hard now to find.
Oh good God! How gentle and how kind
You seemed by your speech and your visage
The day that made was our marriage!

But it is truly said—in any case I find it true,
For in effect it is proven to me—
Love is not the same old as when it is new.
But certainly, lord, for no adversity,
Even if I die in this case, it shall not be
That ever in word or deed I shall repent
That I gave you my heart in whole intent.

My lord, you know well that in my father's place
You stripped my poor clothes from me,
And clad me richly, by your grace.
To you I brought nought else, there is no doubt,
But faith and nakedness and maidenhood.
And here again your clothing I restore,
And also your wedding ring, for evermore.

The remainder of your jewels is prepared
Within your chamber, dare I safely say.
Naked out of my father's house," said she,
"I came, and naked must I return again.
All your pleasure willingly I will follow.
But yet I hope it be not your intent
That smockless out of your palace I should go.

You could not do so dishonest a thing
That this womb in which your children lay
Should before the people, in my walking,

Be seyn al bare; wherfor I yow preye,
Lat me nat lyk a worm go by the weye.
Remembre yow, myn owene lord so dere,
I was your wyf, thogh I unworthy were.

Wherfor, in guerdon of my maydenhede,
Which that I broghte, and noght agayn I bere,
As voucheth sauf to yeve me, to my mede,
But swich a smok as I was wont to were,
That I therwith may wrye the wombe of here
That was your wyf; and heer take I my leve
Of yow, myn owene lord, lest I yow greve."

"The smok," quod he, "that thou hast on thy bak,
Lat it be stille, and ber it forth with thee."
But wel unnethes thilke word he spak,
But wente his wey for rewthe and for pitee.
Biforn the folk hir-selven strepeth she,
And in hir smok, with heed and foot al bare,
Toward hir fader hous forth is she fare.

The folk hir folwe wepinge in hir weye,
And fortune ay they cursen as they goon;
But she fro weping kepte hir yen dreye,
Ne in this tyme word ne spak she noon.
Hir fader, that this tyding herde anoon,
Curseth the day and tyme that nature
Shoop him to been a lyves creature.

For out of doute this olde povre man
Was ever in suspect of hir mariage;
For ever he demed, sith that it bigan,
That whan the lord fulfiled had his corage,
Him wolde thinke it were a disparage
To his estaat so lowe for t'alighte,
And voyden hir as sone as ever he mighte.

Agayns his doghter hastilich goth he,
For he by noyse of folk knew hir cominge,

Be seen all naked; wherefore I you pray,
Let me not like a worm go along the way.
Remember you, my own lord so dear,
I was your wife, though I unworthy were.

Wherefore in recompense for my maidenhood,
That I brought, and not again may bear,
Vouchsafe to give me as my reward
Only such a smock as I was wont to wear,
That I may hide the womb of her
Who was your wife. And here I take my leave
From you, my own lord, lest you I grieve."

"That smock," said he, "that you have on your back,
Let it remain still, and bear it forth with you."
But he could hardly speak those words,
And went his way, in compassion and pity.
Before the folk herself stripped she,
And in her smock, with head and foot all bare,
Toward her father's house forth she fared.

The folk followed her, weeping on their way,
And Fortune ever they cursed as they went.
But she from weeping kept her eyes dry,
Nor in this time did she speak at all.
Her father, who this news heard anon,
Cursed the day and time that nature
Created him to be a living creature.

For certainly this old poor man
Was ever doubtful of her marriage;
For ever he thought, since it began,
That when the lord had fulfilled his desire,
He would think it a disgrace
To his estate so low to alight,
And get rid of her as soon as he might.

Toward his daughter hastily went he,
For by noise of folk he knew her coming,

And with hir olde cote, as it mighte be,
He covered hir, ful sorwefully wepinge;
But on hir body mighte he it nat bringe.
For rude was the cloth, and more of age
By dayes fele than at hir mariage.

Thus with hir fader, for a certeyn space,
Dwelleth this flour of wyfly pacience,
That neither by hir wordes ne hir face
Biforn the folk, ne eek in hir absence,
Ne shewed she that hir was doon offence;
Ne of hir heigh estaat no remembraunce
Ne hadde she, as by hir countenaunce.

No wonder is, for in hir grete estaat
Hir goost was ever in pleyn humylitee;
No tendre mouth, non herte delicaat,
No pompe, no semblant of royaltee,
But ful of pacient benignitee,
Discreet and prydeles, ay honurable,
And to hir housbonde ever meke and stable.

Men speke of Job and most for his humblesse,
As clerkes, whan hem list, can wel endyte,
Namely of men, but as in soothfastnesse,
Thogh clerkes preyse wommen but a lyte,
Ther can no man in humblesse him acquyte
As womman can, ne can ben half so trewe
As wommen been, but it be falle of-newe.

PART SIX

Fro Boloigne is this erl of Panik come,
Of which the fame up-sprang to more and lesse,
And in the peples eres alle and some
Was couth eek, that a newe markisesse
He with him broghte, in swich pompe and richesse,
That never was ther seyn with mannes yë
So noble array in al West Lumbardye.

And with her old cloak, as well as he could,
He covered her full sorrowfully weeping.
But around her body might he it not bring,
For rough was the cloth and she more of age
By many days than at her marriage.

Thus with her father for a certain while,
Dwelt this flower of wifely patience,
Who neither by her words nor her face
Before the folk, or in their absence,
Showed that she was done offense;
Nor of her high estate any remembrance
Had she, to judge by her countenance.

No wonder is, for in her high estate
Her spirit was ever in perfect humility:
No tender palate, no heart delicate,
No pomp, no semblance of royalty,
But full of patient graciousness,
Discreet and prideless, ever honorable,
And to her husband ever meek and constant.

Men speak of Job and most of all of his humility,
As scholars, when they wish, can well write,
Namely of men, but with regard to the truth,
Though scholars praise women very little,
There can no man in humility himself acquit
As women can, nor who can be half so true
As women, unless it be something new.

PART SIX

From Bologna is this Earl of Panico come,
Whose fame became known to great and small,
And in the people's ears all and one
Was known also that a new marquess
He brought with him, in such pomp and richness,
That never was there seen with man's eye
So noble a display in West Lombardy.

The markis, which that shoop and knew al this,
Er that this erl was come, sente his message
For thilke sely povre Grisildis;
And she with humble herte and glad visage,
Nat with no swollen thoght in hir corage,
Cam at his heste, and on hir knees hir sette,
And reverently and wysly she him grette.

"Grisild," quod he, "my wille is outerly,
This mayden, that shal wedded been to me,
Receyved be to-morwe as royally
As it possible is in myn hous to be.
And eek that every wight in his degree
Have his estaat in sitting and servyse
And heigh plesaunce, as I can best devyse.

I have no wommen suffisaunt certayn
The chambres for t'arraye in ordinaunce
After my lust, and therfor wolde I fayn
That thyn were al swich maner governaunce;
Thou knowest eek of old al my plesaunce;
Though thyn array be badde and yvel biseye,
Do thou thy devoir at the leeste weye."

"Nat only, lord, that I am glad," quod she,
"To doon your lust, but I desyre also
Yow for to serve and plese in my degree
With-outen feynting, and shal evermo.
Ne never, for no wele ne no wo,
Ne shal the gost with-in myn herte stente
To love yow best with al my trewe entente."

And with that word she gan the hous to dighte,
And tables for to sette and beddes make;
And peyned hir to doon al that she mighte,
Preying the chambereres, for goddes sake,
To hasten hem, and faste swepe and shake;
And she, the moste servisable of alle,
Hath every chambre arrayed and his halle.

The marquis, who planned and knew all this,
Before this earl had come had sent his messenger
For that same good poor Griselda;
And she with humble heart and glad visage,
With no prideful thought in her soul,
Came at his command, and set herself on her knees,
And reverently and discreetly she him greeted.

"Griselda," said he, "my will is completely
That this maiden, who shall wedded be to me,
Be received tomorrow as royally
As it is possible in my house to be,
And also that every person in his degree,
Have his place at the table and service
And high pleasure, as I can best devise.

I have not women enough, certainly,
The chambers to put in order
After my desire, and therefore would I be pleased
That you would of all such things have governance;
You know of old my preference.
Though your clothing is bad and poor to see,
Fulfill your duty, all the same."

"Not only, lord, am I glad," said she,
"To do your pleasure, but I desire also
To serve you and please you as befits my degree
Without weariness, and shall evermore.
And never, for happiness or woe,
Shall the spirit within my heart stint
To love you best with all my true intent."

And with that word she began the house to prepare,
And tables to set and beds to make;
And took pains to do all that she might,
Praying the chambermaids, for God's sake,
To hurry, and fast sweep and shake.
And she, the most diligent of all,
Had every chamber arranged and his hall.

Abouten undern gan this erl alighte,
That with him broghte thise noble children tweye,
For which the peple ran to seen the sighte
Of hir array, so richely biseye;
And than at erst amonges hem they seye,
That Walter was no fool, thogh that him leste
To chaunge his wyf, for it was for the beste.

For she is fairer, as they demen alle,
Than is Grisild, and more tendre of age,
And fairer fruit bitwene hem sholde falle,
And more plesant, for hir heigh linage;
Hir brother eek so fair was of visage,
That hem to seen the peple hath caught plesaunce,
Commending now the markis governaunce.—

"O stormy peple! unsad and ever untrewe!
Ay undiscreet and chaunging as a vane,
Delyting ever in rumbel that is newe,
For lyk the mone ay wexe ye and wane;
Ay ful of clapping, dere y-nogh a jane;
Your doom is fals, your constance yvel preveth,
A ful greet fool is he that on yow leveth!"

Thus seyden sadde folk in that citee,
Whan that the peple gazed up and doun,
For they were glad, right for the noveltee,
To han a newe lady of hir toun.
Na-more of this make I now mencioun;
But to Grisilde agayn wol I me dresse,
And telle hir constance and hir bisinesse.—

Ful bisy was Grisilde in every thing
That to the feste was apertinent;
Right noght was she abayst of hir clothing,
Though it were rude and somdel eek to-rent.
But with glad chere to the yate is went,
With other folk, to grete the markisesse,
And after that doth forth hir bisinesse.

About midmorn this earl alighted,
Who with him brought these noble children two,
For which the people ran to see the sight
Of their display, so rich to see,
And then for the first time among themselves to say
That Walter was no fool to want
To change his wife, for it was for the best.

For she is fairer, as they judged all,
Than is Griselda, and more young of age,
And fairer fruit of her womb between them should fall,
And more pleasant, due to her high lineage;
Her brother also was so fair of visage
That to see them the people pleased,
Commending now the marquis' decision.

"Oh stormy people! inconstant and ever untrue!
As unwise and changeable as a weathervane!
Delighting ever in rumor that is new,
Just as the moon ever waxes and wanes!
Ever full of chatter, not worth a pence!
Your judgement is false, your constancy untrue,
A full great fool is he who believes in you!"

Thus said steadfast folk in that city,
When that the people gazed up and down,
For they were glad, just for the novelty,
To have a new lady of their town.
No more of this make I now mention,
But to Griselda will I myself address,
And tell her constancy and her goodness.

Full busy was Griselda in everything
That to the feast appertained;
Right not was she of her clothing ashamed,
Though it was rude and somewhat torn.
But with glad cheer to the gate she went
With other folk, to greet the marquess,
And after that continued her business.

With so glad chere his gestes she receyveth,
And conningly, everich in his degree,
That no defaute no man apercyveth;
But ay they wondren what she mighte be
That in so povre array was for to see,
And coude swich honour and reverence;
And worthily they preisen hir prudence.

In al this mene whyle she ne stente
This mayde and eek hir brother to commende
With al hir herte, in ful benigne entente,
So wel, that no man coude hir prys amende.
But atte laste, whan that thise lordes wende
To sitten doun to mete, he gan to calle
Grisilde, as she was bisy in his halle.

"Grisilde," quod he, as it were in his pley,
"How lyketh thee my wyf and hir beautee?"
"Right wel," quod she, "my lord; for, in good fey,
A fairer say I never noon than she.
I prey to god yeve hir prosperitee;
And so hope I that he wol to yow sende
Plesance y-nogh un-to your lyves ende.

O thing biseke I yow and warne also,
That ye ne prikke with no tormentinge
This tendre mayden, as ye han don mo;
For she is fostred in hir norishinge
More tendrely, and, to my supposinge,
She coude nat adversitee endure
As coude a povre fostred creature."

And whan this Walter say hir pacience,
Hir glade chere and no malice at al,
And he so ofte had doon to hir offence,
And she ay sad and constant as a wal,
Continuing ever hir innocence overal,
This sturdy markis gan his herte dresse
To rewen up-on hir wyfly stedfastnesse.

With glad cheer his guests she received,
And so skillfully, each in his degree,
That no fault could any man perceive;
But ever they wondered who she might be
Who in such poor clothing appeared,
And yet knew such honor and reverence;
And worthily they praised her prudence.

In all this while she did not cease
This maid and her brother to commend
With all her heart, in full benign intent,
So well that no man could her praise exceed.
But at last, when this lord thought
To sit down to the feast, he began to call
Griselda, as she was busy in the hall.

"Griselda," said he, quite playfully,
"How do you like my wife and her beauty?"
"Right well," said she, "my lord, for in good faith,
A fairer saw I never any than she.
I pray to God give her prosperity,
And so I hope that he will to you send
Pleasure enough until your lives' end.

One thing I beseech you, and warn also
That you neither goad nor torment
This tender maiden, as you have to others done.
For she was raised in her upbringing
More tenderly, and to my supposing,
She could not adversity endure
As could a poverty-raised creature."

And when this Walter saw her patience,
Her glad cheer and no malice at all—
And though he so often had done to her offence,
She was ever firm and constant as a wall,
Continuing ever her innocence in every way—
This cruel marquis did his heart turn
To take pity on her wifely constancy.

"This is y-nogh, Grisilde myn," quod he,
"Be now na-more agast ne yvel apayed;
I have thy feith and thy benignitee,
As wel as ever womman was, assayed,
In greet estaat, and povreliche arrayed.
Now knowe I, dere wyf, thy stedfastnesse,"—
And hir in armes took and gan hir kesse.

And she for wonder took of it no keep;
She herde nat what thing he to hir seyde;
She ferde as she had stert out of a sleep,
Til she out of hir masednesse abreyde.
"Grisilde," quod he, "by god that for us deyde,
Thou art my wyf, ne noon other I have,
Ne never hadde, as god my soule save!

This is thy doghter which thou hast supposed
To be my wyf; that other feithfully
Shal be myn heir, as I have ay purposed;
Thou bare him in thy body trewely.
At Boloigne have I kept hem prively;
Tak hem agayn, for now maystow nat seye
That thou hast lorn non of thy children tweye.

And folk that otherweyes han seyd of me,
I warne hem wel that I have doon this dede
For no malice ne for no crueltee,
But for t'assaye in thee thy wommanhede,
And nat to sleen my children, god forbede!
But for to kepe hem prively and stille,
Til I thy purpos knewe and al thy wille."

Whan she this herde, aswowne doun she falleth
For pitous joye, and after hir swowninge
She bothe hir yonge children un-to hir calleth,
And in hir armes, pitously wepinge,
Embraceth hem, and tendrely kissinge
Ful lyk a mooder, with hir salte teres
She batheth bothe hir visage and hir heres.

"This is enough, Griselda mine," said he,
"Be now no more afraid or ill-pleased;
I have your faith and your steadfastness,
As well as any woman who ever was tested.
In both great estate, and poorly dressed,
Now I know, dear wife, your faithfulness,"
And took her in his arms and began her to kiss.

And she for wonder took of it no heed;
She heard not what thing he to her said;
She acted as if she had started out of a sleep,
Until she out of her bewilderment awoke.
"Griselda," said he, "by God who for us died,
You are my wife, no other do I have,
Nor ever had, as God my soul save!

This is your daughter whom you have supposed
To be my wife; that other faithfully
Shall be my heir, as I have ever intended;
You bore him in your body truly.
At Bologna I have kept him secretly;
Take him again, for now may you not say
That you have lost either of your children two.

And folk who otherwise have said of me,
I advise them that I have done this deed
For no malice nor for cruelty,
But to test you in your womanhood,
And not to slay my children, God forbid!
But to keep them secretly and in silence,
Until I your purpose knew and all your will."

When she this heard, fainting down she fell
For piteous joy, and after her swooning
She both her young children to her called,
And in her arms, piteously weeping,
Embraced them, and tenderly kissing,
Full like a mother, with her salt tears
She bathed both their faces and their hair.

O, which a pitous thing it was to see
Hir swowning, and hir humble voys to here!
"Grauntmercy, lord, that thanke I yow," quod she,
"That ye han saved me my children dere!
Now rekke I never to ben deed right here;
Sith I stonde in your love and in your grace,
No fors of deeth, ne whan my spirit pace!

O tendre, o dere, o yonge children myne,
Your woful mooder wende stedfastly
That cruel houndes or som foul vermyne
Hadde eten yow; but god, of his mercy,
And your benigne fader tendrely
Hath doon yow kept;" and in that same stounde
Al sodeynly she swapte adoun to grounde.

And in her swough so sadly holdeth she
Hir children two, whan she gan hem t'embrace,
That with greet sleighte and greet difficultee
The children from hir arm they gonne arace.
O many a teer on many a pitous face
Doun ran of hem that stoden hir bisyde;
Unnethe abouten hir mighte they abyde.

Walter hir gladeth, and hir sorwe slaketh;
She ryseth up, abaysed, from hir traunce.
And every wight hir joye and feste maketh,
Til she hath caught agayn hir contenaunce.
Walter hir dooth so feithfully plesaunce,
That it was deyntee for to seen the chere
Bitwixe hem two, now they ben met y-fere.

Thise ladyes, whan that they hir tyme say,
Han taken hir, and in-to chambre goon,
And strepen hir out of hir rude array,
And in a cloth of gold that brighte shoon,
With a coroune of many a riche stoon
Up-on hir heed, they in-to halle hir broghte,
And ther she was honoured as hir oghte.

Oh what a piteous thing it was to see
Her swooning, and her piteous voice to hear!
"Great thanks, lord, God reward you," said she,
"That you have saved me my children dear!
Now I do not care if I should die right here;
Since I stand in your love and your grace
Death has no force, nor do I care when!

Oh tender, oh dear, oh young children mine,
Your woeful mother thought steadfastly
That cruel hounds or some foul beast
Had eaten you; but God of his mercy,
And your gracious father, tenderly
Had you cared for;" and then
All suddenly fell she to the ground.

And in her swoon so firmly held she
Her children two, when she them embraced,
That with great skill and great difficulty
The children from her arms away they tore.
Oh many a tear on many a piteous face
Down ran of them who stood there beside;
Scarcely about her might they abide.

Walter comforted her and her sorrow eased;
She rose up, embarrassed, from her trance,
And every person for her made gladness
Until she composed again her countenance.
Walter so faithfully did her kindness
That it was a delight to see the happiness
Between the two, now that they were together.

These ladies, when they their time saw,
Had taken her and into chamber went,
And removed her rude apparel,
And in a cloth of gold that bright shone,
With a crown of many a rich stone
Upon her head, they into hall her brought,
And there she was honored as they ought.

Thus hath this pitous day a blisful ende,
For every man and womman dooth his might
This day in murthe and revel to dispende
Til on the welkne shoon the sterres light.
For more solempne in every mannes sight
This feste was, and gretter of costage,
Than was the revel of hir mariage.

Ful many a yeer in heigh prosperitee
Liven thise two in concord and in reste,
And richely his doghter maried he
Un-to a lord, oon of the worthieste
Of al Itaille; and than in pees and reste
His wyves fader in his court he kepeth,
Til that the soule out of his body crepeth.

His sone succedeth in his heritage
In reste and pees, after his fader day;
And fortunat was eek in mariage,
Al putte he nat his wyf in greet assay.
This world is nat so strong, it is no nay,
As it hath been in olde tymes yore,
And herkneth what this auctour seith therfore.

This storie is seyd, nat for that wyves sholde
Folwen Grisilde as in humilitee,
For it were importable, though they wolde;
But for that every wight, in his degree,
Sholde be constant in adversitee
As was Grisilde; therfor Petrark wryteth
This storie, which with heigh style he endyteth.

For, sith a womman was so pacient
Un-to a mortal man, wel more us oghte
Receyven al in gree that god us sent;
For greet skile is, he preve that he wroghte.
But he ne tempteth no man that he boghte,
As seith seint Jame, if ye his pistel rede;
He preveth folk al day, it is no drede,

Thus had this piteous day a blissful end,
For every man and woman did his best
This day in mirth and revel to spend
Until in the sky shone the stars' light.
For more splendid in every man's sight
This feast was, and greater of cost,
Than was the revel of her marriage.

Full many a year in high prosperity
Lived these two in concord and in rest,
And richly his daughter married he
Unto a lord, one of the worthiest
Of all Italy, and then in peace and rest
His wife's father in his court he kept,
Until the soul out of his body crept.

His son succeeded in his heritage,
In rest and peace, after his father's day,
And fortunate was also in marriage,
Although put he not his wife in great trial.
This world is not so strong, it cannot be denied,
As it was in times of yore.
And listen to what this Petrarch said therefore:

This story is told, not that wives should
Follow Griselda in humility,
For it would be unbearable if they did;
But so that every person in his degree
Should be constant in adversity
As was Griselda. Therefore Petrarch wrote
This story, which with high style he composed.

For since a woman was so patient
Unto a mortal man, well more we ought
Receive in good will what God us sends.
There is reason for him to test what he created,
But he tempts no man whom he has saved—
As said Saint James, if you his epistle read.
He tests folk all day, doubtless,

And suffreth us, as for our exercyse,
With sharpe scourges of adversitee
Ful ofte to be bete in sondry wyse;
Nat for to knowe our wil, for certes he,
Er we were born, knew al our freletee;
And for our beste, is al his governaunce;
Lat us than live in vertuous suffraunce.

But o word, lordinges, herkneth er I go:—
It were ful hard to finde now a dayes
In al a toun Grisildes three or two;
For, if that they were put to swiche assayes,
The gold of hem hath now so badde alayes
With bras, that thogh the coyne be fair at yö,
It wolde rather breste a-two than plye.

For which heer, for the wyves love of Bathe,
Whos lyf and al hir secte god mayntene
In heigh maistrye, and elles were it scathe,
I wol with lusty herte fresshe and grene
Seyn yow a song to glade yow, I wene,
And lat us stinte of ernestful matere:—
Herkneth my song, that seith in this manere.

The Envoy

Grisilde is deed, and eek hir pacience,
And bothe atones buried in Itaille;
For which I crye in open audience,
No wedded man so hardy be t'assaille
His wyves pacience, in hope to finde
Grisildes, for in certein he shal faille!

O noble wyves, ful of heigh prudence,
Lat noon humilitee your tonge naille,
Ne lat no clerk have cause or diligence
To wryte of yow a storie of swich mervaille
As of Grisildis pacient and kinde;
Lest Chichevache yow swelwe in hir entraille!

And allows us, for our discipline,
With sharp scourges of adversity
Full often to be beaten in sundry ways,
Not to know our will, for certain he,
Before we were born, knew all our frailty.
And for our best is all his governance:
Let us then live in virtuous patience.

But one word, lordings, listen before I go:
It is full hard to find nowadays
In an entire town Griseldas three or two;
For if they were put to such tests,
The gold of them has now such bad alloy
With brass, that though the coin be fair to see,
It would rather break in two than bend.

For which right now, for love of the Wife of Bath—
Whose life and all her sect God maintains
In high mastery, and otherwise would be a pity—
I will with glad heart fresh and green
Sing you a song to gladden you, I think,
And let us stop talking now of serious matter.
Listen to my song, that says in this manner:

The Envoy[4]

Griselda is dead, and also her patience,
And both together buried in Italy.
For which I cry in open hearing:
No wedded man so bold be to try
His wife's patience, in hope to find
Griselda, for in certain he shall fail!

Oh noble wives, full of high prudence,
Let no humility your tongue nail down,
Nor let any scholar have cause or diligence
To write of you a story of such a marvel
As Griselda, patient and kind in her travail,
Lest Chichevache[5] swallow you into her entrails!

Folweth Ekko, that holdeth no silence,
But evere answereth at the countretaille;
Beth nat bidaffed for your innocence,
But sharply tak on yow the governaille.
Emprinteth wel this lesson in your minde
For commune profit, sith it may availle.

Ye archewyves, stondeth at defence,
Sin ye be stronge as is a greet camaille;
Ne suffreth nat that men yow doon offence.
And sclendre wyves, feble as in bataille,
Beth egre as is a tygre yond in Inde;
Ay clappeth as a mille, I yow consaille.

Ne dreed hem nat, do hem no reverence;
For though thyn housbonde armed he in maille,
The arwes of thy crabbed eloquence
Shal perce his brest, and eek his aventaille;
In jalousye I rede eek thou him binde,
And thou shalt make him couche as dooth a quaille.

If thou be fair, ther folk ben in presence
Shew thou thy visage and thyn apparaille;
If thou be foul, be free of thy dispence,
To gete thee freendes ay do thy travaille;
Be ay of chere as light as leef on linde,
And lat him care, and wepe, and wringe, and waille!

Follow Echo, who holds no silence,
But ever answers in counterreply;
Be not made a fool through your innocence,
But sharply take control.
Imprint well this lesson in your mind
For common profit, since it may avail.

You archwives, stand up in self-defense—
Since you be strong as is a camel—
Suffer not that men do you offense.
And slender wives, feeble in battle,
Be fierce as is an Indian tiger;
And chatter as loudly as a mill.

Fear them not, do them no honor;
For though your husband be armed in mail,
The arrows of your crabbed eloquence
Shall pierce his breast, and his visor as well.
In jealousy I advise you also him bind,
And you shall make him cower as does a quail.

If you be fair, where folk be present
Show your face and your apparel;
If you be ugly, be free spending
To get your friends ever to take your side.
Be cheerful and light as a leaf of the linden tree,
And let him worry, and weep, and wring, and wail!

The Marchantes Tale

The Prologue

"WEPING AND WAYLING, CARE, and other sorwe
I know y-nogh, on even and a-morwe,"
Quod the Marchaunt, "and so don othere mo
That wedded been, I trowe that it be so.
For, wel I woot, it fareth so with me.
I have a wyf, the worste that may be;
For thogh the feend to hir y-coupled were,
She wolde him overmacche, I dar wel swere.
What sholde I yow reherce in special
Hir hye malice? she is a shrewe at al.
Ther is a long and large difference
Bitwix Grisildis grete pacience
And of my wyf the passing crueltee.
Were I unbounden, al-so moot I thee!
I wolde never eft comen in the snare.
We wedded men live in sorwe and care;
Assaye who-so wol, and he shal finde
I seye sooth, by seint Thomas of Inde,
As for the more part, I sey nat alle.
God shilde that it sholde so bifalle!
A! good sir hoost! I have y-wedded be
Thise monthes two, and more nat, pardee;
And yet, I trowe, he that al his lyve
Wyflees hath been, though that men wolde him ryve
Un-to the herte, ne coude in no manere
Tellen so muchel sorwe, as I now here
Coude tellen of my wyves cursednesse!"

"Now," quod our hoost, "Marchaunt, so god yow blesse,
Sin ye so muchel knowen of that art,
Ful hertely I pray yow telle us part."

"Gladly," quod he, "but of myn owene sore,
For sory herte, I telle may na-more."

370

The Merchant's Tale

The Prologue

"WEEPING AND WAILING, CARE and other sorrow
I know enough, evening and morning,"
Said the Merchant, "and so do others more
Who have wedded been. I believe that it be so,
For well I know it fares so with me.
I have a wife, the worst that may be;
For though the fiend to her coupled were,
She would him overmatch, I dare well swear.
Why should I rehearse in special
Her high malice? She is a shrew in every way.
There is a long and large difference
Between Griselda's great patience
And of my wife the surpassing cruelty.
Were I unbound, and may I flourish,
I would never again myself snare.
We wedded men live in sorrow and care.
Try whoso will, and he shall find
That I say truth, by Saint Thomas of India,[1]
As for the greater part—I say not all.
God shield that it should so befall!
Ah, good sir Host, I have wedded been
These months two, and not more, by God,
And yet I believe, he that all his life
Wifeless has been, though that men would him stab
Unto the heart, could in no manner
Tell so much sorrow as I now here
Could tell of my wife's cursedness!"

　　"Now," said our Host, "Merchant, so God you bless,
Since you know so much of that art
Full heartily I pray you tell us part."

　　"Gladly," said he, "but of my own sore,
For sorry heart, I may tell no more."

The Tale

Whylom ther was dwellinge in Lumbardye
A worthy knight, that born was of Pavye,
In which he lived in greet prosperitee;
And sixty yeer a wyflees man was he,
And folwed ay his bodily delyt
On wommen, ther-as was his appetyt,
As doon thise foles that ben seculeer.
And whan that he was passed sixty yeer,
Were it for holinesse or for dotage,
I can nat seye, but swich a greet corage,
Hadde this knight to been a wedded man,
That day and night he dooth al that he can
T'espyen where he mighte wedded be;
Preyinge our lord to granten him, that he
Mighte ones knowe of thilke blisful lyf
That is bitwixe an housbond and his wyf;
And for to live under that holy bond
With which that first god man and womman bond.
"Non other lyf," seyde he, "is worth a bene;
For wedlok is so esy and so clene,
That in this world it is a paradys."
Thus seyde this olde knight, that was so wys.

    And certeinly, as sooth as god is king,
To take a wyf, it is a glorious thing,
And namely whan a man is old and hoor;
Thanne is a wyf the fruit of his tresor.
Than sholde he take a yong wyf and a feir,
On which he mighte engendren him an heir,
And lede his lyf in joye and in solas,
Wher-as thise bacheleres singe "allas,"
Whan that they finden any adversitee
In love, which nis but childish vanitee.
And trewely it sit wel to be so,
That bacheleres have often peyne and wo;
On brotel ground they builde, and brotelnesse
They finde, whan they wene sikernesse.
They live but as a brid or as a beste,

The Tale

Once there was dwelling in Lombardy
A worthy knight, who was born of Pavia,
In which he lived in great prosperity;
And sixty years a wifeless man was he,
And followed ever his bodily delight
With women, wherever led his appetite,
As do these fools who are secular.[2]
And when he was passed sixty years,
Were it for holiness or for dotage
I can not say, but such a great desire
Had this knight to be a wedded man
That day and night he did all he could
T'espy where he might wedded be,
Praying our lord to grant him that he
Might once know of that same blissful life
That is between a husband and his wife,
And for to live under that holy bond
With which that first God man and woman bound.
"No other life," said he, "is worth a bean,
For wedlock is so easy and so clean,
That in this world it is a paradise."
Thus said this old knight, who was so wise.

And certainly, as true as God is king,
To take a wife it is a glorious thing,
And namely when a man is old and white-haired;
Then is a wife the flower of his treasure.
Then should he take a wife young and fair,
On which he might engender him an heir,
And lead his life in joy and solace,
Whereas these bachelors sing "Alas,"
When they find any adversity
In love, which is but childish vanity.
And truly it sits well to be so,
That bachelors have often pain and woe;
On shifting ground they build, and shiftiness
They find where they expected a firm foundation.
They live but as a bird or as a beast,

In libertee, and under non areste,
Ther-as a wedded man in his estaat
Liveth a lyf blisful and ordinaat,
Under the yok of mariage y-bounde;
Wel may his herte in joye and blisse habounde.
For who can be so buxom as a wyf?
Who is so trewe, and eek so ententyf
To kepe him, syk and hool, as is his make?
For wele or wo, she wol him nat forsake.
She nis nat wery him to love and serve,
Thogh that he lye bedrede til he sterve.
And yet somme clerkes seyn, it nis nat so,
Of whiche he, Theofraste, is oon of tho.
What force though Theofraste, liste lye?
"Ne take no wyf," quod he, "for housbondrye,
As for to spare in household thy dispence;
A trewe servant dooth more diligence,
Thy good to kepe, than thyn owene wyf.
For she wol clayme half part al hir lyf;
And if that thou be syk, so god me save,
Thy verray frendes or a trewe knave
Wol kepe thee bet than she that waiteth ay
After thy good, and hath don many a day.
And if thou take a wyf un-to thyn hold,
Ful lightly maystow been a cokewold."
This sentence, and an hundred thinges worse,
Wryteth this man, ther god his bones corse!
But take no kepe of al swich vanitee;
Deffye Theofraste and herke me.
    A wyf is goddes yifte verraily;
Alle other maner yiftes hardily,
As londes, rentes, pasture, or commune,
Or moebles, alle ben yiftes of fortune,
That passen as a shadwe upon a wal.
But dredelees, if pleynly speke I shal,
A wyf wol laste, and in thyn hous endure,
Wel lenger than thee list, paraventure.
    Mariage is a ful gret sacrement;
He which that hath no wyf, I holde him shent

In liberty and under no restraint,
Whereas a wedded man in his estate
Lives a life blissful and orderly
Under this yoke of marriage bond.
Well may his heart in joy and bliss abound,
For who can be so obedient as a wife?
Who is so true, and so attentive
To keep him, in health and sickness, as his mate?
For well or woe she will him not forsake;
She wearies not to him love and serve,
Though he lie bedridden until he dies.
And yet some scholars say it is not so,
Of which Theofrastus is one of those.
But so what if Theofrastus[3] wants to lie?
"Take no wife," said he, "for housekeeping,
To be frugal in your household expense.
A true servant does more diligence
Your goods to keep than your own wife,
For she will claim half part all her life.
And if you be sick, so God me save,
Your true friends, or a true servant,
Will keep you better than she who waits ever
For your goods and has done many a day.
And if you take a wife into your hold
Full easily may you be a cuckold."
This sentence, and a hundred things worse,
Wrote this man, God his bones curse!
But take no heed of all such vanity;
Defy Theofrastus, and listen to me.

A wife is God's gift verily;
All other manner of gifts surely,
As lands, rents, pasture, or commons,
Or movable goods—all be gifts of Fortune
That pass as a shadow upon a wall.
But doubt not, if plainly speak I shall;
A wife will last, and in your house endure,
Well longer than you wish, perchance.

Marriage is a full great sacrament.
He who has no wife, I hold him ruined;

He liveth helplees and al desolat,
I speke of folk in seculer estaat.
And herke why, I sey nat this for noght,
That womman is for mannes help y-wroght.
The hye god, whan he hadde Adam maked,
And saugh him al allone, bely-naked,
God of his grete goodnesse seyde than,
"Lat us now make an help un-to this man
Lyk to him-self;" an thanne he made him Eve.
Heer may ye se, and heer-by may ye preve,
That wyf is mannes help and his confort,
His paradys terrestre and his disport
So buxom and so vertuous is she,
They moste nedes live in unitee.
O flesh they been, and o flesh, as I gesse,
Hath but on herte, in wele and in distresse.
        A wyf! a! Seinte Marie, *ben'cite!*
How mighte a man han any adversitee
That hath a wyf! certes, I can nat seye.
The blisse which that is bitwixe hem tweye
Ther may no tonge telle, or herte thinke.
If he be povre, she helpeth him to swinke;
She kepeth his good, and wasteth never a deel;
Al that hir housbonde lust, hir lyketh weel;
She seith not ones "nay," when he seith "ye."
"Do this," seith he; "al redy, sir," seith she.
O blisful ordre of wedlok precious,
Thou art so mery, and eek so vertuous,
And so commended and appreved eek,
That every man that halt him worth a leek,
Up-on his bare knees oghte al his lyf
Thanken his god that him hath sent a wyf;
Or elles preye to god him for to sende
A wyf, to laste un-to his lyves ende.
For thanne his lyf is set in sikernesse;
He may nat be deceyved, as I gesse,
So that he werke after his wyves reed;
Than may he boldly beren up his heed,
They been so trewe and ther-with-al so wyse;

He lives helpless and all desolate—
I speak of folk in secular estate.
And listen why—I say not this for nought—
That woman is for man's help wrought.
The high God, when he had Adam made,
And saw him all alone, belly-naked,
God of his great goodness said then,
"Let us now make a helpmate unto this man
Like to himself "; and then he made Eve.
Here may you see, and here may you prove,
That wife is man's help and his comfort,
His paradise terrestrial, and his disport.
So obedient and virtuous is she,
They must needs live in unity.
One flesh they be, and one flesh, as I guess,
Has but one heart, in health and in distress.
      A wife! Ah, Saint Mary, *benedicite!*
How might a man have any adversity
Who has a wife? Certainly, I cannot say.
The bliss that is between the two
There may no tongue tell, or heart think.
If he be poor, she helps him to work;
She keeps his goods, and wastes nothing;
All that her husband wishes, she also wishes;
She never says "no," when he says "yes."
"Do this," says he; "All ready, sire," says she.
Oh blissful order of wedlock precious,
You are so merry, and so virtuous,
And so commended and proven also
That every man who holds himself worth a leek
Upon his bare knees ought all his life
Thank his God who him has sent a wife,
Or else pray to God him to send
A wife to last until his life's end.
For then his life is set in sureness;
He may not be deceived, as I guess,
If he takes his wife's advice.
Then may he surely hold up his head,
They be so true and at the same time so wise;

For which, if thou wolt werken as the wyse,
Do alwey so as wommen wol thee rede.
   Lo, how that Jacob, as thise clerkes rede,
By good conseil of his moder Rebekke,
Bond the kides skin aboute his nekke;
Thurgh which his fadres benisoun he wan.
   Lo, Judith, as the storie eek telle can,
By wys conseil she goddes peple kepte,
And slow him, Olofernus, whyl he slepte.
   Lo Abigayl, by good conseil how she
Saved hir housbond Nabal, whan that he
Sholde han be slayn; and loke, Ester also
By good conseil delivered out of wo
The peple of god, and made him, Mardochee
Of Assuere enhaunced for to be.
   Ther nis no-thing in gree superlatyf,
As seith Senek, above an humble wyf.
   Suffre thy wyves tonge, as Caton bit;
She shal comande, and thou shalt suffren it;
And yet she wol obeye of curteisye.
   A wyf is keper of thyn housbondrye;
Wel may the syke man biwaille and wepe,
Ther-as ther nis no wyf the hous to kepe.
I warne thee, if wysly thou wolt wirche,
Love wel thy wyf, as Crist loveth his chirche.
If thou lovest thy-self, thou lovest thy wyf;
No man hateth his flesh, but in his lyf
He fostreth it, and therfore bidde I thee,
Cherisse thy wyf, or thou shalt never thee.
Housbond and wyf, what so men jape or pleye,
Of worldly folk holden the siker weye;
They been so knit, ther may noon harm bityde:
And namely, up-on the wyves syde.
   For which this Januarie, of whom I tolde,
Considered hath, inwith his dayes olde,
The lusty lyf, the vertuous quiete,
That is in mariage hony-swete;
And for his freendes on a day he sente,
To tellen hem th'effect of his entente.

By which, if you will do as the wise do,
Do always as women advise you.

Look, how Jacob, as these scholars advise,
By good counsel of his mother Rebecca,
Bound the kidskin about his neck,
By which his father's blessing he won.

Look at Judith, as the stories also tell,
By wise counsel she God's people kept,
And slew Holofernes, while he slept.

Look at Abigail, by good counsel how she
Saved her husband Nabal when he
Should have been slain; and look, Esther[4] also
By good counsel delivered out of woe
The people of God, and made Mordecai
Of Ahasuerus to be exalted.

There is nothing more virtuous,
As said Seneca,[5] than a humble wife.

Suffer your wife's tongue, as Cato[6] bid;
She shall command, and you shall endure it,
And yet she will obey of courtesy.

A wife is keeper of your household;
Well may the sick man bewail and weep,
Where there is no wife the house to keep.
I warn you, if wisely you would work,
Love well your wife, as Christ loved his church.
If you love yourself, you love your wife;
No man hates his flesh, but in his life
He fosters it, and therefore I bid you
To cherish your wife, or you shall never prosper.
Husband and wife, what so men joke or mock,
Of secular folk hold the surest way;
They be so knit there may no harm betide,
And namely upon the wife's side.

For which this January, of whom I told,
Considered once, in his days old,
The pleasant life, the virtuous quiet,
That is in marriage honey-sweet,
And for his friends on a day he sent,
To tell them the gist of his intent.

With face sad, his tale he hath hem told;
He seyde, "freendes, I am hoor and old,
And almost, god wot, on my pittes brinke;
Up-on my soule somwhat moste I thinke.
I have my body folily despended;
Blessed be god, that it shal been amended!
For I wol be, certeyn, a wedded man,
And that anoon in al the haste I can,
Un-to som mayde fair and tendre of age.
I prey yow, shapeth for my mariage
Al sodeynly, for I wol nat abyde;
And I wol fonde t'espyen, on my syde,
To whom I may be wedded hastily.
But for-as-muche as ye ben mo than I,
Ye shullen rather swich a thing espyen
Than I, and wher me best were to allyen.

But o thing warne I yow, my freendes dere,
I wol non old wyf han in no manere.
She shal nat passe twenty yeer, certayn;
Old fish and yong flesh wolde I have ful fayn.
Bet is," quod he, "a pyk than a pikerel;
And bet than old boef is the tendre veel.
I wol no womman thritty yeer of age,
It is but bene-straw and greet forage.
And eek thise olde widwes, god it woot,
They conne so muchel craft on Wades boot,
So muchel broken harm, whan that hem leste,
That with hem sholde I never live in reste.
For sondry scoles maken sotil clerkis;
Womman of manye scoles half a clerk is.
But certeynly, a yong thing may men gye,
Right as men may warm wex with handes plye.
Wherfore I sey yow pleynly, in a clause,
I wol non old wyf han right for this cause.
For if so were, I hadde swich mischaunce,
That I in hir ne coude han no plesaunce,
Thanne sholde I lede my lyf in avoutrye,
And go streight to the devel, whan I dye.
Ne children sholde I none up-on hir geten;

With face serious his tale he has told.
He said, "Friends, I am white-haired and old,
And almost, God knows, upon my pit's brink;
Upon my soul somewhat must I think.
I have my body foolishly expended;
Blessed be God that it shall be amended!
For I will be, certainly, a wedded man,
And that anon in all the haste I can.
Unto some maid fair and tender of age,
I pray you, plan for my marriage
All suddenly, for I will not abide;
And I will try to discover, on my side,
To whom I may be wedded hastily.
But inasmuch as you be more than I,
You shall rather such a thing espy
Than I, who I were best to ally.

"But one thing I warn you, my friends dear,
I will no old wife have in any manner.
She shall not have passed twenty years, certainly;
Old fish and young flesh would I have gladly.
Better is," said he, "a pike than a pickerel,
And better than old beef is the tender veal.
I want no woman thirty years of age;
It is but dried beanstalks and rough forage.
And also these old wives, God knows,
They know so much craft on Wade's boat,
So much mischief, when they wish,
That with them should I never lie in rest.
For sundry schools make clever scholars;
Woman of many schools half a scholar is.
But certainly, a young thing may men guide,
Right as men may warm wax with hands ply.
Wherefore I say to you plainly, in a clause,
I will no old wife have right for this cause.
For if I had such mischance
That in her could I have no pleasure,
Then should I lead my life in adultery
And go straight to the devil when I die.
Nor children should I any upon her beget;

Yet were me lever houndes had me eten,
Than that myn heritage sholde falle
In straunge hand, and this I tell yow alle.
I dote nat, I woot the cause why
Men sholde wedde, and forthermore wot I,
Ther speketh many a man of mariage,
That woot na-more of it than woot my page,
For whiche causes man sholde take a wyf.
If he ne may nat liven chast his lyf,
Take him a wyf with greet devocioun,
By-cause of leveful procreacioun
Of children, to th'onour of god above,
And nat only for paramour or love;
And for they sholde lecherye eschue,
And yelde hir dettes whan that they ben due;
Or for that ech of hem sholde helpen other
In meschief, as a suster shal the brother;
And live in chastitee ful holily.
But sires, by your leve, that am nat I.
For god be thanked, I dar make avaunt,
I fele my limes stark and suffisaunt
To do al that a man bilongeth to;
I woot my-selven best what I may do.
Though I be hoor, I fare as dooth a tree
That blosmeth er that fruyt y-woxen be;
A blosmy tree nis neither drye ne deed.
I fele me nowher hoor but on myn heed;
Myn herte and alle my limes been as grene
As laurer thurgh the yeer is for to sene.
And sin that ye han herd al myn entente,
I prey yow to my wil ye wole assente."
      Diverse men diversely him tolde
Of mariage manye ensamples olde.
Somme blamed it, somme preysed it, certeyn;
But atte laste, shortly for to seyn,
As al day falleth altercacioun
Bitwixen freendes in disputisoun,
Ther fil a stryf bitwixe his bretheren two,
Of whiche that oon was cleped Placebo,

I would rather that hounds had me eaten
Than my heritage should fall
Into a stranger's hands, and this I tell you all.
I dote not; I know the causes why
Men should wed, and furthermore I know
There speaks many a man of marriage
Who knows no more of it than knows my page
For what reasons a man should take a wife.
If he may not live chaste his life,
He should take him a wife in holy devotion,
And for lawful procreation
Of children, to the honor of God above,
Not as a paramour or lover;
And by so doing they would lechery eschew,
And yield their debt when it is due;
And each of them might help the other
In mischance, as a sister shall the brother,
And live in chastity full holily.
But sires, by your leave, that am not I.
For—God be thanked!—I dare make boast
I feel my limbs strong and sufficient
To do all that a man needs to do;
I know myself best what I may do.
Though I be white-haired, I fare as does a tree
That blooms before the fruit grown be;
And a blossoming tree is neither dry nor dead.
I feel myself nowhere hoary but on my head;
My heart and all my limbs be as green
As laurel through the year is to be seen.
And since that you have heard all my intent,
I pray you to my will you will assent."
    Diverse men diversely him told
Of marriage many examples old.
Some blamed it, some praised it, certainly,
But at last, shortly to say,
As every day fall into altercation
Friends in disputation,
There fell a strife between his brothers two,
Of which one was called Placebo;[7]

Justinus soothly called was that other.

Placebo seyde, "o Januarie, brother,
Ful litel nede had ye, my lord so dere,
Conseil to axe of any that is here;
But that ye been so ful of sapience,
That yow ne lyketh, for your heighe prudence,
To weyven fro the word of Salomon.
This word seyde he un-to us everichon:
'Wirk alle thing by conseil,' thus seyde he,
'And thanne shaltow nat repente thee.'
But though that Salomon spak swich a word,
Myn owene dere brother and my lord,
So wisly god my soule bringe at reste,
I hold your owene conseil is the beste.
For brother myn, of me tak this motyf,
I have now been a court-man al my lyf.
And god it woot, though I unworthy be,
I have stonden in ful greet degree
Abouten lordes of ful heigh estaat;
Yet hadde I never with noon of hem debaat.
I never hem contraried, trewely;
I woot wel that my lord can more than I.
What that he seith, I holde it ferme and stable;
I seye the same, or elles thing semblable.
A ful gret fool is any conseillour,
That serveth any lord of heigh honour,
That dar presume, or elles thenken it,
That his conseil sholde passe his lordes wit.
Nay, lordes been no foles, by my fay;
Ye han your-selven shewed heer to-day
So heigh sentence, so holily and weel,
That I consente and conferme every-deel
Your wordes alle, and your opinioun.
By god, ther nis no man in al this toun
N'in al Itaille, that coude bet han sayd;
Crist halt him of this conseil wel apayd.
And trewely, it is an heigh corage
Of any man, that stapen is in age,
To take a yong wyf; by my fader kin,

Justinus truly was called the other.
    Placebo said, "Oh January, brother,
Full little need have you, my lord so dear,
Counsel to ask of any who is here,
But you are so full of wisdom
That you do not like, for your high prudence,
To waiver from the word of Solomon.[8]
This word said he to every one:
'Do all things by counsel,' thus said he,
'And you shall not repentant be.'
But though Solomon spoke such a word,
My own dear brother and my lord,
So wisely God my soul brings to rest,
I hold your own counsel is the best.
For, brother mine, of me take this advice:
I have now been a courtier all my life,
And, God knows, though I unworthy be,
I have stood in full great degree
With lords of full high estate;
Yet had I never with them any debate.
I never them contraried, truly;
I know well that my lord knows more than I.
What he says, I hold it truth unshakable;
I say the same, or else something it resembles.
A full great fool is any counselor
Who serves any lord of high honor,
Who dares presume, or else thinks it,
That his counsel should exceed his lord's wit.
Nay, lords be no fools, by my faith!
You have yourself shown here today
Such good judgement, so holily and well,
That I consent and confirm everything
Your words all and your opinion.
By God, there is no man in all this town,
Nor in Italy, who could have better spoken!
Christ considers himself of this counsel full well satisfied.
And truly, it is a bold thing
For any man who is advanced in years
To take a young wife; by my father's kin,

Your herte hangeth on a joly pin.
Doth now in this matere right as yow leste,
For finally I holde it for the beste."
　　Justinus, that ay stille sat and herde,
Right in this wyse to Placebo answerde:
"Now brother myn, be pacient, I preye,
Sin ye han seyd, and herkneth what I seye.
Senek among his othere wordes wyse
Seith, that a man oghte him right wel avyse,
To whom he yeveth his lond or his catel.
And sin I oghte avyse me right wel
To whom I yeve my good awey fro me,
Wel muchel more I oghte avysed be
To whom I yeve my body; for alwey
I warne yow wel, it is no childes pley
To take a wyf with-outen avysement.
Men moste enquere, this is myn assent,
Wher she be wys, or sobre, or dronkelewe,
Or proud, or elles other-weys a shrewe;
A chydester, or wastour of thy good,
Or riche, or poore, or elles mannish wood.
Al-be-it so that no man finden shal
Noon in this world that trotteth hool in al,
Ne man ne beest, swich as men coude devyse;
But nathelees, it oghte y-nough suffise
With any wyf, if so were that she hadde
Mo gode thewes than hir vyces badde:
And al this axeth leyser for t'enquere.
For god it woot, I have wept many a tere
Ful prively, sin I have had a wyf.
Preyse who-so wole a wedded mannes lyf,
Certein, I finde in it but cost and care,
And observances, of alle blisses bare.
And yet, god woot, my neighebores aboute,
And namely of wommen many a route,
Seyn that I have the moste stedefast wyf,
And eek the mekeste oon that bereth lyf.
But I wot best wher wringeth me my sho.
Ye mowe, for me, right as yow lyketh do;

Your heart hangs on a jolly pin!
Do now in this matter right as you wish,
For finally I hold it for the best."
      Justinus, who ever sat still and heard,
Right in this way he to Placebo answered:
"Now brother mine, be patient, I pray,
Since you have spoken, listen to what I say.
Seneca, among other words wise,
Says that a man ought him consider well
To whom he gives his land or his goods.[9]
And since I ought consider right well
To whom I give my property,
So much more ought I thoughtful be
With regard to whom I give my body.
I warn you well, it is no child's play
To take a wife without deliberation.
Men must inquire—this is my opinion—
Whether she be wise, or sober, or a drinker,
Or proud, or else otherwise a shrew,
A scold or a waster of your goods,
Or fierce, or poor, or else man-crazy.
Albeit that no man shall find
One in this world who is without fault,
Neither man, nor beast, such as man can imagine;
But nevertheless it ought enough suffice
With any wife, if she has
More virtues good than vices bad;
And all this requires leisure for to inquire.
For, God knows, I have wept many a tear
Full privately, since I have had a wife.
Praise whoso will a wedded man's life,
Certainly in it I find but cost and care
And duties, of all blisses bare.
And yet, God knows, my neighbors nearabout,
And namely of women many a crowd,
Say that I have the most steadfast wife,
And also the meekest one alive;
But I know best where pinches me my shoe.
You may, so far as I care, do as you choose;

Avyseth yow, ye been a man of age,
How that ye entren in-to mariage,
And namely with a yong wyf and a fair.
By him that made water, erthe, and air,
The yongest man that is in al this route
Is bisy y-nogh to bringen it aboute
To han his wyf allone, trusteth me.
Ye shul nat plese hir fully yeres three,
This is to seyn, to doon hir ful plesaunce.
A wyf axeth ful many an observaunce.
I prey yow that ye be nat yvel apayd."

     "Wel," quod this Januarie, "and hastow sayd?
Straw for thy Senek, and for thy proverbes,
I counte nat a panier ful of herbes
Of scole-termes; wyser men than thow,
As thou hast herd, assenteden right now
To my purpos; Placebo, what sey ye?"

     "I seye, it is a cursed man," quod he,
"That letteth matrimoine, sikerly."
And with that word they rysen sodeynly,
And been assented fully, that he sholde
Be wedded whanne him list and wher he wolde.

     Heigh fantasye and curious bisinesse
Fro day to day gan in the soule impresse
Of Januarie aboute his mariage.
Many fair shap, and many a fair visage
Ther passeth thurgh his herte, night by night.
As who-so toke a mirour polished bright,
And sette it in a commune market-place,
Than sholde he see many a figure pace
By his mirour; and, in the same wyse,
Gan Januarie inwith his thoght devyse
Of maydens, whiche that dwelten him bisyde.
He wiste nat wher that he mighte abyde.
For if that oon have beautee in hir face,
Another stant so in the peples grace
For hir sadnesse, and hir benignitee,
That of the peple grettest voys hath she.
And somme were riche, and hadden badde name.

Take heed—you be a man of age—
How you enter into marriage,
And namely a young wife and fair.
By him who made water, earth and air,
The youngest man who is in all this company
Is busy enough to bring it about
To have his wife to himself alone. Trust me,
You shall not please her fully years three—
This is to say, to do her full pleasure.
A wife asks full many a duty.
I pray you that you be not displeased."

    "Well," said this January, "and are you finished?
Straw for your Seneca, and for your proverbs!
I give not a basket full of herbs
For a scholar's words. Wiser men than you,
As you may have heard, agree right now
To my purpose. Placebo, what say you?"

    "I say it is a cursed man," said he,
"Who hinders matrimony, certainly."
And with that word they rose suddenly,
And were agreed fully that he should
Be wedded when he wanted and where he would.

    High imagination and long thought
From day to day began to fasten the mind
Of January about his marriage.
Many a fair shape and many a fair visage
There passed through his heart night by night,
And whoso took a mirror, polished bright,
And set it in a common market-place,
Then should he see many a visage pace
By his mirror; and in the same way
Began January within his thought to imagine
Maidens who dwelt him nearby.
He knew not where or how he might decide.
For if one had beauty in her face,
Another stood so in the people's grace
For her seriousness and her benignity
That of the people greatest praise had she;
And some were rich and had bad names.

But nathelees, bitwixe ernest and game,
He atte laste apoynted him on oon,
And leet alle othere from his herte goon,
And chees hir of his owene auctoritee;
For love is blind al day, and may nat see.
And whan that he was in his bed y-broght,
He purtreyed, in his herte and in his thoght,
Hir fresshe beautee and hir age tendre,
Hir myddel smal, hir armes longe and sclendre,
Hir wyse governaunce, hir gentillesse,
Hir wommanly beringe and hir sadnesse.
And whan that he on hir was condescended,
Him thoughte his chois mighte nat ben amended.
For whan that he him-self concluded hadde,
Him thoughte ech other mannes wit so badde,
That impossible it were to replye
Agayn his chois, this was his fantasye.
His freendes sente he to at his instaunce,
And preyed hem to doon him that plesaunce,
That hastily they wolden to him come;
He wolde abregge hir labour, alle and some.
Nedeth na-more for him to go ne ryde,
He was apoynted ther he wolde abyde.

    Placebo cam, and eek his freendes sone,
And alderfirst he bad hem alle a bone,
That noon of hem none argumentes make
Agayn the purpos which that he hath take;
"Which purpos was plesant to god," seyde he,
"And verray ground of his prosperitee."

    He seyde, ther was a mayden in the toun,
Which that of beautee hadde greet renoun,
Al were it so she were of smal degree;
Suffyseth him hir youthe and hir beautee.
Which mayde, he seyde, he wolde han to his wyf,
To lede in ese and holinesse his lyf.
And thanked god, that he mighte han hire al,
That no wight of his blisse parten shal.
And preyde hem to labouren in this nede,
And shapen that he faille nat to spede;

But nevertheless, between earnest and play,
He at last settled his heart on one,
And let all others from his heart go,
And chose her on his own;
For love is blind always, and cannot see.
And when he had gone to bed,
He portrayed in his heart and in his thought
Her fresh beauty and her age tender,
Her middle small, her arms long and slender,
Her discretion, her gentility,
Her womanly bearing, and her seriousness.
And when he on her was decided,
He thought his choice might not be amended.
For when he himself had concluded,
He thought each other man's wit so bad
That impossible it were to reply
Against his choice; this was his fantasy.
His friends he sent to, at his request,
And prayed them to do him the pleasure
That hastily they would to him come;
He would shorten their labor, all and some.
Needed no more for him to go or ride;
He was decided where he would abide.

    Placebo came, and his friends soon,
And first of all he asked of them a favor,
That none of them should arguments make
Against the decision that he had taken,
Which decision was pleasing to God, said he,
And of his welfare the true foundation.

    He said there was a maiden in the town,
Who for her beauty had great renown,
Albeit she was of small degree;
Sufficed him her youth and her beauty.
Which maid, he said, he would have for his wife,
To lead in ease and holiness his life;
And thanked God that he might have her all,
That no person his bliss should share.
And prayed them to labor in this need,
And arrange that toward it he would speed;

For thanne, he seyde, his spirit was at ese.
"Thanne is," quod he, "no-thing may me displese,
Save o thing priketh in my conscience,
The which I wol reherce in your presence.
    I have," quod he, "herd seyd, ful yore ago,
Ther may no man han parfite blisses two,
This is to seye, in erthe and eek in hevene.
For though he kepe him fro the sinnes sevene,
And eek from every branche of thilke tree,
Yet is ther so parfit felicitee,
And so greet ese and lust in mariage,
That ever I am agast, now in myn age,
That I shal lede now so mery a lyf,
So delicat, with-outen wo and stryf,
That I shal have myn hevene in erthe here.
For sith that verray hevene is boght so dere,
With tribulacioun and greet penaunce,
How sholde I thanne, that live in swich plesaunce
As alle wedded men don with hir wyvis,
Come to the blisse ther Crist eterne on lyve is?
This is my drede, and ye, my bretheren tweye,
Assoilleth me this questioun, I preye."
    Justinus, which that hated his folye,
Answerde anon, right in his japerye;
And for he wolde his longe tale abregge,
He wolde noon auctoritee allegge,
But seyde, "sire, so ther be noon obstacle
Other than this, god of his hye miracle
And of his mercy may so for yow wirche,
That, er ye have your right of holy chirche,
Ye may repente of wedded mannes lyf,
In which ye seyn ther is no wo ne stryf.
And elles, god forbede but he sente
A wedded man him grace to repente
Wel ofte rather than a sengle man!
And therfore, sire, the beste reed I can,
Dispeire yow noght, but have in your memorie,
Paraunter she may be your purgatorie!
She may be goddes mene, and goddes whippe;

For then, he said, his spirit was at ease.
"There is," said he, "nothing that may me displease,
Save one thing pricks in my conscience,
Which I will rehearse in your presence.

"I have," said he, "heard said, full long ago,
That no man may have perfect blisses two—
That is to say, on earth and also in heaven.
For though he keeps himself from the sins seven,
And also from every branch of that tree,
Yet is there perfect felicity
And so great ease and pleasure in marriage
That ever I am afraid now in my age
That I shall lead now so merry a life,
So delicious, without woe and strife,
That I shall have my heaven on earth here.
For since that true heaven is bought so dear
With tribulation and great penance,
How should I then, who lives in such pleasure
As wedded men do with their wives,
Come to the bliss where with Christ eternal life is?
This is my dread, and you, my brethren two,
Resolve for me this question, I pray you."

Justinus, who hated his folly,
Answered anon right in mockery;
And in order to his long tale abridge,
He would no authority allege,
But said, "Sire, may there be no obstacle
Other than this, God of his high miracle
And of his mercy may so for you work
That, before your last rites of holy church,
You may repent of the wedded man's life,
In which you say there is no woe or strife.
Or to say it another way: God forbid but that he sends
A wedded man his grace to repent
More often than a single man!
And therefore, sire—the best I know—
Despair you not, but have in your memory,
Peradventure she may be your purgatory!
She may be God's instrument and God's whip;

Than shal your soule up to hevene skippe
Swifter than dooth an arwe out of the bowe!
I hope to god, her-after shul ye knowe,
That their nis no so greet felicitee
In mariage, ne never-mo shal be,
That yow shal lette of your savacioun,
So that ye use, as skile is and resoun,
The lustes of your wyf attemprely,
And that ye plese hir nat to amorously,
And that ye kepe yow eek from other sinne.
My tale is doon:—for my wit is thinne.
Beth nat agast her-of, my brother dere."—
(But lat us waden out of this matere.
The Wyf of Bathe, if ye han understonde,
Of mariage, which we have on honde,
Declared hath ful wel in litel space).—
"Fareth now wel, god have yow in his grace."
     And with this word this Justin and his brother
Han take hir leve, and ech of hem of other.
For whan they sawe it moste nedes be,
They wroghten so, by sly and wys tretee,
That she, this mayden, which that Maius highte,
As hastily as ever that she mighte,
Shal wedded be un-to this Januarie.
I trowe it were to longe yow to tarie,
If I yow tolde of every scrit and bond,
By which that she was feffed in his lond;
Or for to herknen of hir riche array.
But finally y-comen is the day
That to the chirche bothe be they went
For to receyve the holy sacrement.
Forth comth the preest, with stole aboute his nekke,
And bad hir be lyk Sarra and Rebekke,
In wisdom and in trouthe of mariage;
And seyde his orisons, as is usage,
And crouched hem, and bad god sholde hem blesse,
And made al siker-y-nogh with holinesse.
     Thus been they wedded with solempnitee,
And at the feste sitteth he and she

Then shall your soul up to heaven skip
Swifter than does an arrow from a bow.
I hope to God, hereafter shall you know
That there is never so great felicity
In marriage, nor ever more shall be,
That shall keep you from your salvation,
So that you use, as proper is and reason,
The pleasures of your wife temperately,
And that you please her not too amorously,
And that you keep you also from other sin.
My tale is done, for my wit is thin.
Be not afraid, my brother dear,
But let us wade out of this matter.
The Wife of Bath, if you have understood,[10]
Of marriage, which we have on hand,
Declared full well in little space.
Farewell now. God have you in his grace."
    And with this word Justin and his brother
Have taken their leave, and each of them the other.
For when they saw that it must needs be,
They wrought so, by clever and prudent negotiation,
That she, this maid who May was called,
As hastily as ever that she might
Shall wedded be unto this January.
I believe it would too long you to tarry,
If I you told of every document and bond
By which she was endowed with his land,
Or for to hear of her rich raiment.
But finally come was the day
That to the church they both went
To receive the holy sacrament.
Forth came the priest, with stole about his neck,
And bade her be like Sarah and Rebecca[11]
In prudence and devotion in marriage;
And said his orisons, as is customary,
And crossed them, and bade God should them bless,
And made all secure enough with holiness.
    Thus were they wedded with solemnity,
And at the feast sat he and she

With other worthy folk up-on the deys.
Al ful of joye and blisse is the paleys,
And ful of instruments and of vitaille,
The moste deyntevous of al Itaille.
Biforn hem stoode swiche instruments of soun,
That Orpheus, ne of Thebes Amphioun,
Ne maden never swich a melodye.
　　At every cours than cam loud minstraleye,
That never tromped Joab, for to here,
Nor he, Theodomas, yet half so clere,
At Thebes, whan the citee was in doute.
Bacus the wyn hem skinketh al aboute,
And Venus laugheth up-on every wight.
For Januarie was bicome hir knight,
And wolde bothe assayen his corage
In libertee, and eek in mariage;
And with hir fyrbrond in hir hand aboute
Daunceth biforn the bryde and al the route.
And certeinly, I dar right wel seyn this,
Ymenëus, that god of wedding is,
Saugh never his lyf so mery a wedded man.
Hold thou thy pees, thou poete Marcian,
That wrytest us that ilke wedding murie
Of hir, Philologye, and him, Mercurie,
And of the songes that the Muses songe.
To smal is bothe thy penne, and eek thy tonge,
For to descryven of this mariage.
Whan tendre youthe hath wedded stouping age,
Ther is swich mirthe that it may nat be writen;
Assayeth it your-self, than may ye witen
If that I lye or noon in this matere.
　　Maius, that sit with so benigne a chere,
Hir to biholde it seemed fayëryë;
Quene Ester loked never with swich an yë
On Assauer, so meke a look hath she.
I may yow nat devyse al hir beautee;
But thus muche of hir beautee telle I may,
That she was lyk the brighte morwe of May,
Fulfild of alle beautee and plesaunce.

With other worthy folk upon the dais.
All full of joy and bliss was the palace,
And full of music and victuals,
The most delicious of all Italy.
Before them stood instruments of such sound
That neither Orpheus, nor Amphioun,
Ever made such a melody.

    With every course there came loud minstrelsy
That trumpeted such as Joab never heard,
Nor did Theodamas,[12] even half so clear
At Thebes when its fate was in doubt.
Bacchus the wine poured all about,
And Venus smiled upon every person,
For January had become her knight
And would both try his courage
In liberty, and also in marriage;
And with her torch in her hand about
Danced before the bride and all the crowd.
And certainly, I dare right well say this,
Hymen, who god of wedding is,
Saw never in his life so merry a wedded man.
Hold you your peace, you poet Martianus,[13]
Who writes of such a wedding merry
Of Philology and Mercury,
And of the songs the Muses sang!
Too small are both your pen, and your tongue,
For to describe this marriage.
When tender youth has married stooping age,
There is such mirth that it may not be written.
Try it yourself; then may you know
If I lie or not in this matter.

    May, who sat with a look so gracious,
It seemed enchantment to behold her face.
Queen Esther[14] never looked with such an eye
On Ahasuerus, so meek a look as had she.
I may you not describe all her beauty.
But this much of her beauty I may tell,
That she was like the bright morning of May,
Filled with beauty and delight.

This Januarie is ravisshed in a traunce
At every time he loked on hir face;
But in his herte he gan hir to manace,
That he that night in armes wolde hir streyne
Harder than ever Paris dide Eleyne.
But nathelees, yet hadde he greet pitee,
That thilke night offenden hir moste he;
And thoughte, "allas! o tendre creature!
Now wolde god ye mighte wel endure
Al my corage, it is so sharp and kene;
I am agast ye shul it nat sustene.
But god forbede that I dide al my might!
Now wolde god that it were woxen night,
And that the night wolde lasten evermo.
I wolde that al this peple were ago."
And finally, he doth al his labour,
As he best mighte, savinge his honour,
To haste hem fro the mete in subtil wyse.
     The tyme cam that reson was to ryse;
And after that, men daunce and drinken faste,
And spyces al aboute the hous they caste;
And ful of joye and blisse is every man;
All but a squyer, highte Damian,
Which carf biforn the knight ful many a day.
He was so ravisshed on his lady May,
That for the verray peyne he was ny wood;
Almost he swelte and swowned ther he stood.
So sore hath Venus hurt him with hir brond,
As that she bar it daunsinge in hir hond.
And to his bed he wente him hastily;
Na-more of him as at this tyme speke I.
But ther I lete him wepe y-nough and pleyne,
Til fresshe May wol rewen on his peyne.
     O perilous fyr, that in the bedstraw bredeth!
O famulier foo, that his servyce bedeth!
O servant traitour, false hoomly hewe,
Lyk to the naddre in bosom sly untrewe,
God shilde us alle from your aqueyntaunce!
O Januarie, dronken in plesaunce

This January was ravished in a trance
Every time he looked on her face;
But in his heart he began her to menace
That he that night in his arms would her press
Harder than ever Helen was by Paris.
Yet nevertheless had he great pity
That that night injure her must he,
And thought, "Alas! O tender creature,
Now would to God you might endure
All my ardor, it is so sharp and keen!
I am afraid that you shall it not sustain.
But God forbid that I use all my might!
Now would to God that it were night,
And that the night would last for evermore.
I wish that all these people were gone."
And finally he did all he could
As best he could, as etiquette permitted,
To hasten them from the meal in subtle ways.

    The time came when it was right to rise;
And after that men danced and drank,
And spices all about the house they cast,
And full of joy and bliss was every man—
All but a squire, called Damian,
Who carved before the knight full many a day.
He was so ravished by his lady May
That for the pain of love he was almost mad.
He almost fainted and swooned where he stood,
So sore had Venus hurt him with her torch,
As she bore it dancing in her hand;
And he went hastily to his bed.
No more of him at this time speak I,
But there I let him weep enough and complain
Till fresh May will take pity on his pain.

    Oh perilous fire, that in the bedstraw smolders!
Oh home-breaker, who his service offers!
Oh traitorous, domestic false,
Like to the adder in the bosom untrue,
God shield us all from your acquaintance!
Oh January, drunk in delight

Of mariage, see how thy Damian,
Thyn owene squyer and thy borne man,
Entendeth for to do thee vileinye.
God graunte thee thyn hoomly fo t'espye.
For in this world nis worse pestilence
Than hoomly foo al day in thy presence.

    Parfourned hath the sonne his ark diurne,
No lenger may the body of him sojourne
On th'orisonte, as in that latitude.
Night with his mantel, that is derk and rude,
Gan oversprede the hemisperie aboute;
For which departed is this lusty route
Fro Januarie, with thank on eevry syde.
Hom to hir houses lustily they ryde,
Wher-as they doon hir thinges as hem leste,
And whan they sye hir tyme, goon to reste.
Sone after that, this hastif Januarie
Wolde go to bedde, he wolde no lenger tarie.
He drinketh ipocras, clarree, and vernage
Of spyces hote, t'encresen his corage;
And many a letuarie hadde he ful fyn,
Swiche as the cursed monk dan Constantyn
Hath writen in his book *de Coitu;*
To eten hem alle, he nas no-thing eschu.
And to his privee freendes thus seyde he:
"For goddes love, as sone as it may be,
Lat voyden al this hous in curteys wyse."
And they han doon right as he wol devyse.
Men drinken, and the travers drawe anon;
The bryde was broght a-bedde as stille as stoon;
And whan the bed was with the preest y-blessed,
Out of the chambre hath every wight him dressed.
And Januarie hath faste in armes take
His fresshe May, his paradys, his make.
He lulleth hir, he kisseth hir ful ofte
With thikke bristles of his berd unsofte,
Lyk to the skin of houndfish, sharp as brere,
For he was shave al newe in his manere.
He rubbeth hir aboute hir tendre face,

In marriage, see how your Damian,
Your own squire and your man born,
Intends for to do you villainy.
God grant that you your servant foe espy!
For in this world there is no worse pestilence
Than a household foe all day in your presence.

    Performed has the sun his arc diurnal;
No longer may his body sojourn
On the horizon, as in that latitude
Night with his mantle, that is dark and rude,
Began overspreading the hemisphere about;
For which departed was this lively crowd
From January, with thank you on every side.
Home to their houses lively they rode,
Where they did their things as they wished,
And when they saw it time, went to rest.
Soon after that, this urgent January
Would go to bed; he would no longer tarry.
He drank cordials, clarets and liqueurs
Spiced hot to increase his ardor;
And many an elixir had he full fine,
Such as the cursed monk, Sir Constantine,[15]
Had written in his book *De Coitu*;
To eat them all he has nothing eschewed.
And to his close friends thus said he:
"For God's love, as soon as it may be,
Please leave this house in a courteous way."
And they did right as he contrived.
They drank a toast and drew the curtains soon.
The bride was brought to bed still as a stone;
And when the bed was by the priest blessed,
Out of the chamber has every person himself expressed,
And January has hard in his arms taken
His fresh May, his paradise, his mate.
He lulled her, he kissed her full often;
With thick bristles of his beard unsoft,
Like to the skin of a dogfish, sharp as briars—
For he was shaven all new in his manner—
He fondled her about her tender face,

And seyde thus, "allas! I moot trespace
To yow, my spouse, and yow gretly offende,
Er tyme come that I wil doun descende.
But nathelees, considereth this," quod he,
"Ther nis no werkman, what-so-ever he be,
That may bothe werke wel and hastily;
This wol be doon at leyser parfitly.
It is no fors how longe that we pleye;
In trewe wedlok wedded be we tweye;
And blessed be the yok that we been inne,
For in our actes we mowe do no sinne.
A man may do no sinne with his wyf,
Ne hurte him-selven with his owene knyf;
For we han leve to pleye us by the lawe."
Thus laboureth he til that the day gan dawe;
And than he taketh a sop in fyn clarree,
And upright in his bed than sitteth he,
And after that he sang ful loude and clere,
And kiste his wyf, and made wantoun chere.
He was al coltish, ful of ragerye,
And ful of jargon as a flekked pye.
The slakke skin aboute his nekke shaketh,
Whyl that he sang; so chaunteth he and craketh.
But god wot what that May thoughte in hir herte,
Whan she him saugh up sittinge in his sherte,
In his night-cappe, and with his nekke lene;
She preyseth nat his pleying worth a bene.
Than seide he thus, "my reste wol I take;
Now day is come, I may no lenger wake."
And doun he leyde his head, and sleep til pryme.
And afterward, whan that he saugh his tyme,
Up ryseth Januarie; but fresshe May
Holdeth hir chambre un-to the fourthe day,
As usage is of wyves for the beste.
For every labour som-tyme moot han reste,
Or elles longe may he nat endure;
This is to seyn, no lyves creature,
Be it of fish, or brid, or beest, or man.
    Now wol I speke of woful Damian,

And said thus, "Alas! I must injure
You, my spouse, and you greatly offend
Before I will down descend.
But nevertheless, consider this," said he,
"There is no workman, whatsoever he be,
Who may work both well and hastily;
This will be done at leisure perfectly.
It matters not how long we play;
In true wedlock coupled be we two,
And blessed be the yoke that we be in,
For in our acts we may do no sin.
A man may do no sin with his wife,
Nor hurt himself with his own knife,
For we have leave to play together by the law."
Thus labored he until day began to dawn;
And then he took a sip of fine claret,
And upright in his bed then he sat,
And after that he sang full loud and clear,
And kissed his wife, his look all lechery.
He was all coltish, full of wantonness,
And full of chatter as a spotted magpie.
The slack skin about his neck shook
While that he sang, so crooned he and croaked.
But God knows what May thought in her heart,
When she saw him sitting up in his shirt,
In his night-cap, and with his neck lean;
She praised not his performance worth a bean.
Then said he thus, "My rest will I take;
Now day is come, I may no longer wake."
And down he laid his head and slept till prime.
And afterward, when he saw his time,
Up rose January; but fresh May
Held her chamber unto the fourth day.
As custom is of wives for the best.
For every laborer sometime must have rest,
Or else long may he not endure—
This is to say, every creature needs respite,
Be it fish, or bird, or bird, or beast, or man.
    Now will I speak of woeful Damian,

That languissheth for love, as ye shul here;
Therfore I speke to him in this manere:
I seye, "O sely Damian, allas!
Answere to my demaunde, as in this cas,
How shaltow to thy lady fresshe May
Telle thy wo? She wole alwey seye "nay";
Eek if thou speke, she wol thy wo biwreye;
God be thyn help, I can no bettre seye."

This syke Damian in Venus fyr
So brenneth, that he dyeth for desyr;
For which he putte his lyf in aventure,
No lenger mighte he in this wyse endure;
But prively a penner gan he borwe,
And in a lettre wroot he al his sorwe,
In manere of a compleynt or a lay,
Un-to his faire fresshe lady May.
And in a purs of silk, heng on his sherte,
He hath it put, and leyde it at his herte.

The mone that, at noon, was, thilke day
That Januarie hath wedded fresshe May,
In two of Taur, was in-to Cancre gliden;
So longe hath Maius in hir chambre biden,
As custume is un-to thise nobles alle.
A bryde shal nat eten in the halle,
Til dayes foure or three dayes atte leste
Y-passed been; than lat hir go to feste.
The fourthe day compleet fro noon to noon,
Whan that the heighe masse was y-doon,
In halle sit this Januarie, and May
As fresh as is the brighte someres day.
And so bifel, how that this gode man
Remembred him upon this Damian,
And seyde, "Seinte Marie! how may this be,
That Damian entendeth nat to me?
Is he ay syk, or how may this bityde?"
His squyeres, whiche that stoden ther bisyde,
Excused him by-cause of his siknesse,
Which letted him to doon his bisinesse;
Noon other cause mighte make him tarie.

Who languishes for love, as you shall hear;
Therefore I speak to him in this manner:
I say, "Oh, wretched Damian, alas!
Answer to my demand, as in this case.
How shall you to your lady, fresh May,
Tell your woe? She will always say nay.
And if you speak, she will you betray.
God be your help! I can no better say."
        This sick Damian in Venus' fire
So burned that he died for desire,
For which he put his life in danger.
No longer might he in this way endure,
But secretly a pen he borrowed,
And in a letter wrote he all his sorrow,
In manner of a lament or lay,
Unto his fresh, fair lady May;
And in a purse of silk hung in his shirt
He had put it, and laid it at his heart.
        The moon, that at noon was that day
That January had wedded fresh May
In the second degree of Taurus, was into Cancer gliding;[16]
So long had May in her chamber abided,
As custom was unto these nobles all.
A bride shall not eat in the hall
Till days four, or three days at least,
Passed have been; then let her go to the feast.
The fourth day complete from noon to noon,
When the high mass was done,
In hall sits this January and May,
As fresh as is the bright summer's day.
And so it befell that this good man
Remembered him upon this Damian,
And said, "Saint Mary! How may this be,
That Damian attends not on me?
Is he still sick, or how may this betide?"
His squires, who stood there beside,
Excused him by cause of his sickness,
Which prevented him from doing his business;
No other cause might make him tarry,

"That me forthinketh," quod this Januarie,
"He is a gentil squyer, by my trouthe!
If that he deyde, it were harm and routhe;
He is as wys, discreet, and as secree
As any man I woot of his degree;
And ther-to manly and eek servisable,
And for to been a thrifty man right able.
But after mete, as sone as ever I may,
I wol my-self visyte him and eek May,
To doon him al the confort that I can."
And for that word him blessed every man,
That, of his bountee and his gentillesse,
He wolde so conforten in siknesse
His squyer, for it was a gentil dede.
"Dame," quod this Januarie, "tak good hede,
At-after mete ye, with your wommen alle,
Whan ye han been in chambre out of this halle,
That alle ye go see this Damian;
Doth him disport, he is a gentil man;
And telleth him that I wol him visyte,
Have I no-thing but rested me a lyte;
And spede yow faste, for I wole abyde
Til that ye slepe faste by my syde."
And with that word he gan to him to calle
A squyer, that was marchal of his halle,
And tolde him certeyn thinges, what he wolde.

    This fresshe May hath streight hir wey y-holde,
With alle hir wommen, un-to Damian.
Doun by his beddes syde sit she than,
Confortinge him as goodly as she may.
This Damian, whan that his tyme he say,
In secree wise his purs, and eek his bille,
In which that he y-writen hadde his wille,
Hath put in-to hir hand, with-outen more,
Save that he syketh wonder depe and sore,
And softely to hir right thus seyde he:
"Mercy! and that ye nat discovere me;
For I am deed, if that this thing be kid."
This purs hath she inwith hir bosom hid,

"That grieves me," said this January,
"He is a gentle squire, by my troth!
If he died, it were harm and pity.
He is as wise, discreet and trustworthy
As any man I know of his degree,
And also manly and willing,
And to be a success right able.
But after dinner, as soon as ever I may,
I will myself visit him, and also May,
To do him all the comfort that I can."
And for that word blessed him every man,
Who of his bounty and his gentleness
He would so comfort in sickness
His squire, for it was a gentle deed.
"Dame," said this January, "take good heed,
After dinner you with your women all,
When you have departed hall,
That all you go see this Damian.
Give him comfort—he is a gentle man;
And tell him that I will him visit,
As soon as I have rested me a little;
And speed you fast, for I will abide
Till you sleep fast by my side."
And with that word he began to call
A squire, who was marshall of his hall,
And told him certain things, that he wished.
    Thus fresh May has straight her way made
With all her women unto Damian.
Down by his bedside she sat then,
Comforting him as well as she could.
This Damian, when his time he saw,
In secret his purse and also his billet-doux,
In which he had written his desire,
Has put into her hand, without more,
Save that he sighed wondrous deep and sore,
And softly to her right thus said he:
"Mercy! And that you not reveal me
For I am dead if this thing be known."
This purse has she in her bosom hid

And wente hir wey; ye gete namore of me.
But un-to Januarie y-comen is she,
That on his beddes syde sit ful softe.
He taketh hir, and kisseth hir ful ofte,
And leyde him doun to slepe, and that anon.
She feyned hir as that she moste gon
Ther-as ye woot that every wight mot nede.
And whan she of this bille hath taken hede,
She rente it al to cloutes atte laste,
And in the privee softely it caste.

    Who studieth now but faire fresshe May?
Adoun by olde Januarie she lay,
That sleep, til that the coughe hath him awaked;
Anon he preyde hir strepen hir al naked;
He wolde of hir, he seyde, han som plesaunce,
And seyde, hir clothes dide him encombraunce,
And she obeyeth, be hir lief or looth.
But lest that precious folk be with me wrooth,
How that he wroghte, I dare nat to yow telle;
Or whether hir thoughte it paradys or helle;
But here I lete hem werken in hir wyse
Til evensong rong, and that they moste aryse.

    Were it by destinee or aventure,
Were it by influence or by nature,
Or constellacion, that in swich estat
The hevene stood, that tyme fortunat
Was for to putte a bille of Venus werkes
(For alle thing hath tyme, as seyn thise clerkes)
To any womman, for to gete hir love,
I can nat seye; but grete god above,
That knoweth that non act is causelees,
He deme of al, for I wol holde my pees.
But sooth is this, how that this fresshe May
Hath take swich impression that day,
For pitee of this syke Damian,
That from hir herte she ne dryve can
The remembraunce for to doon him ese.
"Certeyn," thoghte she, "whom that this thing displese,
I rekke noght, for here I him assure,

And went her way; you get no more of me.
But unto January she is come,
Who on his bedside sits full quietly,
He took her, and kissed her full often,
And laid himself down to sleep, and that anon.
She pretended that she had to go
There where every person must needs visit;
And when of this billet-doux she had read,
She tore it all into pieces little
And into the privy them quietly cast.

　　Who ponders now but fair fresh May?
Adown by old January she lay,
Who slept until a cough has him awakened,
Anon he asked that she strip herself all naked;
He would of her, he said, have some play;
He said her clothes got in the way,
And she obeyed, be her willing or loathe.
But lest that precious folk be with me wroth,
How that he wrought, I dare not you tell,
Or whether she thought it paradise or hell.
But here I leave them work in their ways
Till evensong rang and that they must arise.

　　Were it destiny or by chance,
Were it by nature or influence,
Or constellation, that in such estate
The heavens stood that time fortunate
To present a petition for Venus' work—
For everything has its time, as say these scholars—
For any woman to get her love,
I cannot say; but great God above,
Who knows that no act is causeless,
May he judge all, for I will hold my peace.
But the truth is this, how this fresh May
Has had such a feeling that day
Of pity for this sick Damian
That from her heart drive she could not
The thought of giving him some comfort.
"Certainly," thought she, "who this thing displeases
I care not, for here I him pledge

To love him best of any creature,
Though he na-more hadde than his sherte."
Lo, pitee renneth sone in gentil herte.

Heer may ye se how excellent franchyse
In wommen is, whan they hem narwe avyse.
Som tyrant is, as ther be many oon,
That hath an herte as hard as any stoon,
Which wolde han lete him sterven in the place
Wel rather than han graunted him hir grace;
And hem rejoysen in hir cruel pryde,
And rekke nat to been an homicyde.

This gentil May, fulfilled of pitee,
Right of hir hande a lettre made she,
In which she graunteth him hir verray grace;
Ther lakketh noght but only day and place,
Wher that she mighte un-to his lust suffyse:
For it shal be right as he wol devyse.
And whan she saugh hir time, up-on a day,
To visite this Damian goth May,
And sotilly this lettre doun she threste
Under his pilwe, rede it if him leste.
She taketh him by the hand, and harde him twiste
So secrely, that no wight of it wiste,
And bad him been al hool, and forth she wente
To Januarie, whan that he for hir sente.

Up ryseth Damian the nexte morwe,
Al passed was his siknesse and his sorwe.
He kembeth him, he proyneth him and pyketh,
He dooth al that his lady lust and lyketh;
And eek to Januarie he gooth as lowe
As ever died a dogge for the bowe.
He is so plesant un-to every man,
(For craft is al, who-so that do it can)
That every wight is fayn to speke him good;
And fully in his lady grace he stood.
Thus lete I Damian aboute his nede,
And in my tale forth I wol procede.

Somme clerkes holden that felicitee
Stant in delyt, and therfor certeyn he,

To love him best of any creature,
Though he no more has than his shirt."
Look, how pity runs soon in a gentle heart!
Here you may see how excellent generosity
In women is, when they consider carefully.
There are tyrants, as there many be,
Who have a heart as hard as any stone,
Who would have let him die in the place
Rather than have granted him her grace,
And they would rejoice in their cruel pride,
And consider not their homicide.
     This gentle May, full of pity,
Right of her hand a letter made she,
In which she granted him her grace.
There lacked only but day and place
Where she might satisfy his desire,
For it should be as he aspired.
And when she saw her time, upon a day
To visit this Damian went May,
And discreetly this letter down she thrust
Under his pillow; to read it if he wished.
She took him by the hand and tightly it clasped
So secretly that no person of it guessed,
And bade him get well soon, and forth she went
To January, when he for her sent.
     Up rose Damian the next morning,
All passed was his sickness and his sorrow.
He combed, he groomed and he washed,
He did all that his lady might like and desire,
And also to January did he go as low
As ever did a dog for the hunter's bow.
He was so pleasant unto every man
(For craft is all, as whoso has it knows)
That every person was glad to speak of him good,
And fully in his lady's grace he stood.
Thus leave I Damian about his needs,
And in my tale forth I will proceed.
     Some scholars hold that felicity
Consists in sensuality, and therefore certainly,

This noble Januarie, with al his might,
In honest wyse, as longeth to a knight,
Shoop him to live ful deliciously.
His housinge, his array, as honestly
To his degree was maked as a kinges.
Amonges othere of his honest thinges,
He made a gardin, walled al with stoon;
So fair a gardin woot I nowher noon.
For out of doute, I verraily suppose,
That he that wroot the Romance of the Rose
Ne coude of it the beautee wel devyse;
Ne Priapus ne mighte nat suffyse,
Though he be god of gardins, for to telle
The beautee of the gardin and the welle,
That stood under a laurer alwey grene.
Ful ofte tyme he, Pluto, and his quene,
Prosperpina, and al hir fayërye
Disporten hem and maken melodye
Aboute that welle, and daunced, as men tolde.
This noble knight, this Januarie the olde,
Swich deintee hath in it to walke and pleye,
That he wol no wight suffren bere the keye
Save he him-self; for of the smale wiket
He bar alwey of silver a smal cliket,
With which, whan that him leste, he it unshette.
And whan he wolde paye his wyf hir dette
In somer seson, thider wolde he go,
And May his wyf, and no wight but they two;
And thinges whiche that were nat doon a-bedde,
He in the gardin parfourned hem and spedde.
And in this wyse, many a mery day,
Lived this Januarie and fresshe May.
But worldly joye may nat alwey dure
To Januarie, ne to no creature.

   O sodeyn hap, o thou fortune instable,
Lyk to the scorpioun so deceivable,
That flaterest with thyn heed when thou wolt stinge;
Thy tayl is deeth, thurgh thyn enveniminge.
O brotil joye! o swete venim queynte!

This noble January, with all his might,
In respectable ways, as befitted a knight,
Tried to live full deliciously.
His house, his finery were
For his rank as respectable as a king's.
Among other of his respectable things,
He made a garden, walled all with stone;
So fair a garden know I nowhere one.
For, without doubt, I truly suppose
That he who wrote the Romance of the Rose[17]
Could not of it the beauty well imagine;
Nor that Priapus[18] might suffice,
Though he be god of gardens, to tell
The beauty of the garden and the spring
That stood under a laurel evergreen.
Full oftentime Pluto and his queen,
Proserpina, and all their fairy crew,[19]
Disported them and made melody
About that spring, and danced, as men told.
This noble knight, this January the old,
Such delight had in it to walk and play,
That he would no person suffer to bear the key
Save for himself; for of the small wicket gate
He carried always of silver a latchkey,
With which, when he wished, he it opened.
And when he would pay his wife her debt
In summer season, there would he go,
And May his wife, and no person but they two;
And things which that were not done abed,
He in the garden performed them with success.
And in this way, many a merry day,
Lived this January and fresh May.
But worldly joy may not always endure
For January, nor for any creature.
     Oh sudden chance! Oh you Fortune unstable!
Like to the scorpion so deceitful,
That flatters with his head when his tail will sting;
Your tail is death, through your poisoning.
Oh unstable joy! Oh sweet sly venom!

O monstre, that so subtilly canst peynte
Thy yiftes, under hewe of stedfastnesse,
That thou deceyvest bothe more and lesse!
Why hastow Januarie thus deceyved,
That haddest him for thy ful frend receyved?
And now thou hast biraft him bothe hise yën,
For sorwe of which desyreth he to dyen.

    Allas! this noble Januarie free,
Amidde his lust and his prosperitee,
Is woxen blind, and that al sodeynly.
He wepeth and he wayleth pitously;
And ther-with-al the fyr of jalousye,
Lest that his wyf sholde falle in som folye,
So brente his herte, that he wolde fayn
That som man bothe him and hir had slayn.
For neither after his deeth, nor in his lyf,
Ne wolde he that she were love ne wyf,
But ever live as widwe in clothes blake,
Soul as the turtle that lost hath hir make.
But atte laste, after a monthe or tweye,
His sorwe gan aswage, sooth to seye;
For whan he wiste it may noon other be,
He paciently took his adversitee;
Save, out of doute, he may nat forgoon
That he nas jalous evermore in oon;
Which jalousye it was so outrageous,
That neither in halle, n'in noon other hous,
Ne in noon other place, never-the-mo,
He nolde suffre hir for to ryde or go,
But-if that he had hand on hir alway;
For which ful ofte wepeth fresshe May,
That loveth Damian so benignely,
That she mot outher dyen sodeynly,
Or elles she mot han him as hir leste;
She wayteth whan hir herte wolde breste.

    Up-on that other syde Damian
Bicomen is the sorwefulleste man
That ever was; for neither night ne day
Ne mighte he speke a word to fresshe May,

Oh monster, that so subtly can paint
Your gifts under guise of steadfastness,
That deceive both more and less!
Why have you January thus deceived,
Whom you had as your friend received?
And now you have bereft him both his eyes,
For sorrow of which desires he to die.
   Alas, this January unconstrained,
Amid his pleasure and prosperity,
Was struck blind, and that all suddenly.
He weeped and wailed piteously;
And at once the fire of jealousy,
Lest that his wife should fall in some folly,
So burned his heart that he would rather
That some man had slain both him and her.
For neither after his death nor in his life
Would he have her be another's paramour or wife,
But ever live as widow in clothes black,
Solitary as the turtledove that has lost her mate.
But at last, after a month or two,
His sorrow began to assuage, truth to tell
For when he knew it might not otherwise be,
He patiently took his adversity,
Save, doubtless, that he could not forgo
His constant jealousy,
Which jealousy was so outrageous
That neither in hall, nor any other room,
Nor in any other place, evermore,
Would he suffer her to ride or go,
Unless he had hand on her always;
For which full often wept fresh May,
Who loved Damian so benignly
That she must either die suddenly
Or she must have him as she wished.
She thought that her heart would burst.
   Upon the other side Damian
Became the sorrowfullest man
Who ever was, for neither night nor day
Might he speak a word to fresh May,

As to his purpos, of no swich matere,
But-if that Januarie moste it here,
That hadde an hand up-on hir evermo.
But nathelees, by wryting to and fro
And privee signes, wiste he what she mente;
And she knew eek the fyn of his entente.

O Januarie, what mighte it thee availle,
Thou mightest see as fer as shippes saille?
For also good is blind deceyved be,
As be deceyved whan a man may see.
Lo, Argus, which that hadde an hondred yën,
For al that ever he coude poure or pryen,
Yet was he blent; and, god wot, so ben mo,
That wenen wisly that it be nat so.
Passe over is an ese, I sey na-more.

This fresshe May, that I spak of so yore,
In warme wex hath emprented the cliket,
That Januarie bar of the smale wiket,
By which in-to his gardin ofte he wente.
And Damian, that knew al hir entente,
The cliket countrefeted prively;
Ther nis na-more to seye, but hastily
Som wonder by this cliket shal bityde,
Which ye shul heren, if ye wole abyde.

O noble Ovyde, ful sooth seystou, god woot!
What sleighte is it, thogh it be long and hoot,
That he nil finde it out in som manere?
By Piramus and Tesbee may men lere;
Thogh they were kept ful longe streite overal,
They been accorded, rouninge thurgh a wal,
Ther no wight coude han founde out swich a sleighte.

But now to purpos; er that dayes eighte
Were passed, er the monthe of Juil, bifil
That Januarie hath caught so greet a wil,
Thurgh egging of his wyf, him for to pleye
In his gardin, and no wight but they tweye,
That in a morwe un-to this May seith he:
"Rys up, my wyf, my love, my lady free;
The turtles vois is herd, my douve swete;

About his purpose, of no such matter,
For fear that January might it hear,
Who had his hand on hers evermore.
But nevertheless, by writing to and fro
By secret signs knew he what she meant,
And she knew also the object of his intent.

Oh January, what might it you avail,
Though you might see as far as ships sail?
For it is just as good to be deceived when blind
As to be deceived when a man may see.
Look, Argus,[20] who had a hundred eyes,
For all that ever he could pore or pry,
Yet he was blind and, God knows, so be more
Who are so sure that it be not so.
What you don't see won't hurt you, I say no more.

This fresh May, whom I spoke of before,
In warm wax has imprinted the key
That January bore of the small gate,
By which into his garden he often went;
And Damian, who knew all her intent,
The key counterfeited secretly.
There is no more to say, but hastily
Some miracle will this key betide,
Which you shall hear, if you will abide.

Oh noble Ovid, full truth say you, God knows,
What magic it is, through effort hot and long,
By which Love will find a way somehow?
By Pyramus and Thisbe may men learn;
Though they were kept apart by measures strict,[21]
They agreed, whispering through a wall,
Where no one could imagine such a trick.

But now to the point: before eight days
Were passed in June, befell
That January had caught a desire so great,
Through the urging of his wife, him for to play
In his garden, and no person but they two,
That in a morning unto his May said he:
"Rise up, my wife, my love, my lady free!
The turtledove's voice is heard, my dove sweet;

The winter is goon, with alle his reynes wete;
Com forth now, with thyn eyën columbyn!
How fairer been thy brestes than is wyn!
The gardin is enclosed al aboute;
Com forth, my whyte spouse; out of doute,
Thou hast me wounded in myn herte, o wyf!
No spot of thee ne knew I al my lyf.
Com forth, and lat us taken our disport;
I chees thee for my wyf and my confort."
    Swiche olde lewed wordes used he;
On Damian a signe made she,
That he sholde go biforen with his cliket:
This Damian thanne hath opened the wiket,
And in he stirte, and that in swich manere,
That no wight mighte it see neither y-here;
And stille he sit under a bush anoon.
    This Januarie, as blind as is a stoon,
With Maius in his hand, and no wight mo,
In-to his fresshe gardin is ago,
And clapte to the wiket sodeynly.
    "Now, wyf," quod he, "heer nis but thou and I,
That art the creature that I best love.
For, by that lord that sit in heven above,
Lever ich hadde dyen on a knyf,
Than thee offende, trewe dere wyf!
For goddes sake, thenk how I thee chees,
Noght for no coveityse, doutelees,
But only for the love I had to thee.
And thogh that I be old, and may nat see,
Beth to me trewe, and I shal telle yow why.
Three thinges, certes, shul ye winne ther-by;
First, love of Crist, and to your-self honour,
And al myn heritage, toun and tour;
I yeve it yow, maketh chartres as yow leste;
This shal be doon to-morwe er sonne reste.
So wisly god my soule bringe in blisse,
I prey yow first, in covenant ye me kisse.
And thogh that I be jalous, wyte me noght.
Ye been so depe enprented in my thoght,

The winter is gone with all his rains wet.
Come forth now, with your dovelike eyes!
How fairer be your breasts than is wine!
The garden is enclosed all about;
Come forth, my lily-white spouse! Without doubt
You have me wounded in my heart, Oh wife!
No fault in you have I known in all my life.[22]
Come forth, and let us take our disport;
I choose you for my wife and my comfort."
   Such old lewd words used he.
To Damian a sign made she,
That he should go before with his key.
This Damian then opened the gate,
And in he went, and that in such manner
That no person might him see or hear,
And still he sat under a bush anon.
   This January, as blind as is a stone,
With May in his hand, and no person more,
Into his fresh garden is a-gone,
And shut the wicket suddenly.
   "Now wife," said he, "here are but you and I,
You are the creature that I best love.
For by that Lord who sits in heaven above,
I would rather die upon a knife
Than you offend, true dear wife!
For God's sake, think how I you chose,
Without doubt not for cupidity,
But only for the love I had for you.
And though I am old and cannot see,
Be to me true, and I will tell you why.
Three things, certainly, shall you gain thereby:
First, love of Christ, and to yourself honor,
And all my inheritance, town and tower;
I give to you, make contracts as you wish;
This shall be done tomorrow before the sun rests,
So surely God my soul brings in bliss.
I pray you first, in covenant you me kiss;
And though I be jealous, blame me not.
You be so deep imprinted in my thought

That, whan that I considere your beautee,
And ther-with-al the unlykly elde of me
I may nat, certes, thogh I sholde dye,
Forbere to been out of your companye
For verray love; this is with-outen doute.
Now kis me, wyf, and lat us rome aboute."
    This fresshe May, whan she thise wordes herde,
Benignely to Januarie answerde,
But first and forward she bigan to wepe,
"I have," quod she, "a soule for to kepe
As wel as ye, and also myn honour,
And of my wyfhod thilke tendre flour,
Which that I have assured in your hond,
Whan that the preest to yow my body bond;
Wherfore I wole answere in this manere
By the leve of yow, my lord so dere:
I prey to god, that never dawe the day
That I ne sterve, as foule as womman may,
If ever I do un-to my kin that shame,
Or elles I empeyre so my name,
That I be fals; and if I do that lakke,
Do strepe me and put me in a sakke,
And in the nexte river do me drenche.
I am a gentil womman and no wenche.
Why speke ye thus? but men ben ever untrewe,
And wommen have repreve of yow ay newe.
Ye han non other contenance, I leve,
But speke to us of untrust and repreve."
    And with that word she saugh wher Damian
Sat in the bush, and coughen she bigan,
And with hir finger signes made she,
That Damian sholde climbe up-on a tree,
That charged was with fruit, and up he wente;
For verraily he knew al hir entente,
And every signe that she coude make
Wel bet that Januarie, hir owene make.
For in a lettre she had told him al
Of this matere, how he werchen shal.
And thus I lete him sitte up-on the pyrie,

That, when I consider your beauty
And at the same time the unsuitability of my age,
I may not, certainly, though I should die,
Forebear to be out of your company
For true love; this is without doubt.
Now kiss me, wife, and let us roam about."

    This fresh May, when she these words heard,
Graciously to January answered,
But first of all she began to weep.
"I have," said she, "a soul for to keep
As well as you, and also my honor,
And of my wifehood the tender flower,
Which I have entrusted in your hand,
When the priest to you my body bound;
Therefore I will answer in this manner,
By leave of you, my lord so dear:
I pray to God that never dawns the day
That I die, as foul women may,
If I ever do unto my kin that shame,
Or else I damage so my name,
That I am false; and if I do that offense,
Do strip me and put me in a sack,
And in the next river do me drown.
I am a gentle woman and no wench.
Why speak you thus? But men are ever untrue,
And women have reproof always of you.
You have no other way, I believe,
But to speak to us of faithlessness and reproof."

    And with that word she saw where Damian
Sat in the bush, and coughing she began,
And with her finger signs made she
That Damian should climb upon a tree
That laden was with fruit, and up he went.
For truly he knew all her intent,
And every design that she could make,
Well better than January, her own mate,
For in a letter she had told him all
Of this matter, how work he shall.
And thus I let him sit upon the pear tree,

And Januarie and May rominge myrie.
   Bright was the day, and blew the firmament,
Phebus of gold his stremes doun hath sent,
To gladen every flour with his warmnesse.
He was that tyme in *Geminis*, as I gesse,
But litel fro his declinacioun
Of Cancer, Jovis exaltacioun.
And so bifel, that brighte morwe-tyde,
That in that gardin, in the ferther syde,
Pluto, that is the king of fayërye,
And many a lady in his companye,
Folwinge his wyf, the quene Proserpyne,
Ech after other, right as any lyne—
Whyl that she gadered floures in the mede,
In Claudian ye may the story rede,
How in his grisly carte he hir fette:—
This king of fairye thanne adoun him sette
Up-on a bench of turves, fresh and grene,
And right anon thus seyde he to his quene.
   "My wyf," quod he, "ther may no wight sey nay;
Th'experience so preveth every day
The treson whiche that wommen doon to man.
Ten hondred thousand [stories] telle I can
Notable of your untrouthe and brotilnesse.
O Salomon, wys, richest of richesse,
Fulfild of sapience and of worldly glorie,
Ful worthy been thy wordes to memorie
To every wight that wit and reson can.
Thus preiseth he yet the bountee of man:
"Amonges a thousand men yet fond I oon,
But of wommen alle fond I noon."
Thus seith the king that knoweth your wikkednesse;
And Jesus *filius Syrak*, as I gesse,
Ne speketh of yow but selde reverence.
A wilde fyr and corrupt pestilence
So falle up-on your bodies yet to-night!
Ne see ye nat this honurable knight,
By-cause, allas! that he is blind and old,
His owene man shal make him cokewold;

And January and May roaming merry.
    Bright was the day, and blue the firmament;
Phoebus had of gold his streams down sent
To gladden every flower with his warmness.
He was that time in *Gemini*,[23] as I guess,
But little from his declination
Of Cancer, Jupiter in exaltation.
And so befell, that bright morningtide
That in that garden, in the further side,
Pluto, who is king of the Underworld,
And many a lady in his company,
Following his wife, the queen Proserpina,
Whom he carried off from Aetna
While she gathered flowers in the meadow—
In Claudian you may the stories read,
How in his horrid chariot he her fetched—
This king of the Underworld down him set
Upon a bench of turf, fresh and green,
And right anon thus said he to his queen:
    'My wife," said he, "there may no one say nay;
As experience proves every day
Of the treasons that women do to men.
Ten hundred thousand tales I can tell
Notable for your untruth and fickleness.
Oh Solomon,[24] wise and richest of the rich,
Full of knowledge and worldly glory,
Full worthy are your words for remembrance
By every person whose wit and reason can.
Thus praised he yet the goodness of man:
"Among a thousand men yet found I one,
But of women all found I none."
Thus said the king who knows your wickedness.
And Jesus, *filius Syrak*,[25] as I guess,
Speaks of you but seldom reverence.
A burning rash and pestilence
So fall upon your bodies yet tonight!
See you not this honorable knight,
Because, alas, that he is blind and old,
His own man shall make him cuckold.

Lo heer he sit, the lechour, in the tree.
Now wol I graunten, of my magestee,
Un-to this olde blinde worthy knight
That he shal have ayeyn his eyen sight,
Whan that his wyf wold doon him vileinye;
Than shal he knowen al hir harlotrye
Both in repreve of hir and othere mo."
    "Ye shal," quod Proserpyne, "wol ye so;
Now, by my modres sires soule I swere,
That I shal yeven hir suffisant answere,
And alle wommen after, for hir sake;
That, though they be in any gilt y-take,
With face bold they shulle hem-self excuse,
And bere hem doun that wolden hem accuse.
For lakke of answer, noon of hem shal dyen.
Al hadde man seyn a thing with bothe his yën,
Yit shul we wommen visage it hardily,
And wepe, and swere, and chyde subtilly,
So that ye men shul been as lewed as gees.
What rekketh me of your auctoritees?
    I woot wel that this Jew, this Salomon,
Fond of us wommen foles many oon.
But though that he ne fond no good womman,
Yet hath ther founde many another man
Wommen ful trewe, ful gode, and vertuous.
Witnesse on hem that dwelle in Cristes hous,
With martirdom they preved hir constance.
The Romayn gestes maken remembrance
Of many a verray trewe wyf also.
But sire, ne be nat wrooth, al-be-it so,
Though that he seyde he fond no good womman,
I prey yow take the sentence of the man;
He mente thus, that in sovereyn bontee
Nis noon but god, that sit in Trinitee.
    Ey! for verray god, that nis but oon,
What make ye so muche of Salomon?
What though he made a temple, goddes hous?
What though he were riche and glorious?
So made he eek a temple of false goddis,

Look, where he sits, the lecher, in a tree!
Now will I grant, of my majesty,
Unto this old, blind, worthy knight
That he shall have ever his eyesight,
When his wife should do him villainy.
Then shall he know all her harlotry,
Both in reproof of her and others more."

    "You shall?" said Proserpina, "Will say so?
Now by my mother's sire's soul I swear
That I shall give her sufficient answer,
And all women after, for her sake,
That, even if they are in the act taken,
With faces bold they shall themselves excuse,
And bear down on those who would them accuse.
For lack of answer none of them shall die.
Albeit had a man seen a thing with both his eyes,
Yet shall women keep a brave face,
And weep, and promise, and chide subtly,
So that men shall be dumb as geese.
What care I of your authorities?

    "I know well that this Jew, this Solomon,
Found among us women fools many a one.
But though he found no good woman,
Yet have there found many another man
Women full true, full good, and virtuous.
Witness those who dwell in Christ's house;
With martyrdom they prove their constancy.
The Roman histories also make remembrance
Of many a true wife also.
But sire, be not wroth, albeit so,
Though that he found no good woman,
I pray you take the gist of the man;
He meant thus, that in perfect goodness
Is none but God, and neither he nor she.

    "Eh! by the true God and no other,
Why make you so much of Solomon?
What though he made a temple, God's house?
What though he was rich and glorious?
So made he also a temple of false gods.

How mighte he do a thing that more forbode is?
Pardee, as faire as ye his name emplastre.
He was a lechour and an ydolastre;
And in his elde he verray god forsook.
And if that god ne hadde, as seith the book,
Y-spared him for his fadres sake, he sholde
Have lost his regne rather than he wolde.
I sette noght of al the vileinye,
That ye of wommen wryte, a boterflye.
I am a womman, nedes moot I speke,
Or elles swelle til myn herte breke.
For sithen he seyde that we ben jangleresses,
As ever hool I mote brouke my tresses,
I shal nat spare, for no curteisye,
To speke him harm that wolde us vileinye."

    "Dame," quod this Pluto, "be no lenger wrooth;
I yeve it up; but sith I swoor myn ooth
That I wolde graunten him his sighte ageyn,
My word shal stonde, I warne yow, certeyn.
I am a king, it sit me noght to lye."

    "And I," quod she, "a queene of fayërye.
Hir answere shal she have, I undertake;
Lat us na-more wordes heer-of make.
For sothe, I wol no lenger yow contrarie."

    Now lat us turne agayn to Januarie,
That in the gardin with his faire May
Singeth, ful merier than the papejay,
"Yow love I best, and shal, and other noon."
So longe aboute the aleyes is he goon,
Til he was come agaynes thilke pyrie,
Wher-as this Damian sitteth ful myrie
An heigh, among the fresshe leves grene.

    This fresshe May, that is so bright and shene,
Gan for to syke, and seyde, "allas, my syde!
Now sir," quod she, "for aught that may bityde,
I moste han of the peres that I see,
Or I mot dye, so sore longeth me
To eten of the smale peres grene.
Help, for hir love that is of hevene quene!

How could he have done a thing that more forbidden was?
By God, as fair as you wash his name white with plaster,
He was an idolator and a lecher,
And in his age he the true God forsook;
And if God had not, as says the book,
Spared him for his father's sake, he would
Have lost his reign sooner than he wanted.
I care not, for all the villainy
That you of women write, a butterfly!
I am a woman, needs must I speak,
Or else swell till my heart breaks.
For since he said that we be chatterboxes,
As long as I will braid my tresses,
I shall not spare, for any courtesy,
To speak harm of him who depicts us shamefully."

   "Dame," said this Pluto, "be no longer wroth;
I give it up! But since I swore my oath
That I would grant him his sight again,
My word shall stand, I warn you certain.
I am a king; it suits me not to lie."

   "And I," said she, "a queen of the Underworld!
Her answer shall she have, I undertake.
Let us no more words hereof make;
For truth, I will no longer you contrary."

   Now let us turn again to January,
Who in the garden with his fair May
Singing full merrier than a popinjay,
"You love I best, and shall, and other none."
So long about the paths did he go,
Till he was come again to that pear tree
Where this Damian sat full merry
On high among the fresh leaves green.

   This fresh May, who is so bright and shining,
Began for to sigh, and said, "Alas, my side!
Now sir," said she, "no matter what,
I must have of the pears that I see,
If I must die, so sore do I yearn
To eat of the small pears green.
Help, for her love that is of Heaven's queen!

I telle yow wel, a womman in my plyt
May han to fruit so greet an appetyt,
That she may dyen, but she of it have."

    "Allas!" quod he, "that I ne had heer a knave
That coude climbe; allas! allas!" quod he,
"That I am blind." "Ye, sir, no fors," quod she:
"But wolde ye vouche-sauf, for goddes sake,
The pyrie inwith your armes for to take,
(For wel I woot that ye mistruste me)
Thanne sholde I climbe wel y-nogh," quod she,
"So I my foot mighte sette upon your bak."

    "Certes," quod he, "ther-on shal be no lak,
Mighte I yow helpen with myn herte blood."
He stoupeth doun, and on his bak she stood,
And caughte hir by a twiste, and up she gooth.
Ladies, I prey yow that ye be nat wrooth;
I can nat glose, I am a rude man.
And sodeynly anon this Damian
Gan pullen up the smok, and in he throng.

    And whan that Pluto saugh this grete wrong,
To Januarie he gaf agayn his sighte,
And made him see, as wel as ever he mighte.
And whan that he hadde caught his sighte agayn,
Ne was ther never man of thing so fayn.
But on his wyf his thought was evermo;
Up to the tree he caste his eyen two,
And saugh that Damian his wyf had dressed
In swich manere, it may nat ben expressed
But if I wolde speke uncurteisly:
And up he yaf a roring and a cry
As doth the moder whan the child shal dye:
"Out! help! allas! harrow!" he gan to crye,
"O stronge lady store, what dostow?"

    And she answerde, "sir, what eyleth yow?
Have pacience, and reson in your minde,
I have yow holpe on bothe your eyen blinde.
Up peril of my soule, I shal nat lyen,
As me was taught, to hele with your yën,
Was no-thing bet to make yow to see

I tell you well, a woman in my condition
May have for fruit so great an appetite
That she may die unless she has it."

"Alas," said he, "That I have not here a knave
Who could climb! Alas, alas," said he,
"For I am blind!" "Yea, sir, no matter," said she;
"But would you vouchsafe, for God's sake,
The pear tree in your arms for to take,
For well I know that you mistrust me,
Then should I climb well enough," said she,
"So I my foot might set upon your back."

"Certainly," said he, "thereon shall be no lack,
Might I you help with my heart's blood."
He stooped down, and on his back she stood,
And caught herself a branch, and up she went—
Ladies, I pray you not be wroth;
I cannot gloss, I am a rude man—
And suddenly anon this Damian
Pulled up her smock, and in he thrust.

And when that Pluto saw this great wrong,
To January he gave his sight again,
And made him see as well as ever he might.
And when he had again caught his sight,
There was never a man of anything so glad,
But on his wife his thought was evermore.
Up to the tree he cast his eyes two,
And saw that Damian his wife had addressed
In such manner it may not be expressed,
Unless I would speak indecorously;
And up he gave a roaring and a cry,
As does a mother when the child shall die:
"Help! Help! Alas! Help!" he began to cry,
"Oh bold, crude hussy, what do you do?"

And she answered, "Sir, what ails you?
Have patience and reason in your mind.
I have you helped with both your eyes blind.
On peril of my soul, I shall not lie,
As I was taught, to heal your eyes,
Was nothing better to make you see,

Than strugle with a man up-on a tree.
God woot, I dide it in ful good entente."
    "Strugle!" quod he, "ye, algate in it wente!
God yeve yow bothe on shames deeth to dyen!
He swyved thee, I saugh it with myne yën,
And elles be I hanged by the hals!"
    "Thanne is," quod she, "my medicyne al fals;
For certeinly, if that ye mighte see,
Ye wolde nat seyn thise wordes un-to me;
Ye han som glimsing and no parfit sighte."
    "I see," quod he, "as wel as ever I mighte,
Thonked be god! with bothe myne eyen two,
And by my trouthe, me thoughte he dide thee so."
    "Ye maze, maze, gode sire," quod she,
"This thank have I for I have maad yow see;
Allas!" quod she, "that ever I was so kinde!"
    "Now, dame," quod he, "lat al passe out of minde.
Com doun, my lief, and if I have missayd,
God help me so, as I am yvel apayd.
But, by my fader soule, I wende has seyn,
How that this Damian had by thee leyn,
And that thy smok had leyn up-on his brest."
    "Ye, sire," quod she, "ye may wene as yow lest;
But, sire, a man that waketh out of his sleep,
He may nat sodeynly wel taken keep
Up-on a thing, ne see it parfitly,
Til that he be adawed verraily;
Right so a man, that longe hath blind y-be,
Ne may nat sodeynly so wel y-see,
First whan his sighte is newe come ageyn,
As he that hath a day or two y-seyn.
Til that your sighte y-satled be a whyle,
Ther may ful many a sighte yow bigyle.
Beth war, I prey yow; for, by hevene king,
Ful many a man weneth to seen a thing,
And it is al another than it semeth.
He that misconceyveth, he misdemeth."
And with that word she leep doun fro the tree.
    This Januarie, who is glad but he?

Than struggle with a man upon a tree.
God knows, I did it in full good intent."
    "Struggle?" said he, "Yea, entirely in it went!
God give you both a shameless death to die!
He paired with you; I saw it with my eyes,
Or else I be hanged by the neck!"
    "Then is," said she, "my medicine false;
For certainly, if that you might see,
You would not say these words unto me.
You have some glimpsing, and no perfect sight."
    "I see," said he, "as well as ever I might,
Thanks be God. With both my eyes two,
And by my troth, I thought he did you."
    "You are bewildered, dazed, good sir," said she;
"These thanks I have for having made you see.
Alas," said she, "that ever I was so kind!"
    "Now Dame," said he, "let that all pass out of mind.
Come down, my beloved, and if I have misspoken,
God help me so, as I am evil paid.
But by my father's soul, I supposed I saw
How this Damian had by you lain,
And that your smock lay upon his breast."
    "Yea, sir," said she, "you may suppose as you wish.
But sir, a man who wakes out of his sleep,
He may not suddenly well take heed
Upon a thing, or see it perfectly,
Till he be awakened fully.
Right so a man who long has blind been,
May not suddenly so well see,
First when his sight is new come again,
As he who has a day or two seen.
Until your sight settled be awhile
There may full many a sight you beguile.
Beware, I pray you, for by heaven's king,
Full many a man supposes to see something,
And it is other than what it seemed.
He who misconceives, misjudges."
And with that word she leapt down from the tree.
    This January, who is glad but he?

He kisseth hir, and clippeth hir ful ofte,
And on hir wombe he stroketh hir ful softe,
And to his palays hoom he hath hir lad.
Now, gode men, I pray yow to be glad.
Thus endeth heer my tale of Januarie;
God blesse us and his moder Seinte Marie!

The Epilogue

"Ey! goddes mercy!" seyde our Hoste tho,
"Now swich a wyf I pray god kepe me fro!
Lo, whiche sleightes and subtilitees
In wommen been! for ay as bisy as bees
Ben they, us sely men for to deceyve,
And from a sothe ever wol they weyve;
By this Marchauntes Tale it preveth weel.
But doutelees, as trewe as any steel
I have a wyf, though that she povre be;
But of hir tonge a labbing shrewe is she,
And yet she hath an heep of vyces mo;
Ther-of no fors, lat alle swiche thinges go.
But, wite ye what? in conseil be it seyd,
Me reweth sore I am un-to hir teyd.
For, and I sholde rekenen every vyce
Which that she hath, y-wis, I were to nyce,
And cause why; it sholde reported be
And told to hir of somme of this meynee;
Of whom, it nedeth nat for to declare,
Sin wommen connen outen swich chaffare;
And eek my wit suffyseth nat ther-to
To tellen al; wherfor my tale is do."

He kissed her and embraced her full often,
And on her belly her stroked her full softly,
And to his palace home he has her led.
Now, good men, I pray you to be glad.
Thus ends here my tale of January;
God bless us, and his mother Saint Mary!

The Epilogue

"Hey! God's mercy!" said our Host then,
"Now such a wife I pray God keep me from!
Lo, what tricks and deceits
In women be! For ever as busy as bees
Be they, us naïve men to deceive,
And from the truth ever will they weave;
By this Merchant's tale it proves well.
But doubtless, as true as any steel
I have a wife, though a poor one she be,
But of her tongue, a blabbing shrew is she,
And yet she has a heap of vices more;
And so what! Let all such things go.
But do you know? Confidentially let it be said,
I repent sorely that I am to her tied.
But if I recounted every vice
That she has, I'd be a fool.
And why? I would reported be
And told on to her by some of this company—
Of whom, it needs not to name,
Some women can display such wares;
And I know enough to not
Tell all; therefore ended is my tale."

The Frankeleyns Tale

The Introduction

"IN FEITH, SQUIER, THOU hast thee wel y-quit,
And gentilly I preise wel thy wit,"
Quod the Frankeleyn, "considering thy youthe,
So feelingly thou spekest, sir, I allow thee!
As to my doom, there is non that is here
Of eloquence that shal be thy pere,
If that thou live; god yeve thee good chaunce,
And in vertu sende thee continuaunce!
For of thy speche I have greet deyntee.
I have a sone, and, by the Trinitee,
I hadde lever than twenty pound worth lond,
Though it right now were fallen in myn hond,
He were a man of swich discrecioun
As that ye been! fy on possessioun
But-if a man be vertuous with-al.
I have my sone snibbed, and yet shal,
For he to vertu listeth nat entende;
But for to pleye at dees, and to despende,
And lese al that he hath, is his usage.
And he hath lever talken with a page
Than to commune with any gentil wight
Ther he mighte lerne gentillesse aright."

    "Straw for your gentillesse," quod our host;
"What, frankeleyn? pardee, sir, wel thou wost
That eche of yow mot tellen atte leste
A tale or two, or breken his biheste."
"That knowe I wel, sir," quod the frankeleyn;
"I prey yow, haveth me nat in desdeyn
Though to this man I speke a word or two."

    "Telle on thy tale with-outen words mo."
"Gladly, sir host," quod he, "I wol obeye
Un-to your wil; now herkneth what I seye.
I wol yow nat contrarien in no wyse
As fer as that my wittes wol suffyse;

434

The Franklin's Tale

The Introduction

"IN FAITH, SQUIRE, YOU have yourself well acquitted
And like a gentleman. I praise well your wit,"
Said the Franklin. "Considering your youth,
So feelingly you speak, sir, I commend you:
In my judgement, there is none that is here
Of eloquence who shall be your peer,
If you live. God give you good fortune,
And in virtue send you continuance,
For of your speech I have great pleasure.
I have a son, and by the Trinity,
I would rather than land paying yearly twenty pounds—
Though it right now were fallen in my hand—
That he were a man of such discretion
As you be. Fie on property,
Unless a man be virtuous withal!
I have my son rebuked, and yet shall,
For he of virtue cares not at all;
But to play at dice, and to spend,
And lose all he has, has become his custom.
And he would rather talk with a servant
Than with any gentlemanly person
From whom he might learn gentility aright."

   "Straw for your gentleness!" said our Host.
"What, Franklin! By God, sir, well you know
That each of you must tell at least
A tale or two, or break his promise."
"That know I well, sir," said the Franklin;
"I pray you, hold me not in disdain
Though to this man I speak a word or two."

   "Tell your tale without words more."
"Gladly, sir Host," said he, "I will obey
Unto your will; now listen to what I say.
I will not oppose you in any way
As far as my wits will suffice.

I prey to god that it may plesen yow,
Than woot I wel that it is good y-now."

The Prologue

Thise olde gentil Britons in hir dayes
Of diverse aventures maden layes,
Rymeyed in hir firste Briton tonge;
Which layes with hir instruments they songe,
Or elles redden hem for hir plesaunce;
And oon of hem have I in remembraunce,
Which I shal seyn with good wil as I can.
    But sires, by-cause I am a burel man,
At my biginning first I yow biseche
Have me excused of my rude speche;
I lerned never rethoryk certeyn;
Thing that I speke, it moot be bare and pleyn.
I sleep never on the mount of Pernaso,
Ne lerned Marcus Tullius Cithero,
Colours ne knowe I none, with-outen drede,
But swiche colours as growen in the mede,
Or elles swiche as men dye or peynte.
Colours of rethoryk ben me to queynte;
My spirit feleth noght of swich matere.
But if yow list, my tale shul ye here.

The Tale

In Armorik, that called is Britayne,
Ther was a knight that loved and dide his payne
To serve a lady in his beste wyse;
And many a labour, many a greet empryse
He for his lady wroghte, er she were wonne.
For she was oon, the faireste under sonne,
And eek therto come of so heigh kinrede,
That wel unnethes dorste this knight, for drede,
Telle hir his wo, his peyne, and his distresse.
But atte laste, she, for his worthinesse,
And namely for his meke obeysaunce,
Hath swich a pitee caught of his penaunce,
That prively she fil of his accord

I pray to God that it may please you:
Then would I know that it is good enough."

The Prologue

Those old gentle Bretons[1] in their days
Of diverse adventures made lays,
Rhymed in their old Breton tongue;
Which verses with their instruments they sung,
Or else read them for their pleasure;
And one of them have I in remembrance,
Which I shall say with as good will as I can.
    But, sirs, because I am an untutored man,
At my beginning first I you beseech
Excuse me for my rough speech.
I learned never rhetoric, certainly:
Things that I speak must be bare and plain.
I slept never on the Mount of Parnassus,
Nor learned Marcus Tullius Cicero.[2]
Rhetorical flourishes know I none—no fear of that,
But only such flowers as grow in the meadow,
Or else such as men dye or paint.
Colors of rhetoric be to me too rarified:
My spirit has no feeling for such matter.
But if you wish, my tale shall you hear.

The Tale

In Armorica, that is called Brittany,
There was a knight who loved and took pains
To serve a lady as best he knew;
And many a labor, and many a great exploit
He for his lady performed, before she was won.
For she was one of the fairest under the sun,
And also came of such high lineage,
That scarcely dared this knight, for fear,
To tell her his woe, his pain, and his distress.
But at last she, for his worthiness,
And especially for his meek obedience,
Had such pity felt for his suffering
That secretly she consented

To take him for hir housbonde and hir lord,
Of swich lordshipe as men han over hir wyves;
And for to lede the more in blisse hir lyves,
Of his free wil be swoor hir as a knight,
That never in al his lyf he, day ne night,
Ne sholde up-on him take no maistrye
Agayn hir wil, ne kythe hir jalousye,
But hir obeye, and folwe hir wil in al
As any lovere to his lady shal;
Save that the name of soveraynetee,
That wolde he have for shame of his degree.
     She thanked him, and with ful greet humblesse
She seyde, "sire, sith of your gentillesse
Ye profre me to have so large a reyne,
Ne wolde never god bitwixe us tweyne,
As in my gilt, were outher werre or stryf.
Sir, I wol be your humble trewe wyf,
Have heer my trouthe, til that myn herte breste."
Thus been they bothe in quiete and in reste.
     For o thing, sires, saufly dar I seye,
That frendes everich other moot obeye,
If they wol longe holden companye.
Love wol nat been constreyned by maistrye;
Whan maistrie comth, the god of love anon
Beteth hise winges, and farewel! he is gon!
Love is a thing as any spirit free;
Wommen of kinde desiren libertee,
And nat to ben constreyned as a thral;
And so don men, if I soth seyen shal.
Loke who that is most pacient in love,
He is at his avantage al above.
Pacience is an heigh vertu certeyn;
For it venquisseth, as thise clerkes seyn,
Thinges that rigour sholde never atteyne.
For every word men may nat chyde or pleyne.
Lerneth to suffre, or elles, so moot I goon,
Ye shul it lerne, wher-so ye wole or noon.
For in this world, certein, ther no wight is,
That he ne dooth or seith som-tyme amis.

To take him for her husband and her lord,
Of such lordship as men have over their wives.
And for to lead the more in bliss their lives,
Of his free will he swore to her as a knight
That never in all his life he, day or night,
Would upon himself take any domination
Against her will, nor display to her jealousy,
But obey her and follow her will in all
As any lover to his lady must—
Save in the appearance of sovereignty,
That he would retain, lest it reflect on his rank.
　　She thanked him, and with full great humbleness
She said, "Sir, since of your gentleness
You offer me to have so free a reign,
God forbid there should be between us,
Through fault of mine, any war or strife.
Sir, I will be your humble true wife:
Have here my loyal pledge until my heart bursts."
Thus were they both in quiet and at rest.
　　For one thing, sirs, safely I dare say,
That friends each other must obey,
If they will long hold company.
Love will not be constrained by mastery.
When mastery comes, the God of Love at once
Beats his wings, and farewell, he is gone!
Love is a thing like any spirit free.
Women by nature desire liberty,
And not to be constrained as a slave;
And so do men, if the truth I shall say.
Consider the man who is most patient in love:
He has the advantage above all others.
Patience is a high virtue, certainly,
For it vanquishes, as these scholars say,
Things that harshness will never attain.
About every word men may not chide or complain:
Learn to suffer, or else, as I may live,
You shall it learn, whether you wish to or not.
For in this world, certainly, there no person is
Who never says or does something amiss.

Ire, siknesse, or constellacioun,
Wyn, wo, or chaunginge of complexioun
Causeth ful ofte to doon amis or speken.
On every wrong a man may nat be wreken;
After the tyme, moste be temperaunce
To every wight that can on governaunce.
And therfore hath this wyse worthy knight,
To live in ese, suffrance hir bihight,
And she to him ful wisly gan to swere
That never sholde ther be defaute in here.

Heer may men seen an humble wys accord;
Thus hath she take hir servant and hir lord,
Servant in love, and lord in mariage;
Than was he bothe in lordship and servage;
Servage? nay, but in lordshipe above,
Sith he hath bothe his lady and his love;
His lady, certes, and his wyf also,
The which that lawe of love acordeth to.
And whan he was in this prosperitee,
Hoom with his wyf he gooth to his contree,
Nat fer fro Penmark, ther his dwelling was,
Wher-as he liveth in blisse and in solas.

Who coude telle, but he had wedded be,
The joye, the ese, and the prosperitee
That is bitwixe an housbonde and his wyf?
A yeer and more lasted this blisful lyf,
Til that the knight of which I speke of thus,
That of Kayrrud was cleped Arveragus,
Shoop him to goon, and dwelle a yeer or tweyne
In Engelond, that cleped was eek Briteyne,
To seke in armes worship and honour;
For al his lust he sette in swich labour;
And dwelled ther two yeer, the book seith thus.

Now wol I stinte of this Arveragus,
And speken I wole of Dorigene his wyf,
That loveth hir housbonde as hir hertes lyf.
For his absence wepeth she and syketh,
As doon thise noble wyves whan hem lyketh,
She moorneth, waketh, wayleth, fasteth, pleyneth;

Anger, illness, or his stars,
Wine, woe, or temperament
Cause us full often to do or speak amiss.
For every wrong a man may not be avenged:
Suited for the circumstances must be moderation
As every man who self-governance understands.
And therefore did this wise, worthy knight,
To live in ease, promise her his forebearance,
And she to him full truly did swear
That it never should be lacking in her.

Here men may see a humble, wise accord:
Thus did she take her servant and her lord,
Servant in love, and lord in marriage;
Then he was both in lordship and servitude.
Servitude? Nay, but in lordship above,
Since he had both his lady and his love;
His lady, certainly, and his wife also,
To which that law of love accords.
And when he was in this prosperity,
Home with his wife he went to his country,
Not far from Penmarch, where his dwelling was,
Where he lived in bliss and joy.

Who could tell, unless he wedded be,
The joy, the ease, the prosperity
That is between a husband and his wife?
A year and more lasted this blissful life,
Until the knight of whom I speak of thus,
Who from Kerru was called Averagus,
Prepared himself to go and dwell a year or two
In England, that was also called Britain,
To seek in arms worship and honor—
For all his pleasure he took in such labor—
And dwelled there two years, the book said thus.

Now will I cease concerning this Averagus,
And speak I will of Dorigen his wife,
Who loved her husband as her heart's life.
For his absence wept she and sighed,
As do these noble wives when them it pleases.
She mourned, kept vigil, wailed, fasted, lamented;

Desyr of his presence hir so distreyneth,
That al this wyde world she sette at noght.
His frendes, whiche that knewe hir hevy thoght,
Conforten hir in al that ever they may;
They prechen hir, they telle hir night and day,
That causelees she sleeth hir-self, allas!
And every confort possible in this cas
They doon to hir with al hir bisinesse,
Al for to make hir leve hir hevinesse.

By proces, as ye knowen everichoon,
Men may so longe graven in a stoon,
Til som figure ther-inne emprented be.
So longe han they conforted hir, til she
Receyved hath, by hope and by resoun,
Th'emprenting of hir consolacioun,
Thurgh which hir grete sorwe gan aswage;
She may nat alwey duren in swich rage.

And eek Arveragus, in al this care,
Hath sent hir lettres hoom of his welfare,
And that he wol come hastily agayn;
Or elles hadde this sorwe hir herte slayn.

Hir freendes sawe hir sorwe gan to slake,
And preyde hir on knees, for goddes sake,
To come and romen hir in companye,
Awey to dryve hir derke fantasye.
And finally, she graunted that requeste;
For wel she saugh that it was for the beste.

Now stood hir castel faste by the see,
And often with hir freendes walketh she
Hir to disporte up-on the bank an heigh,
Wher-as she many a ship and barge seigh
Seilinge hir cours, wher-as hem liste go;
But than was that a parcel of hir wo.
For to hir-self ful ofte "allas!" seith she,
"Is ther no ship, of so manye as I see,
Wol bringen hom my lord? than were myn herte
Al warisshed of his bittre peynes smerte."

Another tyme ther wolde she sitte and thinke,
And caste hir eyen dounward fro the brinke.

Desire of his presence so her distressed
That all this wide world she held to be nought.
Her friends, those who knew her heavy thought,
Comforted her in all that ever they might:
They preached to her, they told her day and night,
That causelessly she was killing herself, alas!
And every comfort possible in this case
They did to her with all their diligence,
All for to make her leave her heaviness.

Over the course of time, as you all know,
Men may so long engrave a stone
Until some figure therein imprinted be.
So long did they comfort her until she
Received had, by hope and by reason,
The imprint of their consolation,
Through which her great sorrow was assuaged:
She might not always continue in such passion.

And also Averagus, in all this care,
Had sent her letters home of his welfare,
And that he would come hastily again;
Or else had this sorrow her heart slain.

Her friends saw her sorrow began to abate,
And prayed to her on their knees, for God's sake,
To come and walk in their company,
To drive away her dark imaginings.
And finally, she granted that request,
For well she saw that it was for the best.

Now her castle stood close by the sea,
And often with her friends walked she,
Herself to amuse upon the bank on high,
Where she many a ship and barge saw
Sailing their courses, where they wished to go.
But then was that a portion of her woe,
For to herself full oft "Alas!" said she,
"Is there no ship, of so many as I see,
Will bring home my lord? Then were my heart
All cured of its bitter pains sharp."

Another time she would sit there and think,
And cast her eyes downward from the brink.

But whan she saugh the grisly rokkes blake,
For verray fere so wolde hir herte quake,
That on hir feet she mighte hir noght sustene.
Than wolde she sitte adoun upon the grene,
And pitously in-to the see biholde,
And seyn right thus, with sorweful sykes colde:
    "Eterne god, that thurgh thy purveyaunce
Ledest the world by certein governaunce,
In ydel, as men seyn, ye no-thing make;
But, lord, thise grisly feendly rokkes blake,
That semen rather a foul confusioun
Of werk than any fair creacioun
Of swich a parfit wys god and a stable,
Why han ye wroght this werk unresonable?
For by this werk, south, north, ne west, ne eest,
Ther nis y-fostred man, ne brid, ne beest;
It dooth no good, to my wit, but anoyeth.
See ye nat, lord, how mankinde it destroyeth?
An hundred thousand bodies of mankinde
Han rokkes slayn, al be they nat in minde,
Which mankinde is so fair part of thy werk
That thou it madest lyk to thyn owene merk.
Than seemed it ye hadde a greet chiertee
Toward mankinde; but how than may it be
That ye swiche menes make it to destroyen,
Whiche menes do no good, but ever anoyen?
I woot wel clerkes wol seyn, as hem leste,
By arguments, that al is for the beste,
Though I ne can the causes nat y-knowe.
But thilke god, that made wind to blowe,
As kepe my lord! this my conclusioun;
To clerkes lete I al disputisoun.
But wolde god that alle thise rokkes blake
Were sonken in-to helle for his sake!
Thise rokkes sleen myn herte for the fere."
Thus wolde she seyn, with many a pitous tere.
    Hir freendes sawe that it was no disport
To romen by the see, but disconfort;
And shopen for to pleyen somwher elles.

But when she saw the grisly rocks black,
For real fear so would her heart quake
That to stand on her feet she could not sustain.
Then would she sit down upon the green,
And piteously into the sea behold,
And say right thus, with sorrowful sighs cold:
    "Eternal God, who through your providence
Guides the world by certain governance,
In vain, as men say, you nothing make.
But Lord, these grisly, fiendish rocks black,
That appear to be rather a foul confusion
Of work, than any fair creation
Of such a perfect, wise and steadfast God,
Why have you wrought this work confounding reason?
For by this work, neither south, north, west, nor east,
There is served any man, nor bird, nor beast.
It does no good, that I can see, but only injury.
See you not, Lord, how mankind it destroys?
A hundred thousand bodies of mankind
Have rocks slain, albeit unnamed:
Which mankind is so fair a part of your work
That you made it like to your own image.
Then seemed it you had great affection
Toward men; but how then may it be
That you make such means that could destroy it,
Such means that do no good, but ever injure?
I know well scholars will say as they please,
By arguments, that all is for the best,
Though I cannot their logic follow.
But that same God that made wind to blow,
May He protect my lord! This is my conclusion.
To scholars leave I all disputation,
But would God that all these black rocks
Were sunk into hell for his sake!
These rocks slay my heart with fear."
This would she say, with many a piteous tear.

    Her friends saw that for her it was no pleasure
To roam by the sea, but discomfort,
And arranged to play somewhere else.

They leden hir by riveres and by welles,
And eek in othere places delitables;
They dauncen, and they pleyen at ches and tables.
    So on a day, right in the morwe-tyde,
Un-to a gardin that was ther bisyde,
In which that they had maad hir ordinaunce
Of vitaille and of other purveyaunce,
They goon and pleye hem al the longe day.
And this was on the sixte morwe of May,
Which May had peynted with his softe shoures
This gardin ful of leves and of floures;
And craft of mannes hand so curiously
Arrayed hadde this gardin, trewely,
That never was ther gardin of swich prys,
But-if it were the verray paradys.
Th' odour of floures and the fresshe sighte
Wolde han maad any herte for to lighte
That ever was born, but-if to gret siknesse,
Or to gret sorwe helde it in distresse;
So ful it was of beautee with plesaunce.
At-after diner gonne they to daunce,
And singe also, save Dorigen allone,
Which made alwey hir compleint and hir mone;
For she ne saugh him on the daunce go,
That was hir housbonde and hir love also.
But nathelees she moste a tyme abyde,
And with good hope lete hir sorwe slyde.
    Up-on this daunce, amonges othere men,
Daunced a squyer biforen Dorigen,
That fressher was and jolyer of array,
As to my doom, than is the monthe of May.
He singeth, daunceth, passinge any man
That is, or was, sith that the world bigan.
Ther-with he was, if men sholde him discryve,
Oon of the beste faringe man on-lyve;
Yong, strong, right vertuous, and riche and wys,
And wel biloved, and holden in gret prys.
And shortly, if the sothe I tellen shal,
Unwiting of this Dorigen at al,

They led her by rivers and by springs,
And also in other places delightful;
They danced, and they played at chess and backgammon.
    So on a day, right in the morning,
Unto a garden that was there beside,
In which they had made their arrangements
For food and other supplies,
They went and played all the long day.
And this was on the sixth morning of May,
Which May had painted with his soft showers
This garden full of leaves and flowers;
And craft of man's hand had so skillfully
Adorned this garden truly,
That never was there a garden so priceless,
Unless it was itself the true Paradise.
The odor of flowers and the fresh sight
Would have made any heart light
That ever was born, unless too great sickness
Or too great sorrow held it in distress,
So full it was of beauty with delight.
In afternoon they began to dance,
And sing also, save Dorigen alone,
Who made always her complaint and her moan,
For she saw him not on the dance go,
Who was her husband and her love also.
But nevertheless she must a time abide,
And with good hope let her sorrow slide.
    In this dance, among other men,
Danced a squire before Dorigen,
Who fresher was and jollier of dress,
In my judgement, than is the month of May.
He sang, he danced, surpassing any man
That is, or was, since that the world began.
He was, if men should him describe,
One of the handsomest men alive:
Young, strong, right virtuous, and rich and wise,
And well beloved, and held in great esteem.
And shortly, if the truth I shall tell,
Unknown to this Dorigen at all,

This lusty squyer, servant to Venus,
Which that y-cleped was Aurelius,
Had loved hir best of any creature
Two yeer and more, as was his aventure,
But never dorste he telle hir his grevaunce;
With-outen coppe he drank al his penaunce.
He was despeyred, no-thing dorste he seye,
Save in his songes somwhat wolde he wreye
His wo, as in a general compleyning;
He seyde he lovede, and was biloved no-thing.
Of swiche matere made he manye layes,
Songes, compleintes, roundels, virelayes,
How that he dorste nat his sorwe telle,
But languissheth, as a furie dooth in helle;
And dye he moste, he seyde, as dide Ekko
For Narcisus, that dorste nat telle hir wo.
In other manere than ye here me seye,
Ne dorste he nat to hir his wo biwreye;
Save that, paraventure, som-tyme at daunces,
Ther yonge folk kepen hir observaunces,
It may wel be he loked on hir face
In swich a wyse, as man that asketh grace;
But no-thing wiste she of his entente.
Nathelees, it happed, er they thennes wente,
By-cause that he was hir neighebour,
And was a man of worship and honour,
And hadde y-knowen him of tyme yore,
They fille in speche; and forth more and more
Un-to his purpos drough Aurelius,
And whan he saugh his tyme, he seyde thus:
      "Madame," quod he, "by god that this world made,
So that I wiste it mighte your herte glade,
I wolde, that day that your Arveragus
Wente over the see, that I, Aurelius,
Had went ther never I sholde have come agayn;
For wel I woot my service is in vayn.
My guerdon is but bresting of myn herte;
Madame, reweth upon my peynes smerte;
For with a word ye may me sleen or save,

This joyful squire, servant to Venus,
Who was called Aurelius,
Had loved her best of any creature
Two years or more, as was his lot,
But never dared he tell her his sorrow:
Drinking his penance straight from the bottle.
He was in despair; nothing dared he say,
Save in his songs somewhat would he reveal
His woe, as in a general lamentation;
He said he loved, and was beloved not at all.
Of such matter made he many ballads,
Songs, complaints, roundels, lays,
How that he dared not his sorrow tell,
But languished as a fury does in hell;
And die he must, he said, as did Echo
For Narcissus, who dared not tell her woe.
In other manner than you hear me say,
He dared not to her his woe betray,
Save that, perchance, sometimes at dances,
Where young folk may speak in glances,
It may well be he looked on her face
In such a way as a man who asks for grace,
But nothing knew she of his intention.
Nevertheless, it happened, before they departed,
Because that he was her neighbor,
And was a man of worship and honor,
And she had known him for a long time,
They fell into conversation; and forth more and more
Unto his purpose drew Aurelius,
And when he saw his time, he said thus:
  "Madam," said he, "by God that this world made,
If only I knew that it might your heart gladden,
I would that when your Averagus
Went over the sea, that I, Aurelius,
Had gone there and never again returned.
For well I know my service is in vain:
My reward is but a breaking of my heart.
Madame, take pity on my pains sharp,
For with a word you may me slay or save.

Heer at your feet god wolde that I were grave!
I ne have as now no leyser more to seye;
Have mercy, swete, or ye wol do me deye!"
    She gan to loke up-on Aurelius:
"Is this your wil," quod she, "and sey ye thus?
Never erst," quod she, "ne wiste I what ye mente
But now, Aurelie, I knowe your entente,
By thilke god that yaf me soule and lyf,
Ne shal I never been untrewe wyf
In word ne werk, as fer as I have wit:
I wol ben his to whom that I am knit;
Tak this for fynal answer as of me."
But after that in pley thus seyde she:
    "Aurelie," quod she, "by heighte god above,
Yet wolde I graunte yow to been your love,
Sin I yow see so pitously complayne;
Loke what day that, endelong Britayne,
Ye remoeve alle the rokkes, stoon by stoon,
That they ne lette ship ne boot to goon—
I seye, whan ye han maad the coost so clene
Of rokkes, that ther nis no stoon y-sene,
Than wol I love yow best of any man;
Have heer my trouthe in al that ever I can."
"Is ther non other grace in yow?" quod he.
"No, by that lord," quod she, "that maked me!
For wel I woot that it shal never bityde.
Lat swiche folies out of your herte slyde.
What deyntee sholde a man han in his lyf
For to go love another mannes wyf,
That hath hir body whan so that him lyketh?"
    Aurelius ful ofte sore syketh;
Wo was Aurelie, whan that he this herde,
And with a sorweful herte he thus answerde:
    "Madame," quod he, "this were an impossible!
Than moot I dye of sodein deth horrible."
And with that word he turned him anoon.
Tho com hir othere freendes many oon,
And in the aleyes romeden up and doun,
And no-thing wiste of this conclusioun,

Here at your feet would that I were in my grave!
I have no chance any more to say:
Have mercy, sweet, or you will make me die!"
    She stared upon Aurelius:
"Is this your will," said she, "and say you thus?
Never before," said she, "Knew I what you meant.
But now, Aurelius, I know your intent,
By that same God who gave me soul and life,
Never shall I be an untrue wife,
In word or deed, as far as I have wit.
I will be his to whom that I am knit:
Take this for final answer as of me."
But after that in play thus said she:
    "Aurelius, by high god above,
Yet would I grant you to be your love,
Since I see you so piteously complain;
On whatever day that, Brittany all along,
You remove all the rocks, stone by stone,
That they no ship prevent from going—
I say, when you have made the coast so clean
Of rocks, that there is no stone seen—
Then will I love you best of any man;
Have here my pledge, in all that ever I can."
"Is there no other mercy in you?" said he.
"No, by that Lord," said she, "who made me!
For well I know that it shall happen never.
Let such follies out of your heart slide.
What delight should a man have in his life
To go love another man's wife,
Who has her body when he likes?"
    Aurelius full sore painfully sighed;
Woe was him, when he this heard,
And with a sorrowful heart he thus answered:
    "Madame," said he, "this is an impossibility!
Then must I die a horrible, sudden death."
And with that word he turned away anon.
Then came to her other friends many a one,
And in the garden paths roamed up and down,
And none knew of this outcome;

But sodeinly bigonne revel newe
Til that the brighte sonne loste his hewe;
For th'orisonte hath reft the sonne his light;
This is as muche to seye as it was night.
And hoom they goon in joye and in solas,
Save only wrecche Aurelius, allas!
He to his hous is goon with sorweful herte;
He seeth he may nat fro his deeth asterte.
Him semed that he felte his herte colde;
Up to the hevene his handes he gan holde,
And on his knowes bare he sette him doun,
And in his raving seyde his orisoun.
For verray wo out of his wit he breyde.
He niste what he spak, but thus he seyde;
With pitous herte his pleynt hath he bigonne
Un-to the goddes, and first un-to the sonne:
    He seyde, "Appollo, god and governour
Of every plaunte, herbe, tree and flour,
That yevest, after thy declinacioun,
To ech of hem his tyme and his sesoun,
As thyn herberwe chaungeth lowe or hye,
Lord Phebus, cast thy merciable yë
On wrecche Aurelie, which that am but lorn.
Lo, Lord! my lady hath my deeth y-sworn
With-oute gilt, but thy benignitee
Upon my dedly herte have som pitee!
For wel I woot, lord Phebus, if yow lest,
Ye may me helpen, save my lady, best.
Now voucheth sauf that I may yow devyse
How that I may been holpe and in what wyse.
    Your blisful suster, Lucina the shene,
That of the see is chief goddesse and quene,
Though Neptunus have deitee in the see,
Yet emperesse aboven him is she:
Ye knowen wel, lord, that right as hir desyr
Is to be quiked and lightned of your fyr,
For which she folweth yow ful bisily,
Right so the see desyreth naturelly
To folwen hir, as she that is goddesse

But suddenly began revelry anew
Until the bright sun lost his hue,
For the horizon had taken from the sun his light—
This is as much to say as it was night—
And home they went in joy and solace,
Save only wretched Aurelius, alas!
He to his house is gone with sorrowful heart.
He sees he may not from his death escape:
He thought he felt his heart grow cold.
Up to the heavens his hands he held,
And on his knees bare he set him down,
And in his raving said his prayer,
For sheer grief out of his mind gone.
He knew not what he spoke, but this he said;
With piteous heart his complaint did he begin
Unto the gods, and first unto the sun:

   He said, "Apollo,[3] god and governor
Of every plant, herb, tree and flower,
Who gives, according to your distance from the equator,
To each of them his time and season,
As your lodging changes low or high,
Lord Phoebus, cast your merciful eye
On wretched Aurelius, who is lost.
Look, lord! My lady has my death sworn
Without guilt, unless your kindness
Upon my dying heart has some pity!
For well I know, lord Phoebus, if you it pleases,
You may help me, except for my lady, best.
Now vouchsafe that I may you describe
How I may be helped and in what way.

   Your blissful sister, Lucina the bright,
Who of the sea is chief goddess and queen—
Though Neptune has deity in the sea,
Yet empress above him is she—
You know well, lord, that right as her desire
Is to be quickened and lighted by your fire,
For which she follows you full busily,
Just so the sea desires naturally
To follow her, as she who is goddess

Bothe in the see and riveres more and lesse.
Wherfore, lord Phebus, this is my requeste—
Do this miracle, or do myn herte breste—
That now, next at this opposicioun,
Which in the signe shal be of the Leoun,
As preyeth hir so greet a flood to bringe,
That fyve fadme at the leeste it overspringe
The hyeste rokke in Armorik Briteyne;
And lat this flood endure yeres tweyne;
Than certes to my lady may I seye:
'Holdeth your heste, the rokkes been aweye.'

Lord Phebus, dooth this miracle for me;
Preye hir she go no faster cours than ye;
I seye, preyeth your suster that she go
No faster cours than ye thise yeres two.
Than shal she been evene atte fulle alway,
And spring-flood laste bothe night and day.
And, but she vouche-sauf in swiche manere
To graunte me my sovereyn lady dere,
Prey hir to sinken every rok adoun
In-to hir owene derke regioun
Under the ground, ther Pluto dwelleth inne,
Or never-mo shal I my lady winne.
Thy temple in Delphos wol I barefoot seke;
Lord Phebus, see the teres on my cheke,
And of my peyne have som compassioun."
And with that word in swowne he fil adoun,
And longe tyme he lay forth in a traunce.

His brother, which that knew of his penaunce,
Up caughte him and to bedde he hath him broght.
Dispeyred in this torment and this thoght
Lete I this woful creature lye;
Chese he, for me, whether he wol live or dye.

Arveragus, with hele and greet honour,
As he that was of chivalrye the flour,
Is comen hoom, and othere worthy men.
O blisful artow now, thou Dorigen,
That hast thy lusty housbonde in thyne armes,
The fresshe knight, the worthy man of armes,

Both of the sea and rivers more and less.
Wherefore, lord Phoebus, this is my request:
Do this miracle—or make my heart burst—
That at the next opposition of moon and sun,
Which in the sign shall be of the Lion,
Pray her so great a flood to bring
That by five fathoms at least it covers
The highest rock in Brittany;
And let this flood endure years two.
Then certainly to my lady may I say:
'Keep your promise, the rocks be away.'
    Lord Phoebus, do this miracle for me!
Pray her that she go no faster course than you;
I say, pray your sister that she go
No faster course than you these years two.
Then shall she be at full always,
And spring-flood last both night and day.
And unless she agrees in such manner
To grant me my sovereign lady dear,
Pray her to sink every rock down
Into her own dark region
Under the ground, where Pluto dwells in,
Or never more shall I my lady win.
The temple in Delphi will I barefoot seek.
Lord Phoebus, see the tears on my cheek,
And of my pain have some compassion."
And with that word in swoon he fell down,
And long time he lay thereafter in a trance.
    His brother, who knew of his suffering,
Picked him up and to bed he brought him.
Despairing in this torment and this thought
Let I—the storyteller—let this woeful creature lie:
Let *Aurelius* choose—for all I care—if he lives or dies.
    Averagus, with health and great honor,
As that he was of chivalry the flower,
Came home, and other worthy men.
Oh blissful are you now, Dorigen,
Who have your lusty husband in your arms,
The lively knight, the worthy man of arms,

That loveth thee, as his owene hertes lyf.
No-thing list him to been imaginatyf
If any wight had spoke, whyl he was oute,
To hire of love; he hadde of it no doute.
He noght entendeth to no swich matere,
But daunceth, justeth, maketh hir good chere;
And thus in joye and blisse I lete hem dwelle,
And of the syke Aurelius wol I telle.

In langour and in torment furious
Two yeer and more lay wrecche Aurelius,
Er any foot he mighte on erthe goon;
Ne confort in this tyme hadde he noon,
Save of his brother, which that was a clerk;
He knew of al this wo and al this werk.
For to non other creature certeyn
Of this matere he dorste no word seyn.
Under his brest he bar it more secree
Than ever dide Pamphilus for Galathee.
His brest was hool, with-oute for to sene,
But in his herte ay was the arwe kene.
And wel ye knowe that of a sursanure
In surgerye is perilous the cure,
But men mighte touche the arwe, or come therby.
His brother weep and wayled prively,
Til atte laste him fil in remembraunce,
That whyl he was at Orliens in Fraunce,
As yonge clerkes, that been likerous
To reden artes that been curious,
Seken in every halke and every herne
Particuler sciences for to lerne,
He him remembered that, upon a day,
At Orliens in studie a book he say
Of magik naturel, which his felawe,
That was that tyme bacheler of lawe,
Al were he ther to lerne another craft,
Had prively upon his desk y-laft;
Which book spak muche of the operaciouns,
Touchinge the eighte and twenty mansiouns
That longen to the mone, and swich folye,

Who loves you as his own heart's life.
He had not the slightest imagining
That any person had spoken, while he was away,
To her of love; he had no fear of it.
He paid no attention to such a thing,
But danced, jousted, made her good cheer;
And thus in joy and bliss I let him dwell,
And of the sick Aurelius will I tell.

 In sickness and in torment furious
Two years or more lay wretched Aurelius,
Before he could walk any step on earth.
No comfort in this time had he,
Save of his brother, who was a scholar:
He knew of all this woe and this affair,
For to no other creature, certainly,
Of this matter dare he a word say.
Within his breast he bore it more secretly
Than ever did Pamphilus for Galatea.[4]
His breast was whole from without seen,
But in his heart ever was the arrow keen;
And well you know that to cure an infection deep
By surgery is perilous,
In case men might touch the arrow, or come near it.
His brother wept and wailed secretly,
Until at last he recalled,
That while he was at Orleans in France,[5]
Because young scholars desiring
To read arts that be recondite
Seek in every corner and nook
Abstruse sciences for to learn—
He remembered that, upon a day,
At Orleans in study a book he saw
Of magic astronomical, that his colleague,
Who was at that time a bachelor of law—
Although he was there to learn another craft—
Had secretly left it upon his desk:
Which book spoke much of the operations
Touching the eight and twenty mansions
That belong to the moon[6]—and such folly

As in our dayes is nat worth a flye;
For holy chirches feith in our bileve
Ne suffreth noon illusion us to greve.
And whan this book was in his remembraunce,
Anon for joye his herte gan to daunce,
And to him-self he seyde prively:
"My brother shal be warisshed hastily;
For I am siker that ther be sciences,
By whiche men make diverse apparences
Swiche as thise subtile tregetoures pleye.
For ofte at festes have I wel herd seye,
That tregetours, with-inne an halle large,
Have maad come in a water and a barge,
And in the halle rowen up and doun.
Somtyme hath semed come a grim leoun;
And somtyme floures springe as in a mede;
Somtyme a vyne, and grapes whyte and rede;
Somtyme a castel, al of lym and stoon;
And whan hem lyked, voyded it anoon.
Thus semed it to every mannes sighte.
    Now than conclude I thus, that if I mighte
At Orliens som old felawe y-finde,
That hadde this mones mansions in minde,
Or other magik naturel above,
He sholde wel make my brother han his love.
For with an apparence a clerk may make
To mannes sighte, that alle the rokkes blake
Of Britaigne weren y-voyded everichon,
And shippes by the brinke comen and gon,
And in swich forme endure a day or two;
Than were my brother warisshed of his wo.
Than moste she nedes holden hir biheste,
Or elles he shal shame hir atte leste."
    What sholde I make a lenger tale of this?
Un-to his brotheres bed he comen is,
And swich confort he yaf him for to gon
To Orliens, that he up stirte anon,
And on his wey forthward thanne is he fare,
In hope for to ben lissed of his care.

As in our days is not worth a fly;
For our faith in holy church's belief
Permits no such illusions to make us grieve.
And when this book was in his remembrance,
Anon for joy his heart began to dance,
And to himself he said secretly:
"My brother shall be cured hastily;
For I am sure that there be sciences
By which men make diverse illusions
Such as are made by these subtle magicians.
For often at feasts have I well heard said
That magicians within a hall large
Have conjured up water and a barge,
And in the hall rowed up and down;
Sometimes a grim lion has appeared;
And sometimes flowers spring as in a meadow;
Sometimes a vine, and grapes white and red;
Sometimes a castle, all of lime and stone—
And when they liked, vanished it anon.
Thus it seemed to every man's sight.

   Now then conclude I thus, that if I might
At Orleans some old companion find
Who had this moon's mansions in mind,
Or other magic even higher,
Should well make my brother have his love.
For with an illusion a scholar may make
It appear that all the black rocks
Of Brittany were removed every one,
And ships by the coast come and go,
And in such form endure a week or two.
Then were my brother cured of his woe;
Then she needs must keep her promise,
Or else he shall blame her at the least."

   Why should I make a longer tale of this?
Unto his brother's bed he went,
And comforted with advice to go
To Orleans, that he leapt up anon,
And set off to travel there,
In hope for to be eased of his care.

Whan they were come almost to that citee,
But-if it were a two furlong or three,
A yong clerk rominge by him-self they mette,
Which that in Latin thriftily hem grette,
And after that he seyde a wonder thing:
"I knowe," quod he, "the cause of your coming";
And er they ferther any fote wente,
He told hem al that was in hir entente.

This Briton clerk him asked of felawes
The whiche that he had knowe in olde dawes;
And he answerde him that they dede were,
For which he weep ful ofte many a tere.

Doun of his hors Aurelius lighte anon,
And forth with this magicien is he gon
Hoom to his hous, and made hem wel at ese.
Hem lakked no vitaille that mighte hem plese;
So wel arrayed hous as ther was oon
Aurelius in his lyf saugh never noon.

He shewed him, er he wente to sopeer,
Forestes, parkes ful of wilde deer;
Ther saugh he hertes with hir hornes hye,
The gretteste that ever were seyn with yë.
He saugh of hem an hondred slayn with houndes,
And somme with arwes blede of bittre woundes.
He saugh, whan voided were thise wilde deer
Thise fauconers upon a fair river,
That with hir haukes han the heron slayn.
Tho saugh he knightes justing in a playn;
And after this, he dide him swich plesaunce,
That he him shewed his lady on a daunce
On which him-self he daunced, as him thoughte.
And whan this maister, that this magik wroughte,
Saugh it was tyme, he clapte his handes two,
And farewel! al our revel was ago.
And yet remoeved they never out of the hous,
Whyl they saugh al this sighte merveillous,
But in his studie, ther-as his bookes be,
They seten stille, and no wight but they three
To him this maister called his squyer,

When they were come almost to that city,
All but a furlong or two or three,
A young scholar roaming by himself they met,
Who suitably greeted them in Latin,
And after that he said a wondrous thing:
"I know," said he, "the cause of your coming."
And before they a step further went,
He told them all that was in their intent.

    This Breton scholar asked him about colleagues
Whom he had known in the old days;
And he answered him that they dead were,
For which he wept full often many a tear.

    Down from his horse Aurelius alighted anon,
And forth with this magician he did go
Home to his house, and made themselves at ease.
They lacked no food that might them please;
So well furnished a house was it that
Aurelius had never seen one better.

    He showed him, before he went to supper,
Forests, parks full of wild deer:
There saw he harts with their horns high,
The greatest that ever were seen with eyes;
He saw of them a hundred slain with hounds,
And some of arrows bled from bitter wounds.
He saw, when departed were these wild deer,
These falconers upon a river fair,
Who with their hawks had the heron slain.
Then saw he knights jousting on a plain;
And after this he did him such pleasure
That he showed him his lady in a dance
In which he himself danced, or so it seemed.
And when this master who this magic wrought
Saw it was time, he clapped his hands two,
And farewell! all our revel was gone.
And yet moved they never out of the house
While they saw all this sight marvelous,
But in his study, there where his books were,
They sat still, and no person but they three.

    This master called his squire,

And seyde him thus: "is redy our soper?
Almost an houre it is, I undertake,
Sith I yow bad our soper for to make,
Whan that thise worthy men wenten with me
In-to my studie, ther-as my bookes be."
    "Sire," quod this squyer, "whan it lyketh yow,
It is al redy, though ye wol right now."
"Go we than soupe," quod he, "as for the beste;
This amorous folk som-tyme mote han reste."
    At-after soper fille they in tretee,
What somme sholde this maistres guerdon be,
To remoeven alle the rokkes of Britayne,
And eek from Gerounde to the mouth of Sayne.
    He made it straunge, and swoor, so god him save,
Lasse than a thousand pound he wolde nat have,
Ne gladly for that somme he wolde nat goon.
    Aurelius, with blisful herte anoon,
Answerde thus, "fy on a thousand pound!
This wyde world, which that men seye is round,
I wolde it yeve, if I were lord of it.
This bargayn is ful drive, for we ben knit.
Ye shal be payed trewely, by my trouthe!
But loketh now, for no necligence or slouthe,
Ye tarie us heer no lenger than to-morwe."
    "Nay," quod this clerk, "have heer my feith to borwe."
    To bedde is goon Aurelius whan him leste,
And wel ny al that night he hadde his reste;
What for his labour and his hope of blisse,
His woful herte of penaunce hadde a lisse.
    Upon the morwe, whan that it was day,
    To Britaigne toke they the righte way,
Aurelius, and this magicien bisyde,
And been descended ther they wolde abyde;
And this was, as the bokes me remembre,
The colde frosty seson of Decembre.
    Phebus wax old, and hewed lyk latoun,
That in his hote declinacioun
Shoon as the burned gold with stremes brighte;
But now in Capricorn adoun he lighte,

And said this, "Is ready our supper?
Almost an hour it is, I declare,
Since I bade you our supper for to make,
When these worthy men went with me
Into my study, there as my books be."

"Sire," said this squire, "when it pleases you,
It is all ready, should you want it right now."
"Go we for supper," said he, "as for the best:
These amorous folk must sometimes have rest."

At after-supper fell they into negotiations
What sum should the master's reward be,
To remove all the rocks of Brittany,
And also from the Gironde to the mouth of the Seine.

He made it difficult, and swore, so God him save,
Less than a thousand pounds he would not have,
And not gladly for that sum would he go.

Aurelius with blissful heart anon
Answered thus, "Fie on a thousand pounds!
This wide world, which that men say is round,
I would give, if I were lord of it.
This bargain is concluded, for we be agreed.
You shall be paid truly, by my troth!
But look now, for no negligence or sloth,
Should you delay us here, no longer than tomorrow."

"Nay," said the scholar, "have here my faith as pledge."

To bed went Aurelius when he wished,
And well nigh all that night he had his rest:
What with his labor and his hope of bliss,
His woeful heart from suffering had relief.

Upon the morrow, when it was day,
To Brittany took they the right way,
Aurelius and this magician beside,
And dismounted there where they would stay;
And this was, as these books remind me,
The cold frosty season of December.

Phoebus waxed old,[7] and colored like brass,
That in his hot declination
Shone as burnished gold with beams bright;
But now in Capricorn down he alighted,

Wher-as he shoon ful pale, I dar wel seyn.
The bittre frostes, with the sleet and reyn,
Destroyed hath the grene in every yerd.
Janus sit by the fyr, with double berd,
And drinketh of his bugle-horn the wyn.
Biforn him stant braun of the tusked swyn,
And "Nowel" cryeth every lusty man.

   Aurelius, in al that ever he can,
Doth to his maister chere and reverence,
And preyeth him to doon his diligence
To bringen him out of his peynes smerte,
Or with a swerd that he wolde slitte his herte.

   This subtil clerk swich routhe had of this man,
That night and day he spedde him that he can,
To wayte a tyme of his conclusioun;
This is to seye, to make illusioun,
By swich an apparence or jogelrye,
I ne can no termes of astrologye,
That she and every wight sholde wene and seye,
That of Britaigne the rokkes were aweye,
Or elles they were sonken under grounde.
So atte laste he hath his tyme y-founde
To maken his japes and his wrecchednesse
Of swich a supersticious cursednesse.
His tables Toletanes forth he broght,
Ful wel corrected, ne ther lakked noght,
Neither his collect ne his expans yeres,
Ne his rotes ne his othere geres,
As been his centres and his arguments,
And his proporcionels convenients
For his equacions in every thing.
And, by his eighte spere in his wirking,
He knew ful wel how fer Alnath was shove
Fro the heed of thilke fixe Aries above
That in the ninthe speere considered is;
Ful subtilly he calculed al this.

   Whan he had founde his firste mansioun,
He knew the remenant by proporcioun;
And knew the arysing of his mone weel,

Where he shone pale, I dare well say.
The bitter frosts, with the sleet and rain,
Destroyed hath the green in every garden.
Janus sat by the fire with double beard,
And drank of his ox-horn goblet the wine;
Before him stood meat of the tusked swine,
And "Noel" cried every lusty man.

    Aurelius, in all that ever he could,
Made to this master good cheer and reverence,
And prayed him to do his diligence
To bring him out of his pains sharp,
Or with a sword would he slit his heart.

    This subtle scholar such compassion had for this man
That night and day he worked as fast as he could,
To watch for a time this matter to conclude;
This is to say, to make illusion,
By such an apparition of magic—
I do not know terms of astrology—
That she and every person should suppose and say
That of Brittany the rocks were away,
Or else they were sunken underground.
So at last he has his time found
To make his tricks and his wretched business
From such a superstitious cursedness.
His tables Toledan[8] forth he brought,
Full well corrected, there lacked nought,
Neither his collect nor his expanse years,
Nor his statistics nor his other gear,
As were his centers and his arguments,
And his proportionals convenient
For his equations in every thing.
And by his eighth sphere in his working
He knew full well how far Alnath was advanced
From that head of that same fixed Aries above
That in the ninth sphere considered is:
Full subtly he calculated all this.

    When he had found his first mansion,
He knew the remainder by proportion,
And he knew the rising of his moon well,

And in whos face, and terme, and every-deel;
And knew ful weel the mones mansioun
Accordaunt to his operacioun,
And knew also his othere observaunces
For swiche illusiouns and swiche meschaunces
As hethen folk used in thilke dayes;
For which no lenger maked he delayes,
But thurgh his magik, for a wyke or tweye,
It semed that alle the rokkes were aweye.

Aurelius, which that yet despeired is
Wher he shal han his love or fare amis,
Awaiteth night and day on this miracle;
And whan he knew that ther was noon obstacle,
That voided were thise rokkes everichon,
Doun to his maistres feet he fil anon,
And seyde, "I woful wrecche, Aurelius,
Thanke yow, lord, and lady myn Venus,
That me han holpen fro my cares colde:"
And to the temple his wey forth hath he holde,
Wher-as he knew he sholde his lady see.
And whan he saught his tyme, anon-right he,
With dredful herte and with ful humble chere,
Salewed hath his sovereyn lady dere:

"My righte lady," quod this woful man,
"Whom I most drede and love as I best can,
And lothest were of al this world displese,
Nere it that I for yow have swich disese,
That I moste dyen heer at your foot anon,
Noght wolde I telle how me is wo bigon;
But certes outher moste I dye or pleyne;
Ye slee me giltelees for verray peyne.
But of my deeth, thogh that ye have no routhe,
Avyseth yow, er that ye breke your trouthe.
Repenteth yow, for thilke god above,
Er ye me sleen by-cause that I yow love.
For, madame, wel ye woot what ye han hight;
Nat that I chalange any thing of right
Of yow my sovereyn lady, but your grace;
But in a gardin yond, at swich a place,

And in whose face, and the division, and everything;
And he knew full well the moon's mansion,
According to his operation,
And he knew also his other ceremonies
For such illusions and mischiefs,
As heathen folk used in those days.
For which no longer made he delays,
But through his magic, for a week or two,
It seemed that all the rocks were away.

    Aurelius, who yet despairing was
Whether he shall have his love or fare amiss,
Awaited night and day on this miracle;
And when he knew that there was no obstacle—
That removed were these rocks every one—
Down to his master's feet he fell anon
And said, "I woeful wretch, Aurelius,
Thank you, lord, and my lady Venus,
Who have helped me from my cares cold."
And to the temple forth his way did he hold,
Where he knew he should his lady see.
And when he saw his time, right away he,
With fearful heart and with full humble manner,
Greeted his sovereign lady dear:

    "My right lady," said this woeful man,
"Whom I most fear and love as best I can,
And most loathe of all this world to displease,
Were it not for you that I have such misery
That I must die here at your foot anon,
I would not tell how woebegone I am.
But certainly must I die or complain;
You slay me, guiltless, with real pain.
But of my death, though of that you have no pity,
Take heed, before you break your pledge.
Repent, for the sake of God above,
Before you slay me because I love you.
For, madame, well you know what you have promised—
Not that I claim anything by right
Of you, my sovereign lady, but your grace—
But in a garden yonder, at such a place,

Ye woot right wel what ye bihighten me;
And in myn hand your trouthe plighten ye
To love me best, god woot, ye seyde so,
Al be that I unworthy be therto.
Madame, I speke it for the honour of yow,
More than to save myn hertes lyf right now;
I have do so as ye comanded me;
And if ye vouche-sauf, ye may go see.
Doth as yow list, have your biheste in minde,
For quik or deed, right ther ye shul me finde;
In yow lyth al, to do me lyve or deye;—
But wel I woot the rokkes been aweye!"

He taketh his leve, and she astonied stood,
In al hir face nas a drope of blood;
She wende never han come in swich a trappe:
"Allas!" quod she, "that ever this sholde happe
For wende I never, by possibilitee,
That swich a monstre or merveille mighte be!
It is agayns the proces of nature:"
And hoom she goeth a sorweful creature.
For verray fere unnethe may she go,
She wepeth, wailleth, al a day or two,
And swowneth, that it routhe was to see;
But why it was, to no wight tolde she;
For out of toune was goon Arveragus.
But to hir-self she spak, and seyde thus,
With face pale and with ful sorweful chere,
In hir compleynt, as ye shul after here:

"Allas," quod she, "on thee, Fortune,
I pleyne,
That unwar wrapped hast me in thy cheyne;
For which, t'escape, woot I no socour
Save only deeth or elles dishonour;
Oon of thise two bihoveth me to chese.
But nathelees, yet have I lever lese
My lyf than of my body have a shame,
Or knowe my-selven fals, or lese my name,
And with my deth I may be quit, y-wis.
Hath ther nat many a noble wyf, er this,

You know right well that you promised me;
And in my hand your troth you pledged
To love me best. God knows, you said so,
Albeit that I unworthy be thereto.
Madame, I speak it for the honor of you
More than to save my heart's life right now.
I have done as you commanded me;
And if you are willing, you may go see.
Do as you wish, have your promise in mind,
For, quick or dead, you shall there me find.
In you lies all to make me live or die:
But well I know the rocks be away!"

    He took his leave, and she astonished stood;
In all her face was not a drop of blood.
She thought never to have come in such a trap.
"Alas!" said she, "that this should ever happen!
For thought I never, by possibility,
That such a strange thing or marvel might be!
It is against the course of nature."
And home she went a sorrowful creature.
For deep fear hardly could she walk.
She wept, she wailed, a whole day or two,
And swooned, that it pitiful was to see;
But why it was, to no person told she,
For out of town was gone Averagus.
But to herself she spoke, and said thus,
With pale face and with sorrowful mien,
In her lament, and you shall after hear:

    "Alas," said she, "To you, Fortune, I make my
        complaint,
Who unaware has wrapped me in your chain,
From which to escape I know no succor
Save only death or else dishonor;
One of these two must I choose.
But nevertheless would I rather lose
My life, than of my body to have a shame,
Or know myself false, or lose my good name;
And with my death I may be quit, I know.
Has there not many a noble wife before now,

And many a mayde y-slayn hir-self, allas!
Rather than with hir body doon trespas?
    Yis, certes, lo, thise stories beren witnesse;
Whan thretty tyraunts, ful of cursednesse,
Had slayn Phidoun in Athenes, atte feste,
They comanded his doghtres for t'areste,
And bringen hem biforn hem in despyt
Al naked, to fulfille hir foul delyt,
And in hir fadres blood they made hem daunce
Upon the pavement, god yeve hem mischaunce!
For which thise woful maydens, ful of drede,
Rather than they wolde lese hir maydenhede,
They prively ben stirt in-to a welle,
And dreynte hem-selven, as the bokes telle.
    They of Messene lete enquere and seke
Of Lacedomie fifty maydens eke,
On whiche they wolden doon hir lecherye;
But was ther noon of al that companye
That she nas slayn, and with a good entente
Chees rather for to dye than assente
To been oppressed of hir maydenhede.
Why sholde I thanne to dye been in drede?
    Lo, eek the tiraunt Aristoclides
That loved a mayden, heet Stimphalides,
Whan that hir fader slayn was on a night,
Un-to Dianes temple goth she right,
And hente the image in hir handes two,
Fro which image wolde she never go.
No wight ne mighte hir handes of it arace,
Til she was slayn right in the selve place.
Now sith that maydens hadden swich despyt
To been defouled with mannes foul delyt,
Wel oghte a wyf rather hir-selven slee
Than be defouled, as it thinketh me.
    What shal I seyn of Hasdrubales wyf,
That at Cartage birafte hir-self hir lyf?
For whan she saugh that Romayns wan the toun,
She took hir children alle, and skipte adoun
In-to the fyr, and chees rather to dye

And many a maid, slain herself, alas!
Rather than with her body do trespass?
   Yes, certainly, these stories bear witness;[9]
When thirty tyrants, full of cursedness,
Had slain Phidon in Athens at the feast,
They commanded his daughters for to be seized,
And brought them before them to scorn
All naked, to fulfill their foul delight,
And in their father's blood they made them dance
Upon the pavement, God give them mischance!
For which these woeful maidens, full of dread,
Rather than they would lose their maidenhood,
They secretly leapt into a well,
And drowned themselves, as the books tell.
   The men of Messena had inquiries made and sought
From Sparta fifty maidens also,
On whom they would perform their lechery;
But there was none of all that company who
Was not slain, and with good will
Chose to die rather than assent
To be ravished of her maidenhood.
Why should I then to die be in dread?
   Look also at the tyrant Aristoclides
Who loved a maiden, named Stimphalades,
When that her father slain was on a night,
Unto Diana's temple went she right,
And clasped the holy image in her hands two,
From which image would she never go.
No person might her hands of it tear away,
Until she was slain right in the place.
Now since that maidens had such scorn
To be defiled with man's foul delight,
Well ought a wife rather herself slay
Than be defiled, as it seems to me.
   What shall I say of Hasdrubal's wife,
Who at Carthage took from herself her life?
From when she saw that Romans won the town,
She took her children all, and jumped down
Into the fire, and chose rather to die

Than any Romayn dide hir vileinye.
　　Hath nat Lucresse y-slayn hir-self, allas!
At Rome, whanne she oppressed was
Of Tarquin, for hir thoughte it was a shame
To liven whan she hadde lost hir name?
　　The sevene maydens of Milesie also
Han slayn hem-self, for verray drede and wo,
Rather than folk of Gaule hem sholde oppresse.
Mo than a thousand stories, as I gesse,
Coude I now telle as touchinge this matere.
　　Whan Habradate was slayn, his wyf so dere
Hirselves slow, and leet hir blood to glyde
In Habradates woundes depe and wyde,
And seyde, 'my body, at the leeste way,
Ther shal no wight defoulen, if I may.'
　　What sholde I mo ensamples heer-of sayn,
Sith that so manye han hem-selven slayn
Wel rather than they wolde defouled be?
I wol conclude, that it is bet for me
To sleen my-self, than been defouled thus.
I wol be trewe un-to Arveragus,
Or rather sleen my-self in som manere,
As dide Demociones doghter dere,
By-cause that she wolde nat defouled be.
　　O-Cedasus! it is ful greet pitee,
To reden how thy doghtren deyde, allas!
That slowe hem-selven for swich maner cas.
　　As greet a pitee was it, or wel more,
The Theban mayden, that for Nichanore
Hir-selven slow, right for swich maner wo.
　　Another Theban mayden dide right so;
For oon of Macedoine hadde hir oppressed,
She with hir deeth hir maydenhede redressed.
What shal I seye of Nicerates wyf,
That for swich cas birafte hir-self hir lyf?
How trewe eek was to Alcebiades
His love, that rather for to dyen chees
Than for to suffre his body unburied be!
　　Lo which a wyf was Alcestè," quod she.

Than any Roman should do her villainy.
    Did not Lucretia slay herself, alas!
At Rome, when she violated was
By Tarquin, for to her seemed it was a shame
To live when she had lost her name?
    The seven maidens of Miletus also
Slew themselves, for great dread and woe,
Rather than folk of Gaul should them oppress.
More than a thousand stories, as I guess,
Could I now tell as touching this matter.
    When Abradates was slain, his wife so dear
Herself slew, and let her blood glide
In Abradates' wounds deep and wide,
And said, 'My body, at least
There shall no person defile, if I may it prevent.'
    Why should I more examples here recite,
Since so many have themselves slain
Rather than be defiled?
I will conclude that it is better for me
To slay myself than be defiled thus.
I will be true unto Averagus,
Or rather slay myself in some manner—
As did Demotion's daughter dear,
By cause that she would not defiled be.
    Oh Scedasus! It is full great pity
To read how your daughter died, alas!
Who slew herself for such a kind of case.
    As great a pity was it, or well more,
The Theban maiden who for Nicanor
Herself slew for such kind of woe.
    Another Theban maiden did right so:
Because one of Macedonia had her oppressed,
She with her death her maidenhood redressed.
What shall I say of Niceratus' wife
Who for such case bereft herself her life?
How true also was to Alcibiades
His love, who chose to die rather
Than for to suffer his body unburied be!
    Look, what a wife was Alcestis," said she.

"What seith Omer of gode Penalopee?
Al Grece knoweth of hir chastitee.

    Pardee, of Laodomya is writen thus,
That whan at Troye was slayn Protheselaus,
No lenger wolde she live after his day.
The same of noble Porcia telle I may;
With-oute Brutus coude she nat live,
To whom she hadde al hool hir herte yive.
The parfit wyfhod of Arthemesye
Honoured is thurgh al the Barbarye.

    O Teuta, queen! thy wyfly chastitee
To alle wyves may a mirour be.
The same thing I seye of Bilia,
Of Rodogone, and eek Valeria."

    Thus pleyned Dorigene a day or tweye,
Purposing ever that she wolde deye.

    But nathelees, upon the thridde night,
Hom came Arveragus, this worthy knight,
And asked hir, why that she weep so sore?
And she gan wepen ever lenger the more.

    "Allas!" quod she, "that ever was I born!
Thus have I seyd," quod she, "thus have I sworn'—
And told him al as ye han herd bifore;
It nedeth nat reherce it yow na-more.

    This housbond with glad chere, in freendly wyse,
Answerde and seyde as I shal yow devyse:
"Is ther oght elles, Dorigen, but this?"

    "Nay, nay," quod she, "god help me so, as wis;
This is to muche, and it were goddes wille."

    "Ye, wyf," quod he, "lat slepen that is stille;
It may be wel, paraventure, yet to-day.
Ye shul your trouthe holden, by my fay!
For god so wisly have mercy on me,
I hadde wel lever y-stiked for to be,
For verray love which that I to yow have,
But-if ye sholde your trouthe kepe and save.
Trouthe is the hyeste thing that man may kepe:"—
But with that word he brast anon to wepe,
And seyde, "I yow forbede, up peyne of deeth,

"What said Homer of good Penelope?
All Greece knew of her chastity.

By God, of Laodamia is written thus,
Who when at Troy was slain Protesilaus,
No longer would she live after his day.
The same of noble Portia tell I may:
Without Brutus could she not live,
To whom she had wholly her heart given.
The perfect wifehood of Artemisia
Honored is through all Barbary.

Oh Teuta, queen! your wifely chastity
To all wives may a mirror be.
The same thing I say of Bilia,
Of Rhodogune, and also Valeria."

Thus lamented Dorigen a day or two,
Intending ever that she would die.

But nevertheless, upon the third night,
Home came Averagus, this worthy knight,
And asked her why she wept so painfully;
And she began weeping ever longer and more.

"Alas!" said she, "that ever I was born!
Thus have I said," said she, "thus have I sworn,"
And told him all as you have heard before;
I need not repeat it anymore.

Her husband, in a kind manner,
Answered and said as I shall you relate:
"Is there nought else, Dorigen, but this?"

"Nay, nay," said she, "God help me;
This is too much, if it were God's will."

"Yea, wife," said he, "let sleep what is still.
It may well yet turn out all right today.
You should your pledge keep, by my faith!
For, God have mercy on me,
I would rather be stabbed,
For the true love I for you have,
Than have you not keep your word.
Fidelity is the highest thing that man may keep."
But with that, he burst at once into tears,
And said, "I forbid you, upon pain of death,

That never, whyl thee lasteth lyf ne breeth,
To no wight tel thou of this aventure.
As I may best, I wol my wo endure,
Ne make no contenance of hevinesse,
That folk of yow may demen harm or gesse."

And forth he cleped a squyer and a mayde:
"Goth forth anon with Dorigen," he sayde,
"And bringeth hir to swich a place anon."
They take hir leve, and on hir wey they gon;
But they ne wiste why she thider wente.
He nolde no wight tellen his entente.

Paraventure an heep of yow, y-wis,
Wol holden him a lewed man in this,
That he wol putte his wyf in jupartye;
Herkneth the tale, er ye up-on hir crye.
She may have bettre fortune than yow semeth;
And whan that ye han herd the tale, demeth.

This squyer, which that highte Aurelius,
On Dorigen that was so amorous,
Of aventure happed hir to mete
Amidde the toun, right in the quikkest strete,
As she was boun to goon the wey forth-right
Toward the gardin ther-as she had hight.
And he was to the gardinward also;
For wel he spyed, whan she wolde go
Out of hir hous to any maner place.
But thus they mette, of aventure or grace;
And he saleweth hir with glad entente,
And asked of hir whiderward she wente?

And she answerde, half as she were mad,
"Un-to the gardin, as myn housbond bad,
My trouthe for to holde, allas! allas!"

Aurelius gan wondren on this cas,
And in his herte had greet compassioun
Of hir and of hir lamentacioun,
And of Arveragus, the worthy knight,
That bad hir holden al that she had hight,
So looth him was his wyf sholde breke hir trouthe;
And in his herte he caughte of this greet routhe,

Ever, while you draw breath,
To tell anyone of this—
As I may best, I will my woe endure—
Nor look sad,
So that folk suspect something is amiss."

And forth he called a squire and a maid:
"Go forth anon with Dorigen," he said,
"And bring her to a certain place anon."
They took their leave, and on their way they went,
But they knew not why she thither went:
He would no one tell of his intent.

Perhaps many of you, certainly,
Will hold him a foolish man in this,
That he would put his wife in jeopardy.
Listen to the tale entire, before you complain.
She may have better fortune than you think,
So when you have heard the tale, then decide.

This squire, who was called Aurelius,
Of Dorigen who was so amorous,
By chance happened her to meet
Amid the town, right in the busiest street,
As she was on her way
To the garden as she had promised;
And he was headed to the garden also,
For he watched closely when she would go
Out of her house to any kind of place.
But thus they met, by chance or fate;
And he saluted her cheerfully,
And asked her whither she went;

And she answered, half as if she were mad,
"Unto the garden, as my husband bade,
My pledge for to hold, alas! alas!"

Aurelius fell to wondering on this event,
And in his heart had great compassion
For her and for her lamentation,
And for Averagus, the worthy knight,
Who bade her hold to all she had said,
So loath he was that his wife should break her pledge.
And in his heart he took great pity on this,

Consideringe the beste on every syde,
That fro his lust yet were him lever abyde
Than doon so heigh a cherlish wrecchednesse
Agayns franchyse and alle gentillesse;
For which in fewe wordes seyde he thus:
    "Madame, seyth to your lord Arveragus,
That sith I see his grete gentillesse
To yow, and eek I see wel your distresse,
That him were lever han shame (and that
    were routhe)
Than ye to me sholde breke thus your trouthe,
I have wel lever ever to suffre wo
Than I departe the love bitwix yow two.
I yow relesse, madame, in-to your hond
Quit every surement and every bond,
That ye han maad to me as heer-biforn,
Sith thilke tyme which that ye were born.
My trouthe I plighte, I shal yow never repreve
Of no biheste, and here I take my leve,
As of the treweste and the beste wyf
That ever yet I knew in al my lyf.
But every wyf be-war of hir biheste,
On Dorigene remembreth atte leste.
Thus can a squyer doon a gentil dede,
As well as can a knight, with-outen drede."
    She thonketh him up-on hir knees al bare,
And hoom un-to hir housbond is she fare,
And tolde him al as ye han herd me sayd;
And be ye siker, he was so weel apayd,
That it were impossible me to wryte;
What sholde I lenger of this cas endyte?
    Arveragus and Dorigene his wyf
In sovereyn blisse leden forth hir lyf.
Never eft ne was ther angre hem bitwene;
He cherisseth hir as though she were a quene;
And she was to him trewe for evermore.
Of thise two folk ye gete of me na-more.
    Aurelius, that his cost hath al forlorn,
Curseth the tyme that ever he was born:

Considering the best on every side,
So that his desire he thought it better to deny
Than do so great a churlish wretched thing
Against generosity and all nobility;
For which in few words said he thus:
    "Madame, say to your lord Averagus,
That since I see his great nobility
To you, and also I see well your distress,
That he would rather have shame (and that would be
    a pity)
Than you should break your pledge,
I would rather ever suffer woe
Than divide the love between you two.
I release you, madame, into your own hands,
Discharged of every oath and every bond
That you had made to me before,
Since that same time that you were born.
My troth I pledge, I shall never you reprove
Of any promise, and here I take my leave,
Of the truest and best wife
That ever yet I knew in all my life.
But every wife be careful of her behest!
Of Dorigen remember at the least.
Thus can a squire do a gentle deed
As well as can a knight, without a doubt."
    She thanked him upon her knees all bare,
And home unto her husband she did fare,
And told him all as you have heard me say;
And you can be sure, he was so well pleased
That it were impossible for me to write.
What should I longer of this case relate?
    Averagus and Dorigen his wife
In sovereign bliss led forth their lives.
Never again was there anger them between:
He cherished her as if she were a queen,
And she was to him true for evermore.
Of these two folk you hear from me no more.
    Aurelius, who his expense has all lost,
Cursed the time that ever he was born:

"Allas," quod he, "allas! that I bihighte
Of pured gold a thousand pound of wighte
Un-to this philosophre! how shal I do?
I see na-more but that I am fordo.
Myn heritage moot I nedes selle,
And been a begger; heer may I nat dwelle,
And shamen al my kinrede in this place,
But I of him may gete bettre grace.
But nathelees, I wol of him assaye,
At certeyn dayes, yeer by yeer, to paye,
And thanke him of his grete curteisye;
My trouthe wol I kepe, I wol nat lye."

    With herte soor he gooth un-to his cofre,
And broghte gold un-to this philosophre,
The value of fyve hundred pound, I gesse,
And him bisecheth, of his gentillesse,
To graunte him dayes of the remenaunt,
And seyde, "maister, I dar wel make avaunt,
I failled never of my trouthe as yit;
For sikerly my dette shal be quit
Towardes yow, how-ever that I fare
To goon a-begged in my kirtle bare.
But wolde ye vouche-sauf, up-on seurtee,
Two yeer or three for to respyten me,
Than were I wel; for elles moot I selle
Myn heritage; ther is na-more to telle."

    This philosophre sobrely answerde,
And seyde thus, whan he thise wordes herde:
"Have I nat holden covenant un-to thee?"
"Yes, certes, wel and trewely," quod he.
"Hastow nat had thy lady as thee lyketh?"
"No, no," quod he, and sorwefully he syketh.
"What was the cause? tel me if thou can."
Aurelius his tale anon bigan,
And tolde him al, as ye han herd bifore;
It nedeth nat to yow reherce it more.

    He seide, "Arveragus, of gentillesse,
Had lever dye in sorwe and in distresse
Than that his wyf were of hir trouthe fals."

"Alas," said he, "alas! that I promised
Of refined gold a thousand pounds by weight
To this philosopher! How shall I do?
I see no more but that I am ruined.
My inheritance must I needs sell
And be a beggar; here I may not dwell,
And shame all my kin in this place,
Unless I of him may have a period of grace.
But nevertheless, I will with him try to arrange
At certain days, year by year, to pay,
And thank him for his great courtesy;
My pledge will I keep, I will not lie."

    With heart sore he went unto his coffer,
And brought gold unto this philosopher
The value of five hundred pounds, I guess,
And him beseeched out of his gentleness
To grant him time to pay the rest,
And said, "Master, I dare well make boast
I failed never of my word as yet;
For surely my debt shall be paid
Toward you, even if I must
Go a-begging in my shirt bare.
If you will grant, upon surety,
Two years or three of respite for me,
Then I will be well; otherwise must I sell
My heritage; there is no more to tell."

    This philosopher soberly answered,
And said thus, when he these words heard:
"Have I not kept covenant with you?"
"Yes, certainly, well and truly," said he.
"Have you had your lady as you wished?"
"No, no," said he, and sorrowfully he sighed.
"And what was the cause, tell me if you can."
Aurelius his tale anon began,
And told him all, as you have heard before:
I need not recite it any more.

    He said, "Averagus, of gentleness,
Would rather have died in sorrow and in distress
Than that his wife were of her pledge false."

The sorwe of Dorigen he tolde him als,
How looth hir was to been a wikked wyf,
And that she lever had lost that day hir lyf,
And that hir trouthe she swoor, thurgh innocence:
She never erst herde speke of apparence;
"That made me han of hir so greet pitee.
And right as frely as he sente hir me,
As frely sente I hir to him ageyn.
This al and som, ther is na-more to seyn."

    This philosophre answerde, "leve brother,
Everich of yow dide gentilly til other.
Thou art a squyer, and he is a knight;
But god forbede, for his blisful might,
But-if a clerk coude doon a gentil dede
As wel as any of yow, it is no drede!

    Sire, I relesse thee thy thousand pound,
As thou right now were cropen out of the ground,
Ne never er now ne haddest knowen me.
For sire, I wol nat take a peny of thee
For al my craft, ne noght for my travaille.
Thou hast y-payed wel for my vitaille;
It is y-nogh, and farewel, have good day:"
And took his hors, and forth he gooth his way.

    Lordinges, this question wolde I aske now,
Which was the moste free, as thinketh yow?
Now telleth me, er that ey ferther wende.
I can na-more, my tale is at an ende.

The sorrow of Dorigen he told him also,
How loath she was to be a wicked wife,
And that she would rather have lost that day her life,
And that her promise she swore through innocence,
She never before heard speak of illusions.
"That made me have of her so great pity;
And just as generously as he sent her to me
As freely I sent her to him again.
This is the whole, there is no more to say."

    This philosopher answered, "Dear brother,
Each of you did gently toward the other.
You are a squire, and he is a knight;
But God forbid, for his blissful might,
That a scholar could not do a gentle deed
As well as any of you, without a doubt!

    Sir, I release you your thousand pounds,
As if you right now had crept out of the ground,
And never before had you known me.
For sir, I will not take a penny from you
For all my craft, nor anything for my labor.
You have paid well for my victuals and play;
It is enough. And farewell, have a good day."
And took his horse, and forth he went his way.

    Lordings, this question then would I ask now:
Who was the most generous, as think you?
Now tell me, before we further wend.
I know no more: my tale is at an end.

The Pardoners Tale

The Introduction

"By corpus bones! but I have triacle,
Or elles a draught of moyste and corny ale,
Or but I here anon a mery tale,
Myn herte is lost for pitee of this mayde.
Thou bel amy, thou Pardoner," he seyde,
"Tel us som mirth or japes right anon."
"It shal be doon," quod he, "by seint Ronyon!
But first," quod he, "heer at this ale-stake
I wol both drinke, and eten of a cake."
    But right anon thise gentils gonne to crye,
"Nay! lat him telle us of no ribaudye;
Tel us som moral thing, that we may lere
Som wit, and thanne wol we gladly here."
"I graunte, y-wis," quod he, "but I mot thinke
Up-on som honest thing, whyl that I drinke."

The Prologue

Radix malorum est Cupiditas: Ad Thimotheum, sexto

"Lordings," quod he, "in chirches whan I preche,
I preyne me to han an hauteyn speche,
And ringe it out as round as gooth a belle,
For I can al by rote that I telle.
My theme is alwey oon, and ever was—
'Radix malorum est Cupiditas.'
First I pronounce whennes that I come,
And than my bulles shewe I, alle and somme.
Our lige lordes seel on my patente,
That shewe I first, my body to warente,
That no man be so bold, ne preest ne clerk,
Me to destourbe of Cristes holy werk;
And after that than telle I forth my tales,
Bulles of popes and of cardinales,
Of patriarkes, and bishoppes I shewe;

The Pardoner's Tale

The Introduction

[. . . The Host speaking]
"By CORPUS BONES![1] UNLESS I have medicine,
Or else a draught of fresh and malty ale,
Or unless I hear anon a merry tale,
Mine heart is lost for pity of this maid.
You sweet friend, you Pardoner,"[2] he said,
"Tell us some mirth or jokes right anon."
"It shall be done," said he, "by Saint Runyan![3]
But first," said he, "here at this tavern
I will both drink and eat cake."

But right anon the gentle folk raised a cry,
"Nay, let him tell us of no ribaldry;
Tell us some moral thing, that we may learn
Something improving, and then will we listen gladly."
"I grant, certainly," said he, "but I must think
Upon some proper thing while I drink."

The Prologue

Greed is the root of all evil [the Bible, 1 Timothy 6:10].

"LORDINGS," SAID HE, "IN churches when I preach,
I take pains to have an elevated speech,
And ring it out as round as sounds a bell,
For I know by rote all that I tell.
My theme is always one, and ever was—
Radix malorum est Cupiditas.[4]
First I proclaim from where I come,
And then my writs of indulgence show I, all and one.
Our bishop's seal on my license,
That show I first, my person to authorize,
That no man be so bold, neither priest nor scholar,
To disturb me while I do Christ's holy work;
And after that then forth I tell my tales.
Writs of indulgence from popes and cardinals,
From patriarchs, and bishops I show,

And in Latyn I speke a wordes fewe,
To saffron with my predicacioun,
And for to stire men to devocioun.
Than shewe I forth my longe cristal stones,
Y-crammed ful of cloutes and of bones;
Reliks been they, as wenen they echoon.
Than have I in latoun a sholder-boon
Which that was of an holy Jewes shepe.
'Good men,' seye I, 'tak of my wordes kepe;
If that this boon he wasshe in any welle,
If cow, or calf, or sheep, or oxe swelle
That any worm hath ete, or worm y-stonge,
Tak water of that welle, and wash his tonge,
And it is hool anon; and forthermore,
Of pokkes and of scabbe, and every sore
Shal every sheep be hool, that of this welle
Drinketh a draughte; tak kepe eek what I telle.
If that the good-man that the bestes oweth,
Wol every wike, er that the cok him croweth,
Fastinge, drinken of this welle a draughte,
As thilke holy Jewe our eldres taughte,
His bestes and his stoor shal multiplye.
And, sirs, also it heleth jalousye;
For, though a man be falle in jalous rage,
Let maken with this water his potage,
And never shal be more his wyf mistriste,
Though he the sooth of hir defaute wiste;
Al had she taken preestes two or three.

    Heer is a miteyn eek, that ye may see.
He that his hond wol putte in this miteyn,
He shal have multiplying of his greyn,
Whan he hath sowen, be it whete or otes,
So that he offre pens, or elles grotes.

    Good men and wommen, o thing warne I yow,
If any wight be in this chirche now,
That hath doon sinne horrible, that he
Dar nat, for shame, of it y-shriven be,
Or any womman, be she yong or old,
That hath y-maad hir housbond cokewold,

And in Latin I speak a words few,
To spice my presentation,
And to stir them to devotion.
Then show I forth my crystal reliquaries,
Crammed full of rags and bones—
Saints' relics they are,[5] or so they suppose.
Then have I in brass a shoulder bone
Of a holy Jew's sheep.
'Good men,' say I, 'of my words take heed:
If this bone be washed in any well,
If cow, or calf, or sheep, or ox swell,
That any worm has eaten, or by viper stung,
Take water of that well, and wash his tongue,
And it is healed anon; and furthermore,
Of pox and of scab and every sore
Shall every sheep be healed, that of this well
Drinks a draft. Take heed also what I tell:
If the good man who the beast owns
Will every week, before the cock crows,
While fasting, drink of this well a draft—
As Jacob our elders taught—
His beasts and his stock shall multiply.
And, sirs, also it heals jealousy:
For though a man be fallen in a jealous rage,
Let him make with this water his broth,
And never shall he more his wife mistrust,
Though he the truth of her should see—
Albeit she takes priests two or three.
    Here is a mitten also, that you may see:
He who his hand will put in this mitten,
He shall have multiplying of his grain
When he has sown, be it wheat or oats,
Provided that he gives me pennies or groats.
    Good men and women, one thing I warn you:
If any person be in this church now,
Who has done sin so horrible that he
Dare not for shame of it shriven be,
Or any woman, be she young or old,
Who has made her husband a cuckold,

Swich folk shul have no power ne no grace
To offren to my reliks in this place.
And who-so findeth him out of swich blame,
He wol com up and offre in goddes name,
And I assoille him by the auctoritee
Which that by bulle y-graunted was to me.'
     By this gaude have I wonne, yeer by yeer,
An hundred mark sith I was Pardoner.
I stonde lyk a clerk in my pulpet,
And whan the lewed peple is doun y-set,
I preche, so as ye han herd bifore,
And telle an hundred false japes more.
Than peyne I me to strecche forth the nekke,
And est and west upon the peple I bekke,
As doth a dowve sitting on a berne.
Myn hondes and my tonge goon so yerne,
That it is joye to see my bisinesse.
Of avaryce and of swich cursednesse
Is al my preching, for to make hem free
To yeve her pens, and namely un-to me.
For my entente is nat but for to winne,
And no-thing for correccioun of sinne.
I rekke never, whan that they ben beried,
Though that her soules goon a-blakeberied!
For certes, many a predicacioun
Comth ofte tyme of yvel entencioun;
Som for plesaunce of folk and flaterye,
To been avaunced by ipocrisye,
And som for veyne glorie, and som for hate.
For, whan I dar non other weyes debate,
Than wol I stinge him with my tonge smerte
In preching, so that he shal nat asterte
To been defamed falsly, if that he
Hath trespased to my brethren or to me.
For, though I telle noght his propre name,
Men shal wel knowe that it is the same
By signes and by othere circumstances.
Thus quyte I folk that doon us displesances;
Thus spitte I out my venim under hewe

Such folk shall have no power or grace
To offer money to my relics in this place.
And whoso finds himself deserving not such blame,
He will come up and make an offering in God's name,
And I will absolve him by the authority
That by those writs was granted to me.'
 By this trick have I won, year by year,
A hundred marks since I was pardoner.
I stand like a scholar in my pulpit,
And when the ignorant people have sat down,
I preach, so as you heard before,
And tell a hundred false stories more.
Then I take pains to stretch forth my neck,
And east and west upon the people I nod
As does a dove, sitting in a barn.
My hands and my tongue move so fast
That it is a joy to see me at my business.
Of avarice and such cursedness
Is all my preaching, to make them generous
To give their pence, and namely unto me.
For my intent is not but to profit,
And not at all for correction of sin:
I care never, when they be buried,
If their souls go a-blackberrying!
For certainly, many a sermon,
Comes oftentimes of evil intention:
Some for amusement of folk and flattery,
To be advanced by hypocrisy,
And some for vainglory, and some for hate.
For when I dare no other way to attack,
Then will I sting my enemy with my tongue sharp
In preaching, so that he may not leap up to protest
At being defamed falsely, if he
Has wronged my fellow pardoners or me.
For, though I tell not his own name,
Men shall well know that it is the same
By signs and other circumstances.
Thus requite I folk who do offenses;
Thus I spit out venom under hue

Of holynesse, to seme holy and trewe.
    But shortly myn entente I wol devyse;
I preche of no-thing but for coveityse.
Therfor my theme is yet, and ever was—
'*Radix malorum est cupiditas.*'
Thus can I preche agayn that same vyce
Which that I use, and that is avaryce.
But, though my-self be gilty in that sinne,
Yet can I maken other folk to twinne
From avaryce, and sore to repente.
But that is nat my principal entente.
I preche no-thing but for coveityse;
Of this matere it oughte y-nogh suffyse.
    Than telle I hem ensamples many oon
Of olde stories, longe tyme agoon:
For lewed peple loven tales olde;
Swich thinges can they wel reporte and holde.
What? trowe ye, the whyles I may preche,
And winne gold and silver for I teche,
That I wol live in povert wilfully?
Nay, nay, I thoghte it never trewely!
For I wol preche and begge in sondry londes;
I wol not do no labour with myn hondes,
Ne make baskettes, and live therby,
Because I wol nat beggen ydelly.
I wol non of the apostles counterfete;
I wol have money, wolle, chese, and whete,
Al were it yeven of the povrest page,
Or of the povrest widwe in a village,
Al sholde hir children sterve for famyne.
Nay! I wol drinke licour of the vyne,
And have a joly wenche in every toun.
But herkneth, lordings, in conclusioun;
Your lyking is that I shall telle a tale.
Now, have I dronke a draughte of corny ale,
By god, I hope I shal yow telle a thing
That shal, by resoun, been at your lyking.
For, though myself be a ful vicious man,
A moral tale yet I yow telle can,

Of holiness, to seem holy and true.
    But briefly my intent I will describe:
I preach of nothing but out of covetousness.
Therefore my theme is yet, and ever was,
Radix malorum est cupiditas.
Thus can I preach against that same vice
Which I practice, and that is avarice.
But though I myself be guilty of that sin,
Yet can I make other folk depart
From avarice, and ardently to repent.
But that is not my principal intent:
I preach nothing but for covetousness.
Of this matter it ought enough suffice.
    Then I tell them examples many a one
Of old stories of time long gone,
For unlearned people love stories told;
Such things can they well repeat and hold.
What? Do you believe that as long as I can preach
And win gold and silver because I teach,
That I will live by choice in poverty?
Nay, nay, I considered it never, truly!
For I will preach and beg in sundry lands,
I will do no labor with my hands,
Neither make baskets, and live thereby,
Because I will not beg unprofitably.
I will none of the apostles imitate:
I will have money, wool, cheese and wheat,
Even if it were given by the poorest page,
Or by the poorest widow in a village,
Even though her children die of famine.
Nay! I will drink liquor of the vine,
And have a jolly wench in every town.
But listen, lordings, in conclusion:
Your liking is that I shall tell a tale.
Now have I drunk a draft of malty ale,
By God, I hope I shall you tell a thing
That shall with reason be to your liking.
For though I am a full vice-ridden man,
A moral tale yet tell you I can,

Which I am wont to preche, for to winne.
Now holde your pees, my tale I wol beginne."

The Tale

In Flaundres whylom was a companye
Of yonge folk, that haunteden folye,
As ryot, hasard, stewes, and tavernes,
Wher-as, with harpes, lutes, and giternes,
They daunce and pleye at dees bothe day and night,
And ete also and drinken over hir might,
Thurgh which they doon the devel sacrifyse
With-in that develes temple, in cursed wyse,
By superfluitee abhominable;
Hir othes been so grete and so dampnable,
That it is grisly for to here hem swere;
Our blissed lordes body they to-tere;
Hem thoughte Jewes rente him noght y-nough;
And ech of hem at otheres sinne lough.
And right anon than comen tombesteres
Fetys and smale, and yonge fruytesteres,
Singers with harpes, baudes, wafereres,
Whiche been the verray develes officeres
To kindle and blowe the fyr of lecherye,
That is annexed un-to glotonye;
The holy writ take I to my witnesse,
That luxurie is in wyn and dronkenesse.

Lo, how that dronken Loth, unkindely,
Lay by his doghtres two, unwitingly;
So dronke he was, he niste what he wroghte.

Herodes, (who-so wel the stories soghte,)
Whan he of wyn was replet at his feste,
Right at his owene table he yaf his heste
To sleen the Baptist John ful giltelees.

Senek seith eek a good word doutelees;
He seith, he can no difference finde
Bitwix a man that is out of his minde
And a man which that is dronkelewe,
But that woodnesse, y-fallen in a shrewe,
Persevereth lenger than doth dronkenesse.

Which I am wont to preach for profit.
Now hold your peace, my tale I will begin."

The Tale

In Flanders once there was a company
Of young folk, who to folly gave themselves—
Such as revelry, dice, taverns and brothels,
There with harps, lutes, and guitars,
They danced and played at dice both night and day,
And ate and drank beyond their capacity,
Through which they did unto the devil sacrifice
Within the devil's temple, in a cursed way,
To excess abominable.
Their oaths were so great and damnable,
That it was grisly to hear them swear.
Our blessed Lord's body they into pieces tore[6]—
They thought the Jews had not torn Him enough—
And each of them at the others' sins laughed.
And right anon then came acrobats and dancers,
Shapely and slender, and young fruitpeddlars,
Singers with harps, bawds, pastryvendors,
Who were the very devil's officers
To kindle and blow the fire of lechery
That is attached to gluttony:
The Holy Writ take I to my witness
That lechery is in wine and drunkenness.

    Look, how the drunken Lot[7] unnaturally
Lay by his daughters two, unwittingly;
So drunk he was, he knew not what he did.

    Herod, who well the stories should pursue,
When he of wine was replete at his feast,
Right at his own table at his behest
Slew John the Baptist[8] though he was guiltless.

    Seneca[9] said a good word doubtless:
He said, he could no difference find
Between a man who is out of his mind
And a man who is soused,
Except that madness, having begun,
Lasts longer than inebriation.

O glotonye, ful of cursednesse,
O cause first of our confusioun,
O original of our dampnacioun,
Til Crist had boght us with his blood agayn!
Lo, how dere, shortly for to sayn,
Aboght was thilke cursed vileinye;
Corrupt was al this world for glotonye!
    Adam our fader, and his wyf also,
For Paradys to labour and to wo
Were driven for that vyce, it is no drede;
For whyl that Adam fasted, as I rede,
He was in Paradys; and whan that he
Eet of the fruyt defended on the tree,
Anon he was out-cast to wo and peyne.
O glotonye, on thee wel oghte us pleyne!
    O, wiste a man how many maladyes
Folwen of excesse and glotonyes,
He wolde been the more mesurable
Of his diete, sittinge at his table.
Allas! the shorte throte, the tendre mouth,
Maketh that, Est and West, and North and South,
In erthe, in eir, in water men to-swinke
To gete a glotoun deyntee mete and drinke!
Of this matere, o Paul, wel canstow trete,
"Mete un-to wombe, and wombe eek un-to mete,
Shal god destroyen bothe," as Paulus seith.
Allas! a foul thing is it, by my feith,
To seye this word, and fouler is the dede,
Whan man so drinketh of the whyte and rede,
That of his throte he maketh his privee,
Thurgh thilke cursed superfluitee.
    The apostel weping seith ful pitously,
"Ther walken many of whiche yow told have I,
I seye it now weping with pitous voys,
[That] they been enemys of Cristes croys,
Of whiche the ende is deeth, wombe is her god."
O wombe! O bely! O stinking cod,
Fulfild of donge and of corrupcioun!
At either ende of thee foul is the soun.

Oh gluttony, full of cursedness!
Oh first cause of our ruination!
Oh origin of our damnation,
Until Christ had bought us with his blood again!
Look, at what cost, to make it brief,
Was bought that same cursed, evil deed;
Corrupted was all this world for gluttony!
    Adam our father and his wife also
From Paradise to labor and to woe
Were driven for that vice, it is no doubt.
For while Adam fasted, as I read,
He was in Paradise, and when he
Ate of the fruit forbidden on the tree,
Anon he was cast out to woe and pain.
Oh gluttony, of you we ought to complain!
    Oh, if only a man knew how many maladies
Followed from excess and gluttony,
He would be more temperate
In his diet, sitting at his table.
Alas! the brief sip, the tastebuds refined,
Cause, east and west, north and south,
On earth, in air, on water, men to labor
To get a glutton dainty meat and drink!
Of this matter, Paul, well can you treat:
"Meat unto stomach,[10] and stomach unto meat,
Shall God destroy both," as Paul said.
Alas! a foul thing is it, by my faith,
To say this word, and fouler is the deed,
When man so drinks of the white and red
That of his throat he makes his privy,
Through that same superfluity.
    The apostle, weeping, said full piteously,[11]
"There walk many of you whom I have told"—
I say it now weeping with piteous voice—
"Who be enemies of Christ's cross,
For whom the end is death: stomach is their god!"
Oh stomach! Oh belly! Oh stinking gut!
Filled full with dung and rot!
At either end of you foul is the sound.

How greet labour and cost is thee to finde!
Thise cokes, how they stampe, and streyne, and grinde,
And turnen substaunce in-to accident,
To fulfille al thy likerous talent!
Out of the harde bones knokke they
The mary, for they caste noght a-wey
That may go thurgh the golet softe and swote;
Of spicerye, of leef, and bark, and rote
Shal been his sauce y-maked by delyt,
To make him yet a newer appetyt.
But certes, he that haunteth swich delyces
Is deed, whyl that he liveth in tho vyces.
    A lecherous thing is wyn, and dronkenesse
Is ful of stryving and of wrecchednesse.
O dronke man, disfigured is thy face,
Sour is thy breeth, foul artow to embrace,
And thurgh thy dronke nose semeth the soun
As though thou seydest ay "Sampsoun, Sampsoun";
And yet, god wot, Sampsoun drank never no wyn.
Thou fallest, as it were a stiked swyn;
Thy tonge is lost, and al thyn honest cure;
For dronkenesse is verray sepulture
Of mannes wit and his discrecioun.
In whom that drinke hath dominacioun,
He can no conseil kepe, it is no drede.
Now keep yow fro the whyte and fro the rede,
And namely fro the whyte wyn of Lepe,
That is to selle in Fish-strete or in Chepe.
This wyn of Spayne crepeth subtilly
In othere wynes, growing faste by,
Of which ther ryseth swich fumositee,
That whan a man hath dronken draughtes three,
And weneth that he be at hoom in Chepe,
He is in Spayne, right at the toune of Lepe,
Nat at the Rochel, ne at Burdeux toun;
And thanne wol he seye, "Sampsoun, Sampsoun."
    But herkneth, lordings, o word, I yow preye,
That alle the sovereyn actes, dar I seye,
Of victories in th'olde testament,

How great the labor and cost to provide for you!
These cooks, how they pound, and strain, and grind,
And turn substance into accident,[12]
To fulfill all your gluttonous desire!
Out of the hard bones knock they
The marrow, for they cast nothing away
That may go through the gullet soft and sweet;
Of spices, of leaf, and bark, and root
Shall sauce be made to its delight,
To make it yet a newer appetite.
But truly, he who gives himself up to such delights
Is dead, while he lives in those vices.

    A lecherous thing is wine, and drunkenness
Is full of quarreling and of wretchedness.
Oh drunk man, disfigured is your face,
Sour is your breath, foul are you to embrace,
And through your drunken nose snorts the sound
As though you said ever "Samson, Samson";[13]
And yet, God knows Samson never drank any wine.
You fall down, like a stuck swine;
Your tongue is lost, and all your decency,
For drunkenness is the true tomb
Of man's wit, and his discretion.
He over whom drink has domination,
Can no counsel keep, it is no doubt.
Now keep you from the white and from the red—
And namely from the white wine of Lepe
That is for sale in Cheapside or on Fish Street.
This wine of Spain creeps subtly
Into other wines growing nearby,
From which there rises such vapor,
That when a man has drunk drafts three
And thinks that he is at home in Cheapside,
He is in Spain, right at the town of Lepe,
Not at La Rochelle, or Bordeaux town;
And then will he snore, "Samson, Samson."

    But listen, lordings, to one word I pray you:
All the supreme deeds, dare I say,
Of victories in the Old Testament,

Thurgh verray god, that is omnipotent,
Were doon in abstinence and in preyere;
Loketh the Bible, and ther ye may it lere.
  Loke, Attila, the grete conquerour,
Deyde in his sleep, with shame and dishonour,
Bledinge ay at his nose in dronkenesse;
A capitayn shoulde live in sobrenesse.
And over al this, avyseth yow right wel
What was comaunded un-to Lamuel—
Nat Samuel, but Lamuel, seye I—
Redeth the Bible, and finde it expresly
Of wyn-yeving to hem that han justyse.
Na-more of this, for it may wel suffyse.
  And now that I have spoke of glotonye,
Now wol I yow defenden hasardrye.
Hasard is verray moder of lesinges,
And of deceite, and cursed forsweringes,
Blaspheme of Crist, manslaughtre, and wast also
Of catel and of tyme; and forthermo,
It is repreve and contrarie of honour
For to ben holde a commune hasardour.
And ever the hyër he is of estaat,
The more is he holden desolaat.
If that a prince useth hasardrye,
In alle governaunce and policye
He is, as by commune opinioun,
Y-holde the lasse in reputacioun.
  Stilbon, that was a wys embassadour,
Was sent to Corinthe, in ful greet honour,
Fro Lacidomie, to make hir alliaunce.
And whan he cam, him happede, par chaunce,
That alle the grettest that were of that lond,
Pleyinge atte hasard he hem fond.
For which, as sone as it mighte be,
He stal him hoom agayn to his contree,
And seyde, "ther wol I nat lese my name;
Ne I wol nat take on me so greet defame,
Yow for to allye un-to none hasardours.
Sendeth othere wyse embassadours;

Through the true God, who is omnipotent,
Were done in abstinence and in prayer:
Look in the Bible, and there you may it learn.

    Consider that Attila,[14] the great conqueror,
Died in his sleep, in shame and dishonor,
Bleeding at his nose from drunkenness:
A captain should live in soberness.
And over all this, be you well advised
What was commanded unto Lemuel[15]—
Not Samuel, but Lemuel, say I—
Read the Bible, and find it speaks explicitly
About giving wine to those who decide justice.
No more of this, for it may well suffice.

    And now that I have spoken of gluttony,
Now will I forbid you gambling at dice.
Gambling is the true mother of lies,
And of deceit and cursed perjuries,
Blasphemy of Christ, manslaughter and waste also
Of goods and time; and furthermore,
It is a reproach and contrary to honor
To be held a common gambler.
And the higher he is of rank
The more is he held debased:
If a prince gambles,
In all governance and policy
Common opinion holds him,
The less in reputation.

    Stilbon, who was a wise ambassador,
Was sent to Corinth in full great honor,
From Sparta to win their alliance.
And when he arrived, it happened by chance
That all the great men of that land
He found playing at dice.
For which, as soon as could be,
He stole away again to his country,
And said, "There will I not lose my name,
Nor will I take on me so great dishonor,
To ally you with a company of gamblers.
Send other wise ambassadors—

For, by my trouthe, me were lever dye,
Than I yow sholde to hasardours allye.
For ye that been so glorious in honours
Shul nat allyen yow with hasardours
As by my wil, ne as by my tretee."
This wyse philosophre thus seyde he.

Loke eek that, to the king Demetrius
The king of Parthes, as the book seith us,
Sente him a paire of dees of gold in scorn,
For he hadde used hasard ther-biforn;
For which he heeld his glorie or his renoun
At no value or reputacioun.
Lordes may finden other maner pley
Honeste y-nough to dryve the day awey.

Now wol I speke of othes false and grete
A word or two, as olde bokes trete.
Gret swering is a thing abhominable,
And false swering is yet more reprevable.
The heighe god forbad swering at al,
Witnesse on Mathew; but in special
Of swering seith the holy Jeremye,
"Thou shalt seye sooth thyn othes, and nat lye,
And swere in dome, and eek in
    rightwisnesse;"
But ydel swering is a cursednesse.
Bihold and see, that in the firste table
Of heighe goddes hestes honurable,
How that the seconde heste of him is this—
"Tak nat my name in ydel or amis."
Lo, rather he forbedeth swich swering
Than homicyde or many a cursed thing;
I seye that, as by ordre, thus it stondeth;
This knowen, that his hestes understondeth,
How that the second heste of god is that.
And forther over, I wol thee telle al plat,
That vengeance shal nat parten from his hous,
That of his othes is to outrageous.
"By goddes precious herte, and by his nayles,
And by the blode of Crist, that it is in Hayles,

For by my troth, I would rather die
Than to gamblers I should you ally.
For you who are so glorious in honors
Shall not ally yourself with gamblers
Neither by my will nor my negotiations."
This wise philosopher, thus said he.

    Look also to the king Demetrius,[16]
The king of Parthia, as the book tells us,
Sent a pair of golden dice in scorn,
For he had gambled there before;
For which he held his glory or his renown
At no value or reputation.
Lords may find other kinds of play
Honorable enough to drive the day away.

    Now will I speak of oaths false and great
A word or two, as old books treat.
Great cursing is a thing abominable,
And false swearing is yet more reproachable.
The high God forbade swearing at all—
Witness on Matthew—but in special
Of swearing says the holy Jeremiah,[17]
"Thou shalt swear truly your oaths and not lie,
And swear in good judgement, and also in
    righteousness;"
But vain swearing is a wickedness.
Behold and see, in Moses' first tablet
Of high God's ten commandments,
That the second commandment of him is this:
"Take not my name wrongly or in vain."
Look, he forbade such swearing even
Before homicide or many a cursed thing—
I say that, in terms of order, thus it stands—
He knows this, who his commandments understands,
How the second commandment of God is that.
And furthermore, I will tell you flat
That vengeance shall not depart from his house
Who of his oaths is too outrageous.
"By God's precious heart," and "By his nails,"
And "By the blood of Christ that is in Hayles.[18]

Seven is my chaunce, and thyn is cink and treye;
By goddes armes, if thou falsly pleye,
This dagger shal thurgh-out thyn herte go"—
This fruyt cometh of the bicched bones two,
Forswering, ire, falsnesse, homicyde.
Now, for the love of Crist that for us dyde,
Leveth your othes, bothe grete and smale;
But, sirs, now wol I telle forth my tale.

    Thise ryotoures three, of whiche I telle,
Longe erst er pryme rong of any belle,
Were set hem in a taverne for to drinke;
And as they satte, they herde a belle clinke
Biforn a cors, was caried to his grave;
That oon of hem gan callen to his knave,
"Go bet," quod he, "and axe redily,
What cors is this that passeth heer forby;
And look that thou reporte his name wel."
    "Sir," quod this boy, "it nedeth never-a-del.
It was me told, er ye cam heer, two houres;
He was, pardee, an old felawe of youres;
And sodeynly he was y-slayn to-night,
For-dronke, as he sat on his bench upright;
Ther cam a privee theef, men clepeth Deeth,
That in this contree al the peple sleeth,
And with his spere he smoot his herte a-two,
And wente his wey with-outen wordes mo.
He hath a thousand slayn this pestilence:
And, maister, er ye come in his presence,
Me thinketh that it were necessarie
For to be war of swich an adversarie:
Beth redy for to mete him evermore.
Thus taughte me my dame, I sey na-more."
"By seinte Marie," seyde this taverner,
"The child seith sooth, for he hath slayn this yeer,
Henne over a myle, with-in a greet village,
Both man and womman, child and hyne, and page
I trowe his habitacioun be there;
To been avysed greet wisdom it were,

Seven is my chance, and yours is five and three;
By God's arms, if you falsely play,
This dagger shall through your heart go!"
This fruit comes from the bitchy bones two[19]—
Perjury, anger, falseness, homicide.
Now for the love of Christ who for us died,
Cease your oaths, both great and small.
But, sirs, now will I tell forth my tale.

These three revelers of whom I tell
Long before prime rang of any bell,
Had set themselves down in a tavern to drink;
And as they sat, they heard a bell clink
Before a corpse being carried to his grave.
The one of them began calling to his knave,
"Go quick," he said, "and ask straightaway,
What corpse is this that passes by;
And look that you get his name right."
    "Sir," said this boy, "no need to inquire.
I learned it two hours before you arrived.
He was, by God, an old companion of yours;
And suddenly he was slain last night,
Dead drunk, as he sat on his bench upright.
There came a secret thief that men call Death,
Who has slain many in this region,
And with his spear he smote his heart in two,
And went his way without words more.
He has a thousand slain during this plague.[20]
And master, before you come in his presence,
Methinks that it is necessary
For to be aware of such an adversary:
Be ready for to meet him at any hour.
Thus taught me my mother, I say no more."
"By Saint Mary," said this tavernkeeper,
"The child says the truth, for he has slain this year,
For a mile around, within a great village,
Both man and woman, child, and servant, and laborer;
I believe his habitation to be there.
Be advised to be careful that he

Er that he dide a man a dishonour."
"Ye, goddes armes," quod this ryotour,
"Is it swich peril with him for to mete?
I shal him seke by wey and eek by strete,
I make avow to goddes digne bones!
Herkneth, felawes, we three been al ones;
Lat ech of us holde up his hond til other,
And ech of us bicomen otheres brother,
And we wol sleen this false traytour Deeth;
He shal be slayn, which that so many sleeth,
By goddes dignitee, er it be night."

    Togidres han thise three her trouthes plight,
To live and dyen ech of hem for other,
As though he were his owene y-boren brother.
And up they sterte al dronken, in this rage,
And forth they goon towardes that village,
Of which the taverner had spoke biforn,
And many a grisly ooth than han they sworn,
And Cristes blessed body they to-rente—
"Deeth shal be deed, if that they may him hente."

    Whan they han goon nat fully half a myle,
Right as they wolde han troden over a style,
An old man and a povre with hem mette.
This olde man ful mekely hem grette,
And seyde thus, "now, lordes, god yow see!"

    The proudest of thise ryotoures three
Answerde agayn, "what? carl, with sory grace,
Why artow al forwrapped save thy face?
Why livestow so longe in so greet age?"

    This olde man gan loke in his visage,
And seyde thus, "for I ne can nat finde
A man, though that I walked in-to Inde,
Neither in citee nor in no village,
That wolde chaunge his youthe for myn age;
And therfore moot I han myn age stille,
As longe time as it is goddes wille.

    Ne deeth, allas! ne wol nat han my lyf;
Thus walke I, lyk a restelees caityf,
And on the ground, which is my modres gate,

Has to dishonor you no opportunity."
"God's arms!" said this reveler,
"Is it such peril with him to meet?
I shall him seek by road and also by street,
I make a vow of it by God's worthy bones!
Harken, fellows, let's we three be agreed:
Let each of us hold up his hand to the other,
And each of us become the other's brother,
And we will slay this false traitor Death.
He shall be slain, he who so many slays,
By God's worthiness, before it be night."

Together have these three their troths plighted
To live and die each of them for the other,
As though they were their own born brothers.
And up they started, all drunk in this passion,
And forth they went toward that village
Of which the tavernkeeper had before spoken,
And many a grisly oath then did they swear,
And Christ's blessed body they tore to pieces—
Death would be dead, if they could him seize.

When they had gone not fully half a mile,
Just as they would have stepped over a stile,
An old and poor man they did meet.
This old man full meekly them greeted,
And said thus, "Now lords, may God you protect!"

The proudest of these revelers three
Answered again, "What, fellow, confound you!
Why are you all wrapped up except your face?
Why do you live so long to such great age?"

This old man looked him in the eye,
And said thus, "Because I cannot find
A man, though I walk to India,
Neither in city or in village,
Who would change his youth for my age;
And therefore must I have my age still,
As long time as it is God's will.

Nor will Death take my life.
Thus walk I, like a restless captive,
And on the ground, which is my mother's gate,

I knokke with my staf, bothe erly and late,
And seye, 'leve moder, leet me in!
Lo, how I vanish, flesh, and blood, and skin!
Allas! whan shul my bones been at reste?
Moder, with yow wolde I chaunge my cheste,
That in my chambre longe tyme hath be,
Ye! for an heyre clout to wrappe me!'
But yet to me she wol nat do that grace,
For which ful pale and welked is my face.

But, sirs, to yow it is no courteisye
To speken to an old man vileinye,
But he trespasse in worde, or elles in dede.
In holy writ ye may your-self wel rede,
'Agayns an old man, hoor upon his heed,
Ye sholde aryse;' wherfor I yeve yow reed,
Ne dooth un-to an old man noon harm now,
Na-more than ye wolde men dide to yow
In age, if that ye so longe abyde;
And god be with yow, wher ye go or ryde.
I moot go thider as I have to go."

"Nay, olde cherl, by god, thou shalt nat so,"
Seyde this other hasardour anon;
"Thou partest nat so lightly, by seint John!
Thou spak right now of thilke traitour Deeth,
That in this contree alle our frendes sleeth.
Have heer my trouthe, as thou art his aspye,
Tel wher he is, or thou shalt it abye,
By god, and by the holy sacrament!
For soothly thou art oon of his assent,
To sleen us yonge folk, thou false theef!"

"Now, sirs," quod he, "if that yow be so leef
To finde Deeth, turne up this croked wey,
For in that grove I lafte him, by my fey,
Under a tree, and ther he wol abyde;
Nat for your boost he wol him no-thing hyde.
See ye that ook? right ther ye shul him finde.
God save yow, that boghte agayn mankinde,
And yow amende!"—thus seyde this olde man.
And everich of thise ryotoures ran,

I knock with my staff both early and late,
And say, 'Dear mother, let me in!
Look, how I am wasting, flesh, and blood, and skin!
Alas! When shall my bones be at rest?
Mother, with you would I exchange my chest
Of clothes that in my chamber long time has been,
Yes, for a haircloth shroud to wrap me in!'
But yet to me she will not do that grace,
For which full pale and withered is my face.

    But sirs, it is not polite of you
To speak to an old man in a manner so rude,
Unless he has offended you in word or deed.
In Holy Writ you may yourselves well read,[21]
'Before an old man, hoarfrost upon his head,
You should arise.' I therefore give you this advice:
Do no harm unto an old man now,
No more than you would have men do to you
When old, if you shall so long abide.
And God be with you, where you walk or ride;
I must go thither where I have to go."

    "No, old fellow, by God, you shall not so,"
Said this other gambler anon;
"You won't get away so lightly, by Saint John!
You speak right now of that same traitor Death
Who in this country all our friends slays.
Have here my pledge, since you are his spy,
Tell where he is, or you shall for it pay,
By God, and by the holy sacrament!
For truly you are his agent
To slay us young folk, you false thief!"

    "Now, sirs," said he, "if you so much desire
To find Death, turn up this crooked way,
For in that grove I left him, by my faith,
Under a tree, and there he will abide:
Your boast will not make him hide.
See that oak? Right there you shall him find.
God save you, who redeemed mankind,
And you improve!" Thus said this old man.
And each of these revelers ran,

Til he cam to that tree, and ther they founde
Of florins fyne of golde y-coyned rounde
Wel ny an eighte busshels, as hem thoughte.
No lenger thanne after Deeth they soughte,
But ech of hem so glad was of that sighte,
For that the florins been so faire and brighte,
That doun they sette hem by this precious hord.
The worste of hem he spake the firste word.

    "Brethren," quod he, "tak kepe what I seye;
My wit is greet, though that I bourde and pleye.
"This tresor hath fortune un-to us yiven,
In mirthe and jolitee our lyf to liven,
And lightly as it comth, so wol we spende.
Ey! goddes precious dignitee! who wende
To-day, that we sholde han so fair a grace?
But mighte this gold be caried fro this place
Hoom to myn hous, or elles un-to youres—
For wel ye woot that al this gold is oures—
Than were we in heigh felicitee.
But trewely, by daye it may nat be;
Men wolde seyn that we were theves stronge,
And for our owene tresor doon us honge.
This tresor moste y-caried be by nighte
As wysly and as slyly as it mighte.
Wherfore I rede that cut among us alle
Be drawe, and lat see wher the cut wol falle;
And he that hath the cut with herte blythe
Shal renne to the toune, and that ful swythe,
And bringe us breed and wyn ful prively.
And two of us shul kepen subtilly
This tresor wel; and, if he wol nat tarie,
Whan it is night, we wol this tresor carie
By oon assent, wher-as us thinketh best."
That oon of hem the cut broughte in his fest,
And bad hem drawe, and loke wher it wol falle;
And it fill on the yongeste of hem alle;
And forth toward the toun he wente anon.
And al-so sone as that he was gon,
That oon of hem spak thus un-to that other,

Till he came to that tree, and there they found
Of florins fine of gold coined round
Well nigh eight bushels, or so it seemed.
No longer then after Death they sought,
Each of them so glad was of that sight—
For the florins were so fair and bright—
That down they set them by this precious hoard.
The worst of them spoke the first word.

"Brothers," said he, "take heed of what I say:
My understanding is great, though I jest and play.
This treasure has Fortune unto us given
Our lives in mirth and jollity to live,
And lightly as it comes, so will we spend.
Hey! God's precious dignity! Who would have guessed
Today that we should find so fair a grace?
If only might this gold be carried from this place
Home to my house—or else unto yours—
For well we know that all this gold is ours—
Then were we in high felicity.
But truly, by day it may not be done:
Men would say that we were thieves,
And for our own treasure have us hung.
This treasure must be carried by night,
As wisely and as slyly as we might.
Therefore I suggest that lots among us all
Be drawn, and let's see to whose lot it shall fall;
And he who has the lot with heart blithe
Shall run to the town, in quick time,
And secretly bring us bread and wine.
And two of us shall guard with care
This treasure well; and if he will not tarry,
When it is night we will this treasure carry,
By one assent, where we think best."
The fellow brought the cut in his fist,
And he bade them draw, and look where it would fall;
And it fell on the youngest of them all,
And forth toward the town he went anon.
But as soon as he was gone,
One of the other two spoke thus to the other:

"Thou knowest wel thou art my sworne brother,
Thy profit wol I telle thee anon.
Thou woost wel that our felawe is agon;
And heer is gold, and that ful greet plentee,
That shal departed been among us three.
But natheles, if I can shape it so
That it departed were among us two,
Hadde I nat doon a freendes torn to thee?"

That other answerde, "I noot how that may be;
He woot how that the gold is with us tweye,
What shal we doon, what shal we to him seye?"

"Shal it be conseil?" seyde the firste shrewe,
"And I shal tellen thee, in wordes fewe,
What we shal doon, and bringe it wel aboute."

"I graunte," quod that other, "out of doute,
That, by my trouthe, I wol thee nat biwreye."

"Now," quod the firste, "thou woost wel we be tweye,
And two of us shul strenger be than oon.
Look when that he is set, and right anoon
Arys, as though thou woldest with him pleye;
And I shal ryve him thurgh the sydes tweye
Whyl that thou strogelest with him as in game,
And with thy dagger look thou do the same;
And than shal al this gold departed be,
My dere freend, bitwixen me and thee;
Than may we bothe our lustes al fulfille,
And pleye at dees right at our owene wille."
And thus acorded been thise shrewes tweye
To sleen the thridde, as ye han herd me seye.

This yongest, which that wente un-to the toun,
Ful ofte in herte he rolleth up and doun
The beautee of thise florins newe and brighte.
"O lord!" quod he, "if so were that I mighte
Have al this tresor to my-self allone,
Ther is no man that liveth under the trone
Of god, that sholde live so mery as I!"
And atte laste the feend, our enemy,
Putte in his thought that he shold poyson beye,
With which he mighte sleen his felawes tweye;

"You well know that you are my sworn brother;
So something to your advantage will I tell you anon.
You know well that our companion is gone,
And here is gold, and plenty of it,
That shall be divided between us three.
But nevertheless, if I can arrange it so
That it divided were between us two,
Would I not have done a friend's turn to you?"

The other answered, "I know not how that may be:
He knows how the gold is with us two.
What shall we do? What shall we say?"

"Can you keep a secret?" said the first wretch;
"And I shall tell in words few
What we shall do, to bring it about."

"I grant it," said that other, "you can be sure,
That, by my word of honor, I will not betray you."

"Now," said the first, "you know well we be two,
And two of us are stronger than one.
As soon as he has sat down, then right away
Arise as though you would with him play;
And I shall stab him through both sides
While you struggle with him as if in play,
And with your dagger you do the same;
And then shall all this gold divided be,
My dear friend, between you and me.
Then may we both our desires fulfill,
And play at dice whenever we will."
And thus these cursed fellows two agreed
To slay the third, as you have heard me say.

This youngest, who went into the town,
Full often in his mind's eye rolled up and down
The beauty of those florins new and bright.
"Oh Lord," said he, "if it were that I might
Have all this treasure to myself alone,
There is no man who lives under the throne
Of God who should live so merry as I!"
And at the last the devil, our enemy,
Put in his thought that he should poison buy,
With which he might slay his fellows two—

For-why the feend fond him in swich lyvinge,
That he had leve him to sorwe bringe,
For this was outrely his fulle entente
To sleen hem bothe, and never to repente.
And forth he gooth, no lenger wolde he tarie,
Into the toun, un-to a pothecarie,
And preyed him, that he him wolde selle
Som poyson, that he mighte his rattes quelle;
And eek ther was a polcat in his hawe,
That, as he seyde, his capouns hadde y-slawe,
And fayn he wolde wreke him, if he mighte,
On vermin, that destroyed him by nighte.

The pothecarie answerde, "and thou shalt have
A thing that, al-so god my soule save,
In al this world ther nis no creature,
That ete or dronke hath of this confiture
Noght but the mountance of a corn of whete,
That he ne shal his lyf anon forlete;
Ye, sterve he shal, and that in lasse whyle
Than thou wolt goon a paas nat but a myle;
This poyson is so strong and violent."

This cursed man hath in his hond y-hent
This poyson in a box, and sith he ran
In-to the nexte strete, un-to a man,
And borwed [of] him large botels three;
And in the two his poyson poured he;
The thridde he kepte clene for his drinke.
For al the night he shoop him for to swinke
In caryinge of the gold out of that place.
And whan this ryotour, with sory grace,
Had filled with wyn his grete botels three,
To his felawes agayn repaireth he.

What nedeth it to sermone of it more?
For right as they had cast his deeth bifore,
Right so they han him slayn, and that anon.
And whan that this was doon, thus spak that oon,
"Now lat us sitte and drinke, and make us merie,
And afterward we wol his body berie."
And with that word it happed him, par cas,

Because the fiend found him living in such a way
That he had God's permission to bring him sorrow:
For this was his full intent,
To slay them both, and never to repent.
And forth he went—no longer would he tarry—
Into the town, unto an apothecary,
And prayed him to sell
Some poison, that he might his rats quell,
And also there was a weasel in his yard,
That, as he said, upon his chickens gnawed,
And gladly would he avenge himself, if he might,
On vermin, that were ruining him by night.

    The apothecary answered, "And you shall have
Something that, so God my soul save,
In all this world there is no creature,
That having eaten or drunk of this mixture
No more than amounts to a grain of wheat,
Then shall he anon his life forfeit.
Yes, die he shall, and that in less time
Than at walking pace you should go a mile,
This poison is so strong and vile."

    This cursed man in his hand grasped
This poison in a box, and then he ran
Into the next street unto a man
And borrowed from him large bottles three,
And in the two his poison poured he—
The third he kept clean for his own drink—
For all the night he himself readied
For carrying the gold out of that place.
And when this reveler, by evil blessed,
Had filled with wine his great bottles three,
To his fellows again returned he.

    Why need we speak of it more?
For right as they had planned his death before,
Right so they did him slay, and that anon.
And when this was done, thus spoke that one:
"Now let us sit and drink, and make us merry,
And afterward we will his body bury."
And with that word it befell him, by chance,

To take the botel ther the poyson was,
And drank, and yaf his felawe drinke also,
For which anon they storven bothe two.
　But, certes, I suppose that Avicen
Wroot never in no canon, ne in no fen,
Mo wonder signes of empoisoning
Than hadde thise wrecches two, er hir ending.
Thus ended been thise homicydes two,
And eek the false empoysoner also.

　O cursed sinne, ful of cursednesse!
O traytours homicyde, o wikkednesse!
O glotonye, luxurie, and hasardrye!
Thou blasphemour of Crist with vileinye
And othes grete, of usage and of pryde!
Allas! mankinde, how may it bityde,
That to thy creatour which that thee wroghte,
And with his precious herte-blood thee boghte,
Thou art so fals and so unkinde, allas!
　Now, goode men, god forgeve yow your trespas,
And ware yow fro the sinne of avryce.
Myn holy pardoun may yow alle waryce,
So that ye offre nobles or sterlinges,
Or elles silver broches, spones, ringes.
Boweth your heed under this holy bulle!
Cometh up, ye wyves, offreth of your wolle!
Your name I entre heer in my rolle anon;
In-to the blisse of hevene shul ye gon;
I yow assoile, by myn heigh power,
Yow that wol offre, as clene and eek as cleer
As ye were born; and, lo, sirs thus I preche.
And Jesu Crist, that is our soules leche,
So graunte yow his pardon to receyve;
For that is best; I wol yow nat deceyve.

The Epilogue

But sirs, o word forgat I in my tale;
I have relikes and pardon in my male,
As faire as any man in Engelond,

To take the bottle where the poison was,
And drank, and gave his fellow drink also,
For which anon they died both two.
    But certainly, I suppose that Avicenna[22]
Described never, in any chapter or treatise,
More awful symptoms of poisoning
Than had these wretches two, before their ending.
Thus ended these murderers two,
And also the false poisoner as well.

    Oh cursed sin of all cursedness!
Oh traitorous murderers, oh wickedness!
Oh gluttony, lechery and gambling!
You blasphemer of Christ with vile words
And oaths great, out of pride and habit!
Alas! mankind, how may it happen
That to your Creator who you wrought,
And with his precious heart blood you redeemed,
You are so false and so unnatural, alas!
    Now, good men, may God forgive you your trespasses,
And protect you from the sin of avarice.
My holy pardon may all you cure—
So long as you offer coin of gold or sterling,
Or else silver brooches, spoons or rings.
Bow your head under this holy bull!
Come up, you wives, offer of your wool!
Your names I enter here in my list anon:
Into the bliss of heaven you shall go.
I you absolve, by my high power—
You who will make an offering—as clean and pure
As you were born. And look, sirs, thus I preach.
And Jesus Christ, who is our souls' healer,
May He grant you His pardon to receive,
For that is best; I will you not deceive.

The Epilogue

But sirs, one word forgot I in my tale:
I have relics and pardons in my pouch
As fair as any man in England,

Whiche were me yeven by the popes hond.
If any of yow wol, of devocioun,
Offren, and han myn absolucioun,
Cometh forth anon, and kneleth heer adoun,
And mekely receyveth my pardoun:
Or elles, taketh pardon as ye wende,
Al newe and fresh, at every tounes ende,
So that ye offren alwey newe and newe
Nobles and pens, which that be gode and trewe.
It is an honour to everich that is heer,
That ye mowe have a suffisant pardoneer
T'assoille yow, in contree as ye ryde,
For aventures which that may bityde.
Peraventure ther may falle oon or two
Doun of his hors, and breke his nekke atwo.
Look which a seuretee is it to yow alle
That I am in your felaweship y-falle,
That may assoille yow, bothe more and lasse,
Whan that the soule shal fro the body passe.
I rede that our hoste heer shal biginne,
For he is most envoluped in sinne.
Com forth, sir hoste, and offre first anon.
And thou shalt kisse the reliks everichon,
Ye, for a grote! unbokel anon thy purs.

        "Nay, nay," quod he, "than have I Cristes curs!
Lat be," quod he, "it shal nat be, so thee'ch!
Thou woldest make me kisse thyn old breech,
And swere it were a relik of a seint,
Thogh it were with thy fundement depeint!
But by the croys which that seint Eleyne fond,
I wolde I hadde thy coillons in myn hond
In stede of relikes or of seintuarie;
Lat cutte hem of, I wol thee helpe hem carie;
They shul be shryned in an hogges tord."

        This pardoner answerde nat a word;
So wrooth he was, no word ne wolde he seye.

        "Now," quod our host, "I wol no lenger pleye
With thee, ne with noon other angry man."
But right anon the worthy Knight bigan,

Which were given to me by the Pope's hand.
If any of you will out of devotion
Offer and have my absolution,
Come forth now, and kneel here down,
And meekly receive my pardon;
Or else, take pardon as you travel,
All new and fresh, at every mile's end—
So long as you make an offering anew each time
Of gold coins or pence, which be good and true.
It is an honor to everyone who is here
To have such an able pardoner
To absolve you, as you ride the countryside,
For anything that may you betide.
Perhaps there may fall one or two
Down off his horse, and break his neck in two.
Look what a security it is to you all
That I am in your fellowship befallen,
Who may absolve you, both great and small,
When the soul shall from the body pass.
I advise our Host here to begin,
For he is the most wrapped up in sin.
Come forth, sir Host, and offer first now,
And you shall kiss the relics every one,
Yes, for a groat: unbuckle now your purse.

    "No, no," said he, "then have I Christ's curse!
Let be," said he, "it shall not be so as I hope to prosper!
You would make me kiss your old breeches
And swear they are the relic of a saint,
Though by your fundament they be stained!
But by the true cross that Saint Helena found,
I would I had your balls in my hand
Instead of relics or things holy.
Let them be cut off! I will help you them carry.
They shall be enshrined in a hog's turd!"

    This Pardoner answered not a word;
So angry he was, no word would he say.

    "Now," said our Host, "I will no longer play
With you, nor with any other angry man."
But right anon the worthy Knight began,

Whan that he saugh that al the peple lough,
"Na-more of this, for it is right y-nough;
Sir Pardoner, be glad and mery of chere;
And ye, sir host, that been to me so dere,
I prey yow that ye kisse the Pardoner.
And Pardoner, I prey thee, drawe thee neer.
And, as we diden, lat us laughe and pleye."
Anon they kiste, and riden forth hir weye.

When he saw all the people laugh,
"No more of this, for it is quite enough!
Sir Pardoner, be glad and merry of cheer;
And you, sir Host, who is to me so dear,
I pray that you kiss the Pardoner.
And Pardoner, I pray you, draw yourself near,
And, as we did, let us laugh and play."
Anon they kissed, and rode forth on their way.

The Prioresses Tale

The Prologue

DOMINE, DOMINUS NOSTER
O Lord our Lord, thy name how merveillous
Is in this large worlde y-sprad—quod she:—
For noght only thy laude precious
Parfourned is by men of dignitee,
But by the mouth of children thy bountee
Parfourned is, for on the brest soukinge
Some tyme shewen they thyn heryinge.

Wherfor in laude, as I best can or may,
Of thee, and of the whyte lily flour
Which that thee bar, and is a mayde alway,
To telle a storie I wol do my labour;
Not that I may encresen hir honour;
For she hir-self is honour, and the rote
Of bountee, next hir sone, and soules bote.—

O moder mayde! o mayde moder frec!
O bush unbrent, brenninge in Moyses sighte,
That ravisedest doun fro the deitee,
Thurgh thyn humblesse, the goost that in
  th'alighte,
Of whos vertu, whan he thyn herte lighte,
Conceived was the fadres sapience,
Help me to telle it in thy reverence!

Lady! thy bountee, thy magnificence,
Thy vertu, and thy grete humilitee
Ther may no tonge expresse in no science;
For som-tyme, lady, er men praye to thee,
Thou goost biforn of thy benignitee,
And getest us the light, thurgh thy preyere,
To gyden us un-to thy sone so dere.

The Prioress's Tale

The Prologue

DOMINE, DOMINUS NOSTER
Oh Lord, our Lord, your name so marvelous
Is in this world spread—said she—
For not only your praise precious
Celebrated is by men of dignity,
But by the mouths of children your bounty
Celebrated is, for suckling at the breast
Do they celebrate your praise.[1]

Therefore in praise, as I best can or may,
Of you and of the white lily flower
Who bore you, and is a maid always,[2]
To tell a story will I do my labor;
Not that I may increase her honor,
For she herself is honor and the root
Of bounty, next to her son, and soul's healer.

Oh mother Maid, Oh maid Mother of grace!
Oh bush unburned, burning in Moses' sight,[3]
Who ravished down from the Deity,
Through your humility, the Holy Spirit who within
    you alighted,
Of whose virtue, when he your heart made light,
Conceived was the Father's knowledge,[4]
Help me tell it in your reverence!

Lady, your bounty, your magnificence,
Your virtue and your great humility
There may no tongue know how to say,
For sometimes, Lady, before men pray to you,
You go before them in your graciousness,
And bring us the light, through your prayer,
To guide us unto your Son so dear.

My conning is so wayk, o blisful quene,
For to declare thy grete worthinesse,
That I ne may the weighte nat sustene,
But as a child of twelf monthe old, or lesse,
That can unnethes any word expresse,
Right so fare I, and therfor I yow preye,
Gydeth my song that I shal of yow seye.

The Tale

Ther was in Asie, in a greet citee,
Amonges Cristen folk, a Jewerye,
Sustened by a lord of that contree
For foule usure and lucre of vilanye,
Hateful to Crist and to his companye;
And thurgh the strete men mighte ryde or wende,
For it was free, and open at either ende.

A litel scole of Cristen folk ther stood
Doun at the ferther ende, in which ther were
Children an heep, y-comen of Cristen blood,
That lerned in that scole yeer by yere
Swich maner doctrine as men used there,
This is to seyn, to singen and to rede,
As smale children doon in hir childhede.

Among thise children was a widwes sone,
A litel clergeon, seven yeer of age,
That day by day to scole was his wone,
And eek also, wher-as he saugh th'image
Of Cristes moder, hadde he in usage,
As him was taught, to knele adoun and seye
His *Ave Marie*, as he goth by the weye.

Thus hath this widwe hir litel sone y-taught
Our blisful lady, Cristes moder dere,
To worshipe ay, and he forgat it naught,
For sely child wol alday sone lere;
But ay, whan I remembre on this matere,
Seint Nicholas stant ever in my presence,
For he so yong to Crist did reverence.

My power is weak, Oh blissful Queen,
To declare your great worthiness
I may not the weight sustain;
But as a child of twelve months old, or less,
Who cannot any word express,
Right so fare I, and therefore I pray you,
Guide my song that I shall of you say.

The Tale

There was in Asia, in a great city,
Among Christian folk a Jewish ghetto,
Sustained by a lord of that country
For foul usury and profits shameful,
Hateful to Christ and all his company;
And through the street men might ride or wend,
For it was free and open at either end.

A little school of Christian folk there stood
Down at the further end, in which there were
Children many, of Christian blood,
Who learned in that school year by year
Such lessons as men taught there,
That is to say, to sing and read,
As small children do in their childhood.

Among these children was a widow's son,
A little schoolboy, seven years of age,
Who day by day to school he went,
And also, where he saw the image
Of Christ's mother, observed the custom,
As he was taught, to kneel down and say
His *Ave Maria*,[5] as he went along his way.

Thus had this widow her little son taught
Our blissful Lady, Christ's mother dear,
To worship ever, and he forgot it not,
For innocent children will ever soon learn.
But, whenever I think upon this matter,
Saint Nicholas[6] stands ever in my presence,
For he so young to Christ did revere.

This litel child, his litel book lerninge,
As he sat in the scole at his prymer,
He *Alma redemptoris* herde singe,
As children lerned hir antiphoner;
And, as he dorste, he drough him ner and ner,
And herkned ay the wordes and the note,
Til he the firste vers coude al by rote.

Noght wiste he what this Latin was to seye,
For he so yong and tendre was of age;
But on a day his felaw gan he preye
T'expounden him this song in his langage,
Or telle him why this song was in usage;
This preyde he him to construe and declare
Ful ofte tyme upon his knowes bare.

His felaw, which that elder was than he,
Answerde him thus: "this song, I have herd seye,
Was maked of our blisful lady free,
Hir to salue, and eek hir for to preye
To been our help and socour whan we deye.
I can no more expounde in this matere;
I lerne song, I can but smal grammere."

"And is this song maked in reverence
Of Cristes moder?" seyde this innocent;
"Now certes, I wol do my diligence
To comme it al, er Cristemasse is went;
Though that I for my prymer shal be shent,
And shal be beten thryës in an houre,
I wol it conne, our lady for to honoure."

His felaw taughte him homward prively,
Fro day to day, til he coude it by rote,
And than he song it wel and boldely
Fro word to word, acording with the note;
Twyës a day it passed thurgh his throte,
To scoleward and homward whan he wente;
On Cristes moder set was his entente.

This little child, his little book studying,
As he sat in the school with his primer,
He *Alma redemptoris*[7] heard sing,
As older children learned their antiphon;
And much as he dared, he to them drew close,
And harkened to the words and notes,
Till he the first verse knew by rote.

Not knew he what this Latin said,
For he so young and tender was of age.
But on a day his fellow student he began to ask
To expound for him the song in his tongue,
Or tell him why this song was sung;
This prayed he him to translate and declare
Full often time upon his knees bare.

His fellow, who older was than he,
Answered him thus: "This song, I have heard say,
Was made of our blissful lady gracious,
To salute her, and also to pray to her
To be our help and succor when we die.
I can no more expound on this matter.
I learn to sing it, but I know little grammar."[8]

"And is this song made in reverence
Of Christ's mother?" said this innocent.
"Now, certainly, I will do my best
To learn it before Christmas be here.
Though I shall neglect my primer,
And shall be beaten thrice an hour,
I will it learn to honor Our Lady!"

His fellow taught him walking home,
From day to day, till it he knew by rote,
And then he sang it well and boldly,
From word to word, and note for note,
Twice a day it passed through his throat,
To school and homeward when he went;
On Christ's mother set was his intent.

As I have seyd, thurgh-out the Jewerye
This litel child, as he cam to and fro,
Ful merily than wolde he singe, and crye
O Alma redemptoris ever-mo.
The swetnes hath his herte perced so
Of Cristes moder, that, to hir to preye,
He can nat stinte of singing by the weye.

Our firste fo, the serpent Sathanas,
That hath in Jewes herte his waspes nest,
Up swal, and seide, "O Hebraik peple, allas!
Is this to yow a thing that is honest,
That swich a boy shal walken as him lest
In your despyt, and singe of swich sentence,
Which is agayn your lawes reverence?"

Fro thennes forth the Jewes han conspyred
This innocent out of this world to chace;
An homicyde ther-to han they hyred,
That in an aley hadde a privee place;
And as the child gan for-by for to pace,
This cursed Jew him hente and heeld him faste,
And kitte his throte, and in a pit him caste.

I seye that in a wardrobe they him threwe
Wher-as these Jewes purgen hir entraille.
O cursed folk of Herodes al newe,
What may your yvel entente yow availle?
Mordre wol out, certein, it wol nat faille,
And namely ther th'onour of god shal sprede,
The blood out cryeth on your cursed dede.

"O martir, souded to virginitee,
Now maystou singen, folwing ever in oon
The whyte lamb celestial," quod she,
"Of which the grete evangelist, seint John,
In Pathmos wroot, which seith that they that goon
Biforn this lamb, and singe a song al newe,
That never, fleshly, wommen they ne knewe."

As I have said, throughout the ghetto
This little child, as he went to and fro,
Full merrily would he sing and cry
O Alma redemptoris evermore.
The sweetness his heart pierced so
Of Christ's mother that, to pray to her,
He cannot stint of singing along the way.

Our first foe, the serpent Satan,
Who had in Jews' hearts his wasp's nest,
Upswelled, and said, "Oh Hebrew people, alas!
Is this to you a thing that is decent,
That such a brat shall walk as he pleases
In your disrespect, and sing of such subjects,
To which your laws object?"

From thenceforth the Jews have conspired
This innocent out of this world to chase.
A murderer thereto have they hired,
Who in an alley had a secret place;
And as the child began past there to pace,
This cursed Jew him seized, and held him fast,
And cut his throat, and in a pit him cast.

I say that in a privy they him threw
Where these Jews purged their bowels.
Oh cursed folk of Herods[9] new,
What may your evil intent avail?
Murder will out, certainly, it will not fail,
And namely there the honor of God shall spread;
The blood cries out against your cursed deed.

Oh martyr, consecrated to virginity,
Now may you sing, following ever
The white Lamb celestial—said she—
Of which the great evangelist, Saint John,
In Patmos wrote,[10] who says that they go
Before this Lamb and sing a song all new,
Who never earthly women knew.

This povre widwe awaiteth al that night
After hir litel child, but he cam noght;
For which, as sone as it was dayes light,
With face pale of drede and bisy thoght,
She hath at scole and elles-wher him soght,
Til finally she gan so fere espye
That he last seyn was in the Jewerye.

With modres pitee in hir brest enclosed,
She gooth, as she were half out of hir minde,
To every place wher she hath supposed
By lyklihede hir litel child to finde;
And ever on Cristes moder meke and kinde
She cryde, and atte laste thus she wroghte,
Among the cursed Jewes she him soghte.

She frayneth and she preyeth pitously
To every Jew that dwelte in thilke place,
To telle hir, if hir child wente oght for-by.
They seyde, "nay"; but Jesu, of his grace,
Yaf in hir thought, inwith a litel space,
That in that place after hir sone she cryde,
Wher he was casten in a pit bisyde.

O grete god, that parfournest thy laude
By mouth of innocents, lo heer thy might!
This gemme of chastitee, this emeraude,
And eek of martirdom the ruby bright,
Ther he with throte y-corven lay upright,
He "*Alma redemptoris*" gan to singe
So loude, that al the place gan to ringe.

The Cristen folk, that thurgh the strete wente,
In coomen, for to wondre up-on this thing,
And hastily they for the provost sente;
He cam anon with-outen tarying,
And herieth Crist that is of heven king,
And eek his moder, honour of mankinde,
And after that, the Jewes leet he binde.

This poor widow awaited all that night
For her little child, but he came not;
For which, as soon as it was daylight,
With face pale with dread and anxious thought,
She has at school and elsewhere him sought,
Till finally she began to learn
That he in the Jewery was last seen.

With mother's pity in her breast enclosed,
She went, as she was half out of her mind,
To every place where she has supposed
By likelihood her little child to find;
And ever to Christ's mother meek and kind
She cried, and at last thus she wrought:
Among the cursed Jews she him sought.

She asked and she prayed piteously
To every Jew who dwelt in that place,
To tell her if her child anywhere there went.
They said "nay;" but Jesus of his grace
Has in her thought in a little while
Led her to that place where for her son she cried,
Where he was cast in the pit beside.

Oh great God, who manifests your praise
In the mouths of innocents, behold your might!
This gem of chastity, this emerald,
And also of martyrdom the ruby bright,
There with throat cut lay face upright,
He *Alma redemptoris* began to sing
So loud that all the place began to ring.

The Christian folk who along the street went
Came in to wonder upon this thing,
And hastily they for the magistrate sent;
He came anon without tarrying,
And praised Christ who is of heaven king,
And also his mother, honor of mankind,
And after that the Jews he bound.

This child with pitous lamentacioun
Up-taken was, singing his song alway;
And with honour of grete processioun
They carien him un-to the nexte abbay.
His moder swowning by the bere lay;
Unnethe might the people that was there
This newe Rachel bringe fro his bere.

With torment and with shamful deth echon
This provost dooth thise Jewes for to sterve
That of this mordre wiste, and that anon;
He nolde no swich cursednesse observe.
Yvel shal have, that yvel wol deserve.
Therfor with wilde hors he dide hem drawe,
And after that he heng hem by the lawe.

Up-on his bere ay lyth this innocent
Biforn the chief auter, whyl masse laste,
And after that, the abbot with his covent
Han sped hem for to burien him ful faste;
And whan they holy water on him caste,
Yet spak this child, whan spreynd was holy water,
And song—"*O Alma redemptoris mater!*"

This abbot, which that was an holy man
As monkes been, or elles oghten be,
This yonge child to conjure he bigan,
And seyde, "o dere child, I halse thee,
In vertu of the holy Trinitee,
Tel me what is thy cause for to singe,
Sith that they throte is cut, to my seminge?"

"My throte is cut un-to my nekke-boon,"
Seyde this child, "and, as by wey of kinde,
I sholde have deyed, ye, longe tyme agoon,
But Jesu Crist, as ye in bokes finde,
Wil that his glorie laste and be in minde;

This child with piteous lamentation
Uptaken was, singing his song always,
And with honor of great procession
They carried him unto the next abbey.
His mother swooning by his bier lay;
Hardly might the people who were there
This new Rachel bring from his bier.[11]

With torture and with shameful death,
This magistrate put those Jews to death
Who of this murder knew, and that anon.
He had never permitted such cursedness.
"Evil shall have what evil deserves";
Therefore with wild horses he did them draw,
And then he them hung as held the law.[12]

Upon this bier ever lay this innocent
Before the chief altar, while the mass lasted;
And after that, the abbot with his monks
Made haste to bury him full fast;
And when they holy water on him cast,
Yet spoke this child, when sprinkled with holy water,
And sang, *O Alma redemptoris mater!*

This abbot, who was a holy man,
As monks be—or else ought to be—
This young child to entreat he began,
And said, "Oh dear child, I beseech you,
In virtue of the holy Trinity,
Tell me what is the cause of your singing,
Since your throat was cut as it seems to me?"

"My throat is cut unto my neck bone,"
Said this child, "and by natural law
I should have died, yea, long time ago.
But Jesus Christ, as you in books find,
May his glory last and be in mind,

And, for the worship of his moder dere,
Yet may I singe 'O Alma' loude and clere.

This welle of mercy, Cristes moder swete,
I lovede alwey, as after my conninge;
And whan that I my lyf sholde forlete,
To me she cam, and bad me for to singe
This antem verraily in my deyinge,
As ye han herd, and, whan that I had songe,
Me thoughte, she leyde a greyn up-on my tonge.

Wherfor I singe, and singe I moot certeyn
In honour of that blisful mayden free,
Til fro my tonge of-taken is the greyn;
And afterward thus seyde she to me,
'My litel child, now wol I fecche thee
Whan that the greyn is fro thy tonge y-take;
Be nat agast, I wol thee nat forsake.' "

This holy monk, this abbot, him mene I,
Him tonge out-caughte, and took a-wey the greyn,
And he yaf up the goost ful softely.
And whan this abbot had this wonder seyn,
His salte teres trikled doun as reyn,
And gruf he fil al plat up-on the grounde,
And stille he lay as he had been y-bounde.

The covent eek lay on the pavement
Weping, and herien Cristes moder dere,
And after that they ryse, and forth ben went,
And toke awey this martir fro his bere,
And in a tombe of marbul-stones clere
Enclosen they his litel body swete;
Ther he is now, god leve us for to mete.

O yonge Hugh of Lincoln, slayn also
With cursed Jewes, as it is notable,
For it nis but a litel whyle ago;

And for the worship of his Mother dear
Yet may I sing *O Alma* loud and clear.

"This well of mercy, Christ's mother sweet,
I loved always, as after my understanding;
And when I my life forfeited,
To me she came, and bade me to sing
This psalm truly in my dying,
As you have heard, and when I had sung,
I thought she laid a seed upon my tongue.

"Therefore I sing, and sing most certain,
In honor of that blissful Maid of mercy
Till from my tongue removed is the seed;
And after that thus she said to me:
'My little child, now will I fetch you,
When the seed is from your tongue taken.
Be not afraid, I will not you forsake.'"

This holy monk, this abbot, I mean,
His tongue grasped, and took away the seed,
And he gave up the ghost full softly.
And when this abbot had this wonder seen,
His salt tears trickled down as rain,
And face down he fell flat upon the ground,
And still he lay as if he were bound.

These monks they lay upon the pavement
Weeping, and praising Christ's mother dear,
And after that they rose, and forth they went,
And took away this martyr from his bier;
And in a tomb of marble shining bright
Enclosed they his little body sweet.
There he is now, God grant that we may meet!

Oh young Hugh of Lincoln,[13] slain also
By cursed Jews, as it is well known,
For it was but a little while ago,

Preye eek for us, we sinful folk unstable,
That, of his mercy, god so merciable
On us his grete mercy multiplye,
For reverence of his moder Marye. Amen.

Pray also for us, we sinful folk unstable,
Who in his mercy may God so merciful
Toward us his great mercy multiply,
In reverence of his mother Mary. Amen.

The Nonne Preestes Tale

The Prologue

"Ho!" QUOD THE KNIGHT, "good sir, na-more of this,
That ye han seyd is right y-nough, y-wis,
And mochel more; for litel hevinesse
Is right y-nough to mochel folk, I gesse.
I seye for me, it is a greet disese
Wher-as men han ben in greet welthe and ese,
To heren of hir sodeyn fal, allas!
And the contrarie is joie and greet solas,
As whan a man hath been in povre estaat,
And clymbeth up, and wexeth fortunat,
And ther abydeth in prosperitee,
Swich thing is gladson, as it thinketh me,
And of swich thing were goodly for to telle."
"Ye," quod our hoste, "by seint Poules belle,
Ye seye right sooth; this monk, he clappeth loude,
He spak how 'fortune covered with a cloude'
I noot never what, and als of a 'Tragedie'
Right now ye herde, and parde! no remedie
It is for to biwaille ne compleyne
That that is doon, and als it is a peyne,
As ye han seyd, to here of hevinesse.
Sir monk, na-more of this, so god yow blesse!
Your tale anoyeth al this companye;
Swich talking is nat worth a boterflye;
For ther-in is ther no desport ne game.
Wherfor, sir Monk, or dan Piers by your name,
I preye yow hertely, telle us somwhat elles
For sikerly, nere clinking of your belles,
That on your brydel hange on every syde,
By heven king, that for us alle dyde,
I sholde er this han fallen doun for slepe,
Although the slough had never been so depe;
Than had your tale al be told in vayn.
For certeinly, as that thise clerkes seyn,
'Wher-as a man may have noon audience,

The Nun's Priest's Tale

The Prologue

"STOP!" SAID THE KNIGHT, "good sir, no more of this:[1]
What you have said is right enough, indeed,
And much more than enough, for a little seriousness
Is right enough for many folk, I guess.
I say for me it is a great discomfort,
There where men have been in great wealth and ease,
To hear of their sudden fall, alas!
And the contrary is joy and great solace,
As when a man has been in poverty,
And climbs up, and waxes lucky,
And there abides in prosperity—
Such a thing is gladsome, as it seems to me,
And of such things it is goodly for to tell."
"Yes," said our Host, "by Saint Paul's bell,
You say right truly: this Monk, he chatters loud.
He spoke 'How Fortune covered with a cloud'—
I know not what. And also of 'tragedy'
Right now you heard, and, by God! no remedy
It is for to bewail or complain
That which is done, and besides it is a pain,
As you have said, to hear seriousness.
Sir Monk, no more of this, so God you bless!
Your tale annoys all this company.
Such talking is not worth a butterfly,
For therein there is no pleasure or game.
Wherefore, sir Monk, or sir Piers by your name,
I pray you heartily tell us something else,
For certainly, were it not for the clinking of your bells
That on your bridle hang on every side,
By Heaven's king who for us all died,
I should before this have fallen down, asleep,
Even if the mud had been ever so deep.
Then would your tale have been told all in vain;
For certainly, just as these scholars say,
'There where a man may have no audience,

537

Noght helpeth it to tellen his sentence.'
And wel I woot the substance is in me,
If any thing shal wel reported be.
Sir, sey somwhat of hunting, I yow preye."
"Nay," quod this monk, "I have no lust to pleye;
Now let another telle, as I hav told."
Than spak our host, with rude speche and bold,
And seyde un-to the Nonnes Preest anon,
"Com neer, thou preest, com hider, thou sir John,
Tel us swich thing as may our hertes glade,
Be blythe, though thou ryde up-on a jade.
What though thyn hors be bothe foule and lene,
If he wol serve thee, rekke nat a bene;
Look that thyn herte be mery evermo."
"Yis, sir," quod he, "yis, host, so mote I go,
But I be mery, y-wis, I wol be blamed:"—
And right anon his tale he hath attamed,
And thus he seyde un-to us everichon,
This swete preest, this goodly man, sir John.

The Tale

A povre widwe, somdel stape in age,
Was whylom dwelling in a narwe cotage,
Bisyde a grove, stonding in a dale.
This widwe, of which I telle yow my tale,
Sin thilke day that she was last a wyf,
In pacience ladde a ful simple lyf,
For litel was hir catel and hir rente;
By housbondrye, of such as God hir sente,
She fond hir-self, and eek hir doghtren two.
Three large sowes hadde she, and namo,
Three kyn, and eek a sheep that highte Malle,
Ful sooty was hir bour, and eek hir halle,
In which she eet ful many a sclendre meel.
Of poynaunt sauce hir neded never a deel.
No deyntee morsel passed thurgh hir throte;
Hir dyete was accordant to hir cote.
Repleccioun ne made hir never syk;
Attempree dyete was al hir phisyk,

Nought helps to tell of his message.'
And well I know I understand the meaning,
If anything well reported be.
Sir, say somewhat of hunting, I you pray."
"Nay," said the monk, "I have no desire to play;
Now let another tell, as I have my tale told."
Then spoke our Host, with rude speech and bold,
And said unto the Nun's Priest anon,
"Come nearer, you priest, come hither, you sir John,
Tell us such thing as may our hearts gladden.
Be blithe, though you ride upon a nag!
What though your horse be both foul and lean?
If he will serve you, care not a bean.
Look that your heart be merry evermore."
"Yes, sir," said he. "Yes, Host, as I may thrive,
Unless I be merry, truly, I will be blamed."
And right anon his tale he began,
And thus he said unto us every one,
This sweet priest, this goodly man sir John.

The Tale

A poor widow, somewhat advanced in years,
Was once dwelling in a small cottage,
Beside a grove, standing in a dale.
This widow of whom I tell you my tale,
Since that same day that she was last a wife,
In patience led a full simple life,
For she had little goods or chattel.
By careful making do with what God her sent
She provided for herself and also her daughters two.
Three large sows had she and no more,
Three cows, and a sheep that was called Malle.
Full sooty was her bedchamber, and dining hall,
In which she ate full many a slender meal.
Of pungent sauce she needed never a portion:
No dainty morsel passed through her throat.
Her diet was frugal as her coat—
Surfeit never made her ill.
A temperate diet was her only pill,

And exercyse, and hertes suffisaunce.
The goute lette hir no-thing for to daunce,
N'apoplexye shente nat hir heed;
No wyn ne drank she, neither whyt ne reed;
Hir bord was served most with whyt and blak,
Milk and broun breed, in which she fond no lak,
Seynd bacoun, and somtyme an ey or tweye,
For she was as it were a maner deye.
      A yerd she hadde, enclosed al aboute
With stikkes, and a drye dich with oute,
In which she hadde a cok, hight Chauntecleer,
In al the land of crowing nas his peer.
His vois was merier than the mery orgon
On messe-dayes that in the chirche gon;
Wel sikerer was his crowing in his logge,
Than is a clokke, or an abbey orlogge.
By nature knew he ech ascencioun
Of equinoxial in thilke toun;
For whan degrees fiftene were ascended,
Thanne crew he, that it mighte nat ben amended.
His comb was redder than the fyn coral,
And batailed, as it were a castel-wal.
His bile was blak, and as the jeet it shoon;
Lyk asur were his legges, and his toon;
His nayles whytter than the lilie flour,
And lyk the burned gold was his colour.
This gentil cok hadde in his governaunce
Sevene hennes, for to doon al his plesaunce,
Whiche were his sustres and his paramours,
And wonder lyk to him, as of colours.
Of whiche the faireste hewed on hir throte
Was cleped faire damoysele Pertelote.
Curteys she was, discreet, and debonaire,
And compaignable, and bar hir-self so faire,
Sin thilke day that she was seven night old,
That trewely she hath the herte in hold
Of Chauntecleer loken in every lith;
He loved hir so, that wel was him therwith.
But such a joye was it to here hem singe,

And exercise, and heart's content.
No gout kept her from dancing,
Nor did apoplexy injure her head.
No wine drank she, neither white nor red;
Her table was served most with white and black—
Milk and brown bread, in which she found no fault,
Bacon fried, and sometimes an egg or two,
For she was a kind of dairy woman.
   A yard she had, fenced all about
With sticks, and a dry ditch without,
In which she had a cock called Chanticleer:[2]
In all the land at crowing there was not his peer.
His voice was merrier than the merry organ
On feast days that in the church they play;
More certain was his crowing in his lodge
Than is a clock or the abbey's *horloge*.[3]
By nature knew he each ascension
Of the equinox in that same town.
For when degrees fifteen were ascended,
Then crowed he, so well it might not be amended.
His comb was redder than the fine coral,
And notched as if it were a castle wall.
His bill was black, and jet black it shone;
Like azure were his legs and his toes;
His nails whiter than the lily flower,
And like burnished gold was his color.
This gentle cock had in his governance
Seven hens, for to do all his pleasure,
Which were his sisters and his paramours,
And wonderfully like to him, in color,
Of which the fairest-colored on her throat
Was called *Mademoiselle* Pertelote.
Courteous she was, discreet and gracious,
And sociable, and bore herself so fair,
Since that day she was seven nights old,
That truly she had the heart in hold
Of Chanticleer, locked in every limb;
He loved her so, that therewith well was him.
But such a joy was it to hear them sing,

Whan that the brighte sonne gan to springe,
In swete accord, "my lief is faren in londe."
For thilke tyme, as I have understonde,
Bestes and briddes coude speke and singe.

And so bifel, that in a daweninge,
As Chauntecleer among his wyves alle
Sat on his perche, that was in the halle,
And next him sat this faire Pertelote,
This Chauntecleer gan gronen in his throte,
As man that in his dreem is drecched sore.
And whan that Pertelote thus herde him rore,
She was agast, and seyde, "O herte dere,
What eyleth yow, to grone in this manere?
Ye been a verray sleper, fy for shame!"

And he answerde and seyde thus, "madame,
I pray yow, that ye take it nat a-grief:
By god, me mette I was in swich meschief
Right now, that yet myn herte is sore afright.
Now god," quod he, "my swevene recche
    aright,
And keep my body out of foul prisoun!
Me mette, how that I romed up and doun
Withinne our yerde, wher-as I saugh a beste,
Was lyk an hound, and wolde han maad areste
Upon my body, and wolde han had me deed.
His colour was bitwixe yelwe and reed;
And tipped was his tail, and bothe his eres,
With blak, unlyk the remenant of his heres;
His snowte smal, with glowinge eyen tweye.
Yet of his look for fere almost I deye;
This caused me my groning, doutelees."

"Avoy!" quod she, "fy on yow, hertelees!
Allas!" quod she, "for, by that god above,
Now han ye lost myn herte and al my love;
I can nat love a coward, by my feith.
For certes, what so any womman seith,
We alle desyren, if it mighte be,
To han housbondes hardy, wyse, and free,
And secree, and no nigard, ne no fool,

When that the bright sun began to rise,
In sweet harmony, "my love has gone far away."[4]
For in those days, as I have understood,
Beasts and birds could speak and sing.

    And so it happened, one morning at dawning,
As Chanticleer among his wives all
Sat on his perch that was in the hall,
And next to him sat this fair Pertelote,
This Chanticleer began groaning in his throat
As a man who in his dream is troubled sore.
And when that Pertelote thus heard him roar,
She was afraid, and said, "Heart dear,
What ails you to groan in this manner?
You're a fine sleeper, fie for shame!"

    And he answered and said thus, "Madame,
I pray you, that you take it not amiss:
By God, I dreamed I was in such trouble
Right now, that yet my heart is sore afright.
Now God," said he, "my dream help me understand
    aright,
And keep my body out of foul prison!
I dreamed that I roamed up and down
Within our yard, where I saw a beast,
That was like a hound and would have laid hold
Upon my body, and would have had me dead.
His color was between yellow and red,
And tipped was his tail and both his ears
With black, unlike the rest of his hairs;
His snout small, with glowing eyes two.
Still of his look for fear I almost die:
This caused me my groaning, doubtless."

    "Go on!" said she, "fie on you, gutless!
Alas!" said she, "for, by that God above,
Now have you lost my heart and my love.
I cannot love a coward, by my faith!
For certainly, what so any woman says,
We all desire, if it might be,
To have husbands bold, wise and generous,
And discreet, and no niggard, nor a fool,

Ne him that is agast of every tool,
Ne noon avauntour, by that god above!
How dorste ye seyn for shame unto your love,
That any thing mighte make yow aferd?
Have ye no mannes herte, and han a berd?
Allas! and conne ye been agast of swevenis?
No-thing, god wot, but vanitee, in sweven is.
Swevenes engendren of replecciouns,
And ofte of fume, and of complecciouns,
Whan humours been to habundant in a wight.
Certes this dreem, which ye han met to-night,
Cometh of the grete superfluitee
Of youre rede *colera*, pardee,
Which causeth folk to dreden in here dremes
Of arwes, and of fyr with rede lemes,
Of grete bestes, that they wol hem byte,
Of contek, and of whelpes grete and lyte;
Right as the humour of malencolye
Causeth ful many a man, in sleep, to crye,
For fere of blake beres, or boles blake,
Or elles, blake develes wole hem take.
Of othere humours coude I telle also,
That werken many a man in sleep ful wo;
But I wol passe as lightly as I can.
    Lo Catoun, which that was so wys a man,
Seyde he nat thus, ne do no fors of dremes?
Now, sire," quod she, "whan we flee fro the bemes,
For Goddes love, as tak som laxatyf;
Up peril of my soule, and of my lyf,
I counseille yow the beste, I wol nat lye,
That bothe of colere and of malencolye
Ye purge yow; and for ye shul nat tarie,
Though in this toun is noon apotecarie,
I shal my-self to herbes techen yow,
That shul ben for your hele, and for your prow;
And in our yerd tho herbes shal I finde,
The wiche han of hir propretee, by kinde,
To purgen yow binethe, and eek above.
Forget not this, for goddes owene love!

Nor him who is afraid of every weapon,
Nor a braggart. By that God above,
How dare you say for shame unto your love
That anything might make you afraid?
Have you no man's heart, and have a beard?
Alas! and can you be afraid of dreams?
Nothing, God knows, but foolishness in dreaming is.
Dreams are born of surfeits,
And often of vapors, and of complexion,
When humors be too abundant in a person.
Certainly this dream, which you have had tonight,
Comes of the great superfluity
Of your red humor, by God,
Which causes folk to fear in their dreams
Arrows, and fire with red flames,
Red beasts, that will them bite,
Of conflict, and of dogs great and little;
Right as the humor of melancholy
Causes full many a man in sleep to cry
For fear of black bears, or bulls black,
Or else that black devils will him take.
Of other humors could I tell also
That work many a man in sleep great woe;
But I will pass as lightly as I can.
    Look at Cato,[5] who was so wise a man,
Said he not thus, 'Give dreams no attention'?
Now sir," said she, "when we fly from the beams,
For God's love, take some laxative.
On peril of my soul and of my life
I counsel you the best, I will not lie,
That both of choler and of melancholy
You purge yourself; and so that you shall not tarry,
Though in this town is no apothecary,
I shall myself to herbs direct you,
That shall be for your health and for your good;
And in our yard those herbs shall I find
Which have of their property by nature
To purge you beneath and also above.
Forget not this, for God's own love!

Ye been ful colerik of compleccioun.
Ware the sonne in his ascencioun
Ne fynde yow nat repleet of humours hote;
And if it do, I dar wel leye a grote,
That ye shul have a fevere terciane,
Or an agu, that may be youre bane.
A day or two ye shul have digestyves
Of wormes, er ye take your laxatyves,
Of lauriol, centaure, and fumetere,
Or elles of ellebor, that groweth there,
Of catapuce, or of gaytres beryis,
Of erbe yve, growing in our yerd, that mery is;
Pekke hem up right as they growe, and ete hem in.
Be mery, housbond, for your fader kin!
Dredeth no dreem; I can say yow na-more."
      "Madame," quod he, "*graunt mercy* of your lore.
But nathelees, as touching daun Catoun,
That hath of wisdom such a greet renoun,
Though that he had no dremes for to drede,
By god, men may in olde bokes rede
Of many a man, more of auctoritee
Than ever Catoun was, so mote I thee,
That al the revers seyn of his sentence,
And han wel founden by experience,
That dremes ben significaciouns,
As wel of joye as tribulaciouns
That folk enduren in this lyf present.
Ther nedeth make of this noon argument;
The verray preve sheweth it in dede.
      Oon of the gretteste auctours that men rede
Seith thus, that whylom two felawes wente
On pilgrimage, in a ful good entente;
And happed so, thay come into a toun,
Wher-as ther was swich congregacioun
Of peple, and eek so streit of herbergage
That they ne founde as muche as o cotage
In which they bothe mighte y-logged be.
Wherfor thay mosten, of necessitee,
As for that night, departen compaignye;

You are choleric in your temperament.
Beware the sun in his ascension.
Nor fill yourself with humors hot;
And if you do, I will bet a lot,
That a fever will to you every third day return,
Or an ague, that may be your end.
A day or two you shall have digestives
Of worms, before you take your laxatives,
Of spurge-laurel, centaury, and fumitory,
Or else of hellebore that grows there,
Of caper-spurge, or of dogwood's berries,
Of herb ivy, growing in our yard, where it is pleasant.
Peck them right up as they grow, and eat them in.
Be merry, husband, for your father's kin!
Dread no dream: I can say you no more."

   "*Madame*," said he, "*merci beaucoup*[6] for your lore.
But nevertheless, as touching sir Cato,
Who has of wisdom such a great renown,
Though he bade us no dreams to dread,
By God, men may in old books read
Of many a man, more of authority
Than ever Cato was, as I may prosper,
That all the opposite of his opinion were,
And well founded by experience,
That dreams are signs
As much of joy as tribulations
That folk endure in this life present.
There need be made of this no argument:
The true proof is in the deed.

   One of the greatest authors[7] who men read
Says thus, that once two companions went
On pilgrimage, in a full good intent;
And it happened so that they came into a town
Where there was such crowd
Of people, and such a dearth of lodging,
That they found not so much as a cottage
In which they both might sheltered be.
Wherefore they had to of necessity,
For that night, part company;

And ech of hem goth to his hostelrye,
And took his logging as it wolde falle.
That oon of hem was logged in a stalle,
Fer in a yerd, with oxen of the plough;
That other man was logged wel y-nough,
As was his aventure, or his fortune,
That us governeth alle as in commune.

    And so bifel, that, longe er it were day,
This man mette in his bed, ther-as he lay,
How that his felawe gan up-on him calle,
And seyde, 'allas! for in an oxes stalle
This night I shal be mordred ther I lye.
Now help me, dere brother, ere I dye;
In alle haste com to me,' he sayde.
This man out of his sleep for fere abrayde;
But whan that he was wakned of his sleep,
He turned him, and took of this no keep;
Him thoughte his dreem nas but a vanitee.
Thus twyës in his sleping dremed he.
And atte thridde tyme yet his felawe
Cam, as him thoughte, and seide, 'I am now slawe;
Bihold my blody woundes, depe and wyde!
Arys up erly in the morwe-tyde,
And at the west gate of the toun,' quod he,
'A carte ful of dong ther shaltow see,
In which my body is hid ful prively;
Do thilke carte aresten boldely.
My gold caused my mordre, sooth to sayn;'
And tolde him every poynt how he was slayn,
With a ful pitous face, pale of hewe.
And truste wel, his dreem he fond ful trewe;
For on the morwe, as sone as it was day,
To his felawes in he took the way;
And whan that he cam to this oxes stalle,
After his felawe he bigan to calle.

    The hostiler answered him anon,
And seyde, 'sire, your felawe is agon,
As sone as day he wente out of the toun.'
This man gan fallen in suspecioun,

And each of them went to his hostelry,
And took his lodging as his lot fell.
And one of them was lodged in a stall,
Far off in a yard, with oxen of the plough;
That other man was lodged well enough,
As was his chance or his fortune,
That governs us all in common.
    And so it befell that, long before it was day,
This man dreamed in his bed, there as he lay,
How that first fellow began to him call,
And said, 'Alas! for in an ox's stall
This night I shall be murdered where I lie.
Now help me, dear brother, or I die;
In all haste come back to me,' he said.
This man out of his fear upstarted,
But when that he was wakened from his sleep,
He turned over, and took of this no heed:
He thought his dream was but in vain.
Thus twice in his sleep dreamed he;
And at the third time yet his friend
Came, as he thought, and said, 'I am now slain.
Behold my bloody wounds, deep and wide!
Arise up early in the morningtide,
And at the west gate of the town,' said he,
'A cartful of dung there shall you see,
In which my body is hid full secretly:
Have this cart stopped boldly.
My gold caused my murder, truth to tell;'
And told him every point how he was slain,
With a full piteous face, pale of hue.
And trust well, his dream he found full true,
For on the morrow, as soon as it was day,
To his fellow's inn he took his way;
And when that he came to this ox's stall,
After his fellow he began to call.
    The innkeeper answered him anon,
And said, 'Sir, your fellow is a-gone:
As soon as day he went out of the town.'
This man became suspicious,

Remembring on his dremes that he mette,
And forth he goth, no lenger wolde he lette,
Unto the west gate of the toun, and fond
A dong-carte, as it were to donge lond,
That was arrayed in the same wyse
As ye han herd the dede man devyse;
And with an hardy herte he gan to crye
Vengeaunce and justice of this felonye:—
'My felawe mordred is this same night,
And in this carte he lyth gapinge upright.
I crye out on the ministres,' quod he,
'That sholden kepe and reulen this citee;
Harrow! allas! her lyth my felawe slayn!'
What sholde I more un-to this tale sayn?
The peple out-sterte, and caste the cart to grounde,
And in the middel of the dong they founde
The dede man, that mordred was al newe.

O blisful god, that art so just and trewe!
Lo, how that thou biwreyest mordre alway!
Mordre wol out, that see we day by day.
Mordre is so wlatsom and abhominable
To god, that is so just and resonable,
That he ne wol nat suffre it heled be;
Though it abyde a yeer, or two, or three,
Mordre wol out, this my conclusioun.
And right anoon, ministres of that toun
Han hent the carter, and so sore him pyned,
And eek the hostiler so sore engyned,
That they biknewe hir wikkednesse anoon,
And were an-hanged by the nekke-boon.

Here may men seen that dremes been to drede
And certes, in the same book I rede,
Right in the nexte chapitre after this,
(I gabbe nat, so have I joye or blis,)
Two men that wolde han passed over see,
For certeyn cause, in-to a fer contree,
If that the wind ne hadde been contrarie,
That made hem in a citee for to tarie,
That stood ful mery upon an haven-syde.

Remembering in his dreams whom he saw,
And forth he went, no longer would he delay,
Unto the west gate of the town, and found
A dung-cart, heading out as if to fertilize,
That was arranged in the same way
As you have heard the dead man describe.
And with a bold heart he began to cry,
'Vengeance and justice of this felony!
My fellow murdered is this same night,
And in this cart he lies, eyes with no sight.
I cry out to the officers,' said he,
'Who should care for and rule this city,
Help! Alas! here lies my fellow slain!'
What should I more unto this tale say?
The people came out, and cast the cart to ground,
And in the middle of the dung they found
The dead man, murdered newly.

    Oh blissful God, who is so just and true!
Behold, how you reveal murder always!
Murder will out, that see we day by day.
Murder is so loathsome, and abominable
To God, who is so just and reasonable,
That he would not suffer it to be concealed.
Though it remains hidden a year, or two, or three,
Murder will out, this is my conclusion.
And right away, ministers of that town
Seized the carter and so sore him tortured,
And also the innkeeper so sore racked,
That they owned up to their wickedness soon,
And were hanged by the neck-bone.

    Here may men see that dreams are to be feared.
And certainly, in the same book I read,
Right in the next chapter after this—
I lie not, so may I have joy or bliss—
Two men who wished to travel over sea,
For a certain purpose, to a far country,
If the wind had not been contrary:
That made them in a city for to tarry
That stood full merry upon a harbor side.

But on a day, agayn the even-tyde,
The wind gan chaunge, and blew right as hem leste.
Jolif and glad they wente un-to hir reste,
And casten hem ful erly for to saille;
But to that oo man fil a greet mervaille.
That oon of hem, in sleping as he lay,
Him mette a wonder dreem, agayn the day;
Him thoughte a man stood by his beddes syde,
And him comaunded, that he sholde abyde,
And seyde him thus, 'if thou to-morwe wende,
Thou shalt be dreynt; my tale is at an ende.'
He wook, and tolde his felawe what he mette,
And preyde him his viage for to lette;
As for that day, he preyde him to abyde.
His felawe, that lay by his beddes syde,
Gan for to laughe, and scorned him ful faste.
'No dreem,' quod he, 'may so myn herte agaste,
That I wol lette for to do my thinges.
I sette not a straw by thy dreminges,
For swevenes been but vanitees and japes.
Men dreme al-day of owles or of apes,
And eke of many a mase therwithal;
Men dreme of thing that never was ne shal.
But sith I see that thou wolt heer abyde,
And thus for-sleuthen wilfully thy tyde,
God wot it reweth me; and have good day.'
And thus he took his leve, and wente his way.
But er that he hadde halfe his cours y-seyled,
Noot I nat why, ne what mischaunce it eyled,
But casuelly the shippes botme rente,
And ship and man under the water wente
In sighte of othere shippes it byside,
That with hem seyled at the same tyde.
And therfor, faire Pertelote so dere,
By swiche ensamples olde maistow lere,
That no man sholde been to recchelees
Of dremes, for I sey thee, doutelees,
That many a dreem ful sore is for to drede.
　　Lo, in the lyf of seint Kenelm, I rede,

But on a day, toward eveningtide,
The wind began to shift, and blew as they wished.
Jolly and glad they went unto their rest,
And they planned full early to sail;
But harken! To one man befell a great marvel.
That one of them, in sleeping as he lay,
He dreamed a wonderful dream, toward the day:
He dreamed a man stood by his bedside,
And him commanded that he should abide,
And said to him thus, 'If you tomorrow wend,
You will be drowned: my tale is at an end.'
He woke, and told his fellow what he dreamed,
And prayed him his voyage to delay;
Just for that day, he prayed him to stay.
His fellow, who lay in the next bed,
Began to laugh, and him scorned.
'No dream,' said he, 'may so my heart scare
That I will fail to keep my plans.
I set not a straw by dreams,
For dreams be but illusions and japes.[8]
Men dream all day of owls or apes,
And also of many other things weird;
Men dream of things that never shall be or were.
But since I see that you will here abide,
And thus so slothily waste your time,
God knows I'm sorry, and good day.'
And thus he took his leave, and went his way.
But before he had half his course sailed,
Know not I why, nor what mischance it ailed,
But by chance the ship's bottom was open rent,
And ship and man under water went
In sight of other ships nearby,
That with them sailed on the same tide.
And therefore, fair Pertelote so dear,
By such old examples may you learn
That no man should be too heedless
Of dreams, for I say to you doubtless,
That many a dream is greatly to be feared.
  Look, in the life of Saint Kenelm[9] I read,

That was Kenulphus sone, the noble king
Of mercenrike, how Kenelm mette a thing;
A lyte er he was mordred, on a day,
His mordre in his avisioun he say.
His norice him expouned every del
His sweven, and bad him for to kepe him wel
For traisoun; but he nas but seven yeer old,
And therfore litel tale hath he told
Of any dreem, so holy was his herte.
By god, I hadde lever than my sherte
That ye had rad his legende, as have I.
Dam Pertelote, I sey yow trewely,
Macrobeus, that writ th'avisioun
In Affrike of the worthy Cipioun,
Affermeth dremes, and seith that they been
Warning of thinges that men after seen.

    And forther-more, I pray yow loketh wel
In th'olde testament, of Daniel,
If he held dremes any vanitee.
Reed eek of Joseph, and ther shul ye see
Wher dremes ben somtyme (I sey nat alle)
Warning of thinges that shul after falle.
Loke of Egipt the king, daun Pharao,
His bakere and his boteler also,
Wher they ne felte noon effect in dremes.
Who-so wol seken actes of sondry remes,
May rede of dremes many a wonder thing.

    Lo Cresus, which that was of Lyde king,
Mette he nat that he sat upon a tree,
Which signified he sholde anhanged be?
Lo heer Andromacha, Ectores wyf,
That day that Ector sholde lese his lyf,
She dremed on the same night biforn,
How that the lyf of Ector sholde be lorn,
If thilke day he wente in-to bataille;
She warned him, but it mighte nat availle;
He wente for to fighte nathelees,
But he was slayn anoon of Achilles.
But thilke tale is al to long to telle,

Who was King Cenwulf's son, the noble king
Of Mercia, how Kenelm dreamed a thing
A little before he was murdered on a day.
His murder in his vision he saw.
His nurse expounded every part
Of his dream, and bade him to guard himself
Against treason; but he was only seven years old,
And therefore little did he take note
Of any dream, so holy was his heart.
By God, I'd give you my shirt
If you had read his legend as I did.
Dame Pertelote, I say to you truly,
Macrobius,[10] who wrote the treatise
In Africa of the worthy Scipio,
Affirms dreams, and says that they be
Warnings of things that men afterward see.

    And furthermore, I pray you look well
In the Old Testament, of Daniel,
If he held dreams but vanity.
Read also of Joseph,[11] and there you shall see
Where dreams be sometime (I say not all)
Warnings of things that shall after befall.
Look at the Egyptian king, sir Pharaoh,
His baker and his butler also,
See whether they believed in dreams or no.
Whoso would seek histories of sundry realms
May read of dreams many a wondrous thing.

    Look at Croesus, who was of Lydia king,
Did he not dream that he sat upon a tree,
Which signified that he should hanged be?
Look here at Andromacha, Hector's wife,
That day that Hector would lose his life,
She dreamed on the same night before,
How the life of Hector should be lost
If that day he went into battle;
She warned him, but to no avail;
He went to fight nevertheless,
But he was slain anon by Achilles.
But this tale is all too long to tell,

And eek it is ny day, I may nat dwelle.
Shortly I seye, as for conclusioun,
That I shal han of this avisioun
Adversitee; and I seye forther-more,
That I ne telle of laxatyves no store,
For they ben venimous, I woot it wel;
I hem defye, I love hem never a del.

    Now let us speke of mirthe, and stinte al this;
Madame Pertelote, so have I blis,
Of o thing god hath sent me large grace;
For whan I see the beautee of your face,
Ye ben so scarlet-reed about your yën,
It maketh al my drede for to dyen;
For, also siker as *In principio*,
Mulier est hominis confusio;
Madame, the sentence of this Latin is—
Womman is mannes joye and al his blis.
For whan I fele a-night your softe syde,
Al-be-it that I may nat on you ryde,
For that our perche is maad, so narwe, alas!
I am so ful of joye and of solas
That I defye bothe sweven and dreem."
And with that word he fley doun fro the beem,
For it was day, and eek his hennes alle;
And with a chuk he gan hem for to calle,
For he had founde a corn, lay in the yerd.
Royal he was, he was namore aferd;
He fethered Pertelote twenty tyme,
And trad as ofte, er that it was pryme.
He loketh as it were a grim leoun;
And on his toos he rometh up and doun,
Him deyned not to sette his foot to grounde.
He chukketh, whan he hath a corn y-founde,
And to him rennen thanne his wyves alle.
Thus royal, as a prince is in his halle,
Leve I this Chauntecleer in his pasture;
And after wol I telle his aventure.

    Whan that the month in which the world bigan,
That highte March, whan god first maked man,

And also it is near daybreak, I may not dwell.
Briefly I say, in conclusion,
That I shall have from this vision
Adversity; and I say furthermore,
That I set in laxatives no store,
For they be poisonous, I know it well;
I them defy, I love them not at all.
    Now let us speak of mirth and stop all this;
Madame Pertelote, so I have bliss,
Of one thing God has sent me bounteous grace:
For when I see the beauty of your face—
You be so scarlet red about your eyes—
It makes me fear the more to die.
—Just as surely as *in principio,*
Mulier est hominis confusio.[12]
Madame, the meaning of this Latin is
'Woman is man's joy and all his bliss.'
For when I feel at night your soft side,
Albeit that I may not on you ride,
Because our perch is made so narrow, alas!
I am so full of joy and comfort
That I defy both dream and vision."
And with that word he flew down from the beam,
For it was day, and so did his hens all,
And with a cluck he began them to call,
For he had found grain spread in the yard.
Regal he was, he was no more afraid;
He covered Pertelote with his wings twenty times,
And trod her just as often, before the bell rang prime.
He looked as if he were a proud lion,
And on his toes he roamed up and down—
He deigned not to set his foot to ground.
He clucked when he had a bit of grain found,
And to him ran then his wives all.
Thus royal, as a prince in his hall,
Leave I this Chanticleer at his dinner
And after will I tell of his adventure.
    When the month in which the world began,
That is called March, when God first made man,

Was complet, and passed were also,
Sin March bigan, thritty dayes and two,
Bifel that Chauntecleer, in al his pryde,
His seven wyves walking by his syde,
Caste up his eyen to the brighte sonne,
That in the signe of Taurus hadde y-roone
Twenty degrees and oon, and somwhat more;
And knew by kynde, and by noon other lore,
That it was pryme, and crew with blisful stevene.
"The sonne," he sayde, "is clomben up on hevene
Fourty degrees and oon, and more, y-wis.
Madame Pertelote, my worldes blis,
Herkneth thise blisful briddes how they singe,
And see the fresshe floures how they springe;
Ful is myn herte of revel and solas."
But sodeinly him fil a sorweful cas;
For ever the latter ende of joye is wo.
God woot that worldly joye is sone ago;
And if a rethor coude faire endyte,
He in a cronique saufly mighte it wryte,
As for a sovereyn notabilitee.
Now every wys man, lat him herkne me;
This storie is al-so trewe, I undertake,
As is the book of Launcelot de Lake,
That wommen holde in ful gret reverence.
Now wol I torne agayn to my sentence.

A col-fox, ful of sly iniquitee,
That in the grove hadde woned yeres three,
By heigh imaginacioun forn-cast,
The same night thurgh-out the hegges brast
Into the yerd, ther Chauntecleer the faire
Was wont, and eek his wyves, to repaire;
And in a bed of wortes stille he lay,
Til it was passed undern of the day,
Wayting his tyme on Chauntecleer to falle,
As gladly doon thise homicydes alle,
That in awayt liggen to mordre men.
O false mordrer, lurking in thy den!
O newe Scariot, newe Genilon!

Was complete, and passed were,
Since March began, thirty days and two,
It came to pass that Chanticleer, in all his pride,
His seven wives walking by his side,
Cast up his eyes to the bright sun,
That in the sign of Taurus had then run
Twenty degrees and one, and somewhat more;
And knew by nature, and no other lore,
That it was prime, and crowed with blissful voice.
"The sun," he said, "has climbed up in heaven
Forty degrees and one, and more, I know.
Madame Pertelote, my world's bliss,
Listen to these blissful birds, how they sing,
And see the fresh flowers, how they spring;
Full is my heart of joy and comfort."
But suddenly befell him a sorrowful event,
For ever the latter end of joy is woe.
God knows that worldly joy is soon gone;
And if a rhetorician could it well indite,
He in a chronicle safely might write
That as a sovereign actuality.
Now every wise man, let him hear me:
This story is just as true, I declare,
As is the book of Lancelot de Lake,[13]
That women hold in full great reverence.
Now will I turn again to my main point.
      A black-marked fox, full of sly iniquity,
That in the grove had dwelt years three,
And as foreseen in Chanticleer's dream,
The same night through the hedges burst
Into the yard, where Chanticleer the fair
Was wont, and his wives, to rest;
And in a bed of herbs still he lay,
Till past midmorning of the day
Watching for his time on Chanticleer to fall,
As usually do these murderers all,
Who lie await to murder men.
Oh false murderer, lurking in your den!
Oh new Iscariot, new Ganelon!

False dissimilour, O Greek Sinon,
That broghtest Troye al outrely to sorwe!
O Chauntecleer, acursed be that morwe,
That thou into that yerd flough fro the bemes:
Thou were ful wel y-warned by thy dremes,
That thilke day was perilous to thee.
But what that god forwoot mot nedes be,
After the opinioun of certeyn clerkis.
Witnesse on him, that any perfit clerk is,
That in scole is gret altercacioun
In this matere, and greet disputisoun,
And hath ben of an hundred thousand men.
But I ne can not bulte it to the bren,
As can the holy doctour Augustyn,
Or Boëce, or the bishop Bradwardyn,
Whether that goddes worthy forwiting
Streyneth me nedely for to doon a thing,
(Nedely clepe I simple necessitee);
Or elles, if free choys be graunted me
To do that same thing, or do it noght,
Though god forwoot it, er that it was wroght;
Or if his witing streyneth nevere a del
But by necessitee condicionel.
I wol not han to do of swich matere;
My tale is of a cok, as ye may here,
That took his counseil of his wyf, with sorwe,
To walken in the yerd upon that morwe
That he had met the dreem, that I yow tolde.
Wommennes counseils been ful ofte colde;
Wommannes counseil broghte us first to wo,
And made Adam fro paradys to go,
Ther-as he was ful mery, and wel at ese.—
But for I noot, to whom it mighte displese,
If I counseil of wommen wolde blame,
Passe over, for I seyde it in my game.
Rede auctours, wher they trete of swich matere,
And what thay seyn of wommen ye may here.
Thise been the cokkes wordes, and nat myne;
I can noon harm of no womman divyne.—

False dissembler, Oh Greek Sinon,[14]
Who brought Troy quite utterly to sorrow!
Oh Chanticleer, cursed be that morrow,
That you into that yard flew from the beams!
You were full well warned by your dreams
That that day was perilous to you.
But that which God foreknows must occur,
After the opinion of certain scholars.
Let him be witness, who any perfect scholar is,
That in the schools is great altercation
In this matter, and great disputation,
Carried on by a hundred thousand men.
But I cannot get into the points fine,
As can the holy doctor Augustine,
Or Boethius, or the bishop Bradwardine,[15]
Whether that God's excellent foreknowledge
Constrains me necessarily to do a thing
("Necessarily" call I *simple necessity*);
Or else, if free choice be granted me
To do that same thing or do it not,
Though God foreknew it before I was wrought;
Or if his knowing constrains not at all
But by *necessity conditional*.
I will not have to do with such matters;
My tale is of a cock, as you may hear,
That took advice from his wife, with sorrow,
To walk in the yard upon that morning
That he had dreamt that dream that I told you.
Woman's counsel can be full often fatal;
Woman's counsel brought us first to woe,
And made Adam from Paradise to go,
There where he was full merry and well at ease.
But since I know not whom it might displease,
If women's counsel I were to blame,
Pass over, for I said it in my game.
Read authorities, where they treat in such matters,
And what they say of women you may hear.
These be the cock's words, and not mine;
I can find no harm in any woman.

Faire in the sond, to bathe hir merily,
Lyth Pertelote, and alle hir sustres by,
Agayn the sonne; and Chauntecleer so free
Song merier than the mermayde in the see;
For Phisiologus seith sikerly,
How that they singen wel and merily
And so bifel that, as he caste his yë,
Among the wortes, on a boterflye,
He was war of this fox that lay ful lowe.
No-thing ne liste him thanne for to crowe,
But cryde anon, "cok, cok," and up he sterte,
As man that was affrayed in his herte.
For naturelly a beest desyreth flee
Fro his contrarie, if he may it see,
Though he never erst had seyn it with his yë.
    This Chauntecleer, when he gan him espye,
He wolde han fled, but that the fox anon
Seyde, "Gentil sire, allas! wher wol ye gon?
Be ye affrayed of me that am your freend?
Now certes, I were worse than a feend,
If I to yow wolde harm or vileinye.
I am nat come your counseil for t'espye;
But trewely, the cause of my cominge
Was only for to herkne how that ye singe.
For trewely ye have as mery a stevene
As eny aungel hath, that is in hevene;
Therwith ye han in musik more felinge
Than hadde Boëce, or any that can singe.
My lord your fader (god his soule blesse!)
And eek your moder, of hir gentilesse,
Han in myn hous y-been, to my gret ese;
And certes, sire, ful fayn wolde I yow plese.
But for men speke of singing, I wol saye,
So mote I brouke wel myn eyen tweye,
Save yow, I herde never man so singe
As dide your fader in the morweninge;
Certes, it was of herte, al that he song.
And for to make his voys the more strong,
He wolde so peyne him, that with bothe his yën

Fair in the sand, to bathe herself merrily,
Lay Pertelote, and all her sisters by,
In the sun, and Chanticleer so free
Sang merrier than the mermaid in the sea—
For Physiologus[16] says truly
That they sing well and merrily—
And so it befell that, as he cast his eye
Among the herbs, on a butterfly,
He became aware of this fox that lay full low.
Not at all then did he wish to crow.
But cried anon, "Cock, cock!" and up he leapt
Like someone who was frightened in his heart.
For naturally a beast desires to flee
From his opposite, if he may it see,
Though he never before had seen it with his eye.

    This Chanticleer, when he caught him in his sight,
He would have fled, but that the fox anon
Said, "Gentle sir, alas! where will you go?
Be you afraid of me who is your friend?
Now certainly, I'd be worse than a fiend,
If I to you wished harm or wrong.
I've not come to spy on your privacy,
But truly, the cause of my coming
Was only to listen to how you sing.
For truly you have as nice a voice
As any angel in heaven;
Therewith you have in music more feeling
Than had Boethius,[17] or any who can sing.
My lord your father (God his soul bless!)
And also your mother, because of her gentleness,
Have in my house been, to my great satisfaction;
And certainly, sir, most willingly would I you please.
But since men speak of singing, I will say,
So may I profit by my eyes two,
Except you, I never heard man so sing
As did your father in the morning.
Truly, it was from the heart, all that he sung.
And for to make his voice the more strong,
He would take such pains that both his eyes

He most winke, so loude he wolde cryen,
And stonden on his tiptoon ther-with-al,
And strecche forth his nekke long and smal.
And eek he was of swich discrecioun,
That ther nas no man in no regioun
That him in song or wisdom mighte passe.
I have wel rad in daun Burnel the Asse,
Among his vers, how that ther was a cok,
For that a preestes sone yaf him a knok
Upon his leg, whyl he was yong and nyce,
He made him for to lese his benefyce.
But certeyn, ther nis no comparisoun
Bitwix the wisdom and discrecioun
Of youre fader, and of his subtiltee.
Now singeth, sire, for seinte Charitee,
Let see, conne ye your fader countrefete?"
This Chauntecleer his winges gan to bete,
As man that coude his tresoun nat espye,
So was he ravissed with his flaterye.

    Allas! ye lordes, many a fals flatour
Is in your courtes, and many a losengeour,
That plesen yow wel more, by my feith,
Than he that soothfastnesse unto yow seith.
Redeth Ecclesiaste of flaterye;
Beth war, ye lordes, of hir trecherye.

    This Chauntecleer stood hye up-on his toos,
Strecching his nekke, and heeld his eyen cloos,
And gan to crowe loude for the nones;
And daun Russel the fox sterte up at ones,
And by the gargat hente Chauntecleer,
And on his bak toward the wode him beer,
For yet ne was ther no man that him sewed.
O destinee, that mayst nat been eschewed!
Allas, that Chauntecleer fleigh fro the bemes!
Allas, his wyf ne roghte nat of dremes!
And on a Friday fil al this meschaunce.
O Venus, that art goddesse of plesaunce,
Sin that thy servant was this Chauntecleer,

He had to shut, so loud he would cry,
And stand on his tiptoes at the same time,
And stretch forth his neck long and thin.
And also he was of such wisdom
That there was no man in any region
Who him in song or wisdom might pass.
I have well read in 'Sir Burnel the Ass,'[18]
Among that book's verses, how there was a cock,
Who because a priest's son gave him a knock
Upon his leg, while he was young and foolish,
He made him lose his benefice.
But certainly, there is no comparison
Between the wisdom and discretion
Of your father, and that other rooster.
Now sing, sir, for holy charity!
Let's see, can you your father imitate?"
This Chanticleer his wings began to beat,
As one who could not see the fox's treason,
So ravished was he by his flattery.

Alas! you lords, many a false flatterer
Is in your courts, and many a deceiving liar,
Who please you well more, by my faith,
Than he who truthfulness unto you speaks.
Read Ecclesiastes on flattery;[19]
Beware, you lords, of their treachery.

This Chanticleer stood high upon his toes,
Stretching his neck, and held his eyes closed,
And began to crow loud for the moment;
And Sir Russell the fox started up at once
And by the throat seized Chanticleer,
And on his back carried toward the wood,
With no one yet in pursuit.
Oh destiny, that may not be eschewed!
Alas, that Chanticleer flew from the beams!
Alas, his wife took no heed of dreams!
And on a Friday befell all this mischance.
Oh Venus, who is goddess of pleasure,
Since that your servant was this Chanticleer,

And in thy service dide al his poweer,
More for delyt, than world to multiplye,
Why woldestow suffre him on thy day to dye?
O Gaufred, dere mayster soverayn,
That, whan thy worthy king Richard was slayn
With shot, compleynedest his deth so sore,
Why ne hadde I now thy sentence and thy lore
The Friday for to chyde, as diden ye?
(For on a Friday soothly slayn was he.)
Than wolde I shewe yow how that I coude pleyne
For Chauntecleres drede, and for his peyne.

    Certes, swich cry ne lamentacioun
Was never of ladies maad, whan Ilioun
Was wonne, and Pirrus with his streite swerd,
Whan he hadde hent king Priam by the berd,
And slayn him (as saith us *Eneydos*),
As maden alle the hennes in the clos,
Whan they had seyn of Chauntecleer the sighte.
But sovereynly dame Pertelote shrighte,
Ful louder than dide Hasdrubales wyf,
Whan that hir housbond hadde lost his lyf,
And that the Romayns hadde brend Cartage;
She was so ful of torment and of rage,
That wilfully into the fyr she sterte,
And brende hir-selven with a stedfast herte.
O woful hennes, right so cryden ye,
As, whan that Nero brende the citee
Of Rome, cryden senatoures wyves,
For that hir housbondes losten alle hir lyves;
Withouten gilt this Nero hath hem slayn.
Now wol I torne to my tale agayn:—
This sely widwe, and eek hir doghtres two,
Herden thise hennes crye and maken wo,
And out at dores sterten they anoon,
And seyen the fox toward the grove goon,
And bar upon his bak the cok away;
And cryden, "Out! harrow! and weylaway!
Ha, ha, the fox!" and after him they ran,
And eek with staves many another man;

And in your service did all he could,
More for delight than world to multiply,
Why would you suffer him on your day to die?[20]
Oh Geoffrey, dear sovereign master,[21]
Who when your worthy King Richard was slain by
An arrow, you lamented his death so sorely,
Why do I not have your wisdom and your lore,
To chide Friday, as you did?
(For on Friday truly slain was he.)
Then would I show you that I could lament
For Chanticleer's fear, and for his pain.

    Truly, no such cry or lamentation
Was ever by ladies made when Troy
Was won, and Pyrrhus with his straight sword,
When he had seized king Priam[22] by the beard,
And slain him (as tells us the Aeneid),
As made all the hens in the yard,
When they had seen what happened to Chanticleer.
But above all dame Pertelote shrieked
Full louder than did Hasdrubal's wife,[23]
When her husband had lost his life,
And the Romans had burned Carthage:
She was so full of torment and rage
That willfully into the fire she leapt,
And burned herself to death, with a steadfast heart.
Oh woeful hens, you cried
As did the Roman senators' wives
When Nero burned the city down
And their husbands lost their lives
When, though guiltless, Nero slew them.
Now will I turn to my tale again.
This good widow and her daughters two
Heard these hens crying and making woe,
And out of the door they leapt anon,
And saw the fox toward the grove going,
And carrying upon his back the cock away;
And cried, "Out! Help! and wellaway!
Ha, ha, the fox!" and after him they ran
And also with sticks many another man;

Ran Colle our dogge, and Talbot, and Gerland,
And Malkin, with a distaf in hir hand;
Ran cow and calf, and eek the verray hogges
So were they fered for berking of the dogges
And shouting of the men and wimmen eke,
They ronne so, hem thoughte hir herte breke.
They yelleden as feendes doon in helle;
The dokes cryden as men wolde hem quelle;
The gees for fere flowen over the trees;
Out of the hyve cam the swarm of bees;
So hidous was the noyse, a! *benedicite!*
Certes, he Jakke Straw, and his meynee,
Ne made never shoutes half so shrille,
Whan that they wolden any Fleming kille,
As thilke day was maad upon the fox.
Of bras thay broghten bemes, and of box,
Of horn, of boon, in whiche they blewe and pouped,
And therwithal thay shryked and they houped;
It semed as that heven sholde falle.
Now, gode men, I pray yow herkneth alle!
    Lo, how fortune turneth sodeinly
The hope and pryde eek of hir enemy!
This cok, that lay upon the foxes bak,
In al his drede, un-to the fox he spak,
And seyde, "sire, if that I were as ye,
Yet sholde I seyn (as wis god helpe me),
Turneth agayn, ye proude cherles alle!
A verray pestilence up-on yow falle!
Now am I come un-to this wodes syde,
Maugree your heed, the cok shal heer abyde;
I wol him ete in feith, and that anon."—
The fox answerde, "in feith, it shal be don."—
And as he spak that word, al sodeinly
This cok brak from his mouth deliverly,
And heighe up-on a tree he fleigh anon.
And whan the fox saugh that he was y-gon,
"Allas!" quod he, "O Chauntecleer, allas!
I have to yow," quod he, "y-doon trespas,

Ran Colle the dog, and Talbot, and Gerland,[24]
And Malkin, with a distaff in her hand;
Ran cow and calf, and also the very hogs,
So frightened by the barking of the dogs
And shouting of the men and women too,
They ran so they thought their hearts would burst.
They yelled as fiends do in hell;
The ducks quacked as if men would them kill;
The geese for fear flew over the trees;
Out of the hive came the swarm of bees;
So hideous was the noise, a! *benedicite!*
Certainly, Jack Straw and his company[25]
Never made shouts half so shrill
When they would any Fleming[26] kill,
As that day was made upon the fox.
Of brass they brought trumpets, and of boxwood,
Of horn, of bone, in which they blew and puffed,
And therewith they shrieked and they whooped:
It seemed as if heaven should fall.
Now, good men, I pray you listen all!

   Look, how Fortune overturns suddenly
The hope and pride of her enemy!
This cock, that lay upon the fox's back,
In all his fear unto the fox he spoke,
And said, "Sir, if I were you,
Yet should I say, may God help me,
'Turn again, you proud churls all!
A very pestilence upon you fall!
Now I am coming into this woodside,
Despite your effort, this cock shall here abide;
I will eat him in faith, and that anon.'"
The fox answered, "In faith, it shall be done,"
And as he spoke that word, all suddenly
This cock broke from his mouth quite nimbly,
And high upon a tree he flew anon.
And when the fox saw that the cock was gone,
"Alas!" said he, "O Chanticleer, alas!
I have to you," said he, "done trespass,

In-as-muche as I maked yow aferd,
Whan I yow hente, and broghte out of the yerd;
But, sire, I dide it in no wikke entente;
Com doun, and I shal telle yow what I mente.
I shal seye sooth to yow, god help me so."
"Nay than," quod he, "I shrewe us bothe two,
And first I shrewe my-self, bothe blood and bones,
If thou bigyle me ofter than ones.
Thou shalt na-more, thurgh thy flaterye,
Do me to singe and winke with myn yë.
For he that winketh, whan he sholde see,
Al wilfully, god lat him never thee!"
"Nay," quod the fox, "but god yeve him meschaunce,
That is so undiscreet of governaunce,
That jangleth whan he sholde holde his pees."

　　Lo, swich it is for to be recchelees,
And necligent, and truste on flaterye.
But ye that holden this tale a folye,
As of a fox, or of a cok and hen,
Taketh the moralitee, good men.
For seint Paul seith, that al that writen is,
To our doctryne it is y-write, y-wis.
Taketh the fruyt, and lat the chaf be stille.
Now, gode god, if that it be thy wille,
As seith my lord, so make us alle good men;
And bringe us to his heighe blisse. Amen.

The Epilogue

"Sir Nonnes Preest," our hoste seyde anoon,
"Y-blessed be thy breche, and every stoon!
This was a mery tale of Chauntecleer.
But, by my trouthe, if thou were seculer,
Thou woldest been a trede-foul a-right.
For, if thou have corage as thou hast might,
Thee were nede of hennes, as I wene,
Ya, mo than seven tymes seventene.
See, whiche braunes hath this gentil Preest,
So greet a nekke, and swich a large breest!

Inasmuch as I made you afraid
When I you seized and brought out of the yard.
But sir, I did it with no wicked intent;
Come down, and I shall tell you what I meant.
I tell you the truth, God help me so."
"No, then," said he, "I curse us both two,
And first I curse myself, both blood and bones,
If you deceive me more than once.
You shall no more, through your flattery,
Cause me to sing and close my eyes.
For he who blinks when he should look,
All willfully, may God not give him luck!"
"No," said the fox, "but God give him mischance,
Who is so indiscreet of self-governance
That chatters when he should hold his tongue."

    Look, this is the way it is to be reckless
And negligent, and trust in flattery.
But you that hold this tale a trifle,
As of a fox, or of a cock and hen,
Take the moral of it, good men.
For Saint Paul says all that is written,[27]
Was written for our benefit.
Take the fruit, and let the husks be still.
Now, good God, if that it be your will,
As says my bishop, so make us all good men,
And bring us to his high bliss. Amen.

The Epilogue

"Sir Nun's Priest," our Host said at once,
"Blessed be your loins and your balls!
This was a merry tale of Chanticleer.
But by my troth, if you were secular,
You would have been some rooster.
For if you have spirit as you have strength,
You would need of hens, I would guess,
Yea, more than seventeen times seven.
See, what muscles has this gentle priest,
So great a neck, and such a large breast!

He loketh as a sperhauk with his yën;
Him nedeth nat his colour for to dyen
With brasil, ne with greyn of Portingale.
Now sire, faire falle yow for youre tale!"

He looks as does a sparrowhawk with his eyes;
He need not his complexion to dye
With red powder, nor with red dye from Portugal.
Now sir, may good befall you for your tale!"

The Chanouns Yemannes Tale

WHAN ENDED WAS THE lyf of seint Cecyle,
Er we had ridden fully fyve myle,
At Boghton under Blee us gan atake
A man, that clothed was in clothes blake,
And undernethe he hadde a whyt surplys.
His hakeney, that was al pomely grys,
So swatte, that it wonder was to see;
It semed he had priked myles three.
The hors eek that his yeman rood upon
So swatte, that unnethe mighte it gon.
Aboute the peytrel stood the foom ful hye,
He was of fome al flekked as a pye.
A male tweyfold on his croper lay,
It semed that he caried lyte array.
Al light for somer rood this worthy man,
And in myn herte wondren I bigan
What that he was, til that I understood
How that his cloke was sowed to his hood;
For which, when I had longe avysed me,
I demed him som chanon for to be.
His hat heng at his bak doun by a laas,
For he had riden more than trot or paas;
He had ay priked lyk as he were wood.
A clote-leef he hadde under his hood
For swoot, and for to kepe his heed from hete.
But it was joye for to seen him swete!
His forheed dropped as a stillatorie,
Were ful of plantain and of paritorie.
And whan that he was come, he gan to crye,
"God save," quod he, "this joly companye!
Faste have I priked," quod he, "for your sake,
By-cause that I wolde yow atake,
To ryden in this mery companye."
His yeman eek was ful of curteisye,
And seyde, "sires, now in the morwe-tyde

The Canon's Yeoman's Tale

The Prologue

WHEN ENDED WAS THE life of Saint Cecilia,[1]
Before we had ridden fully five miles,
At Boughton under Blean we were overtaken
By a man who clothed was in clothes black,
And underneath he had a white surplice.
His hackney, that was dappled gray,
So sweated that it wondrous was to see;
It seemed as if he had spurred miles three.
The horse also that his yeoman rode upon
So labored that it could hardly go on.
About the collar stood the foam full high;
He was of foam flecked as a magpie.
A saddlebag on his crupper rested;
It seemed that he not much carried.
All light for summer rode this worthy man,
And in my heart wondering I began
Who he was till I understood
How that his cloak was sewn to his hood,
For which, when I had pondered me,
Some kind of canon[2] I deemed him to be.
His hat hung at his back down by a lace,
For he had ridden more than trot or pace;
He had ever spurred as if he were mad.
A burdock leaf he had under his hood
For sweat and to keep his head from heat.
But it was a joy to see him sweat!
His forehead perspired like a distillery
Full of plantain and pellitory.[3]
And when he drew near, he began to cry,
"God save," said he, "this jolly company!
Fast have I spurred," said he, "for your sake,
Because I would you overtake,
To ride in this merry company."
His yeoman also was full of courtesy,
And said, "Sirs, now in the morningtide

575

Out of your hostelrye I saugh you ryde,
And warned heer my lord and my soverayn,
Which that to ryden with yow is ful fayn,
For his desport; he loveth daliaunce."

    "Freend, for thy warning god yeve thee good chaunce,"
Than seyde our host, "for certes, it wolde seme
Thy lord were wys, and so I may weldeme;
He is ful jocund also, dar I leye.
Can he oght telle a mery tale or tweye,
With which he glade may this companye?"

    "Who, sire? my lord? ye, ye, withouten lye,
He can of murthe, and eek of jolitee
Nat but ynough; also sir, trusteth me,
And ye him knewe as wel as do I,
Ye wolde wondre how wel and craftily
He coude werke, and that in sondry wyse.
He hath take on him many a greet empryse,
Which were ful hard for any that is here
To bringe aboute, but they of him it lere.
As homely as he rit amonges yow,
If ye him knewe, it wolde be for your prow;
Ye wolde nat forgoon his aqueyntaunce
For mochel good, I dar leye in balaunce
Al that I have in my possessioun.
He is a man of heigh discrecioun,
I warne you wel, he is a passing man."

    "Wel," quod our host, "I pray thee, tel me than.
Is he a clerk, or noon? tel what he is."

    "Nay, he is gretter than a clerk, y-wis,"
Seyde this yeman, "and in wordes fewe,
Host, of his craft som-what I wol yow shewe.

    I seye, my lord can swich subtilitee—
(But al his craft ye may nat wite at me;
And som-what helpe I yet to his werking)—
That al this ground on which we been ryding,
Til that we come to Caunterbury toun,
He coude al clene turne it up-so-doun,
And pave it al of silver and of gold."

    And whan this yeman hadde thus y-told

Out of your hostelry I saw you ride,
And warned here my lord and my master,
Who to ride with you would be much obliged,
For his pleasure; he loves stories and such."
    "Friend, for your warning God give you good luck,"
Then said our Host, "for certain it would seem
Your Lord was wise, and so I may well deem.
He is full jocund also, I dare wager!
Can he at least tell a tale or two,
With which he may make glad this company?"
    "Who, sire? My lord? Yea, yea, without lie,
He knows of mirth and jollity
More than enough; also sir, trust me,
And if you knew him as well as do I,
You would wonder how well and skillfully
He could work, and that in sundry ways.
He takes on himself many a great enterprise,
Which would be full hard for any here
To bring about, unless they learned it from him.
Though simply he rides among you,
If you him knew, it would be for your profit.
You would not forgo his acquaintance
For much good, I dare bet
All that I have in my possession.
He is a man of high discretion;
I warn you well, he is an outstanding person."
    "Well," said our Host, "I pray you, tell me then,
Is he a scholar, or no? Tell what he is."
    "Nay, he is greater than a scholar, truly,"
Said this Yeoman, "and in words few,
Host, of his skill something I will you show.
    "I say, my lord knows such subtlety—
But all his skill you may not learn from me,
And somewhat yet I help his workings—
That all this ground on which we be riding,
Till that we come to Canterbury town,
He could all clean turn upside-down,
And pave it all of silver and of gold."
    And when this Yeoman had this tale told

Unto our host, he seyde, *"ben'cite!*
This thing is wonder merveillous to me,
Sin that thy lord is of so heigh prudence,
By-cause of which men sholde him reverence,
That of his worship rekketh he so lyte;
His oversloppe nis nat worth a myte,
As in effect, to him, so mote I go!
It is al baudy and to-tore also.
Why is thy lord so sluttish, I thee preye,
And is of power better cloth to beye,
If that his dede accorde with thy speche?
Telle me that, and that I thee biseche."

      "Why?" quod this yeman, "wherto axe ye me?
God help me so, for he shal never thee!
(But I wol nat avowe that I seye,
And therfor kepe it secree, I yow preye).
He is to wys, in feith, as I bileve;
That that is overdoon, it wol nat preve
Aright, as clerkes seyn, it is a vyce.
Wherfor in that I holde him lewed and nyce.
For whan a man hath over-greet a wit,
Ful oft him happeth to misusen it;
So dooth my lord, and that me greveth sore.
God it amende, I can sey yow na-more."

      "Ther-of no fors, good yeman," quod our host;
"Sin of the conning of thy lord thou wost,
Tel how he dooth, I pray thee hertely,
Sin that he is so crafty and so sly.
Wher dwellen ye, if it to telle be?"

      "In the suburbes of a toun," quod he,
"Lurkinge in hernes and in lanes blinde,
Wher-as thise robbours and thise theves by kinde
Holden hir privee fereful residence,
As they that dar nat shewen hir presence;
So faren we, if I shal seye the sothe."

      "Now," quod our host, "yit lat me talke to the;
Why artow so discoloured of thy face?"

      "Peter!" quod he, "god yeve it harde grace,
I am so used in the fyr to blowe,

Unto our Host, he said, "*Benedicite!*
This thing is wondrous marvelous to me,
Since that your lord has such knowledge,
Because of which men should him reverence,
Who of his distinction makes he so light.
His overcoat is not worth a mite,
Really, to him, so must I say,
It is all dirty and tattered also.
Why is your lord so sloppy, I you pray,
And is able better cloth to buy,
If his works match your speech?
Tell me that, and that I you beseech."

   "Why?" said this Yeoman, "why ask me?
God help me so, for he shall succeed never!
(But I will not reveal it in what I say,
And therefore keep it secret, I you pray.)
He is too knowing, in faith, as I believe.
What is made too much of, it will not
Succeed, as scholars say, it is a vice.
Therefore in that I hold him both simple and wise.
For when a man has too much wit,
Full often he happens to misuse it.
So does my lord, and that grieves me sore;
God it amend! I can tell you no more."

   "Thereof no matter, good Yeoman," said our Host;
"Since the cunning of your lord you know,
Tell how he works, I pray you with all my heart,
Since he is so skillful and so expert.
Where do you live, if you don't mind saying?"

   "In the suburbs of a town," said he,
"Lurking in hiding places and in blind alleys,
Where these robbers and thieving kinds,
Keep their secret, fear-ridden roosts,
As they who dare not show their faces;
So fare we, if I shall say the truth."

   "Now," said our Host, "yet let me talk to you.
Why are you so discolored in your face?"

   "Peter!" said he, "God give it misfortune,
I am so used in the fire to blow

That it hath chaunged my colour, I trowe.
I am nat wont in no mirour to prye,
But swinke sore and lerne multiplye,
We blondren ever and pouren in the fyr.
And for al that we fayle of our desyr.
For ever we lakken our conclusioun.
To mochel folk we doon illusioun,
And borwe gold, be it a pound or two,
Or ten, or twelve, or many sommes mo,
And make hem wenen, at the leeste weye,
That of a pound we coude make tweye!
Yet is it fals, but ay we han good hope
It for to doon, and after it we grope.
But that science is so fer us biforn,
We mowen nat, al-though we hadde it sworn,
It overtake, it slit awey so faste;
It wol us maken beggars atte laste."

     Whyl this yeman was thus in his talking,
This chanoun drough him ncer, and herde al thing
Which this yeman spak, for suspecioun
Of mennes speche ever hadde this chanoun.
For Catoun seith, that he that gilty is
Demeth al thing be spoke of him, y-wis.
That was the cause he gan so ny him drawe
To his yeman, to herknen al his sawe.
And thus he seyde un-to his yeman tho,
"Hold thou thy pees, and spek no wordes mo,
For if thou do, thou shalt it dere abye;
Thou sclaundrest me heer in this companye,
And eek discoverest that thou sholdest hyde."

     "Ye," quod our host, "telle on, what so bityde;
Of al his threting rekke nat a myte!"
"In feith," quod he, "namore I do but lyte."

     And whan this chanon saugh it wolde nat be,
But his yeman wolde telle his privetee,
He fledde awey for verray sorwe and shame.

     "A!" quod the yeman, "heer shal aryse game,
Al that I can anon now wol I telle.
Sin he is goon, the foule feend him quelle!

That it has changed my color, I know.
I am not wont in a mirror to peer,
But work hard and learn alchemy.
We blunder ever and stare into the fire,
And for all that we fail of our desire,
For ever we lack successful conclusion.
To most folk we do illusion,
And borrow gold, be it a pound or two,
Or ten, or twelve, or many sums more,
And make them believe, at least,
That of a pound we could make two.
Yet is it false, but ever we have good hope
It for to do, and after it we grope.
But that science is so far us before,
We accomplish it not, although we had it sworn,
To achieve, it slides away so fast.
It will make us beggars at the last."

　　While this Yeoman was thus in his talking,
This Canon drew him near and heard everything
That this Yeoman said, for suspicion
Of men's speech ever had this Canon.
For Cato says that he who guilty is
Deems everything spoken to be of him.[4]
That was the reason he began to draw
Near his Yeoman, to hear his chatter.
And thus he said unto his Yeoman then:
"Hold you your peace and speak no words more,
For if you do, you shall for it dearly pay.
You slander me here to this company,
And also reveal what you should hide."

　　"Yea," said our Host, "tell on, what so betides.
Of all his threatening reckon not a mite!"
"In faith," said he, "I do but little more."

　　And when this Canon saw it would not be,
But his Yeoman would reveal his secrecy,
He fled away for true sorrow and shame.

　　"Ah," said the Yeoman, "here shall arise the game;
All that I know soon now will I say.
Since he is gone, the foul fiend him slay!

For never her-after wol I with him mete
For peny ne for pound, I yow bihete!
He that me broghte first unto that game,
Er that he dye, sorwe have he and shame!
For it is ernest to me, by my feith;
That fele I wel, what so any man seith.
And yet, for al my smerte and al my grief,
For al my sorwe, labour, and meschief,
I coude never leve it in no wyse.
Now wolde god my wit mighte suffyse
To tellen al that longeth to that art!
But natheles yow wol I tellen part;
Sin that my lord is gon, I wol nat spare;
Swich thing as that I knowe, I wol declare."—

The Tale

PART ONE

With this chanoun I dwelt have seven yeer,
And of his science am I never the neer.
Al that I hadde, I have y-lost ther-by;
And god wot, so hath many mo than I.
Ther I was wont to be right fresh and gay
Of clothing and of other good array,
Now may I were an hose upon myn heed;
And wher my colour was bothe fresh and reed,
Now is it wan and of a leden hewe;
Who-so it useth, sore shal he rewe.
And of my swink yet blered is myn yë,
Lo! which avantage is to multiplye!
That slyding science hath me maad so bare,
That I have no good, wher that ever I fare;
And yet I am endetted so ther-by
Of gold that I have borwed, trewely,
That whyl I live, I shal it quyte never.
Lat every man be war by me for ever!
What maner man that casteth him ther-to,
If he continue, I holde his thrift y-do.

For never hereafter will I with him meet
For penny nor for pound, I promise you.
He who brought me first unto that game,
Before he dies, sorrow have he and shame!
For it is so serious to me, by my faith;
That I feel strongly, whatever any man says.
And yet, for all my pain and my sorrow,
For all my labor, grief and trouble,
I could never leave it though I tried.
Now would to God that my wit sufficed
To tell all that belongs to that art!
But nevertheless I will tell you part.
Since my lord is gone, I will not spare;
Such things that I know, I will declare.—

The Tale

PART ONE

With this Canon have I dwelt seven years,
And of his science I am never the nearer.
All that I had I have lost thereby,
And, God knows, so have many more than I.
Where I was wont to be right fresh and gay
Of clothing and of other good raiment,
Now may I wear a sock upon my head;
And where my color was both fresh and red,
Now it is all wan and of a leaden hue—
Whoso it uses, sore shall he rue!—
And from my work yet is bleared my eye.
Look, what profit be there in alchemy!
That slippery science has me made so bare
That I have no good, whatever I fare;
And yet I am indebted so
For the gold that I have borrowed, truly,
That while I live I shall repay it never.
Let every man be warned by me forever.
Whoever in that way risks his luck,
If he continues, he will end up broke.

So helpe me god, ther-by shal he nat winne,
But empte his purs, and make his wittes thinne.
And whan he, thurgh his madnes and folye,
Hath lost his owene good thurgh jupartye,
Thanne he excyteth other folk ther-to,
To lese hir good as he him-self hath do.
For unto shrewes joye it is and ese
To have hir felawes in peyne and disese;
Thus was I ones lerned of a clerk.
Of that no charge, I wol speke of our werk.

    Whan we been ther as we shul exercyse
Our elvish craft, we semen wonder wyse,
Our termes been so clergial and so queynte.
I blowe the fyr til that myn herte feynte.
What sholde I tellen ech proporcioun
Of thinges whiche that we werche upon,
As on fyve or sixe ounces, may wel be,
Of silver or som other quantitee,
And bisie me to telle yow the names
Of orpiment, brent bones, yren squames,
That into poudre grounden been ful smal?
And in an erthen potte how put is al,
And salt y-put in, and also papeer,
Biforn thise poudres that I speke of heer,
And wel y-covered with a lampe of glass,
And mochel other thing which that ther was?
And of the pot and glasses enluting,
That of the eyre mighte passe out no-thing?
And of the esy fyr and smart also,
Which that was maad, and of the care and wo
That we hadde in our matires sublyming,
And in amalgaming and calcening
Of quik-silver, y-clept Mercurie crude?
For alle our sleightes we can nat conclude.
Our orpiment and sublymed Mercurie,
Our grounden litarge eek on the porphurie,
Of ech of thise of ounces a certeyn
Nought helpeth us, our labour is in veyn.
Ne eek our spirites ascencioun,

For so help me God, thereby shall he not win,
But empty his purse and make his wits thin.
And when he through his madness and folly
Has lost his own goods through jeopardy,
Then he excites other folk thereto,
To lessen their goods as he himself has done.
For unto wretches joy it is and ease
To have their fellows in pain and disease.
Thus taught was I once by a cleric.
Of that no matter; I speak now of our work.

    When we had set ourselves up to exercise
Our elvish craft, we seemed wondrous wise,
Our terms were scholarly and so abstruse.
I blew the fire till my heart burst.
Why should I tell each measure of
Things that we worked upon—
As to five or six ounces, may well be,
Of silver, or some other quantity—
And busy myself to tell you the names
Of arsenic, burnt bones, iron flakes,
That into powder ground were full small;
And in an earthen pot how put is all,
And salt put in, and also paper,
Before these powders that I spoke of here;
And well-covered with a lamp of glass;
And of much other things that there were;
And of the pot and glasses sealing
That of the vapor might pass out nothing;
And of the easy fire, and brisk also,
Which was made, and of the care and woe
That we had in our ingredients purifying,
And in our amalgamation and reduction
Of quicksilver, called raw mercury?
For all our trickery we cannot succeed.
Our arsenic and purified mercury,
Our ground lead oxide on the porphyry,[5]
Of each of these of ounces a certain measure—
Nought helped us; in vain was our labor.
Nor either our vaporized spirits,

Ne our materes that lyen al fixe adoun,
Mowe in our werking no-thing us avayle.
For lost is al our labour and travayle,
And al the cost, a twenty devel weye,
Is lost also, which we upon it leye.
    Ther is also ful many another thing
That is unto our craft apertening;
Though I by ordre hem nat reherce can,
By-cause that I am a lewed man,
Yet wol I telle hem as they come to minde,
Though I ne can nat sette hem in hir kinde;
As bole armoniak, verdegrees, boras,
And sondry vessels maad of erthe and glas,
Our urinales and our descensories,
Violes, croslets, and sublymatories,
Cucurbites, and alembykes eek,
And othere swiche, dere y-nough a leek.
Nat nedeth it for to reherce hem alle,
Watres rubifying and boles galle,
Arsenik, sal armoniak, and brimstoon;
And herbes coude I telle eek many oon,
As egremoine, valerian, and lunarie,
And othere swiche, if that me liste tarie.
Our lampes brenning bothe night and day,
To bringe aboute our craft, if that we may.
Our fourneys eek of calcinacioun,
And of watres albificacioun,
Unslekked lym, chalk, and gleyre of an ey,
Poudres diverse, asshes, dong, pisse, and cley,
Cered pokets, sal peter, vitriole;
And divers fyres maad of wode and cole;
Sal tartre, alkaly, and sal preparat,
And combust materes and coagulat,
Cley maad with hors or mannes heer, and oile
Of tartre, alum, glas, berm, wort, and argoile

Resalgar, and our materes enbibing;
And eek of our materes encorporing,
And of our silver citrinacioun,

Nor our residue sediment stable,
For success in our working nothing us availed,
For lost is all our labor and our travail;
And all the cost, in the devil's name,
Is lost also, that we had outlaid.

    There is also full many another thing
That is unto our craft appertaining.
Though I cannot rehearse them in order,
Because I am an unlearned man,
Yet will I tell them as they come to mind,
Though I cannot set them in their order by kind:
As Armenian bole, copper, borax,
And sundry vessels made of earth and glass,
Our flasks and our retorts,
Vials, crucibles, and sublimatories,[6]
Distillation vessels and alembics also,
And other such, expensive but not worth a leek—
No need for me to rehearse them all—
Fluids reddening, and bull's gall,
Arsenic, sal ammoniac, and brimstone;
And herbs could I tell many a one,
As agrimony, valerian, and moonwart,
And other such, if I wished to tarry;
Our lamps burning both night and day,
To bring about our purpose, if we may;
Our furnace also of calcination,
And of waters albification;
Unslaked lime, chalk, and white of egg,
Powders diverse, ashes, dung, piss and clay,
Waxed small bags, saltpeter, copper sulphate,
And diverse fires made of wood and coal;
Potassium carbonate, alkali, purified salt,
And burned materials and coagulates;
Clay made with horse or man's hair, and oil
Of tarter, potash alum, brewer's yeast, unfermented beer,
    potassium bitartrate,
Arsenic disulphide, and our ingredients absorbant,
And also of our ingredients compounding,
And of our silver lemon-yellow turning,

Our cementing and fermentacioun,
Our ingottes, testes, and many mo.
    I wol yow telle, as was me taught also,
The foure spirites and the bodies sevene,
By ordre, as ofte I herde my lord hem nevene.
The firste spirit quik-silver called is,
The second orpiment, the thridde, y-wis,
Sal armoniak, and the ferthe brimstoon.
The bodies sevene eek, lo! hem heer anoon:
Sol gold is, and Luna silver we threpe,
Mars yren, Mercurie quik-silver we clepe,
Saturnus leed, and Jupiter is tin,
And Venus coper, by my fader kin!
    This cursed craft who-so wol exercyse,
He shal no good han that him may suffyse
For al the good he spendeth ther-aboute,
He lese shal, ther-of have I no doute.
Who-so that listeth outen his folye,
Lat him come forth, and lerne multiplye;
And every man that oght hath in his cofre,
Lat him appere, and wexe a philosofre.
Ascaunce that craft is so light to lere?
Nay, nay, god woot, al be he monk or frere,
Preest or chanoun, or any other wight,
Though he sitte at his book bothe day and night,
In lernying of this elvish nyce lore,
Al is in veyn, and parde, mochel more!
To lerne a lewed man this subtiltee,
Fy! spek nat ther-of, for it wol nat be;
Al conne he letterure, or conne he noon,
As in effect, he shal finde it al oon.
For bothe two, by my savacioun,
Concluden, in multiplicacioun,
Y-lyke wel, whan they han al y-do;
This is to seyn, they faylen bothe two.
    Yet forgat I to maken rehersaille
Of watres corosif and of limaille,
And of bodyes mollificacioun,
And also of hir induracioun,

Our heat fusion and effervescence,
Our ingot molds, crucibles, and many more.
  I will you tell, as was taught me also,
The volatile spirits four and the metals seven,
In order, as often I heard my lord name them.
The first spirit is called quicksilver,
The second arsenic, the third, truly,
Sal ammoniac, and the fourth sulphur.
The bodies seven also, now here they are:
Sun is gold, and Luna silver we affirm,
Mars iron, Mercury quicksilver,
Saturn lead, and Jupiter is tin,
And Venus copper, by my father's kin!
  This cursed craft whose whole exercise,
Shall do no good for whom it engages,
For all the money he on it spends
He shall lose it; thereof have I no doubt.
Whoso wishes to display his folly,
Let him come forth and learn alchemy;
And every man who has anything in his coffer,
Let him present himself and become a philosopher.
You think the craft is so easy to learn?
Nay, nay, God knows, be he monk or friar,
Priest or canon, or any other,
Though he sits at his book both day and night
In learning of this elvish, foolish lore,
He is in vain and, God knows, much more.
To teach an unschooled man this subtlety—
Fie! Speak not thereof, for it will not be.
And know he books or know he none,
In the end, he shall find it all the one.
For the both, by my salvation,
Conclude in transmutation
Much the same, when they are done;
That is to say, they both fail in the end.
  Yet I forget to make rehearsal
Of liquids acidic, and filings of metal,
And of substances softening,
And also of their hardening;

Oiles, ablucions, and metal fusible,
To tellen al wolde passen any bible
That o-wher is; wherfor, as for the beste,
Of alle thise names now wol I me reste.
For, as I trowe, I have yow told y-nowe
To reyse a feend, al loke he never so rowe.

A! nay! lat be; the philosophres stoon,
Elixir clept, we sechen faste echoon;
For hadde we him, than were we siker y-now.
But, unto god of heven I make avow,
For al our craft, whan we han al y-do,
And al our sleighte, he wol nat come us to.
He hath y-maad us spenden mochel good,
For sorwe of which almost we wexen wood,
But that good hope crepeth in our herte,
Supposing ever, though we sore smerte,
To be releved by him afterward;
Swich supposing and hope is sharp and hard;
I warne you wel, it is to seken ever;
That futur temps hath maad men to dissever,
In trust ther-of, from al that ever they hadde.
Yet of that art they can nat wexen sadde,
For unto hem it is a bitter swete;
So semeth it; for nadde they but a shete
Which that they mighte wrappe hem inne a-night,
And a bak to walken inne by day-light,
They wolde hem selle and spenden on this craft;
They can nat stinte til no-thing be laft.
And evermore, wher that ever they goon,
Men may hem knowe by smel of brimstoon;
For al the world, they stinken as a goot;
Her savour is so rammish and so hoot,
That, though a man from hem a myle be,
The savour wol infecte him, trusteth me;
Lo, thus by smelling and threedbare array,
If that men liste, this folk they knowe may.
And if a man wol aske hem prively,
Why they been clothed so unthriftily,
They right anon wol rownen in his ere,

Oils, ablutions, and metals fusible—
To tell all would pass any bible
That ever was; therefore, as for the best,
All these names now will I let rest,
For, as I believe, I have told you enough,
To raise a fiend, though he looks ever so rough.
    Ah! Nay! Let be; the philosopher's stone,
Elixir called, we all seek eagerly;
For if we had it, then now certain would we be.
But unto God of heaven I make a vow,
For all our craft, when we were all done,
And all our cunning, he would not to us come.
He made us spend much of our money,
For sorrow of which we almost went crazy,
But that good hope crept in our hearts,
Supposing ever though we smarted,
To be relieved by him afterwards.
Such supposing and hope is sharp and hard;
I warn you well, it is to seek forever.
That future tense has made men part,
In hope thereof, from all that ever they had.
Yet of that art they cannot find peace,
For unto them it is a bitter sweet—
So seems it—for had they not but a sheet
Which they might wrap themselves in at night,
And a rough cloak to walk in by daylight,
They would spend and sell themselves on this craft.
They cannot stint until they have nothing left.
And evermore, wherever they go,
Men may them know by the smell of brimstone.
For all the world they stink as a goat;
Their odor is so rammish and gross
That though a man from them a mile be,
Their odor will infect him, trust to me.
Look, thus by smelling and threadbare raiment,
If men wish, this folk they may know.
And if a man will ask him privately
Why they be clothed so unhandsomely,
They right anon will whisper in his ear,

And seyn, that if that they espyed were,
Men wolde hem slee, by-cause of hir science;
Lo, thus this folk bitrayen innocence!
     Passe over this; I go my tale un-to.
Er than the pot be on the fyr y-do,
Of metals with a certein quantitee,
My lord hem tempreth, and no man but he—
Now he is goon, I dar seyn boldely—
For, as men seyn, he can don craftily;
Algate I woot wel he hath swich a name,
And yet ful ofte he renneth in a blame;
And wite ye how? ful ofte it happeth so,
The pot to-breketh, and farwell! al is go!
Thise metals been of so greet violence,
Our walles mowe nat make hem resistence,
But if they weren wroght of lym and stoon;
They percen so, and thurgh the wal they goon,
And somme of hem sinken in-to the ground—
Thus han we lost by tymes many a pound—
And somme are scatered al the floor aboute,
Somme lepe in-to the roof; with-outen doute,
Though that the feend noght in our sighte him shewe,
I trowe he with us be, that ilke shrewe!
In helle wher that he is lord and sire,
Nis ther more wo, ne more rancour ne ire.
Whan that our pot is broke, as I have sayd,
Every man chit, and halt him yvel apayd.
     Som seyde, it was long on the fyr-making,
Som seyde, nay! it was on the blowing;
(Than was I fered, for that was myn office);
"Straw!" quod the thridde, "ye been lewed and nyce,
It was nat tempred as it oghte be."
"Nay!" quod the ferthe, "stint, and herkne me;
By-cause our fyr ne was nat maad of beech,
That is the cause, and other noon, so theech!"
I can nat telle wher-on it was long,
But wel I wot greet stryf is us among.
     "What!" quod my lord, "there is na-more to done,
Of thise perils I wol be war eft-sone;

And say that if they were discovered,
Men would slay them because of their science.
Look, how these folk deceive the innocents!
     Pass over this; I go unto my tale.
Before the pot be on the fire set,
Of metals with a certain quantity,
My lord them blended, and no man but he—
Now he is gone, I dare boldly say—
For as men say, he could do so well.
Although I know well he had made a name;
Yet full often he was to blame.
And you know why? Full often it happened so
The pot exploded, and farewell, all is gone!
These metals be of such great violence
Pot walls may not make them resistance,
But if they were wrought of lime or stone;
They pierce them, and through the wall they go.
And some of them sink into the ground—
Thus have we lost betimes many a pound—
And some are scattered all the floor about;
Some leap into the roof. Without doubt,
Though the fiend not to our sight himself reveals,
I believe he was with us, that same devil!
In hell, where he is lord and sire,
There is no more woe, nor rancor nor ire.
When our pot is broken, as I have said,
Every man himself holds paid badly.
     Some said it was too long on the fire heating;
Some said no, it was the blowing—
Then was I afraid, for that was my chore.
"Straw!" said the third, "you be simple and unlearned,
It was not blended as it ought to have been."
"Nay," said the fourth, "shut up and listen:
Because our fire was not made of beechwood,
That is the cause and no other, so help me God!"
I cannot tell why it went wrong,
But well I know the strife was among us.
     "What," said my lord, "there is no more to be done;
Of these perils I will be wary from now on.

I am right siker that the pot was crased.
Be as be may, be ye no-thing amased;
As usage is, lat swepe the floor as swythe,
Plukke up your hertes, and beth gladde and blythe."

    The mullok on an hepe y-sweped was,
And on the floor y-cast a canevas,
And al this mullok in a sive y-throwe,
And sifted, and y-piked many a throwe.

    "Pardee," quod oon, "somwhat of our metal
That we concluden evermore amis.
But, be it hoot or cold, I dar seye this,
Yet is ther heer, though that we han nat al.
Al-though this thing mishapped have as now,
Another tyme it may be wel y-now,
Us moste putte our good in aventure;
A marchant, parde! may nat ay endure
Trusteth me wel, in his prosperitee;
Somtyme his good is drenched in the see,
And somtym comth it sauf un-to the londe."

    "Pees!" quod my lord, "the next tyme I wol fonde
To bringe our craft al in another plyte;
And but I do, sirs, lat me han the wyte;
Ther was defaute in som-what, wel I woot."

    Another seyde, the fyr was over hoot:—
We fayle of that which that we wolden have,
And in our madnesse evermore we rave.
And whan we been togidres everichoon,
Every man semeth a Salomon.
But al thing which that shyneth as the gold
Nis nat gold, as that I have herd it told;
Ne every appel that is fair at yë
Ne is nat good, what-so men clappe or crye.
Right-so, lo! fareth it amonges us;
He that semeth the wysest, by Jesus!
Is most fool, whan it cometh to the preef;
And he that semeth trewest is a theef;
That shul ye knowe, er that I fro yow wende,
But that I of my tale have maad an ende.

I am right sure the pot was cracked.
Be it as it may, by no means be dismayed;
As customary, sweep the floor without delay,
Pluck up your spirits and make a blithe face."
     The rubbish into a heap was swept,
And on the floor was cast a canvas,
And all this mess in a sieve thrown,
And sifted, and thoroughly picked through.
     "By God," said one, "some of our metal
Yet is here, though we have not all.
And though this thing went wrong for now,
Another time it may go well enough,
We must trust to luck.
A merchant, by God, may not ever endure,
Trust me well, in his prosperity.
Sometimes his cargo is drowned in the sea,
And sometimes it safely reaches land."
     "Peace!" said my lord, "the next time I will try
To bring our craft to another ending,
And if I do not, sires, let me have the blame.
There was fault in it somewhat, well I know."
     Another said the fire was over-hot—
But, be it hot or cold, I dare say this,
That we always ended up amiss.
We failed to get what we tried to have,
And in our madness evermore we raved.
And when we were together everyone,
Every man seemed a Solomon.
But every thing that shines as gold
Is not gold, as I have heard told;
Nor every apple that is fair to the eye
Is good, whatsoever men chatter or cry.
Right so, look, fared it among us;
He who seemed the wisest, by Jesus,
Was most the foolish, when it came to the test;
And he was a thief who seemed most true.
That shall you know, before I from you wend,
By when I of my tale have made an end.

PART TWO

Ther is a chanoun of religioun
Amonges us, wolde infecte al a toun,
Though it as greet were as was Ninivee,
Rome, Alisaundre, Troye, and othere three.
His sleightes and his infinit falsnesse
Ther coude no man wryten, as I gesse,
Thogh that he mighte liven a thousand yeer.
In al this world of falshede nis his peer;
For in his termes so he wolde him winde,
And speke his wordes in so sly a kinde,
Whan he commune shal with any wight,
That he wol make him doten anon right,
But it a feend be, as him-selven is.
Ful many a man hath he bigyled er this,
And wol, if that he live may a whyle;
And yet men ryde and goon ful many a myle
Him for to seke and have his aqueyntaunce,
Noght knowinge of his false governaunce.
And if yow list to yeve me audience,
I wol it tellen heer in your presence.

    But worshipful chanouns religious,
Ne demeth nat that I sclaundre your hous,
Al-though my tale of a chanoun be.
Of every ordre som shrewe is, parde,
And god forbede that al a companye
Sholde rewe a singuler mannes folye.
To sclaundre yow is no-thing myn entente,
But to correcten that is mis I mente.
This tale was nat only told for yow,
But eek for othere mo; ye woot wel how
That, among Cristes apostelles twelve,
Ther nas no traytour but Judas him-selve.
Than why sholde al the remenant have blame
That giltlees were? by yow I seye the same.
Save only this, if ye wol herkne me,
If any Judas in your covent be,
Remeveth him bitymes, I yow rede,

PART TWO

There is a canon of religion
Among us, who would infect all a town,
Though it as great were as Nineveh,[7]
Rome, Alexandria, Troy, and others three.
His deceptions and his infinite falseness
There could no man write, as I guess,
Though he might live a thousand year.
In all this world of falsehood none is his peer,
For in his terminology he will so him wind,
And speak his words in so sly a kind,
When he communes with any person,
Then he will make him act dumb,
Unless the man a fiend is, as he himself is.
Full many a man has he beguiled before this,
And will, if he lives longer for awhile;
And yet men ride and go full many a mile
Him to seek and have his acquaintance,
Not knowing of his false intentions.
And if you wish to give me audience,
I will it tell here in your presence.

    But worshipful canons religious,
Deem not that I slander your house,
Although my tale of a canon be.
In every house some wretch is, by God,
And God forbid that all a company
Should rue a single man's folly.
To slander you is in no way my intent,
But to correct what is amiss I mention.
This tale is not only told for you,
But also for others more; you know well how
That among Christ's apostles twelve
There was no traitor but Judas himself.
Then why should all the others have a blemish
Who guiltless were? To you I say the same,
Save only this, if you will harken to me:
If any Judas in your house be,
Remove him soon, I advise you,

If shame or loss may causen any drede.
And beth no-thing displesed, I yow preye,
But in this cas herkneth what I shal seye.
In London was a preest, an annueleer,
That therein dwelled hadde many a yeer,
Which was so pleasaunt and so servisable
Unto the wyf, wher-as he was at table,
That she wolde suffre him no-thing for to paye
For bord ne clothing, wente he never so gaye;
And spending-silver hadde he right y-now.
Therof no fors; I wol procede as now,
And telle forth my tale of the chanoun,
That broghte this preest to confusioun.

 This false chanoun cam up-on a day
Unto this preestes chambre, wher he lay,
Biseching him to lene him a certeyn
Of gold, and he wolde quyte it him ageyn.
"Lene me a mark," quod he, "but dayes three,
And at my day I wol it quyten thee.
And if so be that thou me finde fals,
Another day do hange me by the hals!"

 This preest him took a mark, and that as swythe,
And this chanoun him thanked ofte sythe,
And took his leve, and wente forth his weye,
And at the thridde day broghte his moneye,
And to the preest he took his gold agayn,
Wherof this preest was wonder glad and fayn.

 "Certes," quod he, "no-thing anoyeth me
To lene a man a noble, or two or three,
Or what thing were in my possessioun,
Whan he so trewe is of condicioun,
That in no wyse he broke wol his day;
To swich a man I can never seye nay."

 "What!" quod this chanoun, "sholde I be untrewe?
Nay, that were thing y-fallen al of-newe.
Trouthe is a thing that I wol ever kepe
Un-to that day in which that I shal crepe
In-to my grave, and elles god forbede;
Bileveth this as siker as is your crede.

If shame or loss cause any fear.
And be in no way displeased, I pray you,
But in this case listen to what I shall say.
In London was a chantry priest,[8]
Who there had dwelt many a year,
And who was so pleasant and attentive
Unto the wife, when he was at table,
That she would not allow him to pay
For board nor clothing, though he was well dressed,
And spending silver had he right enough.
No matter; I will proceed as now,
And tell forth my tale of the canon
Who brought this priest to ruin.

    This false canon came upon a day
Unto this priest's chamber, where he lay,
Beseeching him to lend him of gold a certain
Amount, and he would pay him back again.
"Lend me a mark," said he, "for but days three,
And at my day I will repay you.
And if it so be that you find me untrue,
Another day hang me by the neck!"

    This priest he took a mark, right then,
And this canon thanked him again and again,
And took his leave, and went forth his way,
And at the third day brought his money,
And to the priest he repaid his gold he him owed,
Whereof this priest was wondrous eager and glad.

    "Certainly," said he, "in no way does it annoy me
To lend a man a noble, or two, or three,
Or something in my possession,
When he so true is of disposition
That in no way he misses his due day;
To such a man I can never say nay."

    "What!" said this canon, "should I be untrue?
Nay, that would be something new.
Truth is a thing that I will ever keep
Unto that day in which that I shall creep
Into my grave, and otherwise God forbid.
Believe this as surely as your Creed.

God thanke I, and in good tyme be it sayd,
That ther was never man yet yvel apayd
For gold ne silver that he to me lente,
Ne never falshede in myn herte I mente.
And sir," quod he, "now of my privetee,
Sin ye so goodlich han been un-to me,
And kythed to me so greet gentillesse,
Somwhat to quyte with your kindenesse,
I wol yow shewe, and, if yow list to lere,
I wol yow teche pleynly the manere,
How I can werken in philosophye.
Taketh good heed, ye shul wel seen as yë,
That I wol doon a maistrie er I go."

      "Ye," quod the preest, "ye, sir, and wol ye so?
Marie! ther-of I pray yow hertely!"

      "At your comandement, sir, trewely,"
Quod the chanoun, "and elles god forbede!"

      Lo, how this theef coude his servyse bede!
Ful sooth it is, that swich profred servyse
Stinketh, as witnessen thise olde wyse;
And that ful sone I wol it verifye
In this chanoun, rote of al trecherye,
That ever-more delyt hath and gladnesse—
Swich freendly thoughtes in his herte impresse—
How Cristes peple he may to meschief bringe;
God kepe us from his fals dissimulinge!

      Noght wiste this preest with whom that he delte,
Ne of his harm cominge he no-thing felte.
O sely preest! O sely innocent!
With coveityse anon thou shalt be blent!
O gracelees, ful blind is thy conceit,
No-thing ne artow war of the deceit
Which that this fox y-shapen hath to thee!
His wyly wrenches thou ne mayst nat flee.
Wherfor, to go to the conclusioun
That refereth to thy confusioun,
Unhappy man! anon I wol me hye
To tellen thyn unwit and thy folye,
And eek the falsnesse of that other wrecche,

I thank God, fortunately it may be said,
That there was never yet man evilly repaid
For gold or silver that he to me lent,
Nor ever falsehood in my heart I meant.
And sire," said he, "now confidentially,
Since you so good have been to me,
And shown to me such great gentleness,
Somewhat to repay you for your kindness
I will show you, and if you wish to learn,
I will you teach plainly the manner
How I can work in alchemy.
Take good heed; you will see with your own eyes
That masterfully will I perform before I go."

    "Yea," said the priest, "yea, sire, and will you so?
By Saint Mary, thereof I pray you heartily."

    "At your commandment, sir, truly,"
Said the canon, "and anything else may God forbid!"

    Look, how this thief could his service proffer!
For truth it is such favors unasked for
Stink, so say the wise,
And that full soon will I verify
In this canon, root of all treachery,
Who evermore found delight and cheer—
Such fiendish thoughts his heart held near—
Of how to Christ's people he might destruction bring.
God keep us from his false dissembling!

    Not knew this priest with whom he dealt,
Nor of his harm coming he any thing felt.
Oh nice priest! Oh innocent naive!
By covetousness soon will you be fleeced!
Oh unfortunate one, full blind is your mind
In no way are you aware of the deceit
Which this fox has for you prepared!
His wily tricks you may not flee.
Wherefore, to go to the conclusion,
That refers to your ruin,
Unlucky man, anon I will me hie
To tell your unwit and your folly,
And also the falseness of that other wretch,

As ferforth as that my conning may strecche.

    This chanoun was my lord, ye wolden wene?
Sir host, in feith, and by the hevenes quene,
It was another chanoun, and nat he,
That can an hundred fold more subtiltee!
He hath bitrayed folkes many tyme;
Of his falshede it dulleth me to ryme.
Ever whan that I speke of his falshede,
For shame of him my chekes wexen rede;
Algates, they biginnen for to glowe,
For reednesse have I noon, right wel I knowe,
In my visage; for fumes dyverse
Of metals, which ye han herd me reherce,
Consumed and wasted han my reednesse.
Now tak heed of this chanouns cursednesse!

    "Sir," quod he to the preest, "lat your man gon
For quik-silver, that we it hadde anon;
And lat him bringen ounces two or three;
And whan he comth, as faste shul ye see
A wonder thing, which ye saugh never er this."

    "Sir," quod the preest, "it shal be doon, y-wis."
He bad his servant fecchen him this thing,
And he al redy was at his bidding,
And wente him forth, and cam anon agayn
With this quik-silver, soothly for to sayn,
And took thise ounces three to the chanoun;
And he hem leyde fayre and wel adoun,
And bad the servant coles for to bringe,
That he anon mighte go to his werkinge.

    The coles right anon weren y-fet,
And this chanoun took out a crosselet
Of his bosom, and shewed it the preest.
"This instrument," quod he, "which that thou seest,
Tak in thyn hand, and put thy-self ther-inne
Of this quik-silver an ounce, and heer biginne,
In the name of Crist, to wexe a philosofre.
Ther been ful fewe, whiche that I wolde profre
To shewen hem thus muche of my science.
For ye shul seen heer, by experience,

As far as my understanding will stretch.
    This canon was my lord, do you suppose?
Sir Host, in faith, and by heaven's queen,
It was another canon, and not he,
Who knew a hundredfold more subtlety.
He has betrayed folk many times;
Of his falseness it depresses me to rhyme.
Whenever I speak of his falsehood,
For shame of him my cheeks wax red.
At least they begin to glow,
For redness have I none, right well I know,
In my visage; for fumes diverse
Of metals, which you have heard me rehearse,
Consumed and wasted have my redness.
Now take heed of this canon's cursedness!
    "Sire," said he to the priest, "let your man go
For quicksilver, that we have it anon;
And let him bring ounces two or three;
And when he comes, as fast as you shall see
A wondrous thing, which you never saw before this."
    "Sire," said the priest, "it shall be done, truly."
He bade his servant fetch him this thing,
And he already was at his bidding,
And went him forth, and came anon again
With this quicksilver, shortly to say,
And took these ounces three to the canon;
And he them laid fair and well down,
And bade the servant coals to bring,
That he anon might go to his working.
    The coals right anon were fetched,
And this canon took out his crucible
From his bosom, and showed it to the priest.
"This instrument," said he, "which you see,
Take in your hand, and put yourself therein
Of this quicksilver an ounce, and here begin,
In name of Christ, to become an alchemist.
There be full few to whom I would offer
To show them this much of my science.
For you shall see here, by experience,

That this quik-silver wol I mortifye
Right in your sighte anon, withouten lye,
And make it as good silver and as fyn
As ther is any in your purs or myn,
Or elleswher, and make it malliable;
And elles, holdeth me fals and unable
Amonges folk for ever to appere!
I have a poudre heer, that coste me dere,
Shal make al good, for it is cause of al
My conning, which that I yow shewen shal.
Voydeth your man, and lat him be ther-oute,
And shet the dore, whyls we been aboute
Our privetee, that no man us espye
Whyls that we werke in this philosophye."
Al as he bad, fulfilled was in dede,
This ilke servant anon-right out yede,
And his maister shette the dore anon,
And to hir labour speedily they gon.

     This preest, at this cursed chanouns bidding,
Up-on the fyr anon sette this thing,
And blew the fyr, and bisied him ful faste;
And this chanoun in-to the croslet caste
A poudre, noot I wher-of that it was
Y-maad, other of chalk, other of glas,
Or som-what elles, was nat worth a flye
To blynde with the preest; and bad him hye
The coles for to couchen al above
The croslet; "for, in tokening I thee love,"
Quod this chanoun, "thyn owene hondes two
Shul werche al thing which that shal heer be do."

     "Graunt mercy," quod the preest, and was ful glad,
And couched coles as the chanoun bad.
And whyle he bisy was, this feendly wrecche,
This fals chanoun, the foule feend him fecche!
Out of his bosom took a bechen cole,
In which ful subtilly was maad an hole,
And ther-in put was of silver lymaille
An ounce, and stopped was, with-outen fayle,
The hole with wex, to kepe the lymail in.

That this quicksilver I will solidify
Right in your sight anon, without lie,
And make it as good as silver and as fine
As there is any in your purse or mine,
Or elsewhere, and make it malleable;
Or if not hold me false and worthless
Among folk forever to appear.
I have a powder here, that cost me dear,
Shall make it all good, for it is cause of all
My cunning, which I shall show you.
Send away your man, and let him be gone out,
And shut the door, while we be about
Our secrecy, that no man us espy,
Whilst that we work in this philosophy."
All as he bade was fulfilled in deed.
This same servant anon right went out,
And his master anon shut the door,
And speedily went they to their labor.

This priest, at this cursed canon's bidding,
Upon the fire anon set this thing,
And blew the fire, and busied him full fast.
And this canon into the crucible cast
A powder, I know not of what it was
Made, maybe of chalk, maybe of glass,
Or something else, which was not worth a fly,
To blind with this priest; and bade him hie
The coals for to arrange all above
The crucible. "For as a sign that I you love,"
Said this canon, "your own hands two
Shall work all things which we shall here do."

"Grant mercy," said the priest, and was full glad,
And set the coals as the canon bade.
And while he busy was, this fiendish wretch,
This false canon—the foul fiend him fetch!—
Out of his bosom took a beechwood charcoal,
In which full subtly was made a hole,
And therein were put an ounce of silver filings,
And was stopped, without fail,
This hole with wax, to keep the filings in.

And understondeth, that this false gin
Was nat maad ther, but it was maad bifore;
And othere thinges I shal telle more
Herafterward, which that he with him broghte;
Er he cam ther, him to bigyle he thoghte,
And so he dide, er that they wente a-twinne;
Til he had terved him, coude he not blinne.
It dulleth me whan that I of him speke,
On his falshede fayn wolde I me wreke,
If I wiste how; but he is heer and ther:
He is so variaunt, he abit no-wher.

But taketh heed now, sirs, for goddes love!
He took his cole of which I spak above,
And in his hond he baar it prively.
And whyls the preest couched busily
The coles, as I tolde yow er this,
This chanoun seyde, "freend, ye doon amis;
This is nat couched as it oghte be;
But sone I shal amenden it," quod he.
"Now lat me medle therwith but a whyle,
For of yow have I pitee, by seint Gyle!
Ye been right hoot, I see wel how ye swete,
Have heer a cloth, and wype away the wete."
And whyles that the preest wyped his face,
This chanoun took his cole with harde grace,
And leyde it above, up-on the middeward
Of the croslet, and blew wel afterward,
Til that the coles gonne faste brenne.

"Now yeve us drinke," quod the chanoun thenne,
"As swythe al shal be wel, I undertake;
Sitte we doun, and lat us mery make."
And whan that this chanounes bechen cole
Was brent, al the lymaille, out of the hole,
Into the croslet fil anon adoun;
And so it moste nedes, by resoun,
Sin it so even aboven couched was;
But ther-of wiste the preest no-thing, alas!
He demed alle the coles y-liche good,
For of the sleighte he no-thing understood.

And understand that this trick thing
Was not made there, but it was made before;
And other things I shall tell more
Hereafterward, which he with him brought.
Before he came there, him to beguile he thought,
And so he did, before they went apart;
Till he had skinned him, he could not cease.
It depresses me when I of him speak.
On his falsehood gladly would I vengeance wreak,
If I knew how, but he is here and there;
He is so changeable, he abides nowhere.[9]

    But take heed now, sires, for God's love!
He took his charcoal of which I spoke above,
And in his hand he bore it secretly.
And while the priest arranged busily
The coals, as I told you before this,
This canon said, "Friend, you do amiss.
This is not arranged as it ought be;
But soon I shall amend it," said he.
"Now let me meddle with it a little while,
For of you I have pity, by Saint Gile!
You be right eager, I see how you sweat.
Have here a cloth, and wipe away the wet."
And while the priest wiped his face,
This canon took his charcoal—to him no grace!—
And laid it above the middle
Of the crucible, and blew well afterward
Till that the coals began to fast burn.

    "Now give us drink," said the canon then;
"And quickly all shall be well, I undertake.
Sit we down, and let us merry make."
And when that this canon's beechwood coal
Was burnt, all of the filings out of the hole
Into the crucible fell soon adown;
And so it must needs, by reason
Since it was so precisely arranged above.
But alas! the priest nothing knew thereof.
He deemed all the coals alike good,
For of that trick he nothing understood.

And whan this alkamistre saugh his tyme,
"Rys up," quod he, "sir preest, and stondeth by me;
And for I woot wel ingot have ye noon,
Goth, walketh forth, and bring us a chalk-stoon;
For I wol make oon of the same shap
That is an ingot, if I may han hap.
And bringeth eek with yow a bolle or a panne,
Ful of water, and ye shul see wel thanne
How that our bisinesse shal thryve and preve.
And yet, for ye shul han no misbileve
Ne wrong conceit of me in your absence,
I ne wol nat been out of your presence
But go with yow, and come with yow ageyn."
The chambre-dore, shortly for to seyn,
They opened and shette, and wente hir weye.
And forth with hem they carieden the keye,
And come agayn with-outen any delay.
What sholde I tarien al the longe day?
He took the chalk, and shoop it in the wyse
Of an ingot, as I shal yow devyse.

     I seye, he took out of his owene sleve
A teyne of silver (yvele mote he cheve!)
Which that ne was nat but an ounce of weighte;
And taketh heed now of his cursed sleighte!

     He shoop his ingot, in lengthe and eek in brede,
Of this teyne, with-outen any drede,
So slyly, that the preest it nat espyde;
And in his sleve agayn he gan it hyde;
And fro the fyr he took up his matere,
And in th'ingot putte it with mery chere,
And in the water-vessel he it caste
Whan that him luste, and bad the preest as faste,
"Look what ther is, put in thyn hand and grope,
Thow finde shalt ther silver, as I hope;
What, devel of helle! sholde it elles be?
Shaving of silver silver is, pardee!"
He putte his hond in, and took up a teyne
Of silver fyn, and glad in every veyne
Was this preest, whan he saugh that it was so.

And when this alchemist saw his time,
"Rise up," said he, "sir priest, and stand by me;
And for well I know ingot mold have you none,
Go, walk forth, and bring a chalk stone;
For I will make of it the same shape
That is an ingot, if I may have good luck.
And bring also with you a bowl or a pan
Full of water, and you shall see well then
How our business shall thrive and succeed.
And yet, that you shall have no disbelief
Or wrong idea of me in your absence,
I will not be out of your presence,
But go with you and come with you again."
The chamber door, shortly for to say,
They opened and shut, and went their way.
And forth with them they carried the key,
And returned again without delay.
Why should I tarry all the long day?
He took the chalk and made it into the shape
Of an ingot, as I shall you describe.

   I say, he took out of his own sleeve
A small silver ingot—so does he evil!—
That was not but an ounce of weight.
And take heed now of his cursed sleight!

   He shaped his mold in length and breadth
Of this ingot, without any doubt,
So slyly that the priest not it espied,
And in his sleeve again he began it to hide,
And from the fire he took up his material,
And into the mold put it with merry face,
And in the water-vessel he it cast,
When that he desired, and bade the priest at last,
"Look what there is; put it in your hand and test.
You shall find there silver, as I hope."
What, devil of hell, shall it else be?
Shavings of silver, silver is, by God!
He put his hand in and took up an ingot
Of silver fine, and glad in every vein
Was this priest, when he saw it was so.

"Goddes blessing, and his modres also,
And alle halwes have ye, sir chanoun,"
Seyde this preest, "and I hir malisoun,
But, and ye vouche-sauf to techen me
This noble craft and this subtilitee,
I wol be youre, in al that ever I may!"

Quod the chanoun, "yet wol I make assay
The second tyme, that ye may taken hede
And been expert of this, and in your nede
Another day assaye in myn absence
This disciplyne and this crafty science.
Lat take another ounce," quod he tho,
"Of quik-silver, with-outen wordes mo,
And do ther-with as ye han doon er this
With that other, which that now silver is."

This preest him bisieth in al that he can
To doon as this chanoun, this cursed man,
Comanded him, and faste he blew the fyr,
For to come to th'effect of his desyr.
And this chanoun, right in the mene whyle,
Al redy was, the preest eft to bigyle,
And, for a countenance, in his hande he bar
And holwe stikke (tak keep and be war!)
In the ende of which an ounce, and na-more,
Of silver lymail put was, as bifore
Was in his cole, and stopped with wex weel
For to kepe in his lymail every deel.
And whyl this preest was in his bisinesse,
This chanoun with his stikke gan him dresse
To him anon, and his pouder caste in
As he did er; (the devel out of his skin
Him terve, I pray to god, for his falshede;
For he was ever fals in thoght and dede);
And with this stikke, above the croslet,
That was ordeyned with that false get,
He stired the coles, til relente gan
The wex agayn the fyr, as every man,
But it a fool be, woot wel it mot nede,
And al that in the stikke was out yede,

"God's blessing, and his mother's also,
And all saints, have you, sir canon,"
Said the priest, "and I here me curse,
Unless you vouchsafe to teach me
This noble craft and this subtlety,
I will be yours in all that ever I may."

　　Said the canon, "Yet will I make assay
The second time, that you may take heed
And be an expert of this, and as you need
Another day, assay in my absence
This discipline and this crafty science.
Let take another ounce," said he then,
"Of quicksilver, without words more,
And do therewith as you have done before this
With that other, which now silver is."

　　This priest busied himself in all that he could
To do as this canon, this cursed man,
Commanded him, and fast blew the fire,
For to come to the effect of his desire.
And this canon, right in the meanwhile,
Already was this priest again to beguile,
And for the sake of show in his hand he bore
A hollow stick—take care and beware!—
In the end of which an ounce, and no more,
Of silver filings put was, as before
Was in his charcoal, and stopped with wax well
For to keep in his filings every bit.
And while this priest was about his business,
This canon with his wand began to touch
The fire anon, and his powder cast in
As he did before—the devil out his skin
Him flay, I pray to God, for his falsehood!
For he was ever false in thought and deed—
And with this wand above the crucible,
That was prepared with that hollow end,
He stirred the coals until melting began
The wax against the fire, as every man,
But who a fool be, knows well it must needs do,
And all that was in the stick went out,

And in the croslet hastily it fel.
Now gode sirs, what wol ye bet than wel?
Whan that this preest thus was bigyled ageyn,
Supposing noght but trouthe, soth to seyn,
He was so glad, that I can nat expresse
In no manere his mirthe and his gladnesse;
And to the chanoun he profred eftsone
Body and good; "ye," quod the chanoun sone,
"Though povre I be, crafty thou shalt me finde;
I warne thee, yet is ther more bihinde.
Is ther any coper her-inne?" seyde he.
"Ye," quod the preest, "sir, I trowe wel ther be."
"Elles go bye us som, and that as swythe,
Now, gode sir, go forth thy wey and hy the."
    He wente his wey, and with the coper cam,
And this chanoun it in his handes nam,
And of that coper weyed out but an ounce.
Al to simple is my tonge to pronounce,
As ministre of my wit, the doublenesse
Of this chanoun, rote of al cursednesse.
He seemed freendly to hem that knewe him noght,
But he was freendly bothe in herte and thoght.
It werieth me to telle of his falsnesse,
And nathelees yet wol I it expresse,
To th'entente that men may be war therby,
And for noon other cause, trewely.
    He putte his ounce of coper in the croslet,
And on the fyr as swythe he hath it set,
And caste in poudre, and made the preest to blowe,
And in his werking for to stoupe lowe,
As he dide er, and al nas but a jape;
Right as him liste, the preest he made his ape;
And afterward in th'ingot he it caste,
And in the panne putte it at the laste
Of water, and in he putte his owene hond.
And in his sleve (as ye biforn-hond
Herde me telle) he hadde a silver teyne.
He slyly took it out, this cursed heyne—
Unwiting this preest of his false craft—

And into the crucible hastily it fell.
Now, good sirs, what can be better than well?
When this priest thus was beguiled again,
Supposing nought but truth to witness,
He was so glad that I cannot express
In any manner his mirth and his gladness;
And to the canon he offered again
Body and soul. "Yea," said the canon soon,
"Though I poor be, skillful shall you find me.
I warn you, there is yet more to see.
Is there any copper here?" said he.
"Yes," said the priest, "I think—or maybe not."
"Then go buy us some, and right quick;
Now sir, go forth your way and hurry."

    He went his way, and with the copper came,
And this canon took it in his hands,
And of that copper weighed out but an ounce.
All too simple is my tongue to pronounce,
As minister of my wit, the duplicity
Of this canon, root of all cursedness!
He seemed friendly to those who knew him not,
But he was fiendish both in work and thought.
It wearies me to tell of his falseness,
And nevertheless yet will I express it,
With the intent that men may be warned thereby,
And for no other cause, truly.

    He put this ounce of copper in the crucible,
And on the fire immediately he has it set,
And cast in the powder, and made the priest to blow,
And in his working for to stoop low,
As he did before—and all was but a jape;
Right as he wished, the priest he made his ape!
And afterward in the mold he it cast,
And in the pan put it at the last
Of water, and in he put his own hand,
And in his sleeve (as you beforehand
Heard me tell) he had a silver ingot.
He slyly took it out, this cursed wretch,
Ignorant this priest of his false craft,

And in the pannes botme he hath it laft;
And in the water rombled to and fro,
And wonder prively took up also
The coper teyne, noght knowing this preest,
And hidde it, and him hente by the breest,
And to him spak, and thus seyde in his game,
"Stoupeth adoun, by god, ye be to blame,
Helpeth me now, as I dide yow whyl-er,
Putte in your hand, and loketh what is ther."
This preest took up this silver teyne anon,
And thanne seyde the chanoun, "lat us gon
With thise three teynes, which that we han wroght,
To son goldsmith, and wite if they been oght.
For, by my feith, I nolde, for myn hood,
But-if that they were silver, fyn and good,
And that as swythe preved shal it be."
    Un-to the goldsmith with thise teynes three
They wente, and putte thise teynes in assay
To fyr and hamer; mighte no man sey nay,
But that they weren as hem oghte be.
    This sotted preest, who was gladder than he?
Was never brid gladder agayn the day,
Ne nightingale, in the sesoun of May,
Nas never noon that luste bet to singe;
Ne lady lustier in carolinge
Or for to speke of love and wommanhede,
Ne knight in armes to doon an hardy dede
To stonde in grace of his lady dere,
Than had this preest this sory craft to lere;
And to the chanoun thus he spak and seyde,
"For love of god, that for us alle deyde,
And as I may deserve it un-to yow,
What shal this receit coste? telleth now!"
    "By our lady," quod this chanoun, "it is dere,
I warne yow wel; for, save I and a frere,
In Engelond ther can no man it make."
    "No fors," quod he, "now, sir, for goddes sake,
What shal I paye? telleth me, I preye."
    "Y-wis," quod he, "it is ful dere, I seye;

And in the pan's bottom he has it left;
And in the water groped to and fro,
And wondrous secretly took up also
The copper piece, the priest still deceived,
And hid it, and him grasped by the breast,
And him spoke, and thus said in his game:
"Stoop down, by God, be you to blame!
Help me now, as I did you before;
And put in your hand, and look what is there."
This priest took up this silver ingot anon,
And then said the canon, "Let us go
With these three ingots, that we have wrought,
To some goldsmith and learn if they be what they ought,
For, by my faith, I would not want, by my hood,
That they were anything but silver fine and good,
And that soon shall it tested be."
    Unto the goldsmith with these ingots three
They went and put their ingots in assay
To fire and hammer; might no man say nay,
But that they were as they ought to be.
    This besotted priest, who was gladder than he?
Was never a bird gladder at daybreak,
No nightingale, in the season of May,
Was ever any that lusted better to sing;
Nor lady lustier in caroling,
Or for to speak of love and womanhood,
Nor knight in arms to do a brave deed,
To stand in grace of his lady dear,
Than was this priest this sorry craft to learn.
And to the canon thus he spoke and said:
"For love of God, who for us all died,
And as I may you repay,
What shall this recipe cost? Tell now!"
    "By our lady," said the canon, "it is dear,
I warn you well; for save I and a confrere,
In England there can no man it make."
    "No matter," said he, "no, sire, for God's sake,
What shall I pay? Tell me, I pray."
    "Truly," said he, "it is full dear, I say.

Sir, at o word, if that thee list it have,
Ye shul paye fourty pound, so god me save!
And, nere the freendship that ye did er this
To me, ye sholde paye more, y-wis."

    This preest the somme of fourty pound anon
Of nobles fette, and took hem everichon
To this chanoun, for this ilke receit;
Al his werking nas but fraude and deceit.

    "Sir preest," he seyde, "I kepe han no loos
Of my craft, for I wolde it kept were cloos;
And as ye love me, kepeth it secree;
For, and men knewe al my subtilitee,
By god, they wolden han so greet envye
To me, by-cause of my philosophye,
I sholde be deed, ther were non other weye."

    "God it forbede!" quod the preest, "what sey ye?"
Yet hadde I lever spenden al the good
Which that I have (and elles wexe I wood!)
Than that ye sholden falle in swich mescheef."

    "For your good wil, sir, have ye right good preef."
Quod the chanoun, "and far-wel, grant mercy!"
He wente his wey and never the preest him sy
After that day; and whan that this preest sholde
Maken assay, at swich tyme as he wolde,
Of this receit, far-wel! it wolde nat be!
Lo, thus bijaped and bigyled was he!
Thus maketh he his introduccioun
To bringe folk to hir destruccioun.—

    Considereth, sirs, how that, in ech estaat,
Bitwixe men and gold ther is debaat
So ferforth, that unnethes is ther noon
This multiplying blent so many oon,
That in good feith I trowe that it be
The cause grettest of swich scarsetee.
Philosophres speken so mistily
In this craft, that men can nat come therby,
For any wit that men han now a-dayes.
They mowe wel chiteren, as doon thise jayes,
And in her termes sette hir lust and peyne,

Sir, in a word, if that you wish it to have,
You shall pay forty pounds, so God me save!
And if were not for your kindness before this
To me, you would pay more, I guess."
    This priest the sum of forty pounds anon
Of nobles fetched, and took them every one
To this canon for this recipe.
All his working was nought but fraud and deceit.
    "Sir priest," he said, "I care not for renown
In my craft, for I would it were kept discreet;
And, as you love me, keep it secret.
For, if men knew all my subtlety,
By God, they would have so great envy
Of me by cause of my alchemy
I should be dead; there is no other way."
    "God it forbid," said the priest, "what say you?
I would spend everything
That I have, or go crazy,
Rather than you should fall in such mischief."
    "For your good will, sir, have you right good proof,"
Said the canon, "and farewell, grant mercy!"
He went his way, and never the priest him saw
After that day; and when that the priest should
Make assay, at such time as he would,
Of this recipe, farewell! It would not be.
Look, thus tricked and beguiled was he!
Thus made he his introduction,
To bring folk to their destruction.
    Consider, sires, how that, in each estate,
Between men and gold there is strife
So fierce that of gold there is to be had almost none.
This alchemistry deceives so many
That in good faith I believe it be
The cause greatest of such scarcity.
Alchemists speak so hazily
Of this craft that men cannot learn it thereby,
At least not with the wits that men have nowadays.
They more often chatter as do jays,
And in their terms set their lust and pain,

But to hir purpos shul they never atteyne.
A man may lightly lerne, if he have aught,
To multiplye, and bringe his good to naught!
   Lo! swich a lucre is in this lusty game,
A mannes mirthe it wol torne un-to grame,
And empten also grete and hevy purses,
And maken folk for to purchasen curses
Of hem, that han hir good therto y-lent.
O! fy! for shame! they that han been brent,
Allas! can they nat flee the fyres hete?
Ye that it use, I rede ye it lete,
Lest ye lese al; for bet than never is late.
Never to thryve were to long a date.
Though ye prolle ay, ye shul it never finde;
Ye been as bolde as is Bayard the blinde,
That blundreth forth, and peril casteth noon;
He is as bold to renne agayn a stoon
As for to goon besydes in the weye.
So faren ye that multiplye, I seye.
If that your yën can nat seen aright,
Loke that your minde lakke noght his sight.
For, though ye loke never so brode, and stare,
Ye shul nat winne a myte on that chaffare,
But wasten al that ye may rape and renne.
Withdrawe the fyr, lest it to faste brenne;
Medleth na-more with that art, I mene,
For, if ye doon, your thrift is goon ful clene.
And right as swythe I wol yow tellen here,
What philosophres seyn in this matere.
   Lo, thus seith Arnold of the Newe Toun,
As his Rosarie maketh mencioun;
He seith right thus, with-outen any lye,
"Ther may no man Mercurie mortifye,
But it be with his brother knowleching.
How that he, which that first seyde this thing,
Of philosophres fader was, Hermes;
He seith, how that the dragoun, doutelees,
Ne deyeth nat, but-if that he be slayn
With his brother; and that is for to sayn,

But to their purpose shall they never attain.
A man may easily learn, if he has anything,
To alchemize, and bring himself to nought!
　Look! Such gain is in this fine game,
That a man's mirth it will turn unto shame,
And empty also great and heavy purses,
And make folk for to purchase curses
On those to whom they their goods leant.
Oh, fie, for shame! They who have been burnt,
Alas, can they not flee the fire's heat?
You who it use, I advise you leave it,
Lest you lose all; for better than never is late.
Never to thrive is too long a wait.
Though you prowl forever, you shall never find it.
You be as bold as is Bayard the blind,[10]
Who blunders forth and peril thinks not upon.
He is as likely to run against a stone
As for to go along the road.
So fare you who alchemize, I say.
If your eyes cannot see aright,
Look that your mind lacks not its sight.
For though you look never so hard and stare,
You shall nothing profit in those wares,
But rather lose all that you may acquire.
Dampen the fire, lest it too fast burn;
Meddle no more with that art, I say,
For if you do, your good is gone full clean.
And right as rain I will tell you here
What alchemists say in this matter.
　Look, thus says Arnaldus of Villanova,[11]
As he in his Rosarie made mention;
He says right thus, without any lie:
"There may no man mercury solidify
But it be with his brother sulphur;
How be that he who first said this thing
Of alchemists' father was, Hermes Trismegistus;[12]
He said how the dragon, doubtless,
Dies not unless he be slain
With his brother; or put another way

By the dragoun, Mercurie and noon other
He understood; and brimstoon by his brother,
That out of *sol* and *luna* were y-drawe.
And therfor," seyde he, "tak heed to my sawe,
Let no man bisy him this art for to seche,
But-if that he th'entencioun and speche
Of philosophres understonde can;
And if he do, he is a lewed man.
For this science and this conning," quod he,
"Is of the secree of secrees, parde."

　　Also ther was a disciple of Plato,
That on a tyme seyde his maister to,
As his book Senior wol bere witnesse,
And this was his demande in soothfastnesse:
"Tel me the name of the privy stoon?"

　　And Plato answerde unto him anoon,
"Tak the stoon that Titanos men name."

　　"Which is that?" quod he, "Magnesia is the same,"
Seyde Plato. "Ye, sir, and is it thus?
This is *ignotum per ignotius*.
What is Magnesia, good sir, I yow preye?"

　　"It is a water that is maad, I seye,
Of elementes foure," quod Plato.

　　"Tel me the rote, good sir," quod he tho,
"Of that water, if that it be your wille?"

　　"Nay, nay," quod Plato, "certein, that I nille.
The philosophres sworn were everichoon,
That they sholden discovere it un-to noon,
Ne in no book it wryte in no manere;
For un-to Crist it is so leef and dere
That he wol nat that it discovered be,
But wher it lyketh to his deitee
Man for t'enspyre, and eek for to defende
Whom that him lyketh; lo, this is the ende."

　　Thanne conclude I thus; sith god of hevene
Ne wol nat that the philosophres nevene
How that a man shal come un-to this stoon,
I rede, as for the beste, lete it goon.
For who-so maketh god his adversarie,

By the dragon we mean Mercury, and no other.
And Sulphur, known as brimstone, is his brother,
And these are drawn from Silver and from Gold.
And therefore," said he—"take heed to my screed[13]—
Let no man busy him this art to seek,
Unless he the intention and speech
Of alchemists understands;
And if he does, he is a wretched man.
For this science and this cunning," he said,
"Is of the secret of the secrets, by God."

Also there was a disciple of Plato,[14]
Who once upon a time told his master so,
As in his book Senior Zadith will bear witness,
And this was his request in truthfulness:
"Tell me the name of the secret stone."

And Plato answered him anon,
"Take the stone that Titanos men name."

"Which is that?" said he. "Magnasia is the same,"
Said Plato. "Yea, sire, and is it thus?
This is *ignotum per ignocius.*[15]
What is Magnasia, good sire, I you pray?"

"It is water that is made, I say,
Of elements four," said Plato.

"Tell me the root, good sire," said he then.
"Of that water, if it be your will."

"Nay, nay," said Plato, "certainly, I will not.
The alchemists swear every one
That they should tell it unto no one,
Neither in a book nor write it in any way.
For unto Christ is it so near and dear
Who would not that it discovered be,
Except where it pleases his deity
Men to enlighten, and also to defend
Those whom he likes; look, this is the end."

Then I conclude this, since God of heaven
Wills not that the philosophers name
How a man shall come unto this stone,
I advise, as for the best, let it go.
For whoso makes God his adversary,

As for to werken any thing in contrarie
Of his wil, certes, never shal he thryve,
Thogh that he multiplye terme of his lyve.
And ther a poynt; for ended is my tale;
God sende every trewe man bote of his bale!—Amen

By working anything in contrary
To his will, certainly, never shall he thrive,
Though all his life he alchemize.
And there a stop, for ended is my tale.
God send every true man a cure for what him ails!—Amen

The Freres Tale

The Prologue

THIS WORTHY LIMITOUR, THIS noble Frere,
He made alwey a maner louring chere
Upon the Somnour, but for honestee
No vileyns word as yet to him spak he.
But atte laste he seyde un-to the Wyf,
"Dame," quod he, "god yeve yow right good lyf!
Ye han heer touched, al-so mote I thee,
In scole-matere greet difficultee;
Ye han seyd muchel thing right wel, I seye;
But dame, here as we ryden by the weye,
Us nedeth nat to speken but of game,
And lete auctoritees, on goddes name,
To preching and to scole eek of clergye.
But if it lyke to this companye,
I wol yow of a somnour telle a game.
Pardee, ye may wel knowe by the name,
That of a somnour may no good be sayd;
I praye that noon of you be yvel apayd.
A somnour is a renner up and doun
With mandements for fornicacioun,
And is y-bet at every tounes ende."
  Our host tho spak, "al sire, ye sholde be hende
And curteys, as a man of your estaat;
In companye we wol have no debaat.
Telleth your tale, and lat the Somnour be"
  "Nay," quod the Somnour, "lat him seye to me
What so him list; whan it comth to my lot,
By god, I shal him quyten every grot.
I shal him tellen which a greet honour
It is to be a flateringe limitour;
And eek of many another manere cryme
Which nedeth nat rehercen at this tyme;
And his offyce I shal him telle, y-wis."
  Our host answerde, "pees, na-more of this."

The Friar's Tale

The Prologue

THIS WORTHY LIMITOUR,[1] THIS noble Friar,
He looked always with a sort of scowl
Upon the Summoner, but for politeness' sake
No unpleasant words to him yet spoke he.
But at last he said unto the wife,
"Dame," said he, "God give you right good life!
You have here touched upon, as I swear to thee,
Questions difficult for scholars worthy.
You have said many things right well, I say;
But dame, here as we ride right by the way,
We need not speak but in play,
And leave citing authorities, in God's name,
To preaching and to schools of clergy.[2]
But if it is pleasing to this company,
I will you of a summoner tell a story.
By God, you may well know by the name
That of a summoner no good may be said;
I pray that none of you be displeased.
A summoner is a runner up and down
With summonses for fornication,
And is beaten at every town's end."

Our Host then spoke, "Ah, sir, you should be pleasant
And courteous, as a man of your estate;
In company we will have no debate.
Tell your tale, and let the Summoner be."

"Nay," said the Summoner, "let him say to me
What he wishes; when it comes to my lot,
By God, I shall get even to the last grot.
I shall tell him what a great honor
It is to be a flattering limitour,
And of many other crimes
That we need not mention at this time;
And I shall surely tell how he does his job."

Our Host answered, "Peace, no more of this!"

And after this he seyde un-to the Frere,
"Tel forth your tale, leve maister deere."

The Tale

Whilom ther was dwellinge in my contree
An erchedeken, a man of heigh degree,
That boldely dide execucioun
In punisshinge of fornicacioun,
Of wicchecraft, and eek of bauderye,
Of diffamacioun, and avoutrye,
Of chirche-reves, and of testaments,
Of contractes, and of lakke of sacraments,
And eek of many another maner cryme
Which nedeth nat rehercen at this tyme;
Of usure, and of symonye also.
But certes, lechours dide he grettest wo;
They sholde singen, if that they were hent;
And smale tytheres weren foule y-shent.
If any persone wolde up-on hem pleyne,
Ther mighte asterte him no pecunial peyne.
For smale tythes and for smal offringe
He made the peple pitously to singe.
For er the bisshop caughte hem with his hook,
They weren in the erchedeknes book.
Thanne hadde he, thurgh his jurisdiccioun,
Power to doon on hem correccioun.
He hadde a Somnour redy to his hond,
A slyer boy was noon in Engelond;
For subtilly he hadde his espiaille,
That taughte him, wher that him mighte availle.
He coude spare of lechours oon or two,
To techen him to foure and twenty mo.
For thogh this Somnour wood were as an hare,
To tell his harlotrye I wol nat spare;
For we been out of his correccioun;
They han of us no jurisdiccioun,
Ne never shullen, terme of alle hir lyves.

    "Peter! so been the wommen of the styves,"
Quod the Somnour, "y-put out of my cure!"

And after this he said unto the Friar,
"Tell forth your tale, my master dear."

The Tale

Once there was dwelling in my territory
An archdeacon, a man of high degree,[3]
Who boldly did execution
In punishing of fornication,
Of witchcraft, and also of solicitation,
Of defamation, and of embezzlement, and adultery,
And of violation of wills and contracts for marriage,
Of failure to observe the sacraments,
And also of many another crime
Which we need not rehearse at this time;
Of usury and of simony[4] too.
But certainly, to lechers did he greatest woe;
They had to plead if they were seized;
And unpaid tithes[5] and offerings were punished severely,
If any parson would of them complain.
They would escape no pecuniary pain.
For unpaid tithes and short offerings
He made the people piteously to beg,
For before the bishop caught them with his crook,
They were in the archdeacon's book.
Then had he, through his jurisdiction,
Power to do on them correction.
He had a summoner ready to his hand;
A slyer boyo was none in England;
Full subtly he made use of a ring of spies,
Who let him know where profit might reside.
He could spare of lechers one or two,
To lead him to four and twenty more.
For though this Summoner may go mad as a March hare,
To tell his whoring I will not spare;
For we be exempt from his power.
They have over us no jurisdiction,
Nor ever shall, long as they live.

  "By Saint Peter! so be women of the brothels,"
Said the Summoner, "put beyond our power!"

"Pees, with mischance and with misaventure,"
Thus seyde our host, "and lat him telle his tale.
Now telleth forth, thogh that the Somnour gale,
Ne spareth nat, myn owene maister dere."
    This false theef, this Somnour, quod the Frere,
Hadde alwey baudes redy to his hond,
As any hauk to lure in Engelond,
That tolde him al the secree that they knewe:
For hir acqueyntance was nat come of-newe.
They weren hise approwours prively;
He took him-self a greet profit therby;
His maister knew nat alwey what he wan.
With-outen mandement, a lewed man
He coude somne, on peyne of Cristes curs,
And they were gladde for to fille his purs,
And make him grete festes atte nale.
And right as Judas hadde purses smale,
And was a theef, right swich a theef was he;
His maister hadde but half his duëtee.
He was, if I shal yeven him his laude,
A theef, and eek a Somnour, and a baude.
He hadde eek wenches at his retenue,
That, whether that sir Robert or sir Huwe,
Or Jakke, or Rauf, or who-so that it were,
That lay by hem, they tolde it in his ere;
Thus was the wenche and he of oon assent.
And he wolde fecche a feyned mandement,
And somne hem to the chapitre bothe two,
And pile the man, and lete the wenche go.
Thanne wolde he seye, "frend, I shal for thy sake
Do stryken hir out of our lettres blake;
Thee thar na-more as in this cas travaille;
I am thy freend, ther I thee may availle."
Certeyn he knew of bryberyes mo
Than possible is to telle in yeres two.
For in this world nis dogge for the bowe,
That can an hurt deer from an hool y-knowe,
Bet than this Somnour knew a sly lechour,
Or an avouter, or a paramour.

"Peace! for you mischance and misadventure!"
Thus said our Host, "and let him tell his tale,
Now tell forth, though the Summoner blows a gale;
Nothing spare, my own master dear!"
        This false thief, this summoner, said the Friar,
Had always pimps ready to his hand,
As any hawk to lure in England,
They told him all the secrets that they knew,
For their acquaintance did not come of new.
They were full secretly his agents.
He took himself thereby a great profit.
His master knew not ever what he took from it.
Without a true summons a lewd[6] man
He could summon, on pain of Christ's curse,
And they were glad to fill his purse
And make him great feasts at the alehouse.
And right as Judas he had small sums to him entrusted,
And was a thief, right such a thief was he;
His master received but half what was to him due.
He was, if I shall give him fair credit,
A thief, and a summoner, and a pimp.
He had also wenches in his service,
Who, whether sir Hugh or sir Robert,
Or Jack, or Ralph, or whoso it was
Who lay by them, they told it in his ear.
Thus were the wench and he in league,
And he would fetch a feigned summons,
And summon them to archdeacon's court the two,
And rob the man, and let the wench go.
Then would he say, "Friend, I shall for your sake
Do strike her out of our letters black;
You thereby will no more be troubled by this case.
I am your friend, thereby I may you assist."
Certainly he knew of briberies more
Than is possible to tell in years four.
For certainly there is no hunting hound
That a wounded deer from an unhurt deer can tell
Better than this summoner knew a sly lecher,
Or an adulterer, or a paramour.

And, for that was the fruit of al his rente,
Therfore on it he sette al his entente.
 And so bifel, that ones on a day
This Somnour, ever waiting on his pray,
Rood for to somne a widwe, an old ribybe,
Feyninge a cause, for he wolde brybe.
And happed that he saugh bifore him ryde
A gay yeman, under a forest-syde.
A bowe he bar, and arwes brighte and kene;
He hadde up-on a courtepy of grene;
An hat up-on his heed with frenges blake.
 "Sir," quod this Somnour, "hayl! and wel-a-take!"
"Wel-come," quod he, "and every good felawe!
Wher rydestow under this grene shawe?"
Seyde this yeman, "wiltow fer to day?"
 This Somnour him answerde, and seyde, "nay;
Heer faste by," quod he, "is myn entente
To ryden, for to reysen up a rente
That longeth to my lordes duëtee."
 "Artow thanne a bailly?" "Ye!" quod he.
He dorste nat, for verray filthe and shame,
Seye that he was a somnour, for the name.
 "*Depardieux*," quod this yeman, "dere brother,
Thou art a bailly, and I am another.
I am unknowen as in this contree;
Of thyn aqueyntance I wolde praye thee,
And eek of brotherhede, if that yow leste.
I have gold and silver in my cheste;
If that thee happe to comen in our shyre,
Al shal be thyn, right as thou wolt desyre."
 "Grantmercy," quod this Somnour, "by my feith!"
Everich in otheres hand his trouthe leith,
For to be sworne bretheren til they deye.
In daliance they ryden forth hir weye.
 This Somnour, which that was as ful of jangles,
As ful of venim been thise wariangles,
And ever enquering up-on every thing,
"Brother," quod he, "where is now your dwelling,
Another day if that I sholde yow seche?"

And in that was the fruit of his rent,
Therefore on it was all his intent.
    And so it befell that once upon a day
This summoner, ever waiting on his prey,
Rode for to summon an old widow, an old lady,
Feigning a charge, he would extort.
And it so happened that he saw before him
A gay yeoman, under a forest side.
A bow he bore, and arrows bright and keen;
He wore a jacket of green,[7]
And a hat upon his head with fringes black.
    "Sire," said this summoner, "hail, and well met!"
"Welcome," said he, "and every good fellow!
Where ride you, under this forest greenwood?"
Said this yeoman. "Do you go far today?"
    This summoner him answered and said, "Nay;
Here nearby," said he, "is my intent
To ride, for to obtain a payment
That has long been due my lord."
    "Are you then a bailiff?" "Yes," said he.
He dared not, for the shame and obliquy,
Say that he was a summoner, so bad was the name.
    "*Depardieux*,"[8] said this yeoman, "dear brother,
You are a bailiff, and I am another.
I am unknown in this country;
Your acquaintance I would pray make,
And also brotherhood, if you wish.
I have gold and silver in my chest;
If you happen to come in our shire,
All shall be yours, right as you desire."
    "Thank you," said this summoner, "by my faith!"
And each the other's hand he clasped,
To be sworn brothers till each breathed his last.
With pleasant talk they rode on their way.
    This summoner, who was as full of gossip
As full of venom is a shrike,
And ever inquiring upon everything,
"Brother," said he, "where is now your dwelling
Another day if I should you seek?"

This yeman him answerde in softe speche,
"Brother," quod he, "fer in the north contree,
Wher, as I hope, som-tyme I shal thee see.
Er we departe, I shal thee so wel wisse,
That of myn hous ne shaltow never misse."

"Now, brother," quod this Somnour, "I yow preye,
Teche me, whyl that we ryden by the weye,
Sin that ye been a baillif as am I,
Som subtiltee, and tel me feithfully
In myn offyce how I may most winne;
And sparet nat for conscience ne sinne,
But as my brother tel me, how do ye?"

"Now, by my trouthe, brother dere," seyde he,
"As I shal tellen thee a feithful tale,
My wages been ful streite and ful smale.
My lord is hard to me and daungerous,
And myn offyce is ful laborous;
And therfore by extorcions I live.
For sothe, I take al that men wol me yive;
Algate, by sleyghte or by violence,
Fro yeer to yeer I winne al my dispence.
I can no bettre telle feithfully."

"Now, certes," quod this Somnour, "so fare I;
I spare nat to taken, god it woot,
But-if it be to hevy or to hoot.
What I may gete in counseil prively,
No maner conscience of that have I;
Nere myn extorcioun, I mighte nat liven,
Ne of swiche japes wol I nat be shriven.
Stomak ne conscience ne knowe I noon;
I shrewe thise shrifte-fadres everichoon.
Wel be we met, by god and by seint Jame!
But, leve brother, tel me than thy name,"
Quod this Somnour; and in this mene whyle,
This yeman gan a litel for to smyle.

"Brother," quod he, "wiltow that I thee telle?
I am a feend, my dwelling is in helle.
And here I ryde about my purchasing,
To wite wher men wolde yeve me any thing.

This yeoman him answered in soft speech,
"Brother," said he, "far in the north country[9]
Where I hope sometime I will you see.
Before we part, I shall to it so well you guide
That past my house you shall not ride."

"Now, brother," said this summoner, "I pray you,
Teach me, while that we ride by the way,
Since you be a bailiff as am I,
Some trick of the trade, and tell me faithfully
In my office how I may most gain;
And spare not for conscience or fear of sin,
But as my brother, tell me how you bring it in."

"Now, by my troth, brother dear," said he,
"As I shall tell you a true tale,
My wages be full strait and small.
My lord is hard to me and demanding,
And my office is full laborious,
And therefore by extortions do I live.
For truth, I take all that men will give me,
Anyhow, by sleight or by violence,
From year to year I make my expenses.
I can no better tell, faithfully."

"Now certainly," said this summoner, "so fare I.
I spare not to take, God knows,
Unless it is too hot or heavy.
What I may get secretly,
No manner of conscience for that have I.
Without my extortion, I could not live,
Nor for such tricks will I not be forgiven.
Stomach for conscience have I none;
I curse these confessors[10] every one.
Well be we met, by God and Saint James!
But, dear brother, tell me your name,"
Said this summoner. In the meanwhile
This yeoman began a little for to smile.

"Brother," said he, "would you that I tell you?
I am a fiend, my dwelling is in hell,
And here I ride about my profit-making,
To learn where men will give me something.

My purchas is th'effect of al my rente.
Loke how thou rydest for the same entente,
To winne good, thou rekkest never how;
Right so fare I, for ryde wolde I now
Un-to the worldes ende for a preye."

  "A," quod this Somnour, "*ben'cite*, what sey ye?
I wende ye were a yeman trewely.
Ye han a mannes shap as wel as I;
Han ye figure than determinat
In helle, ther ye been in your estat?"

  "Nay, certeinly," quod he, "ther have we noon;
But whan us lyketh, we can take us oon,
Or elles make yow seme we ben shape
Som-tyme lyk a man, or lyk an ape;
Or lyk an angel can I ryde or go.
It is no wonder thing thogh it be so;
A lousy jogelour can deceyve thee,
And pardee, yet can I more craft than he."

  "Why," quod the Somnour, "ryde ye thanne or goon
In sondry shap, and nat alwey in oon?"

  "For we," quod he, "wol us swich formes make
As most able is our preyes for to take."

  "What maketh yow to han al this labour?"

  "Ful many a cause, leve sir Somnour,"
Seyde this feend, "but alle thing hath tyme.
The day is short, and it is passed pryme,
And yet ne wan I no-thing in this day.
I wol entende to winnen, if I may,
And nat entende our wittes to declare.
For, brother myn, thy wit is al to bare
To understonde, al-thogh I tolde hem thee.
But, for thou axest why labouren we;
For, som-tyme, we ben goddes instruments,
And menes to don his comandements,
Whan that him list, up-on his creatures,
In divers art and in divers figures.
With-outen him we have no might, certayn,
If that him list to stonden ther-agayn.
And som-tyme, at our prayere, han we leve

My profit is the whole part of my rent.
Look how you ride for the same intent.
To gain profit, you care never how;
Right so fare I, for ride would I now
Unto the world's end for my prey."

     "Ah!" said this summoner, "*benedicite!* What do you say?
I thought you were a yeoman truly.
You have a man's shape as much as I do;
Have you another definite shape besides
In hell, where you reside?"

     "No, certainly," said he, "there have we none;
But when we wish we can take us one,
Or else make you think we have a shape;
Sometimes like a man, sometimes like an ape,
Or like an angel can I ride or go.
It is no wondrous thing that it be so;
A poor magician can fool you,
And, by God, I know more craft than they do."

     "Why," said this summoner, "ride you then or go
In sundry shapes, and not always in one?"

     "For we," said he, "will such forms make
As best enable us our prey to take."

     "What makes you have all this labor?"

     "Full many a cause, dear sir summoner,"
Said this fiend, "but all things have their time.
The day is short, and it is past prime,[11]
And yet I have won nothing in this day.
I will attend to winning, if I may,
And not strive for our wits to display.
For, brother mine, your wit is not adequate
To understand, even if I told you more.
But, since you ask why we labor—
Sometimes we are God's instruments
And his means to do his commandments,
When he wishes, upon his creatures,
By diverse methods and in diverse figures.
Without him we have no power, truly,
If he wishes to oppose something we do.
And sometimes, at our request, we have leave

Only the body and nat the soule greve;
Witnesse on Job, whom that we diden wo.
And som-tyme han we might of bothe two,
This is to seyn, of soule and body eke.
And somtyme be we suffred for to seke
Up-on a man, and doon his soule unreste,
And nat his body, and al is for the beste.
Whan he withstandeth our temptacioun,
It is a cause of his savacioun;
Al-be-it that it was nat our entente
He sholde be sauf, but that we wolde him hente.
And som-tyme be we servant un-to man,
As to the erchebisshop Seint Dunstan
And to the apostles servant eek was I."

      "Yet tel me," quod the Somnour, "feithfully,
Make ye yow newe bodies thus alway
Of elements?" the feend answerde, "nay;
Som-tyme we feyne, and som-tyme we aryse
With ded bodies in ful sondry wyse,
And speke as renably and faire and wel
As to the Phitonissa dide Samuel.
And yet wol som men seye it was nat he;
I do no fors of your divinitee.
But o thing warne I thee, I wol nat jape,
Thou wolt algates wite how we ben shape;
Thou shalt her-afterward, my brother dere,
Com ther thee nedeth nat of me to lere.
For thou shalt by thyn owene experience
Conne in a chayer rede of this sentence
Bet than Virgyle, whyl he was on lyve,
Or Dant also; now lat us ryde blyve.
For I wol holde companye with thee
Til it be so, that thou forsake me."

      "Nay," quod this Somnour, "that shal nat bityde;
I am a yeman, knowen in ful wyde;
My trouthe wol I holde as in this cas.
For though thou were the devel Sathanas,
My trouthe wol I holde to my brother,
As I am sworn, and ech of us til other

Only the body and not the soul to grieve;
Witness Job, upon whom we did that woe.
And sometimes have we power over both—
That is to say, of soul and body also.
And sometimes we be suffered for to seek
Upon a man and do his soul unrest
And not his body, and all is for the best.
When he withstands our temptation,
It is a cause of his salvation.
Albeit that it was not our intent
He should be saved, but that we would him seize.
And sometimes we be servants unto man,
As to the archbishop Saint Dunstan,[12]
And to the apostles servant also was I."

   "Yet tell me," said the summoner, "faithfully,
Make you your new bodies thus always
Of elements?" The fiend answered, "Nay.
Sometimes we feign and sometimes we arise
With dead bodies, in full sundry ways,
And speak as readily and fair and well
As to the Witch of Endor did Samuel.[13]
(And yet will some men say it was not he;
I care nothing for your theology.)
But one thing warn I you, I will not joke;
You will surely know how we are made;
You shall hereafter, my brother dear,
Not need from me to learn,
For you shall, by your own experience,
As from a professor's chair lecture on this
Better than Virgil, when he was alive,
Or Dante also. Now let us quickly ride,
For I will hold with your company
Till it be so that you forsake me."

   "Nay!" said the summoner, "that shall not betide!
I am a yeoman, known full widely;
My word will I keep, as in this case.
For though you were the devil Satan,
My pledge I will hold to my brother,
As I am sworn, and each of us to the other,

For to be trewe brother in this cas;
And bothe we goon abouten our purchas.
Tak thou thy part, what that men wol thee yive,
And I shal myn; thus may we bothe live.
And if that any of us have more than other,
Lat him be trewe, and parte it with his brother."

    "I graunte," quod the devel, "by my fey."
And with that word they ryden forth hir wey.
And right at the entring of the tounes ende,
To which this Somnour shoop him for to wende,
They saugh a cart, that charged was with hey,
Which that a carter droof forth in his wey.
Deep was the wey, for which the carte stood.
The carter smoot, and cryde, as he were wood,
"Hayt, Brok! hayt, Scot! what spare ye for the stones.
The feend," quod he, "yow fecche body and bones,
As ferforthly as ever were ye foled!
So muche wo as I have with yow tholed!
The devel have al, bothe hors and cart and hey!"

    This Somnour seyde, "heer shal we have a pley;
And neer the feed he drough, as noght ne were,
Ful prively, and rouned in his ere:
"Herkne, my brother, herkne, by thy feith;
Herestow nat how that the carter seith?
Hent it anon, for he hath yeve it thee,
Bothe hey and cart, and eek hise caples three."

    "Nay," quod the devel, "god wot, never a deel;
It is nat his entente, trust me weel.
Axe him thy-self, if thou nat trowest me,
Or elles stint a while, and thou shalt see."
This carter thakketh his hors upon the croupe,
And they bigonne drawen and to-stoupe;
"Heyt, now!" quod he, "ther Jesu Crist yow blesse
And al his handwerk, bothe more and lesse!
That was wel twight, myn owene lyard boy!
I pray god save thee and sëynt Loy!
Now is my cart out of the slow, pardee!"

    "Lo! brother," quod the feend, "what tolde I thee?
Heer may ye see, myn owene dere brother,

For to be true brothers in this case;
And both we go about our trade.
Take you your part, what men will you give,
And I shall mine; thus may we both live.
And if either of us has more than the other,
Let him be true and share it with his brother."
    "Agreed," said the devil, "by my faith."
And with that word they rode forth their way.
And right at the entrance to the town's edge,
To which this summoner prepared himself to enter,
They saw a cart that was loaded with hay,
Which a carter drove forth on his way.
Deep muddy was the road, in which the cart stood.
The carter smote and cried as if he were crazy,
"Giddap, Brok! Giddap, Scot! Why stop pulling in this mess?
The fiend," said he, "you fetch, body and bones,
As sure as you were foaled,
So much woe as I have with you suffered.
To the devil you all, both horse and cart and hay!"
    This summoner said, "Here shall we have some play."
And near the fiend he drew, as if by it he nothing meant,
And whispered in his ear in private:
"Harken, my brother, harken, by your faith!
Hear you not what the carter says?
Seize it anon, for he has given it to you,
Both hay and cart, and also his horses three."
    "Nay," said the devil, "God knows, in no way!
It is not his intent, trust me well.
Ask him yourself, if you believe not me;
Or else wait awhile, and you shall see."
This carter patted his horses on their cruppers,
And they began to pull with all their muscle.
"Giddap! Now," said he, "there Jesus Christ you bless,
And all his handiwork, both more and less!
That was well pulled, my own dappled boy.
I pray God save you, and Saint Loy!¹⁴
Now is my cart out of the slough, by God!"
    "Look, brother," said the fiend, "what I told you?
Here may you see, my own dear brother,

The carl spak oo thing, but he thoughte another.
Lat us go forth abouten our viage;
Heer winne I no-thing up-on cariage."

Whan that they comen som-what out of toune,
This Somnour to his brother gan to roune,
"Brother," quod he, "heer woneth an old rebekke,
That hadde almost as lief to lese hir nekke
As for to yeve a peny of hir good.
I wol han twelf pens, though that she be wood,
Or I wol sompne hir un-to our offyce;
And yet, god woot, of hir knowe I no vyce.
But for thou canst nat, as in this contree,
Winne thy cost, tak heer ensample of me."

This Somnour clappeth at the widwes gate.
"Com out," quod he, "thou olde viritrate!
I trowe thou hast som frere or prese with thee!"

"Who clappeth?" seyde this widwe, *"ben' cite!*
God save you, sire, what is your swete wille?"

"I have," quod he, "of somonce here a bille;
Up peyne of cursing, loke that thou be
To-morn bifore the erchedeknes knee
T'answere to the court of certeyn thinges."

"Now, lord," quod she, "Crist Jesu, king of kinges,
So wisly helpe me, as I ne may.
I have been syk, and that ful many a day.
I may nat go so fer," quod she, "ne ryde,
But I be deed, so priketh it in my syde.
May I nat axe a libel, sir Somnour,
And answere there, by my procutour,
To swich thing as men wol opposen me?"

"Yis," quod this Somnour, "pay anon, lat se,
Twelf pens to me, and I wol thee acquyte.
I shall no profit han ther-by but lyte;
My maister hath the profit, and nat I.
Com of, and lat me ryden hastily;
Yif me twelf pens, I may no lenger tarie."

"Twelf pens," quod she, "now lady Seinte Marie
So wisly help me out of care and sinne,
This wyde world thogh that I sholde winne,

The carter spoke one thing, but he thought another.
Let us go forth about our endeavor;
Here win I nothing from the carter."
    When they had gone from the town some distance,
This summoner to his brother began to whisper:
"Brother," said he, "Here dwells an old lady
Who would as soon lose her neck
As give a penny of her savings.
I will have twelve pence, no matter if she is mad,
Or I will summon her unto our office;
And yet, God knows, of her I know no vice.
Since you cannot, in this territory,
Make your expenses, take here example from me."
    This summoner knocked at the widow's gate.
"Come out," said he, "you wrinkled old hag!
I believe you have some friar or priest with you."
    "Who knocks?" said this wife, "*benedicite!*
God save you sire, what is your sweet will?"
    "I have," said he, "Of summons here a bill;
Upon pain of excommunication, look that you be
Tomorrow before the archdeacon's knee
To answer to the court about certain things."
    "Now, Lord," said she, "Christ Jesus, king of kings,
So wisely help me, as I pray.
I have been sick, and that full many a day.
I may not go so far," said she, "nor ride,
But I be dead, so hurts it in my side.
May I not ask for a written copy, sir summoner,
And answer through my representer
To whatever men bring against me?"
    "Yes," said this summoner, "pay now—let me see—
Twelve pence to me, and I will you acquit.
I shall no profit have thereby but little;
My master has the profit and not I.
Hurry up, and let me ride hastily;
Give me twelve pence, I may no longer tarry."
    "Twelve pence!" said she, "Now, lady Saint Mary
So wisely help me out of care and sin,
This wide world though I should win,

Ne have I nat twelf pens with-inne myn hold.
Ye knowen wel that I am povre and old;
Kythe your almesse on me povre wrecche."

"Nay than," quod he, "the foule feend me fecche
If I th'excuse, though thou shul be spilt!"

"Alas," quod she, "god woot, I have no gilt."

"Pay me," quod he, "or by the swete seinte Anne,
As I wol bere awey thy newe panne
For dette, which that thou owest me of old,
Whan that thou madest thyn housbond cokewold,
I payde at hoom for thy correccioun."

"Thou lixt," quod she, "by my savacioun!
Ne was I never er now, widwe ne wyf,
Somoned un-to your court in al my lyf;
Ne never I nas but of my body trewe!
Un-to the devel blak and rough of hewe
Yeve I thy body and my panne also!"

And whan the devel herde hir cursen so
Up-on hir knees, he seyde in this manere,
"Now Mabely, myn owene moder dere,
Is this your wil in ernest, that ye seye?"

"The devel," quod she, "so fecche him er he deye,
And panne and al, but he wol him repente!"

"Nay, olde stot, that is nat myn entente,"
Quod this Somnour, "for to repente me,
For any thing that I have had of thee;
I wolde I hadde thy smok and every clooth!"

"Now, brother," quod the devel, "be nat wrooth;
Thy body and this panne ben myne by right.
Thou shalt with me to helle yet to-night,
Where thou shalt knowen of our privetee
More than a maister of divinitee:"
And with that word this foule feend him hente;
Body and soule, he with the devel wente
Wher-as that somnours han hir heritage.
And god, that maked after his image
Mankinde, save and gyde us alle and some;
And leve this Somnour good man to bicome!

Lordinges, I coude han told yow, quod this Frere,

I have not twelve pence within my hold.
You know well that I am poor and old;
Show charity to me, a poor wretch."
    "Nay, then," said he, "the foul fiend me fetch
If I you excuse, though you should be put to death!"
    "Alas!" said she, "God knows, I have no guilt."
    "Pay me," said he, "or by the sweet Saint Anne,[15]
I will bear away your new pan
For debt which you owe me of old.
When you made your husband cuckold,
I paid at home for your correction."
    "You lie!" said she, "by my salvation,
Never was I before or now, widow or wife,
Summoned into your court in all my life;
Nor ever was I but of my body true!
Unto the devil black and rough of hue
Give I your body and my pan also!"
    And when the devil heard her curse so
Upon her knees, he said in this manner,
"Now, Mabel, my own mother dear,
Is this your will in earnest that you say?"
    "The devil," said she, "so fetch him or he die,
And pan and all, unless he will him repent!"
    "Nay, old cow, that is not my intent,"
Said this summoner, "for to repent
For anything that I have had of you.
I would strip from you of every rag and cloth!"
    "Now, brother," said the devil, "be not wroth;
Your body and this pan be mine by right.
You shall go with me to hell yet tonight,
Where you shall know of our secrets
More than a master of divinity."[16]
And with that word this fiend him seized;
Body and soul he with the devil flew
To where summoners have their roost.
And God, who made after his image
Mankind, save and guide us, all and some,
And may these summoners good men become!
    Lordings, I could have told you, said this Friar,

Hadde I had leyser for this Somnour here,
After the text of Crist, Poul and John,
And of our othere doctours many oon,
Swiche peynes, that your hertes mighte agryse,
Al-be-it so, no tonge may devyse,
Thogh that I mighte a thousand winter telle,
The peyne of thilke cursed hous of helle.
But, for to kepe us fro that cursed place,
Waketh, and preyeth Jesu for his grace
So kepe us fro the temptour Sathanas.
Herketh this word, beth war as in this cas;
The leoun sit in his await alway
To slee the innocent, if that he may.
Disposeth ay your hertes to withstonde
The feend, that yow wolde make thral and bonde.
He may nat tempten yow over your might;
For Crist wol be your champion and knight.
And prayeth that thise Somnours hem repente
Of hir misdedes, er that the feend hem hente.

Had I leisure for this summoner here,
After the text of Christ, Paul and John,
And of our other authorities many a one,
Such pains that your hearts might cause to shudder,
Albeit that no tongue may it so utter,
Though that I might a thousand winters tell
The pains of this same cursed house of hell.
But to keep us from that cursed place,
Wake and pray Jesus for his grace
That he may keep us from the tempter Satan.
Harken this word! Beware, as in this case:
"The lion sits in a bush always
To slay the innocent, if he may."[17]
Dispose all your hearts to withstand
This fiend, that you would make servant and slave.
He may not tempt you beyond your power,
For Christ will be your champion and knight protector.
And pray that these summoners repent
Of their misdeeds, or that the fiend them seize!

The Somnours Tale

The Prologue

THIS SOMNOUR IN HIS stiropes hye stood;
Up-on this Frere his herte was so wood,
That lyk an aspen leef he quook for yre.
  "Lordinges," quod he, "but o thing I desyre;
I yow biseke that, of your curteisye,
Sin ye han herd this false Frere lye,
As suffereth me I may my tale telle!
This Frere bosteth that he knoweth helle,
And god it woot, that it is litel wonder;
Freres and feendes been but lyte a-sonder.
For pardee, ye han ofte tyme herd telle,
How that a frere ravisshed was to helle
In spirit ones by a visioun;
And as an angel ladde him up and doun,
To shewen him the peynes that ther were,
In al the place saugh he nat a frere;
Of other folk he saugh y-nowe in wo.
Un-to this angel spak the frere tho:
  'Now, sir,' quod he, 'han freres swich a grace
That noon of hem shal come to this place?'
  'Yis,' quod this angel, 'many a millioun!'
And un-to Sathanas he ladde him doun.
'And now hath Sathanas,' seith he, 'a tayl
Brodder than of a carrik is the sayl.
Hold up thy tayl, thou Sathanas!' quod he,
'Shewe forth thyn ers, and lat the frere see
Wher is the nest of freres in this place!'
And, er that half a furlong-wey of space,
Right so as bees out swarmen from an hyve,
Out of the develes ers ther gonne dryve
Twenty thousand freres in a route,
And thurgh-out helle swarmeden aboute
And comen agayn, as faste as they may gon,
And in his ers they crepten everichon.
He clapte his tayl agayn, and lay ful stille.

The Summoner's Tale

The Prologue

THIS SUMMONER IN HIS stirrups he stood;
Toward this Friar his heart was so wired
That like an aspen leaf he shook for ire.
    "Lordings," said he, "but one thing I desire;
I you beseech that, of your courtesy,
Since you have heard this false Friar lie,
To suffer me that I may my tale tell.
This Friar boasts that he knows hell,
And God knows, it is little wonder;
Friars and fiends be but little asunder.
For, by God, you have oftentime heard tell
How that a friar abducted was to hell[1]
In spirit once by a vision;
And as an angel led him up and down,
To show him the pains that there were,
In all the place saw he not a friar;
Of other folk saw he enough in woe.
Unto this angel spoke the friar then:
    'Now sir,' said he, 'have friars such a grace
That none of them shall come to this place?'
    'Yes,' said the angel, 'many a million!'
And unto Satan he led him down.
'And now has Satan,' said he, 'a tail
Broader than of a carrack is the sail.
Hold up your tail, you Satan!' said he;
'Show forth your arse, and let the friar see
Where is the nest of friars in this place!'
And in but a minute's space,
Right so as bees swarm from a hive,
Out of the devil's arse were expelled
Twenty thousand friars in a crowd,
And throughout hell swarmed all about,
And returned again as fast as they were gone,
And in his arse they crept every one.
He clapped his tail again and lay full still.

This frere, whan he loked hadde his fille
Upon the torments of this sory place,
His spirit god restored of his grace
Un-to his body agayn, and he awook;
But natheles, for fere yet he quook,
So was the develes ers ay in his minde,
That is his heritage of verray kinde.
God save yow alle, save this cursed Frere;
My prologe wol I ende in this manere."

The Tale

Lordinges, ther is in Yorkshire, as I gesse,
A mersshy contree called Holdernesse,
In which ther wente a limitour aboute,
To preche, and eek to begge, it is no doute.
And so bifel, that on a day this frere
Had preched at a chirche in his manere,
And specially, aboven every thing,
Excited he the peple in his preching
To trentals, and to yeve, for goddes sake,
Wher-with men mighten holy houses make,
Ther as divyne service is honoured,
Nat ther as it is wasted and devoured,
Ne ther it nedeth nat for to be yive,
As to possessioners, that mowen live,
Thanked be god, in wele and habundaunce.
"Trentals," seyde he, "deliveren fro penaunce
Hir freendes soules, as wel olde as yonge,
Ye, whan that they been hastily y-songe;
Nat for to holde a preest joly and gay,
He singeth nat but o masse in a day;
Delivereth out," quod he, "anon the soules;
Ful hard it is with fleshhook or with oules
To been y-clawed, or to brenne or bake;
Now spede yow hastily, for Cristes sake."
And whan this frere had seyd al his entente,
With *qui cum patre* forth his wey he wente.
　　Whan folk in chirche had yeve him what hem leste,
He wente his wey, no lenger wolde he reste,

This friar, when he had looked his fill
Upon the torment of this sorry place,
His spirit God restored, of his grace,
Unto his body again, and he awakened.
But nevertheless, for fear yet he quaked,
So was the devil's arse ever in his mind,
That is his lineage in its true kind.
God save you all, save this cursed Friar!
My prologue will I end in this manner."

The Tale

Lordings, there is in Yorkshire, as I guess,
A marshy country called Holderness,
In which there went a limitour about
To preach, and also to beg, it is no doubt.
And so it befell that on a day this friar
Had preached at a church in his manner,
And specially, above everything,
Excited he the people in his preaching
For prayers chanted for the dead, and to give, for God's sake,
The means by which men might holy houses[2] make,
There where divine service is honored,
Not where it is wasted and devoured,
Nor where it needs not to be given,
To secular and monastic clergy, so that they may live,
Thanked be God, in prosperity and abundance.
"Such chanted prayers," said he, "deliver from Purgatory
Your friend's souls, as well old as young—
Even when they be hastily sung,
Not to call a priest jolly and gay—
Though he sings but one mass a day.
Deliver out," said he, "anon the souls!
Full hard it is with meathooks or with awls
To be clawed, or to burn or bake.
Now speed you hastily, for Christ's sake!"
And when this friar had said all his intent,
With but a *qui cum patre*[3] on his way he went.

When folk in church had given him what they wished,
He left; no longer would he stay.

With scrippe and tipped staf, y-tukked hye;
In every hous he gan to poure and prye,
And beggeth mele, and chese, or elles corn.
His felawe hadde a staf tipped with horn,
A peyre of tables al of yvory,
And a poyntel polisshed fetisly,
And wroot the names alwey, as he stood,
Of alle folk that yaf him any good,
Ascaunces that he wolde for hem preye.
"Yeve us a busshel whete, malt, or reye,
A goddes kechil, or a trip of chese,
Or elles what yow list we may nat chese;
A goddes halfpeny or a masse-peny,
Or yeve us of your brawn, if ye have eny;
A dagon of your blanket, leve dame,
Our suster dere, lo! here I write your name;
Bacon or beef, or swich thing as ye finde."
    A sturdy harlot wente ay hem bihinde,
That was hir hostes man, and bar a sak,
And what men yaf hem, leyde it on his bak.
And whan that he was out at dore anon,
He planed awey the names everichon
That he biforn had writen in his tables;
He served hem with nyfles and with fables.
    "Nay, ther thou lixt, thou Somnour," quod the Frere.
    "Pees," quod our Host, "for Cristes moder dere;
Tel forth thy tale and spare it nat at al."
So thryve I, quod this Somnour, so I shal.—
So longe he wente hous by hous, til he
Cam til an hous ther he was wont to be
Refresshed more than in an hundred placis.
Sik lay the gode man, whos that the place is;
Bedrede up-on a couche lowe he lay.
Deus hic, quod he, "O Thomas, freend, good-day,"
Seyde this frere curteisly and softe.
"Thomas," quod he, "god yelde yow! ful ofte
Have I up-on this bench faren ful weel.
Here have I eten many a mery meel;"
And fro the bench he droof awey the cat,

With satchel and metal-tipped staff, and coattails tucked,
In every house he began to pore and peer,
And begged grain and cheese, or else corn.
His partner had a staff tipped with horn,
And folding ivory writing tablets,
And a well-polished stylus,[4]
And wrote the names always, as there he stood,
Of all folk who gave him any good,
As if he would for them pray.
"Give us a bushel of wheat, malt, or rye,
A little almscake, or a bit of cheese;
Or what you wish, we may not choose;
A God's halfpenny, or a mass penny,[5]
Or give us of your meat, if you have any;
A piece of your cloth, dear dame,
Our sister dear—Look! Here I write your name—
Bacon or beef, or such thing as you find."
    A sturdy servant went always them behind,
Who worked for the host at their inn, and bore a sack,
And what men gave them, laid it on his back.
And when he was out of door, anon
He erased away the names every one
That he before had written in his tablets;
He served them with silly stories and with fables.
    "Nay, there you lie, you Summoner!" said the Friar.
    "Peace," said our Host, "for Christ's mother dear!
Tell forth your tale, and spare it not at all."
"So thrive I," said this summoner, "so I shall!"
So along he went, house by house, till he
Came to a house where he was wont to be
Refreshed more than in a hundred other places.
Sick lay the good man whose place it was;
Bedridden upon a couch low he lay.
"*Deus hic!*"[6] said he, "Oh Thomas, friend, good day!"
Said this friar, courteously and soft.
"Thomas," said he, "God reward you! Full often
Have I upon this bench fared full well;
Here have I eaten many a merry meal."
And from the bench he drove away the cat,

And leyde adoun his potente and his hat,
And eek his scrippe, and sette him softe adoun.
His felawe was go walked in-to toun,
Forth with his knave, in-to that hostelrye
Wher-as he shoop him thilke night to lye.
        "O dere maister," quod this syke man,
"How han ye fare sith that March bigan?
I saugh yow noght this fourtenight or more."
"God woot," quod he, "laboured have I ful sore;
And specially, for thy savacioun
Have I seyd many a precious orisoun
And for our othere frendes, god hem blesse!
I have to-day been at your chirche at mese,
And seyd a sermon after my simple wit,
Nat al after the text of holy writ;
For it is hard to yow, as I suppose,
And therfore wol I teche yow al the glose.
Glosinge is a glorious thing, certeyn,
For lettre sleeth, so as we clerkes seyn.
Ther have I taught hem to be charitable,
And spende hir good ther it is resonable,
And ther I saugh our dame; a! wher is she?"
        "Yond in the yerd I trowe that she be,"
Seyde this man, "and she wol come anon."
        "Ey, maister! wel-come be ye, by seint John!"
Seyde this wyf, "how fare ye hertely?"
        The frere aryseth up ful curteisly,
And hir embraceth in his armes narwe,
And kiste hir swete, and chirketh as a sparwe
With his lippes: "dame," quod he, "right weel,
As he that is your servant every deel.
Thanked be god, that yow yaf soule and lyf,
Yet saugh I nat this day so fair a wyf
In al the chirche, god so save me!"
        "Ye, god amende defautes, sir," quod she,
"Algates wel-come be ye, by my fey!"
"Graunt mercy, dame, this have I founde alwey.
But of your grete goodnesse, by your leve,
I wolde prey yow that ye nat yow greve,

And laid down his walking stick and his hat,
And also his tablets, and set himself soft adown.
His fellow was gone walking into town
Forth with his servant, into that hostelry
Where he intended that night to stay.
   "Oh dear master," said this sick man,
"How have you fared since March began?
I saw you not this fortnight or more."
"God knows," said he, "labored have I full sore,
And specially for your salvation
Have I said many a precious orison,[7]
And for our other friends, God them bless!
I have today been at your church at mass,
And said a sermon after my simple wit—
Not all after the text of holy writ,
For it is hard for you, as I suppose,
And therefore will I interpret it for you.
Interpretation is glorious, certainly,
The letters slay,[8] so we clerics say—
There have I taught them to be charitable
And spend their money where it is reasonable;
And there I saw our dame—Ah! Where is she?"
   "Yonder in the yard I believe that she be,"
Said this man, "and she will come anon."
   "Aye, master, welcome be you, by Saint John!"
Said this wife, "How fare you, I ask?"
   The friar arose full courteously,
And her embraced tightly in his arms,
And kissed her sweet, and made chirping sounds, like a sparrow,
With his lips. "Dame," said he, "right well,
As he who is your servant in every way,
Thanks be God, that you have soul and life!
Yet saw I not this day so fair a wife
In all the church, God so me save!"
   "Well, God amend my defects," said she.
"Anyway, welcome be you, by my faith!"
"Grant mercy, dame, this have I found always.
But by your kindness—if I may
Take advantage—you are so kind—

I wol with Thomas speke a litel throwe.
Thise curats been ful necligent and slowe
To grope tendrely a conscience.
In shrift, in preching is my diligence,
And studie in Petres wordes, and in Poules.
I walke, and fisshe Cristen mennes soules,
To yelden Jesu Crist his propre rente;
To sprede his word is set al myn entente."
   "Now, by your leve, o dere sir," quod she,
"Chydeth him weel, for seinte Trinitee.
He is as angry as a pissemyre,
Though that he have al that he can desyre.
Though I him wrye a-night and make him warm,
And on hym leve my leg outher myn arm,
He groneth lyk our boor, lyth in our sty.
Other desport right noon of him have I;
I may nat plese him in no maner cas."
   "O Thomas! *Je vous dy*, Thomas! Thomas!
This maketh the feend, this moste ben amended.
Ire is a thing that hye god defended,
And ther-of wol I speke a word or two."
   "Now maister," quod the wyf, "er that I go,
What wol ye dyne? I wol go ther-aboute."
   "Now dame," quod he, *"Je vous dy sanz doute,*
Have I nat of a capon but the livere,
And of your softe breed nat but a shivere,
And after that a rosted pigges heed,
(But that I nolde no beest for me were deed),
Thanne hadde I with yow hoomly suffisaunce.
I am a man of litel sustenaunce.
My spirit hath his fostring in the Bible.
The body is ay so redy and penyble
To wake, that my stomak is destroyed.
I prey yow, dame, ye be nat anoyed,
Though I so freendly yow my conseil shewe;
By god, I wolde nat telle it but a fewe."
   "Now, sir," quod she, "but o word er I go;
My child is deed with-inne thise wykes two,
Sone after that ye wente out of this toun."

I would with Thomas speak a little while.
These curates be full negligent and slow
To plumb tenderly a conscience
In confession;[9] in preaching is my diligence,
And study in Peter's words and Paul's.
I roam and fish Christian men's souls
To give to Jesus Christ his proper rent;
To spread his word is set all my intent."

    "Now, by your leave, oh dear sir," said she,
"Chide him well, for saint Trinity!
He is as angry as an ant,
Though he has all that he can want;
Though I him cover at night and make him warm,
And over him lay my leg or my arm,
He groans like our pig that lies in our sty.
Other sport right none of him have I;
I may not please him in any way."

    "Oh Thomas, *je vous dis*,[10] Thomas! Thomas!
This strengthens the fiend, this must be amended.
Ire is a thing that high God has forbidden,
And thereof will I speak a word or two."

    "Now master," said the wife, "before I go,
What will you have for dinner? I will cook it now."

    "Now dame," said he, "now *je vous dis sans doute*,
May I have of a capon but the liver,
And of your soft bread not but a sliver,
And after that a roasted pig's head—
Though I would that no beast for me were dead—
That would be fare comforting and sufficient.
I am a man who eats but little;
My spirit has its nourishment in the Bible.
The body is ever so ready and accustomed to suffer,
From nights spent in prayer, that destroyed is my stomach.
I pray you, dame, be not annoyed,
Though I so friendly my counsel show you.
By God! I would not tell it to but a few."

    "Now, sire," said she, "one word before I go.
My child is dead within these weeks two,
Soon after that you went out of this town."

"His deeth saugh I by revelacioun,"
Seith this frere, "at hoom in our dortour.
I dar wel seyn that, er that half an hour
After his deeth, I saugh him born to blisse
In myn avisioun, so god me wisse!
So did our sexteyn and our fermerer,
That han been trewe freres fifty yeer;
They may now, god be thanked of his lone,
Maken hir jubilee and walke allone.
And up I roos, and al our covent eke,
With many a tere trikling on my cheke,
Withouten noyse or clateringe of belles;
Te deum was our song and no-thing elles,
Save that to Crist I seyde an orisoun,
Thankinge him of his revelacioun.
For sir and dame, trusteth me right weel,
Our orisons been more effectueel,
And more we seen of Cristes secree thinges
Than burel folk, al-though they weren kinges.
We live in povert and in abstinence,
And burel folk in richesse and despence
Of mete and drinke, and in hir foul delyt.
We han this worldes lust al in despyt.
Lazar and Dives liveden diversly,
And diverse guerdon hadden they ther-by.
Who-so wol preye, he moot faste and be clene,
And fatte his soule and make his body lene.
We fare as seith th'apostle; cloth and fode
Suffysen us, though they be nat ful gode.
The clennesse and the fastinge of us freres
Maketh that Crist accepteth our preyeres.

Lo, Moyses fourty dayes and fourty night
Fasted, er that the heighe god of might
Spak with him in the mountain of Sinay.
With empty wombe, fastinge many a day,
Receyved he the lawe that was writen
With goddes finger; and Elie, wel ye witen,
In mount Oreb, er he hadde any speche
With hye god, that is our lyves leche,

"His death saw I by revelation,"
Said the friar, "at home in our monastery.
I dare well say that, before half an hour
After his death, I saw him borne to bliss
In my vision, so God me guide!
So did our sexton and our infirmary manager,
Who have been for fifty years true friars;
They may now—God be thanked for his grace!—
Mark their jubilee and walk alone.[11]
And up I rose, and all our brothers also,
With many a tear trickling on my cheek,
Without noise or clattering of bells;
Te Deum[12] was our song and nothing else,
Only that to Christ I said an orison,
Thanking him for his revelation.
For, sire and dame, trust me right well,
Our orisons be more effectual,
And more we see of Christ's secret things,
Than secular folk, even though they may be kings.
We live in poverty and abstinence,
And secular folk in richness and extravagance
Of meat and drink, and in their foul delight.
We all this world's lusts despise.
Lazar and Dives lived differently,[13]
And different rewards had they thereby.
Whoso will pray, he must fast and be chaste,
And fatten his soul, and make his body lean.
We fare as says the apostle; clothing and food
Suffice us, though they be not fancy.
The chastity and the fasting of us friars
Makes that Christ accepts our prayers.
    "Look, Moses forty days and forty nights
Fasted, before the high God of might
Spoke with him on the mount of Sinai.[14]
With empty stomach, fasting many a day,
Received he the law that was written
With God's finger; and Elijah, well you know,
On Mount Horeb, before he made any speech
With high God, who is our lives' healer,

He fasted longe and was in contemplaunce.
    Aaron, that hadde the temple in governaunce,
And eek the othere preestes everichon,
In-to the temple whan they sholde gon
To preye for the peple, and do servyse,
They nolden drinken, in no maner wyse,
No drinke, which that mighte hem dronke make,
But there in abstinence preye and wake,
Lest that they deyden; tak heed what I seye.
But they be sobre that for the peple preye,
War that I seye; namore! for it suffyseth,
Our lord Jesu, as holy writ devyseth,
Yaf us ensample of fastinge and preyeres.
Therfor we mendinants, we sely freres,
Been wedded to poverte and continence,
To charitee, humblesse, and abstinence,
To persecucion for rightwisnesse,
To wepinge, misericorde, and clennesse.
And therfor may ye see that our preyeres—
I speke of us, we mendinants, we freres—
Ben to the hye god more acceptable
Than youres, with your festes at the table.
Fro Paradys first, if I shal nat lye,
Was man out chaced for his glotonye;
And chaast was man in Paradys, certeyn.
    But herkne now, Thomas, what I shal seyn.
I ne have no text of it, as I suppose,
But I shall finde it in a maner glose,
That specially our swete lord Jesus
Spak this by freres, whan he seyde thus:
'Blessed be they that povre in spirit been.'
And so forth al the gospel may ye seen,
Wher it be lyker our professioun,
Or hirs that swimmen in possessioun.
Fy on hir pompe and on hir glotonye!
And for hir lewednesse I hem diffye.
    Me thinketh they ben lyk Jovinian,
Fat as a whale, and walkinge as a swan;
Al vinolent as botel in the spence.

He fasted long and was in contemplation.[15]
    "Aaron, who had the temple in governance,
And also the other priests every one,
Into the temple when they should go
To pray for the people and do service,
They would not drink in any way
Any drink which might them drunken make,
But there in abstinence pray and hold vigil,
Lest they die.[16] Take heed what I say!
Unless they be sober who for the people pray,
Beware—I say no more, for it suffices.
Our Lord Jesus, as holy writ describes,
Gave us examples of fasting and prayers.
Therefore we mendicants, we blessed friars,
Be wedded to poverty and continence,
To charity, humility, and abstinence,
To persecution too for righteousness,
To weeping, mercy, and chastity.
And therefore may you see that our prayers—
I speak of us, we mendicants, we friars—
Be to the high God more acceptable
Than yours, with your feasts at the table.
From Paradise first, if I shall not lie,
Was man out-chased for his gluttony;
And chaste was man in Paradise, certainly.
    "But harken now, Thomas, to what I shall say.
I have no text for it, as I suppose,
But I shall find it in some gloss,
That specially our sweet Lord Jesus
Spoke of friars, when he said thus:
'Blessed be they who poor in spirit be.'
And so forth in all the gospel may you see,
That it more resembles our profession,
Than those who swim in possessions.
Fie on pomp and on their gluttony!
And for their ignorance I them revile.
    "Methinks they be like Jovinianus,
Fat as a whale, and waddling like a duck,[17]
And like old wine bottles their drunkard's breath.

Hir preyer is of ful gret reverence;
Whan they for soules seye the psalm of Davit,
Lo, 'buf!' they seye, *'cor meum eructavit!'*
Who folweth Cristes gospel and his fore,
But we that humble been and chast and pore,
Werkers of goddes word, not auditours?
Therfore, right as an hauk up, at a sours,
Up springeth in-to their, right so prayeres
Of charitable and chaste bisy freres
Maken hir sours to goddes eres two.
Thomas! Thomas! so mote I ryde or go,
And by that lord that clepid is seint Yve,
Nere thou our brother, sholdestou nat thryve!
In our chapitre praye we day and night
To Crist, that he thee sende hele and might,
Thy body for to welden hastily."

    "God woot," quod he, "no-thing ther-of fele I;
As help me Crist, as I, in fewe yeres,
Han spended, up-on dyvers maner freres,
Ful many a pound; yet fare I never the bet.
Certeyn, my good have I almost biset.
Farwel, my gold! for it is al ago!"

    The frere answerde, "O Thomas, dostow so?
What nedeth yow diverse freres seche?
What nedeth him that hath a parfit leche
To sechen othere leches in the toun?
Your inconstance is your confusioun.
Holde ye than me, or elles our covent,
To praye for yow ben insufficient?
Thomas, that jape nis nat worth a myte;
Your malayde is for we han to lyte.
'A! yif that covent half a quarter otes!'
'A! yif that covent four and twenty grotes!'
'A! yif that frere a peny, and lat him go!'
Nay, nay, Thomas! it may no-thing be so.
What is a ferthing worth parted in twelve?
Lo, ech thing that is oned in him-selve
Is more strong than whan it is to-scatered.
Thomas, of me thou shalt nat been y-flatered;

Their prayer is of full great reverence,
When they for souls say the psalm of David:
Look, 'hic!' they say, '*cor meum eructavit!*'[18]
Are not we who follow in Christ's footsteps,
Though that we humble be, and chaste, and poor,
Workers of God's word, not auditors?
Therefore, right as a hawk soars
Upward into the air, right so prayers
By charitable and chaste busy friars
Soar upward to God's two ears.
Thomas, Thomas! So may my prayers fly,
By that lord who is called Saint Ives,[19]
For you our lay brother, that you may thrive.
In our chapel we pray day and night
To Christ, that he send you health and might
Your body to move with ease."
      "God knows," said he, "nothing thereof do I feel!
So help me Christ, have I in the past few years
Spent on diverse kinds of friars
Full many a pound; yet fare I none the better.
Certainly, my assets have I almost spent.
Farewell my gold, for it is all gone!"
      The friar answered, "Oh Thomas, did you so?
Why needed you such diverse friars?
Why needs he who has the perfect healer
To seek other healers in the town?
Your inconstancy has brought you down,
Believe you that I, or my brothers,
To pray for you be not enough?
Thomas, that trick is not worth a mite.
For your malady we have had too little.
'Ah! Give that monastery half a quarter oats!'
'Ah! Give that convent four and twenty groats!'
'Ah! Give that friar a penny, and let him go!'
Nay, nay, Thomas, it may no way be so!
What is a farthing worth split twelve ways?
Look, each thing that is united in itself
Is stronger than when it is scattered.
Thomas, by me you shall not be flattered;

Thou woldest han our labour al for noght.
The hye god, that al this world hath wroght,
Seith that the werkman worthy is his hyre.
Thomas! noght of your tresor I desyre
As for my-self, but that al our covent
To preye for yow is ay so diligent,
And for to builden Cristes owene chirche.
Thomas! if ye wol lernen for to wirche,
Of buildinge up of chirches may ye finde
If it be good, in Thomas lyf of Inde.
Ye lye heer, ful of anger and of yre,
With which the devel set your herte a-fyre,
And chyden heer this sely innocent,
Your wyf, that is so meke and pacient.
And therfor, Thomas, trowe me if thee leste,
Ne stryve nat with thy wyf, as for thy beste;
And ber this word awey now, by thy feith,
Touchinge this thing, lo, what the wyse seith:
'With-in thyn hous ne be thou no leoun;
To thy subgits do noon oppressioun;
Ne make thyne aqueyntances nat to flee.'
And Thomas, yet eft-sones I charge thee,
Be war from hir that in thy bosom slepeth;
War fro the serpent that so slyly crepeth
Under the gras, and stingeth subtilly.
Be war, my sone, and herkne paciently,
That twenty thousand men han lost hir lyves,
For stryving with hir lemmans and hir wyves.
Now sith ye han so holy and meke a wyf,
What nedeth yow, Thomas, to maken stryf?
Ther nis, y-wis, no serpent so cruel,
Whan man tret on his tayl, ne half so fel,
As womman is, whan she hath caught an ire;
Vengeance is thanne al that they desyre.
Ire is a sinne, oon of the grete of sevene,
Abhominable un-to the god of hevene;
And to him-self it is destruccion.
This every lewed viker or person
Can seye, how Ire engendreth homicyde.

You would have our labor all for nought.
The high God, who all this world has wrought,
Says that the workman is worthy of his hire.
Thomas, nought of your treasure I desire
As for myself, but that all our convent
To pray for you be ever so diligent,
And for to build Christ's own church.
Thomas, if you would learn to do good works,
Of the building up of churches may you find it
Well in the life of Saint Thomas of India.
You lie here full of anger and of ire,
With which the devil set your heart afire,
And you chide here the naïve innocent,
Your wife, who is so meek and patient.
And therefore, Thomas, believe me if you wish,
Let go strife with your wife, as for your best,
And bear this word away now, by your faith;
Touching such things, look, what the wise say:
'Within your house be not a lion;
To your subjects do no oppression,
Nor make your acquaintances want to flee.'[20]
And, Thomas, again I command you,
Beware of ire that in your bosom sleeps;
Beware of the serpent that so slyly creeps
Under the grass and stings full subtly.
Beware, my son, and harken patiently
That twenty thousand men have lost their lives
For fighting with their sweethearts and their wives.
Now since you have so wholly meek a wife,
What need you, Thomas, to make strife?
There is, truth to tell, no serpent so cruel,
As when men tread on its tail, nor half so dangerous
As woman is, when she has been made angry;
Vengeance is then all that they desire.
Anger is a sin, one of the great of seven,
Abominable unto the God of heaven;
And to himself it is destruction.
This every unlearned vicar or parson
Can say, how ire engenders homicide.

Ire is, in sooth, executour of pryde.
I coude of Ire seye so muche sorwe,
My tale sholde laste til to-morwe.
And therfor preye I god bothe day and night,
An irous man, god sende him litel might!
It is greet harm and, certes, gret pitee,
To sette an irous man in heigh degree.

Whilom ther was an irous potestat,
As seith Senek, that, duringe his estaat,
Up-on a day out riden knightes two,
And as fortune wolde that it were so,
That oon of hem cam hoom, that other noght.
Anon the knight bifore the juge is broght,
That seyde thus, 'thou hast thy felawe slayn,
For which I deme thee to the deeth, certayn.'
And to another knight comanded he,
'Go lede him to the deeth, I charge thee.'
And happed, as they wente by the weye
Toward the place ther he sholde deye,
The knight cam, which men wenden had be deed.
Thanne thoughte they, it was the beste reed,
To lede hem bothe to the juge agayn.
They seiden, 'lord, the knight ne hath nat slayn
His felawe; here he standeth hool alyve.'
'Ye shul be deed,' quod he, 'so moot I thryve!
That is to seyn, bothe oon, and two, and three!'
And to the firste knight right thus spak he,
'I dampned thee, thou most algate be deed.
And thou also most nedes lese thyn heed,
For thou art cause why thy felawe deyth.'
And to the thridde knight right thus he seyth,
'Thou hast nat doon that I comanded thee.'
And thus he dide don sleen hem alle three.

Irous Cambyses was eek dronkelewe,
And ay delyted him to been a shrewe.
And so bifel, a lord of his meynee,
That lovede vertuous moralitee,
Seyde on a day bitwix hem two right thus:
'A lord is lost, if he be vicious;

Ire is, in truth, the arm of pride.
I could of ire say so much sorrow,
My tale would last until tomorrow.
And therefore I pray God both day and night
An angry man, God send him little might!
It is great harm and certainly a great pity
To set an angry man in a high place.
    "Once there was an angry ruler
As said Seneca,[21] who, during his reign,
Upon a day rode out knights two,
And as Fortune would that it were so,
That one of them came home, the other not.
Anon the knight before the judge was brought,
And said thus, 'You have your fellow slain,
For which I sentence you to death, certainly.'
And to another knight commanded he,
"Go lead him to the death, I charge thee."
And it so happened, as they went by the way
Toward the place where he should die,
The knight came who men thought dead.
Then they thought it would be best
To lead them both to the judge again.
They said, 'Lord, your knight has not slain
His fellow; here he stands alive.'
'You shall be dead,' said he, 'so might I thrive!
That is to say, both one, and two, and three!'
And to the first knight right thus spoke he,
'I condemned; you must therefore die.'
And to the second: 'You must needs also lose your head,
For you are the cause of your fellow's death.'
And to the third knight right thus he said,
'You have not done what I commanded you.'
And thus he did slay them all three.
    "Angry Cambises was also a drunkard,
And ever delighted him to be a shrew.[22]
And so it befell, a lord of his household
Who loved virtuous morality
Said on a day between the two of them right thus:
"A lord is lost, if he be vicious;

And dronkenesse is eek a foul record
Of any man, and namely in a lord.
Ther is ful many an eye and many an ere
Awaiting on a lord, and he noot where.
For goddes love, drink more attemprely;
Wyn maketh man to lesen wrecchedly
His minde, and eek his limes everichon.'

   'The revers shaltou see,' quod he, 'anon;
And preve it, by thyn owene experience,
That wyn ne dooth to folk no swich offence.
Ther is no wyn bireveth me my might
Of hand ne foot, ne of myn eyen sight'—
And, for despyt, he drank ful muchel more
An hondred part than he had doon bifore;
And right anon, this irous cursed wrecche
Leet this knightes sone bifore him fecche,
Comandinge him he sholde bifore him stonde.
And sodeynly he took his bowe in honde,
And up the streng he pulled to his ere,
And with an arwe he slow the child right there:
'Now whether have I a siker hand or noon?'
Quod he, 'is al my might and minde agoon?
Hath wyn bireved me myn eyen sight?'

   What sholde I telle th'answere of the knight?
His sone was slayn, ther is na-more to seye.
Beth war therfor with lordes how ye pleye.
Singeth *Placebo*, and I shal, if I can,
But-if it be un-to a povre man.
To a povre man men sholde hise vyces telle,
But nat to a lord, thogh he sholde go to helle.

   Lo irous Cirus, thilke Percien,
How he destroyed the river of Gysen,
For that an hors of his was dreynt ther-inne,
Whan that he wente Babiloigne to winne.
He made that the river was so smal,
That wommen mighte wade it over-al.
Lo, what seyde he, that so wel teche can?
'Ne be no felawe to an irous man.
Ne with no wood man walke by the weye,

And drunkenness is also a foul reputation
For any man, and especially for a lord.
There are full many eyes and ears
Observing a lord, and he knows not where.
For God's love, drink more temperately!
Wine makes a man to lose governance of
His mind and also his limbs every one.'
    "The reverse shall you see,' said he, 'anon,
And prove it by your own experience,
That wine does to folk no such offence.
There is no wine that bereaves me of my might
Of hand or foot, nor of my eyesight.'
And for spite he drank full much more,
A hundred parts, than he had done before;
And right anon this angry, cursed wretch
Had his knight's son before him fetched,
Commanding that he should before him stand.
And suddenly he took his bow in hand,
And up the string he pulled to his ear,
And with an arrow he slew the child right there.
'Now have I a weakened hand or no?'
Said he; 'Is all my might and all my mind gone?
Has wine bereaved me of my eyesight?'
    What should I tell the answer of the knight?
His son was slain; there is no more to say.
Beware, therefore, with lords how you play.
Sing *Placebo* and 'I shall, if I can,'
Unless it be unto a poor man.
To a poor man should men his vices tell,
But not to a lord, though he should go to hell.
    "Look how Cyrus the Great, the Persian,[23]
How he destroyed the river of Gyndes,
Because a horse of his was drowned therein,
When he went to win Babylon.
He made the river become so small
That women might wade over it all.
Look, what said Solomon who so well taught:
'Be not a companion to an angry man,[24]
Nor with a madman walk by the way,

Lest thee repente;' ther is na-more to seye.
  Now Thomas, leve brother, lef thyn ire;
Thou shalt me finde as just as is a squire.
Hold nat the develes knyf ay at thyn herte;
Thyn angre dooth thee al to sore smerte;
But shewe to me al thy confessioun."
   "Nay," quod the syke man, "by Seint Simoun!
I have be shriven this day at my curat;
I have him told al hooly myn estat;
Nedeth na-more to speke of it," seith he,
"But if me list of myn humilitee."
   "Yif me thanne of thy gold, to make our cloistre,"
Quod he, "for many a muscle and many an oistre,
Whan other men han ben ful wel at eyse,
Hath been our fode, our cloistre for to reyse.
And yet, god woot, unnethe the fundement
Parfourned is, ne of our pavement
Nis nat a tyle yet with-inne our wones;
By god, we owen fourty pound for stones!
Now help, Thomas, for him that harwed helle!
For elles moste we our bokes selle.
And if ye lakke our predicacioun,
Than gooth the world al to destruccioun.
For who-so wolde us fro this world bireve,
So god me save, Thomas, by your leve,
He wolde bireve out of this world the sonne.
For who can teche and werchen as we conne?
And that is nat of litel tyme," quod he;
"But sith that Elie was, or Elisee,
Han freres been, that finde I of record,
In charitee, y-thanked be our lord.
Now Thomas, help, for seinte Charitee!"
And doun anon he sette him on his knee.
   This syke man wex wel ny wood for ire;
He wolde that the frere had been on-fire
With his false dissimulacioun.
"Swich thing as is in my possessioun,"
Quod he, "that may I yeven, and non other.
Ye sey me thus, how that I am your brother?"

Lest you repent;' I will no further say.
    "Now Thomas, dear brother, leave your anger;
You should me find as true as a carpenter's square.
Hold not the devil's knife at your own heart—
Your anger does you all too sore smart—
But show to me all your confession."
    "Nay," said the sick man, "by Saint Simon!
I have been confessed this day by my curate.
I have told him everything of my condition;
There needs no more speak of it," said he,
"Unless I wish, from humility."
    "Give me of your gold, to make our cloister,"
Said he, "for many a mussel and many an oyster,
After other men have been full well filled,
Have been our food, our cloister for to build.
And yet, God knows, nothing but the foundation
Completed is, nor of pavement
Is there yet a tile within our convent.
By God, we owe forty pounds for stones.
Now help, Thomas, for he who harrowed hell![25]
Otherwise must we our books sell.
And if you lack our preaching
Then goes all the world to destruction.
For whoso would us from the world remove,
So God me save, Thomas, by your leave,
He would bereave the world of the sun.
For who can teach and work as we can?
And that has been not just for a brief while," said he,
"But since Elijah was, or Elisha,
Have friars been—that I find of record—
In service,[26] thanked be our Lord!
Now Thomas, help, for saint charity!"
And down anon he set him on his knee.
    This sick man waxed well nigh mad for ire;
He would that the friar had been on fire
With his false dissimulation.
"What things that are in my possession,"
Said he, "those I will give, I have none other.
You told me just before—how that I am your lay brother?"

"Ye, certes," quod the frere, "trusteth weel;
I took our dame our lettre with our seel."

"Now wel," quod he, "and som-what shal I yive
Un-to your holy covent whyl I live,
And in thyn hand thou shalt it have anoon;
On this condicioun, and other noon,
That thou departe it so, my dere brother,
That every frere have also muche as other.
This shaltou swere on thy professioun,
With-outen fraude or cavillacioun."

"I swere it," quod this frere, "upon my feith!"
And ther-with-al his hand in his he leith:
"Lo, heer my feith! in me shal be no lak."

"Now thanne, put thyn hand doun by my bak,"
Seyde this man, "and grope wel bihinde;
Bynethe my buttok ther shaltow finde
A thing that I have hid in privetee."

"A!" thoghte this frere, "this shal go with me!"
And doun his hand he launcheth to the clifte,
In hope for to finde ther a yifte.
And whan this syke man felte this frere
Aboute his tuwel grope there and here,
Amidde his hand he leet the frere a fart.
Ther nis no capul, drawinge in a cart,
That mighte have lete a fart of swich a soun.

The frere up starte as doth a wood leoun:
"A! false cherl," quod he, "for goddes bones,
This hastow for despyt doon, for the nones!
Thou shalt abye this fart, if that I may!"

His meynee, whiche that herden this affray,
Cam lepinge in, and chaced out the frere;
And forth he gooth, with a ful angry chere,
And fette his felawe, ther-as lay his stoor.
He looked as it were a wilde boor;
He grinte with his teeth, so was he wrooth.
A sturdy pas doun to the court he gooth,
Wher-as ther woned a man of greet honour,
To whom that he was alwey confessour;
This worthy man was lord of that village.

"Yes, certainly," said the friar, "trust well.
I brought your wife our sealed fraternal letter."

"Now well," said he, "and a bit shall I give
Unto your holy convent while I live;
And in your hand you shall have it anon,
On this condition, and other none,
That you divide it so, my dear brother,
That every friar shall have as much as the other.
This shall you swear on your vows holy,
Without fraud or equivocation."

"I swear it," said this friar, "by my faith!"
And therewith his hand in his he placed,
"Look, here by my faith, in me shall be no lack."

"Now then, put your hand down by my back,"
Said this man, "and grope well behind.
Beneath my buttock there shall you find
A thing that I have hidden in secrecy."

"Ah!" thought this friar, "That shall go with me!"
And down his hand he slid to the cleft
In hope for to find there a gift.
And when this sick man felt this friar
About his bum groped he here and there;
And into the friar's hand he let fly a fart;
There is no nag, hitched to a cart,
That might have let a fart of such a sound.

The friar upstarted as does a maddened lion—
"Ah, false churl," said he, "for God's sake!
You have for spite done such a jape.
You shall pay for this fart, if I have my way!"

His servants, who heard this affray,
Came leaping in and chased out the friar;
And forth he went, with a full angry face,
And fetched his brother, there where lay his donations.
He looked as if he were a wild boar;
He ground his teeth, such was his ire.
A quick pace down to the manor house he went,
Where there dwelt a man of great honor,
To whom he was always confessor.
This worthy man was lord of that village.

This frere cam, as he were in a rage,
Wher-as this lord sat eting at his bord.
Unnethes mighte the frere speke a word,
Til atte laste he seyde: "god yow see!"
    This lord gan loke, and seide, "*ben'cite!*
What, frere John, what maner world is this?
I see wel that som thing ther is amis.
Ye loken as the wode were ful of thevis,
Sit doun anon, and tel me what your greef is,
And it shal been amended, if I may."
    "I have," quod he, "had a despyt this day,
God yelde yow! adoun in your village,
That in this world is noon so povre a page,
That he nolde have abhominacioun
Of that I have receyved in your toun.
And yet ne greveth me no-thing so sore,
As that this olde cherl, with lokkes hore,
Blasphemed hath our holy covent eke."
    "Now, maister," quod this lord, "I yow biseke."
    "No maister, sire," quod he, "but servitour,
Thogh I have had in scole swich honour.
God lyketh nat that "Raby" men us calle,
Neither in market ne in your large halle."
    "No fors," quod he, "but tel me al your grief."
    "Sire," quod this frere, "an odious meschief
This day bitid is to myn ordre and me,
And so *per consequens* to ech degree
Of holy chirche, god amende it sone!"
    "Sir," quod the lord, "ye woot what is to done.
Distempre yow noght, ye be my confessour;
Ye been the salt of the erthe and the savour.
For goddes love your pacience ye holde;
Tel me your grief:" and he anon him tolde,
As ye han herd biforn, ye woot wel what.
    The lady of the hous ay stille sat,
Til she had herd al what the frere sayde:
"Ey, goddes moder," quod she, "blisful mayde!
Is ther oght elles? telle me feithfully."
    "Madame," quod he, "how thinketh yow her-by?"

This friar came as if in a rage,
Where this lord sat eating at his board;
Hardly might the friar speak a word,
Till at last he said, "May God look over you!"
    The lord looked up, and said, "*Benedicite!*
What, friar John, what in the world is this?
I see well that something is amiss;
You look as if the woods were full of thieves.
Sit down anon, and tell me what your grief is,
And it shall be amended, if I may."
    "I have," said he, "had an insult this day,
May God reward you, down in your village,
That in the world is none so poor a page
That he would suffer the abomination
That I have received in your town.
Yet grieves me nothing so sore,
As that this churl with locks hoary
Blasphemed has our order holy."
    "Now, master," said this lord, "I you beseech—"
    "No master, sire," said he, "but servant,
Though I have had in school that honor.
God likes not that 'Rabbi' men us call,
Neither in the market nor your large hall."
    "No matter," said he, "but tell me all your grief."
    "Sire," said this friar, "an odious mischief
This day happened to my order and me,
And so, *per consequens*, to each degree
Of holy church—God amend it soon!"
    "Sire," said the lord, "you know what to do.
Anger yourself not; you be my confessor;
You be the salt of the earth and the delight.
For God's love, your patience keep!
Tell me your grief!" And he anon him told,
As you have heard before—you know well what.
    The lady of the house ever still sat
Till she had heard what the friar said.
"Eh, God's mother," said she, "Blissful maid!
Is there anything else? Tell me faithfully."
    "Madame," said he, "what do you think of this?"

"How that me thinketh?" quod she; "so god me speede,
I seye, a cherl hath doon a cherles dede.
What shold I seye? god lat him never thee!
His syke heed is ful of vanitee,
I hold him in a maner frenesye."

"Madame," quod he, "by god I shal nat lye;
But I on other weyes may be wreke,
I shal diffame him over-al ther I speke,
This false blasphemour, that charged me
To parte that wol nat departed be,
To every man y-liche, with meschaunce!"

The lord sat stille as he were in a traunce,
And in his herte he rolled up and doun,
"How hadde this cherl imaginacioun
To shewe swich a probleme to the frere?
Never erst er now herde I of swich matere;
I trowe the devel putte it in his minde.
In ars-metryke shal ther no man finde,
Biforn this day, of swich a questioun.
Who sholde make a demonstracioun,
That every man sholde have y-liche his part
As of the soun or savour of a fart?
O nyce proude cherl, I shrewe his face!
Lo, sires," quod the lord, with harde grace,
"Who ever herde of swich a thing er now?
To every man y-lyke? tel me how.
It is an impossible, it may nat be!
Ey, nyce cherl, god lete him never thee!
The rumblinge of a fart, and every soun,
Nis but of eir reverberacioun,
And ever it wasteth lyte and lyte awey.
Ther is no man can demen, by my fey,
If that it were departed equally.
What, lo, my cherl, lo, yet how shrewedly
Un-to my confessour to-day he spak!
I holde him certeyn a demoniak!
Now ete your mete, and lat the cherl go pleye,
Lat him go honge himself, a devel weye!"

Now stood the lordes squyer at the bord,

"How do I think?" said she. "So God me speed,
I say a churl has done a churl's deed.
What should I say? God deny him prosperity!
His sick head is full of vanity;
I hold him to be in some way crazy."

"Madame," said he, "I shall not lie,
But I in some other way shall be avenged,
I shall slander him wherever I speak,
This false blasphemer who commanded me
To share what may not divided be
Equally to every man, with bad luck!"

The lord sat still as if he were in a trance,
And in his heart he thought it over,
"How had this churl the imagination
To ask such a question of logic of the friar?
Never before now heard I of such a matter.
I believe the devil put it in his mind.
In the art of mathematics[27] may no man find,
Before this day, anything of such a question.
Who could prove through logical demonstration
That every man should have equally his share
As of the sound or odor of a fart?
Oh clever, proud churl, I curse his face!
Look, sires," said the lord, "at such sorry grace!
Whoever heard of such a thing before now?
To every man alike? Tell me how.
It is an impossibility, it may not be.
Eh, clever churl, God send him misery!
The rumbling of a fart, and every sound,
Is not but of air reverberating,
And diminishes little by little away.
There is no man who can tell, by my faith,
If that it were shared equally.
Why, look, my churl, look, yet how shrewdly
Unto my confessor today he has spoken!
I hold him certainly possessed by a demon!
Now eat your meal, and let the churl go play;
Let him go hang himself in the Devil's name!"

Now stood the lord's squire at the table,

That carf his mete, and herde, word by word,
Of all thinges of which I have yow sayd.
"My lord," quod he, "be ye nat yvel apayd;
I coude telle, for a goune-clooth,
To yow, sir frere, so ye be nat wrooth,
How that this fart sholde even deled be
Among your covent, if it lyked me."

    "Tel," quod the lord, "and thou shalt have anon
A goune-cloth, by god and by Seint John!"

    "My lord," quod he, "whan that the weder is fair,
With-outen wind or perturbinge of air,
Lat bringe a cartwheel here in-to this halle,
But loke that it have his spokes alle.
Twelf spokes hath a cartwheel comunly.
And bring me than twelf freres, woot ye why?
For thrittene is a covent, as I gesse.
The confessour heer, for his worthinesse,
Shal parfourne up the nombre of his covent.
Than shal they knele doun, by oon assent,
And to every spokes ende, in this manere,
Ful sadly leye his nose shal a frere.
Your noble confessour, ther god him save,
Shal holde his nose upright, under the nave.
Than shal this cherl, with bely stif and toght
As any tabour, hider been y-broght;
And sette him on the wheel right of this cart,
Upon the nave, and make him lete a fart.
And ye shul seen, up peril of my lyf,
By preve which that is demonstratif,
That equally the soun of it wol wende,
And eek the stink, un-to the spokes ende;
Save that this worthy man, your confessour,
By-cause he is a man of greet honour,
Shal have the firste fruit, as reson is;
The noble usage of freres yet is this,
The worthy men of hem shul first be served;
And certeinly, he hath it weel deserved.
He hath to-day taught us so muchel good
With preching in the pulpit ther he stood,

Who carves his meat, and heard word for word
Of all things which I have you said.
"My lord," said he, "be not displeased,
I could tell, for a gown-cloth,
To you, sir friar, so you be not wroth,
How this fart evenly should divided be
Among your convent, if I cared."

"Tell," said the lord, "and you shall have anon
A gown-cloth, by God and by Saint John!"

"My lord," said he, "when the weather is fair,
Without wind or disturbance of air,
Let bring a cartwheel into this hall;
But look that it have its spokes all—
Twelve spokes has a cartwheel commonly.
And bring me then twelve friars. Do you know why?
For thirteen is a convent, as I guess.
Your confessor here, for his worthiness,
Shall complete the number of his convent.
Then shall they kneel down, by agreement,
And to every spoke's end, in this manner,
Full firmly lay his nose shall a friar.
Your noble confessor—there God him save!—
Shall hold his nose upright under the hub.
Than shall this churl, with belly stiff and taut
As any drum, hither be brought;
And set him on the wheel right of this cart,
Upon the hub, and make him let a fart.
And you shall see, upon peril of my life,
By proof which is demonstrable,
That equally the sound of it will wend,
And also the stink, unto the spoke ends,
Save that this worthy man, your confessor,
Because he is a man of great honor,
Shall have the first fruit, as is reasonable.
The noble custom of friars yet is this,
The worthiest of them shall first be served;
And certainly he has it well deserved.
He has today taught us so much good
With preaching in his pulpit there he stood,

That I may vouche-sauf, I sey for me,
He hadde the firste smel of fartes three,
And so wolde al his covent hardily;
He bereth him so faire and holily."
　　The lord, the lady, and ech man, save the frere,
Seyde that Jankin spak, in this matere,
As wel as Euclide or [as] Ptholomee.
Touchinge this cherl, they seyde, subtiltee
And heigh wit made him speken as he spak;
He nis no fool, ye no demoniak.
And Janik hath y-wonne a newe goune.—
My tale is doon; we been almost at toune.

That I would allow, if it were up to me,
That he had the first smell of farts three;
And so would agree all his convent surely,
He bears himself so fair and holily."
    The lord, the lady, and each man, save the friar,
Said that Jankyn spoke, in this matter,
As well as did Euclid or Ptolomy.[28]
Touching the churl, they said, subtlety
And high wit made him speak as he spoke;
He was no fool, or demoniac.
And Jankyn has won a new gown—
My tale is done; we be almost to town.

The Tale of the Man of Lawe

The Introduction

Our Hoste sey wel that the brighte sonne
Th'ark of his artificial day had ronne
The fourthe part, and half an houre, and more;
And though he were not depe expert in lore,
He wiste it was the eightetethe day
Of April, that is messager to May;
And sey wel that the shadwe of every tree
Was as in lengthe the same quantitee
That was the body erect that caused it.
And therfor by the shadwe he took his wit
That Phebus, which that shoon so clere and brighte,
Degrees was fyve and fourty clombe on highte;
And for that day, as in that latitude,
It was ten of the clokke, he gan conclude,
And sodeynly he plighte his hors aboute.

"Lordinges," quod he, "I warne yow, al this route,
The fourthe party of this day is goon;
Now, for the love of god and of seint John,
Leseth no tyme, as ferforth as ye may;
Lordinges, the tyme wasteth night and day,
And steleth from us, what prively slepinge,
And what thurgh neeligence in our wakinge,
As dooth the streem, that turneth never agayn,
Descending fro the montaigne in-to playn.
Wel can Senek, and many a philosophre
Biwailen tyme, more than gold in cofre.
'For los of catel may recovered be,
But los of tyme shendeth us,' quod he.
It wol nat come agayn, with-outen drede,
Na more than wol Malkins maydenhede,
Whan she hath lost it in hir wantownesse;
Lat us nat moulen thus in ydelnesse.
Sir man of lawe," quod he, so hae ye blis,
Tel us a tale anon, as forward is;
Ye been submitted thurgh your free assent

The Man of Law's Tale

The Introduction

OUR HOST SAW WELL that the bright sun
His daylight arc had run
The first quarter, and half an hour and more,[1]
And though not learned deeply in such lore,
He knew it was the eighteenth day
Of April, that is messenger to May;
And saw well that the shadow of every tree
Was in length the same quantity
That was the body that caused it.
And therefore by the shadow made his judgement
That Phoebus, which shone so clear and bright,
Degrees was five and forty ascended on high,
And for that day, in that latitude,
It was ten o'clock, he began to conclude,
And suddenly he pulled his horse about.

    "Lordings," said he, "I warn you, all this company,
The fourth part of the day is gone.
Now for the love of God and of Saint John,
Lose no time, insofar as you may.
Lordings, time is wasting night and day,
And steals from us, what with sleeping,
And through negligence in our waking,
As does the stream that never turns again,
Descending from the mountain into the plain.
Well can Seneca and many a philosopher
Bewail time more than gold in a coffer;
For 'Loss of property may recovered be,
But loss of time ruins us,'[2] said he.
It will not come again, without doubt,
No more than will Malkin's maidenhead,
When she lost it in her wantonness.
Let us not grow moldy thus in idleness.
Sir Man of Law," said he, "so have you bliss,
Tell us a tale anon, as we agreed.
You be submitted, through your free assent,

To stonde in this cas at my jugement.
Acquiteth yow, and holdeth your biheste,
Than have ye doon your devoir atte leste."

    "Hoste," quod he, "*depardieux* ich assente,
To breke forward is not myn entente.
Biheste is dette, and I wol holde fayn
Al my biheste; I can no better seyn.
For swich lawe as man yeveth another wight,
He sholde him-selven usen it by right;
Thus wol our text; but natheles certeyn
I can right now no trifty tale seyn,
But Chaucer, though he can but lewedly
On metres and on ryming craftily,
Hath seyd hem in swich English as he can
Of olde tyme, as knoweth many a man.
And if he have not seyd hem, leve brother,
In o bok, he hath seyd hem in another.
For he hath told of loveres up and doun
Mo than Ovyde made of mencioun
In his Epistelles, that been ful olde.
What sholde I tellen hem, sin they ben tolde?
In youthe he made of Ceys and Alcion,
And sithen hath he spoke of everichon,
Thise noble wyves and thise loveres eke.
Who-so that wol his large volume seke
Cleped the Seintes Legende of Cupyde,
Ther may be seen the large woundes wyde
Of Lucresse, and of Babilan Tisbee;
The swerd of Dido for the false Enee;
The tree of Phillis for hir Demophon;
The pleinte of Dianire and Hermion,
Of Adriane and of Isiphilee;
The bareyne yle stonding in the see;
The dreynte Leander for his Erro;
The teres of Eleyne, and eek the wo
Of Brixseyde, and of thee, Ladomëa;
The crueltee of thee, queen Medëa,
Thy litel children hanging by the hals
For thy Jason, that was of love so fals!

To stand in this case at my judgement.
Acquit yourself now of your obligation;
Then you will have at least your duty done."
   "Host," said he, "*depardieux*, I assent;
To break my promise is not my intent.
A promise is a duty, and I would keep
All my promises, I can no better say.
For such law as a man gives another,
He should himself obey it, by right;
Thus says our text. But nevertheless, certainly,
I can right now no fitting tale say
That Chaucer, though he knows but little
Of meters and skillful rhyming,
Has said them in such English as he can
Long ago, as knows many a man;
And if he has not said them, dear brother,
In one book, he has said them in another.
For he has told of lovers up and down
More than Ovid made of mention
In his Epistles [3] that be full old.
Why should I tell them, since they have been told?
In youth he wrote of Ceyx and Alcion,[4]
And since then he has spoken of everyone,
These noble wives and these lovers also.
Whoso will his large volume seek,
Called the Legend of Good Women,[5]
There may he see the large wounds wide
Of Lucretia, and of Thisbe of Babylon;
The sword of Dido for the false Aeneas;
The tree of Phyllis for her Demophon,
The plaint of Deianira and of Hermione,
Of Ariadne, and of Hypsipyle—
The barren isle standing in the sea—
The drowned Leander for his Hero;
The tears of Helen, and also the woe
Of Briseyde, and of you, Laodomia;
The cruelty of the queen Medea,
Her little children hanging by the neck,
For your Jason, who was in love so false!

O Ypermistra, Penelopee, Alceste,
Your wyfhod he comendeth with the beste!
    But certeinly no word ne wryteth he
Of thilke wikke ensample of Canacee,
That lovede hir owne brother sinfully;
Of swiche cursed stories I sey 'fy';
Or elles of Tyro Apollonius,
How that the cursed king Antiochus
Birafte his doghter of hir maydenhede,
That is so horrible a tale for to rede,
Whan he hir threw up-on the pavement.
And therfore he, of ful avysement,
Nolde never wryte in none of his sermouns
Of swiche unkinde abhominaciouns,
Ne I wol noon reherse, if that I may.
    But of my tale how shal I doon this day?
Me were looth be lykned, doutelees,
To Muses that men clepe Pierides—
Metamorphoseos wot what I mene:—
But nathelees, I recche noght a bene
Though I come after him with hawe-bake;
I speke in prose, and lat him rymes make."
And with that word he, with a sobre chere,
Bigan his tale, as ye shal after here.

The Prologue

O hateful harm! condicion of poverte!
With thurst, with cold, with hunger so confounded!
To asken help thee shameth in thyn herte;
If thou noon aske, with nede artow so wounded,
That verray nede unwrappeth al thy wounde hid!
Maugree thyn heed, thou most for indigence
Or stele, or begge, or borwe thy despence!

Thou blamest Crist, and seyst ful bitterly,
He misdeparteth richesse temporal;
Thy neighebour thou wytest sinfully,
And seyst thou hast to lyte, and he hath al.

Oh Hypermnestra, Penelope, Alcestis,
Your fidelity he commends with the best!
    "But certainly no word writes he
Of that wicked example of Canacee, [6]
Who loved her own brother sinfully—
Of such cursed stories I say fie!
Or else of Apollonius of Tyre,[7]
How that cursed king Antiochus
Bereft his daughter of her maidenhead,
That is so horrible a tale for to read,
When he her threw upon the pavement.
And therefore Chaucer, after careful thought,
Would never write in any of his sermons
Of such unnatural abominations,
Nor will I any rehearse, if I may.
    "But of my tale how shall I do this day?
I am loath to be likened, doubtless,
To Muses whom men call Pierides[8]—
The Metamorphoses know what I mean;
But nevertheless, I do not care a bean
Though I come after him with poor fare.
I speak in prose, and let him rhymes make."
And with that word he, with sober face,
Began his tale, as you shall after hear.

The Prologue

Oh hateful misfortune, condition of poverty![9]
With thirst, with cold, with hunger so distressed!
To ask help you feel shame in your heart;
If you none ask, you are with need so wounded
That need lays bare all your hidden want!
Against your will, you must from indigence
Either steal, beg, or borrow your sustenance!

You blame Christ and say full bitterly
He wrongly divides riches temporal;
Your neighbor you accuse sinfully,
And say you have too little and he has all.

"Parfay," seistow, "somtyme he rekne shal,
Whan that his tayl shal brennen in the glede,
For he noght helpeth needfulle in hir nede."

Herkne what is the sentence of the wyse:—
"Bet is to dyën than have indigence;"
"Thy selve neighebour wol thee despyse;"
If thou be povre, farwel thy reverence!
Yet of the wyse man tak this sentence:—
"Alle the dayes of povre men ben wikke;"
Be war therfor, er thou come in that prikke!

"If thou be povre, thy brother hateth thee,
And alle thy freendes fleen fro thee, alas!"
O riche marchaunts, ful of wele ben ye,
O noble, o prudent folk, as in this cas!
Your bagges been nat filled with *ambes* as,
But with *sis cink*, that renneth for your chaunce;
At Cristemasse merie may ye daunce!

Ye seken lond and see for your winninges,
As wyse folk ye knowen al th'estaat
Of regnes; ye ben fadres of tydinges
And tales, bothe of pees and of debat.
I were right now of tales desolat,
Nere that a marchaunt, goon is many a yere,
Me taughte a tale, which that ye shal here.

The Tale

PART ONE

In Surrie whylom dwelte a companye
Of chapmen riche, and therto sadde and trewe,
That wyde-wher senten her spycerye,
Clothes of gold, and satins riche of hewe;
Her chaffar was so thrifty and so newe,
That every wight hath deyntee to chaffare
With hem, and eek to sellen hem hir ware.

"By my faith," you say, "sometime he shall take account,
When his tail shall burn in live coals,
For he helps not the needy in their need."

Harken to what is the judgement of the wise:
"Better is to die than to live in need,
Such that your very neighbor will you despise."
If you be poor, farewell your respect!
Yet of the wise men take this opinion:
"All the days of poor men be miserable."
Beware, therefore, that you come to that condition!

If you are poor, your brother hates you,
And all your friends flee from you, alas!
Oh rich merchants, full of prosperity be you,
Oh noble, oh prudent folk, as in this case!
Your cups be not filled with snake eyes,
But with six and five, a winning throw of the dice,
At Christmas merry may you dance!

You seek over land and sea for your profit;
As wise folk you know all the estate
Of reigns; you be fathers of tidings
And tales, both of peace and conflict.
I would be right now of tales desolate,
Were it not for one that a merchant, gone many a year,
Taught me, which you shall hear.

The Tale

PART ONE

In Syria once dwelt a company
Of merchants rich, and therefore trustworthy and true,
Who far and wide sent their silk and spice,
Cloth of gold, and satins rich of hue.
Their merchandise was so good and so new
That every person wanted to trade
With them, and also to sell them their wares.

Now fel it, that the maistres of that sort
Han shapen hem to Rome for to wende;
Were it for chapmanhode or for disport,
Non other message wolde they thider sende,
But comen hem-self to Rome, this is the ende;
And in swich place, as thoughte hem avantage
For her entente, they take her herbergage.

Sojourned han thise marchants in that toun
A certein tyme, as fel to hir plesance.
And so bifel, that th'excellent renoun
Of th'emperoures doghter, dame Custance,
Reported was, with every circumstance,
Un-to thise Surrien marchants in swich wyse,
Fro day to day, as I shal yow devyse.

This was the commune vois of every man—
"Our Emperour of Rome, god him see,
A doghter hath that, sin the world bigan,
To rekne as wel hir goodnesse as beautee,
Nas never swich another as is she;
I prey to god in honour hir sustene,
And wolde she were of al Europe the quene.

In hir is heigh beautee, with-oute pryde,
Yowthe, with-oute grenehede or folye;
To alle hir werkes vertu is hir gyde,
Humblesse hath slayn in hir al tirannye.
She is mirour of alle curteisye;
Hir herte is verray chambre of holinesse,
Hir hand, ministre of fredom for almesse."

And al this vois was soth, as god is trewe,
But now to purpos lat us turne agayn;
Thise marchants han doon fraught hir shippes newe,
And, whan they han this blisful mayden seyn,
Hoom to Surryë been they went ful fayn,
And doon her nedes as they han don yore,
And liven in wele; I can sey yow no more.

Now it befell that the masters of that sort
Had arranged themselves to Rome to wend;
Whether for business or pleasure,
No other messenger would they thither send,
But go themselves to Rome; that was their end.
And in such place as they thought advantageous
For their purposes, they took their lodging.

Sojourned have these merchants in that town
A certain time, as they wished.
And so it befell that the excellent renown
Of the Emperor's daughter, dame Constance,
Reported was, with every detail,
Unto these Syrian merchants in such a way,
From day to day, as I shall for you describe.

This was the common opinion of every man:
"Our Emperor of Rome—God him protect!—
A daughter has who, since the world began,
To reckon as well her goodness as beauty,
Was never such another as she.
I pray to God to sustain her in honor,
And would she were of Europe all the queen.

"In her is high beauty, without pride,
Youth, without callowness or folly;
In all her works virtue is her guide;
Humility has slain in her all tyranny.
She is mirror of all courtesy;
Her heart is the very chamber of holiness,
Her hand, minister of charity generous."

And all this report was true, as God is true.
But now to the point let us turn again.
These merchants have laden their ships anew,
And when they had this blissful maiden seen,
Home to Syria went they full gladly,
And conducted their business as they had done before,
And lived in prosperity; I can tell you no more.

Now fel it, that thise marchants stode in grace
Of him, that was the sowdan of Surrye;
For whan they came from any strange place,
He wolde, of his benigne curteisye,
Make hem good chere, and bisily espye
Tydings of sondry regnes, for to lere
The wondres that they mighte seen or here.

Amonges othere thinges, specially
Thise marchants han him told of dame Custance,
So gret noblesse in ernest, ceriously,
That this sowdan hath caught so gret plesance
To han hir figure in his remembrance,
That al his lust and al his bisy cure
Was for to love hir whyl his lyf may dure.

Paraventure in thilke large book
Which that men clepe the heven, y-writen was
With sterres, whan that he his birthe took,
That he for love shulde han his deeth, allas!
For in the sterres, clerer than is glas,
Is writen, god wot, who-so coude it rede,
The deeth of every man, withouten drede.

In sterres, many a winter ther-biforn,
Was written the deeth of Ector, Achilles,
Of Pompey, Julius, er they were born;
The stryf of Thebes; and of Ercules,
Of Sampson, Turnus, and of Socrates
The deeth; but mennes wittes been so dulle,
That no wight can wel rede it atte fulle.

This sowdan for his privee conseil sente,
And, shortly of this mater for to pace,
He hath to hem declared his entente,
And seyde hem certein, "but he mighte have grace
To han Custance with-inne a litel space,
He nas but deed;" and charged hem, in hye,
To shapen for his lyf som remedye.

Now befell it that these merchants stood in the good graces
Of he who was the Sultan of Syria;
And when they came from any foreign place,
He would, of gracious courtesy,
Make them welcome, and eagerly sought
Tidings of sundry reigns, to learn
The wonders that they might have heard or seen.

Among other things, specially,
These merchants had told him of dame Constance
And of her nobility, especially, and in such detail
That this Sultan derived great pleasure
To see her image in his mind's eye,
So that all his hope and all his pleasure
Was to love her so long as his life endured.

Perhaps in that large book
Which men call the heavens, written was
In the stars, that when he his birth took,
He was destined to die for love, alas!
For in the stars, clearer than is glass,
Is written, God knows, whoso could it decipher,
The fate of every man, without doubt.

In stars, many a winter therebefore,
Was written the death of Hector, Achilles,
Of Pompey the Great, of Julius Caesar,[10] before they were born;
The siege of Thebes,[11] and of Hercules,
Of Sampson, Turnus[12] and of Socrates
Their deaths, but men's wits be so dull
That no man can read it in full.

This Sultan for his closest advisors sent,
And, briefly of this matter to look over,
He has to them declared his intent,
And told them, certainly, unless he had the grace
Of Constance within a short time,
He was as good as dead; and ordered them in haste
To devise for his life some remedy.

Diverse men diverse thinges seyden;
They argumenten, casten up and doun
Many a subtil resoun forth they leyden,
They speken of magik and abusioun;
But finally, as in conclusioun,
They can not seen in that non avantage,
Ne in non other wey, save mariage.

Than sawe they ther-in swich difficultee
By wey of resoun, for to speke al playn,
By-cause that ther was swich diversitee
Bitwene hir bothe lawes, that they sayn,
They trowe "that no cristen prince wolde fayn
Wedden his child under oure lawes swete
That us were taught by Mahoun our prophete."

And he answerde, "rather than I lese
Custance, I wol be cristned doutelees;
I mot ben hires, I may non other chese,
I prey yow holde your arguments in pees;
Saveth my lyf, and beeth noght recchelees
To geten hir that hath my lyf in cure;
For in this wo I may not longe endure."

What nedeth gretter dilatacioun?
I seye, by tretis and embassadrye,
And by the popes mediacioun,
And al the chirche, and al the chivalrye,
That, in destruccioun of Maumetrye,
And in encrees of Cristes lawe dere,
They ben acorded, so as ye shal here;

How that the sowdan and his baronage
And alle his liges shulde y-cristned be,
And he shal han Custance in mariage,
And certein gold, I noot what quantitee,
And her-to founden suffisant seurtee;
This same acord was sworn on eyther syde;
Now, faire Custance, almighty god thee gyde!

Different men different things said;
They argued, considered ups and downs;
Many a subtle reason forth they laid;
They spoke of magic and deception.
But finally, in conclusion,
They could not see any advantage
Nor any other way, save in marriage.

Then saw they therein such difficulty
By way of reason, for to speak all plain,
Because there was such difference
Between their religions, that they said
They believed that no "Christian prince would care to
Wed his child under our law sweet
That was taught us by our prophet, Mahomet."

And he answered, "Rather than I lose
Constance, I will be christened, doubtless.
I must be hers, I may no other choose.
I pray you hold your arguments in peace;
Save my life, and be not negligent
To get her—in whose hands lies my fate—
For in this woe I may not long endure."

Need I with words more elaborate?
I say, by treaty and negotiation,
And by the pope's mediation,
And supported by all the church, and all the chivalry,
To further the destruction of idolatry,
And to increase the reign of Christ's law dear,
They came to an accord, as you shall hear:

Whereby the Sultan and his barons
And all his lieges should christened be,
And he should have Constance in marriage,
And certain gold, I know not what quantity;
For this provided sufficient surety.
This same accord was sworn on either side;
Now, fair Constance, almighty God you guide!

Now wolde som men waiten, as I gesse,
That I shulde tellen al the purveyance
That th'emperour, of his grete noblesse,
Hath shapen for his doghter dame Custance.
Wel may men knowe that so gret ordinance
May no man tellen in a litel clause
As was arrayed for so heigh a cause.

Bisshopes ben shapen with hir for to wende,
Lordes, ladyes, knightes of renoun,
And other folk y-nowe, this is the ende;
And notifyed is thurgh-out the toun
That every wight, with gret devocioun,
Shulde preyen Crist that he this mariage
Receyve in gree, and spede this viage.

The day is comen of hir departinge,
I sey, the woful day fatal is come,
That ther may be no lenger taryinge,
But forthward they hem dressen, alle and some;
Custance, that was with sorwe al overcome,
Ful pale arist, and dresseth hir to wende;
For wel she seeth ther is non other ende.

Allas! what wonder is it though she wepte,
That shal be sent to strange nacioun
Fro freendles, that so tendrely hir kepte,
And to be bounden under subieccioun
Of oon, she knoweth not his condicioun.
Housbondes been alle gode, and han ben yore,
That knowen wyves, I dar say yow no more.

"Fader," she sayde, "thy wrecched child Custance,
Thy yonge doghter, fostred up so softe,
And ye, my moder, my soverayn plesance
Over alle thing, out-taken Crist on-lofte,
Custance, your child, hir recomandeth ofte
Un-to your grace, for I shal to Surryë,
Ne shal I never seen yow more with yë.

Now would some expect, as I guess,
That I should tell all the preparations
That the emperor, in his great nobility,
Had planned for his daughter, dame Constance.
Well may men know that such great preparation
May no man tell in a little clause
As was arranged for so high a cause.

Bishops were appointed with her for to wend,
Lords, ladies, knights of renown,
And other folk enough; this is the end;
And made known was throughout the town
That every person, with great devotion,
Should pray to Christ that he this marriage
Receive favorably and speed this voyage.

The day came for her departure;
I say, the woeful fatal day arrived,
That there might be no longer tarrying,
But forward they prepared themselves, all and some.
Constance, who was with sorrow all overcome,
Full pale arose, and prepared herself to wend;
For well she saw there was no other end.

Alas, what wonder that she wept,
Who should be sent to a strange nation
From friends who so tenderly her kept,
And to be bound under subjection
Of one who—she knew not his disposition?
Husbands be all good, and have been of yore;
That know wives, I dare say you no more.

"Father," she said, "your wretched child Constance,
Your young daughter raised so tenderly,
And you, my mother, my sovereign pleasure
Above everything, except Christ above,
Constance your child commends herself often
Unto your grace, for I shall go to Syria,
Never shall my eyes see you again.

Allas! un-to the Barbre nacioun
I moste anon, sin that it is your wille;
But Crist, that starf for our redempcioun,
So yeve me grace, his hestes to fulfille;
I, wrecche womman, no fors though I spille.
Wommen are born to thraldom and penance,
And to ben under mannes governance."

I trowe, at Troye, whan Pirrus brak the wal
Or Ylion brende, at Thebes the citee,
Nat Rome, for the harm thurgh Hanibal
That Romayns hath venquisshed tymes three,
Nas herd swich tendre weping for pitee
As in the chambre was for hir departinge;
Bot forth she moot, wher-so she wepe or singe.

O firste moeving cruel firmament,
With thy diurnal sweigh that crowdest ay
And hurlest al from Est til Occident,
That naturelly wolde holde another way,
Thy crowding set the heven in swich array
At the beginning of this fiers viage,
That cruel Mars hath slayn this mariage.

Infortunat ascendent tortuous,
Of which the lord is helples falle, allas!
Out of his angle in-to the derkest hous.
O Mars, O Atazir, as in this cas!
O feble mone, unhappy been thy pas!
Thou knittest thee ther thou art nat receyved,
Ther thou were weel, fro thennes artow weyved.

Imprudent emperour of Rome, allas!
Was ther no philosophre in al thy toun?
Is no tyme bet than other in swich cas?
Of viage is ther noon eleccioun,
Namely to folk of heigh condicioun,
Nat whan a rote is of a birthe y-knowe?
Allas! we ben to lewed or to slowe.

"Alas, unto the Berber nation[13]
I most go anon, since that is your will;
But Christ, who died for our redemption
So give me grace his heedings to fulfill!
I, wretched woman, no matter if I die!
Women are born to thralldom and penance,
And to be under man's governance."

Not at Troy, when Pyrrhus[14] broke the wall
And the city burned, nor at Thebes,
Nor at Rome, when it was poised to fall
To Hannibal, who thrice vanquished the Romans,
Was heard such tender weeping for pity
As in the chamber was for her departing;
But go she must, weeping or singing.

O primum mobile![15] Cruel firmament,
With your diurnal sway that crowds ever
And hurls all from east to west
That naturally would go another way,
Your force set the heavens in such array
At the beginning of this dangerous voyage,
That cruel Mars will slay this marriage.

Inauspicious ascendent tortuous,[16]
Of which the lord was helplessly fallen, alas,
Out of his angle into the darkest house!
Oh Mars, oh atazir, as in this case!
Oh feeble moon, unhappy are your steps!
You conjoin where you are not well-received;
From where you were well, you are now banished.

Imprudent Emperor of Rome, alas!
Was there no astrologer in all your town?
Was no time better than another in that case?
For a voyage is there no choice,
Especially for folk of high position?
Not when a date of birth is known?
Alas, we be too unlearned or too slow!

To shippe is brought this woful faire mayde
Solempnely, with every circumstance.
"Now Jesu Crist be with yow alle," she sayde;
Ther nis namore but "farewel! faire Custance!"
She peyneth hir to make good countenance,
And forth I lete hir sayle in this manere,
And turne I wol agayn to my matere.

The moder of the sowdan, welle of vyces,
Espyëd hath hir sones pleyn entente,
How he wol lete his olde sacrifyces,
And right anon she for hir conseil sente;
And they ben come, to knowe what she mente.
And when assembled was this folke in-fere,
She sette hir doun, and sayde as ye shal here.

"Lordes," quod she, "ye knowen everichon,
How that my sone in point is for to lete
The holy lawes of our Alkaron,
Yeven by goddes message Makomete.
But oon avow to grete god I hete,
The lyf shal rather out of my body sterte
Than Makometes lawe out of myn herte!

What shulde us tyden of this newe lawe
But thraldom to our bodies and penance?
And afterward in helle to be drawe
For we reneyed Mahoun our creance?
But, lordes, wol ye maken assurance,
As I shal seyn, assenting to my lore,
And I shall make us sauf for evermore?"

They sworen and assenten, every man,
To live with hir and dye, and by hir stonde;
And everich, in the beste wyse he can,
To strengthen hir shal alle his freendes fonde;
And she hath this empryse y-take on honde,
Which ye shal heren that I shal devyse,
And to hem alle she spak right in this wyse.

To ship was brought this woeful fair maid
Solemnly, with every ceremony.
"Now Jesus Christ be with you all!" she said;
There was no more, but, "Farewell, Constance!"
She tried to put on a brave face;
And forth I let her sail in this manner,
And turn I will again to my matter.

The mother of the Sultan, well of vices,
Espied has her son's plain intent,
How he would abandon his old sacrifices;
And right anon she for her private counsel sent,
And they came to know what she meant.
And when assembled were this folk together,
She set herself down, and said as you shall hear.

"Lords," said she, "you know every one,
How my son is about to forsake
The holy laws of the Koran,
Given by God's messenger Mahomet.
But one vow to great God I promise,
The life shall rather out of my body depart
Before Mahomet's law departs my heart!

"What should happen to us with this new law
But thralldom for our bodies and remorse,
And afterward in hell to be drawn,
If we renounce our belief in Mahomet?
But lords, will you make assurance,
To follow what I shall say, assenting to my advice,
And I shall thereby make us safe for evermore?"

They swore and assented, every man,
To live with her and die, and by her stand,
And every one, in the best way he could,
To strengthen her would persuade all his friends;
And she has this enterprise taken in hand,
Which you shall hear that I shall describe,
And to them all she spoke right in this way:

"We shul first feyne us cristendom to take,
Cold water shal not greve us but a lyte;
And I shal swich a feste and revel make,
That, as I trowe, I shal the sowdan quyte.
For though his wyf be cristned never so whyte
She shal have nede to wasshe awey the rede,
Thogh she a font-ful water with hir lede."

O sowdanesse, rote of iniquitee,
Virago, thou Semyram the secounde,
O serpent under femininitee,
Lyk to the serpent depe in helle y-bounde,
O feyned womman, al that may confounde
Vertu and innocence, thurgh thy malyce,
Is bred in thee, as nest of every vyce!

O Satan, envious sin thilke day
That thou were chased from our heritage,
Wel knowestow to wommen the olde way!
Thou madest Eva bringe us in servage.
Thou wolt fordoon this cristen mariage.
Thyn instrument so, weylawey the whyle!
Makestow of wommen, whan thou wolt begyle.

This sowdanesse, whom I thus blame and warie,
Leet prively hir conseil goon hir way.
What sholde I in this tale lenger tarie?
She rydeth to the sowdan on a day,
And seyde him, that she wolde reneye hir lay,
And cristendom of preestes handes fonge,
Repenting hir she hethen was so longe,

Biseching him to doon hir that honour,
That she moste han the cristen men to feste;
"To plesen hem I wol do my labour."
The sowdan seith, "I wol don at your heste,"
And kneling thanketh hir of that requeste.
So glad he was, he niste what to seye;
She kiste hir sone, and hoom she gooth hir weye.

"We shall first feign us Christianity to take—
Cold water shall not grieve us but a little—
And I shall such a feast and revel make
That, as I believe, shall the Sultan revenge.
For though his wife be christened ever so white,
She shall have need to wash away the red,
Though she bring a baptismal font."

Oh Sultaness, root of iniquity!
Virago, you Semiramis the second!
Oh serpent disguised as femininity,
Like to Satan deep in hell bound!
O feigned woman, all that may destroy
Virtue and innocence, through your malice,
Is bred in you, a nest of every vice!

Oh Satan, envious since that day
That you were chased from our Garden,
Well know you women in the old way!
You made Eve bring us into servitude;
You would destroy this Christian marriage.
Your instrument—alas!—
Make you of women, when you would beguile.

This Sultaness, whom I thus blame and curse,
Secretly dismissed her counsel to go their ways.
Why should I in this tale longer tarry?
She rode to the Sultan on a day,
And said that she would renounce her faith,
And Christianity at the priest's hands accept,
Repenting that she had Mahomet so long worshiped,

And beseeching him that he would do her the honor,
That she might have the Christian folk to feast—
"To please them will I make an effort."
The sultan said, "I will comply with your behest."
And kneeling thanked her for that request.
So glad he was, he knew not what to say.
She kissed her son, and home she went her way.

PART TWO

Arryved ben this Cristen folk to londe,
In Surrie, with a greet solempne route,
And hastily this sowdan sente his sonde,
First to his moder, and al the regne aboute,
And seyde, his wyf was comen, out of doute,
And preyde hir for to ryde agayn the quene,
The honour of his regne to sustene.

Gret was the prees, and riche was th'array
Of Surriens and Romayns met y-fere;
The moder of the sowdan, riche and gay,
Receyveth hir with al-so glad a chere
As any moder mighte hir doghter dere,
And to the nexte citee ther bisyde
A softe pas solempnely they ryde.

Noght trowe I the triumphe of Julius,
Of which that Lucan maketh swich a bost,
Was royaller, ne more curious
Than was th'assemblee of this blisful host.
But this scorpioun, this wikked gost,
The sowdanesse, for al hir flateringe,
Caste under this ful mortally to stinge.

The sowdan comth him-self sone after this
So royally, that wonder is to telle,
And welcometh hir with alle joye and blis.
And thus in merthe and joye I lete hem dwelle.
The fruyt of this matere is that I telle.
Whan tyme cam, men thoughte it for the beste
That revel stinte, and men goon to hir reste.

The tyme cam, this olde sowdanesse
Ordeyned hath this feste of which I tolde,
And to the feste Cristen folk hem dresse
In general, ye! bothe yonge and olde
Here may men feste and royaltee biholde,

PART TWO

Arrived were this Christian folk to land
In Syria, with a great solemn company,
And hastily this Sultan sent his message
First to his mother, and all the reign about,
And said his wife was coming, with no doubt,
And prayed for her to ride toward the queen,
The honor of his reign to sustain.

Great was the crowd, and rich was the raiment
Of Syrians and Romans met together;
The mother of the Sultan, rich and gay,
Received her also with a glad face
As any mother might her daughter dear,
And to the next city there beside
Slowly and solemnly they rode.

I believe that Caesar's triumphal march,
Of which Lucan makes such a boast,[17]
Was not more royal or elaborate
Than was the assembly of this blissful host.
But this scorpion, this wicked spirit,
The Sultaness, for all her flattery,
Planned under this full mortally to sting.

The Sultan came himself soon after this
So royally that it wondrous is to tell,
And welcomed her with all joy and bliss.
And thus in mirth and joy I let him dwell;
The heart of this matter is what I tell.
When the time came, men thought it for the best
The revels to end, and men went to their rest.

The time came that this old Sultaness
Ordained this feast of which I told,
And to the feast Christian folk attended
In general, yea, both young and old.
Here may men feast and royalty behold,

And deyntees mo than I can yow devyse,
But al to dere they boughte it er they ryse.

O sodeyn wo! that ever art successour
To worldly blisse, spreynd with bitternesse;
Th'ende of the joye of our worldly labour;
Wo occupieth the fyn of our gladnesse.
Herke this conseil for thy sikernesse,
Up-on thy glade day have in thy minde
The unwar wo or harm that comth bihinde.

For shortly for to tellen at o word,
The sowdan and the Cristen everichone
Ben al to-hewe and stiked at the bord,
But it were only dame Custance allone.
This olde sowdanesse, cursed crone,
Hath with hir frendes doon this cursed dede,
For she hir-self wolde al the contree lede.

Ne ther was Surrien noon that was converted
That of the conseil of the sowdan woot,
That he nas al to-hewe er he asterted.
And Custance han they take anon, foot-hoot,
And in a shippe al sterelees, god woot,
They han hir set, and bidde hir lerne sayle
Out of Surrye agaynward to Itayle.

A certein tresor that she thider ladde,
And, sooth to sayn, vitaille gret plentee
They han hir yeven, and clothes eek she hadde.
And forth she sayleth in the salte see.
O my Custance, ful of benignitee,
O emperoures yonge doghter dere,
He that is lord of fortune be thy stere!

She blesseth hir, and with ful pitous voys
Un-to the croys of Crist thus seyde she,
"O clere, o welful auter, holy croys,
Reed of the lambes blood full of pitee,

And dainties more than I can for you describe;
But all too dear they bought it before they rose.

Oh sudden woe, that ever is successor
To worldly bliss, sprinkled with bitterness,
The end of the joy of our worldly labor!
Woe occupies the end of our gladness.
Harken to this counsel for your safety:
Upon the glad day have in your mind
The unknown woe or harm that comes behind.

For shortly for to tell, in a word,
The Sultan and the Christians every one
Were hacked and stabbed at the table,
Except for dame Constance alone.
This old Sultaness, cursed crone,
Has with her friends done this cursed deed,
For she herself would all the country lead.

None of the Syrians who were converted,
Who of the counsel of the Sultan knew,
Were not stabbed or to pieces hewn.
And Constance they took anon with hot feet,
And in a rudderless old hulk, God knows,
They her set, and bid her learn to sail
From Syria back to Italy again.

A certain treasure she thither carried,
And, truth to tell, of food great plenty
They have her given, and clothes also she had,
And forth she sailed in the salt sea.
Oh my Constance, full of benignity,
Oh Emperor's young daughter dear,
He who is lord of Fortune may your ship steer!

She blessed herself, and with full piteous voice
Unto the cross of Christ said she:
"Oh pure, oh blessed altar, holy cross,
Red with the Lamb's blood full of pity,

That wesh the world fro the olde iniquitee,
Me fro the feend, and fro his clawes kepe,
That day that I shal drenchen in the depe.

Victorious tree, proteccioun of trewe,
That only worthy were for to bere
The king of heven with his woundes newe,
The whyte lamb, that hurt was with the spere,
Flemer of feendes out of him and here
On which thy limes feithfully extenden,
Me keep, and yif me might my lyf t'amenden."

Yeres and dayes fleet this creature
Thurghout the see of Grece un-to the strayte
Of Marrok, as it was hir aventure;
On many a sory meel now may she bayte;
After her deeth ful often may she wayte,
Er that the wilde wawes wol hir dryve
Un-to the placë, ther she shal arryve.

Men mighten asken why she was not slayn?
Eek at the feste who mighte hir body save?
And I answere to that demaunde agayn,
Who saved Daniel in the horrible cave,
Ther every wight save he, maister and knave,
Was with the leoun frete er he asterte?
No wight but god, that he bar in his herte.

God liste to shewe his wonderful miracle
In hir, for we sholde seen his mighty werkes;
Crist, which that is to every harm triacle,
By certein menes ofte, as knowen clerkes,
Doth thing for certein ende that ful derk is
To mannes wit, that for our ignorance
Ne conne not knowe his prudent purveyance.

Now, sith she was not at the feste y-slawe,
Who kepte hir fro the drenching in the see?
Who kepte Jonas in the fisshes mawe

That washes the world of old iniquity,
Me from the fiend and from his claws keep,
That day that I shall drown in the deep.

"Victorious cross, protector of the faithful,
That alone was worthy for to bear
The King of Heaven with his wounds new,
The white lamb, that was wounded with a spear,
Banisher of fiends from him and her
Over which your limbs faithfully extend,
Me keep, and me give the power my life to amend."

Years and days drifted this creature
Through the Sea of Greece unto the Straits
Of Gibraltar, as it was her luck.
On many a sorry meal now may she dine;
For her death full often may she wait,
Before that the wild waves will her drive
Unto the place where she shall arrive.

Men might ask why she was not slain
Also at the feast? Who might her body save?
And I answer to that demand again,
Who saved Daniel in the horrible cave[18]
Where every person save he, master and servant,
Was by the lion devoured before he escaped?
No person but God whom he bore in his heart.

God chose to show his wonderful miracle
In her, that we should see his mighty works;
Christ, who is to every harm the medicine,
By certain means often, as know scholars,
Does things for certain ends that full dark are
To men's wit, that in our ignorance
We can not know his prudent providence.

Now since she was not at the feast slain,
Who kept her from drowning in the sea?
Who kept Jonas in the fish's maw[19]

Til he was spouted up at Ninivee?
Wel may men knowe it was no wight but he
That kepte peple Ebraik fro hir drenchinge,
With drye feet thurgh-out the see passinge.

Who bad the foure spirits of tempest,
That power han t'anoyen land and see,
"Bothe north and south, and also west and est,
Anoyeth neither see, ne land, ne tree?"
Sothly, the comaundour of that was he,
That fro the tempest ay this womman kepte
As wel whan [that] she wook as whan she slepte.

Wher mighte this womman mete and drinke-have?
Three yeer and more how lasteth hir vitaille?
Who fedde the Egipcien Marie in the cave,
Or in desert? no wight but Crist, sans faille.
Fyve thousand folk it was as gret mervaille
With loves fyve and fisshes two to fede.
God sente his foison at hir grete nede.

She dryveth forth in-to our occean
Thurgh-out our wilde see, til; atte laste,
Under an hold that nempnen I ne can,
Fer in Northumberlond the wawe hir caste,
And in the sond hir ship stiked so faste,
That thennes wolde it noght of al a tyde,
The wille of Crist was that she shulde abyde.

The constable of the castel doun is fare
To seen this wrak, and al the ship he soghte,
And fond this wery womman ful of care;
He fond also the tresor that she broghte.
In hir langage mercy she bisoghte
The lyf out of hir body for to twinne,
Hir to delivere of wo that she was inne.

A maner Latin corrupt was hir speche,
But algates ther-by was she understonde;

Till he was spouted up at Nineveh?
Well may men know that it was no person but he
Who kept the Hebrew people from their drowning,
With dry feet passing through the sea.[20]

Who bade the four angels of tempest[21]
Who have the power to trouble land and sea,
Both north and south, and also west and east,
"Trouble neither sea, nor land, nor cross"?
Truly, the commander of that was he
Who from the tempest ever this woman kept
As well when she woke as when she slept.

Where might this woman food and drink have
Three years and more? How lasted her provisions?
Who fed Saint Mary the Egyptian in the cave,[22]
Or in the desert? No one but Christ, without doubt.
It was as miraculous as when with two loaves and fishes
Five thousand folk he fed.
God sent his plenty at her great need.

She drove forth into our ocean
Throughout our wild sea, till at last
Under a castle that I cannot name,
Far in Northumberland the waves her cast,
And in the sand her ship stuck so fast
That thence would it not float for all a tide;
The will of Christ was that she should abide.

The constable of this castle down is fared
To see the wreck, and all the ship he searched,
And found this very woman full of sorrow;
He found also the treasure that she brought.
In her language mercy she besought,
The life out of her body to take,
Her to deliver of the woe that she was in.

A kind of corrupted Latin was her speech,
But nevertheless thereby was she understood.

The constable, whan him list no lenger seche,
This woful womman broghte he to the londe;
She kneleth doun, and thanketh goddes sonde.
But what she was, she wolde no man seye,
For foul ne fair, thogh that she shulde deye.

She seyde, she was so massed in the see
That she forgat hir minde, by hir trouthe;
The constable hath of hir so greet pitee,
And eek his wyf, that they wepen for routhe,
She was so diligent, with-outen slouthe,
To serve and plesen everich in that place,
That alle hir loven that loken on hir face.

This constable and dame Hermengild his wyf
Were payens, and that contree everywhere;
But Hermengild lovede hir right as hir lyf,
And Custance hath so longe sojourned there,
In orisons, with many a bitter tere,
Til Jesu hath converted thurgh his grace
Dame Hermengild, constablesse of that place.

In al that lond no Cristen durste route,
Alle Cristen folk ben fled fro that contree
Thurgh payens, that conquereden al aboute
The plages of the North, by land and see;
To Walis fled the Cristianitee
Of olde Britons, dwellinge in this yle;
Ther was hir refut for the mene whyle.

But yet nere Cristen Britons so exyled
That ther nere somme that in hir privetee
Honoured Crist, and hethen folk bigyled;
And ny the castel swiche ther dwelten three.
That oon of hem was blind, and mighte nat see
But it were with thilke yën of his minde,
With whiche men seen, after that they ben blinde.

The constable, when he was done his search,
This woeful woman brought he to the land.
She knelt down and thanked God's providence;
But who she was she would no man tell,
For foul nor fair, though she should die.

She said that she was so bewildered in the sea
That she lost her memory, by her troth.
The constable had for her such great pity,
And also his wife, that they wept for compassion.
She was so diligent, without sloth,
To serve and please everyone in that place
That all her loved who looked upon her face.

This constable and dame Hermengyld, his wife,
Were pagans, as was that country everywhere;
But Hermengyld loved her right as her life,
And Constance so long sojourned there,
Giving herself to prayer, with many a bitter tear,
Till Jesus converted through his grace
Dame Hermengyld, the constable's wife of that place.

In all that land no Christians dared gather;
All Christian folk were fled from that country
Because of the pagans, who conquered all about
The coasts of the north, by land and sea.[23]
To Wales fled the Christian
Old Britons dwelling in that isle;
There was their refuge for the meanwhile.

But yet were not Christian Britons so exiled
That there were not some who in secret
Honored Christ and heathen folk beguiled,
And near the castle there dwelt three.
And one of them was blind and might not see,
Except with those eyes of his mind
With which men may see, after they go blind.

Bright was the sonne as in that someres day,
For which the constable and his wyf also
And Custance han y-take the righte way
Toward the see, a furlong wey or two,
To pleyen and to romen to and fro;
And in hir walk this blinde man they mette
Croked and old, with yën faste y-shette.

"In name of Crist," cryde this blinde Britoun,
"Dame Hermengild, yif me my sighte agayn."
This lady wex affrayed of the soun,
Lest that hir housbond, shortly for to sayn,
Wolde hir for Jesu Cristes love han slayn,
Til Custance made hir bold, and bad hir werche
The wil of Crist, as doghter of his chirche.

The constable wex abasshed of that sight,
And seyde, "what amounteth al this fare?"
Custance answerde, "sire, it is Cristes might,
That helpeth folk out of the feendes snare."
And so ferforth she gan our lay declare,
That she the constable, er that it were eve,
Converted, and on Crist made him bileve.

This constable was no-thing lord of this place
Of which I speke, ther he Custance fond,
But kepte is strongly, many wintres space,
Under Alla, king of al Northumberlond,
That was ful wys, and worthy of his hond
Agayn the Scottes, as men may wel here,
But turne I wol agayn to my matere.

Sathan, that ever us waiteth to bigyle,
Saugh of Custance al hir perfeccioun,
And caste anon how he mighte quyte hir whyle,
And made a yong knight, that dwelte in that toun,
Love hir so hote, of foul affeccioun,
That verraily him thoughte he shulde spille
But he of hir mighte ones have his wille.

Bright was the sun in that summer's day,
For which the constable and his wife also
And Constance had taken the right way
Toward the sea a furlong length or two,
To play and roam to and fro,
And in their walk this blind man they met,
Crooked and old, with eyes fast shut.

"In name of Christ," cried this blind Briton,
"Dame Hermengyld, give me my sight again!"
This lady waxed afraid of the sound,
Lest that her husband, shortly for to tell,
Would her for Jesus Christ's love have slain,
Till Constance made her bold, and bade her work
The will of Christ, as daughter of his church.

The constable waxed abashed at that sight,
And said, "What does all this mean?"
Constance answered, "Sire, it is Christ's might,
Who helps folk out of the fiend's snare."
And so much she began our religion to declare
That she the constable, before it was evening
Converted, and in Christ made him believe.

This constable was not lord of this place
Of which I speak, where he Constance found,
But kept it strongly many a winter's space
Under Alla, king of all Northumberland,
Who was full wise, and brave in battle
Against the Scots, as men may well hear;
But turn I will again to my matter.

Satan, who ever waits us to beguile,
Saw of Constance all her perfection,
And plotted anon how he might repay her soon,
And made a young knight who dwelt in that town
Love her so hotly, with such passion,
That verily he thought he should die,
Unless he of her might once have his will.

He woweth hir, but it availleth noght,
She wolde do no sinne, by no weye;
And, for despyt, he compassed in his thoght
To maken hir on shamful deth to deye.
He wayteth whan the constable was aweye,
And prively, up-on a night, he crepte
In Hermengildes chambre whyl she slepte.

Wery, for-waked in her orisouns,
Slepeth Custance, and Hermengild also.
This knight, thurgh Sathanas temptaciouns,
Al softely is to the bed y-go,
And kitte the throte of Hermengild a-two,
And leyde the blody knyf by dame Custance,
And wente his wey, ther god yeve him meschance!

Sone after comth this constable hoom agayn,
And eek Alla, that king was of that lond,
And saugh his wyf despitously y-slayn,
For which ful ofte he weep and wrong his hond,
And in the bed the blody knyf he fond
By dame Custance; allas! what mighte she seye?
For verray wo hir wit was al aweye.

To king Alla was told al this meschance,
And eek the tyme, and where, and in what wyse
That in a ship was founden dame Custance,
As heer-biforn that ye han herd devyse.
The kinges herte of pitee gan agryse,
Whan he saugh so benigne a creature
Falle in disese and in misaventure.

For as the lomb toward his deeth is broght,
So stant this innocent bifore the king;
This false knight that hath this tresoun wroght
Berth hir on hond that she hath doon this thing.
But nathelees, ther was [ful] greet moorning

He wooed her, but it availed not;
She would do no sin, in no way.
And for spite he plotted in his thought
To make her in shameful death to die.
He waited when the constable was away,
And privately upon a night he crept
Into Hermengyld's chamber, while she slept.

Weary, exhausted from prayer,
Slept Constance, and Hermengyld also.
This knight, through Satan's temptation,
All softly is to the bed gone,
And cut the throat of Hermengyld in two,
And laid the bloody knife by dame Constance,
And went his way, may God give him mischance!

Soon after came this constable home again,
And also Alla, who king was of that land,
And the constable saw his wife cruelly slain,
For which full oft he wept and wrung his hands,
And in the bed the bloody knife he found
Beside Dame Constance. Alas, what might she say?
In her woe her wit was all away.

To King Alla was told all this mischance,
And also the time, and where, and in what way
That in a ship was found this Constance,
As herebefore you have heard described.
The king's heart of pity began to tremble,
When he saw so benign a creature
Fall in distress and misadventure.

For as the lamb toward its death is brought,
So stood this innocent before the king.
This false knight, who has this treason wrought,
Falsely accused her of having done this thing.
But nevertheless, there was great mourning

Among the peple, and seyn, "they can not gesse
That she hath doon so greet a wikkednesse.

For they han seyn hir ever so vertuous,
And loving Hermengild right as her lyf."
Of this bar witnesse everich in that hous
Save he that Hermengild slow with his knyf,
This gentil king hath caught a gret motyf
Of this witnesse, and thoghte he wolde enquere
Depper in this, a trouthe for to lere.

Allas! Custance! thou hast no champioun,
Ne fighte canstow nought, so weylawey!
But he, that starf for our redempcioun
And bond Sathan (and yit lyth ther he lay)
So be thy stronge champioun this day!
For, but-if Crist open miracle kythe,
Withouten gilt thou shalt be slayn as swythe.

She sette her doun on knees, and thus she sayde,
"Immortal god, that savedest Susanne
Fro false blame, and thou, merciful mayde,
Mary I mene, doghter to Seint Anne,
Bifore whos child aungeles singe Osanne,
If I be giltlees of this felonye,
My socour be, for elles I shal dye!"

Have ye nat seyn some tyme a pale face,
Among a prees, of him that hath be lad
Toward his deeth, wher-as him gat no grace,
And swich a colour in his face hath had,
Men mighte knowe his face, that was bisted,
Amonges alle the faces in that route:
So stant Custance, and loketh hir aboute.

O quenes, livinge in prosperitee,
Duchesses, and ye ladies everichone,
Haveth som routhe on hir adversitee;

Among the people, and said they could not guess
That she had done so great a wickedness,

For they had seen her ever so virtuous,
And loving Hermengyld right as her life.
Of this bore witness everyone in that house,
Save he who slew Hermengyld with his knife.
This gentle king was deeply moved
By this witnessing, and thought he would inquire
Deeper into this, for to learn the truth.

Alas! Constance, you have no champion,
Nor can you fight, so wellaway!
But he who died for our redemption,
And bound Satan (who yet lies there still),
So be your strong champion this day!
For, unless Christ an open miracle reveals,
Guiltless you shall be slain and soon.

She knelt down, and thus she said:
"Immortal God, who saved Susanna
From false blame,[24] and you, merciful maid,
Mary I mean, daughter to Saint Anne,
Before whose child angels sing Hosanna,
If I be guiltless of this felony,
My succor be, for else shall I die!"

Have you not seen sometime a pale face,
Among a crowd, of him who is led
Toward his death, who has received no grace,
And who has such a color in his face that
Men might see that trouble standing out
Of all the faces in the crowd?
So stood Constance, as she looked her about.

Oh queens, living in prosperity,
Duchesses, and you ladies everyone,
Have some pity on her adversity!

An emperoures doghter stant allone;
She hath no wight to whom to make hir mone.
O blood royal, that stondest in this drede,
Fer ben thy freendes at thy grete nede!

This Alla king hath swich compassioun,
As gentil herte is fulfild of pitee,
That from his yën ran the water doun.
"Now hastily do fecche a book," quod he,
"And if this knight wol sweren how that she
This womman slow, yet wole we us avyse
Whom that we wole that shal ben our justyse."

A Briton book, writen with Evangyles,
Was fet, and on this book he swoor anoon
She gilty was, an in the mene whyles
A hand him smoot upon the nekke-boon,
That doun he fil atones as a stoon,
And bothe his yën broste out of his face
In sight of every body in that place.

A vois was herd in general audience,
And seyde, "thou hast desclaundred giltelees
The doghter of holy chirche in hey presence;
Thus hastou doon, and yet holde I my pees."
Of this mervaille agast was al the prees;
As mased folk they stoden everichone,
For drede of wreche, save Custance allone.

Greet was the drede and eek the repentance
Of hem that hadden wrong suspeccioun
Upon this sely innocent Custance;
And, for this miracle, in conclusioun,
And by Custances mediacioun,
The king, and many another in that place,
Converted was, thanked be Cristes grace!

This false knight was slayn for his untrouthe
By jugement of Alla hastily;

An Emperor's daughter stands alone;
She has no one to whom she can make her moan.
Oh blood royal, who stands in this dread,
Far be your friends at your great need!

This Alla king has such compassion,
As a gentle heart is filled with pity,
That from his eyes ran the water down.
"Now hastily do fetch a book," said he,
"And if this knight will swear how that she
This woman slew, yet will we think carefully
Who shall be her executioner."

A British book, written with Gospels,
Was fetched, and in this book he swore anon
She guilty was, and in the meanwhile
A hand him smote upon the neck-bone,
And down he fell as a stone,
And both his eyes burst out of his face
In sight of everybody in that place.

A voice was heard by everyone there,
That said, "You have slandered, guiltless,
The daughter of holy church in God's presence;
Thus have you done, and yet I held my peace!"
By this miracle astonished was all the gathering;
As bewildered folk they stood every one,
For dread of vengeance, save Constance alone.

Great was the dread and also the repentance
Of those who had wrongly suspected
This true innocent, Constance;
And for this miracle, in conclusion,
And by Constance's mediation,
The king—and many another in that place—
Converted was, thanked be Christ's grace!

This false knight was slain for his untruth
By judgement of Alla swiftly;

And yet Custance hadde of his deeth gret routhe.
And after this Jesus, of his mercy,
Made Alla wedden ful solempnely
This holy mayden, that is so bright and shene,
And thus hath Crist y-maad Custance a quene.

But who was woful, if I shal nat lye,
Of this wedding but Donegild, and na mo,
The kinges moder, ful of tirannye?
Hir thoughte hir cursed herte brast a-two;
She wolde noght hir sone had do so;
Hir thoughte a despit, that he sholde take
So strange a creature un-to his make.

Me list nat of the chaf nor of the stree
Maken so long a tale, as of the corn.
What sholde I tellen of the royaltee
At mariage, or which cours gooth biforn,
Who bloweth in a trompe or in an horn?
The fruit of every tale is for to seye;
They ete, and drinke, and daunce, and singe, and pleye.

They goon to bedde, as it was skile and right;
For, thogh that wyves been ful holy thinges,
They moste take in pacience at night
Swich maner necessaries as been plesinges
To folk that han y-wedded hem with ringes,
And leye a lyte hir holinesse asyde
As for the tyme; it may no bet bityde.

On hir he gat a knave-child anoon,
And to a bishop and his constable eke
He took his wyf to kepe, whan he is goon
To Scotland-ward, his fo-men for to seke;
Now faire Custance, that is so humble and meke,
So longe is goon with childe, til that stille
She halt hir chambre, abyding Cristes wille.

And yet Constance had of his death great pity.
And after this Jesus, of his mercy,
Made Alla wed full solemnly
This holy maiden, who was so bright and shining;
And thus Christ made Constance a queen.

But who was woeful, if I shall not lie,
Of this wedding but Donegild, and no others,
The king's mother, full of tyranny?
She thought her cursed heart would break in two.
She would not that her son had done so;
She thought it an insult that he should take
So strange a creature to be his mate.

I care not about the chaff, nor the straw,
Of this long tale—only the kernel.
What should I tell of the royalty
At marriage, or which course went before;
Or who blew a trumpet or a horn?
The heart of every tale is what we should tell:
They ate, and drank, and danced, and sung, and played.

They went to bed, as it was reasonable and right;
For though wives be full holy things,
They must take in patience at night
Such necessities as be pleasing
To folk who have wedded them with rings,
And lay a little of their holiness aside,
For awhile—that is in life the way.

On her he begot a boy child anon,
And to a bishop, and his constable also,
He gave his wife to keep, while he was gone
To Scotland-ward, his enemies to seek.
Now fair Constance, who is so humble and meek,
So long is gone with child, that still
She stayed in her chamber, awaiting Christ's will.

The tyme is come, a knave-child she ber;
Mauricius at the font-stoon they him calle;
This constable dooth forth come a messager,
And wroot un-to his king, that cleped was Alle,
How that this blisful tyding is bifalle,
And othere tydings speedful for to seye;
He tak'th the lettre, and forth he gooth his weye.

This messager, to doon his avantage,
Un-to the kinges moder rydeth swythe,
And salueth hir ful faire in his langage,
"Madame," quod he, "ye may be glad and blythe,
And thanke god an hundred thousand sythe;
My lady quene hath child, with-outen doute,
To joye and blisse of al this regne aboute.

Lo, heer the lettres seled of this thing,
That I mot bere with al the haste I may;
If ye wol aught un-to your sone the king,
I am your servant, bothe night and day."
Donegild answerde, "as now at this tyme, nay;
But heer al night I wol thou take thy reste,
Tomorwe wol I seye thee what me leste."

This messager drank sadly ale and wyn,
And stolen were his lettres prively
Out of his box, whyl he sleep as a swyn;
And countrefeted was ful subtilly
Another lettre, wroght ful sinfully,
Un-to the king direct of this matere
Fro his constable, as ye shal after here.

The lettre spak, "the queen delivered was
Of so horrible a feendly creature,
That in the castel noon so hardy was
That any whyle dorste ther endure.
The moder was an elf, by aventure

The time came that a boy child she bore;
Maurice at the baptismal font they him called.
This constable sent for a messenger,
And wrote to his king, who was called Alla,
How this blissful tiding had occurred,
And other tidings useful for to say.
He took the letter, and went forth his way.

This messenger, to do himself good,
Unto the king's mother swiftly rode,
And saluted her full fair in his language:
"Madame," said he, "you may be glad and blithe,
And thank God a hundred thousand times!
My lady queen has a child, without doubt,
To the joy and bliss of this reign about.

"Look, here the letters sealed of this thing,
That I might bear with all the haste that I may.
If you wish to send something to your son the king,
I am your servant, both night and day."
Donegild answered, "At this time, nay;
But here all night I would you take your rest.
Tomorrow will I tell you what I wish."

This messenger drank steadily ale and wine,
And stolen were his letters secretly
From his box, while he slept as a swine;
And counterfeited was full subtly
Another letter, wrought full sinfully,
Unto the king direct of this matter
From his constable, as you shall after hear.

The letter said the queen delivered was
Of so horrible a fiendish creature
That in the castle no one so hardy was
Who for any while dared they endure.
The mother was an evil spirit, by chance

Y-come, by charmes or by sorcerye,
And every wight hateth hir companye."

Wo was this king whan he this lettre had seyn,
But to no wighte he tolde his sorwes sore,
But of his owene honde he wroot ageyn,
"Welcome the sonde of Crist for evermore
To me, that am now lerned in his lore;
Lord, welcome be thy lust and thy plesaunce,
My lust I putte al in thyn ordinaunce!

Kepeth this child, al be it foul or fair,
And eek my wyf, un-to myn hoom-cominge;
Crist, whan him list, may sende me an heir
More agreable than this to my lykinge."
This lettre he seleth, prively wepinge,
Which to the messager was take sone,
And forth he gooth, ther is na more to done.

O messager, fulfild of dronkenesse,
Strong is thy breeth, thy limes faltren ay,
And thou biwreyest alle secreenesse.
Thy mind is lorn, thou janglest as a jay,
Thy face is turned in a newe array!
Ther dronkenesse regneth in any route,
Ther is no conseil hid, with-outen doute.

O Donegild, I ne have noon English digne
Un-to thy malice and thy tirannye!
And therfor to the feend I thee resigne,
Let him endyten of thy traitorye!
Fy, mannish, fy! o nay, by god, I lye,
Fy, *feendly* spirit, for I dar wel telle,
Though thou heer walke, thy spirit is in helle!

This messager comth fro the king agayn,
And at the kinges modres court he lighte,
And she was of this messager ful fayn,

Come, by charms or sorcery,
And every person hated her company.

Woe was this king when he this letter had seen,
But to no person he told his sorrows sore,
But in his own hand he wrote again,
"Welcome the dispensation of Christ for evermore
To me who knows his lore!
Lord, welcome be your wish and pleasure;
My will I put all in your hands.

"Keep this child, albeit foul or fair,
And also my wife, until my homecoming.
Christ, when he wishes, may send me an heir
More agreeable than this to my liking."
This letter he sealed, privately weeping,
Which to the messenger was taken anon,
And forth he went; there was no more to be done.

Oh messenger, filled with drunkenness,
Strong is your breath, your limbs falter ever,
And you betray all secrecy.
Your mind is lost, you chatter as a jay,
Your face has a new look.
Your drunkenness reigns with any group,
There are no secrets kept, without doubt.

Oh Donegild, I have no English fit
For your malice and your tyranny!
And therefore to the fiend I you commend;
Let him indite of your treachery!
Fie, mannish, fie!—oh nay, by God, I lie—
Fie, fiendish spirit, for I dare well tell,
Though you here walk, your spirit is in hell!

This messenger came from the king again,
And at the king's mother's court he alighted,
And she was of this messenger full eager,

And plesed him in al that ever she mighte.
He drank, and wel his girdel underpighte.
He slepeth, and he snoreth in his gyse
Al night, un-til the sonne gan aryse.

Eft were his lettres stolen everichon
And countrefeted lettres in this wyse;
"The king comandeth his constable anon,
Up peyne of hanging, and on heigh juyse,
That he ne sholde suffren in no wyse
Custance in-with his regne for t'abyde
Thre dayes and a quarter of a tyde;

But in the same ship as he hir fond,
Hir and hir yonge sone, and al hir gere,
He sholde putte, and croude hir fro the lond,
And charge hir that she never eft come there."
O my Custance, wel may thy goost have fere
And sleping in thy dreem been in penance,
When Donegild caste al this ordinance!

This messager on morwe, whan he wook,
Un-to the castel halt the nexte wey,
And to the constable he the lettre took;
And whan that he this pitous lettre sey,
Ful ofte he seyde "allas!" and "weylawey!"
"Lord Crist," quod he, "how may this world endure?
So ful of sinne is many a creature!

O mighty god, if that it be thy wille,
Sith thou art rightful juge, how may it be
That thou wolt suffren innocents to spille,
And wikked folk regne in prosperitee?
O good Custance, allas! so wo is me
That I mot be thy tormentour, or deye
On shames deeth; ther is noon other weye!"

Wepen bothe yonge and olde in al that place,
Whan that the king this cursed lettre sente,

And pleased him in every way that she might.
He drank, and put them down,
He slept, and snorted in his way
All night, till the sun began to rise.

Again his letters were stolen every one,
"And counterfeited letters in this way:
The king commands his constable anon,
Upon pain of hanging, and by high court,
That he should suffer in no way
Constance in his realm to abide
More than three days and a quarter tide;

"But in the same ship as he her found,
Her, and her young son, and all her gear,
He should put, and drive her from the land,
And charge her that she never should return."
Oh my Constance, well may your spirit fear,
And, sleeping, in your dream be misery,
When Donegild plotted this ordinance.

This messenger in the morning, when he woke,
Unto the castle took the shortest way,
And to the constable he the letter took;
And when that he this piteous letter saw,
Full often he said, "Alas and wellaway!"
"Lord Christ," said he, "how may this world endure,
So full of sin is many a creature?

"Oh mighty God, if it be your will,
Since you are rightful judge, how may it be
That you would suffer innocence to die,
And wicked folk reign in prosperity?
Oh good Constance, alas, so woe is me
That I must be your tormentor, or die
Myself; there is no other way."

Wept both young and old in all that place
When the king this cursed letter sent,

And Custance, with a deedly pale face,
The ferthe day toward hir ship she wente.
But natheles she taketh in good entente
The wille of Crist, and, kneling on the stronde,
She seyde, "lord! ay wel-com be thy sonde!

He that me kepte fro the false blame
Whyl I was on the londe amonges yow,
He can me kepe from harme and eek fro shame
In salte see, al-thogh I see nat how.
As strong as ever he was, he is yet now.
In him triste I, and in his moder dere,
That is to me my seyl and eek my stere."

Her litel child lay weping in hir arm,
And kneling, pitously to him she seyde,
"Pees, litel sone, I wol do thee non harm."
With that hir kerchef of hir heed she breyde,
And over his litel yën she it leyde;
And in hir arm she lulleth it ful faste,
And in-to heven hir yën up she caste.

"Moder," quod she, "and mayde bright, Marye,
Sooth is that thurgh wommannes eggement
Mankind was lorn and damned ay to dye,
For which thy child was on a croys y-rent;
Thy blisful yën sawe al his torment;
Than is ther no comparison bitwene
Thy wo and any wo man may sustene.

Thou sawe thy child y-slayn bifor thyn yën,
And yet now liveth my litel child, parfay!
Now, lady bright, to whom alle woful cryën,
Thou glorie of wommanhede, thou faire may,
Thou haven of refut, brighte sterre of day,
Rewe on my child, that of thy gentillesse
Rewest on every rewful in distresse!

And Constance, with a deathly pale face,
The fourth day toward the ship she went.
But nevertheless she took in good intent
The will of Christ, and kneeling on the strand,
She said, "Lord, ever welcome be what you will!

"He who kept me from false blame
While I was in the land among you,
He can keep me from harm and from shame
In salt sea, although I see not how.
As strong as ever he was, he is yet now.
In him I trust, and in his mother dear,
Who is to me my sail and also my rudder."

Her little child lay weeping in her arm,
And kneeling, piteously to him she said,
"Peace, little son, I will do you no harm."
With that her kerchief she removed from her head,
And over his little eyes she it laid,
And in her arms she lulled it full fast,
And unto heaven her eyes up she cast.

"Mother," said she, "and maid bright, Mary,
True it is that through woman's urging
Mankind was lost, and doomed ever to die,
For which your child was on a cross torn.
Your blissful eyes saw all his torment;
There is no comparison between
Your woe and any woe man may sustain.

"You saw your child slain before your eyes,
And yet now lives my little child, by my faith!
Now, lady bright, to whom all woeful cry,
You glory of womanhood, you fair maid,
You haven of refuge, bright star of day,
Take pity on my child, who in your gentleness
Pities every soul in distress.

O litel child, allas! what is thy gilt,
That never wroughtest sinne as yet, pardee,
Why wil thyn harde fader han thee spilt?
O mercy, dere constable!" quod she;
"As lat my litel child dwelle heer with thee;
And if thou darst not saven him, for blame,
So kis him ones in his fadres name!"

Ther-with she loketh bakward to the londe,
And seyde, "far-wel, housbond routhelees!"
And up she rist, and walketh doun the stronde
Toward the ship; hir folweth al the prees,
And ever she preyeth hir child to holde his pees;
And taketh hir leve, and with an holy entente
She blesseth hir; and in-to ship she wente.

Vitailled was the ship, it is no drede,
Habundantly for hir, ful longe space,
And other necessaries that sholde nede
She hadde y-nogh, heried be goddes grace!
For wind and weder almighty god purchace,
And bringe hir hoom! I can no bettre seye;
But in the see she dryveth forth hir weye.

PART THREE

Alla the king comth hoom, sone after this,
Unto his castel of the which I tolde,
And axeth wher his wyf and his child is.
The constable gan aboute his herte colde,
And pleynly al the maner he him tolde
As ye han herd, I can telle it no bettre,
And sheweth the king his seel and [eek] his lettre,

And seyde, "lord, as ye comaunded me
Up peyne of deeth, so have I doon, certein."
This messager tormented was til he
Moste biknowe and tellen, plat and plein,
Fro night to night, in what place he had leyn.

"Oh little child, alas! what is your guilt,
Who never wrought sin as yet, by God?
Why will your hard father have you killed?
O mercy, dear constable," said she,
"Grant that my little child dwell here with you;
And if you dare not save him, for blame,
So kiss him once in his father's name!"

Therewith she looked backward to the land,
And said, "Farewell, husband ruthless!"
And up she rose, and walked down the strand
Toward the ship—her followed all the crowd—
And ever she prayed her child to hold his peace;
And took her leave, and with holy intent
She blessed herself, and into the ship she went.

Provisioned was the ship, it is no doubt,
Abundantly for a long voyage,
And of other necessities
She had enough—praise be God's grace!
For wind and weather almighty God provide,
And bring her home! I can no better say,
But in the sea she sailed forth her way.

PART THREE

Alla the king came home soon after this
Unto his castle, of which I told,
And asked where his wife and child were.
The constable felt his heart turn cold,
And plainly everything he him told
As you have heard—I can tell it no better—
And showed the king his seal and also his letter,

And said, "Lord, as you commanded me
Upon pain of death, so have I done, certainly."
This messenger tortured was until he
Must reveal and tell, bluntly and plain,
From night to night, in what place he had lain;

And thus, by wit and subtil enqueringe,
Ymagined was by whom this harm gan springe.

The hand was knowe that the lettre wroot,
And al the venim of this cursed dede,
But in what wyse, certeinly I noot.
Th'effect is this, that Alla, out of drede,
His moder slow, that men may pleinly rede,
For that she traitour was to hir ligeaunce.
Thus endeth olde Donegild with meschaunce.

The sorwe that this Alla, night and day,
Maketh for his wyf and for his child also,
Ther is no tonge that it telle may.
But now wol I un-to Custance go,
That fleteth in the see, in peyne and wo,
Fyve yeer and more, as lyked Cristes sonde,
Er that hir ship approched un-to londe.

Under an hethen castel, atte laste,
Of which the name in my text noght I finde,
Custance and eek hir child the see upcaste.
Almighty god, that saveth al mankinde,
Have on Custance and on hir child some minde,
That fallen is in hethen land eft-sone,
In point to spille, as I shal telle yow sone.

Doun from the castel comth ther many a wight
To gauren on this ship and on Custance.
But shortly, from the castel, on a night,
The lordes styward—god yeve him meschaunce!—
A theef, that had reneyed our creaunce,
Com in-to ship allone, and seyde he sholde
Hir lemman be, where-so she wolde or nolde.

Wo was this wrecched womman tho bigon,
Hir child cryde, and she cryde pitously;
But blisful Marie heelp hir right anon;
For with hir strugling wel and mightily

And thus, by wit and subtle inquiring,
Imagined was by whom this harm had sprung.

The hand was known who had the letter written,
And all the venom of this cursed deed,
But in what way, certainly, I do not know.
The effect was: that Alla, with no doubt,
His mother slew—that men may plainly read—
For she was traitor to her allegiance.
Thus ended old Donegild, with mischance!

The sorrow that this Alla night and day
Made for his wife, and for his child also,
There is no tongue that tell it may.
But now will I unto Constance go,
Who floated in the sea, in pain and woe,
Five years and more, by Christ's command,
Before her ship approached unto land.

Under a heathen castle, at last,
Of which the name in my text I find not,
Constance, and also her child, the sea upcast.
Almighty God, who saves all mankind,
Have for Constance and her child some mind,
Who fallen are in heathen hands again.
To the point of death, as I shall tell you anon.

Down from the castle came there many a person
To stare at this ship and also on Constance.
But shortly, from the castle, on a night,
The lord's steward—God give him mischance!—
A thief, who had renounced our belief,
Came into the ship alone, and said he should
Her lover be, whether she would or no.

Woe was this wretched woman's plight;
Her child cried, and she cried piteously.
But blissful Mary helped her right anon;
For with her struggling well and mightily

The theef fil over bord al sodeinly,
And in the see he dreynte for vengeance;
And thus hath Crist unweummed kept Custance.

O foule lust of luxurie! lo, thyn ende!
Nat only that thou feyntest mannes minde,
But verraily thou wolt his body shende;
Th'ende of thy werk or of thy lustes blinde
Is compleyning, how many-oon may men finde
That noght for werk som-tyme, but for th'entente
To doon this sinne, ben outher sleyn or shente!

How may this wayke womman han this strengthe
Hir to defende agayn this renegat?
O Golias, unmesurable of lengthe,
How mighte David make thee so mat,
So yong and of armure so desolat?
How dorste he loke up-on thy dredful face?
Wel may men seen, if nas but goddes grace!

Who yaf Judith corage or hardinesse
To sleen him, Olofernus, in his tente,
And to deliveren out of wrecchednesse
The peple of god? I seye, for this entente,
That, right as god spirit of vigour sente
To hem, and saved hem out of meschance,
So sente he might and vigour to Custance.

Forth goth hir ship thurgh-out the narwe mouth
Of Jubaltar and Septe, dryving ay,
Som-tyme West, som-tyme North and South,
And som-tyme Est, ful many a wery day,
Til Cristes moder (blessed be she ay!)
Hath shapen, thurgh hir endelees goodnesse,
To make an ende of al hir hevinesse.

Now lat us stinte of Custance but a throwe,
And speke we of the Romain Emperour,

The thief fell overboard all suddenly,
And in the sea he drowned for vengeance;
And thus has Christ undefiled kept Constance.

Oh foul lust of lechery, look at your end!
Not only do you weaken men's minds,
But truly will you his body ruin.
The end of your work, or of your lusts blind,
Is lamentation. How many a time may men find
That not for the deed sometimes, but for the intent
To do this sin, be they either ruined or slain!

How may this weak woman have the strength
Herself to defend against this renegade?
Oh Goliath, immeasurable of length,[25]
How may David make you so defeated,
So young and of armor so desolate?
How dared he look upon your dreadful face?
Well may men see, it was not but by God's grace.

Who gave Judith courage or strength
To slay Holofernes in his tent,[26]
And to deliver out of wretchedness
The people of God? I say, for this intent,
That right as God the spirit of vigor sent
To them and saved them out of mischance,
So sent he might and vigor to Constance.

Forth went her ship through the narrow mouth
Of Gibraltar and Morocco, sailing ever
Sometimes westward, sometimes north and south,
And sometimes east, full many a weary day,
Till Christ's mother—blessed be she ever!—
Has planned—through her endless goodness,
To make an end to all her sorrow.

Now let us stint of Constance but a short while,
And speak we of the Roman Emperor,

That out of Surrie hath by lettres knowe
The slaughtre of Cristen folk, and dishonour
Don to his doghter by a fals traitour,
I mene the cursed wikked sowdanesse,
That at the feste leet sleen both more and lesse.

For which this emperour hath sent anoon
His senatour, with royal ordinance,
And othere lordes, got wot, many oon,
On Surriens to taken heigh vengeance.
They brennen, sleen, and bringe hem to meschance
Ful many a day; but shortly, this is the ende,
Homward to Rome they shapen hem to wende.

This senatour repaireth with victorie
To Rome-ward, sayling ful royally,
And mette the ship dryving, as seith the storie,
In which Custance sit ful pitously.
No-thing ne knew he what she was, ne why
She was in swich array; ne she nil seye
Of hir estaat, althogh she sholde deye.

He bringeth hir to Rome, and to his wyf
He yat hir, and hir yonge sone also;
And with the senatour she ladde her lyf.
Thus can our lady bringen out of wo
Woful Custance, and many another mo.
And longe tyme dwelled she in that place,
In holy werkes ever, as was hir grace.

The senatoures wyf hir aunte was,
But for al that she knew hir never the more;
I wol no lenger tarien in this cas,
But to king Alla, which I spak of yore,
That for his wyf wepeth and syketh sore,
I wol retourne, and lete I wol Custance
Under the senatoures governance.

Who had from Syria by letters known
The slaughter of Christian folk, and dishonor
Done to his daughter by a false traitor,
I mean the cursed wicked Sultaness
Who at the feast had ordered slain both more and less.

For which this Emperor had sent anon
His senator, with royal ordinance,
And other lords, God knows, many a one,
On Syrians to take high vengeance.
They them burned, slew, and brought to mischance
Full many a day, but shortly—this is the end—
Homeward to Rome they began to wend.

This senator repaired with victory
Toward Rome, sailing full royally,
And met the ship driving, as says the story,
In which Constance sat full piteously.
He knew not who she was, nor why
She was in such a condition, nor would she say,
Not even upon threat of death.

He brought her to Rome, and to his wife
He gave her, and her young son also;
And with the senator she led her life.
Thus can Our Lady bring out of woe
Woeful Constance, and many another more.
And long time dwelled she in that place,
In holy works ever, as was her grace.

The senator's wife her aunt was,
But despite that she knew her never the more.
I will not longer tarry in this case,
But to king Alla, of whom I spoke before,
Who for his wife wept and sickened sore,
I will return, and I will leave Constance
Under the senator's governance.

King Alla, which that hadde his moder slayn,
Upon a day fil in swich repentance,
That, if I shortly tellen shal and plain,
To Rome he comth, to receyven his penance;
And putte him in the popes ordinance
In heigh and low, and Jesu Crist bisoghte
Foryeve his wikked werkes that he wroghte.

The fame anon thurgh Rome toun is born,
How Alla king shal come in pilgrimage,
By herbergeours that wenten him biforn;
For which the senatour, as was usage,
Rood him ageyn, and many of his linage,
As wel to shewen his heighe magnificence
As to don any king a reverence.

Greet chere dooth this noble senatour
To king Alla, and he to him also;
Everich of hem doth other greet honour;
And so bifel that, in a day or two,
This senatour is to king Alla go
To feste, and shortly, if I shal nat lye,
Custances sone wente in his companye.

Som men wolde seyn, at requeste of Custance,
This senatour hath lad this child to feste;
I may nat tellen every circumstance,
Be as be may, ther was he at the leste.
But soth is this, that, at his modres heste,
Biforn Alla, during the metres space,
The child stood, loking in the kinges face.

This Alla king hath of this child greet wonder,
And to the senatour he seyde anon,
"Whos is that faire child that stondeth yonder?"
"I noot," quod he, "by god, and by seint John!
A moder he hath, but fader hath he non

King Alla, who had his mother slain,
Upon a day fell into such repentance
That, if I shall tell it short and plain,
To Rome he went to receive his penance;
And put himself in the Pope's command
In all things, and Jesus Christ besought
To forgive the wicked works that he had wrought.

The news anon through Rome town was borne,
How Alla the king should come in pilgrimage,
By servants who travelled him before;
And so the senator, as was his custom,
Rode toward Alla, with many of his retinue,
As much to show his own noble estate,
As to do any king a reverence.

Great greeting did this noble senator
To king Alla, and he to him also;
Each of them did to the other great honor.
And so it befell that in a day or two
This senator was to Alla gone
To feast, and shortly, if I shall not lie,
Constance's son went in his company.

Some men would say at request of Constance
This senator had brought this child to the feast;
I may not tell every circumstance—
Be it as it may, there was he at the least.
But the truth is this, that at his mother's behest
Before Alla, during the dinner time,
The child stood, looking in the king's face.

This Alla king had of this child great wonder,
And to the senator he said anon,
"Who is that fair child who stands yonder?"
"I know not," said he, "By God, and Saint John!
A mother he has, but father has he none

That I of woot"—but shortly, in a stounde,
He tolde Alla how that this child was founde.

"But god wot," quod this senatour also,
"So vertuous a livere in my lyf,
Ne saugh I never as she, ne herde of mo
Of worldly wommen, mayden, nor of wyf;
I dar wel seyn hir hadde lever a knyf
Thurgh-out her breste, than been a womman wikke;
Ther is no man coude bringe hir to that prikke."

Now was this child as lyk un-to Custance
As possible is a creature to be.
This Alla hath the face in remembrance
Of dame Custance, and ther-on mused he
If that the childes moder were aught she
That was his wyf, and prively he sighte,
And spedde him fro the table that he mighte.

"Parfay," thoghte he, "fantome is in myn heed!
I oghte deme, of skilful jugement,
That in the salte see my wyf is deed."
And afterward he made his argument—
"What woot I, if that Crist have hider y-sent
My wyf by see, as wel as he hir sente
To my contree fro thennes that she wente?"

And, after noon, hoom with the senatour
Goth Alla, for to seen this wonder chaunce.
This senatour dooth Alla greet honour,
And hastifly he sente after Custaunce.
But trusteth weel, hir liste nat to daunce
Whan that she wiste wherefor was that sonde.
Unnethe up-on hir feet she mighte stonde.

When Alla saugh his wyf, faire he hir grette,
And weep, that it was routhe for to see.
For at the firste look he on hir sette
He knew wel verraily that it was she.

That I know of"—and shortly, in a little while,
He told Alla how this child was found.

"But God knows," said this senator also,
"So virtuous a being in my life
Never saw I ever as she, nor heard of more,
Of worldly women, maid, nor wife.
I dare well say she would rather a knife
Through her breast, than be a woman wicked;
There is no man who could bring her to that point."

Now was this child as like unto Constance
As possible is a creature to be.
This Alla had the face in remembrance
Of dame Constance, and thereon mused he
If this child's mother were she
Who was his wife, and inwardly he sighed,
And left the table as soon as he might.

"By my faith," thought he, "I am seeing phantoms!
I ought deem, by all good judgement,
That in the salt sea my wife is dead."
And afterward he made his argument:
"What know I if Christ has hither sent
My wife by sea, as he her sent
To my country from thence she went?"

And in the afternoon, home with the senator
Went Alla, for to see this wondrous chance.
This senator did Alla great honor,
And hastily he sent after Constance.
But trust well, she did not with joy dance
When she learned why she was sent for;
Upon her feet she could scarcely stand.

When Alla saw his wife, fair he her greeted,
And wept so that it was a pity for to see;
For at the first look he upon her set
He knew well verily that it was she.

And she for sorwe as domb stant as a tree;
So was hir herte shet in hir distresse
Whan she remembred his unkindnesse.

Twyës she swoned in his owne sighte;
He weep, and him excuseth pitously:—
"Now god," quod he, "and alle his halves brighte
So wisly on my soule as have mercy,
That of your harm as giltelees am I
As is Maurice my sone so lyk your face;
Elles the feend me fecche out of this place!"

Long was the sobbing and the bitter peyne
Er that hir woful hertes mighte cesse;
Greet was the pitee for to here hem pleyne,
Thurgh whiche pleintes gan hir wo encresse.
I prey yow al my labour to relesse;
I may nat telle hir wo un-til tomorwe,
I am so wery for to speke of sorwe.

But fynally, when that the sooth is wist
That Alla giltelees was of hir wo,
I trowe an hundred tymes been they kist,
And swich a blisse is ther bitwix hem two
That, save the joye that lasteth evermo,
Ther is non lyk, that any creature
Hath seyn or shal, whyl that the world may dure.

Tho preyde she hir housbond mekely,
In relief of hir longe pitous pyne,
That he wold preye hir fader specially
That, of his magestee, he wolde enclyne
To vouche-sauf som day with him to dyne;
She preyde him eek, he sholde by no weye
Un-to hir fader no word of hir seye.

Som men wold seyn, how that the child Maurice
Doth this message un-to this emperour;
But, as I gesse, Alla was nat so nyce

And she, for sorrow, as silent stood as a tree,
So was her heart shut in her distress,
When she remembered his unkindness.

Twice she swooned in his own sight;
He wept, and excused himself piteously.
"Now God," said he, "and his saints bright
Surely on my soul have mercy,
That of your harm guiltless am I
As is Maurice my son, so like your face;
Else the fiend me fetch out of this place!"

Long was the sobbing and the bitter pain,
Before their woeful hearts might cease;
Great was the pity for to hear them lament,
Though that lamentation made their woe increase.
I pray you all my labor to release;
I would need to tell all their woe until tomorrow,
And I am so weary for to speak of sorrow.

But finally, when the truth was known
That Alla guiltless was of her woe,
I believe a hundred times have they kissed,
And such a bliss was between the two
That, save the joy that lasts evermore,
There is nothing like that any creature
Has seen or shall, while the world may endure.

Then requested she of her husband meekly,
In repayment for her long, piteous suffering,
That he would invite her father specially
If in his majesty he would incline
To vouchsafe some day with him to dine.
She prayed him also that he should in no way
Unto her father any word of her say.

Some men would say that the child Maurice
Brought this message unto the Emperor;
But, as I guess, Alla was not so foolish

To him, that was of so sovereyn honour
As he that is of Cristen folk the flour,
Sente any child, but it is bet to deme
He wente him-self, and so it may wel seme.

This emperour hath graunted gentilly
To come to diner, as he him bisoghte;
And wel rede I, he loked bisily
Up-on this child, and on his doghter thoghte.
Alla goth to his in, and, as him oghte,
Arrayed for this feste in every wyse
As ferforth as his conning may suffyse.

The morwe cam, and Alla gan him dresse,
And eek his wyf, this emperour to mete;
And forth they ryde in joye and in gladnesse.
And when she saugh hir fader in the strete,
She lighte doun, and falleth him to fete.
"Fader," quod she, "your yonge child Custance
Is now ful clene out of your remembrance.

I am your doghter Custance," quod she,
"That whylom ye han sent un-to Surrye.
It am I, fader, that in the salte see
Was put allone and dampned for to dye.
Now, gode fader, mercy I yow crye,
Send me namore un-to non hethenesse,
But thonketh my lord heer of his kindenesse."

Who can the pitous joye tellen al
Bitwix hem three, sin they ben thus y-mette?
But of my tale make an ende I shal;
The day goth faste, I wol no lenger lette.
This glade folk to diner they hem sette;
In joye and blisse at mete I lete hem dwelle
A thousand fold wel more than I can telle.

This child Maurice was sithen emperour
Maad by the pope, and lived Cristenly.

Toward him who was of such sovereign honor
And who was of Christian folk the flower,
To have sent any child, but it is better deemed
He went himself, Maurice in his retinue.

This emperor has granted genteely
To come to dinner, as he him besought;
And well read I in my book that he looked intently
Upon this child, and on his daughter thought.
Alla went to his inn, and as he ought,
Prepared for this feast in every way
As far as his skill might suffice.

The morrow came, and Alla began to dress,
And also his wife, this Emperor to meet;
And forth they rode in joy and gladness.
And when she saw her father in the street,
She alighted, and fell to his feet.
"Father," said she, "your young child Constance
Is now full clean out of your remembrance.

"I am your daughter Constance," said she,
"Who once you sent unto Syria.
It is I, father, who in the salt sea
Was put alone and damned for to die.
Now, good father, mercy I you cry!
Send me no more unto heathens,
But thank my lord of his kindness."

Who can the piteous joy tell all
Between the three, since they were thus met?
But of my tale I shall make an end;
The day goes fast, I will no longer delay.
These glad folk to dinner they them set;
In joy and bliss at dinner I let them dwell
A thousandfold more well than I can tell.

This child Maurice was in time Emperor
Made by the Pope, and lived Christianly;

To Cristes chirche he dide greet honour;
But I lete al his storie passen by,
Of Custance is my tale specially.
In olde Romayn gestes may men finde
Maurices lyf; I bere it noght in minde.

This king Alla, whan he his tyme sey,
With his Custance, his holy wyf so swete,
To Engelond been they come the righte wey,
Wher-as they live in joye and in quiete.
But litel whyl it lasteth, I yow hete,
Joye of this world, for tyme wol nat abyde;
Fro day to night it changeth as the tyde.

Who lived ever in swich delyt o day
That him ne moeved outher conscience,
Or ire, or talent, or som kin affray,
Envye, or pryde, or passion, or offence?
I ne seye but for this ende this sentence,
That litel whyl in joye or in plesance
Lasteth the blisse of Alla with Custance.

For deeth, that taketh of heigh and low his rente,
When passed was a yeer, even as I gesse,
Out of this world this king Alla he hente,
For whom Custance hath ful gret hevinesse.
Now lat us preyen god his soule blesse!
And dame Custance, fynally to seye,
Towards the toun of Rome gooth hir weye.

To Rome is come this holy creature,
And fyndeth ther hir frendes hole and sounde:
Now is she scaped al hir aventure;
And whan that she hir fader hath y-founde,
Doun on hir kneës falleth she to grounde;
Weping for tendrenesse in herte blythe,
She herieth god an hundred thousand sythe.

To Christ's church he did great honor.
But I let all his story pass by;
Of Constance is my tale especially.
In the old Roman histories may men find
Maurice's life; I bear it not in mind.

This king Alla, when he his time saw,
With his Constance, his holy wife so sweet,
To England were they come the shortest way,
Where they lived in joy and quiet.
But a little while it lasted, I may tell you,
Joy of this world, for not long will abide;
From day to day it changes as the tide.

Who lived ever in such delight one day
That he never felt another sensation,
Either anger, or desire, or some kind of fear,
Envy, pride, or passion, or offence?
I say but this sentence:
That little while in joy or in leisure
Lasted the bliss of Alla with Constance.

For Death, who takes of high and low his rent,
When passed had many a year, even as I guess,
Out of this world this king Alla he seized,
For whom Constance had full great sorrow.
Now let us pray to God his soul to bless!
And dame Constance, finally to say,
Toward the town of Rome went her way.

To Rome is come this holy creature,
And found her friends whole and sound;
Now has she escaped all her adventure.
And when she her father found,
Down on her knees she fell to the ground;
Weeping for tenderness in heart blithe,
She praised God a hundred thousand times.

In vertu and in holy almes-dede
They liven alle, and never a-sonder wende;
Til deeth departed hem, this lyf they lede.
And fareth now weel, my tale is at an ende.
Now Jesu Crist, that of his might may sende
Joye after wo, governe us in his grace,
And kepe us alle that ben in this place! Amen.

In virtue and in holy alms-deeds,
They lived all, and never parted were;
Till death separated them, this life they lead.
And fare now well! My tale is at an end.
Now Jesus Christ, who of his might may send
Joy after woe, govern us in his grace,
And keep us all who have been in this place! Amen.

The Maunciples Tale

WITE YE NAT WHER ther stant a litel toun
Which that y-cleped is Bob-up-and-doun,
Under the Blee, in Caunterbury weye?
Ther gan our hoste for to jape and pleye,
And seyde, "sirs, what! Dun is in the myre!
Is ther no man, for preyere ne for hyre,
That wol awake our felawe heer bihinde?
A theef mighte him ful lightly robbe and binde.
See how he nappeth! see, for cokkes bones,
As he wol falle from his hors at ones.
Is that a cook of Londoun, with meschaunce?
Do him com forth, he knoweth his penaunce,
For he shal telle a tale, by my fey!
Al-though it be nat worth a botel hey.
Awake, thou cook," quod he, "god yeve thee sorwe,
What eyleth thee to slepe by the morwe?
Hastow had fleen al night, or artow dronke,
Or hastow with som quene al night y-swonke,
So that thou mayst nat holden up thyn heed?"

    This cook, that was ful pale and no-thing reed,
Seyde to our host, "so god my soule blesse,
As ther is falle on me swich hevinesse,
Noot I nat why, that ne were lever slepe
Than the beste galoun wyn in Chepe."

    "Wel," quod the maunciple, "if it may doon ese
To thee, sir cook, and to no wight displese
Which that heer rydeth in this companye,
And that our host wol, of his curteisye,
I wol as now excuse thee of thy tale;
For, in good feith, thy visage is ful pale,
Thyn yën daswen eek, as that me thinketh,
And wel I woot, thy breeth ful soure stinketh,
That sheweth wel thou art not wel disposed;
Of me, certein, thou shalt nat been y-glosed.
Se how he ganeth, lo, this dronken wight,

The Manciple's Tale

KNOW YOU NOT WHERE there stands a little town
Which is called Bob-up-and-down,[1]
Under the Blean Wood, on Canterbury Way?
There began our Host for to joke and play,
And said, "Sires, what! We're stuck in the mire![2]
Is there no man, for prayer or hire,
Who will awaken our fellow all behind?
A thief might him full easily rob and bind.
See how he naps! See how, for cock's bones,
He will fall from his horse at once!
Is that a cook of London, worse luck for us?
Do him come forth, he knows his penance;
For he shall tell a tale, by my faith,
Although it be not worth a bale of hay.
Awaken, you Cook," said he, "God give you sorrow!
What ails you to sleep in the morning?
Have you had fleas all night, or are you soused?
Or have you with some queen all night caroused,
So that you may not hold up your head?"

This Cook, who was full pale and nothing red,
Said to our Host, "So God my soul bless,
There is fallen on me such drowsiness,
Know I not why, that I would rather have sleep
Than the best gallon of wine in Cheap."[3]

"Well," said the Manciple, "if it may do ease
To you, sir Cook, and no person displease,
Who rides here in this company,
And our Host agrees, of his courtesy,
I will now excuse you of your tale.
For, in good faith, your visage is full pale,
Your eyes are bleary, so that I think,
And well I know, your breath full sour stinks:
That shows well that you are not well disposed.
By me, certainly, you shall not be flattered.
See how you yawn, look, this drunken fellow,

As though he wolde us swolwe anon-right.
Hold cloos thy mouth, man, by thy fader kin!
The devel of helle sette his foot ther-in!
Thy cursed breeth infecte wol us alle;
Fy, stinking swyn, fy! foule moot thee falle!
A! taketh heed, sirs, of this lusty man.
Now, swete sir, wol ye justen atte fan?
Ther-to me thinketh ye been wel y-shape!
I trowe that ye dronken han wyn ape,
And that is whan men pleyen with a straw."
And with this speche the cook wex wrooth and wraw,
And on the maunciple he gan nodde faste
For lakke of speche, and doun the hors him caste,
Wher as he lay, til that men up him took;
This was a fayr chivachee of a cook!
Allas! he nadde holde him by his ladel!
And, er that he agayn were in his sadel,
Ther was greet showving bothe to and fro,
To lifte him up, and muchel care and wo,
So unweldy was this sory palled gost.
And to the maunciple thanne spak our host,
"By-cause drink hath dominacioun
Upon this man, by my savacioun
I trowe he lewedly wolde telle his tale.
For, were it wyn, or old or moysty ale,
That he hath dronke, he speketh in his nose,
And fneseth faste, and eek he hath the pose.
He hath also to do more than y-nough
To kepe him and his capel eut of slough;
And, if he falle from his capel eft-sone,
Than shul we alle have y-nough to done,
In lifting up his hevy dronken cors.
Telle on thy tale, of him make I no fors.

    But yet, maunciple, in feith thou art to nyce,
Thus openly repreve him of his vyce.
Another day he wol, peraventure,
Reclayme thee, and bringe thee to lure;
I mene, he speke wol of smale thinges,
As for to pinchen at thy rekeninges,

As though he would us swallow.
Hold closed your mouth, man, by my father's kin!
The devil of hell set his foot therein!
Your cursed breath will infect us all.
Fie, stinking swine! Foul must you fall!
Ah, take heed, sires, of this lively fellow.
Now, sweet sir, would you a bull's eye hit?
For that I think you be well prepared!
I believe that you are very drunk[4]
And that is when men do all things wrong."
And with this speech the Cook waxed wroth and raw,
And to the Manciple he began to shake his head
For lack of speech, and down the horse him cast,
Where he lay, until men picked him up.
This was the horsemanship of a cook!
Alas, he could not prop himself up with his ladle![5]
And before he was again in the saddle,
There was great shoving both to and fro
To lift him up, and much care and woe,
So unwieldy was this sorry pallid ghost.
And to the Manciple then spoke our Host:
"Because drink has domination
Upon this man, by my salvation,
I believe he poorly would tell his tale.
For, were it wine or old or new ale
That he has drunk, he speaks in his nose,
And sneezes fast, and has a cold.
He has also to do more than enough
To keep himself and his horse out of the mud;
And if he falls from his horse again,
Then shall we all have enough to do
In lifting up his heavy drunken corpse.
Tell on your tale; to him I pay no heed.

    "But yet, Manciple, in faith you are not so nice,
Thus openly to reprove him of his vice.
Another day he will, peradventure,
Return the favor;
I mean, he will speak of small things,
For example your reckonings,

That wer not honeste, if it cam to preef."
    "No," quod the maunciple, "that were a greet mescheef!
So mighte he lightly bringe me in the snare.
Yet hadde I lever payen for the mare
Which he rit on, than he sholde with me stryve;
I wol nat wratthe him, al-so mote I thryve!
That that I spak, I seyde it in my bourde;
And wite ye what? I have heer, in a gourde,
A draught of wyn, ye, of a rype grape,
And right anon ye shul seen a good jape.
This cook shal drinke ther-of, if I may;
Up peyne of deeth, he wol nat seye me nay!"
    And certeinly, to tellen as it was,
Of this vessel the cook drank faste, allas!
What neded him? he drank y-nough biforn.
And whan he hadde pouped in this horn,
To the maunciple he took the gourde agayn;
And of that drinke the cook was wonder fayn,
And thanked him in swich wyse as he coude.
    Than gan our host to laughen wonder loude,
And seyde, "I see wel, it is necessarie,
Wher that we goon, good drink we with us carie;
For that wol turne rancour and disese
T'acord and love, and many a wrong apese.
    O thou Bachus, y-blessed be thy name,
That so canst turnen ernest in-to game!
Worship and thank be to thy deitee!
Of that matere ye gete na-more of me.
Tel on thy tale, maunciple, I thee preye."
    "Wel, sir," quod he, "now herkneth what I seye."

The Tale

Whan Phebus dwelled her in this erthe adoun,
As olde bokes maken mencioun
He was the moste lusty bachiler
In al this world, and eek the beste archer;
He slow Phitoun, the serpent, as he lay
Slepinge agayn the sonne upon a day;
And many another noble worthy dede

That were not honest, if it came to proof."

"No," said the Manciple, "that were a great mischief!
So might he easily bring me into the snare.
Yet I would rather pay for the mare
That he rides upon, than he should with me have strife.
I will not provoke him, also may I thrive!
That which I speak, I say it in jest.
And do you know what? I have here in a flask
A draft of wine, of a ripe grape,
And right anon you shall see a good jape.
This Cook shall drink thereof, if I may.
Upon pain of death, he will not say me nay."

And certainly, to tell as it was,
Of this vessel the Cook drank fast, alas!
Why needed he? He drank enough before.
And when he had tooted in this horn,
To the Manciple he gave the flask again;
And of that drink the Cook was wondrous grateful,
And thanked him in such way as he could.

Then began our Host to laugh wondrous loud,
And said, "I see well it is necessary,
Where we go, that good drink we with us carry;
For that will turn rancor and discord
To accord and love, and many a wrong appease.

"Oh Bacchus, blessed be your name,
Who can turn earnest into game!
Worship and thanks be to your deity!
Of that matter you get no more of me.
Tell on your tale, Manciple, I you pray."

"Well, sire," said he, "now harken to what I say."

The Tale

When Phoebus[6] dwelt here in this earth adown,
As old books make mention,
He was the most lusty bachelor
In all this world, and also the best archer.
He slew Python, the serpent,[7] as he lay
Sleeping in the sun upon a day;
And many another noble deed

He with his bowe wroghte, as men may rede.
    Pleyen he coude on every minstralcye,
And singen, that it was a melodye,
To heren of his clere vois the soun.
Certes the king of Thebes, Amphioun,
That with his singing walled that citee,
Coude never singen half so wel as he.
Therto he was the semelieste man
That is or was, sith that the world bigan.
What nedeth it his fetures to discryve?
For in this world was noon so fair on lyve.
He was ther-with fulfild of gentillesse,
Of honour, and of parfit worthinesse.
    This Phebus, that was flour of bachelrye,
As wel in fredom as in chivalrye,
For his desport, in signe eek of victorie
Of Phitoun, so as telleth us the storie,
Was wont to beren in his hand a bowe.
    Now had this Phebus in his hous a crowe,
Which in a cage he fostred many a day,
And taughte it speken, as men teche a jay.
Whyt was this crowe, as is a snow-whyt swan,
And countrefete the speche of every man
He coude, whan he sholde telle a tale.
Ther-with in al this world no nightingale
Ne coude, by an hondred thousand deel,
Singen so wonder merily and weel.
    Now had this Phebus in his hous a wyf,
Which that he lovede more than his lyf,
And night and day dide ever his diligence
Hir for to plese, and doon hir reverence,
Save only, if the sothe that I shal sayn,
Jalous he was, and wolde have kept hir fayn;
For him were looth by-japed for to be.
And so is every wight in swich degree;
But al in ydel, for it availleth noght,
A good wyf, that is clene of werk and thoght,
Sholde nat been kept in noon await, certayn;
And trewely, the labour is in vayn

He with his bow wrought, as men may read.
    Play he could on every instrument,
And sing so that it was melodious
To hear the sound of his clear voice.
Certainly the king of Thebes, Amphioun,
Who with his singing walled that city,
Could never sing half so well as he.
And in addition he was the handsomest man
Who is or was since the world began.
Why need we his features to describe?
For in this world there was none so fair alive.
He was fulfilled of gentleness,
Of honor and of perfect worthiness.
    This Phoebus, who was the flower of knighthood,
As well in character as in chivalry,
For his pleasure, and as a sign also of his victory
Over Python, as tells us the story,
Was wont to bear in his hand a bow.
    Now had this Phoebus in his house a crow
That in a cage he fostered many a day,
And taught it to speak, as men teach a jay.
White was this crow as is a snow white swan,
And counterfeit the speech of every man
He could, when he should tell a tale.
And also in all this world no nightingale
Could, by a hundred thousandth part,
Sing so wondrous merrily and well.
    Now had this Phoebus in his house a wife
Whom he loved more than his life,
And night and day did ever his diligence
Her for to please and do her reverence,
Save only, if the truth I shall say,
Jealous he was, and would have kept her under lock and key.
For he was loath betrayed to be,
And so is every person in such estate,
But all in vain, for it avails not.
A good woman, who is clean of work and thought,
Should not be kept under watch, certainly;
And truly the labor is in vain

To kepe a shrewe, for it wol nat be.
This holde I for a verray nycetee,
To spille labour, for to kepe wyves;
Thus writen olde clerkes in hir lyves.

But now to purpos, as I first bigan:
This worthy Phebus dooth all that he can
To plesen hir, weninge by swich plesaunce,
And for his manhede and his governaunce,
That no man sholde han put him from hir grace.
But god it woot, ther may no man embrace
As to destreyne a thing, which that nature
Hath naturelly set in a creature.

Tak any brid, and put it in a cage,
And do al thyn entente and thy corage
To fostre it tendrely with mete and drinke,
Of alle deyntees that thou canst bithinke,
And keep it al-so clenly as thou may;
Al-though his cage of gold be never so gay,
Yet hath this brid, by twenty thousand fold,
Lever in a forest, that is rude and cold,
Gon ete wormes and swich wrecchednesse.
For ever this brid wol doon his bisinesse
To escape out of his cage, if he may;
His libertee this brid desireth ay.

Lat take a cat, and fostre him wel with milk,
And tendre flesh, and make his couche of silk,
And lat him seen a mous go by the wal;
Anon he weyveth milk, and flesh, and al,
And every deyntee that is in that hous,
Swich appetyt hath he to ete a mous.
Lo, here hath lust his dominacioun,
And appetyt flemeth discrecioun.

A she-wolf hath also a vileins kinde;
The lewedeste wolf that she may finde,
Or leest of reputacion wol she take,
In tyme whan hir lust to han a make.

Alle thise ensamples speke I by thise men
That been untrewe, and no-thing by wommen.
For men han ever a likerous appetyt

To keep a shrew, for it will not be.
This hold I to be pure folly,
To waste labor for to keep wives:
Thus wrote old scholars in their lives.
    But now to the point, as I first began:
This worthy Phoebus did all he could
To please her, supposing that for such pleasure,
And for his character and his behavior,
That no man should put him from her grace.
But, God knows, there may no man embrace
To restrain a thing that nature
Has naturally set in a creature.
    Take any bird, and put it in a cage,[8]
And do all your intent and all your strength
To foster it tenderly with meat and drink
Of all the dainties that you can bethink,
And keep it all so carefully as you may,
Although his cage of gold be never so gay,
Yet would this bird, by twenty thousand fold,
Rather in a forest that is rude and cold
Go eat worms and such wretchedness.
For ever this bird will do his business
To escape out of his cage, if he may.
His liberty this bird desires always.
    Or take a cat, and foster him well with milk
And tender flesh, and make his couch of silk,
And let him see a mouse go by the wall,
Anon he waives milk and meat and all,
And every dainty that is in that house,
Such appetite has he to eat a mouse.
Look, here has lust his domination,
And appetite overcomes discretion.
    A she-wolf is also of an evil kind.
The lewdest wolf that she may find
Of least reputation, will she take,
In times when she lusts to have a mate.
    All these examples I mention of men
Who have been untrue, and nothing of women,
For men have ever a lecherous appetite

On lower thing to parfourne hir delyt
Than on hir wyves, be they never so faire,
Ne never so trewe, ne so debonaire.
Flesh is so newefangel, with meschaunce,
That we ne conne in no-thing han plesaunce
That souneth in-to vertu any whyle.

This Phebus, which that thoghte upon no gyle,
Deceyved was, for al his jolitee;
For under him another hadde she,
A man of litel reputacioun,
Noght worth Phebus in comparisoun.
The more harm is; it happeth ofte so,
Of which ther cometh muchel harm and wo.

And so bifel, whan Phebus was absent,
His wyf anon hath for hir lemman sent;
Hir lemman? certes, this is a knavish speche!
Foryeveth it me, and that I yow biseche.

The wyse Plato seith, as ye may rede,
The word mot nede accorde with the dede.
If men shal telle proprely a thing,
The word mot cosin be to the werking.
I am a boistous man, right thus seye I,
Ther nis no difference, trewely,
Bitwixe a wyf that is of heigh degree,
If of hir body dishonest she be,
And a povre wenche, other than this—
If it so be, they werke bothe amis—
But that the gentile, in estaat above,
She shal be cleped his lady, as in love;
And for that other is a povre womman,
She shal be cleped his wenche, or his lemman.
And, god it woot, myn owene dere brother,
Men leyn that oon as lowe as lyth that other.

Right so, bitwixe a titlelees tiraunt
And an outlawe, or a theef erraunt,
The same I seye, ther is no difference.
To Alisaundre told was this sentence;
That, for the tyrant is of gretter might,
By force of meynee for to sleen doun-right,

For lower things to perform their delight
Than on their wives, be they ever so fair,
Or ever so true, or ever so debonair.
Flesh is so fond of novelty, worse luck for us,
That we can in no way have enjoyment
With anything that makes us virtuous.

This Phoebus, who thought not of guile,
Deceived was, for all his handsomeness.
For under him another had she,
A man of little reputation,
Not worthy of Phoebus in comparison.
And more's the harm it happens often so,
And from which comes much misery and woe.

And so it happened, when Phoebus was absent,
His wife anon has for her stallion sent.
Her stallion? Certainly, this is knavish speech!
Forgive me it, I you beseech.

The wise Plato says, as you may read,
The word must needs accord with the deed.
If men shall tell properly a thing,
The word must cousin be to the working.
I am a plain man, right thus say I:
There is no difference, truly,
Between a wife who is of high degree,
If of her body she dishonest be,
And a poor wench, other than this—
If it so be they both work amiss—
Except that the gentlewoman, estate above,
She shall be called his lady, as in love;
And if the other is a woman poor,
She shall be called his trollop or his whore.
And, God knows, my own dear brother,
Men lay as low with one as with the other.

Right so between a titleless tyrant
And an outlaw or thief arrant,
The same I say: there is no difference.
To Alexander was told this sentence,[9]
That, though the tyrant is of greater might
In his army's strength for to slay downright,

And brennen hous and hoom, and make al plain,
Lo! therfor is he cleped a capitain;
And, for the outlawe hath but smal meynee,
And may nat doon so greet an harm as he,
Ne bringe a contree to so greet mescheef,
Men clepen him an outlawe or a theef.
But, for I am a man noght textuel,
I wol noghte telle of textes never a del;
I wol go to my tale, as I bigan.

Whan Phebus wyf had sent for hir lemman,
Anon they wroghten al hir lust volage.

The whyte crowe, that heng ay in the cage,
Biheld hir werk, and seyde never a word.
And whan that hoom was come Phebus, the lord,
This crowe sang "cokkow! cokkow! cokkow!"

"What, brid?" quod Phebus, "what song singestow?
Ne were thow wont so merily to singe
That to myn herte it was a rejoisinge
To here thy vois? allas! what song is this?"

"By god," quod he, "I singe nat amis;
Phebus," quod he, "for al thy worthinesse,
For al thy beautee and thy gentilesse,
For al thy song and al thy minstralcye,
For al thy waiting, blered is thyn yë
With oon of litel reputacioun,
Noght worth to thee, as in comparisoun,
The mountance of a gnat; so mote I thryve!
For on thy bed thy wyf I saugh him swyve."

What wol ye more? the crowe anon him tolde,
By sadde tokenes and by wordes bolde,
How that his wyf had doon hir lecherye,
Him to gret shame and to gret vileinye;
And tolde him ofte, he saugh it with his yën.
This Phebus gan aweyward for to wryen,
Him thoughte his sorweful herte brast a-two;
His bowe he bente, and sette ther-inne a flo,
And in his ire his wyf thanne hath he slayn.
This is th'effect, ther is na-more to sayn;
For sorwe of which he brak his minstralcye,

And burn houses and homes, and lay to waste,
Look, therefore he is called a captain;
And though the outlaw has not but a few men,
And may not do so great a harm as he,
Nor bring a country to so great mischief,
Men call him an outlaw or a thief.
But I am not learned from books,
In no way will I cite their texts;
I will tell my tale, as I began.

   When Phoebus' wife had sent for her stud,
Anon they wrought all their foolish lust.

   The white crow, that ever in the cage perched,
Beheld their work, and said never a word.
And when home was come Phoebus, the lord,
This crow sang, "Cuckoo! Cuckoo! Cuckoo!"[10]

   "What, bird?" said Phoebus. "What song sing you?
Were you not wont so merrily to sing
That to my heart it was a rejoicing
To hear your voice? Alas, what song is this?"

   "By God," said he, "I sing not amiss.
Phoebus," said he, "for all your worthiness,
For all your beauty and your gentleness,
For all your song and all your minstrelsy,
For all your waiting, bleared is your eye
By one of little reputation,
Not worthy of you in comparison.
The value of a gnat, so may I thrive!
For on your bed I saw him enjoy your wife!"

   What would you more? The crow anon him told,
By strong proofs and words bold,
How his wife had done her lechery,
Him to great shame and to great villainy,
And told him he saw it often with his own eyes.
This Phoebus began away to turn,
And thought his sorrowful heart would burst in two.
His bow he bent, and sent thereby an arrow,
And in his ire his wife then has he slain.
This is the effect, there is no more to say;
For sorrow of which he broke his instruments,

Bothe harpe, and lute, and giterne, and sautrye;
And eek he brak his arwes and his bowe.
And after that, thus spak he to the crowe:
    "Traitour," quod he, "with tonge of scorpioun,
Thou hast me broght to my confusioun!
Allas! that I was wroght! why nere I deed?
O dere wyf, O gemme of lustiheed,
That were to me so sad and eek so trewe,
Now lystow deed, with face pale of hewe,
Ful giltelees, that dorste I swere, y-wis!
O rakel hand, to doon so foule amis!
O trouble wit, O ire recchelees,
That unavysed smytest giltelees!
O wantrust, ful of fals suspecioun,
Where was thy wit and thy discrecioun?
O every man, be-war of rakelnesse,
Ne trowe no-thing with-outen strong witnesse;
Smyt nat to sone, er that ye witen why,
And beeth avysed wel and sobrely
Er ye doon any execucioun,
Up-on your ire, for suspecioun.
Allas! a thousand folk hath rakel ire
Fully fordoon, and broght hem in the mire.
Allas! for sorwe I wol my-selven slee!"
    And to the crowe, "O false theef!" seyde he,
"I wol thee quyte anon thy false tale!
Thou songe whylom lyk a nightingale;
Now shaltow, false theef, thy song forgon,
And eek thy whyte fetheres everichon,
Ne never in al thy lyf ne shaltou speke.
Thus shal men on a traitour been awreke;
Thou and thyn of-spring ever shul be blake,
Ne never swete noise shul ye make,
But ever crye agayn tempest and rayn,
In tokeninge that thurgh thee my wyf is slayn."
And to the crowe he stirte, and that anon,
And pulled his whyte fetheres everichon,
And made him blak, and refte him al his song,
And eek his speche, and out at dore him slong

Both harp, and lute, and zither and psaltery;
And also he broke his arrows and his bow,
And after that spoke he to the crow:
    "Traitor," said he, "with tongue of scorpion,
You have me brought to my ruin;
Alas, that I was made! Why am I not dead?
O dear wife! O gem of delight!
You who were to me so steady and so true,
Now lie you dead, with face pale of hue,
Full guiltless, that dare I swear, truly!
Oh rash hand, to do so foul a wrong!
Oh troubled mind, oh ire reckless,
That thoughtlessly slew the guiltless!
Oh distrust, full of false suspicion,
Where was your wit and your discretion?
Oh every man, beware of rashness!
Believe nothing without strong evidence.
Smite not too soon, before you know why,
And be advised well and soberly
Before you do any execution
In your ire out of suspicion.
Alas, a thousand folk in rash ire
Fully be undone, and bring themselves into the mire.
Alas! For sorrow I will myself slay!"
    And to the crow, "Oh false thief!" said he,
"I will you requite anon for your false tale.
You sang once like a nightingale;
Now shall you, false thief, your song forego,
And also your white feathers every one,
Nor ever in your life shall you speak.
Thus men shall on a traitor vengeance wreak;
You and your offspring ever shall be black
Nor ever sweet noise shall you make,
But ever cry against tempest and rain,
As a sign that through you my wife is slain."
And to the crow he started, and that anon,
And pulled his white feathers every one,
And made him black, and bereft him of his song,
And also of his speech, and out the door him slung

Un-to the devel, which I him bitake;
And for this caas ben alle crowes blake.—
    Lordings, by this ensample I yow preye,
Beth war, and taketh kepe what I seye:
Ne telleth never no man in your lyf
How that another man hath dight his wyf;
He wol yow haten mortally, certeyn.
Daun Salomon, as wyse clerkes seyn,
Techeth a man to kepe his tonge wel;
But as I seyde, I am noght textuel.
But nathelees, thus taughte me my dame:
"My sone, thenk on the crowe, a goddes name;
My sone, keep wel thy tonge and keep thy freend.
A wikked tonge is worse than a feend.
My sone, from a feend men may hem blesse;
My sone, god of his endelees goodnesse
Walled a tonge with teeth and lippes eke,
For man sholde him avyse what he speke.
My sone, ful ofte, for to muche speche,
Hath many a man ben spilt, as clerkes teche;
But for a litel speche avysely
Is no men shent, to speke generally.
My sone, thy tonge sholdestow restreyne
At alle tyme, but whan thou doost thy peyne
To speke of god, in honour and preyere.
The firste vertu, sone, if thou wolt lere,
Is to restreyne and kepe wel thy tonge.—
Thus lerne children whan that they ben yonge.—
My sone, of muchel speking yvel-avysed,
Ther lasse speking hadde y-nough suffysed,
Comth muchel harm, thus was me told and taught.
In muchel speche sinne wanteth naught.
Wostow wher-of a rakel tonge serveth?
Right as a swerd forcutteth and forkerveth
An arm a-two, my dere sone, right so
A tonge cutteth frendship al a-two.
A jangler is to god abhominable;
Reed Salomon, so wys and honurable;
Reed David in his psalmes, reed Senekke.

Unto the devil, to whom I him commit;
And for this case be all crows black.

   Lordings, by this example I you pray,
Beware, and take heed what I say:
Never tell any man in your life
How another man had his wife;
He will hate you mortally, for certain.
Lord Solomon, as wise scholars say,
Teaches a man to keep his tongue well.[11]
But, as I say, I am not learned in books.
Nevertheless, thus taught me my mother:
"My son, think on a crow, in God's name!
My son, hold well your tongue, and keep your friends.
A wicked tongue is worse than a fiend;
My son, from a fiend men may them bless.
My son, God of his endless goodness
Walled a tongue with teeth and lips also,
For man should consider before he speaks.
My son, full often, for too much speech
Has many a man died, as scholars teach,
But for speech little and discreet
Is no man ruined, to speak generally.
My son, your tongue you should restrain
At all times, except when you devote yourself
To speak of God, in honor and prayer.
The first virtue, son, if you will learn,
Is to restrain and keep well your tongue;
Thus learn children when they be young.
My son, of much talking ill-advised,
When less speaking would have sufficed,
Comes much harm; thus I was told and taught.
In much chatter sin lacks not.
Know you what a rash tongue can do?
Right as a sword cuts
An arm in two, my dear son, right so
A tongue cuts a friendship apart.
A tongue-wagger is to God abominable.
Read Solomon, so wise and honorable;
Read David in his psalms, read Seneca.

My sone, spek nat, but with thyn heed thou bekke
Dissimule as thou were deef, if that thou here
A jangler speke of perilous matere.
The Fleming seith, and lerne it, if thee leste,
That litel jangling causeth muchel reste.
My sone, if thou no wikked word hast seyd,
Thee thar nat drede for to be biwreyd;
But he that hath misseyd, I dar wel sayn,
He may by no wey clepe his word agayn.
Thing that is seyd, is seyd; and forth it gooth,
Though him repente, or be him leef or looth.
He is his thral to whom that he hath sayd
A tale, of which he is now yvel apayd.
My sone, be war, and be non auctour newe
Of tydinges, whether they ben false or trewe.
Wher-so thou come, amonges hye or lowe,
Kepe wel thy tonge, and thenk up-on the crowe."

My son, speak not, but with your head you nod.
Dissimulate as if you were deaf, if you hear
A chatterbox speak of perilous matter.
The Fleming says, and learn if you wish,
That to talk less will give you more rest.
My son, if you no wicked word have said,
You then need not dread to be betrayed;
But if you have missaid, I dare well say,
You may by no way recall your word again.
Something that is said is said, and forth it goes,
Though you repent, or be ever so loath.
He is in thrall to whom he has told
A tale for which he is now evilly repaid.
My son, beware, and be no author new
Of tidings, whether they be false or true.
Whereso you go, among high or low,
Keep well your tongue and think upon the crow."

The Squieres Tale

The Prologue

"Squire, com neer, if it your wille be,
And sey somwhat of love; for, certes, ye
Connen ther-on as muche as any man."
"Nay, sir," quod he, "but I wol seye as I can
With hertly wille; for I wol nat rebelle
Agayn your lust; a tale wol I telle.
Have me excused if I speke amis,
My wil is good; and lo, my tale is this."

The Tale

PART ONE

At Sarray, in the land of Tartarye,
Ther dwelte a king, that werreyed Russye,
Thurgh which ther deyde many a doughty man.
This noble king was cleped Cambinskan,
Which in his tyme was of so greet renoun
That ther nas no-wher in no regioun
So excellent a lord in alle thing;
Him lakked noght that longeth to a king.
As of the secte of which that he was born
He kepte his lay, to which that he was sworn;
And ther-to he was hardy, wys, and riche,
And piëtous and just, alwey- y-liche;
Sooth of his word, benigne and honurable,
Of his corage as any centre stable;
Yong, fresh, and strong, in armes desirous
As any bacheler of al his hous.
A fair persone he was an fortunat,
And kepte alwey so wel royal estat,
That ther was nowher swich another man.
This noble king, this Tartre Cambinskan
Hadde two sones on Elpheta his wyf,
Of whiche th'eldeste highte Algarsyf,

The Squire's Tale

The Prologue

"SQUIRE, COME NEAR, IF it your will be,
And say something of love, for certainly you
Know thereof as much as any man."
"Nay, sir," said he, "but I will say as I can
With hearty will, for I will not rebel
Against your wish; a tale will I tell.
Have me excused if I speak amiss;
My will is good, and lo, my tale is this."

The Tale

PART ONE

In Tsarev, in the land of Tartary,[1]
There dwelt a king who waged war on Russia,
Through which there died many a doughty man.
This noble king was called Genghis Khan,
Who in his time was of so great renown
That there was nowhere in any region
So excellent a lord in all things:
He lacked nothing wanted by a king.
In accord with the religion to which he was born
He kept his laws, to which he was sworn;
And also he was brave, wise and rich,
And merciful and just,
True to his word, benign, and honorable;
Of his courage as any center stable;
Young, fresh and strong, in arms ambitious
As any young knight of all his house.
A fair person he was and fortunate,
And kept always so well royal estate
That there was nowhere such another man.
This noble king, this Tartar Ghengis Khan,
Had two sons by Elpheta his wife,
Of which the eldest was called Algarsyf;

771

That other sone was cleped Cambalo.
A doghter hadde this worthy king also,
That yongest was, and highte Canacee.
But for to telle yow al hir beautee,
It lyth nat in my tonge, n'in my conning;
I dar nat undertake so heigh a thing.
Myn English eek is insufficient;
It moste been a rethor excellent,
That coude his colours longing for that art,
If he sholde hir discryven every part.
I am non swich, I moot speke as I can.
　　And so bifel that, whan this Cambinskan
Hath twenty winter born his diademe,
As he was wont fro yeer to yeer, I deme,
He leet the feste of his nativitee
Don cryen thurghout Sarray his citee,
The last Idus of March, after the yeer.
Phebus the sonne ful joly was and cleer;
For he was neigh his exaltacioun
In Martes face, and in his mansioun
In Aries, the colerik hote signe.
Ful lusty was the weder and benigne,
For which the foules, agayn the sonne shene,
What for the seson and the yonge grene,
Ful loude songen hir affecciouns;
Hem semed han geten hem protecciouns
Agayn the swerd of winter kene and cold.
　　This Cambinskan, of which I have yow told,
In royal vestiment sit on his deys,
With diademe, ful heighe in his paleys,
And halt his feste, so solempne and so riche
That in this world ne was ther noon it liche.
Of which if I shal tellen al th'array,
Than wolde it occupye a someres day;
And eek it nedeth nat for to devyse
At every cours the ordre of hir servyse.
I wol nat tellen of hir strange sewes,
Ne of hir swannes, ne of hir heronsewes.
Eek in that lond, as tellen knightes olde,

The other son was called Cambalo.
A daughter had this worthy king also,
Who youngest was, and called Canacee.
But to tell you all her beauty,
It lies not in my tongue, nor in my skill,
I dare not undertake so high a thing.
My English also is insufficient.
It would require an excellent rhetorician
Who would need all the devices of that art,
If he should her describe in every part.
I am none such, I must speak as I can.

   And so it befell that when this Genghis Khan
Had for twenty winters borne his diadem,
As he was wont from year to year, I deem,
He ordered a feast of his nativity
Proclaimed throughout Tsarev, his city,
The Ides of March, that year exactly.
Phoebus the sun full jolly was and clear,
For he was near his exaltation
In Mars' face and in his mansion
In Aries, the coleric hot sign.[2]
Full lusty was the weather and benign,
For which the birds, facing the sun,
What with the season and the young green,
Full loud sang their passions.
They seemed to have had protection
Against the sword of winter, keen and cold.

   This Genghis Khan, of whom I have you told,
In royal vestment sat on his dais,
With diadem, full high in his palace,
And held his feast so solemn and so rich
That in this world there was none like it;
Of which if I shall tell all the display,
Then would it occupy a summer's day,
And also we need not describe
At every course the order of their service.
I will not tell of their strange stews,
Nor of their swans, nor of their young herons.
Also in that land, as tell knights of old,

Ther is som mete that is ful deyntee holde,
That in this lond men recche of it but smal;
Ther nis no man that may reporten al.
I wol nat tarien yow, for it is pryme,
And for it is no fruit but los of tyme;
Un-to my firste I wol have my recours.
　　And so bifel that, after the thridde cours,
Whyl that this king sit thus in his nobleye,
Herkninge his minstralles hir thinges pleye
Biforn him at the bord deliciously,
In at the halle-dore al sodeynly
Ther cam a knight up-on a stede of bras,
And in his hand a brood mirour of glas.
Upon his thombe he hadde of gold a ring,
And by his seyde a naked swerd hanging;
And up he rydeth to the heighe bord.
In al the halle ne was ther spoke a word
For merveille of this knight; him to biholde
Ful bisily ther wayten yonge and olde.
　　This strange knight, that cam thus sodeynly,
Al armed save his heed ful richely,
Saluëth king and queen, and lordes alle,
By ordre, as they seten in the halle,
With so heigh reverence and obeisaunce
As wel in speche as in contenaunce,
That Gawain, with his olde curteisye,
Though he were come ageyn out of Fairye,
Ne coude him nat amende with a word.
And after this, biforn the heighe bord,
He with a manly voys seith his message,
After the forme used in his langage,
With-outen vyce of sillable or of lettre;
And, for his tale sholde seme the bettre,
Accordant to his wordes was his chere,
As techeth art of speche hem that it lere;
Al-be-it that I can nat soune his style,
Ne can nat climben over so heigh a style,
Yet seye I this, as to commune entente,
Thus muche amounteth al that ever he mente,

There is some food that is full dainty held
That in this land men regard it but little;
There is no man who may report it all.
I will not tarry you, for it is prime
And because it is no fruit but loss of time;
Unto my first I will return.

    And so it befell that after the third course,
While the king sat thus in his nobility,
Listening to his minstrels their instruments play
Before him at the table so deliciously,
At the hall door all suddenly
There came a knight upon a steed of brass,
And in his hand a broad mirror of glass.
Upon his thumb he had of gold a ring,
And by his side a naked sword hanging;
And up he rode to the head table.
In all the hall there was spoken not a word
For marvel of this knight; him to behold
Full busily they waited, young and old.

    This strange knight, who came thus suddenly,
All armed, save his head, full richly,
Saluted the king and queen and lords all,
In order, as they were seated in the hall,
With such high reverence and obeisance,
As well in speech as in countenance,
That Gawain,[3] with his old courtesy,
Though he were coming out of Fairyland,
Could not him amend with a word.
And after this, before the head table,
He with a manly voice said his message,
After the form used in his language,
Without vice of syllable or letter;
And so that his tale should seem the better,
According to his words was his face,
As the art of rhetoric teaches those who learn it.
Albeit that I can not repeat his style,
Nor can I climb over so high a stile,
Yet I say this, in language plain:
This much says what he meant,

If it so be that I have it in minde.
　　He seyde, "the king of Arabie and of Inde,
My lige lord, on this solempne day
Saluëth yow as he best can and may,
And sendeth yow, in honour of your feste,
By me, that am al redy at your heste,
This stede of bras, that esily and wel
Can, in the space of o day naturel,
This is to seyn, in foure and twenty houres,
Wher-so yow list, in droghte or elles shoures,
Beren your body in-to every place
To which your herte wilneth for to pace
With-outen wem of yow, thurgh foul or fair;
Or, if yow list to fleen as hye in the air
As doth an egle, whan him list to sore,
This same stede shal bere yow ever-more
With-outen harm, til ye be ther yow leste,
Though that ye slepen on his bak or reste;
And turne ayeyn, with wrything of a pin.
He that it wroghte coude ful many a gin;
He wayted many a constellacioun
Er he had doon this operacioun;
And knew ful many a seel and many a bond.
　　This mirour eek, that I have in myn hond,
Hath swich a might, that men may in it see
Whan ther shal fallen any adversitee
Un-to your regne or to your-self also;
And openly who is your freend or foo.
And over al this, if any lady bright
Hath set hir herte on any maner wight,
If he be fals, she shal his treson see,
His newe love and al his subtiltee
So openly, that ther shal no-thing hyde.
Wherfor, ageyn this lusty someres tyde,
This mirour and this ring, that ye may see,
He hath sent to my lady Canacee,
Your excellente doghter that is here.
　　The vertu of the ring, if ye wol here,
Is this; that, if hir lust it for to were

If I have well remembered its content.
   He said, "The king of Arabia and of India,
My liege lord, on this solemn day
Salutes you, as best he can and may,
And sends you, in honor of your feast,
By me, who am all ready at your behest,
This steed of brass, that easily and well
Can in the space of a day natural—
That is to say, in four and twenty hours—
Wherever you wish, in drought or else in showers,
Bear your body into every place
To which your heart wills to go,
Without harm of you, though foul or fair;
Or if you wish to fly as high in the air
As does an eagle when he wishes to soar,
This same steed shall bear you ever the more,
Without harm, until you be where you wish,
Though you sleep on his back or rest,
And return again with the turning of a peg.
He who wrought it made many a device ingenious.
He waited many a constellation[4]
Before he had done this operation,
And knew full well many a seal and many a bond.
   "This mirror also, that I have in my hand,
Has such a might that men may in it see
When there shall fall any adversity
Unto your reign or to yourself also,
And openly who is your friend or foe.
"And over all this, if any lady bright
Has set her heart on any manner of person,
If he be false, she shall his treason see,
His new love, and all his subtlety,
So openly that there shall no thing hide.
And so, in anticipation of this lusty summer's tide,
This mirror and this ring, that you may see,
He has sent to my lady Canacee,
Your excellent daughter who is here.
   "The virtue of this ring, if you will hear,
Is this; that if she wishes to wear it

Up-on hir thombe, or in hir purs it bere,
Ther is no foul that fleeth under the hevene
That she ne shal wel understonde his stevene,
And knowe his mening openly and pleyn,
And answere him in his langage ageyn.
And every gras that groweth up-on rote
She shal eek knowe, and whom it wol do bote,
Al be his woundes never so depe and wyde.

This naked swerd, that hangeth by my syde,
Swich vertu hath, that what man so ye smyte,
Thurgh-out his armure it wol kerve and byte,
Were it as thikke as is a branched ook;
And what man that is wounded with the strook
Shal never be hool til that yow list, of grace,
To stroke him with the platte in thilke place
Ther he is hurt: this is as muche to seyn
Ye mote with the platte swerd ageyn
Stroke him in the wounde, and it wol close;
This is a verray sooth, with-outen glose,
It failleth nat whyl it is in your hold."

And whan this knight hath thus his tale told,
He rydeth out of halle, and doun he lighte.
His stede, which that shoon as sonne brighte,
Stant in the court, as stille as any stoon.
This knight is to his chambre lad anon,
And is unarmed and to mete y-set.

The presents been ful royally y-fet,
This is to seyn, the swerd and the mirour,
And born anon in-to the heighe tour
With certeine officers ordeyned therfore;
And un-to Canacee this ring was bore
Solempnely, ther she sit at the table.
But sikerly, with-outen any fable,
The hors of bras, that may nat be remewed,
It stant as it were to the ground y-glewed.
Ther may no man out of the place it dryve
For noon engyn of windas or polyve;
And cause why, for they can nat the craft.
And therefore in the place they han it laft

Upon her thumb or carry it in her purse,
There is no bird that flies under the heaven
That she shall not understand his voice,
And know his meaning openly and plain,
And answer him in his language again;
And every grass that grows upon root
She shall also know, and whom it will heal,
Though his wounds be ever so deep and wide.

"This naked sword, that hangs by my side,
Such virtue has that whatever man so you smite
Through his armor it will carve and bite,
Though it be thick as is a branched oak;
And whatever man is wounded with the stroke
Shall never be whole until you wish, of grace,
To stroke him with the flat side in the place
Where he is hurt; that is to say,
You must with the flat of the sword again
Stroke him on the wound, and it will close.
This is the absolute truth, without gloss;
It fails not while it is in your hold."

And when this knight had thus his tale told,
He rode out of the hall and down he alighted.
His steed, which shone sun-bright,
Stood in the court, still as any stone.
This knight to his chamber was led anon,
And was unarmed, and for him food set.

The presents were royally fetched—
That is to say, the sword and the mirror—
And borne anon into the high tower
With certain officers ordained therefore;
And unto Canacee this ring was borne
Solemnly, where she sat at the table.
But truly, without any fable,
The horse of brass, that could not be removed,
It stood as if it were to the ground glued.
There could no man drive it out of the place
Neither with pulley nor windlass;
And why? Because they knew not the craft.
And therefore in the place they have left it

Til that the knight hath taught hem the manere
To voyden him, as ye shal after here.
    Greet was the prees, that swarmeth to and fro,
To gauren on this hors that stondeth so;
For it so heigh was, and so brood and long,
So wel proporcioned for to ben strong,
Right as it were a stede of Lumbaryde;
Ther-with so horsly, and so quik of yë
As it a gentil Poileys courser were.
For certes, fro his tayl un-to his ere,
Nature ne art ne coude him nat amende
In no degree, as al the peple wende.
But evermore hir moste wonder was,
How that it coude goon, and was of bras;
It was of Fairye, as the peple semed.
Diverse folk diversely they demed;
As many hedes, as many wittes ther been.
They murmureden as dooth a swarm of been,
And maden skiles after hir fantasyes,
Rehersinge of thise olde poetryes,
And seyden, it was lyk the Pegasee,
The hors that hadde winges for to flee;
Or elles it was the Grekes hors Synon,
That broghte Troye to destruccion,
As men may in thise olde gestes rede.
"Myn herte," quod oon, "is evermore in drede;
I trowe som men of armes been ther-inne,
That shapen hem this citee for to winne.
It were right good that al swich thing were knowe."
Another rowned to his felawe lowe,
And seyde, "he lyeth, it is rather lyk
An apparence y-maad by som magyk,
As jogelours pleyen at thise festes grete."
Of sondry doutes thus they jangle and trete,
As lewed peple demeth comunly
Of thinges that ben maad more subtilly
Than they can in her lewednes comprehende;
They demen gladly to the badder ende.
    And somme of hem wondred on the mirour,

Till the knight taught them the manner
To move him, as you shall after hear.
    Great was the crowd that swarmed to and fro
To gaze on this horse that stood so.
For it so high was, and so broad and long,
So well proportioned to be strong,
Right as if it were a steed of Lombardy;
A horsely horse, and so lively of eye,
As if it were a gentle Apulian courser.
For truly, from his tail unto his ear
Neither nature nor art could him improve
In any way, as all the people knew.
But evermore their greatest wonder was
How that it could go, and yet was of brass;
It was an illusion, as the people imagined.
Diverse folk diversely they deemed;[5]
As many heads, as many were there ideas.
They murmured as does a swarm of bees,
And made reasons for their fantasies,
Recalling the old poetry,
And said it was like Pegasus,[6]
The horse that had wings to fly;
Or else it was the Greek horse of Synon,[7]
That brought Troy to destruction,
As in these old tales men read.
"My heart," said one, "is evermore in dread;
I believe some men of arms be therein,
Who intend this city to win.
It were right good that all such things were known."
Another whispered to his fellow low,
And said, "He lies, for it is rather like
An illusion made by some magic,
As conjurors play at these feasts great."
Of sundry guesses thus they chattered and debated,
As unlearned people often pass judgement
On things that be made more subtley
Than they can in their ignorance comprehend;
They judge usually to the badder end.
    And some of them wondered on the mirror,

That born was up in-to the maister-tour,
How men mighte in it swiche thinges see.
Another answerde, and seyde it mighte wel be
Naturelly, by composiciouns
Of angles and of slye reflexiouns,
And seyden, that in Rome was swich oon.
They speken of Alocen and Vitulon,
And Aristotle, that writen in hir lyves
Of queynte mirours and of prospectyves,
As knowen they that han hir bokes herd.

    And othere folk han wondred on the swerd
That wolde percen thurgh-out every-thing;
And fille in speche of Thelophus the king,
And of Achilles with his queynte spere,
For he coude with it bothe hele and dere,
Right in swich wyse as men may with the swerd
Of which right now ye han your-selven herd.
They speken of sondry harding of metal,
And speke of medicynes ther-with-al,
And how, and whanne, it sholde y-harded be;
Which is unknowe algates unto me.

    Tho speke they of Canacëes ring,
And seyden alle, that swich a wonder thing
Of craft of ringes herde they never non,
Save that he, Moyses, and king Salomon
Hadde a name of konning in swich art.
Thus seyn the peple, and drawen hem apart.
But nathelees, somme seyden that it was
Wonder to maken of fern-asshen glas,
And yet nis glas nat lyk asshen of fern;
But for they han y-knowen it so fern,
Therfore cesseth her jangling and her wonder.
As sore wondren somme on cause of thonder,
On ebbe, on flood, on gossomer, and on mist,
And alle thing, til that the cause is wist.
Thus jangle they and demen and devyse,
Til that the king gan fro the bord aryse.

    Phebus hath laft the angle meridional,
And yet ascending was the beest royal,

That was borne up into the master-tower,
How men might in it such things see.
Another answered and said it might well be
Naturally, by arrangements
Of angels and of sly reflections,
And said that in Rome there was such a one.
They spoke of Alhazen, and Vitulon,[8]
And Aristotle, who wrote in their lives
Of ingenious mirrors and perspectives,
As they know who have them heard.

 And other folk wondered on the sword
That would pierce through every thing.
And fell into talk of Telephus the king,[9]
And of Achilles with his wondrous spear,
For he could with it both harm and heal,
Right in such ways as men may with the sword
Of which right now you have yourselves heard.
They spoke of sundry tempering of metal,
And spoke also of chemicals,
And how and when it should hardened be,
Which is unknown, at least unto me.

 They spoke of Canacee's ring,
And all said that such a wondrous thing
In making rings they had never known,
Save that Moses and King Solomon
Had a name for cunning in such art.
Thus said the people in groups scattered about.
But nevertheless some of them said that it was
Wondrous to make glass from fern ash,
And yet glass is not like the ash of fern;
But, because they had known of it before,
They ceased their chattering and their wonder.
As deeply wondered some on the cause of thunder,
On ebb, on flood, on spider webs, and on mist,
And all things, till that the cause is known.
Thus chattered they, and judged, and described
Till the king began from the table to arise.

 Phoebus had left the angle meridional,
And yet ascending was the beast royal,

The gentil Leon, with his Aldiran,
Whan that this Tartre king, this Cambinskan,
Roos fro his bord, ther that he sat ful hye.
Toforn him gooth the loude minstralcye,
Til he cam to his chambre of parements,
Ther as they sownen diverse instruments,
That it is lyk an heven for to here.
Now dauncen lusty Venus children dere,
For in the Fish hir lady sat ful hye,
And loketh on hem with a freendly yë.

    This noble king is set up in his trone.
This strange knight is fet to him ful sone,
And on the daunce he gooth with Canacee.
Heer is the revel and the jolitee
That is nat able a dul man to devyse.
He moste han knowen love and his servyse,
And been a festlich man as fresh as May,
That sholde yow devysen swich array.

    Who coude telle yow the forme of daunces,
So uncouthe and so fresshe contenaunces,
Swich subtil loking and dissimulinges
For drede of jalouse mennes aperceyvinges?
No man but Launcelot, and he is deed.
Therefor I passe of al this lustiheed;
I seye na-more, but in this jolynesse
I lete hem, til men to the soper dresse.

    The styward bit the spyces for to hye,
And eek the wyn, in al this melodye.
The usshers and the squyers ben y-goon;
The spyces and the wyn is come anoon.
They ete and drinke; and whan this hadde an ende,
Un-to the temple, as reson was, they wende.

    The service doon, they soupen al by day.
What nedeth yow rehercen hir array?
Ech man wot wel, that at a kinges feeste
Hath plentee, to the moste and to the leeste,
And deyntees mo than been in my knowing.
At-after soper gooth this noble king
To seen this hors of bras, with al the route

The gentle Lion, with his Aldiran,[10]
When this Tartar king, Genghis Khan,
Rose from his table, there where he sat full high.
Before him went the loud minstrelsy
Until he came to his official chamber,
There where they played diverse instruments
That were like a heaven for to hear.
Now danced Venus' lusty children dear,[11]
For in Pisces their lady sat full high,
And looked on them with a friendly eye.

    This noble king set upon his throne.
This strange knight was fetched to him full soon,
And in the dance he went with Canacee.
Here is the revelry and the jollity
That a dull man is not able to describe.
He must have known love and its service
And been a convivial man as fresh as May,
That you should imagine such a display.

    Who could tell you the form of dances
So exotic, and such fresh countenances,
Such subtle lookings and dissimulations
For fear of jealous men's interpretations?
No man but Lancelot, and he is dead.
Therefore I pass over all this lustihood,
I say no more, but in this jollyness
I leave them till men to supper go.

    The steward bid the spiced cakes be brought quickly,
And also the wine, in all this melody.
The ushers and the squires were gone,
The spiced cakes and the wine were come anon.
They ate and drank, and when this had an end,
Unto the temple, as reason was, they wended.

    The service done, they breakfasted at daybreak.
Who needs rehearse their scene?
Each man knows well that a king's feast
Has plenty for the greatest and for the least,
And dainties more than be in my knowing.
At after-breakfast went this noble king
To see this horse of brass, with all a crowd

Of lordes and of ladyes him aboute.
Swich wondring was ther on this hors of bras
That, sin the grete sege of Troye was,
Ther-as men wondreden on an hors also,
Ne was ther swich a wondring as was tho.
But fynally the king axeth this knight
The vertu of this courser and the might,
And preyede him to telle his governaunce.
This hors anoon bigan to trippe and daunce,
Whan that this knight leyde hand up-on his reyne,
And seyde, "sir, ther is na-more to seyne,
But, whan yow list to ryden any-where,
Ye moten trille a pin, stant in his ere,
Which I shall telle yow bitwix vs two.
Ye mote nempne him to what place also
Or to what contree that yow list to ryde.
And whan ye come ther as yow list abyde,
Bidde him descende, and trille another pin,
For ther-in lyth the effect of al the gin,
And he wol doun descende and doon your wille;
And in that place he wol abyde stille,
Though al the world the contrarie hadde y-swore;
He shal nat thennes ben y-drawe n'y-bore.
Or, if yow liste bidde him thennes goon,
Trille this pin, and he wol vanisshe anoon
Out of the sighte of every maner wight,
And come agayn, be it by day or night,
When that yow list to clepen him ageyn
In swich a gyse as I shal to yow seyn
Bitwixe yow and me, and that ful sone.
Ryde whan yow list, ther is na-more to done."
Enformed whan the king was of that knight,
And hath conceyved in his wit aright
The maner and the forme of al this thing,
Thus glad and blythe, this noble doughty king
Repeireth to his revel as biforn.
The brydel is un-to the tour y-born,
And kept among his jewels leve and dere.
The hors vanisshed, I noot in what manere,

Of lords and ladies him about.
    Such wondering was there about this horse of brass
Not unlike at the great siege of Troy,
There where men also wondered about a horse;
Never since then was there a horse so astonishing.
But finally the king asked this knight
The virtue of this courser and the might,
And prayed him to explain its governance.
    This horse anon began to trip and dance,
When this knight laid hand upon the rein,
And said, "Sire, there is no more to say,
But when you wish to ride anywhere,
You must turn a peg, standing in his ear,
Which I shall tell you between us two.
You must tell him to what place also,
Or to what country, that you wish to ride.
And when you come where you wish to abide,
Bid him descend, and turn another peg,
For within lies the guidance of all the contrivance,
And he will descend and do your will,
And in that place he will abide still.
Though all the world contrary has sworn,
He shall not be from there drawn or borne.
Or, if you wish to bid him to go,
Turn this peg, and he will vanish anon
Out of the sight of everyone,
And come again, be it day or night,
When you wish to call him again
In such a manner as I shall you say.
Between you and me, and that full soon.
Ride when you wish, there is no more to do."
    Informed when the king was by that knight,
And having conceived in his wit aright
The manner and form of all these things,
Full glad and blithe, this noble doughty king
Repaired to his revel as before.
The bridle was unto the tower borne
And kept among the jewels and treasures dear.
The horse vanished, I know not in what manner,

Out of hir sighte; ye gete na-more of me.
But thus I lete in lust and Iolitee
This Cambynskan his lordes festeyinge,
Til wel ny the day bigan to springe.

PART TWO

The norice of digestioun, the slepe,
Gan on hem winke, and bad hem taken kepe,
That muchel drink and labour wolde han reste;
And with a galping mouth hem alle he keste,
And seyde, "it was tyme to lye adoun,
For blood was in his dominacioun;
Cherissheth blood, natures freend," quod he.
They thanken him galpinge, by two, by three,
And every wight gan drawe him to his reste,
As slepe hem bad; they toke it for the beste.
Hir dremes shul nat been y-told for me;
Ful were hir hedes of fumositee,
That causeth dreem, of which ther nis no charge.
They slepen til that it was pryme large,
The moste part, but it were Canacee;
She was ful mesurable, as wommen be.
For of hir fader hadde she take leve
To gon to reste, sone after it was eve;
Hir liste nat appalled for to be,
Nor on the morwe unfestlich for to see;
And slepte hir firste sleep, and thanne awook.
For swiche a joye she in hir herte took
Both of hir queynte ring and hir mirour,
That twenty tyme she changed hir colour;
And in hir slepe, right for impressioun
Of hir mirour, she hadde a visioun.
Wherfore, er that the sonne gan up glyde,
She cleped on hir maistresse hir bisyde,
And seyde, that hir liste for to ryse.

    Thise olde wommen that been gladly wyse,
As is hir maistresse, answerde hir anoon,
And seyde, "madame, whider wil ye goon

Out of their sight; you get no more of me.
But thus I leave in joy and jollity
This Genghis Khan and his lords feasting
Till well nigh the day began to spring.

PART TWO

The nourishment of digestion, the sleep,
Began on them to wink and bade them take heed
That much drink and labor will have rest;
And with a gaping yawn he all them kissed,
And said that it was time to lie adown,
For blood was in his domination.
"Cherish blood, nature's friend," said he.
They thanked him, yawning, by two, by three,
And every person began to draw him to rest,
As sleep them bade; they took it for the best.
Their dreams shall not now be told by me;
Full were their heads of fumosity,
That causes dreams with no meaning.
They slept until it was prime,
The most part, except for Canacee.
She was full moderate, as women be;
For of her father had she taken leave
To go to rest soon after it was eve.
She wished not to be pale,
Nor on the morrow unfestive to appear,
And slept her sleep, and then awoke.
For such a joy she in her heart took
Both of her magic ring and her mirror,
That twenty times she changed her color;
And in her sleep, right from the impression
Made by her mirror, she had a vision.
Therefore, before that the sun began up to glide,
She called her governess to her side,
And said that she wished to rise.
    These old women who are often wise,
As was her governess, answered her anon,
And said, "Madam, whither will you go

Thus erly? for the folk ben alle on reste."
"I wol," quod she, "aryse, for me leste
No lenger for to slepe, and walke aboute."
     Hir maistresse clepeth wommen a gret route,
And up they rysen, wel a ten or twelve;
Up ryseth fresshe Canacee hir-selve,
As rody and bright as dooth the yonge sonne,
That in the Ram is four degrees up-ronne;
Noon hyer was he, whan she redy was;
And forth she walketh esily a pas,
Arrayed after the lusty seson sote
Lightly, for to pleye and walke on fote;
Nat but with fyve or six of hir meynee;
And in a trench, forth in the park, goth she.
The vapour, which that fro the erthe glood,
Made the sonne to seme rody and brood;
But nathelees, it was so fair a sighte
That it made alle hir hertes for to lighte,
What for the seson and the morweninge,
And for the foules that she herde singe;
For right anon she wiste what they mente
Right by hir song, and knew al hir entente.
     The knotte, why that every tale is told,
If it be taried til that lust be cold
Of hem that han it after herkned yore,
The savour passeth ever lenger the more,
For fulsomnesse of his prolixitee.
And by the same reson thinketh me,
I sholde to the knotte condescende,
And maken of hir walking sone an ende.
     Amidde a tree fordrye, as whyt as chalk,
As Canacee was pleying in hir walk,
Ther sat a faucon over hir heed ful hye,
That with a pitous voys so gan to crye
That all the wode resouned of hir cry.
Y-beten hath she hir-self so pitously
With bothe hir winges, til the rede blood
Ran endelong the tree ther-as she stood.
And ever in oon she cryde alwey and shrighte,

This early, for the folk be all at rest?"
"I will," said she, "arise, for I wish
No longer for to sleep, and walk about."
    Her governess called the women in a rout,
And up they rose, some ten or twelve;
And up rose fresh Canacee herself,
As ruddy and bright as shines the young sun,
That in the Ram is four degrees uprisen[12]—
No higher when she ready was—
And forth she walked with easy step,
Arrayed for the lusty, fragrant season
Lightly, for to play and walk on foot,
Not but with five or six of her many;
And in a path forth in the park went she.
The vapor that from the earth rose
Made the sun seem ruddy and broad;
But nevertheless it was so fair a sight
That it made all their hearts light,
What for the season and the morning,
And for the birds that she heard sing.
For right anon she knew what they meant
Right by their song, and knew all their intent.
    The gist of every tale that is told,
If delayed until the curiosity is cold
Among those who have it heard before,
So diminishes its enjoyment ever the more
With the fulsomeness of its prolixity,
That for that reason, I think,
I should to the essence quickly wend,
And make of her walking soon an end.
    Amid a tree, from dryness as white as chalk,
As Canacee was playing in her walk,
There sat a falcon over her head full high,
That with a piteous voice so began to cry
That all the wood resounded of her cry.
She had bitten herself so piteously
Upon both her wings till the red blood
Ran endlong the tree there where she stood.
And again and again she cried and shrieked,

And with hir beek hir-selven so she prighte,
That ther nis tygre, ne noon so cruel beste,
That dwelleth either in wode or in foreste
That nolde han wept, if that he wepe coude,
For sorwe of hir, she shrighte alwey so loude.
For ther nas never yet no man on lyve—
If that I coude a faucon wel discryve—
That herde of swich another of fairnesse,
As wel of plumage as of gentillesse
Of shap, and al that mighte y-rekened be.
A faucon peregryn that semed she
Of fremde land; and evermore, as she stood,
She swowneth now and now for lakke of blood,
Til wel neigh is she fallen fro the tree.

This faire kinges doghter, Canacee,
That on hir finger bar the queynte ring,
Thurgh which she understood wel every thing
That any foul may in his ledene seyn,
And coude answere him in his ledene ageyn,
Hath understonde what this faucon seyde,
And wel neigh for the rewthe almost she deyde.
And to the tree she gooth ful hastily,
And on this faucon loketh pitously,
And heeld hir lappe abrood, for wel she wiste
The faucon moste fallen fro the twiste,
When that it swowned next, for lakke of blood.
A long while to wayten hir she stood
Till atte laste she spak in this manere
Un-to the hauk, as ye shul after here.

"What is the cause, if it be for to telle,
That ye be in this furial pyne of helle?"
Quod Canacee un-to this hauk above.
"Is this for sorwe of deeth or los of love?
For, as I trowe, thise ben causes two
That causen moost a gentil herte wo;
Of other harm it nedeth nat to speke.
For ye your-self upon your-self yow wreke,
Which proveth wel, that either love or drede
Mot been encheson of your cruel dede,

And with her beak she herself so pricked
That there was no tiger, nor any other cruel beast
That dwelt either in wood or forest,
That would not have wept, if weep it could,
For sorrow of her, she shrieked always so loud.
For there is yet no man alive,
If I could a falcon well describe,
Who has heard such another so fair,
As well of plumage as gentleness
Of shape, of all that might reckoned be.
A falcon peregrine then seemed she
Of foreign land; and evermore, as she stood,
She swooned now and then for lack of blood,
Till well nigh was she fallen from the tree.
    This fair king's daughter, Canacee,
Who on her finger bore the magic ring,
Through which she understood well every thing
That any bird might in his language say,
And could answer him in his language again,
Now understood what this falcon said,
And well nigh for pity she almost died.
And to the tree she went full hastily,
And on this falcon looked piteously,
And spread her skirt broad, for well she knew
The falcon must fall from the wood,
When it swooned next, for lack of blood.
A long while waiting there she stood
Till she spoke at last in this manner
Unto the hawk, as you shall after hear:
    "What is the cause, if you can tell,
That you be in the Furies' pain of hell?"
Said Canacee unto this hawk above.
"Is this for sorrow of death or loss of love?
For, as I believe, these be the causes two
That cause most a gentle heart woe;
Of other harm we need not speak.
For you upon yourself you wreak,
Which proves well that either ire or dread
Must be the reason for your cruel deed,

Sin that I see non other wight yow chace.
For love of god, as dooth your-selven grace
Or what may ben your help; for west nor eest
Ne sey I never er now no brid ne beest
That ferde with him-self so pitously.
Ye slee me with your sorwe, verraily;
I have of yow so gret compassioun.
For goddes love, com fro the tree adoun;
And, as I am a kinges doghter trewe,
If that I verraily the cause knewe
Of your disese, if it lay in my might,
I wolde amende it, er that it were night,
As wisly helpe me gret god of kinde!
And herbes shal I right y-nowe y-finde
To hele with your hurtes hastily."
    Tho shrighte this faucon mor pitously
Than ever she dide, and fil to grounde anoon,
And lyth aswowne, deed, and lyk a stoon,
Til Canacee hath in hir lappe hir take
Un-to the tyme she gan of swough awake.
And, after that she of hir swough gan breyde,
Right in hir haukes ledene thus she seyde:—
"That pitee renneth sone in gentil herte,
Feling his similitude in peynes smerte,
Is preved al-day, as men may it see,
As wel by werk as by auctoritee;
For gentil herte kytheth gentillesse.
I see wel, that ye han of my distresse
Compassioun, my faire Canacee,
Of verray wommanly benignitee
That nature in your principles hath set.
But for non hope for to fare the bet,
But for to obeye un-to your herte free,
And for to maken other be war by me,
As by the whelp chasted is the leoun,
Right for that cause and that conclusioun,
Whyl that I have a leyser and a space,
Myn harm I wol confessen, er I pace."
And ever, whyl that oon hir sorwe tolde,

Since I see no other person you chase.
For love of God, have on yourself grace,
Or how may I help you? For west nor east
Never saw I ever until now any bird or beast
That fared with itself so piteously.
You slay me with your sorrow verily,
I have of you so great compassion.
For God's love, come from the tree adown;
And as I am a king's daughter true,
If I verily the cause knew
Of your misery, if it lay in my might,
I would amend it before night,
So wisely help me great God of nature!
And herbs shall I right enough find
To heal your hurts hastily!"

    Then shrieked this falcon yet more piteously
Than ever she did, and fell to the ground anon,
And lay aswoon, dead and like a stone,
Till Canacee had in her lap her taken
Until she began from the swoon to awaken.
And after that she from her swoon upstarted,
Right in her hawk's language thus she said:
"That pity runs soon in a gentle heart,
Feeling its compassion in pains smart,
Is proved always, as men may it see,
As well by work as by authority;
For a gentle heart makes known gentleness.
I see well that you have of my distress
Compassion, my fair Canacee,
Of very womanly benignity
That Nature in your disposition has set.
And with no hope to fare better,
But to respond to your generosity,
And to make others beware by me,
As by the whelp chastened is the lion,
Right for that cause and that conclusion
While I have the leisure and time,
My pain I will confess before I fly."
And ever, while that one her sorrow told,

That other weep, as she to water wolde,
Til that the faucon bad hir to be stille;
And, with a syk, right thus she seyde hir wille.
    "Ther I was bred (allas! that harde day!)
And fostred in a roche of marbul gray
So tendrely, that nothing eyled me,
I niste nat what was adversitee,
Til I coude flee ful hye under the sky.
Tho dwelte a tercelet me faste by,
That semed welle of alle gentillesse;
Al were he ful of treson and falsnesse,
It was so wrapped under humble chere,
And under hewe of trouthe in swich manere,
Under plesance, and under bisy peyne,
That no wight coude han wend he coude feyne,
So depe in greyn he dyed his coloures.
Right as a serpent hit him under floures
Til he may seen his tyme for to byte,
Right so this god of love, this ypocryte,
Doth so his cerimonies and obeisaunces,
And kepeth in semblant alle his observances
That sowneth in-to gentillesse of love.
As in a toumbe is al the faire above,
And under is the corps, swich as ye woot,
Swich was this ypocryte, bothe cold and hoot,
And in this wyse he served his entente,
That (save the feend) non wiste what he mente.
Til he so longe had wopen and compleyned,
And many a yeer his service to me feyned,
Til that myn herte, to pitous and to nyce,
Al innocent of his crouned malice,
For-fered of his deeth, as thoughte me,
Upon his othes and his seuretee,
Graunted him love, on this condicioun,
That evermore myn honour and renoun
Were saved, bothe privee and apert;
This is to seyn, that, after his desert,
I yaf him al myn herte and al my thoght—
God woot and he, that otherwyse noght—

The other wept as if she would dissolve,
Till the falcon bade her to be still,
And, with a sigh, right thus she said her will:
    "There I was bred—alas that day!—
And fostered in a rock of marble gray
So tenderly that no thing ailed me,
I knew not what was adversity
Till I could fly full high under the sky.
Then dwelt a tercelet me nearby,
That seemed a spring of all gentleness;
Although he was full of treason and falseness,
It was so wrapped behind a humble manner,
And under a hue of truth in such a way,
Under a seeming eagerness to please,
That no person could have known it for a disguise,
So deep in grain he dyed his colors.
Right as a serpent hides himself under flowers
Till he may see his time for to bite,
Right so this god of love's hypocrite
Did so his ceremonies and obeisances,
And kept in semblance all his observances
That imitate the gentleness of love.
As in a tomb is all the fair above,
And under is the corpse, such as you know,
Such was this hypocrite, both cold and hot.
And in this way he served his intent
That, save the fiend, none knew what he meant,
Till he so long had wept and complained,
And many a year his service to me feigned,
Till my heart, too piteous and too nice,
All innocent of his sovereign malice,
Feared his death, as I thought,
And believing his oaths and surety,
Granted him love, upon this condition,
That evermore my honor and renown
Were saved, both privately and otherwise;
That is to say, that after his desire,
I gave him all my heart and all my thought—
God knows and he, nor would have done any other way—

And took his herte in chaunge for myn for ay.
But sooth is seyd, gon sithen many a day,
'A trew wight and a theef thenken nat oon'
And, whan he saugh the thing so fer y-goon
That I had graunted him fully my love,
In swich a gyse as I have seyd above,
And yeven him my trewe herte, as free
As he swoor he his herte yaf to me;
Anon this tygre, ful of doublenesse,
Fil on his knees with so devout humblesse,
With so heigh reverence, and, as by his chere,
So lyk a gentil lovere of manere,
So ravisshed, as it semed, for the joye,
That never Jason, ne Parys of Troye,
Jason? certes, ne non other man,
Sin Lameth was, that alderfirst bigan
To loven two, as writen folk biforn,
Ne never, sin the firste man was born,
Ne coude man, by twenty thousand part,
Countrefete the sophimes of his art;
Ne were worthy unbokele his galoche,
Ther doublenesse or feyning sholde approche,
Ne so coude thanke a wight as he did me!
His maner was an heven for to see
Til any womman, were she never so wys;
So peynted he and kembde at point-devys
As wel his wordes as his contenaunce.
And I so lovede him for his obeisaunce,
And for the trouthe I demed in his herte,
That, if so were that any thing him smerte,
Al were it never so lyte, and I it wiste,
Me thoughte, I felte deeth myn herte twiste.
And shortly, so forforth this thing is went,
That my wil was his willes instrument;
This is to seyn, my wil obeyed his wil
In alle thing, as fer as reson fil,
Keping the boundes of my worship ever.
Ne never hadde I thing so leef, ne lever,
As him, god woot! ne never shal na-mo.

And took his heart in exchange for my own forever.
But truth to tell, for many a day,
'A true person and a thief think not the same way.'
And when he saw the thing so far gone
That I had granted him fully my love
In such a guise as I have said above,
And given him my true heart as freely
As he swore he had given his heart to me,
Anon this tiger, full of doubleness,
Fell on his knees with such devout humbleness,
With such high reverence, and, as by his face,
So like a gentle lover in manner,
So carried away by joy
That neither Jason nor Paris of Troy[13]—
Jason? Certainly, no other man
Since Lamech[14] was, who first of all began
To love two, as wrote folk before—
No never, since the first man was born,
Could any man, by twenty thousand parts,
Counterfeit the sophisms of his art,
Nor would be worthy to unbuckle his sandals,
Compared to his doubleness and feigning,
Nor could so thank a person as he did me!
His manner was a heaven for to see
To any woman, were she ever so wise,
He so concealed his true intent
As well in his words as his countenance.
And I so loved him for his obeisance,
And for the truth I deemed in his heart,
That if anything him smarted,
Albeit ever so little, and I it knew,
I thought I felt death my heart twist.
And shortly, so far this thing went
That my will was his will's instrument;
That is to say, my will obeyed his will
In all things, as far as reason went,
Keeping the bounds of my honor ever.
Never had I loved anything so much,
As him, God knows, nor shall evermore.

This lasteth lenger than a yeer or two,
That I supposed of him noght but good.
But fynally, thus atte laste it stood,
That fortune wolde that he moste twinne
Out of that place which that I was inne.
Wher me was wo, that is no questioun;
I can nat make of it discripcioun;
For o thing dar I tellen boldely,
I knowe what is the peyne of deth ther-by;
Swich harm I felte for he ne mighte bileve.
So on a day of me he took his leve,
So sorwefully eek, that I wende verraily
That he had felt as muche harm as I,
Whan that I herde him speke, and saugh his hewe.
But nathelees, I thoughte he was so trewe,
And eek that he repaire sholde ageyn
With-inne a litel whyle, sooth to seyn;
And reson wolde eek that he moste go
For his honour, as ofte it happeth so,
That I made vertu of necessitee,
And took it wel, sin that it moste be.
As I best mighte, I hidde fro him my sorwe,
And took him by the hond, seint John to borwe,
And seyde him thus: 'lo, I am youres al;
Beth swich as I to yow have been, and shal.'
What he answerde, it nedeth noght reherce,
Who can sey bet than he, who can do werse?
Whan he hath al wel seyd, thanne hath he doon.
'Therfor bihoveth him a ful long spoon
That shal ete with a feend,' thus herde I seye.
So atte laste he moste forth his weye,
And forth he fleeth, til he cam ther him leste.
Whan it cam him to purpos for to reste,
I trowe he hadde thilke text in minde,
That 'alle thing, repeiring to his kinde,
Gladeth him-self'; thus seyn men, as I gesse;
Men loven of propre kinde newfangelnesse,
As briddes doon that men in cages fede.
For though thou night and day take of hem hede,

"This lasted longer than a year or two,
That I supposed of him nought but good.
But finally, thus at last it stood,
That Fortune willed he must depart
Out of the place where I was in.
I was in woe, that is no question;
I cannot make of it description.
But one thing I dare tell boldly;
I know what is the pain of death thereby;
Such hurt I felt for him that he would not stay.
So on a day he took his leave of me,
So sorrowfully also that I truly believed
That he felt as much pain as I,
When I heard him speak and change his hue.
But nevertheless, I thought he was so true,
And also that he return should again
Within a little while, truth to tell;
And reason said that he must go
For his honor, as often it happens so,
That I made virtue of necessity,
And took it well, since that it must be.
As I best might, I hid from him my sorrow,
And took him by the hand, and by Saint John
Said him thus: 'Lo, I am yours all;
Both as I have been to you and shall.'
What he answered, I need not rehearse;
Who can say better than he, who can do worse?
When he has all well said, then he has done.
'If you dine with the devil
Use a full long spoon,' thus have I heard said.
So at last he must go his way,
And forth he flew until he went where he wished.
When it came time for him to rest,
I believe he had in mind this text,
That 'all things, according to their nature,
Seek their pleasure;' thus say men, I guess.
Men by their nature love newfangledness,
As birds do that men in cages feed.[15]
For though they night and day take of them heed,

And strawe hir cage faire and softe as silk,
And yeve hem sugre, hony, breed and milk,
Yet right anon, as that his dore is uppe,
He with his feet wol spurne adoun his cuppe,
And to the wode he wol and wormes ete;
So newefangel been they of hir mete,
And loven novelryes of propre kinde;
No gentillesse of blood [ne] may hem binde.
So ferde this tercelet, allas the day!
Though he were gentil born, and fresh and gay,
And goodly for to seen, and humble and free,
He saugh up-on a tyme a kyte flee,
And sodeynly he loved this kyte so,
That al his love is clene fro me ago,
And hath his trouthe falsed in this wyse;
Thus hath the kyte my love in hir servyse,
And I am lorn with-outen remedye!"
And with that word this faucon gan to crye,
And swowned eft in Canaceës barme.

    Greet was the sorwe, for the haukes harme,
That Canacee and alle hir wommen made;
They niste how they mighte the faucon glade.
But Canacee hom bereth hir in hir lappe,
And softely in plastres gan hir wrappe,
Ther as she with hir beek had hurt hir-selve.
Now can nat Canacee but herbes delve
Out of the grounde, and make salves newe
Of herbes precious, and fyne of hewe,
To helen with this hauk; fro day to night
She dooth hir bisinesse and al hir might.
And by hir beddes heed she made a mewe,
And covered it with veluëttes blewe,
In signe of trouthe that is in wommen sene.
And al with-oute, the mewe is peynted grene,
In which were peynted alle thise false foules,
As beth thise tidifs, tercelets, and oules,
Right for despyt were peynted hem bisyde,
And pyes, on hem for to crye and chyde.

    Thus lete I Canacee hir hauk keping;

And straw their cage fair and soft as silk,
And give them sugar, honey, bread and milk,
Yet as soon as his door is up
He with his feet will kick adown his cup,
And to the wood he will go and on worms sup;
So newfangled would they have their food,
And love of novelties in their blood,
No gentleness of nature may them bind.
"So fared this tercelet, alas the day!
Though he was gentle born, and fresh and gay,
And goodly for to see, and humble and free,
He saw upon a time a kite fly,
And suddenly he loved this kite so
That all his love is clean from me gone,
And has his pledge betrayed in this way.
Thus has the kite my love in her service,
And I am lorn without remedy!"
And with that word this falcon began to cry
And swooned at once into Canacee's lap.

    Great was the sorrow for this hawk's pain
That Canacee and all her women made;
They knew not how they might this falcon comfort.
But Canacee home bore her in her lap,
And softly in bandages began her to wrap,
There where she had with her beak hurt herself.
Now Canacee cannot but delve herbs
Out of the ground, and make new salves
Of herbs precious and fine of hue
To heal this hawk. From day to night
She did her business with all her might,
And by her bed's head she made a mews
And covered it with cloth of velvet blue,
In sign of devotion that is in women seen.
And all without the mews was painted green,
On which were painted all these false fowls,
As be these small birds, tercelets and owls;
Right for spite were painted them beside,
Magpies, on them to cry and chide.

    Thus leave I Canacee her hawk keeping;

I wol na-more as now speke of hir ring,
Til it come eft to purpos for to seyn
How that this faucon gat hir love ageyn
Repentant, as the storie telleth us,
By mediacioun of Cambalus,
The kinges sone, of whiche I yow tolde.
But hennes-forth I wol my proces holde
To speke of aventures and of batailles,
That never yet was herd so grete mervailles.

    First wol I telle yow of Cambinskan,
That in his tyme many a citee wan;
And after wol I speke of Algarsyf,
How that he wan Theodora to his wyf,
For whom ful ofte in greet peril he was,
Ne hadde he ben holpen by the stede of bras;
And after wol I speke of Cambalo,
That faught in listes with the bretheren two
For Canacee, er that he mighte hir winne.
And ther I lefte I wol ageyn biginne.

I will no more now speak of her ring
Till it comes time to say
How this falcon got her love again
Repentant, as the story tells us,
By mediation of Cambalus,
The king's son, of whom I told.
But henceforth I will my story hold
To speak of adventures and battles
Of which never yet were heard so great marvels.
    First will I tell you of Genghis Khan,
Who in his time many a city won;
And after will I speak of Algarsyf,
How he won Theodora to become his wife,
For whom full often in great peril he was,
Nor had he help by a steed of brass;
And after I will speak of Cambalo,
Who fought in lists with brethren two
For Canacee, to prove their mettle to win her.
And where I left I will again begin.

The Phisiciens Tale

THER WAS, AS TELLETH Titus Livius,
A knight that called was Virginius,
Fulfild of honour and of worthinesse,
And strong of freendes and of greet richesse.

   This knight a doghter hadde by his wyf,
No children hadde he mo in al his lyf.
Fair was this mayde in excellent beautee
Aboven every wight that man may see;
For nature hath with sovereyn diligence
Y-formed hir in so greet excellence,
As though she wolde seyn, "lo! I, Nature,
Thus can I forme and peynte a creature,
Whan that me list; who can me countrefete?
Pigmalion noght, though he ay forge and bete,
Or grave, or peynte; for I dar wel seyn,
Apelles, Zanzis, sholde werche in veyn,
Outher to grave or peynte or forge or bete,
If they presumed me to countrefete.
For he that is the former principal
Hath maked me his vicaire general,
To forme and peynten erthely creaturis
Right as me list, and ech thing in my cure is
Under the mone, that may wane and waxe,
And for my werk right no-thing wol I axe;
My lord and I ben ful of oon accord;
I made hir to the worship of my lord.
So do I alle myne othere creatures,
What colour that they han, or what figures."—
Thus semeth me that Nature wolde seye.

   This mayde of age twelf yeer was and tweye,
In which that Nature hadde swich delyt.
For right as she can peynte a lilie whyt
And reed a rose, right with swich peynture
She peynted hath this noble creature
Er she were born, up-on hir limes free,
Wher-as by right swiche colours sholde be;
And Phebus dyed hath hir tresses grete

The Physician's Tale

THERE WAS, AS LIVY tells,[1]
A knight who was called Virginius,
Fulfilled of honor and of worthiness,
And strong of friends, and of great richness.
    This knight a daughter had he by his wife;
No children had he more in all his life.
Fair was this maid in excellent beauty
Above every person that man may see;
For Nature had with sovereign diligence
Formed her in so great excellence,
As though she would say, "Lo! I, Nature,
Thus can I form and paint a creature,
When I wish; who can me counterfeit?
Pygmalion[2] nought, though he forge and beat,
Or carve or paint; I dare well say
Apelles, Zeuxis,[3] should work in vain
Either to carve, or paint, or forge, or beat,
If they presumed me to counterfeit,
For he who is the principal maker
Has made me his vicar general,
To form and paint earthly creatures
Right as I wish, and each thing is in my power
Under the moon, that may wane and wax,
And for my work nothing will I ask;
My lord and I be fully of one accord.
I made her to the worship of my lord;
So do I all my other creatures,
What color they have or what figures."
Thus it seems to me that Nature would say.
    This maid of age twelve years was and two,
In which Nature had such delight.
For right as she can paint a lily white,
And red a rose, right with such colors
She had painted this noble creature,
Before she was born, upon her limbs freely,
Where by right such colors should be;
And Phoebus[4] had dyed her tresses long

Lyk to the stremes of his burned hete.
And if that excellent was hir beautee,
A thousand-fold more vertuous was she.
In hir ne lakked no condicioun,
That is to preyse, as by discrecioun.
As wel in goost as body chast was she;
For which she floured in virginitee
With alle humilitee and abstinence,
With alle attemperaunce and pacience,
With mesure eek of bering and array.
Discreet she was in answering alway;
Though she were wys as Pallas, dar I seyn,
Hir facound eek ful wommanly and pleyn,
No countrefeted termes hadde she
To seme wys; but after hir degree
She spak, and alle hir wordes more and lesse
Souninge in vertu and in gentillesse.
Shamfast she was in maydens shamfastnesse,
Constant in herte, and ever in bisinesse
To dyrve hir out of ydel slogardye.
Bacus hadde of hir mouth right no maistrye;
For wyn and youthe doon Venus encrece,
As men in fyr wol casten oile or grece.
And of hir owene vertu, unconstreyned,
She hath ful ofte tyme syk hir feyned,
For that she wolde fleen the companye
Wher lykly was to treten of folye,
As is at festes, revels, and at daunces.
That been occasions of daliaunces
Swich thinges maken children for to be
To sone rype and bold, as men may see,
Which is ful perilous, and hath ben yore.
For al to sone may she lerne lore
Of boldnesse, whan she woxen is a wyf.
    And ye maistresses in your olde lyf,
That lordes doghtres han in governaunce,
Ne taketh of my wordes no displesaunce;
Thenketh that ye ben set in governinges
Of lordes doghtres, only for two thinges;

Like unto the streams of his burnished heat.
And if excellent was her beauty,
A thousand-fold more virtuous was she.
In her lacked no feature
That is to praise, in her character.
As well in spirit as body chaste was she,
For which she flowered in virginity
With all humility and abstinence,
With all temperance and patience,
With measure also of bearing and appearance.
Discreet was she in answering always;
Though she was wise as Pallas,[5] dare I say,
Her speech was also full womanly and plain.
No counterfeited terms had she
To seem wise, but after her degree
She spoke, and all her words, more and less,
Conducive to virtue and gentleness.
Modest was she in maiden's modesty,
Constant in heart, and ever busy
To drive her out of idle sluggardy.
Bacchus had of her mouth no mastery;
For wine and youth does desire increase,
As men into a fire will cast oil or grease.
And by her own virtue, unconstrained,
She had full oftentime sickness feigned,
For she would flee the company
Where likely was to speak of folly,
As is at feasts, revels and at dances,
That be occasions of dalliances.
Such things make children be
Too soon ripe and bold, as men may see,
Which is full perilous and has been of yore.
For all too soon she may learn lore
Of boldness, when she has become a wife.

    And you governesses, in your old life,
Who lords' daughters have in governance,
Take of my words no offence.
Think that you be set as governesses
Of lords' daughters only for two things:

Outher for ye han kept your honestee,
Or elles ye han falle in freletee,
And knowen wel y-nough the olde daunce,
And han forsaken fully swich meschaunce
For evermo; therefore, for Cristes sake,
To teche hem vertu loke that ye ne slake.
A theef of venisoun, that hath forlaft
His likerousnesse, and al his olde craft,
Can kepe a forest best of any man.
Now kepeth hem wel, for if ye wol, ye can;
Loke wel that ye un-to no vice assente,
Lest ye be dampned for your wikke entente;
For who-so doth, a traitour is certeyn.
And taketh kepe of that that I shal seyn;
Of alle tresons sovereyn pestilence
Is whan a wight bitrayseth innocence.

Ye fadres and ye modres eek also,
Though ye han children, be it oon or two,
Your is the charge of al hir surveyaunce,
Whyl that they been under your governaunce.
Beth war that by ensample of your livinge,
Or by your necligence in chastisinge,
That they ne perisse; for I dar wel seye,
If that they doon, ye shul it dere abeye.
Under a shepherde softe and necligent
The wolf hath many a sheep and lamb to-rent.
Suffyseth oon ensample now as here,
For I mot turne agayn to my matere.

This mayde, of which I wol this tale expresse,
So kepte hir-self, hir neded no maistresse;
For in hir living maydens mighten rede,
As in a book, every good word or dede,
That longeth to a mayden vertuous;
She was so prudent and so bountevous.
For which the fame out-sprong on every syde
Bothe of hir beautee and hir bountee wyde;
That thurgh that land they preysed hir echone,
That loved vertu, save envye allone,
That sory is of other mennes wele,

Either because you have kept your honesty,
Or else you have fallen in frailty,
And know well enough the old dance,[6]
And have forsaken fully such mischance
For evermore; therefore, for Christ's sake,
To teach them virtue look that you do not slacken.
A thief of venison, who has forsaken
His greed and all his old craft,
Can keep a forest best of any man.
Now keep well, for if you will, you can.
Look well that you unto no vice assent,
Lest you be damned for your wicked intent;
For whoso does, a traitor is, certainly.
And take heed of what I shall say:
Of all treasons sovereign pestilence
Is when a person betrays innocence.

　　You mothers and you fathers also,
Though you have children, be it one or more,
Yours is the duty of all their protection,
While they be under your governance.
Beware, if by example of your living,
Or by your negligence in chastising,
They perish; for I dare well say
If they do, you shall for it dearly pay.
Under a shepherd soft and negligent
The wolf has many a sheep and many a lamb rent.
Suffice one example here,
For I must turn again to my matter.

　　This maid, of whom I will this tale express,
So kept herself that she needed no mistress,
For in her living maidens might read,
As in a book, every good word or deed
That belongs to a maiden virtuous,
She was so prudent and so bounteous.
For which the fame sprang out on every side,
Both of her beauty and her bounty wide,
That through that land they praised her each one
Who loved virtue, save envy alone,
Who sorry is of other men's weal

And glad is of his sorwe and his unhele;
(The doctour maketh this descripcioun).
This mayde up-on a day wente in the toun
Toward a temple, with hir moderdere,
As is of yonge maydens the manere.

    Now was ther thanne a justice in that toun,
That governour was of that regioun.
And so bifel, this juge his eyen caste
Up-on this mayde, avysinge him ful faste,
As she cam forby ther this juge stood.
Anon his herte chaunged and his mood,
So was he caught with beautee of this mayde;
And to him-self ful prively he sayde,
"This mayde shal be myn, for any man."

    Anon the feend in-to his herte ran,
And taughte him sodeynly, that he by slighte
The mayden to his purpos winne mighte.
For certes, by no force, ne by no mede,
Him thoughte, he was nat able for to spede;
For she was strong of freendes, and eek she
Confermed was in swich soverayn bountee,
That wel he wiste he mighte hir never winne
As for to make hir with hir body sinne.
For which, by greet deliberacioun,
He sente after a cherl, was in the toun,
Which that he knew for subtil and for bold.
This juge un-to this cherl his tale hath told
In secree wyse, and made him to ensure,
He sholde telle it to no creature,
And if he dide, he sholde lese his heed.
Whan that assented was this cursed reed,
Glad was this juge and maked him greet chere,
And yaf him yiftes preciouse and dere.

    Whan shapen was al hir conspiracye
Fro point to point, how that his lecherye
Parfourned sholde been ful subtilly,
As ye shul here it after openly,
Hoom gooth the cherl, that highte Claudius.
This false juge that highte Apius,

And glad is of his sorrow and his unheal.
(Saint Augustine made this description.)[7]
This maid upon a day went in the town
Toward a temple, with her mother dear,
As is of young maidens the manner.

Now was there then a justice in that town,
Who governor was of that region.
And so it befell that this judge his eyes cast
Upon this maid, making him to consider full fast,
As she came past where this judge stood.
Anon his heart changed and his mood,
So was he caught with the beauty of this maid.
And to himself privately he said,
"This maid shall be mine, before any man!"

Anon the fiend into his heart ran,
And taught him suddenly that he by sleight
The maiden to his purpose win he might.
For certainly, neither by force or payment,
He thought, would he be able to speed;
For she was strong of friends and also she
Confirmed was in such sovereign bounty
That well he knew he might never succeed
To make her with her body sin.
For which, by great deliberation,
He sent after a churl, who was in the town,
Whom he knew for subtlety and boldness.
This judge unto this churl his tale has told
In secrecy, and made him to assure
That he would tell it to no creature,
And if he did, he should lose his head.
When to this purpose they were agreed
Glad was this judge, and made him great cheer,
And gave to him gifts precious and dear.

When shaped was all their conspiracy
From point to point, how his lechery
Performed should be full subtly,
As you shall hear after openly,
Home went this churl, who was called Claudius.
This false judge, named Apius,

So was his name, (for this is no fable,
But knowen for historial thing notable,
The sentence of it sooth is, out of doute),
This false juge gooth now faste aboute
To hasten his delyt al that he may.
And so bifel sone after, on a day,
This false juge, as telleth us the storie,
As he was wont, sat in his consistorie,
And yaf his domes up-on sondry cas.
This false cherl cam forth a ful greet pas,
And seyde, "lord, if that it be your wille,
As dooth me right up-on this pitous bille,
In which I pleyne up-on Virginius.
And if that he wol seyn it is nat thus,
I wol it preve, and finde good witnesse,
That sooth is that my bille wol expresse."

The juge answerde, "of this, in his absence,
I may nat yeve diffinitif sentence.
Lat do him calle, and I wol gladly here;
Thou shalt have al right, and no wrong here."

Virginius cam, to wite the juges wille,
And right anon was rad this cursed bille;
The sentence of it was as ye shul here.

"To yow, my lord, sire Apius so dere,
Sheweth your povre servant Claudius,
How that a knight, called Virginius,
Agayns the lawe, agayn al equitee,
Holdeth, expres agayn the wil of me,
My servant, which that is my thral by right,
Which fro myn hous was stole up-on a night,
Whyl that she was ful yong; this wol I preve
By witnesse, lord, so that it nat yow greve.
She nis his doghter nat, what so he seye;
Wherfore to yow, my lord the juge, I preye,
Yeld me my thral, if that it be your wille."
Lo! this was al the sentence of his bille.

Virginius gan up-on the cherl biholde,
But hastily, er he his tale tolde,
And wolde have preved it, as sholde a knight,

(So was his name, for this is no fable,
But known as an historical thing notable;
The meaning of it is true, without doubt),
This false judge now went fast about
To hasten his delight all that he may.
And so it befell soon after, on a day,
This false judge, as tells us the story,
As he was wont, sat in his court,
And gave his decisions upon sundry cases.
This false churl came forth at full great pace,
And said, "Lord, if it be your will,
Do me right upon this piteous bill,
In which I complain of Virginius;
And if he will say it is not thus,
I will it prove, and find good witness,
The truth is that which my bill will express."

    The judge answered, "Of this, in his absence,
I may not give definitive sentence.
Have him called, and I will gladly hear;
You shall have justice, and no wrong fear."

    Virginius came to know the judge's will;
And right anon was read this cursed bill;
The meaning of it was as you shall hear:

    "To you, my lord, sir Apius so dear,
Show your poor servant Claudius
How a knight, called Virginius,
Against the law, against all justice,
Holds, expressly against my will,
My servant, who is my thrall by right,
Who from my house was stolen upon a night,
While she was full young; this will I prove
By witness, lord, so that it not you grieves.
She was not his daughter, no matter what he says.
Therefore to you, my lord the judge, I pray,
Yield me my thrall, if it be your will."
Lo, this was all the sentence of his bill.

    Virginius began upon this churl to stare,
But hastily, before he his tale told,
And would have proved it in battle as should a knight,

And eek by witnessing of many a wight,
That it was fals that seyde his adversarie,
This cursed juge wolde no-thing tarie,
Ne here a word more of Virginius,
But yaf his jugement, and seyde thus:—
    "I deme anon this cherl his servant have;
Thou shalt no lenger in thyn hous hir save.
Go bring hir forth, and put hir in our warde,
The cherl shal have his thral, this I awarde."
    And whan this worthy knight Virginius,
Thurgh sentence of this justice Apius,
Moste by force his dere doghter yiven
Un-to the juge, in lecherye to liven,
He gooth him hoom, and sette him in his halle,
And leet anon his dere doghter calle,
And, with a face deed as asshen colde,
Upon hir humble face he gan biholde,
With fadres pitee stiking thurgh his herte,
Al wolde he from his purpos nat converte.
    "Doghter," quod he, "Virginia, by thy name,
Ther been two weyes, outher deeth or shame,
That thou most suffre; allas! that I was bore!
For never thou deservedest wherfore
To deyn with a swerd or with a knyf.
O dere doghter, ender of my lyf,
Which I have fostred up with swich plesaunce,
That thou were never out of my remembraunce!
O doghter, which that art my laste wo.
And in my lyf my laste joye also,
O gemme of chastitee, in pacience
Take thou thy deeth, for this is my sentence.
For love and nat for hate, thou most be deed;
My pitous hand mot smyten of thyn heed.
Allas! that ever Apius thee say!
Thus hath he falsly juged thee to-day"—
And tolde hir al the cas, as ye bifore
Han herd; nat nedeth for to telle it more.
    "O mercy, dere fader," quod this mayde,
And with that word she both hir armes layde

And also by witnessing of many a person,
That all was false that said his adversary,
This cursed judge would no thing tarry,
Nor hear a word more from Virginius,
But gave his judgement, and said thus:

"I deem anon this churl his servant have;
You shall no longer in your house her keep.
Go bring her forth, and put her in our ward.
The churl shall have his thrall, this I award."

And when this worthy knight Virginius
Through sentence of this justice Apius,
Must by force his dear daughter give
Unto the judge, in lechery to live,
He went home, and sat in his hall,
And then had his dear daughter called,
And with a face dead as ashes cold,
Upon her humble face he began to look,
With father's pity striking through his heart,
All would he from his purpose not convert.

"Daughter," said he, "Virginia, by your name,
There be two ways, either death or shame,
That you must suffer; alas, that I was born!
For never you deserved for this reason
To die with a sword or with a knife.
O dear daughter, ender of my life,
Whom I have fostered up with such pleasure
That you were never out of my remembrance!
Oh daughter, who is my last woe,
And in my life my last joy also,
Oh gem of chastity, in patience
Take you your death, for this is my sentence.
For love, and not for hate, you must be dead;
My piteous hand must smite your head.
Alas, that ever Apius you saw!
Thus has he falsely judged you today"—
And told her all the case, as you before
Have heard; I need not tell it more.

"Oh mercy, dear father!" said this maid;
And with that word she both her arms laid

About his nekke, as she was wont to do:
The tres broste out of hir eyen two,
And seyde, "gode fader, shal I dye?
Is ther no grace? is there no remedye?"

    "No, certes, dere doghter myn," quod he.

    "Thanne yif me leyser, fader myn," quod she,
"My deeth for to compleyne a litel space;
For pardee, Jepte yaf his doghter grace
For to compleyne, er he hir slow, allas!
And god it woot, no-thing was hir trespas,
But for she ran hir fader first to see,
To welcome him with greet solempnitee."
And with that word she fil aswoyne anon,
And after, whan hir swowning is agon,
She ryseth up, and to hir fader sayde,
"Blessed be god, that I shal dye a mayde.
Yif me my deeth, er that I have a shame;
Doth with your child your wil, a goddes name!"

    And with that word she preyed him ful ofte,
That with his swerd he wolde smyte softe,
And with that word aswowne doun she fil.
Hir fader, with ful sorweful herte and wil,
Hir heed of smoot, and by the top it hente,
And to the juge he gan it to presente,
As he sat yet in doom in consistorie.
And whan the juge it saugh, as seith the storie,
He bad to take him and anhange him faste.
But right anon a thousand peple in thraste,
To save the knight, for routhe and for pitee,
For knowen was the false iniquitee.
The peple anon hath suspect of this thing,
By manere of the cherles chalanging,
That it was by th'assent of Apius;
They wisten wel that he was lecherous.
For which un-to this Apius they gon,
And caste him in a prison right anon,
Wher-as he slow him-self; and Claudius,
That servant was un-to this Apius,
Was demed for to hange upon a tree;

About his neck, as she was wont to do.
The tears burst out of her eyes two,
And said, "Good father, shall I die?
Is there no grace, is there no remedy?"
    "No, certainly, dear daughter mine," said he.
    "Then give me leisure, father mine," said she,
"My death to complain a little while;
For, by God, Jephtha gave his daughter grace[8]
To complain, before he her slew, alas!
And, God it knows, no thing was her trespass,
But she ran her father first to see,
To welcome him with great solemnity."
And with that word she fell aswoon anon,
And after, when her swooning was gone,
She rose up, and to her father said,
"Blessed be God that I shall die a maid!
Give me my death, before I have a shame;
Do with your child your will, in God's name!"
    And with that word she prayed him full often
That with his sword he would smite soft;
And with that word a-swooning down she fell.
Her father, with full sorrowful heart and will,
Her head off smote, and held it by the hair,
And to the judge he began to present it,
As he sat giving judgement in his court.
And when the judge it saw, as says the story,
He bade to take him and hang him fast;
But right anon a thousand people in thrust,
To save the knight, for mercy and pity,
For known was the false iniquity.
The people had anon suspected this thing,
By reason of the churl's claiming,
That it was by the assent of Apius;
They knew well that he was lecherous.
For which unto Apius they were gone
And cast him in a prison right anon,
There where he slew himself; and Claudius,
Who servant was unto this Apius,
Was deemed to hang upon a tree,

But that Virginius, of his pitee,
So preyde for him that he was exyled;
And elles, certes, he had been bigyled.
The remenant were anhanged, more and lesse,
That were consentant of this cursednesse.—
    Heer men may seen how sinne hath his meryte!
Beth war, for no man woot whom god wol smyte
In no degree, ne in which maner wyse
The worm of conscience may agryse
Of wikked lyf, though it so privee be,
That no man woot ther-of but god and he.
For be he lewed man, or elles lered,
He noot how sone that he shal been afered.
Therfore I rede yow this conseil take,
Forsaketh sinne, er sinne yow forsake.

But Virginius, of his pity,
So prayed for him that he was exiled,
Otherwise, certainly, would he have been killed.
The remainder were hanged, more and less,
Who had consented in this cursedness.

    Here may men see how sin is repaid.
Beware, for no man knows who God will smite
In any way, nor in what manner;
The worm of conscience may writhe inside
The wicked, though it so secret be
That no man knows thereof but God and he.
For be he an unlearned man, or else learned,
He knows not how soon that he shall be stricken.
Therefore I advise you now this counsel take:
Forsake sin, before your sins you forsake.

Endnotes

The General Prologue

1. (p. 3) *The holy blissful martyr:* Saint Thomas Becket, archbishop of Canterbury, was assassinated in Canterbury Cathedral on December 29, 1170. The place where he was martyred quickly became one of Europe's most popular pilgrimage sites.

2. (p. 3) *Tabard:* The Tabard is an inn in Southwark, a district across the Thames from London.

3. (p. 3) *anon:* At once, soon, shortly; the word occurs often in both Chaucer and Shakespeare.

4. (p. 5) *A Knight there was:* The list of battles that follows spans many decades, perhaps more than a single knight could be assumed to have undertaken, but all were places in which English knights fought during the fourteenth century, either as crusaders or in support of the ambitions of English or other rulers.

5. (p. 7) *Flanders, Artois and Picardy:* These are places where the English campaigned during the so-called Hundred Years' War. The references here are probably to an abortive "crusade" against Flemish schismatics led by Bishop Dispencer of Norwich.

6. (p. 9) *Stratford at Bow:* The Benedictine Nunnery of Saint Leonard's was located here, about two miles from London.

7. (p. 11) Amor vincit omnia: This translates from the Latin as "love conquers all" (from Virgil's *Eclogues* 10.69). The phrase originally referred to erotic passion, but also was used in medieval Christian discourse.

8. (p. 11) *The rule of Saint Maurus or of Saint Benedict:* Benedict of Nursia (c.480–c.543) composed the *Rule* that came to be the authoritative document governing the life of Western European Christian monks. Saint Maurus was an influential follower of Benedict.

9. (p. 11) *Augustine:* Saint Augustine of Hippo (354–430), an influential Church father, was the supposed author of a monastic rule followed by the religious order of Augustinian canons.

10. (p. 13) *A Friar:* A member of one of the four fraternal or mendicant orders, founded in the thirteenth century to combat heresy and to preach the faith to the largely ignorant laity of the Catholic Church. Originally they were to live in poverty, constantly moving from place to place and surviving by begging.

11. (p. 13) *power of confession:* During the thirteenth century, the Papacy allowed members of the mendicant orders to hear confessions, modifying the rule that laypeople could confess only to their parish priest. Because it was customary to offer a small donation to one's confessor after confessing one's sins, the parish clergy resented the intrusion of the friars and collaborated in the accusation that friars gave easy penances in return for larger donations (the sin of simony).

12. (p. 15) *And gave a certain payment for the grant:* A friar would be granted by his order a certain area (his "ferme") in which to beg, from which he was expected to raise a certain amount (his "rente"). No other friars could beg in this area, and if the friar made more (his "purchas") than his assigned "rente," he sometimes kept the excess (improperly).

13. (p. 15) *In principio:* "In the beginning . . ." (Latin).

14. (p. 15) *scholar:* Modernized from "Clerk" in Middle English.

15. (p. 17) *Middleburgh and Orowelle:* Dutch and English ports, respectively, crucial to the export of wool and other commodities by English merchants in the late fourteenth century.

16. (p. 19) *Sergeant of the Law:* One of a small group of powerful lawyers entitled to hear and argue the most important legal cases.

17. (p. 19) *parvis:* From the French word *paradise.* The porch of Saint Paul's Cathedral in London, where clients came to consult with sergeants on legal matters.

18. (p. 19) *assizes cases:* Only sergeants could serve on assizes courts, which had jurisdiction over civil cases in English counties.

19. (p. 19) *Franklin:* A landholder of free but not noble status; many such men became rich and prominent after the Plague of 1348–1349 made land available for purchase by survivors.

20. (p. 19) *Of his temperament he was sanguine:* The theory of humors divided people into four groups, each dominated by a specific "humor" (bodily fluid) that determined their physical features and temperament. The Franklin's behavior, as described in his "portrait," accords with the sanguine (blood-dominated) humor.

21. (p. 19) *Saint Julian:* Patron saint of hospitality.

22. (p. 21) *His table . . . for his dinner set:* Boards set upon trestles served as tables for meals in the great hall of a castle. Normally the tables were disassembled after each meal; the Franklin leaves his tables permanently assembled as a sign of his readiness to entertain all comers.

23. (p. 21) *parish guild:* An association of people from one or more trades and professions, attached to a parish church where they hold periodic services

under the protection of the patron saint of the parish. Parish guilds also levied membership fees that were then used to make contributions to the widows of guild members and to support sick and destitute members.

24. (p. 23) *Shipman:* Ship captain.

25. (p. 23) *the signs for his patient:* Medieval medicine made use of astrological lore as well as the theory of humors in its treatment of the sick and injured.

26. (p. 25) *The old Aesculapius . . . and Gilbert:* This passage lists a pantheon of classical and Arabic medieval medical theorists and practitioners.

27. (p. 25) *Of clothmaking . . . Ypres and Ghent:* In the late fourteenth century, English cloth began to be exported in large quantities, in competition with the cloth manufactured in the Flemish towns of Ypres and Ghent. As a cloth-maker or clothier, the Wife of Bath is an entrepreneur who presides over the production of cloth by many cottage workers, then collects and sells the finished product to merchants who will market it in England or abroad.

28. (p. 25) *certain so angry . . . out of charity:* This is a charge frequently made against women in misogynist literary discourse.

29. (p. 25) *Husbands at church door:* In much of medieval Europe, weddings were celebrated with a priest in attendance, but at the front door of the church rather than at the altar.

30. (p. 27) *To Rome she had been . . . :* The list that follows includes several popular European pilgrimage destinations.

31. (p. 27) *excommunicate for his tithes:* Laypeople were expected by the Church to commit a portion of their income (usually one-tenth) to support the parish priest. Many resented the necessity of tithing.

32. (p. 29) *chantry-priest . . . chaplain for a guild:* A chantry-priest was employed by a wealthy family to say masses periodically for deceased members of the family buried within a private (chantry) chapel within a church. Parish guilds required the services of a priest to say mass for the deceased members of the guild. In the years following the plague, some poorly paid country parish priests decamped for London, where they could earn better pay as employees of guilds or well-to-do urban families.

33. (p. 29) *Plowman:* Farmhand.

34. (p. 31) *Reeve:* The head serf of an estate, who functioned as the manager or accountant for the property.

35. (p. 31) *Summoner:* The official who brought wrongdoers before the ecclesiastical court, in this instance having to do with matrimony, adultery, and fornication.

36. (p. 31) *Pardoner:* A pardoner sold papal indulgences (pardons for sinners); some pardoners were frauds.

37. (p. 31) *Manciple:* Steward; purchaser of provisions and keeper of accounts.

38. (p. 35) Questio quid iuris: The question is, what point of law applies? (Latin).

39. (p. 35) *the Archdeacon's curse:* The archdeacon was the diocesan official responsible for the operation of the ecclesiastical courts in that diocese.

40. (p. 37) *Rouncival:* Saint Mary Rouncival was a hospital at Charing Cross, at that time outside London, that used pardoners to raise the money needed for its operation. Donations to the hospital would earn the donor remission of some of the purgatorial pain he or she would otherwise encounter. The system was subject to abuse.

41. (p. 37) *A veronica:* A badge showing that the wearer had made a pilgrimage to Rome. It depicted the cloth that Veronica used to wipe the face of Christ during his Passion; an image of Christ's face was believed to have been imprinted on the cloth.

42. (p. 39) *Bell:* The Bell Inn.

43. (p. 41) *And Plato says . . . The words must be cousin to the deed:* The phrase is originally from Plato's *Timaeus*, which Chaucer could have known in the Latin translation by Calcidius; it is repeated in Boethius' *Consolation of Philosophy*, which Chaucer translated.

44. (p. 45) *Saint Thomas a Watering:* The reference is to a brook a short distance outside London on the Canterbury road.

The Knight's Tale

1. (p. 51) *Fortune and her false wheel:* Medieval images of the goddess Fortune characteristically depict her with an ever-turning wheel on which she places great rulers, who first rise on it, then inevitably fall off it as it revolves.

2. (p. 53) *king Capaneus:* One of seven kings who, according to classical legend, attacked the city of Thebes. The lore about Thebes in "The Knight's Tale" is based on Statius' Roman epic the *Thebaid*, directly or through the mediation of Boccaccio's romance epic *Il Teseida*, on which Chaucer's tale is based.

3. (p. 55) *The Minotaur:* A mythical creature, half human, half bull, slain by Theseus as a young man, with the help of Ariadne, whom he promised to marry but later abandoned on the island of Naxos. The story was widely known in classical antiquity.

4. (p. 61) *Some wicked aspect . . . some constellation:* Astrology is based on the belief that the interaction of planets with the constellations they pass through in the night sky has profound effects on human lives.

5. (p. 65) *A worthy duke named Perotheus:* The friendship of Theseus and Pirithous was reported in a number of classical sources, which do not, however, include a journey to the underworld to rescue a dead friend.

6. (p. 73) *Juno, jealous, angry and wild:* Chaucer derives Juno's hatred of Thebes from the *Thebaid*, where the goddess is depicted as furious with Jupiter for his love affairs with Theban women.

7. (p. 83) *"In hope that I something green may get":* This is an oblique reference to the fact that young men and women went into the woods to celebrate May and along the way managed to get "green" on their clothes from lying on the grass to make love. Compare the famous English carol "Greensleeves."

8. (p. 83) *Seldom is Friday like the week's other days:* In folklore, Friday was the most changeable day of the week.

9. (p. 89) *Who stood in the clearing with a spear:* In hunting ferocious animals, beaters and dogs formed a circle around the beast's lair, leaving a gap through which it would seek to escape, but at which those responsible for killing it would wait with their weapons.

10. (p. 97) benedicite: God bless you (Latin).

11. (p. 103) *a cuckoo sitting on her hand:* In medieval popular culture, the cuckoo, which laid its eggs in other birds' nests, was a symbol of the cuckolded husband.

12. (p. 105) *the mount of Cythaeron:* A confusion with the island of Cytherea, traditional home of Venus in classical legend.

13. (p. 105) *Medea and Circe:* A mortal woman and a goddess, respectively, famous in classical legend as practitioners of sorcery to gain power over mortal lovers.

14. (p. 105) *Turnus:* Aeneas' rival for the hand of Lavinia in Virgil's *Aeneid*.

15. (p. 105) *Croesus:* King of Lydia, fabled in classical civilization for his wealth and bad fortune.

16. (p. 107) *Crime, Treachery, and all the plotting . . . :* The elaborate description of misdeeds and calamities within the temple of Mars reflects the fact that Mars was both the classical god of war and the planetary deity whose astrological influence was widely believed to result in all types of violence, intended or accidental.

17. (p. 109) *Puella . . . Rubeus:* Figures related to Mars in medieval systems of divination.

18. (p. 111) *Callisto:* A nymph, follower of Diana, who was punished by the goddess for becoming pregnant. See Ovid, *Metamorphoses*, 2, 409–507.

19. (p. 111) *Daphne:* Beautiful daughter of a river god, wooed by Apollo and, as she flees his advances, turned into a laurel tree. See Ovid, *Metamorphoses,* 2, 452–567.

20. (p. 111) *Actaeon:* A hunter who saw Diana naked at her bath and was punished by the goddess by being turned into a stag and hunted down by his own hounds. See Ovid, *Metamorphoses,* 3, 138–252.

21. (p. 111) *Lucina:* Diana in her manifestation as the goddess of childbirth.

22. (p. 119) *And in her hour:* Each planet was supposed to govern certain hours of the day, depending upon certain variables. Palamon, Emily, and Arcita all visit the temples of their respective protecting deities at the proper time for the god or goddess in question to have the most influence.

23. (p. 127) *When Vulcan caught you in his net:* In classical myth, Venus and Mars enjoy a love affair until they are discovered by Venus' husband, Vulcan, smith of the gods, who imprisons them in a net for all the inhabitants of Olympus to see and laugh at.

24. (p. 131) *pale Saturn, baleful and cold:* Saturn is the planetary deity (compare "my orbit, that has a circuit so wide to turn") who presides over catastrophe and chaos. His power is especially strong in Leo, "the sign of the lion."

25. (p. 137) *prime:* This is a reference to the system of canonical hours, the ancient division of the hours of the day; monks and clerics said certain prayers at set times during the day. Prime is the "first" hour of the day, 6 A.M.

26. (p. 159) *The First Mover . . . the fair chain of love:* The First (or Unmoved) Mover is the Aristotelian principle of origin for the created world. Classical myth and, later, neoplatonic philosophy imagined the universe held together in a harmony of discordant parts by a great chain extending from the highest heaven to the least animate parts of the earth.

The Miller's Tale

1. (p. 167) *Pilate's voice:* In medieval mystery plays, based on biblical stories and incidents, villains such as Pontius Pilate, the Roman governor who gave up Jesus to be crucified, ranted and raved in a high, loud, hoarse voice, not only at other characters, but at the audience. This is the first of several references in "The Miller's Tale" to characters and episodes from mystery plays.

2. (p. 171) *astrolabe:* An instrument used to measure distances and determine latitude, hence of special use to sailors. Chaucer wrote (more precisely translated) a treatise on the use of the astrolabe.

3. (p. 171) *augrim-stones:* Counting stones for arithmetical calculation.

4. (p. 171) *the king's note:* A song now unknown. It may have symbolic significance in the story, like the Annunciation song "Angelus ad virginem," the situation of which is broadly parodied in Nicholas' wooing of Alison.

5. (p. 175) *Osney:* Suburb of Oxford, site of an Augustinian abbey.

6. (p. 175) *quack:* Pun on a colloquial word for the *pudendum mulieris* (Latin for female external genitalia).

7. (p. 177) *clerk:* Assistant.

8. (p. 177) *Saint Paul's windows cut in his shoes:* The reference is to a design, similar to the pattern of Saint Paul's Cathedral windows, cut into the leather of his shoe uppers.

9. (p. 177) *Well could he let blood . . . .:* Absolon appears to have mastered the often-repeated skills of a barber-surgeon and a notary. Compare the famous Figaro of Beaumarchais' plays and Rossini's opera.

10. (p. 181) *Herod:* He played the loud and boastful character of King Herod in the medieval mystery plays.

11. (p. 183) *Saint Frideswide:* Eighth-century abbess and patron saint of Oxford, reputed to have struck blind, and later cured, a noble suitor when he attempted to ravish her.

12. (p. 183) *astromony:* John mispronounces "astronomy."

13. (p. 185) paternoster: The Latin words *pater noster*, meaning "our Father," are the opening words of the Lord's Prayer.

14. (p. 187) *quarter night:* About 9 P.M.

15. (p. 189) *The troubles of Noah . . . wife to ship:* Noah's difficulties with his shrewish wife, and her resistance to joining him and their children in the Ark, was a popular subject in the mystery plays, in which it usually took the form of knockabout comedy à la Punch and Judy.

16. (p. 193) *curfew-time:* About 8 P.M.

17. (p. 195) *chapel bell:* About 4 A.M.

18. (p. 201) *Saint Neot:* Ninth-century saint, peripherally connected with the Anglo-Saxon King Alfred's supposed founding of Oxford University.

19. (p. 201) *coulter:* Metal part of the plow, sometimes a round disk, that cuts into the earth.

20. (p. 203) *Harrow!:* Cry of distress, legally enjoining assistance by those who hear it.

21. (p. 203) *Noel's flood:* The carpenter confuses Noah with Noel.

The Reeve's Tale

1. (p. 207) *medlar fruit:* A fruit that is inedible until it is almost rotten.
2. (p. 213) *Solar Hall at Cambridge:* Another name for King's Hall, an undergraduate institution that is part of Cambridge University.
3. (p. 219) *cake:* The reference is to a loaf of bread.
4. (p. 221) *Saint Cuthbert:* Seventh-century bishop of Lindisfarne in northern England, hence appropriately invoked by the northerners Allen and John.
5. (p. 229) *holy cross of Bromholm:* Bromholm was a shrine in Norfolk; it contained a supposed relic of the True Cross and as such was an object of pilgrimage and devotion.
6. (p. 229) In manus tuas: These words are the beginning of a Christian Passion prayer: "Into your hands I commend my spirit, oh Lord" (Latin).

The Wife of Bath's Tale

1. (p. 233) "*(If I so often might have wedded be)*": Both the Wife of Bath and Chaucer are deliberately vague here.
2. (p. 233) *degree:* Station in society, rank.
3. (p. 233) *Cana of Galilee:* This is a reference to a passage in the Bible, John 2:1, in which Jesus turns water into wine.
4. (p. 233) *in reproof to the Samaritan:* In the Bible, John 4:6, Jesus encounters a Samaritan woman at a well and speaks the words that follow.
5. (p. 241) *Ptolemy: Read in his Almagest:* Ptolemy, a Greek astronomer and mathematician (second century C.E.), wrote an astronomical treatise to which Arab scholars gave the name *Al-majisti*, "the greatest." The quoted proverb is from an Arabic collection added as a preface to a Latin translation of Ptolemy's treatise.
6. (p. 243) *Essex:* At Dunmow, in Essex, a side of bacon was awarded annually to couples claiming that they had not argued or been unfaithful to each other during the previous year.
7. (p. 245) *the talking bird is crazy:* This is an allusion to a story, like that told in "The Manciple's Tale," in which a talking bird reveals a wife's adultery to a husband. In this version, the wife, by a trick, convinces the husband that the bird is crazy and that its testimony is therefore worthless.
8. (p. 249) *the Apostle's name:* The apostle Paul wrote the following lines in his first letter to Timothy, which appear in the New Testament as 1 Timothy 2:9.
9. (p. 251) *Argus:* Mythical creature with 100 eyes, commissioned by the goddess Juno to keep watch on Io, one of Jupiter's lovers.

10. (p. 257) *the sepulchre of old Darius:* A fictitious tomb for King Darius of Persia, supposedly designed by an equally fictitious Jewish architect, Appelles (not the legendary Greek painter).

11. (p. 259) *my secrets . . . parish priest:* All Christians had to confess their sins, usually to their parish priest, and receive Communion at least once a year to avoid damnation.

12. (p. 263) *the birthmark of Saint Venus' seal:* This kind of birthmark, often in the genital area, was traditionally associated with a libidinous nature.

13. (p. 263) *pudendum:* The wife here is using a polite word for female external genitalia, instead of a word more colloquial but considered vulgar.

14. (p. 263) *My ascendant was Taurus, and Mars therein:* The Wife claims that her sexual voracity is determined by the position of Mars in Taurus (a constellation associated with Venus) at the time of her birth.

15. (p. 265) *Simplicius Gallus:* The incident is taken from Valerius Maximus' popular late-classical collection *Facta et dicta memorabilia* (*Memorable Facts and Sayings*).

16. (p. 267) *Valerie and Theofraste:* Valerius supposedly wrote a letter to his friend Rufinus urging him not to marry. The letter, actually written by Walter Map in the twelfth century, was widely known. Theophrastus, a classical author, wrote an anti-matrimonial tract, *The Golden Book of Theophrastus on Marriage*, that was preserved in Saint Jerome's fourth-century C.E. anti-matrimonial *Letter Against Jovinian*, which is extensively paraphrased and mocked in the first part of the Wife of Bath's prologue.

17. (p. 267) *Tertulian, Chrysippus, Trotula:* Tertulian was an early Christian ascetic theologian; Chrysippus was a misogynist writer quoted by Jerome; Trotula was an eleventh-century female physician at Salerno, site of a famous medical school in Italy.

18. (p. 267) *Who painted the lion:* In one of Aesop's fables, a lion challenges a man painting a picture of a hunter killing a lion; the lion claims the picture would look quite different if painted by him.

19. (p. 269) *The children of Mercury and of Venus:* That is, people born under the astrological influence of those planets.

20. (p. 269) *Hercules and his Deianira:* Deianira was Hercules' second wife. She gave him a poisoned shirt, mistakenly thinking it would restore his love; it killed him instead.

21. (p. 269) *Pasiphae:* The wife of King Minos of Crete, she fell in love with a bull and gave birth to the monster Minotaur (compare with note 3 of "The Knight's Tale").

22. (p. 271) *Clytemnestra:* The wife of King Agamemnon of Greece, she killed her husband on his return from the Trojan War along with a concubine he had brought home with him.

23. (p. 271) *Amphiaraus:* This Greek warrior was betrayed by his wife into fighting against Thebes (compare with "The Knight's Tale," which begins with Theseus's attack on Thebes as part of that war).

24. (p. 271) *Latumius . . . Arrius:* The reference is to the story of the hanging tree, which is widely quoted in misogamous literature.

25. (p. 275) *Sittingbourne:* Town on the road to Canterbury.

26. (p. 277) *beggars and other holy friars:* The lines that follow are a compendium of satirical commonplaces directed against the mendicant friars.

27. (p. 277) *limitour:* Friar licensed to beg within certain geographical limits or boundaries.

28. (p. 281) *Ovid . . . Midas:* Ovid tells the story of Midas and his ass's ears in *Metamorphoses* 11. In Ovid's version, it is Midas' barber, not his wife, who reveals his secret.

29. (p. 291) *Dante:* Many of the old woman's arguments are taken from Dante's *Il Convivio* (*The Banquet*), book 4.

The Clerk's Tale

1. (p. 299) *Petrarch:* Chaucer may have met Italian poet and philosopher Petrarch (1304–1374) on a trip to Italy in 1373. "The Clerk's Tale" is based in good part on Petrarch's Latin version of Boccaccio's story of Griselda, the last novella of his *Decameron*.

2. (p. 299) *Legnano:* Giovanni da Legnano, a fourteenth-century Italian legal scholar.

3. (p. 341) *papal bulls:* A bull was an official papal letter, closed with a leaden seal (*bulla*).

4. (p. 367) *The Envoy:* An envoy (or envoi) is an explanatory concluding section of a poem or prose work.

5. (p. 367) *Chichevache:* In stories, Chichevache was a cow that fed only on patient wives and so was very lean.

The Merchant's Tale

1. (p. 371) *Saint Thomas of India:* Thomas the Apostle was reputed in medieval legend to have traveled to India to evangelize its inhabitants.

2. (p. 373) *fools who are secular:* Here "secular" is used in the sense of "not clergy"; the Merchant is ironic at January's expense.

3. (p. 375) *Theofrastus:* See note 16 to "The Wife of Bath's Tale."

4. (p. 379) *Rebecca . . . Judith . . . Abigail . . . Esther:* In the Hebrew Scriptures, these four women demonstrated their wisdom through trickery, albeit in good causes.

5. (p. 379) *Seneca:* Seneca was a first-century C.E. Roman philosopher, politician, and educator; the saying is actually from Fulgentius' late-classical *Mythologies.*

6. (p. 379) *Cato:* The *Dystichs of Cato,* a collection of maxims and proverbs used in medieval elementary education, has no connection with the Roman philosopher of that name.

7. (p. 383) *Placebo:* In Latin, *placebo* means "I will please"; it is a traditional name for a counselor who offers only advice his lord wants to hear.

8. (p. 385) *Solomon:* To the biblical king Solomon were attributed many statements of proverbial wisdom, including the one that follows.

9. (p. 387) *a man ought him consider well / To whom he gives his land or his goods:* Another false attribution to Seneca, this time from the *Dystichs* falsely attributed to Cato (see note 6, above).

10. (p. 395) *The Wife of Bath, if you have understood:* Only here does a character within a tale refer to an "actual" Canterbury pilgrim.

11. (p. 395) *Sarah and Rebecca:* Sarah, Abraham's wife, and Rebecca, Isaac's wife, are figures in the biblical book of Genesis.

12. (p. 397) *Orpheus, nor Amphioun . . . Joab . . . Theodamas:* Orpheus and Amphioun were legendary musicians of classical antiquity. In the Bible (2 Samuel 2:28), Joab was a trumpeter for Israel. Theodamus was an Argive soothsayer in Statius' *Thebaid,* a first-century C.E. Roman epic of the siege of Thebes.

13. (p. 397) *Martianus:* Martianus Capella, a fifth-century C.E. grammarian, wrote *The Marriage of Mercury and Philology,* a treatise on the liberal arts in the guise of an allegorical marriage celebration.

14. (p. 397) *Queen Esther:* The heroine of the biblical Book of Esther saved the Jews from persecution by King Ahasuerus and his wicked henchman Haman.

15. (p. 401) *Sir Constantine:* Constantine the African was a translator of Arab medical texts, including *De Coitu,* a manual on sexual disorders and their cures.

16. (p. 405) *The moon . . . was into Cancer gliding:* The moon has passed from one constellation into the next during the four days of May's restriction to her bedchamber.

17. (p. 413) *That he who wrote the Romance of the Rose:* An allegorical dream vision describing the quest of a young man to achieve sexual union with

his beloved, *Romance of the Rose* was the work of two thirteenth-century authors—first Guillaume de Lorris, then Jean de Meun; it was extremely popular and influential.

18. (p. 413) *Priapus:* The Roman god of sexual desire, as well as gardens, Priapus is usually depicted with an erect phallus.

19. (p. 413) *Pluto and his queen, / Proserpina, and all their fairy crew:* In Roman mythology, Pluto, god of the underworld, kidnapped Proserpina, daughter of Ceres, goddess of the harvest. Medieval Europe knew the story through Claudian's late-classical poem *De raptu Proserpinae* (*The Rape of Proserpina*), mentioned below.

20. (p. 417) *Argus:* After Jupiter seduced Io, she was turned into a cow by the god's jealous consort, Juno, who commissioned Argus, a creature with 100 eyes, to keep eternal watch over her.

21. (p. 417) *By Pyramus and Thisbe . . . kept apart by measures strict:* In Ovid's *Metamorphoses*, Pyramus and Thisbe are young lovers forbidden by their parents from seeing one another; their attempt to elope ends tragically.

22. (p. 419) *"Rise up . . . No fault in you have I known in all my life":* The lines paraphrase the biblical Song of Songs, also known as the Song of Solomon.

23. (p. 423) *Phoebus . . . was that time in* Gemini: These lines describe a date in early May.

24. (p. 423) *Solomon:* The Middle Ages attributed to Solomon several books of the Old Testament (Hebrew scriptures), including Ecclesiastes, from which the saying below is taken (Ecclesiastes 7:28).

25. (p. 423) *Jesus*, filius Syrak: Jesus, the son of Sirach, was the author of the book of Ecclesiasticus in the Vulgate (Latin) Old Testament. Saint Jerome (346–420), translated much of what Christians called the Old Testament from Hebrew into Latin during the last years of the fourth and first years of the fifth centuries. These translations, and Jerome's of the Four Gospels (from Greek), were combined in following centuries with other, older translations to make a complete Latin Bible that came to be called the *versio vulgata*, or common edition.

The Franklin's Tale

1. (p. 437) *Bretons:* The Bretons were famous as storytellers, circulating tales of King Arthur and other legendary Celtic heroes. So-called "Breton lays" were short narrative poems about love and adventure, often featuring supernatural elements.

2. (p. 437) *Marcus Tullius Cicero:* The Roman politician and philosopher Cicero was widely known in medieval Europe for, among other works, his rhetorical treatise *De inventione.*

3. (p. 453) *Apollo:* The sun god, to whom Aurelius prays because of his influence on Lucina, goddess of the moon and thus controller of tides.

4. (p. 457) *Pamphilus for Galatea:* The twelfth-century Latin scholastic "comedy" of Pamphilus' love for Galatea, whom he eventually rapes, circulated widely in small manuscripts from which the modern English word "pamphlet" derives.

5. (p. 457) *Orleans in France:* Seat of a university, and center of astrological studies.

6. (p. 457) *eight and twenty mansions / That belong to the moon:* In astrology, the division of the lunar month into twenty-eight equal divisions, in order to make calculations about human fortunes.

7. (p. 463) *Phoebus waxed old . . . . :* A description of December and its characteristic activities, taken from the medieval tradition of the "labors of the months"; however, Janus, the two-faced god, is taken from descriptions of January.

8. (p. 465) *tables Toledan . . . :* The following lines reveal the Franklin's knowledge of astrological procedures, even as he mocks them. The temporary "disappearance" of the rocks may only be a natural result of an exceptionally high tide.

9. (p. 471) *these stories bear witness:* Dorigen calls to mind a series of classical stories and legends of women who killed themselves rather than submit to sexual degradation. Chaucer would have found these stories in a section of Jerome's treatise against the monk Jovinian (see note 17 to "The Wife of Bath's Tale").

The Pardoner's Tale

1. (p. 485) *corpus bones:* Christ's bones.

2. (p. 485) *"You sweet friend, you Pardoner":* There appears to be a sexually derogatory element in the Host's summons; compare the narrator's comment in "The General Prologue" that he believes the Pardoner to be a gelding or a mare.

3. (p. 485) *"by Saint Runyan!":* The Pardoner is mimicking the Host, who has used this oath a few lines before. This is a pun on Ronan, an Irish saint, and "runyan," kidney; the latter word also has sexual overtones.

4. (p. 485) *Radix malorum est Cupiditas:* Greed is the root of all evil (Latin).

5. (p. 487) *Saints' relics they are:* The relics of holy men and women were highly prized (and often fabricated) in medieval Europe, as they were considered to possess some of the power that the saints had during their lifetime, as conduits of divine grace and power.

6. (p. 493) *Our blessed Lord's body they into pieces tore:* Swearing, and all other sins for which Christ died on the cross, were thought therefore to have contributed to the brutality of his Passion.

7. (p. 493) *Lot:* See the Bible, Genesis 19:30–36.

8. (p. 493) *Herod . . . Slew John the Baptist:* See the Bible, Matthew 14:3–12 and Mark 6:17–29, with no mention of Herod's drunkenness, however.

9. (p. 493) *Seneca:* Roman philosopher, from whose Epistle 83 the lines are taken.

10. (p. 495) *"Meat unto stomach, . . .":* See the Bible, 1 Corinthians 6:13.

11. (p. 495) *The apostle, weeping, said full piteously . . . . :* See the Bible, Philippians 3:18–19.

12. (p. 497) *turn substance into accident:* A punning reference to the doctrine of Transubstantiation, which seeks to explain what happens to the Eucharistic host at the moment of consecration as Christ's body and blood. The definition was contested by religious reformers in Chaucer's day.

13. (p. 497) *Samson:* From the Bible, the great Israelite warrior in the book of Judges.

14. (p. 499) *Attila:* This king of the Huns died in 453 C.E. as a result of drinking too much.

15. (p. 499) *Lemuel:* In the Bible, Proverbs 31:4, Lemuel is advised not to give wine to kings, lest they reveal all the realm's secrets.

16. (p. 501) *Stilbon . . . Demetrius:* Chaucer found the stories of Demetrius and Stilbon in John of Salisbury's *Policraticus,* a twelfth-century treatise on court politics.

17. (p. 501) *Jeremiah:* See the Bible, Jeremiah 4:2.

18. (p. 501) *Hayles:* The reference is to the abbey of Hayles in Gloucestershire, which claimed to have a vial of Christ's blood.

19. (p. 503) *bitchy bones two:* Dice.

20. (p. 503) *this plague:* The so-called Black Death that swept through Europe in the late 1340s, or one of the later outbreaks of the plague that recurred during the fourteenth century and beyond.

21. (p. 507) *In Holy Writ you may yourselves well read:* See the Bible, Leviticus 19:32.

22. (p. 515) *Avicenna:* The reference is to Ibn Sina (980–1037 c.e.), an Arabic medical theorist and author of the widely known textbook the *Canon of Medicine*, which covers poisons in book 4.

The Prioress's Tale

1. (p. 521) *Oh Lord, our Lord . . . Do they celebrate your praise:* The opening stanza recalls the biblical verses of Psalm 8 (Vulgate numbering).

2. (p. 521) *the white lily flower / Who bore you, and is a maid always:* The reference is to the Virgin Mary.

3. (p. 521) *Oh bush unburned, burning in Moses' sight:* In medieval biblical interpretation, the burning bush seen by Moses (Exodus 3:2) was frequently understood to anticipate the virgin birth of Jesus.

4. (p. 521) *Conceived was the Father's knowledge:* In medieval theology Jesus was often spoken of as *Sapientia Dei*, the knowledge or wisdom of God.

5. (p. 523) *Ave Maria:* The prayer Ave Maria (Hail Mary) is based on the Archangel Gabriel's words to Mary (Luke 1:28).

6. (p. 523) *Saint Nicholas:* A fourth-century bishop of Myra in Asia Minor, Saint Nicholas was the subject of many medieval miracle stories that included descriptions of his learning and piety at a young age.

7. (p. 525) *Alma redemptoris:* A liturgical prayer to Mary: Alma Redemptoris Mater (Nurturing Mother of the Redeemer), sung during the Advent and Christmas seasons.

8. (p. 525) *"I know little grammar":* Here "grammar" refers to Latin.

9. (p. 527) *Herods:* In the Gospel of Matthew, Herod, king of Judea, tries to kill the infant Jesus; he is one of the major villains of medieval religious drama.

10. (p. 527) *Of which the great evangelist, Saint John, / In Patmos wrote:* The Book of Revelation (The Apocalypse) claims to have been written by the apostle and evangelist Saint John on the Aegean island of Patmos.

11. (p. 531) *Hardly might the people who were there / This new Rachel bring from his bier:* In the Bible, Jeremiah 31:15 tells of Rachel "weeping for her children . . . because they are no more." The verse is quoted in Matthew 2:18, the gospel passage read on the Feast of the Holy Innocents, December 28.

12. (p. 531) *Therefore with wild horses he did them draw, / And then he them hung as held the law:* The passage describes the medieval punishment for high treason.

13. (p. 533) *Hugh of Lincoln:* A child reputedly killed by Jews in 1255, Hugh of Lincoln was venerated as a martyr for centuries; in modern times the story has been disproved.

The Nun's Priest's Tale

1. (p. 537) *"good sir, no more of this":* These words of the Knight interrupt the Monk's catalog of "tragedies" of fortune.

2. (p. 541) *Chanticleer:* The rooster's name comes from medieval beast fables, descendants of Aesop's fable collection.

3. (p. 541) horloge: Abbey great clock.

4. (p. 543) *"my love has gone far away":* Popular song.

5. (p. 545) *Cato:* Cato's *Distychs*, a popular medieval school-text, consisted of proverbial bits of advice.

6. (p. 547) "merci beaucoup": Thank you very much (French).

7. (p. 547) *One of the greatest authors:* Either Cicero or Valerius Maximus could be intended; both tell the stories that follow.

8. (p. 553) *japes:* Tricks.

9. (p. 553) *Saint Kenelm:* The reference is to the legendary ninth-century king of Mercia in Anglo-Saxon England, who became king at age seven but was murdered at his sister's instigation, after having a predictive dream.

10. (p. 555) *Macrobius:* Sixth-century C.E. author of the *Commentary on the Dream of Scipio*, a widely read allegorical treatise based on the dream of Scipio that concludes Cicero's *De re publica* (*On the Republic*). It includes a taxonomy of dream types.

11. (p. 555) *Daniel . . . Joseph:* Successful interpreters of dreams in the Hebrew Scriptures.

12. (p. 557) In principio, / Mulier est hominis confusio: In the beginning, woman is man's ruin (Latin).

13. (p. 559) *the book of Lancelot de Lake:* A thirteenth-century compendium of Arthurian adventures centered around the love of Lancelot for Arthur's queen, Guinevere, an adulterous liaison that contributed to the downfall of the Round Table.

14. (p. 561) *Iscariot . . . Ganelon . . . Sinon:* These are famous traitors of history and legend. Judas Iscariot betrayed Jesus; Ganelon betrayed Charlemagne and Roland; Sinon fooled the Trojans into allowing a wooden horse full of Greek soldiers within the walls of Troy.

15. (p. 561) *Augustine . . . Boethius . . . Bradwardine:* These are famous contributors to Christian thought and argument about the nature of divine foreknowledge and its implication for the idea of free will.

16. (p. 563) *Physiologus:* A popular medieval text describing the characteristics of real or imaginary animals and birds, and allegorizing these characteristics to illustrate Christian doctrine.

17. (p. 563) *in music more feeling / Than had Boethius:* Boethius, a sixth-century Christian philosopher, wrote a theoretical treatise on music—that is, on universal harmonies—that was well known in medieval Europe.

18. (p. 565) *'Sir Burnel the Ass':* Burnel is the protagonist of Nigel Longchamps' twelfth-century satire *Speculum stultorum*, which, like "The Nun's Priest's Tale," comments on human folly under the guise of an animal fable.

19. (p. 565) *Ecclesiastes on flattery:* Flattery is warned against in the biblical books of Ecclesiastes and Proverbs, and, in the apocrypha, Ecclesiasticus.

20. (p. 567) *on your day to die:* That is, on Friday, Venus' day (compare French *vendredi* and Italian *venerdi*).

21. (p. 567) *Geoffrey, dear sovereign master:* Twelfth-century poet, author, and rhetorical theorist Geoffrey of Vinsauf's *Poetria nova*, a treatise on writing poetry, contains a lament for the death of King Richard I of England as a school exercise.

22. (p. 567) *Pyrrhus . . . seized king Priam:* Pyrrhus, son of Achilles, kills Priam, king of Troy, in the *Aeneid*, book 2.

23. (p. 567) *Hasdrubal's wife:* Hasdrubal was king of Carthage when the Romans burned it in 146 B.C.E.

24. (p. 569) *Colle . . . Talbot . . . Gerland:* These were common names for dogs.

25. (p. 569) *Jack Straw and his company:* Jack Straw was a leader of the Great Rising (also called the Peasants' Revolt) of 1381. When rebel forces broke into London, one of the targets of their hostility was foreigners, such as Flemish textile workers, whom they felt threatened their livelihoods. This is Chaucer's only overt reference in his poetry to the Rising, and one of very few topical references in *The Canterbury Tales.*

26. (p. 569) *Fleming:* Many of those killed in the suppression of the Peasants' Revolt were Flemish weavers.

27. (p. 571) *Saint Paul says all that is written:* See the Bible, Romans 15:4. The Nun's Priest's application of Paul's words to this beast fable is a final comic comment on human attempts to understand life.

The Canon's Yeoman's Tale

1. (p. 575) *the life of Saint Cecilia:* The immensely popular story of the life of Saint Cecilia, based on a fictitious account of her life and martyrdom written at the end of the fifth century, is told in "The Second Nun's Tale," not included in this edition.

2. (p. 575) *canon:* A canon is a member of a religious community who may (as a "regular canon") or may not (as a "secular canon") follow a monastic or other religious rule.

3. (p. 575) *plantain and pellitory:* Two herbs used for distilling.

4. (p. 581) *he who guilty is / Deems everything spoken to be of him:* The allusion is to the *Dystichs of Cato* (1.17). See note 6 to "The Merchant's Tale."

5. (p. 585) *porphyry:* The hard igneous rock called porphyry was used as a surface on which to grind or mix ingredients.

6. (p. 587) *sublimatories:* Vessels used for changing solid substances into vapors.

7. (p. 597) *Nineveh:* Capital of ancient Assyria.

8. (p. 599) *chantry priest:* Chantry priests were hired to say (chant) masses and prayers for the souls of members of a family or association in a special chapel (a chantry) constructed for that purpose within a church or cathedral. See also note 32 to "The General Prologue."

9. (p. 607) *he is here and there; / He is so changeable, he abides nowhere:* Traditional attributes of the Devil.

10. (p. 619) *Bayard the blind:* A traditional name for a horse.

11. (p. 619) *Arnaldus of Villanova:* In the thirteenth century, Arnold of Villanova wrote scientific and alchemical treatises, including *Rosarium philosophorum* (*Rose Garland of the Philosophers*).

12. (p. 619) *Hermes Trismegistus:* "Thrice Great Hermes," the Egyptian god Thoth, credited by the Greeks as the founder of alchemy.

13. (p. 621) *"take heed to my screed":* The several lines that follow are adapted from Arnold of Villanova's *De lapide philosophorum* (*On the Philosopher's Stone*).

14. (p. 621) *there was a disciple of Plato:* The dialogue between Plato and Zadith is adopted from an alchemical treatise by the tenth-century Arab scientific writer Muhammad ibn Umail.

15. (p. 621) ignotum per ignocius: The Latin phrase means "[explaining] the unknown by the even more unknown."

The Friar's Tale

1. (p. 625) *this worthy limitour:* A limitour was a friar who begged and preached within boundaries assigned him by his order. (See note 10 to "The General Prologue.")

2. (p. 625) *leave citing authorities, in God's name, / To preaching and to schools of clergy:* The medieval Church, following the biblical injunctions of the First Epistle to Timothy (2:12), forbade women to preach or teach publicly.

3. (p. 627) *an archdeacon, a man of high degree:* Archdeacons were diocesan officials responsible, among other duties, for the ecclesiastical courts.

4. (p. 627) *simony:* Simony is the sin of selling of ecclesiastical offices or positions. The term is also used for any sale of spiritual favors.

5. (p. 627) *tithes:* An offering of one-tenth of one's wages or produce to the Church. Theoretically required of all laity in medieval Europe, the practice was widely resented and resisted.

6. (p. 629) *lewd:* Here the term means "ignorant."

7. (p. 631) *He wore a jacket of green:* In medieval legends about him, the Devil often wears green.

8. (p. 631) *Depardieux:* The term means "by God."

9. (p. 633) *far in the north country:* The north was traditionally where the Devil dwelled, based on an assumed reference to him in the Bible, Isaiah 14:13.

10. (p. 633) *confessors:* Confessors are priests who hear confessions and assign penances for sins such as those to which the Summoner here "confesses."

11. (p. 635) *prime:* The first hour of the liturgical day.

12. (p. 637) *Saint Dunstan:* A tenth-century archbishop of Canterbury, Dunstan was celebrated in medieval legends for his power over devils.

13. (p. 637) *As to the Witch of Endor did Samuel:* The reference is to the Bible, 1 Samuel 28:7–25.

14. (p. 639) *Saint Loy:* Another name for Saint Eligius, patron saint of carters.

15. (p. 643) *Saint Anne:* The mother of the Virgin Mary, Saint Anne was much revered in late-medieval England.

16. (p. 643) *master of divinity:* A university professor of theology.

17. (p. 645) *"The lion sits in a bush always / To slay the innocent, if he may":* A reference to the Bible, Psalm 10:8–9 (Vulgate).

The Summoner's Tale

1. (p. 647) *you have oftentime heard tell / How that a friar abducted was to hell:* The Summoner here parodies a popular medieval religious genre, the admonitory vision of the afterlife, featuring the pains of Hell and Purgatory.

2. (p. 649) *holy houses:* The reference is to convents for friars, as opposed to priests and monks (secular and monastic clergy, mentioned below), traditionally the enemies of the friars. (See note 10 to "The General Prologue.") Monks took vows of poverty, chastity, and obedience, and lived in communities they were not to leave without special permission; the orders of friars, or medicants, were charged by the institutional Catholic Church with the duty of moving about the world preaching the gospel to Christians of every class and situation. They were supposed to beg for their (simple) needs. Friars sometimes accused monks of living too well, which earned them the enmity of some monastic writers; on the enmity between parish priests and friars, see note 9 on the next page.

3. (p. 649) *qui cum patre:* The Latin phrase translates as "Who with the father" and continues with wording that translates as "reigns in Heaven . . ." The phrase occurred at the conclusion of many liturgical prayers.

4. (p. 651) *folding ivory writing tablets, / And a well-polished stylus:* In medieval Europe, as in classical antiquity, all impermanent writing was done with a stylus on easily erasable, thus reusable, waxed wooden or ivory tablets.

5. (p. 651) *mass penny:* A donation to have a mass said for one's intention (that is, for a favor one wishes to be granted by God).

6. (p. 651) *"Deus hic!":* The Latin phrase translates as "God be here" (that is, in this house).

7. (p. 653) *orison:* The word means "prayer."

8. (p. 653) *The letters slay:* A reference to the Bible, 2 Corinthians 3:6: "the letter [of the law] kills, but the spirit gives life."

9. (p. 655) *These curates be full negligent and slow / To plumb tenderly a conscience / In confession:* Friars were permitted to hear parishioners' confessions, to the annoyance of parish clergy, who were thereby deprived of the offering customarily given to the confessor by the penitent. (See note 11 to "The General Prologue.")

10. (p. 655) *je vous dis:* "I tell you" (see also, below: "I tell you without doubt"). The friar's French is an affectation.

11. (p. 657) *They may now . . . Mark their jubilee and walk alone:* Friars were normally required by their orders to go about begging and preaching in pairs; after fifty years of service they were exempt from this requirement.

12. (p. 657) *Te Deum:* The reference is to "Te Deum laudamus" ("We Praise You, God"), a liturgical hymn of praise.

13. (p. 657) *Lazar and Dives lived differently:* See the Bible, Luke 16:19–31 for this parable of the rich man (Dives) and the poor leper (Lazarus).

14. (p. 657) *Moses . . . on the mount of Sinai:* See the Bible, Exodus 34:28.

15. (p. 659) *Elijah . . . fasted long and was in contemplation:* See the Bible, 1 Kings 19, where Elijah is said to have fasted on Mount Horeb.

16. (p. 659) *They would not drink . . . Lest they die:* See the Bible, Leviticus 10:8–9.

17. (p. 659) *Jovinianus, / Fat as a whale, and waddling like a duck:* Saint Jerome attacked Jovinian, a fourth-century monk with whose views on marriage and virginity he violently disagreed, and whom he derided as fat and overly groomed.

18. (p. 661) *'cor meum eructavit!':* The Latin words are the opening of Psalm 44 (Vulgate); *eructavit* can mean either "proclaimed" or "belched."

19. (p. 661) *Saint Ives:* Several medieval saints were called Saint Yves or Yvo.

20. (p. 663) *'Within your house be not a lion; . . . Nor make your acquaintances want to flee':* The source for this advice is the Vulgate Bible (Ecclesiasticus 4:35), plus other proverbial material.

21. (p. 665) *"Once there was an angry ruler / As said Seneca . . .":* The reference is to the first-century C.E. Roman philosopher, politician, and educator Seneca and his work *Concerning Anger* 1.18.

22. (p. 665) *"Angry Cambises was also a drunkard, / And ever delighted him to be a shrew . . .":* See Seneca's *Concerning Anger* 3.14.

23. (p. 667) *"Look how Cyrus the Great, the Persian . . .":* See Seneca's *Concerning Anger* 3.21.

24. (p. 667) *'Be not a companion to an angry man . . .':* See the Bible, Proverbs 22:24–25.

25. (p. 669) *he who harrowed hell:* In what was described as the Harrowing of Hell, Jesus was believed to have descended to Hell after his death and before his Resurrection, and to have liberated from Hell the righteous souls of the Old Testament.

26. (p. 669) *"But since Elijah was, or Elisha, / Have friars been—that I find of record— / In service":* The Carmelite Friars claimed to have been founded by the Old Testament prophet Elijah when he triumphed over the priests of Baal on Mount Carmel, as described in the Bible, 1 Kings 18:20–40.

27. (p. 675) *art of mathematics:* The Middle English *ars-metrike* contains an obvious pun on Thomas's fart.

28. (p. 679) *Euclid or Ptolomy:* The fourth-century B.C.E. Greek mathematician Euclid invented geometry. The celebrated second-century C.E. Greek astronomer Ptolemy wrote a treatise, the *Almagest*, that was well known in medieval Europe.

The Man of Law's Tale

1. (p. 681) *the bright sun / His daylight arc had run / The first quarter, and half an hour and more:* In keeping with the general wordiness of the tale to follow, this is a very circuitous way of announcing the time (ten o'clock).

2. (p. 681) *'Loss of property may recovered be, / But loss of time ruins us':* The Host cites Seneca (*Moral Epistles* 1.3), but the expression is commonplace.

3. (p. 683) *More than Ovid made of mention / In his Epistles:* The reference is to Ovid's *Heroides*, a collection of letters supposedly written (mostly) by women of classical myth and legend to their lovers and ex-lovers.

4. (p. 683) *"In youth he wrote of Ceyx and Alcion":* The Book of the Duchess, apparently Chaucer's earliest extant long poem, contains a paraphrase of Ovid's story of Ceyx and Alcyone from *Metamorphoses*, book 11.

5. (p. 683) *the Legend of Good Women:* The list of abandoned or mistreated classical heroines that follows includes those who appear in *The Legend of Good Women* and several who do not; the latter may have been slated for inclusion had Chaucer completed the collection.

6. (p. 685) *wicked example of Canacee:* See Ovid, *Heroides* 2.

7. (p. 685) *Apollonius of Tyre:* The story of Apollonius of Tyre was widely known in medieval Europe. Apollonius is a prince who must go into exile when his life is threatened by Antiochus, the incestuous father of the woman Apollonius wishes to marry.

8. (p. 685) *Pierides:* The Pierides (daughters of Pierus) challenged the Muses to a singing contest and for their presumption were transformed into magpies (Ovid, *Metamorphoses* 5). But the term Pierides can also refer to the Muses themselves, who, according to legend, were born in Pieria.

9. (p. 685) *Oh hateful misfortune, condition of poverty!:* The dispraise of poverty is adapted from *On the Misery of the Human Condition* (also known as *De contemptu mundi* [*On Contempt for the World*]), a late-twelfth-century oration by Cardinal Lothario de' Segni, who later became Pope Innocent III. A companion oration on the dignity of humanity was planned but never executed. The Man of Law's subsequent praise of merchants has no connection to Innocent's text.

10. (p. 691) *Hector . . . Julius Caesar:* Hector and Achilles were, respectively, Trojan and Greek heroes of the Trojan War. Pompey the Great and Julius Caesar were first allies, then bitter rivals at the end of the Roman Republic and the beginning of the Empire.

11. (p. 691) *The siege of Thebes:* In classical myth, the city of Thebes was the home of Oedipus, who blinded himself in punishment for unintentionally killing his father and marrying his own mother. After Oedipus' death his two sons, Polynices and Eteocles, agreed to take turns ruling Thebes, but Eteocles broke the agreement, refusing to vacate the throne when his time was up, so Polynices raised an army and besieged the city. Eventually, the two brothers met and killed each other in battle. The story is the subject of the first-century C.E. epic, the *Thebaid*, by Statius.

12. (p. 691) *Turnus:* Prince of the Rutulians, he was Aeneas' rival in the war fought by the exiled Trojans for a place to settle in Latium on the Italian peninsula, as told by Virgil in the *Aeneid*.

13. (p. 697) *the Berber nation:* The Berbers, a north African civilization, are here used broadly to represent non-Christian nations.

14. (p. 697) *Pyrrhus:* The son of Achilles. See the *Aeneid*, book 2.

15. (p. 697) *O primum mobile!*: The *primum mobile* ("prime mover") was the outermost heavenly sphere in the Ptolemaic model of the universe; it was thought to be the force that moved the other spheres from east to west.

16. (p. 697) *Inauspicious ascendent tortuous*: This stanza describes the conditions of the heavens that made Constance's voyage inauspicious. Three lines below, the *atazir* of a planetary configuration was its dominant factor with respect to human affairs.

17. (p. 703) *Caesar's triumphal march, / Of which Lucan makes such a boast*: Lucan's *Pharsalia* (a history of the Roman civil wars) reports Caesar's plans for a triumph (that is, a celebration of his victory) on his return to Rome after defeating Pompey; the triumph never materialized.

18. (p. 707) *Who saved Daniel in the horrible cave*: Daniel is saved from the lions' den, as told in the Bible, Daniel 6:16–24.

19. (p. 707) *Who kept Jonas in the fish's maw*: See the Bible, Jonah 1:17–2:10.

20. (p. 709) *Who kept the Hebrew people from their drowning, / With dry feet passing through the sea*: See the Bible, Exodus 14:21–23.

21. (p. 709) *the four angels of tempest*: See the Bible, Revelation 7:1–3.

22. (p. 709) *Who fed Saint Mary the Egyptian in the cave*: The legend of Saint Mary the Egyptian, a repentant prostitute who lived a solitary life in the desert for forty-seven years, was widely known throughout medieval Europe.

23. (p. 711) *In all that land no Christians dared gather; . . . Because of the pagans, who conquered all about / The coasts of the north, by land and sea*: Chaucer takes these details of early English history from Nicholas Trevet's Anglo-Norman chronicle, his source for the Constance story. Behind Trevet stands Bede's authoritative account in his *Ecclesiastical History of the English* (c.735 C.E.).

24. (p. 717) *saved Susanna / From false blame*: See the Bible, Daniel 13 (Vulgate), the story of Susannah and the Elders who want to have sex with her, and accuse her of fornication when she refuses. Daniel's intervention saves her from being condemned to death.

25. (p. 735) *Oh Goliath, immeasurable of length*: See the Bible, 1 Samuel 17:4–51.

26. (p. 735) *Who gave Judith courage or strength / To slay Holofernes in his tent*: See the Vulgate Bible, Judith 13:1–10.

The Manciple's Tale

1. (p. 751) *Bob-up-and-down*: The reference is probably to the town of Harbledown, outside Canterbury on the road from London.

2. (p. 751) *We're stuck in the mire!:* "Dun is in the mire" is the name of a rural game of strength and a popular expression for getting stuck.

3. (p. 751) *in Cheap:* The reference is to Cheapside, a London district of shops; the name derives from the Old English *ceap*, meaning a bargain or a business dealing.

4. (p. 753) *very drunk:* In medieval popular thought, *wyn ape* ("ape drunk") was one of the four stages of drunkenness; each stage was related to the behavior of a particular animal.

5. (p. 753) *he could not prop himself up with his ladle:* That is, he should have been content to remain a cook instead of trying to imitate a knight on a campaign (*chyvachee*); this is said ironically, of course.

6. (p. 755) *Phoebus:* Apollo, the god of the sun and of music.

7. (p. 755) *Python, the serpent:* See Ovid, *Metamorphoses* 1.438–451.

8. (p. 759) *Take any bird, and put it in a cage:* The following is a popular piece of conventional wisdom, also told in "The Squire's Tale." Chaucer could have found it in Boethius' *Consolation of Philosophy* (sixth century c.e.) or *Romance of the Rose*, both of which he translated.

9. (p. 761) *To Alexander was told this sentence:* This well-known story was available to Chaucer from several sources, including works by Cicero and Saint Augustine.

10. (p. 763) *"Cuckoo! Cuckoo! Cuckoo!":* The cry of the cuckoo was often used to refer to a husband who had been cuckolded by his wife. See also note 11 to "The Knight's Tale."

11. (p. 767) *Lord Solomon, as wise scholars say, / Teaches a man to keep his tongue well:* See the Bible, Proverbs 21:23.

The Squire's Tale

1. (p. 771) *in the land of Tartary:* Tartary was the generic medieval term for the Mongol Empire.

2. (p. 773) *In Mars' face and in his mansion / In Aries, the coleric hot sign:* The sun's relation to the planets and constellations is an important element of an astrological horoscope, here relevant because this is the ruler's birthday (a horoscope is cast based upon the subject's date of birth).

3. (p. 775) *Gawain:* In medieval chivalric romances, Gawain, a knight of Arthur's Round Table, was considered a model of courtesy.

4. (p. 777) *He waited many a constellation:* That is, he waited until the stars were so aligned as to favor his enterprise.

5. (p. 781) *Diverse folk diversely they deemed:* A favorite line of Chaucer's, expressing the inevitable multiplicity of human opinions on most matters in life.

6. (p. 781) *Pegasus:* In classical myth, Pegasus was a winged horse belonging to the hero Bellerophon.

7. (p. 781) *Synon:* The Greek Synon, pretending to be a refugee from persecution by his fellow Greeks besieging Troy, convinced the Trojans to take the wooden horse, its hollow belly full of Greek soldiers, into Troy, assuring the city's destruction. See Virgil, *Aeneid*, book 2.

8. (p. 783) *Alhazen, and Vitulon:* Alhazen was an Arabic author of a treatise on optics. Vitulon (Witelo) was a Polish author of a treatise on perspective.

9. (p. 783) *Telephus the king:* Telephus was an enemy wounded and then healed by Achilles during the Trojan War.

10. (p. 785) *ascending was the beast royal, / The gentle Lion, with his Aldiran:* The gentle lion is the constellation Leo; the precise meaning of "Aldiran" is unclear; the time is after noon.

11. (p. 785) *Now danced Venus' lusty children dear:* Venus' astrological "children" are lovers. Venus is most powerful when favorably located in the constellation of Pisces.

12. (p. 791) *the young sun, / That in the Ram is four degrees uprisen:* That is, it is just after 6 A.M.

13. (p. 799) *neither Jason nor Paris of Troy:* In classical mythology, Jason was the lover and betrayer of Medea. Paris, son of the king of Troy, brought on the Trojan War by abducting Helen from her home in Argos.

14. (p. 799) *Lamech:* In the Bible, Lamech had two wives; see Genesis 4:19–23.

15. (p. 801) *As birds do that men in cages feed:* The piece of conventional wisdom that follows also appears in "The Manciple's Tale" (see note 8).

The Physician's Tale

1. (p. 807) *as Livy tells:* The story of Virginia originates in the history of Rome from its beginnings (*Ab urbe condita*) by Livy (Titus Livius; 59 B.C.E.–17 C.E.), but Chaucer probably knew it from *Romance of the Rose*, lines 5589–5658. It was widely known in the Middle Ages, and is also told by Chaucer's contemporary John Gower in his story collection *Confessio amantis* (*The Lover's Confession*).

2. (p. 807) *Pygmalion:* Pygmalion made a sculpture of a beautiful woman and fell in love with his work of art, so the gods brought her to life for his pleasure. See Ovid, *Metamorphoses* 10.243–297.

3. (p. 807) *Apelles, Zeuxis:* Apelles and Zeuxis were fabled artists of antiquity. Their marvelous works were known to the Middle Ages only from stories about them in various classical texts.

4. (p. 807) *Phoebus:* Apollo, the sun god.

5. (p. 809) *Pallas:* Another name for Athena, the goddess of wisdom.
6. (p. 811) *the old dance:* The "old dance" is a colloquial way of referring to the maneuvers of courtship and seduction as practiced by experts in these matters; the term is also used by Chaucer elsewhere in *The Canterbury Tales* to describe the Wife of Bath, and in his *Troilus and Criseyde* to describe Pandar, the go-between figure who woos Criseyde for Troilus.
7. (p. 813) *Saint Augustine made this description:* See Augustine, *Interpretation of the Psalms* 104.17, on envy.
8. (p. 819) *Jephtha gave his daughter grace:* See the Bible, Judges 11, where Jephtha promises God, in return for victory in battle, to sacrifice to him the first creature he encounters on his return home; it is his daughter, who requests a two-month respite to mourn before dying.

Inspired by Geoffrey Chaucer *and* The Canterbury Tales

The last six centuries have seen an incredible number of specific allusions to Chaucer in canonical world literature—and not exclusively in poetry. In *Chaucer, the Critical Heritage* (1978), Derek Brewer writes, "All the later major poets, and almost all distinguished English and American men of letters up to the first third of the twentieth century have made at least passing allusion to Chaucer." In his own day, Chaucer found favor with groups as diverse as court society, the general public, and other poets; he inspired a number of verse tributes and imitations during that time and immediately following his death. The first recorded instance came from French poet Eustache Deschamps, whose tribute, in the form of a ballad (c.1386), lauds Chaucer as a Socrates in philosophy, a Seneca in morals, and an Ovid in poetry. High praise of Chaucer surfaces in several of his close descendants' works, such as Thomas Hoccleve's *De Regimine Principum* (1412; *Regiment of Princes*), in which Hoccleve refers to Chaucer as "maister deere and fadir reverent" ("worthy and respected master"), and John Lydgate's *The Fall of Princes* (c.1431–1438), in which Lydgate calls the poet the "lodesterre" ("lodestar") of the English language. Two English monarchs sang the praises of Chaucer, including King James I of Scotland, who in *The Kingis Quair* (1423; *The King's Book*), calls Chaucer and John Gower "my maisteris dere" ("my dear masters"), recommending "thair saulis vn-to the blisse of hevin" ("their souls unto the bliss of heaven"). Sir Walter Scott notes in *The Monastery* (1820) that Queen Elizabeth I, too, was fond of quoting Chaucer's aphorism from "The Reeve's Tale" that "the greatest clerks [scholars] are not the wisest men."

Chaucer earned much admiration among fiction writers, particularly during the nineteenth century, when the novel rose to a respected status. Washington Irving, Sir Walter Scott, Charles Dickens, George Eliot, and Elizabeth Gaskell all quote from or allude to Chaucer in their works. In the visual realm, William Blake produced a 54" × 18" tempera painting, *The Canterbury Pilgrims*, in 1808, and Edward Burne-Jones provided illustrations for the Kelmscott edition of Chaucer's writings (1896), which was edited by William Morris. Film adaptations of *The Canterbury Tales* include Italian director Pier Paolo Pasolini's film in 1972 and an animated version in 1998, which was nominated for an Academy Award for Best Animated Short Film. A six-part miniseries also appeared in Britain in 2003.

Chaucer's greatest legacy, however, has always manifested in verse. The first work of the English literary Renaissance, Edmund Spenser's *The Shepheardes Calender* (1579), reflects a strong Chaucerian influence, and Spenser invokes the author by name in the first books of his greatest work, *The Faerie Queene* (1590). William Shakespeare's *A Midsummer Night's Dream* (c.1595–1596) most likely had its beginnings in "The Knight's Tale," and act 3 of *King Lear* (c.1605–1606) has the Fool quoting from "The General Prologue" to *The Canterbury Tales.* Indeed, Chaucer's general influence permeates the works of Shakespeare and of John Milton, who directly alludes to Chaucer in his poem "Il Penseroso" (c.1625–1632; "The Melancholy Man").

At the turn of the eighteenth century, John Dryden published his *Fables, Ancient and Modern* (1700), which includes a highly regarded modernization of *The Canterbury Tales.* Several years later, satirist Alexander Pope modernized "The Prologue of the Wife of Bath's Tale" and likely "The General Prologue" and "The Reeve's Tale," both of which were attributed to Thomas Betterton. *Gulliver's Travels* author Jonathan Swift (1667–1745) composed an imitation of Chaucer, now lost, that Sir Walter Scott mentions in his memoir of Swift. In the latter half of the eighteenth century, English scholar Samuel Johnson (1709–1784) considered creating a major annotated edition of Chaucer's writings similar to his earlier interpretation of Shakespeare, but the project never came to fruition.

As Romanticism dawned at the beginning of the nineteenth century, Chaucer continued to influence writers. William Wordsworth mentions him in the preface to *Lyrical Ballads* (1800) and the *Prelude* (1805); he also modernized "The Prioress's Tale," praising the original in the sonnet "Edward VI" (1821). Around the same time, John Keats imitated Chaucer in the poem "The Eve of Saint Mark" (1819). Henry Wadsworth Longfellow's *Tales of a Wayside Inn* (1863) is an adaptation of the *Canterbury Tales*; the first tale in the collection, told by the host of the inn, which still stands in western Massachusetts, is "The Midnight Ride of Paul Revere." Longfellow also immortalized the *Canterbury Tales* author in the sonnet "Chaucer" (1825):

> An old man in a lodge within a park;
> The chamber walls depicted all around
> With portraitures of huntsman, hawk, and hound,
> And the hurt deer. He listeneth to the lark,
> Whose song comes with the sunshine through the dark
> Of painted glass in leaden lattice bound;
> He listeneth and he laugheth at the sound,
> Then writeth in a book like any clerk.
> He is the poet of the dawn, who wrote
> The Canterbury Tales, and his old age
> Made beautiful with song; and as I read
> I hear the crowing cock, I hear the note
> Of lark and linnet, and from every page
> Rise odors of ploughed field or flowery mead.

George Meredith wrote his own poetic appreciation, "The Poetry of Chaucer" (1851):

> Grey with all honours of age! but fresh-featured and ruddy
> As dawn when the drowsy farm-yard has thrice heard
>   Chaunticlere.
> Tender to tearfulness—childlike, and manly, and motherly;
> Here beats true English blood richest joyance on sweet
>   English ground.

But the best-known Chaucer-inspired lines in poetry appear in T. S. Eliot's landmark *The Waste Land* (1922), the premier poem of the twentieth century. Delineating the horrors of the modern era, Eliot turns on its head the celebration of spring in "The General Prologue." The poem opens with a lament that a winter of hibernation has ended, declaring, "April is the cruellest month, breeding / Lilacs out of the dead land, mixing / Memory and desire, stirring / Dull roots with spring rain." Echoes of Chaucer continue in E. E. Cummings's "honour corruption villainy holiness" (1950), a poem about Chaucer; Margaret Atwood's dystopian novel *The Handmaid's Tale* (1985); and Spencer Reece's *The Clerk's Tale* (2004), a highly regarded collection of Chaucer-influenced poems.

Comments & Questions

In this section, we aim to provide the reader with an array of perspectives on the text, as well as questions that challenge those perspectives. The commentary has been culled from sources as diverse as comments contemporaneous with the work, literary criticism of later generations, and appreciations written throughout the work's history. Following the commentary, a series of questions seeks to filter The Canterbury Tales *through a variety of points of view and bring about a richer understanding of this enduring work.*

Comments

WILLIAM CAXTON

We ought to gyve a synguler laude unto that noble and grete philosopher Gefferey Chaucer, the whiche for his ornate wrytyng in our tongue maye wel have the name of a laureate poete. For tofore that he by hys labour enbelysshyd, ornated and made faire our Englisshe, in thys royame was had rude speche and incongrue, as yet it appiereth by olde bookes whyche at thys day ought not to have place ne be compare emong ne to hys beautevous volumes and aournate writynges; of whom he made many bokes and treatyces of many a noble historye, as wel in metre as in ryme and prose, and them so craftyly made that he comprehended hys maters in short, quyck and hye sentences, eschewyng prolyxyte, castyng away the chaf of superfluyte, and shewyng the pyked grayn of sentence utteryd by crafty and sugred eloquence.

[We ought to give a singular laud unto that noble and great philosopher Geoffrey Chaucer, who for his ornate writing in our tongue may well have the name of a laureate poet. For before he by his labor embellished, ornated, and made fair our English, in this realm speech was rude and incongruous, as yet shown by old books, which at this day ought not to have place nor be compared among, nor to, his beauteous volumes and ornate writings. He made many books and treatises of many a noble history, as gifted in meter as in rhyme and prose; and them so craftly made that he comprehended his matters in short, quick, and high sentences, eschewing prolixity, casting away the chaff of superfluity, and showing the picked grain of sentence uttered by crafty and sugared eloquence.]

—from Proem to *The Canterbury Tales* (1484)

SIR BRIAN TUKE

I . . . have taken great delectation, as the times and leisures might suffer, to read and hear the books of that noble and famous clerk Geoffrey Chaucer, in whose works is so manifest comprobation of his excellent learning in all kinds of doctrines and sciences, such fruitfulness in words well according to the matter and purpose, so sweet and pleasant sentences, such perfection in metre, the composition so adapted, such freshness of invention, compendiousness in narration, such sensible and open style, lacking neither majesty ne mediocrity convenable in disposition, and such sharpness or quickness in conclusion, that it is much to be marvelled how in his time, when doubtless all good letters were laid asleep throughout the world, as the thing which either by the disposition and influence of the bodies above or by other ordinance of God seemed like and was in danger to have utterly perished, such an excellent poet in our tongue should as it were (nature repugning) spring and arise.

—from the Preface to *Works of Geoffrey Chaucer* (1532)

SIR FRANCIS BEAUMONT

So may Chaucer rightly be called the pith and sinews of Eloquence, and very life itself of all mirth and pleasant writing. Besides, one gift he hath above all authors, and that is by excellency of his descriptions to possess his reader with a more forcible imagination of seeing that (as it were) done before their eyes which they read, than any other that ever hath written in any tongue.

—from *Works of Our Ancient and Learned Poet Geoffrey Chaucer* (1602)

EDWARD PHILLIPS

True it is that the style of poetry till Henry the Eighth's time, and partly also within his reign, may very well appear uncouth, strange and unpleasant to those that are affected only with that is familiar and accustomed to them; not but there were even before those times some that had their poetic excellencies, if well examined; and chiefly among the rest Chaucer, who through all the neglect of former aged poets still keeps a name, being by some few admired for his real worth, to others not unpleasing for his facetious way, which, joined with his old English, entertains them with a kind of drollery.

—from *Theatrum Poetarum* (1675)

JOHN DRYDEN

In the first place, as he is the father of English poetry, so I hold him in the same degree of veneration as the Grecians held Homer, or the Romans Virgil. He is a perpetual fountain of good sense; learned in all sciences; and, therefore, speaks properly on all subjects. As he knew what to say, so he knows also when to leave off; a continence which is practised by few writers, and scarcely by any of the ancients, excepting Virgil and Horace. . . .

He must have been a man of a most wonderful comprehensive nature, because, as it has been truly observed of him, he has taken into the compass of his *Canterbury Tales* the various manners and humours (as we now call them) of the whole English nation, in his age. Not a single character has escaped him. All his pilgrims are severally distinguished from each other; and not only in their inclinations, but in their very physiognomies and persons. Baptista Porta could not have described their natures better, than by the marks which the poet gives them. The matter and manner of their tales, and of their telling, are so suited to their different educations, humours, and callings, that each of them would be improper in any other mouth. Even the grave and serious characters are distinguished by their several sorts of gravity: their discourses are such as belong to their age, their calling, and their breeding; such as are becoming of them, and of them only. Some of his persons are vicious, and some virtuous; some are unlearned or (as Chaucer calls them) lewd, and some are learned. Even the ribaldry of the low characters is different: the Reeve, the Miller, and the Cook, are several men, and distinguished from each other as much as the mincing Lady Prioress and the broad-speaking, gaptoothed Wife of Bath. But enough of this; there is such a variety of game springing up before me, that I am distracted in my choice, and know not which to follow. 'Tis sufficient to say according to the proverb, that here is God's plenty. We have our forefathers and greatgrand-dames all before us, as they were in Chaucer's days; their general characters are still remaining in mankind, and even in England, though they are called by other names than those of Monks, and Friars, and Canons, and Lady Abbesses, and Nuns; for mankind is ever the same, and nothing lost out of Nature, though everything is altered.

—from the Preface to *Fables, Ancient and Modern* (1700)

THOMAS WARTON

Hitherto our poets had been persons of a private and circumscribed education; and the art of versifying, like every other kind of composition, had been confined to recluse scholars. But Chaucer was a man of the world; and from this circumstance we are to account, in great measure, for the many new embellishments which he conferred on our language and our poetry. The descriptions of splendid processions and gallant carousals with which his works abound are a proof that he was conversant with the practices and diversions of polite life. Familiarity with a variety of things and objects, opportunities of acquiring the fashionable and courtly modes of speech, connexions with the great at home, and a personal acquaintance with the vernacular poets of foreign countries, opened his mind and furnished him with new lights. . . .

Chaucer's vein of humour, although conspicuous in the *Canterbury Tales*, is chiefly displayed in the characters with which they are introduced. In these his knowledge of the world availed him in a peculiar degree, and enabled him to give such an accurate picture of ancient manners as no contemporary nation has transmitted to posterity. It is here that we view the pursuits and employments, the customs and diversions of our ancestors, copied from the life and represented with equal truth and spirit by a judge of mankind whose penetration qualified him to discern their foibles or discriminating peculiarities, and by an artist who understood that proper selection of circumstances and those predominant characteristics which form a finished portrait. We are surprised to find, in so gross and ignorant an age, such talents for satire and for observation on life, qualities which usually exert themselves at more civilized periods, when the improved state of society, by subtilizing our speculations and establishing uniform modes of behaviour, disposes mankind to study themselves, and renders deviations of conduct and singularities of character more immediately and necessarily the objects of censure and ridicule. These curious and valuable remains are specimens of Chaucer's native genius, unassisted and unalloyed. The figures are all

British, and bear no suspicious signatures of classical, Italian or French imitation.

—from *History of English Poetry* (1774)

WILLIAM BLAKE
Of Chaucer's characters, as described in his Canterbury Tales, some of the names or titles are altered by time, but the characters themselves for ever remain unaltered, and consequently they are the physiognomies or lineaments of universal human life, beyond which Nature never steps. Names alter, things never alter. I have known multitudes of those who could have been monks in the age of monkery, who in this deistical age are deists. As Newton numbered the stars, and as Linneus numbered the plants, so Chaucer numbered the classes of men.

—from *Descriptive Catalogue* (1809)

SAMUEL TAYLOR COLERIDGE
I take unceasing delight in Chaucer. His manly cheerfulness is especially delicious to me in my old age. How exquisitely tender he is, and yet how perfectly free from the least touch of sickly melancholy or morbid drooping! The sympathy of the poet with the subjects of his poetry is particularly remarkable in Shakespeare and Chaucer; but what the first effects by a strong act of imagination and mental metamorphosis, the last does without any effort, merely by the inborn kindly joyousness of his nature. How well we seem to know Chaucer! How absolutely nothing do we know of Shakespeare!

—from *Table Talk* (March 15, 1834)

HENRY DAVID THOREAU
For the most part we read [Chaucer] without criticism, for he does not plead his own cause, but speaks for his readers, and has that greatness of trust and reliance that compels popularity. He confides in the reader, and speaks privily with him, keeping nothing back. And in return the reader has great confidence in him, that he tells no lies, and reads his story with indulgence, as if it were the circumlocution of a child, but often discovers afterwards that he has spoken with more directness and economy of words than a sage.

—from *A Week on the Concord and Merrimack Rivers* (1849)

RALPH WALDO EMERSON

The influence of Chaucer is conspicuous in all our early literature; and, more recently, not only Pope and Dryden have been beholden to him, but, in the whole society of English writers, a large unacknowledged debt is easily traced. One is charmed with the opulence which feeds so many pensioners.

—from *Representative Men* (1850)

JOHN RUSKIN

I think the most perfect type of a true English mind in its best possible temper, is that of Chaucer.

—from *Lectures on Art* (1870)

JAMES RUSSELL LOWELL

Modern imaginative literature has become so self-conscious, and therefore so melancholy, that Art, which should be 'the world's sweet inn,' whither we repair for refreshment and repose, has become rather a watering-place, where one's own private touch of the liver-complaint is exasperated by the affluence of other sufferers whose talk is a narrative of morbid symptoms. Poets have forgotten that the first lesson of literature, no less than of life, is the learning how to burn your own smoke; that the way to be original is to be healthy; that the fresh color, so delightful in all good writing, is won by escaping from the fixed air of self into the brisk atmosphere of universal sentiments; and that to make the common marvelous, as if it were a revelation, is the test of genius. It is good to retreat now and then beyond earshot of the introspective confidences of modern literature, and to lose ourselves in the gracious worldliness of Chaucer. Here was a healthy and hearty man, so genuine that he need not ask whether he was genuine or no, so sincere as quite to forget his own sincerity, so truly pious that he could be happy in the best world that God chose to make, so humane that he loved even the foibles of his kind. Here was a truly epic poet, without knowing it, who did not waste time in considering whether his age were good or bad, but quietly taking it for granted as the best that ever was or ever could be for *him*, has left us such a picture of contemporary life as no man ever painted.

—from *My Study Windows* (1871)

MATTHEW ARNOLD

Chaucer is the father of our splendid English poetry; he is our 'well of English undefiled,' because by the lovely charm of his diction, the lovely charm of his movement, he makes an epoch and founds a tradition. In Spenser, Shakespeare, Milton, Keats, we can follow the tradition of the liquid diction, the fluid movement, of Chaucer; at one time it is his liquid diction of which in these poets we feel the virtue, and at another time it is his fluid movement. And the virtue is irresistible.   —from *The English Poets* (1880)

WILLIAM PATON KER

With regard to some of the strongest parts of Chaucer's poetry, no later writer has been able to add anything essentially new to the estimate given by Dryden. 'Here is God's plenty' is still the best criticism ever uttered on the 'Canterbury Tales'; and Dryden's comparison of Chaucer and Ovid, with his preference of the English author's sanity and right proportions over the Latin poet's ornamental epigrams, is to this day a summary of the whole matter.

—from *The Quarterly Review* (April 1895)

GEORGE SAINTSBURY

Chaucer is perpetually seeing the humorous side, not merely of his emotions but of his interests, his knowledge, his beliefs, his everything. . . .

His good humour is even more pervading. It gives a memorable distinction of kindliness between 'The Wife of Bath's Prologue' and the brilliant following of it by Dunbar in 'The Tua Mariit Wemen and the Wedo'; and it even separates Chaucer from such later humorists as Addison and Jane Austen, who, though never savage, can be politely cruel. Cruelty and Chaucer are absolute strangers.

—from *The Cambridge History of
English Literature* (1908)

WILLIAM BUTLER YEATS

Though I preferred Shakespeare to Chaucer I begrudged my own preference.   —from *The Trembling of the Veil* (1922)

VIRGINIA WOOLF

Chaucer was a poet; but he never flinched from the life that was being lived at the moment before his eyes. A farmyard, with its straw,

its dung, its cocks and its hens, is not (we have come to think) a po-
etic subject; poets seem either to rule out the farmyard entirely or to
require that it shall be a farmyard in Thessaly and its pigs of mytho-
logical origin. . . . He will tell you what his characters wore, how
they looked, what they ate and drank, as if poetry could handle the
common facts of this very moment of Tuesday, the sixteenth day of
April, 1387, without dirtying her hands.

—from *The Common Reader* (1925)

SIR WALTER RALEIGH

Chaucer's strong sanity and critical commonsense, his quick power of
observation, and his distaste for all extravagances and follies helped to
make him a great comic poet. But he is not a railing wit, or a bitter
satirist. His broad and calm philosophy of life, his delight in diversities
of character, his sympathy with all kinds of people, and his zest in all
varieties of experience—these are the qualities of a humorist.

—from *On Writing and Writers* (1926)

G. K. CHESTERTON

The challenge of Chaucer is that he is our one medieval poet, for
most moderns; and he flatly contradicts all that they mean by me-
dieval. Aged and crabbed historians tell them that medievalism was
only filth, fear, gloom, self-torture and the torture of others. Even
medievalist aesthetes tell them it was chiefly mystery, solemnity and
care for the supernatural to the exclusion of the natural. Now
Chaucer is obviously *less* like this than the poets after the Renais-
sance and the Reformation. He is obviously more sane even than
Shakespeare; more liberal than Milton; more tolerant than Pope;
more humorous than Wordsworth; more social and at ease with
men than Byron or Shelley.   —from *All I Survey* (1933)

EZRA POUND

Chaucer had a deeper knowledge of life than Shakespeare.

—from *ABC of Reading* (1934)

HAROLD BLOOM

Chaucer anticipates by centuries the inwardness we associate with
the Renaissance and the Reformation: his men and women begin to
develop a self-consciousness that only Shakespeare knew how to

quicken into self-overhearing, subsequent startlement, and the arousal of the will to change.

—from *The Western Canon* (1994)

Questions

1. Do you find that narratives with subject matters as different as "The Knight's Tale," "The Miller's Tale," and "The Wife of Bath's Tale" share an outlook, worldview, or conception of human nature? If so, how would you describe their outlook?

2. Was Chaucer a misogynist (one who hates women)? Was he a misogamist (one who hates marriage)? Consider especially the Wife of Bath, her tale, and what is said about her.

3. In Chaucer's time the Catholic Church was powerful—spiritually, morally, economically, politically, militarily—and it had a strong influence on art, music, and literature. On the evidence of *The Canterbury Tales*, how pure a Christian would you say Chaucer was? Pick a single tale and think about what, if any, message there is in it regarding Catholicism.

4. Modern readers are sometimes surprised by how powerful and recurrent a motive eros (love or sexual desire) is for Chaucer's characters. Would you say Chaucer is realistic about this matter? Is he a puritan or a libertine, or simply tolerant? In Chaucer, does eros make people funny, sad, or tragic? Does Chaucer offer a cure for tormenting desire? Should there be one?

For Further Reading

Biography

Crow, Martin M., and Clair C. Olson, eds. *Chaucer Life-Records.* Austin: University of Texas Press, 1966.

Howard, Donald R. *Chaucer: His Life, His Works, His World.* New York: E. P. Dutton, 1987.

Pearsall, Derek. *The Life of Geoffrey Chaucer: A Critical Biography.* Oxford, UK, and Cambridge, MA: Blackwell Publishing, 1992.

Sources

Bronfman, Judith. *Chaucer's Clerk's Tale: The Griselda Story Received, Rewritten, Illustrated.* New York: Garland, 1994.

Brown, Peter. *Chaucer at Work: The Making of "The Canterbury Tales."* London and New York: Longman, 1994.

Burnley, J. D. *Chaucer's Language and the Philosophers' Tradition.* Totowa, NJ: Rowman and Littlefield, 1979.

Fyler, John M. *Chaucer and Ovid.* New Haven, CT: Yale University Press, 1979.

Kolve, V. A. *Chaucer and the Imagery of Narrative.* Stanford, CA: Stanford University Press, 1984.

Mann, Jill. *Chaucer and Medieval Estates Satire.* Cambridge: Cambridge University Press, 1973.

Muscatine, Charles. *Chaucer and the French Tradition.* Berkeley: University of California Press, 1957.

Contexts

Bisson, Lillian. *Chaucer and the Late Medieval World.* New York: St. Martin's Press, 1998.

Blamires, Alcuin, ed. *Women Defamed and Women Defended: An Anthology of Medieval Texts.* New York: Oxford University Press, 1992.

Coleman, Janet. *Medieval Readers and Writers, 1350–1400.* New York: Columbia University Press, 1981.

Fisher, John Hurt. *The Importance of Chaucer.* Carbondale: Southern Illinois University Press, 1991.

Green, Richard Firth. *Poets and Princepleasers.* Toronto: University of Toronto Press, 1980.

Hanawalt, Barbara, ed. *Chaucer's England.* Minneapolis: University of Minnesota Press, 1992.

Keen, Maurice. *English Society in the Later Middle Ages, 1348–1500.* New York: Penguin, 1990.

Rickert, Edith, Martin M. Crow, and Clair C. Olson, eds. *Chaucer's World.* New York and London: Columbia University Press, 1948.

Robertson, D. W. *Chaucer's London.* New York: Wiley, 1968.

Saul, Nigel. *Richard II.* New Haven, CT: Yale University Press, 1997.

Strohm, Paul. *Hochon's Arrow.* Princeton, NJ: Princeton University Press, 1992.

Wallace, David, ed. *Cambridge History of Medieval English Literature.* Cambridge and New York: Cambridge University Press, 1998.

Wilson, Katharina M., and Elizabeth M. Makowski. *Wykked Wyves and the Woes of Marriage: Misogamous Literature from Juvenal to Chaucer.* Albany: State University of New York Press, 1990.

Criticism and Explication

Arrathoon, Leigh A., ed. *Chaucer and the Craft of Fiction.* Rochester, MI: Solaris Press, 1986.

Askins, William. "All that Glisters: The Historical Setting of the Tale of Sir Thopas." In *Reading Medieval Culture: Essays in Honor of Robert W. Hanning,* edited by Robert M. Stein and Sandra Pierson Prior. Notre Dame, IN: University of Notre Dame Press, 2005, pp. 271–289.

Beidler, Peter, ed. *The Wife of Bath.* Boston: Bedford Books, 1996.

Benson, C. David, and Elizabeth Robertson, eds. *Chaucer's Religious Tales.* Rochester, NY: Boydell and Brewer, 1990.

Blamires, Alcuin. *"The Canterbury Tales": The Critics Debate.* Atlantic Highlands, NJ: Humanities Press International, 1987.

Cooper, Helen. *Oxford Guides to Chaucer: "The Canterbury Tales."* Second edition. Oxford and New York: Oxford University Press, 1996.

Crane, Susan. *Gender and Romance in Chaucer's "Canterbury Tales."* Princeton, NJ: Princeton University Press, 1994.

Dinshaw, Carolyn. *Chaucer's Sexual Poetics.* Madison: University of Wisconsin Press, 1989.

Donaldson, E. Talbot. *Speaking of Chaucer.* New York: W. W. Norton, 1970.

———. *Chaucer's Poetry: An Anthology for the Modern Reader.* Second edition. New York: Ronald Press, 1975. Includes commentary on *The Canterbury Tales.*

Ganim, John. *Chaucerian Theatricality.* Princeton, NJ: Princeton University Press, 1990.

Hansen, Elaine Tuttle. *Chaucer and the Fictions of Gender.* Berkeley: University of California Press, 1992.

Jost, Jean E., ed. *Chaucer's Humor: Critical Essays.* New York: Garland, 1994.

Kittredge, G. L. *Chaucer and His Poetry.* Cambridge, MA: Harvard University Press, 1915.

Knapp, Peggy. *Chaucer and the Social Contest.* New York: Routledge, 1990.

Lawton, David. *Chaucer's Narrators.* Cambridge, UK: D. S. Brewer, 1985.

Leicester, H. Marshall, Jr. *The Disenchanted Self: Representing the Subject in Chaucer's "Canterbury Tales."* Berkeley: University of California Press, 1990.

Martin, Priscilla. *Chaucer's Women: Nuns, Wives, and Amazons.* Iowa City: University of Iowa Press, 1990.

Patterson, Lee. *Chaucer and the Subject of History.* Madison: University of Wisconsin Press, 1991.

Pearsall, Derek. *Chaucer's "The Canterbury Tales."* London and Boston: George Allen and Unwin, 1985.

Phillips, Helen. *An Introduction to "The Canterbury Tales": Reading, Fiction, Context.* New York: St. Martin's Press, 2000.

Strohm, Paul. *Social Chaucer.* Cambridge, MA: Harvard University Press, 1989.

Wallace, David. *Chaucerian Polity.* Stanford, CA: Stanford University Press, 1997.

Wetherbee, Winthrop. *Chaucer: "The Canterbury Tales."* Cambridge: Cambridge University Press, 1989.

Periodicals Dealing with Chaucer and His Works

Studies in the Age of Chaucer.
The Chaucer Review.
The Chaucer Yearbook.

Edition Based on All Known Manuscripts

Manly, J. M., and Edith Rickert, eds. *The Text of The Canterbury Tales.*
   8 vols. Chicago: University of Chicago Press, 1940.

Look for the following titles, available now from
BARNES & NOBLE CLASSICS

Title	Author	ISBN	Price
Adventures of Huckleberry Finn	Mark Twain	1-59308-112-X	$5.95
The Adventures of Tom Sawyer	Mark Twain	1-59308-139-1	$5.95
The Aeneid	Vergil	1-59308-237-1	$8.95
Aesop's Fables		1-59308-062-X	$7.95
The Age of Innocence	Edith Wharton	1-59308-143-X	$7.95
Agnes Grey	Anne Brontë	1-59308-323-8	$6.95
Alice's Adventures in Wonderland and Through the Looking-Glass	Lewis Carroll	1-59308-015-8	$7.95
The Ambassadors	Henry James	1-59308-378-5	$8.95
Anna Karenina	Leo Tolstoy	1-59308-027-1	$8.95
The Arabian Nights	Anonymous	1-59308-281-9	$9.95
The Art of War	Sun Tzu	1-59308-017-4	$7.95
The Autobiography of an Ex-Colored Man and Other Writings	James Weldon Johnson	1-59308-289-4	$5.95
The Awakening and Selected Short Fiction	Kate Chopin	1-59308-113-8	$6.95
Babbitt	Sinclair Lewis	1-59308-267-3	$8.95
The Beautiful and Damned	F. Scott Fitzgerald	1-59308-245-2	$7.95
Beowulf	Anonymous	1-59308-266-5	$6.95
Billy Budd and The Piazza Tales	Herman Melville	1-59308-253-3	$6.95
Bleak House	Charles Dickens	1-59308-311-4	$9.95
The Bostonians	Henry James	1-59308-297-5	$8.95
The Brothers Karamazov	Fyodor Dostoevsky	1-59308-045-X	$11.95
Bulfinch's Mythology	Thomas Bulfinch	1-59308-273-8	$12.95
The Call of the Wild and White Fang	Jack London	1-59308-200-2	$6.95
Candide	Voltaire	1-59308-028-X	$6.95
The Canterbury Tales	Geoffrey Chaucer	1-59308-080-8	$9.95
A Christmas Carol, The Chimes and The Cricket on the Hearth	Charles Dickens	1-59308-033-6	$6.95
The Collected Oscar Wilde		1-59308-310-6	$9.95
The Collected Poems of Emily Dickinson		1-59308-050-6	$5.95
Common Sense and Other Writings	Thomas Paine	1-59308-209-6	$6.95
The Communist Manifesto and Other Writings	Karl Marx and Friedrich Engels	1-59308-100-6	$5.95
The Complete Sherlock Holmes, Vol. I	Sir Arthur Conan Doyle	1-59308-034-4	$9.95
The Complete Sherlock Holmes, Vol. II	Sir Arthur Conan Doyle	1-59308-040-9	$9.95
Confessions	Saint Augustine	1-59308-259-2	$6.95
A Connecticut Yankee in King Arthur's Court	Mark Twain	1-59308-210-X	$7.95
The Count of Monte Cristo	Alexandre Dumas	1-59308-151-0	$9.95
The Country of the Pointed Firs and Selected Short Fiction	Sarah Orne Jewett	1-59308-262-2	$7.95
Crime and Punishment	Fyodor Dostoevsky	1-59308-081-6	$10.95
Cyrano de Bergerac	Edmond Rostand	1-59308-387-4	$7.95
Daisy Miller and Washington Square	Henry James	1-59308-105-7	$6.95
Daniel Deronda	George Eliot	1-59308-290-8	$9.95

(continued)

Dead Souls	Nikolai Gogol	1-59308-092-1	$9.95
The Deerslayer	James Fenimore Cooper	1-59308-211-8	$10.95
Don Quixote	Miguel de Cervantes	1-59308-046-8	$9.95
Dracula	Bram Stoker	1-59308-114-6	$6.95
Emma	Jane Austen	1-59308-152-9	$6.95
Essays and Poems by Ralph Waldo Emerson		1-59308-076-X	$8.95
Essential Dialogues of Plato		1-59308-269-X	$10.95
The Essential Tales and Poems of Edgar Allan Poe		1-59308-064-6	$8.95
Ethan Frome and Selected Stories	Edith Wharton	1-59308-090-5	$5.95
Fairy Tales	Hans Christian Andersen	1-59308-260-6	$9.95
Far from the Madding Crowd	Thomas Hardy	1-59308-223-1	$7.95
The Federalist	Hamilton, Madison, Jay	1-59308-282-7	$7.95
Founding America: Documents from the Revolution to the Bill of Rights	Jefferson, et al.	1-59308-230-4	$12.95
Frankenstein	Mary Shelley	1-59308-115-4	$6.95
The Good Soldier	Ford Madox Ford	1-59308-268-1	$8.95
Great American Short Stories: From Hawthorne to Hemingway	Various	1-59308-086-7	$9.95
The Great Escapes: Four Slave Narratives	Various	1-59308-294-0	$6.95
Great Expectations	Charles Dickens	1-59308-116-2	$6.95
Grimm's Fairy Tales	Jacob and Wilhelm Grimm	1-59308-056-5	$9.95
Gulliver's Travels	Jonathan Swift	1-59308-132-4	$5.95
Hard Times	Charles Dickens	1-59308-156-1	$6.95
Heart of Darkness and Selected Short Fiction	Joseph Conrad	1-59308-123-5	$5.95
The History of the Peloponnesian War	Thucydides	1-59308-091-3	$11.95
The House of Mirth	Edith Wharton	1-59308-153-7	$7.95
The House of the Dead and Poor Folk	Fyodor Dostoevsky	1-59308-194-4	$9.95
The House of the Seven Gables	Nathaniel Hawthorne	1-59308-231-2	$7.95
The Hunchback of Notre Dame	Victor Hugo	1-59308-140-5	$8.95
The Idiot	Fyodor Dostoevsky	1-59308-058-1	$7.95
The Iliad	Homer	1-59308-232-0	$8.95
The Importance of Being Earnest and Four Other Plays	Oscar Wilde	1-59308-059-X	$7.95
Incidents in the Life of a Slave Girl	Harriet Jacobs	1-59308-283-5	$6.95
The Inferno	Dante Alighieri	1-59308-051-4	$8.95
The Interpretation of Dreams	Sigmund Freud	1-59308-298-3	$9.95
Ivanhoe	Sir Walter Scott	1-59308-246-0	$8.95
Jane Eyre	Charlotte Brontë	1-59308-117-0	$7.95
Journey to the Center of the Earth	Jules Verne	1-59308-252-5	$6.95
Jude the Obscure	Thomas Hardy	1-59308-035-2	$6.95
The Jungle Books	Rudyard Kipling	1-59308-109-X	$7.95
The Jungle	Upton Sinclair	1-59308-118-9	$7.95
King Solomon's Mines	H. Rider Haggard	1-59308-275-4	$7.95
Lady Chatterley's Lover	D. H. Lawrence	1-59308-239-8	$7.95
The Last of the Mohicans	James Fenimore Cooper	1-59308-137-5	$7.95
Leaves of Grass: First and "Death-bed" Editions	Walt Whitman	1-59308-083-2	$11.95
The Legend of Sleepy Hollow and Other Writings	Washington Irving	1-59308-225-8	$6.95
Les Misérables	Victor Hugo	1-59308-066-2	$9.95
Les Liaisons Dangereuses	Pierre Choderlos de Laclos	1-59308-240-1	$8.95
Little Women	Louisa May Alcott	1-59308-108-1	$7.95

(continued)

Lost Illusions	Honoré de Balzac	1-59308-315-7	$9.95
Madame Bovary	Gustave Flaubert	1-59308-052-2	$6.95
Maggie: A Girl of the Streets and Other Writings about New York	Stephen Crane	1-59308-248-7	$8.95
The Magnificent Ambersons	Booth Tarkington	1-59308-263-0	$8.95
Main Street	Sinclair Lewis	1-59308-386-6	$9.95
Man and Superman and Three Other Plays	George Bernard Shaw	1-59308-067-0	$7.95
The Man in the Iron Mask	Alexandre Dumas	1-59308-233-9	$10.95
Mansfield Park	Jane Austen	1-59308-154-5	$5.95
The Mayor of Casterbridge	Thomas Hardy	1-59308-309-2	$7.95
The Metamorphoses	Ovid	1-59308-276-2	$7.95
The Metamorphosis and Other Stories	Franz Kafka	1-59308-029-8	$6.95
Moby-Dick	Herman Melville	1-59308-018-2	$9.95
Moll Flanders	Daniel Defoe	1-59308-216-9	$8.95
My Ántonia	Willa Cather	1-59308-202-9	$6.95
My Bondage and My Freedom	Frederick Douglass	1-59308-301-7	$8.95
Narrative of Sojourner Truth		1-59308-293-2	$6.95
Narrative of the Life of Frederick Douglass, an American Slave		1-59308-041-7	$6.95
Nicholas Nickleby	Charles Dickens	1-59308-300-9	$8.95
Night and Day	Virginia Woolf	1-59308-212-6	$9.95
Nostromo	Joseph Conrad	1-59308-193-6	$9.95
Notes from Underground, The Double and Other Stories	Fyodor Dostoevsky	1-59308-124-3	$9.95
O Pioneers!	Willa Cather	1-59308-205-3	$5.95
The Odyssey	Homer	1-59308-009-3	$7.95
Of Human Bondage	W. Somerset Maugham	1-59308-238-X	$10.95
Oliver Twist	Charles Dickens	1-59308-206-1	$6.95
The Origin of Species	Charles Darwin	1-59308-077-8	$9.95
Paradise Lost	John Milton	1-59308-095-6	$8.95
The Paradiso	Dante Alighieri	1-59308-317-3	$9.95
Père Goriot	Honoré de Balzac	1-59308-285-1	$8.95
Persuasion	Jane Austen	1-59308-130-8	$5.95
Peter Pan	J. M. Barrie	1-59308-213-4	$4.95
The Phantom of the Opera	Gaston Leroux	1-59308-249-5	$6.95
The Picture of Dorian Gray	Oscar Wilde	1-59308-025-5	$6.95
The Pilgrim's Progress	John Bunyan	1-59308-254-1	$7.95
A Portrait of the Artist as a Young Man and Dubliners	James Joyce	1-59308-031-X	$7.95
The Possessed	Fyodor Dostoevsky	1-59308-250-9	$10.95
Pride and Prejudice	Jane Austen	1-59308-201-0	$6.95
The Prince and Other Writings	Niccolò Machiavelli	1-59308-060-3	$5.95
The Prince and the Pauper	Mark Twain	1-59308-218-5	$4.95
Pudd'nhead Wilson and Those Extraordinary Twins	Mark Twain	1-59308-255-X	$7.95
The Purgatorio	Dante Alighieri	1-59308-219-3	$9.95
Pygmalion and Three Other Plays	George Bernard Shaw	1-59308-078-6	$8.95
The Red Badge of Courage and Selected Short Fiction	Stephen Crane	1-59308-119-7	$4.95
Republic	Plato	1-59308-097-2	$7.95
The Return of the Native	Thomas Hardy	1-59308-220-7	$7.95
Robinson Crusoe	Daniel Defoe	1-59308-360-2	$6.95
A Room with a View	E. M. Forster	1-59308-288-6	$7.95
Scaramouche	Rafael Sabatini	1-59308-242-8	$9.95
The Scarlet Letter	Nathaniel Hawthorne	1-59308-207-X	$5.95

(continued)

BARNES & NOBLE CLASSICS

If you are an educator and would like to receive an
Examination or Desk Copy of a Barnes & Noble Classics edition,
please refer to Academic Resources on our website at
WWW.BN.COM/CLASSICS
or contact us at
BNCLASSICS@BN.COM

All prices are subject to change.